BALLAD
OF THE
BLADE

ANDREW P MERITT

Authorial Intrusion

This is not a story for the faint of heart.
This is a story of blood and bone, of love and loss, of rage and regret.
Proceed with caution, for this is no fairy tale. Real stories seldom have happy endings, and I won't promise you one here. The lines between good and evil are rarely easy to identify and usually a matter of perspective. Is this the type of tale for you? If so, then read on.
This is *Ballad of the Blade*, one story of many in *A Serenade of Smoke*.

In Other Words:
Content Warning

The language and imagery depicted in this novel are graphic in nature. If you have any triggers related to violent imagery or explicit language, please proceed with caution. If you would like a more extensive list of trigger warnings that include spoilers, please scan here:

Or go to:
https://andrewpmeritt.com/content-warnings

Dedicated in loving memory to Brian Guritz,
an amazing storyteller and an even greater friend.
Your absence has impacted many of us
more than words on paper can ever convey.

Acknowledgements

A special thanks to Jess Miller,
whose red pen never seems to run dry,
and
Annika Sabella,
who somehow manages to put up with me.

———◆———

A massive shout-out to the editors, readers, and readers who might as well be editors. This book would not be what it is without each of you. Thank you for all you did:

Cassidy Hood, Kathleen Fossum, Brianna Bean, Emily Cummings, Kelly Brown, Eileen Horan, Olivia Buzzacco, Brittany Meléndez, Brooke Allen, Lily Gleeson, Katelyn Sherwood, Rachel Froelich, Aspen Gray, Megan Friebe, Jacqueline Wilson, Patricia Park, Alyssa Kelly, Seth Brown, Caryn Pine, Haley Carbaugh, Robert DeGraaff, Ross Hight, Crystal Rothanburg, Larissa Sattler, Julian Keller-King, Mary Faulkner, Mercedes Malcolm, Jennifer Thornberg, Nicole Koviak, Mary Pierce, Donald Morris, Matt Sabella, Gerry Stevens, Courtney Holmes, Jena Roach, Shea Wilson, Aneva Holleran, Ashley Hamann, Boris Loucel, River Hampton, Brittnie Smith, Paul Meritt, Matthew Leon, Samhita Chitturi, Charlyn Darling, Veronica Jauregui, Bryn Reed, Erin Roney, Alissa Miles, Alexis Byers, Keanna-Mae Bachiller, Katelyn Raney-Plourde, Sara Albertson, J.V. Hilliard, Audrey Ruff, Caroline Krauss, Tammy Thompson, Marcia Moulton, Melissa Connors, Haille Rae Rourke, Janette Ramsey, Molly Chapman, Amanda Doscher, Janaia Fudally, Jordyn Tate, Katelyn Evans, Rayna Wilson, Hillary Smith, Eli Soto, Vanessa Mangini, Kathy Jaeger, Alina Bwy, Tiffany Morse, Gloria Fernandez, Robert Thompson, Haley Luke, Dorothy Emry, Benjamin Pererva, Kenneth Dearmore, Johnny Gould, Ryan Fiedler.

DARIN

DARKLOOM

ARDENDALE

RIVERSPLIT

NORINSPIRE

BLACKBARROW

GRENISPORT

WINDMORE

ELLISFJORD

SWORDBREAK

TERRA

STONEWOOD

RAVENSTAR

RAMOS

EBONSTALL

LANCASTER

CREED

BRINEVEIL

SWIFTBELL

Scan here for a color high resolution map

Or go to:

https://andrewpmeritt.com/maps

1
THOMAS KEMP

M*agic's supposed to be bloody dead.*

A cold, wet wind rushed past Thomas as he fell upward toward the three moons. Precipitation clung to his skin, still thick from the earlier rain. The air felt thin, and he couldn't pull enough of it into his tired lungs. He'd been falling for quite some time. Time enough to think, time enough to regret, and time enough to realize he wasn't about to stop.

Thomas looked skyward. The Trickster moon looked back, eyes gleaming with fresh lava as it took in the carnage below. The bloody bastard was smiling too. Interlaced rivers of magma surrounded black cliffs, filling a mouth with far too many jagged teeth. Aura, its purple sister, was suspiciously absent from the disconcerting equation.

Thomas wanted to scream.

What good will that do? No one will hear.

He looked down. The ground spun, and the bacon stew from earlier threatened to make a reappearance.

The sky held only death, and the ground was no better from this height.

Think, damn it.

Thomas racked his brain, trying to understand what was happening.

How's this possible? Everyone knows magic is dead.

It always came back to those same three words, the three words that started this gods-forsaken evening.

Lilian's and Jarod's faces swam through his mind. He'd been with them such a short time ago, back when everything was normal. His lungs burned, and his head throbbed, but despite it all, he forced himself to think. Bits and pieces of the evening flowed through his mind like sand in an hourglass.

When had it all gone wrong?

Thomas's eyebrows knit together as he concentrated on the plate before him, willing it to move.

It didn't.

Magic is dead, he reminded himself with a sigh.

Besides, what would I've done if it had moved? Point at the nearest gray-cloak, or run like hell?

He shifted his head from side to side, considering.

Why not both?

Thomas chuckled, gave up on the empty plate, and looked around the room. The long hall was filled with gray-cloaked men, candlelight, and muttering. Thomas spun a signet ring around his knuckle.

No, magic isn't dead. It's a beaten-down thought. An idea so flimsy it's been forgotten.

Magic wasn't some mystical force to be reckoned with, not like the Order proclaimed, anyway. It was far more drab than all that. Unlike most, Thomas had seen it. The memory of his father towering above him was etched into his mind like a title on a leather-bound tome.

"If the gift ever manifests for one of you, tell no one," his father had said to Thomas and his siblings after levitating a candle in their dimly lit parlor. "The Order has been weeding the arcane out for a thousand years. Not even the family name will save you if they find it."

That was ten years ago. Thomas was twenty-three now and had seen no magic since. He wasn't sure if he'd ever be able to perform the arcane arts but knew these stuffy old bastards in the Order wouldn't.

"Thomas! Hey, Thomas," Jarod yelled.

Jarod wove his way through the mess hall, careful not to jostle the intellectuals pretending to listen to each other while they waited for their chance to speak. At just under a span, Jarod was slightly shorter than average. He had a tousle of brown hair, a sharp mind, and an even sharper tongue.

Even if that tongue doesn't often make sense, Thomas thought with a smile.

Jarod was great, and not simply because he was the only other acolyte under thirty sent to apprentice here by the Order of Appropriate Magic.

The good ole OAM.

Thomas nearly laughed.

2

Such a silly name for a group whose sole purpose is to exterminate the arcane.

Jarod plopped down on the bench opposite him with a thump.

"You wanna help me with this damn essay the Superior assigned?" Jarod asked, opening a dusty tome and fishing pen and paper from his weathered satchel.

"The one on the archaic writings of Walter Raft?" Thomas asked.

"Yeah." Jarod sighed.

"Hard pass."

"C'mon! This stuff's far too dense for me. You read it, right?"

"That stuff was far too dense for Walter too. I heard his wife did all the research, and he took all the credit. Maybe write your essay on that?"

Jarod scratched his chin. "Nah, I can't do that. The Superior would whip me bloody for writing an essay on a rumor."

"Suit yourself."

"You finish yours?" Jarod asked.

"Yep. Did it in class."

"You already knew about Walter fucking Raft?"

"Yeah, him and his wife. Obviously."

"Ah. Well, we're not all as smart as you, asshole," Jarod said with a wry smile.

"Ouch! Assholes have feelings, too, you know."

Jarod snorted. "What'd you write your essay on?"

"I suggested that Walter's theory on the moons and their effect on the tides was good for its time. However, his wife didn't know nearly enough about Aura's influence."

Jarod scribbled furiously.

"Hey, quit that." Thomas felt a playful scowl tug at his lips. "We can't turn in the same bloody paper, you twit."

Jarod stopped scribbling and looked up. "Did you really claim it was Walter's wife?"

"Fuck no. The Superior would skin me alive for that sort of slander."

"Then why'd you tell me to?"

"I knew you weren't dumb enough to actually do it," Thomas ribbed.

"Ah, the old Thomas special, huh?" Jarod asked.

"What?"

"The backhanded compliment, you putz."

"Oh, I'm the putz?" Thomas raised an eyebrow. "Who's asking for help again?"

"Yeah, yeah, yeah. We all know you're smart. So why does Aura matter so much?" Jarod readied his pen.

"Well, Huna is the biggest of our three moons and—"

"I may not understand Walter Fuckface Raft," Jarod interrupted, "but I'm not a bloody idiot."

"Sorry, never sure where to start with *commoners*." Thomas grinned.

Jarod scowled, tapping pen to page.

"All right, all right." Thomas held up his hands defensively. "You know Huna orbits the planet much slower than we rotate, right?"

"Well, yeah."

"And it's also farther away than the other two moons, so it's *way* bigger." Thomas gestured outward with each hand.

"Yep, got that part."

"Well, Huna's the main reason the tides rise and fall nearly three stories. If it was simply Aura and Sirius, then we'd have much smaller tides, if any at all."

"So where's Raft tie in?" Jarod asked.

"Well, he theorized everything we've been talking about," Thomas explained. "But Raft also claimed Sirius and Aura were null and void in tidal equations."

Jarod frowned, working it out. "The Trickster orbits us at the same speed our planet turns, putting it always overhead. So it shouldn't affect the tides," he muttered, scratching the back of his head. "Why do I sense a 'but'?"

"Two reasons."

"Gods, you're dramatic." Jarod rolled his eyes. "What bloody reasons?"

"Well, when Huna pulls the ocean to the other side of the planet, the Trickster and Aura oppose it. However, when it's on our side, they're additive. That tends to make things all fucky."

"Fucky?" Jarod asked, one eyebrow slowly rising.

"Yeah, it's a word."

Jarod sighed. "And the second reason?"

"We don't know enough about Aura. We know it's the smallest of the three moons, it orbits Sirius, and it pulls at the surrounding light. That's what causes Sirius's face to change and shift. Well, and the volcanoes, in theory."

"Would you quit the mental masturbation?" Jarod asked impatiently. "What in the hells does it have to do with the tides?"

Thomas grinned. "Hypothetically, it could affect the ocean with that pull, the same way it affects the light. That's the theory, anyway."

"So that's why none of the tide tables can ever be completely accurate? They're missing a piece of the equation?" Jarod finished writing and looked up.

"You got it," Thomas replied, pointing an index finger at Jarod.

"Okay, so who proved Walter Raft wrong, then?"

Thomas leaned back in his chair, a sly smile spreading across his face.

"You came up with this!" Jarod accused.

Thomas laughed.

Jarod tossed his notes into the air with a dramatic flourish. "There's no bloody fucking way the Superior will ever believe this came from me."

Thomas laughed some more, and Jarod joined him.

"Gods, you're a smug fuck, aren't you?" Jarod finally asked.

Thomas shrugged. "Hey, write that thing in the morning. Let's hit the Fox."

"You know I can't go for a drink. I gotta get this done, and you just wasted a bunch of my time."

"Come on, it does us good to spend some time with the common folk. Otherwise, you might turn into one of these stuffy old bastards." Thomas gestured at the other gray-robed figures, who were doing a fantastic job looking dull.

"I can't!" Jarod protested.

"C'mon, I'll help you with the assignment after, or maybe in the morning if you find someone willing to take your sorry ass home with 'em." Thomas raised his eyebrows twice and smirked.

Jarod gave him a suspicious side-eye as he looked up from Walter Raft's *Lunar Etchings.*

"Deal," he said, slamming the book shut.

"Yes!" Thomas stood, grin widening.

"Come on." Jarod sighed. "Before I change my mind."

Laughing and joking, they exited the stuffy hall into the frigid night.

The sky was dark, and a storm raged. Waves battered the island's sheer cliffs, louder than a whole section of percussion.

Thomas yanked his hood tight, focusing on the path ahead. Shadows shifted across the cobblestone as oil lamps flickered in the roaring wind three spans above the street.

Span. Who came up with that?

Thomas wasn't sure but decided the subject might warrant more study.

I suppose a measuring system based on the average height makes as much sense as anything else in this silly world. Besides, what else would we use?

He looked around, eyes settling on his shoes as he stepped over a puddle.

A foot? Absurdity. How would you ever measure anything vertically?

Thomas shivered, and looked around.

Seafront lay somewhere off the western side of Darin, but Thomas had never seen a map labeling the exact location and doubted he ever would.

"Must've been a logistical nightmare to build this place." Thomas had to raise his voice to be heard over the heavy wind and rain.

Jarod nodded, pulling his cowl tight as they plodded along.

"I mean, they must've imported labor, materials, everything," Thomas shouted.

"Sure, but why in the fuck do I care?" Jarod asked.

"Don't you think it's odd this place exists at all? I mean, we still don't even know what this outpost is for."

"It's a bloody training facility, Thomas. How much more do you need to know?"

"So, you believe that a secret fortress—built at an insanely exorbitant cost, on an island where sailors fear to sail, with no strategic advantage—is simply a training facility?" Thomas asked.

"Well, when you say it like *that.*"

"There's something more to Seafront. I just can't put my finger on it. Besides, don't tell me you believe all that panther shit they spew about the Forge."

"Yeah, yeah, yeah. You've been sayin' that since we got here. Gonna start callin' you, Thomas Conspiracy Kemp."

"How often am I wrong, though?"

Jarod grunted, and they weathered the storm in silence for a while. They passed the blacksmith and soon arrived in the Residential District.

Two-story houses with steepled roofs and painted exteriors lined the street. Each was similar in cut and style, but the design was pleasing to the eye, and they were all immaculately maintained with OAM funds. The houses even had glass windows instead of shutters, an extravagance normally only afforded to the wealthy. The OAM paid for it all: housing, infrastructure, food and supplies, even the island itself. It was just a drop in the bucket for the Order, but it still struck Thomas as odd.

Amazing, really, for any organization to have so much wealth and power. Especially an organization that only exists to exterminate the nonexistent.

"You gonna talk to her tonight?" Jarod finally asked, startling Thomas back to reality.

"To who?" Thomas took a step closer to avoid yelling.

"You bloody know who, you twat."

Thomas did know who. *Lilian*. She was the innkeeper's daughter, and she was...well, she was perfect.

"I don't know what you're talking about." Thomas felt blood rush to his face and hoped the bad weather sufficiently covered it.

"So you're not gonna talk to her? She's just a girl, Thomas."

No, she's the *girl*.

"I can't," Thomas finally said.

"Why not?"

"What if I screw it up?"

Jarod turned to Thomas, cocked an eyebrow, then laughed. "You never screw anything up. Well, nothing you don't bloody mean to, anyway."

"Thanks, but this is...different."

"Different, how?" Jarod asked.

"If I screw this up, the Fox will be awkward from here on out. Then we'll be stuck in the mess hall with all the other gray-cloaked bastards," Thomas said.

In truth, he wasn't really worried about that. He was much more concerned about screwing up his chances with Lilian.

"You want me to talk to her for—"

"*No!*"

"Then you'd better do it soon, or I'm likely to take matters into my own hands."

Thomas shot him a glare. "You wouldn't dare."

"Or what?" Jarod's smile was as wide as it was mischievous.

Thomas considered saying that he'd no longer help Jarod with his assignments, but the threat was empty.

He's my only friend on this gods-forsaken rock, and I'm not sure I could stand it here without him.

"Let's just get to the fucking Fox," Thomas said. He glanced at Jarod, who was an absolute picture of smug triumph.

All right, you win this one, you little bastard. Thomas smiled and rolled his eyes.

Lightning arced across the sky, and thunder echoed like hammer on anvil as they silently trudged along the main road. Eventually, Thomas led them down two side streets, and they approached a well-lit building. A wrought iron sign shaped like a fox curled in a ball hung above the door with three words etched in metal: The Slippery Fox.

Now, these *are the true people of Darin*.

Thomas preferred the company of the common folk to his fellow OAM members, but it didn't hurt that the drinks were twice as good here, and the girls were more than twice as pretty.

Especially Lilian.

A sweet, melodic voice flooded Thomas's ears, and pipe smoke seeped into his nostrils as he opened the door. Wrought iron chandeliers hung from the rafters, and little towers of melted candle wax littered the tables. The bar was crowded with folk engaged in lively conversation. They were paid to live on the island and support the OAM, but no ship took passengers back to the mainland without the Order's authorization.

Thomas had eyes for none of them. Instead, his gaze fell only on the girl in the middle of the room. She stood on a table, singing and swaying as her delicate fingers moved flawlessly across the strings of a harp.

Heavenly. And I don't believe in gods.

"Move. I'm still getting bloody soaked, you lout," Jarod protested, shoving Thomas into the room. He shut the door behind them and joined a few patrons at a table in the middle of the room. "Mike, two ales, eh?" Jarod yelled.

The sturdy man behind the bar grunted in response, grabbed two empty tankards, and began filling them from a tap. Thomas barely noticed the exchange. Instead, he stood there, eyes glued to the center of the room.

Lilian had an apron tied about her waist, accenting her shapely figure. She wore brown leather pants tucked into black boots and a shirt that matched her bright green eyes. Her auburn hair hung halfway down her back in curls that shimmered as they bounced playfully in the candlelight. She scanned the crowd, smiling as her attention danced from face to face. Her emerald eyes were utterly captivating, almost as if they could pierce all the way to his soul.

In the unlikely event souls exist at all.

Lilian's gaze met his, and suddenly, the question of souls didn't matter in the slightest. The only thing that mattered was her. Then her eyes flitted away, off toward the next patron. She started another verse, filling the whole room with delight.

As beautiful as an entire symphony.

Suddenly, a roaring boom drowned out her voice and music.

That thunder sounds close—

Shingles cracked overhead as something tore through them. A wooden beam buckled and splintered as a boulder the size of a small horse ripped through the building. Thomas ducked, reflexively shielding his face.

The beam collapsed, taking the back half of the roof with it and burying several patrons under the falling structure. A chandelier clattered to the ground in an eruption of wax, metal, and smoke.

Lilian's song morphed into a scream.

The boulder slammed into her, silencing her final falsetto note as it dragged her across the floor. The massive stone slid through the bar and slammed into Mike, pinning him to the wall.

A shocked silence fell over the room. Dust and debris slowly started to settle. Thomas stood, lowering his hands and blinking as he tried to comprehend what had happened. Slowly, he looked around. One survivor coughed, but most were still covering their faces or gaping in horror.

Thomas's gaze fell on what was left of Lilian. It wasn't much.

She can't really be dead, can she? I never even got a chance to say hello. The thought rattled around absently as Thomas blinked, trying to make sense of the red smear. *Am I in shock? Do people in shock know they're in shock?*

Thomas's eyes followed the trail of gore across the splintered wood.

I should've talked to her. Maybe if I had, she wouldn't be...

The red mark ended under the boulder.

He sucked in a breath, tasting smoke, dust, and candle wax.

If I'd just listened to Jarod—Oh shit! Where's Jarod?

Thomas glanced toward the table his friend claimed a mere minute earlier.

Jarod stood there, coughing.

Thomas's slamming heart slowed at the sight of his friend, and he let out a breath.

Mike gurgled out a scream behind the bar, pulling Thomas's attention back to the disaster before him. Thomas shuddered, gathered himself, then staggered forward. He stopped two spans from the man. The boulder was the only thing keeping the barkeep's organs from cascading down the wall.

Nothing I can do for him.

Thomas's head jerked sideways as another thunderous crash sounded down the street. Two heartbeats later, another boom shook Seafront, then a third, a fourth. Thomas lost count as projectiles hammered into the ground, sending overlapping tremors through the keep.

What in fuck's name is going on? Are we under attack, or is this some sort of meteor shower?

Thomas was torn between staring at the aftermath and watching the sky through the enormous hole in the roof.

Surely, an astronomical event.

Nothing else made any sense.

Finally, Seafront stopped shaking, and only Mike's gurgles filled the space. Thomas took a tentative step toward the still squirming barkeep.

I could put him out of his misery.

Thomas bit his lip.

Am I the right man for that?

The sky split open, and lightning arced through the hole in the roof, striking the meteorite pinning Mike to the wall.

"Holy fucking hells!" Thomas lurched away, clamping his hands over his ears.

Mike convulsed, then caught fire. The thunder drowned out all other noise, roaring on forever. Finally, it ended, and Thomas slowly uncovered his ears.

Mike's gurgling had transformed into a wet scream.

The rock sizzled and smoked as the barkeep slapped at the flames with burning hands. The outside of the boulder crumbled away, and Mike fell from the wall. A heap of stone and ash covered him, muffling his screams and extinguishing the flames that fed on his flesh.

A massive gemstone stood in place of the boulder.

The orb was taller than a man, nearly as wide, and was a deep, complex purple. Swirls of black shifted under the surface, swallowing the candlelight.

It's bloody moonstone.

Thomas glanced at Jarod, then back to the glimmering stone.

It must be worth more than all of Seafront.

He took another step, then stopped dead in his tracks.

Did it move?

Thomas shuddered, trying to shake off the ghastly idea. He looked around. Dumb-founded faces stared back. If anyone else had seen the thing shift, they showed no sign of it.

Must've been my imagination.

Thomas took a deep breath and walked to the center of the room. He was a member of the OAM, after all, and despite what he thought about the Order, these people would look to him and Jarod in a time of crisis.

"People of Seafront—"

Everyone in the tavern pointed, gasped, or gaped at something behind him.

Thomas whipped around.

The immense orb of pure moonstone had risen into the air and started to spin.

2
TANYA RINGHOLDER

Tanya sat at the long, lavishly set table, a fake smile plastered on her face, wearing a dress clearly designed by a man.

No one else would make a waist this tight or a neckline so low.

Not that she was complaining. The garment was doing its job, and the nobles were paying far less attention to her face than they should be.

Amen Rocktell raised a glass for yet another toast. Light reflected off his cup, dancing over stone walls and the stuffed animal heads decorating them. The trophies were all predators, bared teeth locked in permanent snarls. Twin lion heads stood over the hearth, bear pelts hung on opposing walls, and an ancient skull of some creature far larger than any Tanya had ever seen loomed over Amen's chair.

"Ladies and gentlemen," the duke began, "as you all know, we are gathered here on my son's twenty-sixth birthday for a momentous occasion. There were times I thought he might never grow up, and I wasn't sure I'd ever convince someone to marry him!"

The duke paused, looking around the room expectantly.

The crowd erupted into laughter.

Robert blushed a deep red but had the good sense not to interrupt his father's speech.

"Of course, I jest. The boy has proven to be a capable man, and soon he will be wed to the most brilliant of beauties, Miss Evelyn Stolle." Amen locked eyes with Tanya, tipping his glass toward her. His lips curled into a smile that showed a few too many teeth. It looked rather predatory and had an uncanny resemblance to the dead animals surrounding him.

Tanya tried to blush, though truthfully, she'd never been very good at faking one. Instead, she settled on giving the duke her meekest smile.

"Ah, see, now I've embarrassed her." The duke looked around the table, drawing even more attention to the spectacle.

Had the blush worked?

Tanya met the man's eye, then looked away.

No, more likely, the duke is simply seeing what he wants to.

"I'm sorry, my dear. Sometimes I do get carried away," Amen continued. "It has been many years since I last saw you, and you have turned into a fine-looking woman!"

He isn't the slightest bit sorry, but it hardly matters. It's all just a dance, and this fool only thinks he knows the steps. In reality, he doesn't even know what song is playing.

Robert shot Tanya an apologetic glance from his seat across the table. She gave him a reassuring smile in return while still trying to maintain the pretense of embarrassment.

A shame, really. The boy's clearly better than his father, though not by much if you listen to the common folk.

The feast and speeches dragged on for some time.

Eventually, Robert leaned across the table. "Would you like to get some air? Maybe find a quieter place to get to know one another?" he whispered.

Tanya sat back in her chair and smiled.

I thought you'd never ask.

She stood, quietly asked the woman sitting next to her if she knew where the privy was, then exited the hall. Once outside, Tanya leaned against the wall and waited.

Robert emerged a few minutes later.

"C'mon, before we're missed," he said, taking her hand. He led Tanya through the keep's winding corridors and up to his private chamber.

Well, that's a bit presumptuous of you, isn't it, little Rocktell? It would likely offend the real Evelyn Stolle. Good thing for us both, she's not here.

Once in his room, Robert guided Tanya to the bed and sat her down.

Even more forward than expected.

Robert grabbed a decanter from a tray by the window and poured a bottle of wine into it. He gave it a swirl, then filled a glass for each of them. Tanya smiled up at him. He unbuttoned the top of his shirt and handed her the glass. As he moved to sit, her expression shifted from smile to objection.

"Would you mind starting a fire?" Tanya asked. "I would hate to end up too...cold." Robert hadn't struck her as particularly bright so far, but even he seemed to grasp the implication. He looked at the hearth, then toward the door.

Trying to decide if he should call a servant or figure it out himself. Typical nobility.

Robert walked to the fireplace, clearly deciding to give it a shot rather than interrupt their time alone. He stacked up five logs, then grabbed the flint and steel without adding any kindling or tinder.

So much for not being missed.

13

Tanya rolled her eyes.

Maybe I should offer to help?

He scraped the stone and metal together, creating sparks with no chance of catching.

No, not in this dress, might catch the damn thing on fire.

Tanya watched him struggle, trying to keep a smile from the corners of her mouth.

Besides, helping might emasculate him, and that could ruin the rest of our night. She breathed out a quiet sigh. *Men are so often idiotic about such things.*

A few minutes went by with no sign of progress, aside from some quiet cursing.

"I can call for a servant if you need," Tanya offered, unable to resist.

"No. I've got it," Robert said with a grunt of frustration.

"Suit yourself."

Tanya glanced around the room, spotting a small chamber pot on a bedside table. Quietly, she cracked the lid, leaned over, and poured her glass of wine into the vessel. She glanced up at the struggling noble, crossed her legs, and examined her fingernails. After a few more muttered curses, Robert finally got a fire going. He downed the last of his wine and walked over to the bed, undoing the next button on his shirt.

"So tell me, what do you do for your father?" Tanya asked.

Robert looked up from his next button, cocking an eyebrow. "Well, I do a lot for him."

"Like what?" Tanya smiled sweetly.

"Well, I oversee much of the estate, and I often visit our farms to ensure everything is being run properly. If it's not, then I decide what needs to be done and assign resources to deal with the situation."

"What kind of resources?"

"I suppose that kind of depends. I might assign a diplomat if relations between us and another noble house are strained. If the slaves are out of line, then I might hire a driver."

"Oh, that does sound exciting," Tanya lied. She stood up, gathered the decanter, and refilled their glasses. Robert smiled at the wine, eyes shifting slowly up to hers. Tanya tapped her glass to his with a devilish smile. "To our long-awaited marriage."

"Long-awaited, indeed."

Tanya looked down at the man's bulging britches. She let her eyes linger, making it painfully obvious. Slowly, Tanya drew her gaze back up, met Robert's stare, and raised an eyebrow.

"Drink up. It won't be very comfy to sip on that in bed," Tanya said with a sly smile.

Robert downed the wine, and she refilled his glass.

"Are you trying to get me drunk, Evelyn?"

"Me? I'm a lady, Robert," Tanya replied with mock indignation. She placed one finger on the bottom of his glass and gently guided it to his lips.

Robert drank it down, grabbed her glass, and set both on the tray. He laid her down on the bed and slid between her legs. His body pressed against hers, and he reached up, gripping her bodice like he meant to rip it off.

"Ah-ah-ah," Tanya warned.

Robert growled, hands still tight on the dress.

"Too expensive," Tanya explained, then flipped him over in one fluid motion and straddled him. Thankfully, that seemed to mollify the man, but Tanya could feel a swelling in the trousers beneath her.

Gotta work fast now.

Tanya leaned down and kissed him. Sweet wine and foul mutton filled her nostrils. She choked back a gag, nearly pulled away, then forced herself to nibble on his upper lip instead. Tanya suffered the stench for a minute longer, then cupped his face and pulled back slightly. He gazed longingly back, pupils growing larger.

Good, the lotus root's taking hold.

Tanya lowered herself, gently bit Robert's lower lip, then turned his head to the side and nibbled on his ear.

Robert let out a groan. His heart was racing.

Not quick enough, though. Time to improvise.

Tanya reached back into the folds of her dress and pulled the razor-sharp stiletto blade from the garter wrapped around her thigh. Robert moaned and grabbed ahold of her hips, clearly impatient. He groped under her dress with one hand, tugging at the laces of his britches with the other.

"Patience," Tanya said. "I'll make it worth your while."

"No."

"No?" Tanya sat up a little, eyes locking with his, as she slid her hand slowly up the bed.

"We have waited long enough. We'll be married soon anyway." Robert's voice was low, insistent, and the wolfish resemblance to his father was suddenly undeniable.

"That's true. Tonight should just be a taste, though. We wouldn't want to spoil the wedding night."

For a moment, Robert seemed to consider. Then he reached for her.

Tanya brought the slender knife in fast—one quick stab through the side of his neck, then a slice across his vocal cords. Robert fumbled, gurgling as he tried to push her off, but quickly stilled as blood poured onto the bed.

"Shhhhh," Tanya said, never looking away.

The surprise slowly left his eyes, replaced with a glassy stare.

Tanya stood from the bed, pulling the curly golden wig from her head and tossing it into the fire. She let her straight black hair down from its tight knot, stretched her neck to each side, then ran her fingernails roughly across her scalp. With a sigh, she gathered her hair back up into a loose bun.

Glad that part's over.

There was an audible rip as Tanya tore away the bottom of her dress and wiped her face clean. She uncurled the rope fastened to the skirt's inner hoops, then deposited the dress into the fireplace in sections. Tanya walked over to the mirror and undid the lacing up the back of the bodice, then fed it to the flames as well. She looked down at the black corset wrapping her torso.

Another male invention.

Still, she'd commissioned the undergarment with steel boning, so it was a bit more practical and had the potential to stop a slashing blade. The corset inhibited movement, but she could still fight in it. Tanya had made sure of that when the seamstress fitted her with the damn thing a few moons ago. She didn't love how much skin it left exposed, but jobs in a dress were uncommon enough to tolerate it.

Tanya walked over to Robert's closet and rummaged around until she found a pair of trousers, a shirt, and a plain black cloak. She slipped into the shirt and pants, rolling up the sleeves and legs, then settled the cloak over her shoulders.

Everyone owns a plain black cloak, even the nobles. What else would they wear to visit a seedy brothel?

Tanya noted the garment's dirty hem as she walked toward the terrace.

Looks like Robert used this one often.

Tanya opened the balcony door and stepped into the crisp night air. She secured the rope to the railing, descended the three stories to a small courtyard, and crept over to a stone wall. Torches bobbed through the night beyond, marking sentries.

Some of the guards followed set paths, while others were less predictable. She'd learned as much watching the estate over the past week but hadn't been able to plan a route without knowing the location of Robert's room. Luckily, only one torch moved between her and the stables tonight.

Tanya waited patiently until the guard's torch revealed him, then ducked behind the wall. He passed by, continuing his loop toward the front gate. She grabbed the top of the wall, hoisted herself up, and dropped silently onto the other side. Tanya slid through the grounds, staying low and out of the red light of the nearly full Trickster as she moved between well-manicured features.

Gotta get through before that guard comes back around.

Tanya crept from a marble statue to an urn near the entrance to the servants' quarters. The stable was just around the corner. She stepped out—

Light flickered on the path ahead.

Tanya pulled back into the shadows.

Too soon. He shouldn't have completed his circuit yet.

Ironclad shoes scraped over dirt as someone walked into the yard. The steps grew steadily louder, and Tanya sucked in a breath. The noise ceased. The only remaining shadow stretched from the pot she leaned against.

Nowhere to go.

The guard stood there for what seemed like forever, then metal rasped against metal.

A sword?

No, the sound of a scabbard was too distinct.

Scrape, scrape. This time, it was metal on stone.

Pipe smoke seeped into Tanya's nostrils.

Really? Havin' a bloody smoke right now—

"Hey! How's the night treating you, Captain?" a male voice asked from the other side of the urn.

Someone shuffled closer.

Not good.

"Quiet." Another voice, female, and apparently the captain.

"Quiet's good, right?"

"I suppose."

Ten heartbeats of silence.

"You ever get bored of this, Captain?"

"Of course. This job's more boring than watching a lacquered hull dry. But it's better than the alternative."

"Yeah, I guess you're right. Still, I wouldn't mind if something happened 'round here. I mean, every once in a while," the man commented.

"You wish there was a little more excitement at the Rocktell estate?" the captain asked dryly.

"Well yeah, might break up the day a little."

"Oh, like a heist? Perhaps a burglary?"

"Yeah, I mean, it wouldn't have to be something so dramatic."

"Do you know anyone dumb enough to try and knock over the Rocktells?"

Silence. Tanya pulled in a single breath through her nose.

"I mean, no. But they certainly do have a lot worth stealing."

"You know what Amen would do if he found someone skulking about his estate? Or worse yet, actually *in* his keep?"

"Uhhh..."

"If Amen caught you, he'd have you dragged to the dungeon, then someone would go to work on you. They'd get out the pliers, the knives, and the fire. That might last for days, maybe even weeks. As long as it took to pump every fuckin' name outta you."

The captain paused, taking a few drags from her pipe before continuing.

"The list of names would include anyone you ever worked for."

Good luck getting that. The Lance would do far worse than the Rocktells ever could.

"All your friends."

Friends—wouldn't that be a luxury?

"Your whole fucking family."

In the dirt.

"Everyone you ever fuckin' knew."

Well, that would be a hell of a list. Good thing there aren't many left alive I give a damn about.

"Then they'd take you, lock you in one of them cages," the captain paused, clearly gesturing at something. "Let the birds go at you for a while as they gather up your whole list and do the exact same thing to them."

Another pause and a few more deep inhales.

"So I ask again: you know anyone dumb enough to try and knock over the Rocktells?"

"I guess not."

I guess so.

"Didn't think so. Now, since you fucked the timing of your circuit up, we are gonna have to reset your round. See Don up there? Wait here until he's at the third tower, then start your loop again."

Tanya heard the same scuff of metal on dirt as the captain walked away. The guard stood there a moment, then leaned against the pot Tanya crouched behind. As he did, the shadow around her shrank, and Tanya held her breath.

Something sloshed around inside the clay vessel.

"Oh, and Bran. Maybe don't lean on the estate's oil supply with a lit fuckin' torch," the captain called back.

Bran straightened, seemed to realize what he was doing, and took a step away from the large clay pot.

Thank the bloody gods. Maybe he'll give me a little space.

As soon as she finished the thought, Bran began to walk around the container.

Fuck, why'd I even think it?

Tanya moved with him, using the light to keep herself opposite the sentry. She stayed crouched, fighting the rigid corset as she silently transferred her weight between each leg. Finally, the man stopped and stared toward the ramparts. Tanya waited, trying to keep her breathing slow and even—not that the corset helped.

Bloody thing.

Bran hesitated a moment longer, then walked away.

Once he neared the edge of the yard, Tanya let out a sigh and stood. She turned, scuffed some loose gravel with her foot, and froze.

A horse whinnied from the stables.

Bran turned, and Tanya darted behind a well-pruned pine tree. Her heart was pounding. She peered out, risking a glance. Bran wandered back in her direction, torch held aloft. He circled the pot they'd been dancing around, then turned toward her. Tanya ducked back behind the tree. She watched the light of the torch shift from one side of the trunk to the other. His footfalls slowly grew louder.

Tanya fingered the narrow blade strapped to her leg. The light crept closer. She pulled the knife free. Her heart was slamming in her chest, but her hands were steady. Her hands were always steady. She'd learned that about herself in the early days pilfering purses in the Severance Quarter. Shaky hands meant getting caught, and getting caught meant not having to worry about shaky hands ever again.

The light peeked around the edge of the tree, and Tanya crept the opposite way. Soon, she was a few steps behind Bran. Killing him was a risk. The captain seemed to have a good handle on the location of her men at any given time.

Still, staying here while he searches is worse.

Bran moved slowly forward, peering around each tree.

Tanya stalked up behind him.

If he calls the captain, and she starts sniffing around, too...

Tanya bit her lip.

That simply won't do.

19

Tanya drew the knife back, then brought it down hard.

The blade pierced skin where neck met shoulder, and Bran sucked in a breath to scream. Tanya snaked her other hand around and clamped it over his mouth, muffling the cry. The knife slid out with a sucking pop, and she brought it back around, carving through his throat in one clean motion.

Bran struggled, even tried to bite her. A few heartbeats later, he was dead weight, slumping to the dirt. Tanya dragged him behind the tree, wiped her bloody hand on his pants, then tossed his still-burning torch toward the base of the tree.

Time to go.

Tanya headed straight for the stables. Jacob stood beside the carriage, a brown bison head emblazoned on its side. As planned, two of the four horses were untethered, saddled, and ready to go.

"Let's move. We need to get out of here now," Tanya said, ducking into the carriage. She removed her cloak and pulled on the servant's garb laid out on the leather seats.

"What happened?" Jacob asked as she emerged from the coach.

"Things got messy. I'll explain once we're out of here."

Jacob nodded. They mounted up and rode to the gate.

"Hold!" a sentry called out as they neared the open portcullis.

They pulled their horses up short.

"Urgent missive from House Stolle," Jacob said, handing down a sealed letter. The bison head sigil of the Stolles was pressed into the wax seal.

The guard looked it over. "Still need to clear it with my superiors."

"What seems to be the problem?" a woman asked, striding over. Tanya recognized the captain's voice. The woman took the letter and examined the seal.

"Urgent message," Jacob provided. "The Lady Evelyn gave explicit instruction that it go out immediately."

The captain glanced back at the letter, then at them skeptically. Tanya had her hood up, but that shouldn't be too odd in the rainy season.

"Fire!" someone yelled near the servants' quarters.

More voices joined the call a moment later.

Tanya turned in her saddle, feigning curiosity.

The captain's eyes shifted from them to something in the distance. She sniffed the air. "If that's fucking Bran," she growled. "Let them pass. Looks like we have bigger problems tonight." The captain handed Jacob back the letter and strode past them.

They heeled their mounts into a trot. A moment later, they were through the gate. Tanya let out a sigh of relief.

Now, we just need to lose the horses and get back to the Lance.

Reynolds wouldn't be pleased when he heard about the fire. Then again, he was never happy when things didn't go to plan. The man used to be an agent, so he should know plans rarely lasted past the first hurdle.

It'll be fine. Reynolds will chastise me then give me my next assignment.

Tanya bit her lip.

Probably be a gods-damned handler job after he finds out about the fire.

Tanya hated that part of the business. Worse yet, Reynolds knew it. Handling was more babysitting than actual work, and amateurs always overestimated their abilities.

3
RIGEL CROSS

I t was dusk, and a wolf let out a long, lonely howl. Cross sat with his back against a huge oak, staring down at a trail of blood. His blood mostly. An enormous panther lay near him in a truly tranquil state. A state only death could bring.

Wide gashes marked Cross's chest and arms. Blood filled his right eye and leaked from dozens of other wounds. It pooled around him, gleaming in the last remnants of sunlight as it mingled with the panther's. Cross watched the two liquids coalesce, knowing soon, he would be dead.

Seems we're all made of the same stuff in the end.

Cross looked to the sky. Elinfall was nowhere to be seen.

Funny. Only a few days ago, I was just a slave to the ring.

He let out a long sigh. Fighting was all he'd done for so long.

Is that all I am anymore, a weapon?

Cross's vision began to fade.

No, all that violence was for others.

He closed his eyes, mind drifting back to the previous weeks as darkness engulfed him.

─◆◇◆─

Need to clear my head.

It wasn't easy. Distracting shouts and cheers rang through the morning air. A pair of guards led him down a narrow hall of rough sandstone, then lowered a small portcullis directly behind him. Cross stood head and shoulders over most men at four hands over a span and weighed nearly double at over thirty brick.

Cross closed his eyes, relaxed his shoulders, unclenched his fists, and took a deep breath.

Whatever's behind that next grate is all that matters. Whatever they—

Click. Click. Click.

Cross's thoughts were interrupted as the metal grate before him began to rise. He felt a little like a rat in a maze. He and the other slave children used to build mazes for rats at night once the work was done. They would release them and bet on whose rat would get to the end first. Pride, or perhaps a chore, was the only thing on the line, but pride for a slave was in short supply.

Click. Click. Click.

Now I'm the rat. Except there's no scrap of cheese at the end of this maze, and there's a whole lot more to lose. Well, and the rats go free in the end.

Click. Click. Click.

Even as cruel boys, they'd treated the rats better than Darins treated their slaves.

The rats never risked getting disemboweled, after all.

Click. Click. Click.

Disemboweled. It was a good word. A good word for a bad thing, and not one he'd ever needed working on the Rocktells' farm.

Funny, never thought those would feel like better times.

Click. Click. Click.

An image of his father's face pressed against the dirt filled Cross's mind. A shiver worked its way up his spine, then the vision fled.

Click. Click. Click.

Maybe the pits aren't much like a maze at all, Cross decided. The differences were too great, too stark.

Another good word. Who taught me that one?

Click. Click. Click.

None of that mattered anymore. Cross ducked under the portcullis as it disappeared into a slot above the doorway.

Click. Click. Click.

All that matters now is the other man.

Almost as if the thought had summoned him, his opponent emerged from the door on the opposite side of the ring. Cross stepped into his proverbial maze.

Click. Click. Grind.

Metal scraped on stone as the portcullis slid back into place behind him. Cross looked up, scanning the crowded stands. People laughed, others jeered, and some were even cheering.

That's odd. The cheers usually start with the violence.

Spectators only had one thing in common—their eagerness for blood. The stone walls of the pit were spattered and smeared with the stuff. The smell of death from the previous battle still lingered in the air, and flies buzzed from red to brown stains in the sweltering heat. Some stains were from fights earlier that day. Most were from countless struggles before that. Nearly all were from Terran men and women who had lost all choice in the matter.

Cross ignored the distractions, focusing all his attention on the man in front of him. He was almost as large as Cross, and his whole body was shaved from scalp to feet. His muscles bunched and rippled in the sun, and his skin was lighter than most.

How long have they had Hairless stuffed in a sunless hole?

The big man grabbed a rusty shield and sword from the wall beside the door, bashing them together. Cross glanced to his left. A bow and quiver were propped against the wall.

Hairless ran at him.

Another deserter.

Cross had fought enough times to recognize the weaving run soldiers were taught to avoid oncoming arrows. He glanced to the right. A gigantic maul that looked like it had seen better days leaned against the wall, its weathered stone head resting in the sand. Hairless was nearly on him.

A hammer's not the best weapon against sword and shield.

Hairless must have seen Cross's dilemma because his pace quickened.

Three spans away.

Cross snatched the maul.

Two spans.

He heaved the weapon in a huge arc.

One.

The head of the maul connected with the charging man's shield as he leapt to strike. Stone smashed into metal, reverberating up the handle and into Cross's bones. Hairless flew across the ring, hit the ground, and tumbled over the bloodstained sand. He tried to rise, failed, then slumped back down and stilled.

The crowd went silent.

Is it over?

Cautiously, Cross took a few steps toward the crumpled form.

Maybe it really is like Guildmaster Marius always says: when in doubt, hit 'em harder.

The crowd began to boo and jeer. They were clearly over their initial shock and quite upset about the match ending before it even started. Cross didn't care how they felt.

They'd come for death, and death had been provided, even if it wasn't as dramatic as they'd have liked. Cross turned in a circle, looking out at the angry faces. He wanted to hate them but found he couldn't. Even with their fancy clothes, even though they killed and enslaved the people of Terra in droves.

I do pity them, though—

Something smashed into the back of Cross's knee, and he crumpled to the ground. The maul tumbled from his grip, thudding to the sand. The booing and hissing fell away, replaced with a dull roar. Cross sputtered, took a breath, then rolled. The maul's stone head grazed Cross's nose as it slammed into the sand. He tried to stand.

A foot filled Cross's vision an instant before it connected with his temple. The world spun, and he landed on his back, squinting into the sun. Hairless stepped in, blotting out the light. He swung the huge hammer behind his back as if to split a log.

Cross rolled.

Thump.

The hammer buried into the rocky ground beneath the sand, two fingers from crushing ribs. Red flooded Cross's sight as the fury took over. The feeling was now familiar, yet no less unsettling.

Hairless snarled as he pulled on the handle of the maul. The hammer's shaft came loose from its stone head. The man lost his balance and took one stumbling step backward. Cross sat up, snatched the end of the wooden handle, and yanked.

Hairless held on and pitched forward, slamming into the dirt. He rolled to his back. Cross leapt at him but got tangled up in the deserter's legs as they wrapped around his waist. With a snarl, he bore down on the man, putting all his weight into a blow with his right hand. Hairless pushed him back with his hips and pulled his arms up defensively. Cross's fist glanced off the other man's forearm, so he threw another punch, then a third.

Hairless struggled beneath him, blocking strikes, as Cross reached for the head of the maul with his other hand. His fingertips brushed stone, then closed around the pitted head. He tugged at it, but the stone was wedged in something beneath the sand. He threw another punch. Hairless blocked, and this time, struck back. The fist connected with Cross's jaw.

Pop.

Pain lanced through Cross's face, and more red flooded his sight. He worked the dirt furiously with his left hand, trying to free the stone. Cross pulled his right elbow over his mouth, sheltering his nose and jaw as Hairless threw blow after blow at his face. Fists connected with either side of Cross's arm, then something slammed into his ribs.

25

Crack.

Red haze seeped into his vision.

Pain, it's only pain.

Cross threw a punch, but it glanced off a raised elbow.

Knuckles connected with his nose.

Crunch.

The smell of iron permeated everything, sloshing around his mouth. Something wet and sticky streamed down Cross's chin. He let go of the maul and roared. Blood and spit spattered Hairless's face as Cross laid into him wildly. The first three strikes were blocked, but the fourth connected with the man's head. The deserter deflected the next blow, and Cross's fist slammed into the dirt. Pain spiraled up his arm, but that didn't matter. Not anymore. He brought his other hand around.

Hairless caught his wrist as it came down. An enormous pressure built against the back of his elbow. The joint strained. It was either move with the hold or let the man break his arm. Cross chose the former and rolled. Hairless moved with him, straddling his waist. Cross pulled his arms up, blocking blows to his face and chest.

Crack.

Pain shot through Cross's ribs again. He managed to deflect the next fist into the sand and threw all his weight into a strike with his right. Knuckles connected with the man's skull, producing a loud crunch, as the bones in Cross's right hand broke. The other man reeled back. Cross reached for the head of the maul and found it still wedged in something under the sand. He pulled desperately.

It wiggled.

Hairless visibly shook away his disorientation, then began pummeling him again. Cross blocked with only his left arm now, and knuckles slammed into his fractured ribs and head. He clenched loosened teeth, enduring the assault.

Crimson painted the world, and everything tasted of hot iron. A fist connected with the side of Cross's head, and his vision swam with more than red. He raised his arm, blearily trying to block a follow-up strike.

Scrape.

The head of the maul came free of its rocky prison. Cross's swelling hand clenched around it as Hairless raised a fist for a final blow. Cross swung the stone in a straight-armed arc. Hairless pulled the arm blocking Cross's face to the side and brought his other fist down.

Cross winced.

This is over.

The head of the maul connected with something. Cross held his breath, jaw tight, bracing for impact.

The blow didn't come.

The grip on his left arm released. Cross slowly opened his eyes. The man on top of him reeled once, then toppled.

Cross wearily got to his knees. Spectators screamed and jumped around in the stands, but he couldn't hear them over the ringing in his ears. Lethargically, Cross straddled the other man's chest. Hairless threw a dazed punch, but Cross didn't even bother blocking the clumsy thing. Hands fumbled against his chest, trying to push him off, but there was no strength behind them. Cross brought the pitted stone down with two hands. It slammed into the other man's forehead.

Hairless's arms flailed as the back of his head hit the blood-soaked sand. He tried to raise his head. Cross brought the stone down again. Blood sprayed as the other man's head hammered backward. Again. This time, it crushed his nose and cracked an eye socket.

Then again.

And again.

And again.

Rage took over completely. The world became a much smaller thing, containing only him, Hairless, and the stone. He couldn't have said how many times he slammed the head of the maul into the other man's face. His ears rang, and Cross knew he was grunting, maybe even screaming, but he couldn't hear any of it. Eventually, the red haze permeating everything began to fade, bringing the world back into focus. The other man's head was completely unrecognizable, a pulpy mass of flesh and bone.

Cross looked around in a daze. He was straddling a lifeless body. Blood was everywhere. He could feel it on his face, see it splattered on his chest and arms, taste it on his lips. Cross's gaze shifted down to the sand. He knelt in a pool of burgundy still pouring from someone's neck.

How does so much blood come from a mass so small?

The ringing in Cross's ears slowly lessened. Someone far away was cheering.

No, that wasn't right.

The ringing slowly morphed into a deafening roar.

"Cross!"

"Cross!"

"Cross!"

Each shout was punctuated with the stomping of feet.

With a wince, Cross staggered up. Blood flowed down his face, dripping off his chin and hitting the sand. There, it joined the blood of so many others, so many Terran slaves who hadn't made it out alive.

The head of the maul rolled from his quaking fingertips, landing with a dull thud.

Cross stood in the middle of the pit, his whole world spinning.

The crowd was pointing, yelling, writhing in celebration.

He wanted to hate these cheering onlookers for what they had done to him and his people. He wanted to hate them for what they just forced him to do. He wanted to hate each and every one, but in truth, he couldn't feel anything at all.

4
DAVID TRUEHEART

David sat at a table in the Rooster, one of his favorite places. Tobacco smoke filled his nostrils, and he sighed contently. He enjoyed the smell yet had no desire to smoke or chew it; he had far worse vices than that. Mostly, he liked it because it reminded him of the bar: a place where people came to enjoy themselves and escape tedious lives. Some escaped with a deck of cards, others between the sheets upstairs, most at the bottom of a bottle.

Either way, people here are happy.

A scuffle broke out nearby.

Well, mostly happy.

"Glen, what have I told you about picking fights with my customers?" Rob yelled from behind the bar.

David smiled. The Rooster was his place of work, but it was work he loved. He traced the engraving on the back of his lute with calloused fingers:

> *For Trueheart, a man as faithful as his name implies,*
> *and the absolute love of my life.*

The lute had been his father's. His mother had given it to him after ten years of marriage. A money collector took his father's right hand a few years later, and he passed the lute on to David a few years after that.

You need to pick your vices, boy. Men typically fall into one of three categories in that regard: money, women, or drink. Choose one and do it right. Just make sure you don't fall into the trap of all three.

The words were a distant memory, but they rang in David's head from time to time. It wasn't necessarily bad advice, but David often wondered why he'd listened at all, especially when the wisdom came from a crusty, washed-up, one-handed musician.

Still, David had listened, even after telling himself he wouldn't. He'd become a gambler, like his father, and now owed a large sum of money to the Freemen's Guild. The type of folk you shouldn't owe the slightest stone. If he didn't start paying, he'd end up just like his father.

Right before the end.

Thankfully, David had inherited more than his father's gambling addiction. He'd got the man's good looks as well. At three fingers over a span, his father was medium height with coal black hair and a small, shapely nose. David could still remember his straight white teeth and mischievous smile. His forearms were muscular from hours honing his craft each day, and his hands were rough, worn, and precise from the lute.

Back when he had them both.

Everyone said David was a spitting image of the man, except for his eyes. They were a deep, stunning blue inherited from his mother. David knew he was an attractive man and used it to his advantage whenever possible.

"Give us a song!" one of the patrons called.

David hadn't planned to play tonight. He had a meeting, after all.

"Song!" Someone thumped a tankard on their table.

Rob set up the soiree after David confided he might need to skip town, but not out of the goodness of his heart. The Rooster's crowd had quadrupled since David started playing here, and the innkeeper was simply trying to hold on to the increased clientele.

"'The Warrior'!" someone else yelled.

What could a ballad or two hurt? Just to pass the time.

Rob had warned him the meeting was with some pretty nefarious folk. Apparently, an organization was willing to pay off David's debt to the Freemen in exchange for something, but Rob was somewhat vague on that point. Still, David would figure it out. He always did.

"All right, all right, but I only have time for a couple. Got it?" David smiled, stood, and gathered his lute.

Some grumbles emanated from the crowd, but there were more murmurs of assent.

A silly song first. Gotta build 'em up before you tear 'em down.

His father's words again. The man was long gone, but his wisdom still resounded often, like a particularly obstinate echo. David strummed the lute with deft fingers, adjusted a few pegs, strummed it again, then began to play. The chord progression sounded out a somber cadence, and he sang the words as if they were a lament to some great king:

"There once was a girl, all curves and curls."

Strum-di-da-la-dum.

"She danced with the earl, twirl after twirl."

Strum.

"Stumble did the girl, bent and hurled."

Strum-di-da-la-dum.

"A step in the hurl, he took a twirl."

Strum.

"He went for a whirl, landed in swirl."

Strum-di-da-la-dum.

"Giggle did the girl, facing the earl."

Strum.

"He glared at the girl, anger unfurled."

Strum.

David stopped for a moment and looked at the crowd with mock sadness.

"Then what did he yell?" he asked as his somber face cracked a smile.

"Off with her head!" the crowd called out as one. David's fingers flew across the frets, and the song picked up into a jaunty tune. The tavern laughed and cheered as he headed into the next verse. His fingers strummed out a rapid progression of chords as his voice alternated between a deep baritone and an absurd falsetto.

"I say off with her head, or she gets in my bed.

But I've just barely bled! So no way till we're wed!

But I'm a figurehead, see look I'm overfed.

Are you all this inbred? To demand I be dead!

Perhaps you I misread, I'm just looking for head.

You best watch where you tread. Then she turned, and she fled."

David jumped onto the nearest table and danced in a circle as his practiced fingers played without thinking. He smiled at a young girl, nodded to a group of established artisans, and nudged a tankard closer to a patron with his foot. The whole tavern swayed to the music, smashed tankards together, and sang. The song went on for three more verses before David headed straight into another lively tune.

This one was about a baker's wife who got sick of the baker, killed him, and baked him into the pies. The song was morbid, but the words were as silly as "The Earl and the Girl," and the people in the bar ate it up.

Just like the pies in the story.

The door opened at the far end of the Rooster.

David turned away, thinking to ignore it, but there was no way to ignore the woman who swaggered in. Her cloak trailed behind her, hips swaying from side to side in time with the music. She was provocative, serious, and her whole demeanor exuded confidence.

Her black ponytail moved back and forth in time with her hips, and she wore tight brown leather pants tucked into knee-high leather boots. A black leather jacket wrapped her upper body, with burnished silver buckles running down one side. The garment's collar went all the way to the bottom of her chin and looked like it could stop a knife.

David was momentarily captivated, and he nearly forgot the progression of his chords. His normally deft fingers stumbled through two notes, then found their rhythm.

The mysterious woman took a seat in a corner, putting her feet up on the table. David glanced over again and found her staring at him. Their eyes met, and she crooked one finger toward him, beckoning. David smiled, cut the last verse short, then gave a little half-bow to the audience as he exited the stage.

Groans and protests echoed through the room.

"I'll give you another song, after my meeting and some ale," David called.

"C'mon, David! You know we don't come here for this swill," an oversized man yelled, holding up his tankard.

"Then you might as well go somewhere else, Sven!" the tavern keeper shouted back.

The raucous patrons had a good laugh at that.

"One more song!" someone started to chant. Another person joined in, then another.

"Let the boy wet his whistle, you animals!" Rob yelled.

There was more laughing and grumbling, but the protests faded as David sat opposite the intriguing woman. He waved Sally over, and the buxom redhead brought two ales with her.

"Thanks," David said.

"'Course, honey." Sally winked, then gave the woman in black a quick once-over with her eyes. Truthfully, she called everyone honey and winked at them, too. It was just good business.

Not sure she ends the night in many other beds, though.

David stole a look at Sally's backside as she walked away, then turned his attention back to the woman across from him. She wasn't even looking at him. Instead, she seemed deep in contemplation on the state of her fingernails.

The woman had well-defined cheekbones, yet her chin and nose were soft. She was undeniably pretty, yet hardness lurked behind those intricate amber eyes.

She did call me over, right?

"You aren't very bright, are you?" she asked without looking up.

That's a hell of a way to start. David opened his mouth to object.

"I'm slightly disappointed," she went on. "We don't usually employ pretty boys who can't keep their mouths shut."

"Nice to meet you, too," David said, plastering an exaggerated smile on his face.

Should I tell her to fuck off? No, that wouldn't do. He needed this job if he ever wanted to clear his debt with the Freemen.

"I think we got off on the wrong foot. Perhaps we start again? I'm David," he said, extending a hand.

"Nice to meet you, boy." The woman finally looked up and took his hand. Her grip was firm, and her hands even rougher than his own.

Not the type of calluses you earn from the strings.

David felt his lips press together.

Perhaps from the hilt of a blade?

He shook his head. It didn't matter right now.

"So, how does this work?" David asked. "Rob told me your organization would make contact, but that was all he was willing to say."

The woman took a sip of her ale, swung her feet off the table, and leaned in close.

"This works by you shutting the fuck up a minute. Gods, do all gamblers talk this much?" she asked. "A common room is far too public to discuss specifics."

"No, it's more of a bard thing," David said.

"What?"

"The talking."

"Oh, for fuck's sake, just shut your mouth and listen a moment."

"Okay, do you want to go up to my room?" David asked, trying to be helpful.

The woman laughed.

David cocked an eyebrow. "I mean to talk."

"Is that what the boys are calling it these days?" She raised an eyebrow of her own.

"I mean...in private. Like, to talk. I mean...about the fucking job!"

"Oh, you were serious? No. We've talked too much already, with too many watching eyes. Meet me at the fountain at midnight."

"The one by the Coliseum?"

"Yes, the one by the bloody Coliseum. What other one would I be talking about?"

"Well, I mean, there are other fountains," David protested.

"I didn't say *a* fountain, now did I? I said *the* fountain, and there's only one fucking *the* fountain in Windmore. Hells, this is gonna be a long job, isn't it?" the woman asked, without looking at him.

"All right, *the* fountain at midnight. Sorry, I'm a little new to this. Isn't the fountain a bit...public?"

"You don't fucking say?" The woman let out a long-suffering sigh, then muttered, "Amateurs." She stood, took another swig of ale, set the tankard back on the table with a sloshing thunk, and turned to leave.

"Wait! I didn't get your name," David said.

"Midnight," the woman repeated without stopping.

"Midnight's your name?" David asked.

The woman didn't respond.

Still, David found it difficult to look away from her swaying hips as she strode to the door, even as Sally came into view at a nearby table.

That might be the sexiest woman I've ever seen. Even if she is a bit scary.

David looked at Sally. She was bent low, cleavage popping out, shamelessly putting on a show. He didn't blame her. It was part of the job, and she made much more stone by showing a little skin.

Hells, I put on a show every night, and it's not any more dignified.

Still, there was something far more appealing about the confidence and swagger seeping from his new contact.

Whoever she is.

David finished his ale and swapped it with her half-full tankard.

Waste not, David thought, taking a swig. It was another of his father's sayings.

I can't seem to escape that old man, can I?

If David eventually skipped town, there'd be no playing his lute, not for a long while.

Maybe not ever.

Finding a practicing minstrel, traveling or not, wouldn't be hard. He'd be lucky to end up like his father with the stone he owed.

An image of a one-handed bard begging in the streets for bits of topaz and scraps of food filled his mind. David dismissed it. Things were looking up. He might not have to skip town after all, and it finally felt as if an anvil was lifting from his chest.

I might just feel like singing.

Cheers rang out as David took to the stage again, and most conversation softened to a whisper. The Rooster had acquired a reputation lately, and the people now came for the music as much as anything else.

David strummed his lute.

Still in tune.

"'The Warrior'!" someone yelled again.

"Yeah, yeah, I got it," David said.

He played a song about a legendary figure named Thorne Squall, who was often referred to as simply the Warrior. This ballad was about Thorne pushing back the evil forces of Terra after they besieged the capital of Darin.

The crowd booed when the Terran armies surrounded Norinspire, then cheered when Thorne sent them packing. Finally, they laughed when he snubbed his nose at the OAM's advice and rallied an army to push the Terrans back to their own continent.

David continued the saga in the next song, "Blood and Betrayal."

Thorne gathered the people of Darin and took the fight across the Great Divide. It was an upbeat tale, half story, half song, with lots of battles. The ballad was full of tactics, and Thorne was always one step ahead of the Terran generals. He constantly outmaneuvered, flanked, and cut off their supply lines. In the end, the Terrans surrendered. They were amidst peace talks and reparations when the Terran nobles had Thorne assassinated.

The tavern-goers cheered for Thorne's every victory, laughed each time he outsmarted the armies of Terra, and somberly drank to his death. There were too many songs to count about Thorne Squall. David doubted many details were accurate, but the War of Iron and Blood was recent enough that the bones were likely true. Thorne was also widely accepted as the greatest military mind of his age.

David played "The Last Dragon" next. The ancient ballad must have been entirely made up, but it always got the crowd swaying. The song was about a knight and his company venturing into a frozen wasteland past the mountains in the far north, where no one had gone before.

The group traveled through wind, sleet, and snow until they found an immense cave. An enormous white dragon ambushed them there, fighting with tooth and fire. The beast killed the entire company except the knight and his minstrel. The knight, of course, slew the dragon but died before making it back over the mountains. Only his traveling minstrel returned to tell the tale.

Rather convenient. Then again, songs so often are.

David finished the third song with a bow.

The crowd clapped and cheered, throwing topaz flakes and even a few ruby chips at the stage. He gathered up the stone and excused himself. The three ballads had taken hours, and he was parched and hungry. Sally brought him a generous helping of vegetable stew ladled over biscuits and topped with shredded beef. Savory steam wafted from the bowl, making David's mouth water as Sally set another tankard of ale near his elbow.

"See you later tonight?" she asked with a sly smile.

"No, not tonight. Got another meeting." David took a deep whiff of the meal.

Sally's eyebrows rose. "A meeting? You?"

"Respectable businessman," David said, tapping a thumb to his chest.

Sally laughed. "Suit yourself, honey. That's not how I'd spend my night. Especially with the weather rollin' in."

"Ugh, I bloody hate fall."

"Well, good luck, sugar." Sally gave him another wink, then headed off to the bar to pick up another order of drinks.

Is she swaying her hips more than usual?

David turned back to his meal, letting the thought drift away. The dinner crowd slowly thinned until the only people left were unlikely to pay for a song.

Must be nearing midnight. Best get going.

David headed to his room on the second floor and over to the closet. He retrieved a belt with multiple loops, wrapped it around his waist, and strung a rope through a central metal ring. He stuffed a dagger into his boot and another into a sheath on the back of his belt. Finally, he settled a long black cloak over his shoulders and tied it at his throat.

His fingers traced the plain cord. A beautiful silver brooch with a tiny sapphire used to hang there, but he'd thrown it into a card game long ago.

Forgive me, Mother.

David had hid the treasure from his father for years, knowing he would've gambled it away. But things always seemed to come full circle, and eventually, he threw it in the pot himself. He'd thought there was no way to lose that hand, but of course, he had.

It was all I had left of her.

David sighed.

Oh well, gone now. After my debt is cleared, maybe I can find it. Buy it back.

David shook his head. Those were problems for another time. He reached into the closet, pulled on the clothes bar, then slowly eased his weight onto it. Satisfied, he looped one end of the rope around the rod and strung it back through the ring on his belt. He walked to the window, opened the shutters, and climbed out. David rappelled the short distance from his window to the ground, unstrung one end of the rope, and pulled it free of the bar. He snatched the end as it came tumbling down and quickly coiled the rope into his bag.

Probably could've walked out the front, but Mystery-Hips seemed a bit twitchy.

David looked each way as he shouldered the pack, then headed toward the main road.

Best be careful tonight. I'm dealing with dangerous folk, after all.

A cold autumn wind clawed at David's cheeks, and he pulled his hood tighter.

The streets were mostly vacant, but occasional townsfolk still made their way home from the many bars and taverns sprinkled throughout the city. As David neared the center of Windmore, travelers became less frequent, and soon, the crown of the Coliseum jutted up in the distance. At nine spans high and over a hundred wide, it was the pride and joy of House Rocktell. Apparently, Norinspire had even taller structures, but it was hard to imagine one wider.

Honestly, gives me the creeps—like someone tried to smash "colossal" and "mausoleum" together.

David shivered and looked away, trying to focus on something else. The fountain was only a few blocks away, and the storm was still just threatening.

Maybe Sally was wrong about the weather.

He took a few more steps before the sky opened up and poured on him. Five steps later, he was soaked to the soul.

Just had to go and think it. I bloody hate fall.

David saw no sign of his contact, so he approached the basin at the square's center. Somehow, the red light of the moon still illuminated the fountain, even through the torrential downpour.

Damn moon always finds a way to peek through.

At least the Trickster was the only one out tonight.

Its sisters must be lurking behind the clouds.

Unfortunately, like in most things, the middle child was the problem.

Just ask my parents.

Standing under the middle moon was rumored to bring misfortune, especially when it was full.

David glanced up.

The Trickster stared down longingly, and it was entirely full.

David shuddered.

Hate that bloody moon. Stupid nickname isn't even accurate. More like Psychopath.

Rain battered David's brow as he looked away from the unwinnable staring contest.

Don't need any more bad luck. The Freemen's ledger can vouch for that.

His eyes settled on the sculpture at the fountain's center. Brass statues of men and women crouched, frozen in a grisly entanglement of human flesh. The whole thing spiraled upward in a mass of bodies and limbs, ending in a carved likeness of Argyle Rocktell. The sculpted slaves at the bottom were being trampled by those higher up. Their faces were tight, agonized—pure desperation. As the slaves climbed, their expressions slowly composed. Those touching Argyle looked downright reverent as they stared up at the onyx rendition of the man who commissioned the Coliseum.

The whole fountain's ghastly as hell. Odd I never noticed that before.

Crimson water flowed from Argyle's upturned palms in an offering to the people of Windmore. The slaves near the bottom of the fountain were supposed to be drinking greedily, but with rain overflowing the basin and the Trickster above, it looked more like they were drowning in blood.

David shuddered again.

Still, something was fitting about Argyle giving the people of Windmore water or blood, depending on their appetites.

"You're late," someone rasped.

David jumped, eyes searching for the voice's source. The woman from the Rooster swayed into view from the dark side of the fountain. She was absolutely soaked, with a slight limp to her swagger.

"Sorry. Took extra precautions getting here," David said. "What happened to you?"

"I've been waitin' over an hour for you in the pouring rain and under the bloody Trickster, no less," she growled.

Again, not the best start. No choice but to push through, I suppose.

"So, how does this work?" David asked, trying to change the subject. "Oh, and what's your name?"

She scowled. "It's pretty simple. I give you the job, then you do the job."

"First your name was Midnight, now it's Pretty Simple," David said. "While I do agree with the pretty part, I must say, this is getting awfully confusing." He flashed a smile.

One of her eyebrows slowly rose, but she didn't respond.

He sighed. "And if I can't?"

"Then you're out of fuckin' luck. What's not making sense? Do I need to sing it?"

"Could you? Might help," David said.

She shook her head. "Unbelievable."

"Also, I've never had any of that to begin with."

"Believability?"

"No, luck. Truehearts are born without it."

She looked away from him, brow furrowing. "Cute. Are you done?"

"Yeah, I think I got that out of my system," David said.

"Good. The name's Tanya. Any other stupid questions before we begin?"

"Just one."

Tanya gave him a long-suffering stare.

Guess the question was rhetorical.

"What do you do for fun?" David asked anyway.

"Gods, you are somethin' fuckin' else. I told the boss this wouldn't work out." Tanya turned to leave.

"Wait," David said, taking a step forward. "Sorry, humor's kind of a defense for me."

Tanya turned back, exasperation filling her features.

How do all women know how to deliver that look with such perfection? They must have schools for such things.

"Do me a favor, will ya?" she finally asked.

"Anything."

"Save your bloody cleverness for the job."

"You think I'm clever?"

"No, I think *you* think you're clever."

There was a short silence.

"What is it?" David asked.

Tanya looked at him skeptically.

"Err, the job, that is," David clarified.

Tanya reached into the satchel at her side, and red light reflected from the fountain, illuminating her face.

She really is stunning, David thought as she rummaged around in the bag.

David tore his eyes from her waistline as she looked back up. The letter wavered in the wind, getting soaked as their eyes met.

"What's that?" David asked.

"Your assignment."

"It's sealed." David warily took the envelope.

"Yep."

"Why?" he asked.

"On a job like this, the less I know, the better," Tanya explained. "That's how these things work. You only know me, and I know nothin' about where you're headed."

"Why?" he asked.

"Good fuck, what are you, a bloody child?"

Another rhetorical question? David stayed silent.

"It's so *when* you get caught," Tanya started, "and before you ask me bloody why again, I say *when* because amateurs like you always get caught."

David clamped his mouth shut.

She's quick. Quicker than the floozies that hang around the Rooster, anyway.

"So, *when* you get caught, you only know me, and I don't have a damn clue what you're doing for the guild."

So, you work for a guild. Which one, though?

"Well, I know what you look like. For a clever man, that'd be enough," David said.

"Good thing we don't have to worry about that then." A wicked smile danced across her lips, but it was gone in a flash.

At least I can still make 'em smile. That's gotta count for something.

"Fuck, you're mean, huh?" David accused.

"Nope, just tired of holding nitwitted folks' hands," Tanya said.

"Does the *guild* give you a lot of these types of assignments?" David asked. It was his turn to smile.

Silence.

She fucked up, and she knows it.

"No, I just seem to get all the fools who are out of their depth. Now read the bloody letter, will you?"

David examined the envelope. The letter was unadorned, except for an unfamiliar insignia pressed into red wax.

Well, in for a chip, in for a shard, I suppose.

More wise words from a one-handed musician.

5
SCARLETT REINHOLM

S carlett sat with her back to the half-completed wall of her little cabin, ears straining against the silence. The howling of wolves had grown closer and closer each night, but their lonely song ceased nearly ten minutes ago.

She looked to the east. Once finished, her cabin would have an incredible view over the edge of the plateau, but it offered little protection for now. Scarlett's green eyes shifted back to the forest, straining for any motion in the moonlight.

Nothing, not a flicker of movement. No sound either, not a peep.

"The waiting's worse than anything else," Scarlett muttered.

When did I start talking to myself?

Sometime in the first six months of isolation, she decided. No culminating event had facilitated the change. Her consciousness had simply started to seep from her mouth.

Movement at the tree line pulled Scarlett from contemplation, and her lean muscles tensed. An enormous animal barreled out of the trees. It was well over a span at the shoulder, easily ten times her weight, and had a thick brown fur coat. It galloped on all fours, similar to a horse, except with two scooped antlers full of sharp points.

Scarlett readied her bow, but drawing an arrow seemed foolish from this distance. She'd been utterly terrible with the tool when she'd first arrived on the plateau, but, like so many things up here:

You either learn, or you die.

So, Scarlett learned. She'd learned how to fletch an arrow, how to string a bow, and how to sight down the shaft. She'd learned to inhale as she pulled back on the string. Most of all, she'd learned not to draw the thing so early that her arms were shaking by the time prey came into range.

They were shaking now, though, and not because she'd drawn the bow.

"That thing's absolutely massive," Scarlett whispered. The creature barreled toward her little structure, long legs eating the distance as its oversized peanut of a head swayed from side to side.

41

"A moose?" Scarlett muttered. She'd read a description of one at the Academy, and it fit. *But holy hells—can they really be that large?*

Scarlett blew out a slow breath, deciding they must be.

More four-legged creatures streamed from the woods.

One, two, three—

Scarlett lost count as a wave of teeth and fur cascaded from the trees.

"Wolves," she muttered.

They were big. Nowhere near the size of the first animal, but there were nearly a dozen of them. The moose was fast, but they were faster, and they gained on it in the open ground. The big creature must have noticed because it slowed, turned, and squared off around fifteen spans from Scarlett's little structure. Most of the wolves veered off, but one tripped and rolled, slamming into the sharp points on the creature's antlers. It bounced off with a whimper and a whine, three large punctures in its side.

The remaining wolves circled the beast, slowly surrounding it. The ones behind slunk closer. The moose spun on them, antlers slashing. They pulled back, and the ones opposite began to tighten the noose. Teeth found flesh where hoof met sinuous muscle. The moose lashed out with a kick. The wolf let go, leaping sideways.

The beast turned again, antlers low. One of the largest wolves lunged, latching onto the same back leg. A hoof cracked into the wolf's side, sending it flying. Two more wolves moved in, jaws clamping on each hind leg. The moose tried another kick, but there was no power behind the strike with a wolf latched on.

The huge creature spun, antlers goring a slinking wolf and tossing it sideways. The predator landed in a heap, tried to rise, then fell back into the knee-high grass. Two more sets of jaws clamped onto the moose's flank, locking it in place. The wolf in front stalked forward, then slunk back as the moose lowered its antlers menacingly.

It was becoming more and more obvious how this would end.

A wrongness settled in the pit of Scarlett's stomach.

This is the way of life up here, isn't it? Kill or be killed?

Scarlett pursed her lips and fingered the string of her bow. These wolves had given her more unease over the last week than she could quantify.

Two more wolves sank their teeth into the moose's haunches, and all six started pulling together to drag the beast down.

They'll feed on it for weeks. No way they won't smell me out.

The two remaining wolves stalked forward, waiting for an opening in the slashing antlers. They licked their lips, eyeing the massive creature's throat.

"This is a bad idea," Scarlett muttered, stepping into the half-built doorway.

She set her feet, blew a strand of auburn hair from her face, and took a deep breath. Scarlett drew back the string, aimed, then loosed. The shaft thudded into the side of a wolf on the moose's flank. The thing yelped and fell away. She let another arrow fly. It sank into the moose's butt.

"Shit!" Scarlett nocked another arrow. "Sorry, big guy."

The five wolves had the moose on the ground now, and it was clearly tiring. The next arrow hammered into the neck of a wolf on the right. Scarlett's next shaft plunged into one on the left. A wolf tried to dart in but got caught on the moose's antlers.

Where'd the other one in front go?

A gray bolt streaked toward her doorway. Scarlett barely had time to think before the wolf was airborne. It was huge, nearly twice the size of any dog back in Terra. She stumbled backward, throwing her bow up to block the creature.

The beast slammed into her chest.

Air fled Scarlett's lungs as her back hit the ground and her head whipped into packed dirt. Paws pressed down on her airless chest as jaws snapped toward her throat. She struggled, pushing the bow against the wolf's neck with all her might.

Scarlett sucked in a frantic breath. Teeth gnashed toward her neck a finger's width at a time. Saliva and tears blurred her vision. Her head throbbed. A tooth grazed her chin. Her stomach tightened, twisting into a knot.

Slowly, Scarlett's brain started working again, and the gut-wrenching sensation subsided. *The Gray Tome* went into wolf encounters extensively, and she'd read those pages a hundred times in the last week of howl-filled nights.

Scarlett let go of the bow and thrust her arm up.

Fangs tore into her forearm.

She screamed through gritted teeth.

The beast opened its jaws wider, trying to get a better grip to crush bone. Scarlett shoved her forearm deeper into its mouth. Teeth pierced new skin. It hurt like the thirteen hells, but the book was right; the wolf couldn't bring nearly as much force to bear with its mouth held wide.

A little confidence flowed back into Scarlett. The wolf tried to pull back, but she wrapped her other arm around the back of its head, free hand gripping her trapped elbow. It growled, pushing with its paws, but she held tight. Scarlett lifted her legs, locking her ankles around the beast's back. In one fluid motion, she pulled down with her legs and pushed forward with her arms.

Snap.

The wolf collapsed.

"Oof." A stuttered breath was forced from Scarlett's chest. "Damn thing...weighs as much...as I do."

Scarlett sucked in another lungful of air, then groaned as she pushed the beast's upper body from her chest. She squirmed, wormed her lower body free of it with a series of grunts, then turned and picked up her bow. Blood streamed down her forearm, slicking her palm.

Her punctured forearm throbbed, but Scarlett lifted the bow, nocked an arrow, and set her jaw. She drew back the string, sighting down the shaft. Three wolves stood in the red-spattered grass around the downed moose. Two clung to the beast's back leg, ripping and tearing at the flesh there. The last approached its head, clearly trying to get at the throat.

The moose let out a bellowing moan and tried to kick, but its legs didn't appear to work properly anymore. It swung its antlers back and forth, still threatening the final wolf. Scarlett let another arrow fly, and it sailed directly into the neck of the front wolf. The next shot went wide.

Scarlett reached for another shaft but found only air. Hands shaking, she turned to the wall of the cabin and picked up her workman's hammer from earlier. Scarlett took a deep breath, bellowed a barbaric cry, and charged. The two remaining wolves stopped their savage mauling, took one look at the screaming form rushing toward them, then tucked tail and bolted for the tree line.

The moose readied its antlers as Scarlett approached, but she stopped short of it. The beast tried to stand but fell back into the grass. Blood was everywhere. Much of it pooled around the half dozen wolf carcasses, but a good deal was from the moose. Scarlett looked the giant creature up and down.

"You're kind of cute...aren't you?" Scarlett asked between labored breaths. "I mean...in a misshapen...silly sort of way. But still...kinda cute."

The moose snorted, tried to stand again, and collapsed.

"Hold still. You're hurt."

Scarlett looked around. She wasn't sure what to do for him or if she even should. The moose would probably feed her for a year if she could keep the meat from spoiling.

"Too late for that. I already admitted he was cute," Scarlett said to no one in particular. "Just don't name him, not yet at least."

Unfortunately, she'd already thought of a name: *Roland.*

Scarlett approached slowly, arms wide, palms down. The big moose let out another snort, antlers tipping forward.

"It's all right, big guy," Scarlett whispered. "I'm here to help."

Roland was clearly not convinced.

Dammit! Not Roland—Moose! Moose is clearly not convinced.

He sure looked like a Roland, though.

Scarlett moved closer, slowly resting her hand on one bloody point of his scooped antlers. He shook her hand off and let out a derisive bellow.

Is that right? Can a moose be derisive?

"All right, all right, I got the message."

Scarlett felt her face scrunch up. She could leave him to fend for himself, but he couldn't even stand. Her eyes drifted to the start of her little cabin, and she snapped her fingers.

"Stay right there, big guy. I'll be right back."

Scarlett took two slow steps back, then turned and ran. She darted around the half-built cabin and into the garden. Planting rows of vegetables was the first thing she'd done after arriving on the plateau nearly ninety days ago. She pulled out two handfuls of carrots, three heads of lettuce, and six radishes. Arms overloaded with produce, Scarlett trotted back around front, dropping the occasional vegetable along the way.

Roland was—*Fuck, not Roland!*

The moose still lay there, apparently trying to decide the best way out of his predicament. Scarlett slowed a couple of strides from the downed creature.

"All right, big boy. You're gonna like these. They won't hurt you, and neither will I."

Scarlett dropped all the veggies except one carrot. She stepped forward slowly, the orange treat held out as far as she could reach. Roland readied his antlers, then his nose twitched. Her hand slowly passed the boney points, and he didn't swing them back and forth. He sniffed the strange orange stick twice, then twice more. A surprisingly long tongue snaked out, scooping up the carrot. Scarlett pulled her hand back as Roland devoured the vegetable in two grinds, stem and all.

"Good?" Scarlett asked, hand hovering slowly forward.

Roland shook his antlers at her, and she pulled back. His eyes shifted from her to the pile of vegetables. She could almost see his face flicker between mistrust and greed.

"All right, let's have some more then, eh?"

Scarlett grabbed another carrot and carefully fed it to the big beast, then another, then some lettuce. He ate it all. Scarlett scooped up a radish and held it out. The moose pulled his nose away with a snort.

"That's okay. Kaylee didn't like radishes either." She smiled at the memory of her younger sister. "Used to say they smelled like an old fart."

Scarlett tossed the red vegetable over her shoulder and grabbed another carrot. The moose's eyes widened. She fed it to him and half the remaining vegetables. Slowly and deliberately, she walked around to his flank.

"Let's see what we can do to get you patched up, big guy."

Scarlett pulled off her shirt and ripped it into strips. She wrapped the sleeve around her bleeding forearm, then got to work on the big moose. Carefully, she pushed skin and tissue back into position, tying pieces of her shirt tight around it. Roland watched her warily out of the corner of his eye. Still, he didn't kick or lash out, so that was something.

Needs stitches, Scarlett thought. But that would be pushing her luck tonight.

"I'm sorry, buddy." Scarlett wrapped one hand around the shaft of the arrow and readied the last piece of her shirt to stanch the blood. "This is gonna hurt."

The head came free with a sickening squelch.

A hoof flew at her.

She dropped the cloth, leaping sideways. Wind blew by as the hoof skimmed her midsection with enough force to crush ribs. Scarlett breathed out a sigh, locking eyes with the big moose. He wasn't kicking but still had the leg raised.

"That was for your own good!" Scarlett protested, holding up the bloody shaft.

Roland snorted, tried to stand, and collapsed back into the grass. Scarlett circled back around and gingerly picked up the rest of her vegetables, minus the radishes, of course. She crept closer and fed the produce to him, alternating between carrots and lettuce.

"See, I'm not so bad. Just shot you in the ass, is all," she soothed.

Tentatively, Scarlett reached forward, touching Roland's nose. His big snout followed her hand, bumping and licking. He was only looking for carrots, but at least he wasn't trying to bite.

After a while, Scarlett worked her way back to his flank and pressed the cloth to his still-bleeding butt cheek. Roland nearly tried to kick her again then, but slowly, and with lots of tender words from Scarlett, he lowered his leg. She sat with the moose a while longer, then stood. The time for sleep had passed, so Scarlett gutted and hung the dead wolves from trees. She wasn't happy they were dead but wouldn't let them go to waste, either.

Scarlett's wounds throbbed, and her stomach growled as she worked. By the time she finished, even the raw meat looked palatable.

"Wow, I've been too long on the edge of the world," she said, pushing the savage thought away. "Food will have to wait until the work is done."

Eventually, as the dawn rose, she fell asleep slumped against the cabin wall.

When Scarlett awoke, her hands were still covered in blood, her skinning knife lay at her side, and the big moose still watched her.

The next few days went by in a similar fashion. Scarlett fed Roland, patched him up, and processed the wolves. Little by little, he began to trust her until she was able to treat his injuries properly. One night, she even fell asleep with her head on the massive creature's chest. A few days later, he stood and walked out of the clearing while Scarlett was skinning a pelt.

Roland was back later that night, though, sniffing around for carrots.

Over the next few months, the moose came around at least once a day until finally, he bedded down in her backyard, and Scarlett decided it was time for a fence. They spent the rest of the summer together, growing closer each day.

The next three years flew by, each one bringing them closer than the last. Scarlett finished her cabin, walled off an area for Roland, and built a secondary fence around her vegetables. The big moose had absolutely no concept of future meals and would decimate the entire garden without a second thought if she let him.

The forest was dark, as if an inky black curtain had been pulled across the world.

Scarlett peered from behind the trunk of an old spruce, heart pounding. Nothing moved, so she darted to the next tree. Her feet were small, but her steps sounded loud and intrusive. Her lungs blazed, heaving in ragged breaths as quietly as possible.

Someone was chasing her. Scarlett wasn't entirely sure who, but they were there. She hadn't seen the man, but she'd felt him. Felt his eyes on her. And felt his hunger. An overwhelming sense of dread had filled her, and she'd run. She'd run as fast and as far as she could and was nearly back to the cabin. There, she would be safe.

A flicker of light danced through glass windows on either side of the little green door. No more trees stood between her and it. The open space meant she was almost home, but it also meant exposure to anyone or anything watching from the shadows. Worse yet, Sirius had decided to peek from the clouds and illuminate the clearing with a red glow.

Scarlett took a deep breath, clenched her little fists, and ran.

Time slowed as she approached the door, each step taking longer than the last.

A shadowy form slipped around the side of the cabin, skulking along the wall. Scarlett skidded to a stop as the hulking man's head turned. He stood, impassable, between her and the door. Moonlight illuminated her face as their eyes locked.

For an eternity, he just gazed down at her, then licked his lips, turned, and pushed silently through the green door. Scarlett exhaled, took one terrified step forward to follow, then heard a scream.

It was her own.

Scarlett sat bolt upright in the piled furs of her bed, inhaling sharply through a throat that felt too small. Cold sweat covered her body. She reached up to her neck, hands clasping around the pendant woven into her twine necklace as she tried to calm her breathing. Slowly, her heart stopped slamming, her breath evened, and the constriction of her throat eased.

The fire in the hearth had long since gone out, and the room was freezing. Scarlett threw off the wolf pelts she'd skinned three years earlier, scampered over to the fireplace, and stoked the coals. She shivered and considered getting back under the covers until the cabin was warm.

"No. I've gotta check on Roland."

Logically, Scarlett knew the moose was fine. Still, she grabbed her old coat and slipped on new fur boots. Her coat always seemed to last, but it felt like she constantly replaced boots and the rest of her clothes. Scarlett opened the door and stepped into the brisk night.

The first snow of the year blanketed the plateau and crunched under her feet in the most satisfying way. The cold nipped at her bare legs as she walked around to the backyard and opened the gate. Roland's head lifted, sniffing the air. He was in his usual spot, bedded down next to the house on the wall closest to the hearth.

Scarlett passed by the cold storage, eyes sliding over the compost pile as she approached her big goofy boy. She plopped down between his front leg and head, sinking fingers into his coarse fur. She pressed her face close, then wrapped her arms around his neck.

"I don't know what I'd do if I ever lost you, big guy," Scarlett said as she clutched him.

The big moose snorted but didn't pull away.

"I know. You don't get it. But I've lost people before. People that I loved. It truly is the worst."

6
UNKNOWN

A dead man lay naked on a small sandbar at the bottom of a canyon. Gulls screeched and spiraled overhead, trying to decide if he'd be their next meal. Suddenly, he sputtered. Water spilled from his lips as the first sweet lungful of life pulled into his chest.

Sand slid through his fingers as he flexed them for what felt like the first time. He groaned and tried to open his eyes but found they were sealed shut. The man got to his knees, rubbing away crusted grains of sand to free his lids. Glorious light flooded in. For a moment, he just knelt, taking in all the colors, smells, and sounds of life. He tried to stand, but the muscles lining his body were stiff.

Almost as if they've atrophied.

With tremendous effort, the man stood and stretched.

Where am I? How did I get here?

A much more pressing realization struck him like a fist to the face.

Who am I?

Icy fingers of panic spread through his skin. He pushed them away.

Lose your nerve, lose your life.

The man wasn't sure how he knew the adage, but he was sure it was true.

Maybe something physical will jog my memory.

He looked down. A well-chiseled body, lined with old scars, held him upright.

More like a sculpture than a man. Am I a warrior? A laborer? A circus performer?

He lifted his hands, inspecting them. They looked as if they could squeeze juice from a stone, and his palms were covered in thick calluses.

Perhaps a circus performer is right. Maybe a guide? That'd make sense.

Physically, it fit and explained why he might be in the middle of nowhere.

But where are my clothes?

That made less sense. Then again, it seemed sense was in short supply.

A tattoo on the back of his right hand stood out like an aggravated wound.

A thirteen-pointed star marked the flesh between thumb and forefinger. Each point was divided: one half dark, the other light. A circle of pure white in the middle of the symbol drank in the light side of each point as it tapered inward. He couldn't remember the tattoo's origin but recognized the symbol. The sign of the one true God.

My God?

The man flexed his fingers, watching the symbol stretch in the light.

Apparently so.

Scars marked the flesh beneath the tattoo, but it was impossible to make out the details with the ink imposed atop it.

The mark tells me nearly nothing, but it's all I have to go on for now.

The man let out a long sigh. His identity would have to wait until more immediate concerns were addressed.

Where am I? And where's the nearest town?

There was no sign of anyone, just a sheer wall of rock over ten spans high. Boulders and short bars of sand broke the shallow water as it flowed steadily through the base of the canyon. He moved to the edge of the stream, running a hand along the wall. The stone was water-worn, smooth, and slippery.

Best get out of here before it starts to rain.

Willing his stagnant muscles into motion again, the man began to walk. His stiff calves complained as they pushed him through the wet sand. The sun hung overhead, and he'd have guessed it was summer, except the cool breeze weaving down the canyon told of something else.

Interesting, I still remember the seasons. The same way I remember how to walk.

The man trailed his hand along the wet wall and realized his name wasn't the only thing that escaped him. He couldn't recall anyone he'd known, places he'd been, or meaningful moments in his life. However, he did remember other things. Odd things.

How to play croxix was a good example. It was a complicated game, played with colored stones on a board. He even knew players could combine two sets to accommodate four people. It was a game of strategy, and great military leaders through the ages swore how effective it was to train a decisive mind.

How do I know all that? Yet things that should be far more ingrained are gone?

His mind felt hazy as if awakening from a nightmare, the dregs of which still tickled the fringes of imagination. The past was still there. He could feel it. It was simply walled off and inaccessible.

Is something blocking my memories?

51

He frowned.

No, only the one true God has that kind of power.

The man eyed the sloping canyon walls, searching for a reason God might deny his memories.

No, a tumble into the ravine or a long ride in the river is more likely.

A few minutes later, the canyon straightened again. Ahead, on the right, was a notch in the canyon wall. His heart beat a little faster as he approached, knowing it might be his best chance of escape. The notch was about two spans square at its base, slowly widened as it rose, then tapered back together near the top.

A chimney.

The man wasn't sure how he remembered the term but knew it was right.

He stood there, studying the stone for a moment. It was too wide to reach both sides at once but holds lined the right, growing sparser as the pitch grew steeper. The left side of the chimney was the opposite, with little to no holds near the bottom and large pockets near the lip of the canyon wall.

The man placed each hand on a hold, settled into the weight with his forearms, then began to climb. He kept his arms straight as much as possible, using his hands as a fulcrum and pushing with his legs to the next hold. He moved quickly, knowing time on the sheer face was limited. Before long, the rock grew overhung, and all the holds vanished.

Looks even worse up close than it did from the bottom.

The opposite wall was nearly two spans away, and there was no way he'd reach it. Large pockets pitted the rock there, only slightly over his head. He considered heading back down, but his stiff arms were already burning, and down was always harder than up.

The top of the canyon is only a few spans away.

The ledge above looked good, and he could reach it from the other side of the chimney. The man bent his knees, lowered to a squat, and silently counted.

One.

He pushed with his legs, rocking up and down, eyes locked on the pocket.

Two.

He sucked in a breath.

Three.

He sprang.

Air rushed past him.

Adrenaline coursed through him.

The wall crashed into him.

His hands slammed into the pocket as his feet kicked into flat stone. Pain shot up his toes and into each calf. The pocket wasn't deep, and what should have been a cup was more of a sloping ledge. His left hand came free. He searched blindly with his feet for anything that might take weight off his other hand.

His right hand slid, and he flung his left toward a small outcropping of rock. He caught the smooth stone between his thumb and two fingers, pinching it with all his might. He grunted, grip failing. His toes curled onto a tiny nub, taking a slight strain off his arms.

A high-pitched whine escaped his lips. His whole body quaked as he slowly raised his right foot, matching it in the pocket with his hand. He let go with that hand, moving it up the wall a finger's width at a time. His fingertips scraped a ledge, and he jammed his hand into it. This one was good.

Thank God.

The man sighed, putting pressure on the ledge and testing the hold. The rock didn't crumble. He released the pinch, brought his hands together, one atop the other, and found better placement for his feet.

The last few spans were all overhung, but the handholds were good. The man kept his hips close to the wall as he worked from one pocket to the next. Finally, his fingers found the edge of the slot canyon. In one dynamic motion, he pulled with his arms and pushed off the ledge below him. His chest crested the edge, and he got an elbow on solid ground. With a grunt, he hooked his right heel on the top of the wall, then pulled himself over the canyon's lip.

A mantle.

Another climbing technique and perhaps another clue to who he really was.

He stood and took a few steps away from the sheer rock wall, eyes widening.

Massive trees lined the top of the gorge. They were easily a dozen stories tall, and ten men couldn't have encompassed their base. Thick yellow moss crept up their ancient trunks, and fluorescent teal leaves ran down each branch. The leaves weaved along the bottom of each limb in a strange, zig-zagging pattern, uncurling like flowers in bloom. The trees had actual flowers, too, blossoming randomly from the bark in bursts of deep purple.

Amazing.

The trees reached out and intertwined in a canopy, almost as if they were one giant organism. Ambient light filtered through the web of branches, but there was no way to use the sun or stars for navigation.

No chance of climbing one of these giants either.

The trees were enormous, and their lowest limbs only sprouted seven spans or so from the ground. The man pulled his attention from the trees and looked up and down the river.

Water means life. Best follow it.

Downriver would lead to the sea, upriver to the mountains.

A fishing village, or a farming town?

He decided to head upriver and spent the rest of the day traveling. Long after sunset, he found a hollow between two large boulders and bedded down. Sleep was slow to come and tense, with only the calls of big cats for company in the unknown forest.

Something rustled, pulling the man from the first deep sleep of the night. Dawn light pierced the thick canopy as his heart pumped jittery energy through his veins. A few spans away, a bush quivered. The man stood, fingers twitching for the hilt of a weapon. For some reason, the absence of a blade made him feel more naked than the lack of clothes.

The bush rustled again, and his fists raised instinctively to either side of his face.

One breath went by. Then two. Then, a third.

Nothing.

A crinkling of leaves. Closer now.

The man coiled into a crouch, legs ready to spring.

A furry little brown rodent rounded the corner between the two boulders, cocked its head, then chirped. It had a round body, beady eyes, and a forked tail nearly as big as the rest of it.

The man slowly lowered his hands.

It jumped toward him, fur puffing up to twice its normal size.

"Whoa there, little buddy. Didn't mean to trespass," the man explained with a laugh.

The creature jumped at him again, letting out a chittering protest.

"Yep, got it. Not my woods," he said, backing slowly away.

He'd barely slept a wink but was awake now, so he said goodbye to the little furball and continued along the river. The tiny mammal followed him, sniffing from a distance and chittering whenever he so much as looked at it.

Perhaps he's never seen a human.

The man found a large stick and broke the end, creating a rough point.

Not the fire-hardened spear I could make with a knife and cookfire, but it should do.

A few hours later, he found a thicket full of exotic berries and hooked thorns. He picked a few and tossed them to the little creature.

The furry rodent grabbed them and greedily stuffed them into his mouth.

Seems he's willing to eat them.

The man's belly rumbled, so he plucked a handful of berries and continued. An hour later, the little creature still followed him, occasionally sniffing the air.

Well, you seem okay.

The man took a berry, tossed it into his mouth, then chewed. It was sweet but with a tang akin to a...

Mustard?

It was undoubtedly odd but should sustain him, at least for a time. When his stomach hadn't turned after a couple hours, he devoured the rest despite the strange taste. Later, he found another bush and carefully gathered more fruit. He tossed one to the little creature.

The rodent snatched the berry up with a chirp, then ran back a few spans into the woods.

Little bugger must not be able to get at them with the thorns.

The man threw him another, and the little furball crammed it into his mouth. The creature was similar to a squirrel but bigger, with far longer toes and a tail that split near the tip, ending in two bushy points.

"What should I call you?" the man asked.

The little creature watched warily, eyes shifting from him to the bush.

"Hmm, if you're sticking with me, you need a name." The man scratched his chin. "How about Scrat?"

The tiny beast chirped at him, clearly affronted.

"All right. Stump?"

More chirping as it glanced between him and the bush.

"Okay, okay." The man grabbed two more berries and tossed them over.

"Steve?"

The little creature shoved a berry into his mouth, chewing contentedly.

"Wanted a human name, huh?"

Steve crammed in another berry.

"Well, Steve it is, then."

The man ate some more berries, threw Steve a few more, then gathered a load in the crook of his elbow and continued on.

Later that day, he found a more gradual path back down into the canyon and drank the cool water until his stomach ached. That night, he slept, but not well, and not much. The next two days passed in a similar fashion. He foraged when he could, sharing the berries with Steve. He went down to the river whenever possible to drink. The days blended in his sleep-deprived state, and the not-so-balanced diet took a toll on his stomach and bowels. Somewhere along the way, Steve began to look rather edible.

"No, you're the only friend I've got," the man said.

Steve just sniffed, little head swiveling in each direction.

Looking for a berry bush, no doubt.

The man resigned himself to the mustard berries and continued on.

After nearly a week, the forest thinned, and the monstrous trees gave way to smaller, more familiar pines. A few hours later, even the spruce grew sparse and pointed stumps marked by axe or saw jutted from the soil.

Hope kindled in the pit of the man's stomach.

Civilization. Real food. Maybe even a full night's sleep.

The man climbed a nearby hill, staying low until he peeked over the final rise. Fifty or so structures dotted a hillside ahead, and an enormous barn of a building stood at the summit. Sharpened logs jutted from the dirt, walling off the entire village and lining the streets.

A bit like a porcupine God forgot to finish making.

The spikes wouldn't do much, though, not practically.

So why make them? Hoping to skewer the occasional child playing a game of moons?

As the man surveyed the landscape, a battle unfolded in his mind.

A row of archers, arrows wrapped in pitch-soaked rags on this hill. One line of cavalry waiting in the woods. God. There'd be no stopping the ensuing bonfire.

Still, even if the defenses were foolish, no one would make them for fun.

Vast, snow-covered mountains jutted up behind the village, forming a plateau, and even larger peaks loomed beyond. He exhaled, unable to shake the feeling that they were the tallest things he'd ever seen.

Down here, it could be summer, but up there, it probably never is.

He stared at the village and let out a long sigh. Steve's head swiveled from him to the settlement several times, then he scampered back into the forest.

"Might as well get this over with," he muttered. "Sure hope they're friendly to savage-looking strangers with real believable stories."

The man took a deep breath, gritted his teeth, then set off toward the settlement, naked as the day he was born.

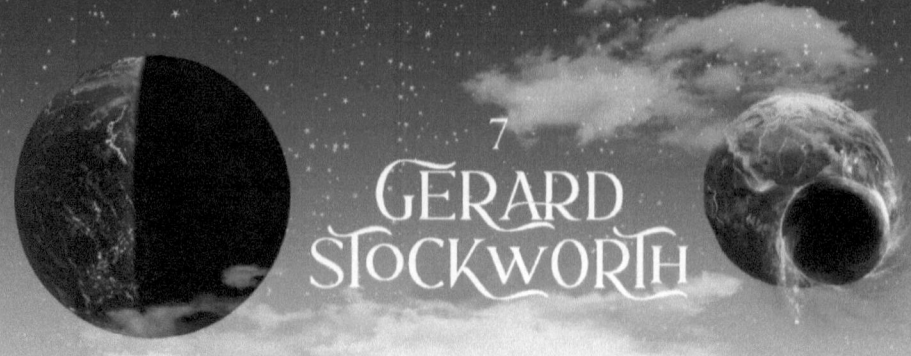

7
GERARD STOCKWORTH

The tracks were everywhere.

Hoofprints churned the mud around a small grouping of trees where horses had been tethered. Boots joined them, then the hooves spread to a full gallop.

Gerard ran a hand over his close-cropped beard, then stood, his piercing blue eyes following the boot prints into camp. They were spread wide, frantically funneling from all over camp toward the mounts. A cookpot lay overturned near the fire, and stew coated the packed ground.

Obviously been some kinda scuffle.

The air smelled of dew, and the tracks were pressed into the dirt after it was churned to mud.

Must've moved last night. Or, perhaps, this morning.

Gerard walked over to a ring of rocks, fingering the small necklace dangling inside his gray flannel shirt: a shield crossed by a sword and spear, the mark of the Justiseer's Guild. The symbol didn't put him above the law but allowed him to circumvent it in pursuit of quarry. He crouched and held a calloused hand over the blackened coals.

Still warm. Only a few hours ahead, then. Half a day at most.

He glanced around the clearing again. Blood spattered the fallen leaves.

Any wound that sprays like that is bound to slow 'em down.

"C'mon, Vigilant, let's go."

The brown-and-white stallion snorted in response.

"I hear you. But we're almost done. Then it's a barrel of oats for you and a nice warm bed for me."

Gerard mounted up.

That isn't what I really want, though…

He scratched the back right side of his neck.

Cut that shit out.

It'd been over a year, and yet the itch persisted. Gerard pushed the notion away.

I haven't slept more than a few hours the last two nights, that's all.

He looked down, focusing on the task at hand instead of ruminating on past mistakes.

The hoofprints were easy to follow. Thirteen horses left camp at a full gallop, and eight veered off into the woods a half mile later.

Giving up the chase? No matter. We're only here for two.

Another half hour passed before the rest of the horses slowed to a stop. Gerard dismounted and circled the tracks, boots squelching in the muddy ground. Bloody bandages lay in the ditch off the side of the road.

He smiled.

Won't be riding much longer with an injury like that.

Vigilant snorted impatiently.

"I know, I know. We're wasting time," Gerard said.

They continued at a trot until the sun fell out of sight behind the rolling hills to the west. Evening quickly turned to night, and Gerard slowed Vigilant to a walk.

Can't have you breakin' a leg, boy. Gerard gave the stallion a pat on the neck.

They traveled for another two hours until a flicker of firelight danced in the distance. Gerard dismounted, and the two of them walked along together. Vigilant was familiar with the routine and almost seemed to soften his hooves as they plodded along.

"You're smarter than most bloody humans, aren't you, old boy?" Gerard muttered.

No response from Vigilant this time.

Gerard led them off the trail and through the trees, circling the campfire. They crossed a babbling brook and crept through the forest, keeping the flickering light barely in sight. Gerard navigated them from the west side of the camp around to the south in a quarter circle, then slowly advanced toward the light.

A few dozen spans from the edge of a clearing, he turned to Vigilant and held up a closed fist. The big stallion stopped and gave his head a shake.

Good boy.

Gerard crept through the bushes toward the crackling light of the fire, stopping a few strides from the edge of a clearing. A small camp was set in the middle of the open ground.

No tents, Gerard noted. *Lookin' to escape quick if the other bandits catch up to 'em.*

The thought of one band of outlaws ambushing another nearly made Gerard laugh, but now was no time for levity.

Three men were still up, and two were sprawled out around the campfire. One was badly injured, with two large punctures in his chest.

Arrows, I'd wager, but it was hard to be sure from here.

Another thug tended to the first man's wounds, tossing bloody bandages into the fire and replacing them with clean dressings. The last brigand leaned against a tree, staring off to the west with a bow in hand.

Lookin' toward the road.

His first mark was one of the two sleepers. The other was the medic, tending to his wounded comrade. Only two men were wanted, but the other three were aiding and abetting outlaws convicted of crimes against House Rocktell.

Windmore's nobility was as ruthless as they come, but they paid promptly and were indisputably the largest source of the guild's income. The OAM was a better client, but contracts with them were rare and had a tendency to get complicated.

Gerard's eyes shifted between the men.

Probably have to kill the other three.

Fortunately, that would be completely legal. House Rocktell only wanted the two alive, but a head would do.

Except a head only pays half the bounty.

A little vineyard filled Gerard's mind—rows of grapes that would always need tending and a big paddock where Vigilant could graze and run.

He let out a long sigh.

It had been Molly's dream originally, but dreams were for the living.

We need to start bringing back more than severed heads, old boy.

Gerard reached out to pat Vigilant's neck but found only air.

He scowled.

Rather bring them back alive anyway.

Removing a head was a bloody business, and carrying one back through the humid bayous was no picnic either. Gerard sighed again. Heads were part of the job, but a part he took no pleasure in.

Sometimes, you gotta get your hands in the mud, though.

Silently, Gerard reached over his shoulder and undid the leather straps holding his bow in place. He checked the string and tips, then slid an arrow from the quiver. The goose-feather fletching was soft and familiar, calming his nerves as he nocked shaft to string. He crept forward toward the edge of the clearing.

Snap.

Gerard's foot found a stick under the layer of leaves.

He froze.

The medic's chin shot up, looking around the clearing. His head cocked to the side, waiting, listening. Slowly, his face relaxed, and he went back to work.

Gerard let out a breath.

Too close, that.

Monotonous snoring competed with the crackling fire.

Safe to assume at least one's asleep.

Gerard inhaled, drew back the string, then loosed. The arrow pierced through the sentry's neck, embedding into the tree he leaned against with a thunk.

The man gurgled, weight sagging onto the shaft.

The bandit tending to his friend looked up.

Gerard's second arrow plunged into his left knee.

He collapsed with a bloodcurdling scream.

The two sleeping men scrambled up in a heartbeat, charging with steel in hand.

Gerard's next arrow thudded into his mark's shoulder, slowing him. The following shaft went wide. The third sank into the man's inner thigh. He took one more step, then toppled headfirst into the packed dirt.

The last man was nearly on him.

I hoped it wouldn't come to this.

Gerard barely got his longsword out as the other blade slashed down. Sparks flew as the swords ground together. The blow tore Gerard's blade from his grip, sending it spinning. He leapt back as the other man's honed edge came back around, nearly cleaving a hunk from his shoulder. The thug stood between him and his blade.

Oh well, never been much good with a sword anyhow.

Gerard gritted his teeth and squared up with the brigand. The thug widened his stance, pulled his sword up, and stepped in. The blade came down again, forcing Gerard back. The man slashed, parallel to the ground. Gerard threw himself back, and the point cut a thin line through the front of his shirt.

Something slammed into his back, knocking the air from his lungs.

Fuck! Where in the eighteen bloody hells—

The sword came down at his neck.

Gerard half rolled, half fell over in desperation.

Thunk.

The blade sank into the bark above him. Gerard sucked in a sputtering breath, trying to regain his bearings. His assailant grunted, yanking on the wedged sword. Gerard pulled himself up and lunged forward, throwing his weight into a kick aimed at the man's groin.

The boot connected, and the brigand doubled over, groaning and swaying. Gerard sucked in another breath, took a second to aim, then brought an elbow down on the back of the man's skull. There was a crack as the bandit dropped to the ground in a heap.

Gerard stepped to the side.

The outlaw stirred, fingers flexing through the soil as he tried to rise.

Gerard brought his heel down on the side of the man's temple.

A sickening crunch filled the night as the bandit's skull caved inward, spraying the forest floor with blood and brain.

Gerard stared at the splatter, chest heaving.

Just like that, the most discernible thing is a messy boot.

He shook his head.

Gods, when did I become less concerned with a life than laundry?

Someone grunted, then cursed, pulling Gerard's attention back to the clearing.

He snatched up his bow and stalked into the camp, bloody boot forgotten.

The bandaged man still sat propped against a pack, his face set in acceptance. Gerard weaved between him and his first mark. The man had an arrow through the thigh and lay in a surprisingly large pool of blood.

Must've hit an artery. At least one head will be swingin' from the saddle.

His second mark, the medic, hopped on his one good leg, attempting to mount a spotted mare. "Fucking son of a cock," the man cursed as the arrow in his knee caught on a stirrup.

Abandoning the friends who stuck their necks out for you?

The thug managed to get his belly onto the saddle, then slipped off the other side and fell in a heap. Gerard approached, pulling the bundle of rope from his belt. As he rounded the horse, spittle hit him in the face. The man had stopped trying to scramble backward and was glaring at him.

Just a vain attempt to keep dignity.

With no change of expression, Gerard wiped off the saliva and kicked the man in the belly. He curled up, clutching his abdomen.

They never do go easy. Even when the chase is clearly up.

Gerard tossed a loop of rope around the man's neck, tightened it, then walked around the horse and threw the rope over the saddle. He hoisted the outlaw up by his neck, ignoring the symphony of gurgles.

"So, you Kal, or Jeff?" Gerard asked conversationally.

No response.

"I mean, what should I call you?"

"Fuck you!"

"Well, that's an odd name, ain't it? Parents didn't like you much?" Gerard asked, dragging on the rope.

"I'm Sigmund!" the man sputtered.

"Ah. Jeff, then, I suppose. Makes no difference to me," Gerard said. "This will all be over in a few days if you don't cause too much trouble. Hells, they might not even kill you."

That was a lie. The Rocktells were practical, brutally efficient, and would never waste food or water on a prisoner for long.

Not when they can just feed him to the birds.

Gerard tossed the rope under the horse's belly, then walked back around it. The man tried to kick him when he bent down for the rope, but Gerard was ready for it. He grabbed the flailing foot and tied the man's neck to his ankles one at a time. With a flick of his wrist, Gerard tossed the rope back under the mare and repeated the process with the man's flailing hands. Once Jeff was fastened to the saddle, he checked to make sure the beast wasn't suffering any discomfort.

"Not your fault that Jeff's been a bad boy," he said, patting the mare on the shoulder.

Gerard walked back into the camp. The injured man was in bad shape. He'd bled out a lot during their ride, and the care he'd been given wasn't strictly professional.

The brigand gurgled something as Gerard approached.

"You're gone, man," Gerard said, squatting and meeting his eye.

The fellow took a deep breath, let it out, then looked away.

"Better a quick death than one lying in the woods till the scavengers find you, right?" Gerard asked.

The man turned back, fear flashing across his face. Slowly, the terror shifted to resolve, though, and the man nodded.

"Do-ith," the brigand sputtered through bloody saliva.

Good, it's always easier when they make the choice.

He wouldn't leave a loose end either way.

Gerard drew his hunting knife and pulled the razor-sharp edge across the dying man's throat in one clean motion. He stepped back as the man's heart pumped what was left of his blood onto the packed dirt in weak spurts.

No point soiling my shirt any more than it already is.

Gerard moved on to his second mark. He was absolutely dead.

"So, you're Kal, huh?" Gerard asked.

No response, of course.

"Well, at least only one of us has to experience this." Gerard bent, unfolded a brown burlap sack, and readied his hunting knife.

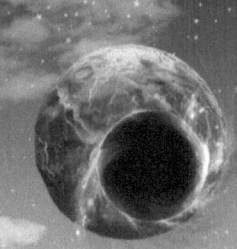

8
THOMAS KEMP

T homas backed away from the spinning purple orb.

The crystal pulsed, and the room imploded. Tankards, bottles, chairs, tables, and even a couple of people hurtled toward the orb. The nearby walls and the roof collapsed inward, slamming into the stone and adding their bulk to its mass.

Thomas grabbed the edge of the nearest table and clung on desperately. His feet lifted from the floor, his body pulling parallel to the ground. The tempest ripped at him as the table he held slowly shifted, rattling across the floor toward the orb.

The patrons were clearly screaming, but there was no sound.

Jarod clung to the back of a chair, body stretched out a span above the floor, hands a ghastly shade of white. The chair wobbled precariously on two legs, the seat wedged under the nearest table.

Their eyes met, and Jarod mouthed the word "Help."

How?

Thomas looked around frantically, but no solution was forthcoming. No theory, no hypothesis, no law of science would get them out of this.

Hells, this isn't obeying laws at—

The wooden legs of Jarod's chair buckled, then broke.

With a soundless scream, Thomas's only friend flew toward the hurricane of energy. He slammed into the conglomeration, followed by the chair, a table, then a piece of the fireplace. Jarod disappeared, lost in the mass of blood and debris.

"No!" Thomas screamed, but even sound seemed to hurtle toward the maelstrom.

A bottle lifted before Thomas's eyes then flew toward him. He tried to jerk his head to the side but was too slow. It struck him in the temple. Dizziness washed over him. His grip loosened, but to let go was to die. Thomas ground his teeth, burning forearms tightening. Two of the table's legs lifted, and his lifeline began to skid across the floor. He clenched his jaw, whole body tensing as he braced for impact.

Everything stopped.

Thomas was weightless, thoughtless, and for once, speechless. Slowly, the rusty cogs of his brain ground back together.

What in the—

He hit the floor with an airless grunt.

The table came down in a clatter of wood and metal. Glass shattered. Timber creaked. Meaty thuds echoed all around as townsfolk fell to the floor. Thomas reached for his head with a groan, then pulled himself up, turning back to the stone.

A monstrosity towered where the crystal once stood.

Chairs, tables, beams, debris, and people all gathered together in one tangled, gruesome mass. The hulking form had no legs, just a torso that rested on the ground, propped up by two immense arms with fists the size of dining tables. A twisted jumble made from the fireplace, an elk trophy, and someone's body formed a head.

The crystal at its center throbbed, casting an eerie purple glow across the ravaged room in a rhythmic pulse. An arm protruded from the thing's side, but the rest of the person was entirely engulfed.

Jarod?

A wail sounded on the left side of the bar, then a wet scream pierced the rubble surrounding the crystal. Thomas took a step toward his friend, then paused.

There's no way he could have lived through—

Black smoke seeped from two cavities in the fiend's head, where eyes should sit.

In a burst of motion, the thing slammed its fists down in a quaking smash. Floorboards splintered, and the stone underneath cracked. Shrapnel and debris flew across the Slippery Fox, colliding with tattered walls and patrons alike.

A board clipped Thomas's leg as it hurtled past, sending him sprawling.

A man abandoned his companions and bolted for the door.

Thomas scrambled back.

The monster's arms bent, bringing its head down to his level. The hulking form stood between him and the gaping hole at the back of the tavern.

He glanced at the door.

Two men sprinted past him.

Bricks from the fireplace, a set of antlers, and charred logs on the monster's head shifted as it opened a lipless mouth and let forth a cataclysmic roar. Gravel and dirt sprayed across the room like spittle from a creature of flesh and blood. Thomas threw his hands up, shielding his face. One of the men attempting to run crumpled to the floor as a stone struck the back of his head.

The temporary awe and wonder finally wore off, replaced by hysteria and dread. Suddenly, everyone was running. Patrons scrambled across the room, hurtled over chairs, and clawed at one another. All relationships evaporated as people headed for the only thing that mattered.

The door.

Thomas sprung to his feet, glancing around the room in utter terror and disbelief. He was at the back of the crowd, with no one between him and the creature.

Is this a dream? Could there—

The hulking fiend shifted, burning black eyes falling on him. Smoke drifted from smoldering embers in the creature's makeshift sockets, searing into his soul.

I don't even believe in souls. The thought was intrusive. *Not fucking helpful.*

The creature stared, relentless eyes assessing.

Intelligence?

Fear wormed through Thomas's skin.

Does it kill for sport? It doesn't appear to have a digestive system—

A gravelly cascade filled the room as the beast lurched into motion. Protrusions broke from its body as the entire wreckage shifted and buckled around the crystal in the middle. It clawed toward him, torso shredding through floorboards as it dragged along the ground.

Thomas turned and bolted toward the nearly clear door, shoving one man aside as he emerged into the chill night air.

The storm had been replaced by pandemonium.

Screams echoed off walls and buildings. Townsfolk ran through the street aimlessly.

Nowhere to go. Except off a cliff into an ocean with no bloody boat for a hundred miles.

Thomas looked around, racking his brain for any other solution.

Nothing came.

Damn the OAM and damn their need to authorize all passage off this island.

He broke into a sprint, deciding to formulate a plan once there was a little distance between him and the monstrosity. He pushed and shoved through common folk who were frantically doing the same.

A crash filled the night.

Thomas risked a glance back. The front of the Slippery Fox was gone, and the two remaining walls were collapsing behind the creature. It scanned the crowd, eyes locking onto him. With a malevolent howl, it lunged forward.

People scrambled, clawing at each other to get out of the way. They weren't quick enough. It flattened men, women, and children with each lurch, smearing them across the cobblestone like jelly across a piece of toast. Thomas pushed the horrendous image away, willing his burning legs on.

Purple light pulsed behind him.

Thomas looked back. The beast was practically on top of him.

Fuck! Won't outrun it in the open.

Thomas ducked into an alleyway, shoving a woman aside as he fled from the hulking formation. A sloppy crunch filled the air behind, and he risked another glance back. The beast lifted its hand, revealing crushed bones and splattered innards. It grabbed the side of a building and tore through the wall, bellowing as it tried to create a path for its immense form.

Thank the fucking gods this alleyway's small.

Thomas sprinted down the narrow path.

With another bloodcurdling roar, the monster hurled itself into the narrow opening. Its bulk scraped along the sides of the alley, collapsing walls and ripping up foundations as relentless hands pulled it ever forward. The alley ended at a cross street ahead.

Thomas darted to the right.

The beast skidded across the ground, hands clinging to nearby roofs, trying to stop its terrible momentum. The massive torso smashed into the wall where the two streets met, and the bottom of the building crumbled. The rest of the structure followed shortly behind, half burying the thing.

Yes! Thomas smiled.

The rubble shifted. A big hand reached out and latched onto a rooftop.

Fuck! His elation quickly fled.

The colossus pulled itself from the rubble, roared, and plowed down the alleyway toward him.

"Fuck, fuck, fuck...fuuuck!" Thomas screamed between labored breaths as the creature's hand smashed down less than a span behind.

The alleyway split ahead. Right led back toward the main street; left led farther into Seafront. He veered left, heading deeper into the labyrinth of narrow streets.

The beast roared, close again.

Gotta get back to the square. The Order will have mounted a defense.

Unfortunately, the OAM's headquarters were a mile or more away.

Why's this thing so intent on me?

Thomas gasped for air as he took three more turns, each one putting a little more distance between him and the monster. He turned another corner and skidded to a stop, nearly slamming into a dead end.

Shit. Thomas turned.

The creature rounded the corner.

Thomas sprinted for the door of a little house on his left. He tried the handle. Locked. He threw his shoulder into it. Pain fissured through his arm, but the door didn't budge.

He glanced back.

A massive hand filled his vision.

Thomas dove sideways.

The creature's hand crashed into the building, nearly flattening him.

Thomas got up as the claw pulled back, taking most of the wall with it. He darted into the now-open building. A woman stood in the kitchen, a cast-iron pan held at the ready. Two exits: a staircase and a back door.

He ran for the door.

The woman swung the frying pan at him.

Thomas ducked. The cast-iron pan clanged into his shoulder. He grunted, shoving the woman off her feet before she could bring the skillet back around for another blow.

We have bigger problems right now, you dirty old coot! He wanted to scream, but there was no time.

Upstairs, a baby let out a wail. Thomas bit his lip, half tempted to do something.

What, though?

The front of the building crumpled inward as the monster barreled inside. Thomas ran through the back door. A moment later, the creature emerged, the structure folded in on itself, and the wailing stopped.

Thomas took turn after turn, running for all he was worth, staying barely ahead of the monster. His side throbbed, his legs ached, and his lungs burned. At some point, he stopped looking back and started judging the creature's distance by the pulsing purple light that bathed the alleyway around him. With each turn, his strength waned, yet the beast never tired.

And why would it? It's not like it's made of flesh and blood. Well, mostly.

Thomas quickly rounded two more corners, widening the gap between him and it. The beast crashed into another building behind him, roaring with frustration. The city square was just a dozen spans past the end of the alley.

Almost there.

Thomas hurtled down the narrow street and into the square.

The OAM headquarters stood across an open field of cobblestone that was oddly empty and void of destruction.

Where's the guard? Where's the resistance? Where's the bloody fucking fountain?

The sculpture of dozens of children throwing water at one another was entirely absent, and large puddles were the only proof it ever existed. Screams and chaos echoed throughout the city, but it was almost quiet here. The door to the barracks hung ajar, swinging back and forth in the wind.

It doesn't make any sense. It should be utter anarchy here.

Thomas pushed the thought away and sprinted toward the open door.

A halberd clattered to the ground to his left.

Good fuck! What now?

He dodged to the right.

A spear nearly landed on his right foot. He jumped away from it. A shield clanged down right in front of him. He vaulted over it, then risked a glance up.

The Trickster loomed above, staring down past hundreds of falling objects.

What in the name of all thirteen bloody gods?

A far-off scream grew loud in an instant.

Clang.

A breastplate hit the ground, cutting the scream off mid-note.

Thomas lurched to the side. "Fucking hells."

Another body, fully clad in metal, slammed into the ground—then another, and another, and another. Thomas weaved back and forth between the plummeting and shrieking people as they smacked into the cobbles. His terror joined theirs as he screamed from lungs with no capacity left for the noise. Bodies continued to rain down, almost landing on him more times than he cared to count.

Thomas glanced back.

Dead OAM soldiers littered the square.

A grinding crunch drew his attention back to the monster as it ripped a chimney from a single-story building at the square's edge. It pulled its arm back with a roar, then brought it forward, releasing the mass of stone and mortar.

Shit.

Thomas planted his heel, splashing up water as he tried to stop. His foot slipped, and he flipped, sprawling onto his back. The chimney soared overhead, gray lines cracking and giving way as the brick structure crumbled. He rolled, ducking as loose material flew overhead.

A deafening clatter sounded as masonry collided with something. Debris pummeled into Thomas's back. Something hard hit the side of his head. He blinked. Dust clouded around him. Something trickled down his temple. He touched it, and his hand came away wet.

Blood?

Thomas's vision swam, and his mind reeled, trying to make sense of the fuzzy red stain.

Mine?

The monstrosity scraped closer.

Where from?

He couldn't tell through the haze and pain. His head throbbed. Nothing made sense. He took a guess—it was all he had left. With tremendous effort, Thomas stood. He stumbled through the rubble, nearly tripping on the corpse of a flattened guard. The door to the barracks materialized a stride ahead, hanging by a single hinge.

Thank the bloody gods.

Thomas lurched through the open door, tripped on a crumpled doormat, and landed in a heap. His eyes flicked to each side, searching the floor for anything useful. He tried to struggle to his feet, then gave up.

What's the point? This was the only place with even a chance of safety.

A pair of dusty black boots, wreathed in smoke, stepped into view.

"Kemp?" someone asked.

Blinking, Thomas looked up. A dark form stood above him. Not only were they dressed in black, but black consumed them. Onyx tendrils writhed from them, and an inky void billowed all around them. Before Thomas could answer, the monster burst through the wall in a shattering of brick and mortar. It raised a fist above him and the stranger. Thomas flinched, eyes closing as he braced for death.

One breath.

Two.

Three.

Nothing happened.

Thomas let one eye peek open. It was frozen. Not just the monster. All of it. Bricks drifted about in the air. Dust lingered without settling. Even splinters lazily floated in the well of weightlessness.

Is this me? Did the magic finally manifest, like Father promised?

Thomas slowly uncurled from his fetal position, trying to maintain concentration. The shadowy stranger held up one smoking hand toward the straining creature, then waved it.

The monster shattered.

Pieces of the Slippery Fox crumbled away in all directions. Jarod's torso thumped to the floor next to Thomas. The purple orb held in stasis for a moment, still pulsing, then plummeted. It crashed through two floors, embedding into the foundation below.

Tears streamed down Thomas's face.

Are those for you?

Jarod's mangled face stared back at him.

Or are they tears of relief?

He wasn't sure. His emotions were all coiled up like a snake in his belly, and it was hard to analyze anything through the throbbing in his head.

"If it's any consolation, I didn't know you would be here," the stranger said in a tone devoid of emotion.

"What?"

"A Kemp. I didn't know you would be here. It doesn't matter. It'll all be over soon."

The words churned through Thomas's mind.

What did they mean? Gods, my head hurts.

"What will all be over soon?" Thomas finally asked.

"Everything."

Everything?

All of a sudden, Thomas was falling.

Wait, that isn't right. I'm on the ground.

But he wasn't. He was falling.

Thomas's orientation shifted, and he fell through the hole the monster had ripped through the roof and plummeted up into the night sky.

Up toward the clouds that recently soaked Jarod and him.

Up toward the three moons Walter fucking Raft had theorized about.

Up toward the same moons he'd postulated on earlier. Postulation that certainly hadn't included anything about this. Thomas hurtled away from Seafront faster and faster, and soon, the island was the same size as the Trickster above.

The moon's eyes gleamed, and for a time, Thomas was lost in frantic thought, trying to reason a way out of an impossible situation.

A moment of weightlessness hit him.

Thomas puked. Then he was falling again.

Truly falling.

His heart hammered frantically against his ribs as gravity reasserted its relentless hold. Thomas prayed now. He prayed to every god he didn't believe in, the old ones and the new. Truthfully, he knew they wouldn't save him—probably *couldn't* save him.

Either way, no one answered.

Thomas tried to scream, but the words were lost, left somewhere far above.

Pull yourself together, man!

Thomas slapped himself in the face.

He tried to concentrate, focusing on the power deep within. He tried to make sense of the crumpled soldiers littering the square. He tried to push against the ground, and for half a second, he thought he might be slowing.

Thomas collided with the cobblestone, and everything went dark.

9
DAVID TRUEHEART

The Coliseum loomed over David as he stared down at the sealed letter. His gaze shifted up, meeting Tanya's. She cocked an eyebrow, watching him expectantly as brass slaves drowned in the fountain behind her.

"Should I open it now?"

"That's the general idea," she said.

David shielded the letter with a hand as he tore it open, eyes consuming the precise, flowery script. The letter was folded into three sections. The first paragraph was scrawled out on the upper third of the page, and another seal held the bottom two-thirds together.

To our potential associate,

We are willing to make good on your debt with the Freemen but require two tasks in return. The first is detailed in this letter below the second seal. The second, simpler task will be given to you after completion of the first. If this does not suit you, return this letter to your contact before reading on, and we will consider our business concluded. Of course, your debt with the Freemen will not be paid, but neither will you incur a new obligation from us. If you decide to continue, be aware that the inability to complete either job will be seen as a sign of insurrection against our organization.

David's eyes settled on the seal.

I rolled the dice to get here. Might as well roll 'em again.

He traced the wax with his thumb, considering all his recent blunders.

Life can only dish out cat eyes so many times.

He flicked open the wax, unfolded the remainder of the letter, and read.

We consider the breaking of the previous seal to be a binding agreement between you and our organization, and we're glad to see you trust us enough to commit without receiving all the details. We will try to honor that trust by giving you a relatively simple second assignment once you have completed the task specified below:

You are to infiltrate the Freemen's Guild and acquire a green ledger for us.

A retired gladiator named Odin is one of two men in charge of the guild. A reliable source confirmed his office is in the highest room of the Freemen's Tower. The document will likely be in that room. However, to be clear, your assignment is not to search Odin's office. Your assignment is to retrieve his ledger. Once you finish this task, return here at midnight to receive your final assignment.

You have forty-eight hours.

BURN AFTER READING.

David reread those final three words, then pulled out flint and steel and sparked the letter.

The parchment ignited easily despite the rain.

Oiled paper or some such.

David watched the letter burn until the flames licked at his thumb and forefinger, then dropped it to the wet cobblestone.

Someone cleared their throat.

He looked up.

Tanya stood there with crossed arms, tapping her foot impatiently. "Anything I need to know about in there?"

"Yep. Said we're supposed to head to the Gauntlet. There's an important client we need to meet," David responded.

"The *Ivory* Gauntlet? Isn't that a gambling hall?"

"Yep, we're goin' undercover," David said, trying to keep a grin from his face. "The note said you're to accompany me and hang all over me until the place closes down. Apparently, we gotta make a big show of it, too."

"The assignment said I should accompany you?" Tanya's face was a mask of skepticism as she glanced down at the burned scrap of paper.

"Yeah, said you need to lay it on thick, too. I mean, really go all in."

"They said 'go all in'?" Tanya asked, eyebrows rising even higher.

"Well, I'm not sure they used those words *exactly*. I don't have a perfect painter's memory, but that was my interpretation."

Tanya fixed him with a stare, eyebrows narrowing.

"You ready? We need to get there soon," David urged.

"You always this full of shit? Or only after midnight in the bloody pouring rain?"

"And under the Trickster," David added.

"That, too."

Silence.

David held it together as long as he could, but a smile finally crept across his face. "Pretty much always, I'd say."

"Fucking bards," Tanya cursed, turned, and began to walk away.

"You're still welcome to join me at the Gauntlet!" David called after her.

Tanya disappeared into the shadows that clawed from the Coliseum.

David chuckled, turned, and headed back to the Rooster.

He went straight through the front door even though folk would still be up. They might even recognize him, but odds were better they'd be too drunk to stand. Besides, he was worried about being followed to the meeting, not from it.

If someone managed to tail me, then those chips are already in the pot.

David decided it didn't matter. No one else could've read the letter.

Best case, they overheard our conversation and are headed to the Gauntlet now.

The Rooster was even less crowded than David anticipated, and the only three people still lingering were ass-over-the-cookfire drunk. He passed through the common room, met Rob's eye, and exchanged a nod. David stopped at the landing, considering the prospect of a drink. Ultimately, he decided against it and trudged up the steps, dripping water onto the worn wood.

A door banged open in front of him.

He jumped back, heart racing, hand tangling on the hilt of his blade.

A night-cat stumbled into the hallway, clutching a tiny piece of fabric in one hand. A single middle button held her shirt together, and she appeared to have misplaced her pants.

"Fuck you, too!" the woman yelled back into the room, then pulled her shirt open and waggled her tits through the door. "Last time you'll be seein' these!"

The woman turned, and their eyes met before David could look away. He didn't recognize her, but there was little doubt she recognized him. The woman smiled, slammed the door, and swaggered over.

"Like what you see, sweetie?" she asked, bending over and slipping on the tiny scrap of fabric that was apparently a skirt.

David smiled. "Very nice. Not in the market, though."

"Never know till you try, darling," she shot back.

"Perhaps another time," David said, slipping past her.

He didn't have anything against night-cats. They were good for business, after all, and attracted men with a bit of stone who weren't real eager to keep it.

Men kinda like me...just with a different sort of vice.

Anyone with a loose chip or two was always good for the musician, though, and a bard was undoubtedly good for them as well. A night-cat's ventures wouldn't be as successful without a tavern, copious amounts of ale, and good spirits.

A symbiotic relationship I have with the ladies of the night.

David smiled.

That might make a good song, but how to title it? Bards and Ladies o' the Night?

No, that was no good.

The Night-cat and the Bard? Better, but not quite.

Chords of Cats and Cocks. He chuckled.

The name wasn't perfect, but like most things in life, it would do until something better wandered along.

David hummed out a new tune as he headed down the corridor, unlocked the door to his room, and stepped in. He scanned the chamber, just as Aunt Jocelin had taught him. Everything appeared untouched, so he stripped off his wet garments, tossed them haphazardly onto the floor, and tumbled into bed.

When David woke, the morning had come and gone.

Not the worst thing, since I'll be up late tonight.

Still, a lot needed doing with not much time to do it. David rolled out of bed, pulled on dry clothes, and headed downstairs.

The common room was already crowded with carpenters, masons, and blacksmiths enjoying their midday meal. They were a raucous bunch, constantly tossing insults from table to table and roaring with laughter.

"Ah, here comes David for a song!" Glen called from the masons' table. He was a monster of a man with a red beard and unkempt hair.

"Not today, Glen. I've got errands to run."

"Well, ain't that some shit," Glen said, looking at his crew.

David walked over to the counter.

"Morning, Eland." David placed his palms on the bar. "You got anything back there I can take for the road?"

The innkeeper's daughter looked up from polishing a glass and gave him a warm smile. "Of course." She pulled a loaf of bread from under the counter, carefully sliced off two pieces, and threw them into a wood-fired oven behind her. "Freshly baked this very morning," she said cheerfully.

"Thank you, Eland. You're the best."

"I know. Honey?"

"Please."

A moment later, Eland peeked inside the oven, pulled out the toast, and drizzled honey across it. She turned to the side, grabbed a metal can, and gave each slice two cinnamon shakes before passing the toast across the bar.

David took a deep breath and felt his mouth water.

"Enjoy." She gave him another sweet smile.

"Thanks again." David turned, walking toward the door. "Oh, and Eland," he said, turning back.

Eland quickly averted her eyes.

Was she just checking me out?

David smiled. "You have a wonderful morning."

"You, too, David," she said with a flush and a cautious twitch of the corner of her mouth.

David tipped his toast to her and left the Rooster, chuckling.

The streets were wet, and the sweet smell of rain lingered in the air. David happily hummed out a new tune between bites of his toast, meandering toward the center of town. He passed by shops, nodded to busy laborers, and smiled at pretty ladies.

His toast was long gone by the time he arrived at the Coliseum.

At least the slaves are no longer drowning.

David took a left at the massive structure and continued until the smell of forges and workshops filled his nostrils. The Industrial District was home to blacksmiths, lumber mills, guildhouses, and other businesses that didn't peddle to the general public. It wasn't a place he frequented often, so he stuck to the main road.

After another half hour, he spotted the Freemen's Guild on the right.

The structure was massive, easily engulfing three warehouse blocks, and looked more like a fortress than a guildhouse.

This will be difficult.

David scratched his head.

What was I expecting? A lovely long hall filled with ale and good cheer?

The guild was made to hold people and train them to kill, not host a banquet.

Hard to get in, even harder to get out.

David walked around the building slowly, inspecting anything and everything.

Four stone walls surrounded the compound, and thorn-covered vines weaved up each sheer face, coiling like thousands of snakes. David reached out, thumb hovering over a glistening red point, then pulled his hand away.

Best not tempt fate. Might be toxic.

Men grunted, and metal clanged inside as steel met steel.

An open courtyard, then.

The only other thing visible from outside was a large tower spiraling upward at the far end of the compound. The spire must've stood ten spans and was easily double the height of the walls.

That must be the tower the letter referenced.

The spire was thankfully free of vines, but there was no way to get to it without scaling the outer wall. Windows were cut into stone at each floor and filled with real glass, unlike the shuttered openings of common folk.

David nearly scoffed.

At least the Freemen are frugal with their blood money.

Breaking those windows would be dangerous and, more importantly, loud.

Still, it's the best point of entry so far.

David circled the rest of the building, searching for better options. Three of the four walls surrounding the courtyard were flat stone with nothing for company except the vines latticing up them. The fourth side housed a great wooden door reinforced with riveted iron. The Freemen's sigil was cast in an iron disc at the door's center, a man on one knee with a hand pressed over his heart and head bowed.

Their sigil does invoke a bit of courage and loyalty, unlike the Freemen's Guild itself.

A smaller door was set into the stone wall next to the enormous oak slab, and a guard stood at attention between the entrances.

This place is tighter than Rula's butthole. No wonder Mystery-Hips doesn't want to infiltrate the compound herself.

David's eyes shifted from the guard to the vine-covered walls and finally settled on the tower.

If I fail, then there's no need to pay off my debt. Smart bet. Either way, they win.

David watched the building for another few hours. Occasionally, the guard would open the door, letting someone in or out with a nod or greeting.

Finally, a cart pulled up to the gate, and the guards came out and chatted with the driver for a while. They pulled apart every barrel and rummaged through the food stores on the man's wagon before finally waving him in.

So, the front gate's pretty much out. I'm gonna need some gear.

On the way back through the Industrial District to the Rooster, David asked around and got the name of a glazier. He went to the little shop and procured a glass cutter, then stopped at a general outfitter and bought a few dozen spans of rope. His feet betrayed him after that, and he found himself in front of the Ivory Gauntlet.

David stared at the gambling hall with undisguised longing.

My debt will be settled soon...or I'll be dead. So, what will a few more bets matter?

A white gauntlet hung above the door, swaying in the afternoon breeze. The paint around each interlocking piece was old, weathered, and chipped.

Maybe just a game or two?

David let out a long sigh.

There's no such thing as a game or two.

With more than a little effort, David pulled his eyes away from the iron mitten and let his feet slowly carry him down the familiar path between the Gauntlet and Rooster.

David spent the rest of the day preparing upstairs, eating, and playing a few songs in the common room. When night finally fell, he excused himself from an upset crowd, gathered his things, and left the Rooster through the front door. David had no intention of going straight to the Freemen's Guild, so he didn't take the same precautions as the night before. He had one dagger in his boot, another tucked up his sleeve, and a straight, short sword at his waist.

Hopefully, I won't need the blade.

David was no expert swordsman, but he knew which end to hold.

Aunt Jocelin made sure of that.

She was a retired city guard and had been like a second mother to him until he started gambling away his life like his father.

David took the back alleys instead of the main roads, slowly weaving toward the Freemen's Guild. The sky was full of clouds again, and the Trickster was completely obscured.

Thank the gods.

David looked down at his normally deft hands. They were already shaking. He flexed each one, trying to calm his nerves.

I guess this one's for all the marbles.

It would be death if he failed. Either from the Freemen or whoever Tanya worked for. The only other option was to get captured and handed over to the Rocktells, which would likely be worse than a blade.

No, definitely worse, he decided.

Something clattered in the alleyway behind.

David wheeled around, eyes scanning the street. A can spun on the cobbles, wobbling, before finally rolling to a stop.

Nothing else moved.

Maybe my cloak brushed it as I walked by?

Despite the justification, a shiver worked its way up David's spine, and a queasiness bedded down in the pit of his stomach.

Tonight's not a night for chances. Especially when chance is what landed me in this mess.

David shook his head. He could still hardly believe he'd lost so much stone on such a winning grip of paper and ink.

It had just felt like such a sure thing.

David pulled his thoughts away from the card table and back to the alleyway.

The narrow street forked ahead. He walked briskly and turned right, eyes darting about in the dim light. A nook filled with refuse caught his attention.

Not a great hiding place, but it'll have to do.

David bent, recoiling as the smell of piss filled his nostrils. He exhaled, grimaced, then pulled back the first layer of garbage and tossed it aside. Quietly, he brushed away an old coat and dug through tattered linens.

"Fuck," David muttered as a mangled scrap of metal clattered to the cobblestone. He glanced back the way he'd come, but nothing lurked in the shadows.

David stepped into the hollow, crouched, and cringed. The smell of urine permeated everything. With a shake of his head, he grabbed the disgusting old coat and pulled it over his head. He pushed the sleeve aside, peered out, and waited.

Silence.

His thudding heart and sharp breath sounded incredibly loud. He covered his nose and mouth with a hand. It didn't seem to help with the noise, but it certainly helped with the smell.

Minutes went by.

Nothing. No movement, no sound, no sign of anyone.

Probably just my cloak, or maybe a rat rooting around in that can.

David patted the dagger in his boot. Touching it filled him with a sliver of control, something he felt so seldom these days.

No one came around the bend.

This is a waste of time, and now I stink.

Still, something held him back. David counted in his head. The seconds dragged by like minutes, and the minutes dragged by like hours. His heart slowly stopped its frantic dance, nearly returning to its regular rhythmic thump.

David took a deep breath, satisfied enough to leave his hiding place.

A slight scuff sounded from behind, like a leather sole on stone.

David's heart began its overexuberant pumping again. His hand tightened around the hilt of his knife. He waited, eyes wide, ears straining.

The Trickster chose that moment to peek through the clouds, shedding a red glow onto the cobblestone.

A shadow crept into the alleyway, then a set of boots stepped into view. The figure stalked forward on silent feet, passing by his hiding place, then stopped. The silhouette's head shifted left, then right. Finally, he turned, hooded gaze locking on him.

Time to fight.

David's grip tightened around the hilt of his knife, and he prepared to spring.

The figure turned away, looking down the alleyway. David's thighs burned, yet he dared not move.

Not yet.

The stranger bent, examining the ground where David might have passed. He scraped his fingers along the stone, then brought them into the moonlight.

He's not gonna leave—time to ante up.

David lifted the old jacket, silently standing on screaming muscles. He glanced up. The Trickster gazed down. Aura was at its right side, pulling the red moon's customary grimace into a sadistic smile. David took a step forward and undid the strap on his sleeve. The dagger slid into his right hand. His heart slammed against his ribs, feeling as if it might burst from his chest at any moment.

The stranger shook his head. David loomed over the hooded figure as the Trickster loomed over him.

Something tugged at his guts.

The silhouette slowly stood.

David's teeth clenched.

The figure looked up and let out a little shiver.

The Trickster leered down knowingly.

David thrust the point of the dagger up into the stranger's ribs. He gurgled and tried to speak, but David cupped a hand over the other man's mouth. Countless hours of work with the strings showed their darker side as sinuous muscles held in a muffled scream.

The stranger reached feebly for a weapon, but there was little strength in the movement. Blood pulsed onto David's hand in rhythmic beats nearly in time with his own heart.

They're dancing together now, our two hearts. The invasive thought drifted unbidden into his mind. *Well, aren't we poetic? Morbid as all fuck, but poetic.*

David glanced up, half expecting the Trickster to be doing a jig of its own.

The moon was gone, though. It had fled, leaving him to hold up the figure by the tip of a blade. David let his arm relax. The body slid off his knife and crumpled to the stone. He stared at the lifeless heap as a dark stain latticed between the cobblestones.

A spiderweb of blood. Guess I'm the spider.

David's hands were somehow steady now. His right was covered in red; his left could have just been washed.

I killed him. Shouldn't I feel something...more?

With a shudder, he stepped away from the body, mind racing almost as fast as his heart.

I'll figure this out later. Write a fucking song about it. Work it out of my system.

Most likely, the stranger was an agent hired by the Freemen.

He would've killed me, given half a chance.

David doubted it was true, but the thought made him feel a little better.

If whoever sent him finds the body, they'll have questions.

It occurred to David that he wasn't even sure this was a man. He hadn't gotten a good look at their face. With the tip of his boot, he rolled the corpse over. There wasn't much light, but the beard was a good indicator.

Was he in the Rooster last night?

David frowned.

Does it even matter anymore?

He dragged the corpse to the pile of refuse, stuffed it into the newly made hole, then grabbed the smelly jacket and tossed it over the body. No doubt someone would find it, but hopefully, whoever did wouldn't know the man was following him. Murders were commonplace in Windmore, and authorities might simply burn the body and move on.

Now, if I'd killed a horse, that'd be another matter.

The Rocktells took equicide pretty seriously.

David let out a long-suffering sigh. The night wasn't off to a great start.

Things usually get a whole lot worse before they get any better.

The intrusive thought didn't even belong to him this time. It was his father's instead. As a teenager, David had rolled his eyes each time his father said it, but as he got older, he'd seen it come true time and time again.

A Trueheart Truism.

He shook his head.

Good thing the old devil never coined that term.

David nearly laughed until his eyes found the corpse again.

He glanced up, expecting to see the Trickster, but the red moon and its purple sister were obscured by clouds again. His eyes shifted back to the blood-smeared cobbles.

This is going to haunt me, isn't it?

A channel of blood slowly pooled against the tip of David's boot. He pulled it away.

I didn't have a choice.

That was a lie. He'd never been a good man, but he hadn't been a killer either, and there was always a choice.

Choices like sweetening the pot or sitting down at the table in the first place.

No one could see what he was about to do tonight, though, not if he wanted to keep his right hand. An image of his father flashed through David's mind. His left hand was outstretched, clutching a cup. His right hand, just a stump, lay useless in his lap—the same hand that used to pluck the strings.

David shook away the image with a shiver.

Just gotta hope the next pool of blood left to dry on the cobbles tonight isn't mine.

10
UNKNOWN

A whistle sounded from up the hill. A dozen paces later, a gong slammed. The sound reverberated through the entire settlement and lingered in his ears.

Doesn't seem good.

The clang should've been the loudest thing he'd ever heard. But deep down, the man knew it wasn't. He'd heard cavalry thundering across a muddy field. He'd heard a thousand swords clattering against wood and steel. He'd heard dams break and the roar that followed. All of them would've put the gong to shame.

Still, he was reasonably sure the clang was for him.

Not much to do except keep walking.

The man only took a few more steps before three people charged down the hill. They ran heedlessly around the sharpened logs embedded in the dirt as if one misstep wouldn't be their last. Two of them carried axes—the kind more suited to chopping wood than to battle. The third, a short and stocky man, dropped what he held and sprinted headlong down the little embankment ahead of the others.

Time slowed to a crawl. The sensation was familiar, though why, he couldn't say.

Could just step to the side. Leave him sputtering in the dirt.

The man let out a long sigh and felt his shoulders loosen.

This needs to happen. The little guy sure is fast—

The stout man slammed into him mid-thought, and they careened through the air. They hit the ground and rolled, tossing up dirt and grass. The stocky man came up on top with a furrowed brow and a fist raised.

"Who are ye...and what's yer business...ye naked git?" His accent was thick, his breath labored.

Good questions. Too bad I've no good answers.

"What's yer name?" the stout man yelled.

At least I understand him.

The men with the axes had closed the distance and were observing the one-sided wrestling match.

"I said, what's yer name?" Spittle flew from the stout man's mouth.

The other two men leaned in, clearly more keen to use their axes than to listen.

"Na—" The man's mind reeled. "Na—Nathan," he stammered. "My name's Nathan."

It probably wasn't, but it was a name, as good as any other.

The burly man balled his fist, eyes narrowing.

"And what's yer purpose...*Naathaan?*" His words dripped with suspicion.

"Actually, I have no idea," the man, now named Nathan, said.

Would I believe that? Doubtful. Just have to hope they see my conviction.

"I woke up on the side of the river and have been searching for some sign of humanity for nearly a week," Nathan explained. "I can't remember anything before that."

More villagers approached, forming a loose circle around them.

"I don't like the way this one talks," the stout fellow growled. "Yer not from 'round here, are ye?"

Is he daft? Nathan wondered, then decided to try again.

"Well, I don't think so, but truthfully, I'm not sure. As I said, I woke up—"

"Aye, I remember what ye said," the man interrupted. "Quite a convenient story that is."

"Convenient?" Nathan repeated.

"I say we kill 'im and be rid of this outsider with 'is silver tongue and 'is fancy stories." The man looked around at the gathering townsfolk. Murmurs of assent rippled through the crowd. Nathan's muscles tensed as he prepared to fight.

I was hoping for a roof over my head, but not one made of dirt.

Nathan got ready to roll onto his side and squirm from beneath the other man.

Tuck and curl. Go for the nose to incapacitate. The one on the left looks less eager. Take the one on the right. Try to maim, not kill. Get the axe. Threaten your way free. Fight the group only if necessary.

The plan flew through Nathan's mind, concrete and logical, yet a fury also built deep behind his eyes. He took a deep breath. It was time, and things were about to get messy. Nathan started to roll.

A loud whistle pierced the air.

Silence fell over the gathered villagers, and Nathan hesitated.

All heads turned back toward the village, including the stubborn bastard straddling him.

Nathan waited, despite his better judgment.

"There won't be any killing today, not unless this man starts it." A middle-aged man stepped from the crowd, draped in the pelts of predators. The hood of his cloak was fashioned from a panther's head and the teeth jutted down, intersecting his eyes. His pants were made from a spotted pelt, and his bare chest was brawny despite his age.

Some sort of shaman? No, too muscular for a typical priest.

Nathan glanced at the man's right hand.

No tattoo, no scar.

"I have heard the voice of Pirel," the man bellowed.

Pirel? Nathan wondered. The name was somehow familiar, yet its meaning eluded him.

The man looked around, letting the message sink in a moment. "She has spoken to me, and I have listened. She told of a man from the forest, a man who would save us from our plight."

There was another pause as Nathan's new name spread through the crowd. Many of the villagers watched him suspiciously. Others' eyes widened. The murmurs were nearly deafening.

"Pirel didn't mention memory loss or…nudity, but our gods work in mysterious ways," the shaman continued. He had an accent, too, but it was far less pronounced than the man still atop him.

"I believe this is that man!" the shaman boomed.

"That's tigershit!" the man on top of Nathan yelled. "He's clearly in league with it!"

"Horinth! I vouch for the one called Nathan and take full responsibility for him and his actions," the shaman said.

"No, I says we vote on it. I don't trust 'im, or 'is story."

"There is no need for a vote, not today," the shaman calmly corrected. "I have vouched, and if that is not enough for you, we can settle this in the ways of old."

The villagers fell silent. Horinth released Nathan, stood, and walked over to the shaman. His jaw was tight, and he leaned forward, jabbing a finger at the other man's chest.

"Fine! But 'e's *yer* responsibility then, *Ray*-lor." Horinth nearly spat the name, then stormed from the circle of villagers.

Nathan stood, dusting himself off as the shaman approached.

"You truly have no idea where you come from?" the shaman quietly asked.

"Not a clue." Nathan stood naked in front of most of the village. The majority of the women pointedly looked away, but some were more bold.

He almost winked at one of them but managed to force back the strange reflex.

What in the hell was that?

"Pirel has smiled on us this day," the shaman raised his voice again.

Chatter rose from the gathered villagers.

"Could he save us?"

"Is he really the one?"

"The culler of darkness?"

The many voices grew to an incomprehensible roar.

What troubles these people? What exactly do they think my role is in this little 'prophecy'? Who's Pirel, and why does that name sound vaguely familiar?

So many questions. So few answers.

Someone stepped forward, handing him a shawl. Nathan accepted the garment and wrapped it around his waist. Suddenly, a wave of exhaustion washed over him, and his stomach growled.

"Is there somewhere we can speak privately?" Nathan asked the shaman. "Maybe over a meal and after a bit of rest? I've been traveling for a week with nearly nothing to eat and no sleep due to the yowling of predators."

More murmurs spiraled through the crowd.

"Unfortunately, there are far more terrible things in the woods than big cats. Worse yet, the forests are no longer ours." The shaman's tone was somber, but he forced a smile onto his lips. "But let's get you a meal and a bed. We can discuss all that tomorrow."

The two men walked up the hill as the crowd dispersed.

"Who do the forests belong to, then?" Nathan asked skeptically. "Pirel?"

If the shaman noticed Nathan's doubt, he showed no sign of it.

"They used to belong to her, but no longer...now, they belong to *it*."

II
TANYA
RINGHOLDER

It really is a terrible likeness of me, Tanya thought as she stared at the Wanted poster pasted to the Coliseum wall.

The flyer displayed a generically beautiful woman with long blond curls, pouty lips, and an overly made-up face. Tanya wasn't surprised they'd gotten her lips and hair all wrong. The wig and fire ant venom were reason enough for that.

How did they screw my nose up so badly, though?

Bold, unadorned script marked the bottom of the page:

WANTED: Alive for questioning. NAME: Unknown.

At least they don't still think I'm Evelyn Stolle.

If they were that daft, it might have caused an all-out war between the Rocktells and the Stolles.

Tanya walked back over to the fountain and sat on the rim. She watched the moon, using it to track the passage of time as the night dragged on. Most people avoided meeting the Trickster's gaze, but it was honestly a good way to tell the time. It would wax through the evening, was full at midnight, then wane until winking out in the morning.

A man wobbled into the square, singing something incomprehensible about a big-breasted bosom and a barrel of barley.

Big-breasted bosom?

Tanya shook her head. It made no sense.

Hopefully, that's just the drunkard's version of the song.

Still, she watched the stranger for a while, ensuring he wasn't there for something more nefarious. Eventually, she decided he was just a drunk who forgot his way home. She was always on the lookout for folk who might be hiding something these days. At first, she thought David was concealing something, but eventually decided his secret was only the bulge in his britches.

Tanya snorted, causing the fresh wound in her side to throb.

Silly boy's in over his head...and these *waters have sharks.*

The shifting silhouette from earlier invaded Tanya's mind, and she pulled her coat tighter.

She wanted to leave and get out of this bloody rain. There was no way David would finish the job in less than twenty-four hours.

Probably no way he'll finish it at all.

Tanya let out a long sigh. She couldn't leave—orders needed to be followed.

Even if those orders are idiotic.

The swaying drunk nearly tipped into the fountain.

Perhaps, especially if they're idiotic.

Tanya took another deep breath. Her wound throbbed again, a constant reminder of earlier mistakes. It was cool to the touch. That was a blessing, at least, and a good sign it was free of infection.

Damn, it hurts like the thirteen hells, though.

Tanya's first assignment had gone according to plan, no thanks to Reynolds. He should've had the bartender tell David to meet her at the fountain, but he was still clearly pissy about the fire at the Rocktell estate.

Her second assignment was another story.

That's when things went off the rails.

She frowned.

Why, though?

Tanya thought back to earlier that afternoon after first meeting the infernal bard.

Knock-knock.

Tanya waited a few heartbeats, then knocked three more times.

A slat opened with a grind. "Spring and fall always stay the same," Tom said, one shallow eye peering out.

"Come on, Tom. It's Tanya, surely you can see that," she replied.

Tom sighed. "Spring and fall always stay the same."

Tanya rolled her eyes. "In everything but color and name."

Damn rhyme doesn't make a bit of sense.

The door swung open, and she walked past Tom into the Lance's long guildhall. Tanya felt Tom's eyes linger on her long after the latch clicked back into place. The looks always made her a little uneasy, but she couldn't show fear in this den of jackals.

Tanya hadn't always looked this way. Once, she'd been a gangly little street rat, cutting purses in the Severance Quarter of the capital.

Me and every other orphan with a lick of dexterity and a dash of boldness.

Jack's and Ted's faces floated through her mind, smiling and full of life. That was before the guards knocked their teeth out, before she'd found them face down in the Channel, and before their faces haunted her dreams. Her childhood best friends had never treated her differently, but that was ages ago, and their bloated bodies had long since gone to the vermin.

Everything changed when Tanya started to develop in her teens. Suddenly, she wasn't a forgettable grime-covered girl anymore, and the men of Norinspire began to take interest. After that, being a pickpocket only got harder.

Boards creaked under Tanya's feet as she headed upstairs, lost in thought. An image of Old Ned's face returned to her, and she shuddered. She could still smell his foul breath, see his yellow teeth, feel his hand pushing her against a wall outside the Cruel Crab.

Once Tanya realized he wasn't the type of man to take no for an answer, she took action instead. She'd given him a kiss, unlaced his britches, then pulled the knife she used for cutting purse straps and took the stones between his legs. He doubled over, and she jammed the stiletto into his exposed neck twice, then ran. A week later, she overheard two men laughing about how Old Ned finally messed with the wrong boy.

A muffled yell down the hall interrupted Tanya's thoughts.

She perked up, creeping forward silently.

"I don't know how it happened! Surely, you see, this was out of my hands. W-we did the work...it just...w-well," someone stammered behind the door to Reynolds's office.

Another voice responded, calm and methodic but too quiet to make out the words.

Tanya smiled as she approached, ears straining. Reynolds had a way about him. He was always cool, calm, and collected, but he sure could make someone squirm. He would simply ask question after question, each harder to answer than the last. Reynolds was the top of the food chain for the Lance in Windmore and still handed out assignments directly to his agents. Tanya had only done a little work for the guild in Norinspire but knew their superiors were far less involved. Reynolds even went on jobs from time to time.

Just to prove he's still got it.

Tanya skulked up to the wooden slab. The low voice hummed on the other side, barely audible, even though the door was slightly ajar. Tanya's eyes lingered on the crack.

I probably shouldn't.

Her mouth shifted from one side to the other, then relaxed into a smile.

Ah, who the fuck am I kidding?

Tanya crouched, peeking through the narrow gap between the thick slab of heartwood and the steel frame.

Low murmuring emanated from a black-cloaked figure leaning over Reynolds's desk, but she couldn't make out who sat on the other side through the narrow slit. Tanya thought she heard the word "repercussions" as a shadowy form slowly sat back down in the chair, revealing the face of the man behind the desk.

Reynolds was as far back in his seat as possible, gripping the arms of the chair as if his life depended on it. Sweat beaded his forehead, and his eyes were wide and wild.

Who on fuckin' Darin could make Reynolds's voice raise three octaves?

"I-I know it's a mess, but we'll deliver! I promise!" Reynolds stammered. "I just—I just need a little more time. We have a contract with the Order already. We-we'll figure it out!"

The stranger uttered something low and menacing.

"I'll send my best this time!" Reynolds pleaded.

More hushed words from the stranger.

"No more excuses, j-just give me one more chance, I'll make it right. The guild won't do anything to tarnish our long-standing relationship."

Whispers from the stranger broke off mid-sentence as their head turned toward the door.

Fuck!

Tanya met their gaze. No, that wasn't right. You needed eyes for a gaze.

Smoke consumed the figure.

The thing's hood was up, but a small chin jutted out of the jet-black gossamer billowing from its cowl. Tanya couldn't see a face, but she knew whatever was behind that veil of smoke was staring directly at her.

Tanya wanted to back away from the door. She wanted to turn and flee like she had with Jack and Ted all those years ago. But she couldn't. Fear gripped every part of her. She'd never felt utterly powerless—not with old man Ned, and not with Weber.

The figure rose and took a step toward her.

"W-what is it?" Reynolds stuttered, still strangling the arms of his poor chair.

Tanya barely heard him; she was too busy shrinking.

It took another step.

Obsidian fog flowed from the thing's hood and sleeves, slowly cascading to the floor in its wake. Each time its boot hit the boards, Tanya thought it would be the last thing she ever heard, yet the thuds kept on coming, and so did it.

After what seemed like an eternity, it finally stepped up to the door.

Tanya shuddered, closing her eyes.

Silence.

She cracked one eyelid open for a last look.

The figure loomed, shrouded gaze boring into her through the billowing veil.

Tanya cringed.

The shadowy form pushed the door shut.

Boot heels clipped lightly against the floor, receding. Tanya took a shuddering breath and scrambled back. Her shoulders hit the opposite wall with a thud, clearing a bit of fog from her brain.

Why'd I just cower like a mouse?

A tiny piece of her still wanted to approach the door and listen. But the curious little voice was a whole lot less demanding than usual.

There's not enough stone in all fucking Darin to face that thing.

The muffled conversation resumed. Tanya considered turning and running.

Maybe they won't know it was me outside the room?

That was panther shit, and she knew it. The thing had seen her.

Still, it's eventually coming out that door if I wait here.

The prospect sent a shiver up her spine and was plenty of reason not to linger. Tanya headed back to the common room, filled a mug with the strongest stuff she could find, and sat.

What in the hells was *that thing? Someone manipulating smoke mechanically?*

It seemed unlikely. Soot could be used to blind a foe or for a quick escape, but it wouldn't look anything like what she had seen. Tanya tried to puzzle it out a bit longer, but that meant trying to picture the thing. With a final shudder and a large swig of ale, she stopped attempting to reason and simply focused on pushing the vision from her head.

Tanya watched the hallway to Reynolds's office as she drank. For half an hour, no one came out. She'd mustered up a little courage: some was mental, but most was liquid. Tanya set down her ale, stood, and cautiously returned to Reynolds's office. There was no sign of the thing, or anyone else, for that matter. She waited for another five minutes without hearing a peep.

Tanya slowly pressed her ear to heartwood.

No sound.

She knocked.

"Come in," Reynolds called out wearily.

Tanya cracked the door, glanced around the room, and let out an audible sigh.

The smoking silhouette was gone.

But they didn't leave through the common room...

There was only one way out of the guild from here, which meant it was still in the building. Tanya shivered, focusing her attention on Reynolds. Her boss's mask of control was firmly reattached, but he fidgeted with the ring on his left hand, and his leather pants rubbed on something as his foot bobbed up and down behind the desk.

Can hardly blame him. Nearly pissed myself.

"Tanya," Reynolds said, pulling her from her thoughts. He held a letter out toward her, elbow propped on the table.

She took one more wary look around the room, then walked in and took the letter. "David's next assignment?"

"Yes." Reynolds paused, furrowing his brow.

"What is it?" Tanya asked, voice betraying her with a slight quaver.

Reynolds pursed his lips. "Never mind." Their eyes locked momentarily, then he added, "It's nothing, Tanya. Really. But I have another task for you. I need you to go to Capper's house. You know him?"

"Yeah, I know the bloke," Tanya said.

"Well, I want you to pay him a little visit. Tell him the Shadow's Lance is disappointed in his recent work. Explain that if he doesn't finish his task, we'll be *very* upset."

"That all?"

"Yes, Tanya, that's all."

"And if he refuses?"

"Oh, he won't do that. But if he does, explain he'll have to deal with me personally."

"All right. When do you need it done?"

"Now."

"Like, *now,* now?"

"Yes, Tanya, now."

Reynolds looked up, meeting her eye. Tanya smiled, but he was having none of it today and simply returned his attention to his paperwork.

"You got it, boss." She turned to leave.

"Oh, and Tanya," Reynolds said. "You know that job for the OAM in Norinspire?"

Tanya turned back hesitantly. "Yeah, Vincent's the contact, right?"

"Put it out of your mind. I'll need you here." He didn't even look up from his page.

"Okay." Tanya drew out the word. "You mind if I ask why?" But she knew the answer.

Reynolds glanced up, an indiscernible emotion flickering across his face.

Was that anger? Pity? Regret?

No. Disappointment seemed more likely.

I just lost some standing for my curiosity, even if he won't come out and say it.

"I need you here instead," Reynolds said. "Something pressing came up, and you are the only agent I trust with the job."

"What's the—"

"Don't push your luck, Tanya," Reynolds cut in. "You're dismissed."

Tanya opened her mouth to ask anyway, then clamped the traitorous thing shut instead and spun on a heel. She exited Reynolds's office and headed toward the common room, glancing over her shoulder every few steps.

At the bottom of the guildhouse stairs, she let out a long sigh and checked the Trickster.

Only a few hours till my meeting at the fountain.

Tanya began the brisk walk toward Capper's house. The clouds were out again, but the rain was only a threat for now.

Still, looks like I'm getting wet tonight.

She shook her head. The Lance often demanded everything from its members, and sitting in the rain was no exception. Sometimes, she got real tired of it all.

Especially the messenger errands.

A flash in the distance and thunder rolled through the night.

At least there's a roof over my head, and every meal doesn't end wondering when the next might come.

Tanya made her way to the Residential District. It was tucked a little way off the main road, probably to keep the stink of the stagnant masses at bay. Before long, she stood in front of Capper's house. The little blue door matched the slatted shutters on the windows to either side.

How cute. Not sure it fits though, considering Capper is anything but.

Tanya couldn't help but chuckle as she rapped on the door.

No response.

Something twitched at the edge of Tanya's vision, pulling her attention to the wooden shutters on the left side of the door. Curtains swung ever so slightly behind the slats.

Tanya's eyebrows narrowed. She licked a finger and raised it.

No wind tonight.

"I know you're in there, Capper." Tanya raised her voice and pounded on the door again. "I'm just here to give you a message."

No response.

Fucking informants. Unreliable at best, a downright liability at worst.

"Reynolds needs you to fulfill your half of the bargain. If you don't, he's gonna be very disappointed," Tanya said.

Still no response.

Maybe no one really is home? Can I justify leaving?

Tanya bit her lip.

I gave the message, after all, and Reynolds didn't say I should kick in the door.

Tanya turned and began to walk away, then stopped and looked back.

I'll get bloody handler jobs for a year if Reynolds finds out that's all the effort I put in.

With a sigh, Tanya strode back to the house. Her knock was harder and more demanding this time.

No answer.

Tanya pulled a pair of lockpicks from the nine lining the inside of her jacket and inserted them into the keyhole. She stepped in close to the door and worked blind.

"Always best to stand if you're good enough."

The picks rattled around in the cylinder as the wise words from her first trainer rattled around in her head.

Dead now, like so many others.

Her first pick scraped over a pin as her mind scraped at the memory.

"While standing, you could be fumbling with a lock instead of doing something nefarious."

She pushed up with the pick and eased the other smoothly in.

Click. The handle turned, and the door swung in with a rusty creak.

A wave of rot invaded her nostrils, and she forced back a gag.

A little blue chair sat in the middle room, facing an unlit hearth. The back of someone's head protruded over the top of the chair, but they made no move to turn or greet her. A blue curtain that functioned as a door hung in one corner of the room, and a set of stairs stood in another. The space was otherwise empty and unadorned.

At least there's nothing to hide behind.

Tanya stepped into the house.

Bang.

The door swung past her, nearly clipping her shoulder, and slammed into the frame. Tanya reached for the dagger strapped to her hip. A firm hand grabbed hers, squeezing hard, but she didn't let go of the blade. A second hand wrapped around her shoulders, clamping over her mouth.

Think I'll try to scream? Good. One less hand to worry about.

"I h-have a message f-f-for your master cu-cu-cully." The voice sounded wet, and the pitches changed from low to high as it chopped the letters up. "T-t-tell him—"

"You're gonna have to tell him yourself, Capper," Tanya growled. Her voice was muffled through his hand, but still coherent. "Also, what in the actual fuck is a cully, you silly twat?"

The man behind her paused, then giggled. The noise carried on far too long and changed pitch too often.

Tanya lifted her boot and brought the heel down on Capper's toe. The man let out a high-pitched yowl, pushing her dagger sideways. Her teeth clenched as the razor-sharp blade sliced through leather and into the skin beneath. Hot blood welled against the hilt of the blade, running down her thumb and forefinger.

How long till I bleed out? Need to end this quick.

Tanya threw an elbow into Capper's stomach, and he doubled over. She spun, gripping her dagger. Capper clung to her arm, but the movement pulled him off balance. His legs tangled, and he let go of her as he toppled, still cackling. Tanya brought her foot around and kicked him square in the side of the head. The maniacal laugh transformed into a whimper.

Tanya pressed a hand to her side; it came away red.

No time for questions.

Tanya pulled her foot back, aiming a second kick for Capper's head.

The wiry man scrambled up, throwing himself at her.

Her boot cracked into his ribs as he barreled into her. His shoulder slammed into her gut, and his arms wrapped around her waist. They went down in a heap. He wriggled past her legs and straddled her torso, swinging wildly. A fist connected with her temple.

Everything went fuzzy. A blur grew as something rushed toward her. Tanya deflected the blow with her right elbow, grabbed the back of Capper's neck, and pulled him close as she drove her knife through the knob in his throat.

The world slowly came back into focus as the madness in Capper's eyes shifted to terror. Tanya pulled the knife free, wincing as blood sprayed her face and jacket.

A weight left her chest. Tanya blinked.

Capper took two staggering steps toward the door, then collapsed.

"Fuck Reynolds! I mean…fuck!"

Tanya stood, wiping the blood from her eyes.

"This was a job for an enforcer, a thug, a blunt fucking instrument," she growled. "Not an agent, not me."

Tanya sighed and looked around the room. Her side throbbed, but the wound didn't feel mortal. With gritted teeth, she peeled off her jacket and looked over her shoulder. A long line of skin was flayed open, but the leather and buckles had probably saved her liver.

Thank the bloody gods. Or better yet, thank the bloody tailor.

The cut wasn't life-threatening, but it needed stitches and would be a bastard to reach. Tanya pulled a needle and thread from her jacket. She occasionally used the sewing kit to fix her gear or jimmy up a disguise, but the curved needle was packed for occasions such as this. Tanya checked the light outside through a slit in the shuttered window. The Trickster was hidden behind the clouds and wouldn't provide enough light for the work. She looked toward the fireplace, noticed the figure still sitting in the chair, and nearly jumped.

"Amara's bloody twat! Forgot about you."

Tanya bit her lip.

Why'd you just sit there while we fought to the literal fucking death?

Slowly, Tanya circled the chair, blade ready. When the face of the figure came into view, she almost jumped again. The corpse of an old woman leaned against the cushions, skin shriveled and papery. Salt spilled from her open mouth, dusting her clothes, chair, and floor.

"Well, if that isn't the creepiest fucking thing I've ever seen," Tanya muttered. "Have I ever got a story for you, Reynolds."

Tanya's eyes moved from the woman to Capper. "I suppose you aren't bothering anyone," she said to the stiff as she stocked and lit a fire.

Once the wood caught, Tanya used the flames to sterilize the curved needle and the light to thread it. She reached back and pinched the skin together with one hand and took the needle in the other. She drew in a deep breath, gritted her teeth, and started to sew. It was slow work, done all by feel, and it hurt like the thirteen hells.

No doubt it won't look much better either.

But it needed to be done, and she trusted no one else enough to do it.

What about David?

The thought was unexpected, unbidden, and nearly made Tanya laugh.

He must be good with those hands, playing that lute all day.

She did laugh at that, causing the needle to stab deep into her left hand.

"Fuck!"

Tanya pushed David from her mind and continued to work. She pricked her fingers a few more times and was forced to repeat stitches where her needle went through the same side of the cut. Eventually, her grisly surgery produced something serviceable.

I probably look like some abhorrent abomination pieced together by an inartistic lunatic.

Tanya smiled.

Does that make me the lunatic too? Guess it would.

She looked down at her blood-smeared hands.

At least it's mine for once.

The corpse sitting next to her had a scarf wrapped around its neck. She pulled the cloth free, used it to clean her hands and jacket, then flipped it over and wiped her face.

"Hopefully, you're with her now, you twisted little fuck." Tanya tossed the scarf over Capper's wide eyes, turned back to the old woman, and cocked her head to the side. A collection of purple stains trailed up the front of the woman's sweater, leading to the hole in her neck.

Burno's bloody balls, this just keeps gettin' fuckin' weirder.

Tanya's eyebrows narrowed as she glanced around the room. She redrew her knife and quietly walked over to the blue curtain. Blade at the ready, she peeked around the side of the drapery, then yanked the screen back.

The little kitchen was a disaster.

The foul odor here was worse than the stiff in the chair.

Cautiously, Tanya stepped into the little room.

Every surface was filled with pots, pans, and dishes, all coated with the same purple substance. They were stacked nearly waist-high, and there were far more than would've ever fit in the cupboards.

Someone used them all, then went out and got more.

Tanya took a little path, weaving through the clutter toward the stove.

A helmet stood atop a pile of pots on the left side of the oven. The only discernible detail through the crusty layer of purple was the roaring lion of House Rocktell.

How in the hells did you get your hands on that, Capper?

A lidless kettle sat on the range, and heat still emanated from the stove. The kettle smelled of decaying lilacs and was filled with the same deep violet sludge. Two brand-new bowls stood empty next to a ladle layered with dull purple crust.

What in the fuck were you doing with all this, Capper? Were you eating it or feeding it to her?

Tanya pictured the salt and the hole in the woman's neck. Her stomach tried to turn, but curiosity pushed through the nausea.

Why? What is this stuff, and what would possess someone to eat it?

Tanya left the kitchen and checked upstairs. The dirty little bedroom was a disaster, bedding all balled up like some sort of nest. She walked back downstairs and over to the window. The Trickster was nearly full.

No time for this right now.

Tanya left Capper's house and made her way to the Coliseum. There, she waited, pondering the day, trying to puzzle out exactly where it had all gone to shit.

So let's see. I saw someone or something I can't even begin to explain. I murdered a madman who keeps old ladies dried out by his fire to feed them purple soup. I lost a job and some standing in the guild—all because of my cursed curiosity.

Worst of all, I still need to meet that daffy-assed fucking bard tonight.

Tanya bit her lip and slowly shook her head.

At least he's kinda cute.

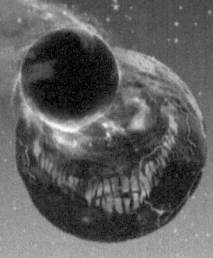

12
RIGEL CROSS

A wave of pain hit Cross, pulling him back to the present. The dead cat still lay in front of him.

How long was I out? How much blood did I lose? Does it matter?

No, it was over. He could barely move, and if anyone found him, they would either kill him or turn him in for being a runaway slave. He looked to the heavens, hoping to see Elinfall one last time, but the sun was still on the horizon.

Maybe I can last a little longer.

His eyelids were heavy, and it was a fight to keep them open.

Perhaps your life never flashes before your eyes. Maybe it's just a few key moments. Or perhaps I simply don't have much worth remembering.

Cross's vision started to fade again. Fighting suddenly felt far too hard.

He let oblivion take him.

◆○◆

Pinpricks of white shone through a crimson curtain.

"Son, do you see that star?" his father said, pointing into the night sky.

Cross shook his head, grass tickling the back of his neck.

"The one that shines so much brighter than the rest." His father leaned over to give Cross the proper perspective on the tip of his finger.

"I see it," Cross murmured. He'd seen the star before but never noticed how it blazed like a tiny bonfire.

"It's named Elinfall, or was by our people in the East. Your great-grandmother and grandfather were from Terra. They were simple farmers, living off the land before Darin invaded."

"What happened to them?" Cross asked.

"Well, when the East fell, everything got harder for our people," his father began. "The conquering Darin army executed our nobles and replaced them with stewards. The cities filled with refugees. Famine and disease ran rampant. The stewards couldn't support the needs of the people, so they gathered up anyone who couldn't pay their taxes and brought them to Darin to work off their debt. That's how the slave trade started."

"Rampant?" Cross asked.

"It means they were commonplace."

Cross nodded. "So the nobles tallied up room and board against the debt and paid next to nothing?" It was a trick they still used to this day. Technically, slaves were supposed to be able to buy their freedom, but no one ever did.

"Our ancestors' farm was destroyed in the war, and they found themselves in Ebonstall as refugees," his father explained. "Without a farm, they had no income and couldn't pay the high taxes, so they were rounded up like cattle and taken as slaves. You're the fourth generation of the Cross family to work on this farm. Your mother and I were going to escape, but after we learned she was pregnant...well, we weren't willing to risk you on the run."

"Wouldn't it have made sense to give it a shot?" Cross asked. "Better to try for a real life, even if it means a little danger."

"More than a little, son, and the road's no place for a woman with a babe in her belly. There are things she would need like medicine and someone to deliver our child. The nobles provide such things. As cruel as they can be otherwise, the Rocktells take a lot of care when it comes to the birth of a new slave. They see it as an investment, and they pay good doctors to protect that investment."

"But they don't give a shit about us. We're enslaved at birth."

"Rigel, don't swear," his father scolded. "You're better than that, and your mother wouldn't tolerate it."

Not sure how much I care. Never even knew her.

"If they have such good doctors, why'd they let her die?" Cross asked.

"Well, with a baby, there can be complications, and the doctors had to choose to either save you or risk losing you both. The Rocktells are practical and ruthless, and they decided to protect their new investment."

"So I killed her?"

"No!" His father met Cross's eye. "Nothing like that, my boy. Sometimes, things just happen. It's not anyone's fault, especially not yours."

"But, maybe if I wasn't so big..." Cross trailed off.

"You weren't real big then, Rigel. Besides, if size were the issue, that'd be my fault, not yours. You got your height and frame from me, after all."

Cross wasn't sure he believed that, but it was a nice lie, so he let it go.

"So what's that star got to do with it?" Cross asked.

"Well, Elinfall points east."

"Toward our homeland?"

"Yes."

"The two of you were going to follow it?" Cross asked.

"We planned to try, but just as the Rocktells spare no expense when it comes to the birth of slaves, they also spare no expense in hunting them down. They would've paid Justiseers to track us. If they caught us, they would have strung us up or racked us in the yard, even if your mother was still carrying you in her belly."

"But you said they valued newborn slaves. Wouldn't they try to protect their...investment?" Cross asked.

"I guess they value their examples even more. If they show they're willing to kill an entire family, even an innocent who hasn't come into this world...well, the rest of the slaves will think twice before running."

"It worked on you and Mom." Cross couldn't keep a hint of bitterness from his voice even though he didn't blame his father, not truly.

Cross's father met his eye, then turned away and nodded. "I guess it did, my boy. I guess it did."

"Let's go now then. I think it's what Mom would want."

His father's laugh had always been a booming thing, but even his chuckle filled the night.

"I'm too old for that, Rigel," his father said. "This body's all used up, and there's no way I'd make the trip."

"How far is it?"

"A very long way. My father used to say you'd need to travel through the Rocktells' estate a thousand times just to get to the Great Divide."

"What's the Great Divide?"

"A vast ocean separating Terra and Darin."

"And what is an O-sean?" Cross asked, puzzling through the word.

"I've never seen one, but I was told it's a lot of water, more than you could ever swim across or even see over."

It sounded impossible, but it also sounded like something Cross wouldn't mind seeing.

"How would you have crossed it?"

"I'm not sure we would have. Apparently, there are enormous waves, and it swells up and down higher than the Rocktells' manor twice a day. Plus, we would've needed a boat. I've heard some captains are willing to sail the Divide to bring goods back and forth from Terra despite the pirates and rough seas, but I guess the fare is steep."

"But the manor house is three stories tall. Can water really do that?"

"I guess so. Though, I'm not sure how," his father said.

They talked about the waves and the pirates for a long while, but the conversation eventually tapered off as they stared into the night sky.

Elinfall was so bright. Cross could hardly believe he'd never noticed it before.

"So why are you telling me all this now if we can't go?" Cross asked.

"Because it's high time I did. You're old enough to make your own decisions, and I won't be around forever. I'm sure your mother would tell you to stay here and live a good life. The Rocktells aren't exactly kind to their slaves, but they're far worse to those caught trying to escape."

"What about you? If you're too old to leave, what would happen to you?"

"Well, no matter what you decide, I'll stay here. I want to be buried next to your mother and spend the rest of whatever comes next right by her side." His father pointed toward the little hill they visited twice a year.

"Won't they hurt you if I leave?" Cross asked.

"No, I don't think so. The Rocktells know I'm still valuable, even if I am getting old."

Liar.

The Rocktells would bring in a Justiseer to hunt Cross down, according to his father's own words. The first thing the hunter would do was question the old man, and he clearly wasn't very good at hiding the truth.

"I'll think about it." It was Cross's turn to lie. He'd never abandon his father.

Cross became a little obsessed with the star after that night. He would work all day and lie in the grass all night, staring at Elinfall and dreaming of a life in Terra. A life where he was no longer a slave. The ritual began to take a toll on him and his work, yet he couldn't seem to stop. The dream was too powerful.

Something shook Cross awake. The sky was still dark, and it felt as if he hadn't slept at all.

"Come on, we're already late," his father warned.

"Just a little longer," Cross grumbled, drifting off again.

Someone shook him again. He opened his eyes, blinking away the night. His father's face filled his vision.

"Got to go. Now."

With a groan, Cross grabbed his shirt and pants, threw them haphazardly onto his body, and followed his father out the door. His father led them up the rolling hills toward a field scheduled to be cleared and tilled near the edge of the estate. As they ascended the last rise, the sun peeked over the horizon, revealing three men standing in the middle of the knoll.

The central man was short, and his belly hung from a tattered coat that looked a size too small. One of his eyes was scarred shut; the other glared over a mocking smile. A whip hung from his left hip, sharp steel from his right.

The other two men were bigger, not as large as Cross and his father, but big nonetheless. They were armored lightly with boiled leather and iron helmets. Short broadswords hung from their belts, pommels glittering in the morning sun.

"You're late!" the shorter man yelled before they were within a reasonable distance for conversation.

"Sorry, we misjudged the time it would take to get all the way across the property," his father boomed back.

There was a short silence as they approached.

"Did he just yell at me?" the man in the center asked, looking back and forth between the two men with swords.

"I think he may have," the one on the right said. He smiled, revealing a mouth full of missing teeth and pulling at a large scar on his right cheek.

"Didn't mean to yell. Only trying to be heard," his father assured. "I'm Barrett, and this is my son, Rigel." Barrett approached the man with a hand extended in greeting. One of the thugs pulled his sword halfway from the scabbard, and Cross's father stopped dead in his tracks.

"Well, *Barrr-ett.*" The central man drew out the name. "I'm Wortack, and we've been hired to keep you worthless dogs in line."

Wortack paused for a long moment. Cross considered responding, then decided it might be a trap. His father must have thought so, too, as he didn't say anything.

"Amen hired us to up efficiency 'round this here farm, and we figured what better place to start than with the oxen," Wortack said. An ugly grin crept across his lips, and he spat on the ground between them.

"Would you like us to start working then, Wortack?" his father asked respectfully.

"I should whip the two of you bloody for not being here before sunup, but then we might not get anything done. In exchange for my leniency, I expect you to fly through that fuckin' field." Cruelty shone in Wortack's eyes, and Cross couldn't help but notice the hand resting on the whip on his side.

Boulders were scattered across the old, neglected pasture and needed to be cleared before they could plow. Cross and his father got to work. Wortack and his men lounged on some farming equipment and watched.

They worked separately, each carrying rocks to the edge of the field. The boulders were immense and would've taken at least two ordinary men to lift a single one, let alone carry it. Wortack and his two hyena-faced cronies occasionally got up and circled Cross and his father while they labored.

After an hour or so, Cross heard a thump and turned. A large stone lay at his father's feet. An ear-splitting crack rippled through the field as Barrett bent to pick up the boulder. His father was upright in an instant, back arched, face painted with pain. A bloody line ran from his shoulder down to the small of his back.

"Best not drop the stones!" Wortack yelled. "No time for that since you weren't here before dawn."

Wortack and his men jeered as Cross's father bent to retrieve the boulder.

Cross felt his blood heat as if someone was stoking a fire in his belly. He wanted to drop his stone and give Wortack a taste of his own lash. Instead, Cross picked up his pace to the edge of the field. As the day drew on, the feeling slowly died away.

Around midday, the crack of the whip split the air again. Cross turned to find his father already on his hands and knees. Cross's eyes narrowed, and the fury in the pit of his stomach reignited.

It's my fault we were late.

The anger burned through his chest and arms, flowing into his head.

I need to fix this.

Cross dropped the boulder he was carrying and turned toward Wortack. Their eyes met, and the slave driver's expression hardened. Wortack stared him down, letting the tip of his whip hit the ground, even though he'd just finished looping it up again.

"That's not helping." Cross didn't yell, but even he could hear the metal in the words.

"Oh, look! It speaks, boys." Wortack checked on his comrades. They chuckled, and Wortack's lips widened in an ugly smile.

"He's getting old and—"

"No!" Wortack interrupted. "He's getting lazy, and he's getting useless. But you know what's worse than laziness or uselessness?"

No one said a thing.

"Disobedience. Ain't that right, boys?"

"The worst," the thug with the missing teeth responded. The other slaver just sneered, nodding along.

Wortack's eyes narrowed, then he pulled the whip back and lashed out.

Instinctively, Cross threw his left arm up. The whip wrapped around it, slashing into his skin with a painful crack. He barely felt it. The red-hot fury coursing through his veins blocked out the pain. Wortack tugged on the whip.

Cross didn't budge.

The slaver pulled again and almost lost his grip. Wortack stepped forward, wrapping the whip around his forearm in frustration. He snarled and yanked on the leather line again.

Cross moved less than a great oak would have. Without thinking, his hand tightened around the whip, and he pulled.

Wortack's feet left the ground. An instant later, his heels were higher than his head, then he was coming down. The slaver spiked into the dirt face first, feet flying forward like a scorpion's tail. His face and belly scraped along the ground until he finally came to a stop.

Everyone stood there in shocked silence as the dust started to settle.

Cross launched himself at Wortack's men. They were still fumbling with the straps on their scabbards as he sank a fist into Toothless's stomach. The man bent, hands giving up on the strap and clutching at his abdomen.

Sneer unsheathed his sword and moved to intervene.

Cross grabbed the back of Toothless's helmet and spun, dragging the man by his head.

Snap.

The strap of the helm gave way. Toothless stumbled into his comrade, then sprawled into the dirt. Sneer staggered but managed to stay upright. Cross hurled the helm at him.

Clang.

The casque on Sneer's head vibrated, and the man wobbled with it. He dropped his sword and tried to pull off the headgear. Cross stepped forward, kicking the man's kneecap.

Crunch.

Bones and cartilage bent backward, breaking and tearing through skin. The man cried out in agony. Cross grabbed the rim of his helmet in both hands and twisted. A series of snaps sounded as something in Sneer's neck gave way. Cross let go, and the man collapsed in a lifeless heap.

How am I doing any of this? The thought was a whisper, an unimportant detail from a part of him that was no longer in control.

Vaguely, Cross was aware that somewhere, someone was screaming.

He ignored it, stalking forward.

Toothless started to rise. Cross brought the heel of his torn-up work boot down on the slaver's unprotected head.

Crack.

The man's skull bounced off the dirt.

Cross stomped on Toothless's head again, and again...and again.

Bit by bit, the red faded from his vision. There wasn't much left of the man's head, just a spray of blood, caved-in bone, and spattering of brain across the long yellow grass. Cross's arms shook, chest moving up and down in shallow breaths.

Wortack shifted and groaned nearby, attempting to stand. "My legs! I can't feel my legs!" he screamed into the still morning air.

Nearly forgot about you.

Cross's fury stormed back in like an autumn monsoon, and suddenly, the two dead men were not enough.

Not enough for the cruelty of the day. Not enough for the suffering of our ancestors. Not enough for a hundred years of oppression.

These slave drivers might not be responsible for all that, but they weren't innocent either.

Wortack stared, eyes widening, as Cross stalked over.

"P-please," Wortack rolled onto his back.

Cross didn't respond. Instead, he knelt, grabbed the man's whip, and looped it twice around his neck.

"It's just a jo—"

Wortacks words were cut short as Cross cinched the leather bullwhip tight.

The little man sputtered, flailing feebly at meaty forearms as he tried to suck in a breath. Cross pulled tighter, muscles bunching as he yanked the ends of the whip in opposite directions. He didn't look away as Wortack's face began to purple. He didn't look away as the man's arms slowly stopped their futile slapping. He didn't even look away as the life slowly drained from Wortack's pleading eyes.

The red-fueled rage began to fade once more, and suddenly, Cross wasn't strangling Wortack, the ruthless slaver, he was just holding a dead man's head in his lap. All the pent-up rage from being pushed around his entire life had finally boiled to the surface, and Cross wasn't sure he could stomach the distillation.

He let go of the whip, feeling like he might be sick.

Part of him knew the three men deserved it, but the other part knew he'd just changed everything, and probably not for the better. Cross wobbled to his feet, shuddered, then looked around, meeting his father's sorrow-filled gaze.

"I'm afraid..." The words caught in his father's throat. "I'm afraid our family line may never see home again." His father gave a smile, a half-hearted attempt, as his eyes welled and tears began to flow.

Cross had never seen his father cry.

"Son, you need to go," his father said. "It's your only chance. When the Rocktells see what you've done...well, there isn't anyone in Darin who can save you then. Your only hope is Terra."

"No, I can't leave you. You didn't leave me. Come with me."

"Listen to reason, Rigel. Don't throw your life away. Go!" his father's voice quavered as he forced out the word.

"We can go together," Cross repeated, a coil of dread settling in his belly.

"I am too old, and I won't leave your mother."

"She is dead, Father!"

"And you will be too if you don't go. Now run!" his father commanded.

"I can't!"

"You must."

"I won't."

Stuck between a plow and untilled ground.

Hooves beat into the packed dirt as Cross and his father stared at each other.

Whatever choice there might've been, it's gone now.

Cross's father fell to his knees, holding his face.

Seven horses breached the ridge at the end of the field. A red lion's head was emblazoned on their armor: the sigil of House Rocktell. Cross's eyes shifted to the edge of the field. It was easily a half mile to the first outcropping of trees.

We'll never make it.

Cross looked from the line of horses to his father, kneeling in the untilled soil.

Stay and fight? Or try to reason with the Rocktells?

No good options.

A moment ago, Cross would have already been charging, but the fire that burned through his veins mere minutes earlier was out. He set his jaw, icy regret sinking its claws into him.

The horses fanned out, surrounding them. Dalton Rocktell rode at the front on a big gray stallion. He was a cousin of Amen and managed the farm for the Rocktells. Dalton pulled his horse up short as the rest of his men closed in. Three of them readied crossbows as the other three tightened the noose.

"What in the hells is going on here?" Dalton shouted.

Neither Cross nor his father said a thing.

"Who killed these men?" Dalton demanded.

Cross opened his mouth.

"I did," Cross's father cut in. "I killed them."

Cross was speechless. He could hardly believe what was happening. For a moment, he considered telling them his father was lying, that it was entirely his doing.

But what good will that do? Are two dead Crosses better than one?

"You know what must be done." Dalton dismounted his horse and unsheathed his sword. "You know we cannot tolerate something like this despite how good of a hand you've been."

Cross's father was already on his knees, but he nodded, tears still streaming.

"Let my son bury me on the hill? Please?" he begged.

"You know I can't do that. You'll be strung up, and what the birds don't finish will go into the sewer with the rest of the waste," Dalton said.

Cross's father let out a low moan but lowered his head anyway.

Dalton brought his sword up.

Cross couldn't take it anymore. He screamed and charged.

Thrum. Crossbows loosed all around him.

A bolt slammed into each shoulder from opposite sides, spinning him like a top. He hit the ground.

"Nooo!" someone screamed.

His father struggled to rise. Dalton's sword came down on the back of Barrett's neck. The blade made it halfway through, and blood sprayed. Cross tried to stand, but an armored boot kicked out his hands.

He groaned, opening his eyes as Dalton's sword came down again. It chopped into Barrett's neck, and the noble had to twist it free to unlock it from the spine. A high-pitched whine poured from his father, confusion filling his face as he still tried to stand.

The blade came down for the last time, taking Barrett's head.

Cross screamed and attempted to rise. Many arms held him fast. He railed against them, trying to get to his father. Cold iron clicked into place around his wrists, yet still he strained. Blood trickled down his hands where they pulled against the metal, but all he could see was his father. Something heavy struck him on the back of the head, and Cross's vision started to fade.

"Take him to the pits. Get what you can for him there. Any loyalty he might have had will be gone after today."

13
GERARD STOCKWORTH

Flames crackled, and nutty smoke rose into the air. Gerard sat on his haunches, stoking the blaze with dead branches. The fire was a risk, but not a major one. Jeff was still tied atop his horse, its reins looped around a limb of a walnut tree.

"How long till we're back to Windmore?" Jeff asked. He clearly shared an accent with the slums but was trying to hide it.

"About a week," Gerard lied. It would be more like two days if the weather held. *Hope he's not real familiar with this part of the country.*

"Why'd you leave him?" Jeff asked.

"Who? Your injured accomplice?"

There was a long silence. Gerard stirred the fire with a stick.

"Harper," Jeff finally said.

"Well, Jeff, if I were you, I'd be more concerned with my own fate than Harper's."

"He was hurt. He's gonna die out there. Alone."

No, he's in the bloody dirt.

But Jeff hadn't seen him cut the kid's throat, and it was hard to think of a good reason to share that little tidbit.

"Either he dies from blood loss, or the critters and the cats is gonna get him," Jeff continued. "Either way, it ain't right."

"Harper's no concern of mine, Jeff. I only came for you and Kal." Gerard glanced at the red-stained bag hanging from Vigilant's saddle. "Harper's lucky I gave him a chance to live at all."

Jeff lowered his gaze and shut up for a bit.

That's what you signed 'em up for when you asked for help.

"I'm sure your legs and back are crampin' after ridin' like that all day," Gerard said. "You gonna cause any trouble if I let you down for the night?"

"No, I don't think I will," Jeff said with a shake of his head.

"All right, but be warned: you try to escape, hurt me or my horse—hells, you even eyeball me wrong—things are going to get a lot harder. That clear?"

Jeff nodded.

"Good. Best remember the Rocktells only care if you're alive or dead, not if you've been dragged behind a horse. You're worth more alive, but cause too much trouble and I'll separate your head from your shoulders. Neither one of us wants that, right?"

Jeff shook his head.

"All right then, let's get you off that horse. I'll retie you so your legs and arms are straight. Then you can sit by the fire. In the morning, assuming all goes well tonight, I'll put you back on your horse in a more dignified fashion. Deal?"

Jeff nodded again. He wasn't sweating, and his eyes were steady.

The truth then, at least for now.

The rope had cinched tight during the ride and was a bear to unbind. Once Jeff's hands were finally free, Gerard retied them behind his back before loosening the rest of the knots. He pulled Jeff from the saddle, bound his swollen feet back together, and helped him hop over to a seat near the fire. He secured the horse to a tree then tied a bit of rope between the mare and man.

"Struggle, and you'll wake her. If she wakes me...well, I think we're past the threats, right?"

Jeff nodded absently, staring straight ahead.

Startin' to realize this is a one-way trip.

Things always got harder once that happened.

Nothin' for it, though.

Gerard focused on preparing the pheasant he'd shot the day before, and it wasn't long before the bird was crackling on a spit and turning a lovely shade of golden brown. He ate, fed some to Jeff, then inspected the wound in the man's knee. He'd never run again, but the puncture was starting to close.

Unlikely to kill him before we're back in Windmore, and death will be mercy after.

With a belly full of roast bird, Gerard's lids were feeling mighty heavy. He took a deep breath, eyes closing. His head tottered, and he pulled it back up once, then twice.

Pop.

A log crackled in the fire, bringing him back to the waking world. He forced his eyes open and checked on Vigilant. The big stallion's teeth were buried in a few blades of grass, but his breathing was slow and even.

You fall asleep during dinner? Maybe we're both gettin' too old for this.

Gerard chuckled, then looked back at Jeff. His eyes were glassy and distant.

Acceptance? Or is a sharp edge starting to sound better than iron bars and birds?

Gerard got up and inspected Jeff's bonds again, ensuring the rope between him and his horse was secure. Satisfied with his handiwork, Gerard hunkered down and laid his head to rest.

The sun was on the rise when Gerard awoke. His eyes snapped open, searching for Jeff, but the man was right where he'd left him. Gerard let out a long sigh, then sucked it back in. Jeff's eyes were already open and still had that glassy, detached look.

Gerard stood and cautiously walked over, checking Jeff's bonds. They were still tight and showed no sign of struggle. Vigilant grazed a little way off, and Jeff's mare was eating the last of the shrubs she could reach from her tether.

Gave my word I'd let him ride in a more dignified fashion if he behaved.

Today, Gerard was having second thoughts about yesterday's promise. Jeff hadn't done anything wrong, but his complacency was becoming unnerving. Gerard could go back on his word, but that was a slippery business, and he'd quickly lose the ability to make even the small deals required to bring Jeff back alive.

Might as well take his head after that and cut the bounty in half.

Gerard shook his head.

No, I'm no fork-tongued noble. Can't just go back on my word.

With his mind made up, Gerard ate some dried meat, drank from his waterskin, and gave some to Jeff.

"First, I'm gonna untie your legs," Gerard began. "Then, we'll get you on your horse. What's her name?"

Jeff shrugged.

"You don't know her name?" Gerard asked.

"No, it's just a horse."

He looked at Vigilant, raising an eyebrow.

Maybe we should just take his head.

Gerard blew out his cheeks.

No, not if we want that little vineyard someday.

"Well fuck, Jeff, you gotta name her."

"Why?" Jeff asked. "It's just an animal."

"Bloody fucking eighty-two hells, she still deserves a name, Jeff." Gerard turned his hands out to each side, waiting for a response. All he got was the same glassy stare. "Spots, then, her name is Spots now."

"Why Spots?" Jeff asked.

"'Cause she's got fucking spots, Jeff! I mean, fuck!" Gerard shook his head. "Now, as I was sayin', I'm gonna help get you on Spots, then I'll retie your feet as promised."

What kind of bloody monster doesn't name his horse?

Gerard shook his head again, glancing over at Vigilant.

Can't wait till we're done with these psychos—just you, me, and some grapevines.

Gerard ran a hand through his hair, let out a long breath, then put two fingers in his mouth and whistled for Vigilant. He helped Jeff over to Spots and up into the saddle, leaving his hands bound as he tied each leg to a stirrup. He tied Spots's reins around the back of Vigilant's saddle with a slip knot. If either horse pulled, the knot would hold, but one yank to the end, and the whole thing would unravel.

They trotted out of camp, making good time once they hit the main road. Half a day later, the beginnings of a storm hit Gerard's brow. He pulled his hood up and gave Vigilant's neck a pat.

Always somethin', ain't it, boy?

An hour later, the rain was coming down in thick, heavy drops. Soon after, a stiff wind picked up, bringing the torrential downpour in sideways. The dirt road turned to mud, slowing their little procession to a crawl. The rain hadn't let up after another hour, and the clouds were so thick it was hard to tell if day had turned to night.

Gerard trekked on.

A chill lingered in the air, and the monsoon threatened to transform into a hailstorm. There was no point stopping in the cold, wet dark, though, especially with no chance of a fire or sleep. Besides, each time Gerard turned back, he was met with the same unsettling stare.

Should just take his head, word be damned.

Visibility only worsened over the next few hours. The ground churned to mud under the horses' hooves, and continuing was starting to feel like a fool's errand. Still, there was nowhere to stop, so Gerard drove them on despite his growing concern about a horse breaking a leg.

Neither horse was complaining, though, or even slowing up. That didn't surprise Gerard in Vigilant's case, but even Spots was being a trooper.

Someone trained her at some point—possibly even the cutthroat behind me.

Gerard scratched his beard.

No, couldn't have been. Psycho didn't even name her.

But Jeff was a bit of a conundrum. He hadn't uttered a single complaint all day despite the harsh conditions, nor had he tried to escape.

The "hard men" usually gripe about everything regardless of—

A flicker of light off the left side of the road pulled Gerard from his thoughts.

What in the sixty-two hells?

Gerard checked the sky. The weather showed no sign of letting up.

Fire? Shelter?

It was a risk, but so was pushing on in this shit.

With a dissatisfied grunt, Gerard turned the horses toward the dot of light and led them off the road. As the ground became more treacherous, he dismounted and walked ahead on foot.

"Don't want you steppin' in somethin' we can't see in the deep grass, buddy," Gerard said, patting Vigilant's neck.

The big stallion snorted in response.

As they approached the light, a structure slowly materialized from the gloom. Gerard had never seen the cabin before, and he'd traveled this path more than most.

Vigilant gave a little whinny.

"I know, buddy. Odd. Shoulda seen that a hundred times before," Gerard muttered.

So why now in the pouring rain and dark?

The light dimmed substantially then, but they were close enough to still make out the cabin. Lightning crashed behind them as they entered the woods, casting fleeting shadows through the trees. Thunder followed, and both horses picked up the pace.

"Hold on, you two," Gerard growled, then sniffed the air.

Woodsmoke?

The rain must have knocked the smell down before, but there was no denying the scent of burning pine as they closed in on the cabin. The light they'd barely seen from the road clawed out from a shuttered window on the side of the house.

No wonder we've never seen it.

Gerard looped Vigilant's reins around the post of a wood-filled lean-to and approached the cabin. A thin line of light shone from under the door and out onto the packed dirt. Gerard raised his hand to knock, then hesitated.

Somethin' tells me these folk ain't interested in company.

Thunder crashed again, and a whinny pierced the night. Gerard turned, expecting to find a spooked Spots. Instead, both horses tugged at their reins, snorting and shifting.

"All right, all right. You two are worse than a couple of lotus pushers."

Gerard scratched the back right side of his neck, then hammered his fist against the oak door.

No response.

He turned, eyeballing his audience.

Vigilant flicked his nose in the air and shook his head back and forth.

Gerard pursed his lips, then slammed his fist into the door again, much harder this time.

Nothing.

He circled the cabin and found another window. The angled slats on the shutters pointed down, shedding light on the dirt. Gerard bent at the waist and peered up through the gaps. Light flickered across the exposed joists of a wooden ceiling, but that was all he could see. He returned to the door despite the tightness in his gut.

"I mean you no harm!" he shouted.

Silence.

"I'm a Justiseer, transporting a fugitive. We need a place to rest and shelter for two horses if you have it!"

More silence.

Somethin's wrong here.

Gerard tried the knob.

Locked.

It wasn't as if Gerard cared too much for the law, but anyone who wouldn't open the door for a Justiseer usually had something nasty to hide. He took out a light club and flipped it around in his hand.

Perhaps they're growin' blue lotus inside?

No, the climate wasn't right for it around here. It needed the arid heat of the desert. Gerard scratched the back of his neck, pulled his hand away, and brought the club down on the door handle with a bang.

Hopefully, we didn't just break into some deaf old woodsman's house.

Gerard pushed the broken handle away.

Oh well, too late for speculation.

He manipulated the mechanism in the door with a small bar and applied pressure to the wood with the tip of his toe.

The latch shifted, and the door swung inward.

Two chairs sat next to a table in the center of the room. A bed stood in one corner, a bookcase in another. A rocking chair rested near the books on a well-used, colorful rug. Two dressers filled one wall, and a hearth took up another.

Nobody home?

Gerard angled his head to either side of the door to get a good view of the room, then pushed it all the way to the wall to ensure no one was lurking behind it.

"Hello!" he called out one more time.

Silence.

Gerard stepped into the cabin.

Vigilant snorted behind him.

"Hold on a damn minute," he said.

Thunder echoed through the woods again, and the horses whinnied in unison. Gerard glanced back. Spots pawed at the ground impatiently, and Vigilant tossed his head.

Gerard looked around again.

No one.

He walked over to the fireplace and crouched. It still blazed with heat.

The logs are fresh, placed in the hearth five...maybe ten minutes ago.

Gerard walked over to the bookcase. An unlit lantern sat on a side table. Gingerly, he touched it. The glass warmed his cold hands. Only a minute or two could have passed since it was burning.

Maybe they just left?

Gerard looked around the room again. There was a spot by the door where shoes should be placed, but none stood there. The door creaked as it swung back and forth in the gusting wind.

Took off in the middle of a bloody monsoon? Unlikely.

Gerard relit the lantern, illuminating the room with a golden glow. His eyes wandered to the bookcase, and his feet followed. He pulled a book titled *Harold and the Empress* from the shelf. The book seemed normal enough as he quickly flipped through it. After replacing it, he reached back and grabbed another: *Tales from Dragon Rock.*

Gerard shook his head, putting the book back. He ran his finger down the spines of three more: *Of Sun and Swords, Rain Drops of Norrington,* and *In the Realm of the Rhinetoryians.*

Strange. All children's books.

Gerard walked back outside and patted Vigilant on the head.

"Sorry, boy, you're not gonna fit in the cabin."

Gerard led the horses to the side of the building most sheltered from the rain. Some tools leaned up against the side of the cabin under an overhang. He situated the two horses, drove a shovel into the ground, and hitched Vigilant's reins around it.

"We'll have to wait for grazing till the morning, boy," Gerard said apologetically. He looked at Jeff. The man slumped in his saddle, a dejected look plastered on his face.

I'll be back for you in a minute.

Gerard cautiously reentered the cabin.

Plunk.

Something hit the roof, nearly causing him to jump. More taps followed the first, slowly growing into a torrent of noise.

Hail. At least the horses are covered.

Gerard walked over to the nearest dresser. The drawers were filled with clothes, but like the books, most were clearly made for children. Some were rags, but more were fancy courtwear. He was no tailor, but most of it could've been the genuine article.

Whoever was here a minute ago should be back already, especially if they have kids.

Gerard's eyebrow raised as he looked around the room again.

Or maybe they didn't leave at all.

The heels of his boots thumped on the floorboards as Gerard walked over to the corner of the room. He threw the colorful rug aside, knocking over the rocking chair atop it. Two thin lines cut through the floorboards, outlining a trapdoor a pace wide.

Gerard glanced over his shoulder, drew his bow, and nocked an arrow. He reached down, cracking the hatch just enough to get the tip of his boot under it. The hail nearly muffled the squeal of the old, rusty hinges as he drew his foot along the seam of the trapdoor, then flicked it open with his boot. Gerard stepped back and drew the arrow, taking aim into the darkness.

He sighted down the shaft, eyes straining for any sign of movement.

Nothing. No sound. No motion. Only a black hole dug deep in the dirt.

The trapdoor hung against a chain stop, shadowing the hole from the lantern's light. Gerard let down the arrow, grabbed the lamp, and cautiously held it over the opening.

Solid ground down there, all right.

Gerard shifted the light, revealing a ladder. He slung his bow across his back and climbed down one-handed. The lantern illuminated a long tunnel for six spans before darkness enveloped the rest.

Huh, well, that's not nefarious or nothin'.

Gerard saw a faint shadow flicker across the dimly lit ground. He spun, instinctively drawing his bow. Jeff stared down from above. His eyes weren't glazed over anymore. Instead, they'd gone cold.

"You shouldn't have left my friend to die alone, mate." Jeff's tone was void of emotion and barely audible over the hail. He kicked the trapdoor shut.

Gerard's arrow thudded into the wooden hatch as it fell. He dropped his bow, scrambling for the ladder.

Crash.

Something hit the floor, producing far more noise than a single object had any right to.

Fuck! The bookcase.

Frantically, Gerard climbed the ladder and threw his shoulder into the wood. It didn't budge. He tried again. Pain shot through his arm, but the hatch didn't move.

Vigilant!

Gerard put his back against the trapdoor, braced his feet on the ladder, and pushed with all his might. Wood creaked as he strained against the door. Suddenly, something gave way, and he found himself in a heap on the packed dirt. He opened his eyes. A rung on the middle of the ladder was snapped in two.

No way I'm getting through that hatch.

Gerard considered yelling all the horrible things he would do if Jeff so much as shaved one hair from Vigilant's coat, but the words died on his lips. Threats might cause the psycho to do something rash.

If he hasn't already.

Gerard drew in a long breath and turned to the enveloping darkness.

"I'm coming for ya, boy."

14
SCARLETT REINHOLM

Thwack. Thunk. Creak.

Thwack. Thunk. Creak.

Thwack. Thunk. Creak.

Chopping wood heated you four times: once when you cut the tree down, again when you hauled the wood back to the cabin, once more when you split the logs, and a final time when the wood made its way into the hearth.

There were a lot of ways to die on the plateau, but the cold was the most reliable threat. It could turn any innocuous situation dire in a heartbeat, and it was constant work to keep it at bay.

Scarlett took a swig of water and wiped the sweat from her brow. She smiled at Roland, and the big moose shook his antlers at her.

"Trying to look cute for a carrot, eh?" Scarlett asked.

Roland's huge ears swiveled up at the word, and he leaned forward. Scarlett walked over to her threadbare coat and pulled a carrot from the right pocket.

"This what you're looking for?" she asked, wiggling the orange spike at him.

The big moose sauntered over and gingerly took the carrot, devouring it in two powerful grinds of his jaw. Scarlett smiled and patted the side of his head. She rested her forehead against his big soft nose and whispered gentle nothings.

"Just you and me, big guy. Hopefully, we can keep it that way."

For a minute, the two of them simply shared breath. Scarlett ran her hands through Roland's coarse fur and gave his ears a scratch.

"All right, break time's up. That wood ain't gonna cut itself," she proclaimed.

Scarlett put a hand on her jacket, considered, then decided against it. She'd gotten a little chilly during the short break but would be too warm for the layer in a few minutes with the axe.

I'll eventually need to find somewhere to resupply.

Scarlett was constantly going through clothes. Skin boots tore, leather pants wore through, and she went through smallclothes so often that she usually chose to go without. For the most part, she'd learned to mend and make new garments herself, but certain articles proved more difficult than others.

A new coat would be welcome, and soon, sharpening the nubs of the saw isn't going to cut it. Literally.

It was a joke her father would've made, and remembering him brought a smile to her lips and a tear to her eye.

Scarlett turned back to the axe. She had enough pelts to trade with most any settlement, but the thought of confronting another human face filled her with anxious dread. She placed a block of wood on the stump, grabbed the axe, and swung it around overhead.

Thwack, the axe split the block. *Thunk*, the metal head buried itself in the stump. *Creak*, the honed edge twisted free.

Scarlett lost herself in the rhythm of the task. She considered where she might find civilization all the way out here. It would be difficult since she'd specifically come to this corner of the world to avoid other people. Hopefully, if she did find someone, they'd be better than the people in Ravenstar.

"Now that's a low bar," she muttered.

Scarlett's mind drifted back to her old life. It had been a life of study, debate, and philosophy—filled with beauty, discovery, and very self-important, crusty old men. Scarlett laughed aloud as she pictured old Luther Raft.

—◆◇◆—

"You can't just change the status quo, Scarlett. These theories were created hundreds of years ago, and they have been proven ti—"

"Time and time again," Scarlett interrupted. "But things change, and I've discovered something amazing!"

Luther eyed her skeptically. "You've discovered something new about the moons? The same moons great men have been studying for hundreds—"

"Yes! I mean, I think so. And I know your great, great, great, great to the umpteenth grandfather came up with all those theories, but they are a bit dated. Don't you think?" Scarlett prodded.

"Well, perhaps...but Scarlett, these things need to be proven, and that takes time. A lot of time, usually."

"Yeah, yeah, yeah, we can work on all that later," Scarlett said, producing a small purple sphere from her pocket. "Look! Regular old moonstone, right?" She held the polished sphere out.

"Scarlett, that should be in the vault!" Luther gasped, cupping his old, weathered hands under her outstretched one.

"Relax, I'm not gonna drop it. Besides, it wasn't doing anyone a bit of good in the vault. You can't learn anything about it through two fingers of iron."

"Scarlett, it's nearly priceless."

"And science isn't?" she countered.

Luther sighed. "The recklessness of youth never ceases to amaze me."

"Yours passed too long ago to remember, eh?" Scarlett shot her kindly tutor a sly smile.

"Sometimes it feels that way...but you go too far, young lady. That stone must be returned to the vault."

"Just look, Luther." Scarlett held up the orb. "Notice anything different about it?"

"Not really. Perhaps it shines a bit brighter than normal? Did you polish it?" Luther asked, his scientific mind finally peeking from behind the curtain of apprehension.

"Exactly! I mean, no, no polish. But exactly. That shine happened after I left it sitting out all day."

"You *what*?"

"After I left it sitting out in the sun!"

His eyes widened. "Scarlett! That thing's worth more than your family's entire house!"

"Calm down, Luther, it's just money." Scarlett tossed the orb back and forth between each hand. She was absolutely giddy about her discovery, and Luther couldn't even be bothered to hear her out.

"Please, for the sake of all mankind, stop throwing it." Luther cringed, trying to keep his cupped hands under the orb.

Scarlett stopped and held out the stone again.

"You see, I'm pretty sure the sun charged it. Now check this out!" Scarlett walked over to Luther's desk, lit a candle, and brought it close to the little stone.

"Do you see it?" she asked.

Luther winced as the flame licked at the flawless gem. Slowly, his face unbunched, and his eyes grew wide. "Now, isn't that something..." he trailed off, leaning in to peer at the orb.

"Told ya," Scarlett said, a smug smile plastered across her face.

Knock-knock-knock.

123

Luther jumped, nearly jostling the candle from Scarlett's hands.

"Put it away," he whispered. "I don't need you getting ostracized. Who would help me fill out all the required forms if you're gone?"

"Gods forbid you might have to do your own job." Scarlett widened her eyes in mock concern.

Luther walked over to the door, then turned back, giving her a pointed look.

With a sigh, she slipped the stone into a pocket and blew out the candle.

He cracked the door, exchanged a few murmured sentences with someone, then let them in. The headmaster and a constable padded quietly into the room.

What've I done this time? Did they finally notice the gem missing from the vault?

Scarlett glanced at Luther but found no reassurance in his eyes.

Why is a constable here? The university wouldn't get the law involved for a missing jewel...would they?

"Scarlett?" the constable asked.

"Yes. Is something the matter, sir?"

"When was the last time you were home, Scarlett?" he asked, ignoring the question.

"Um, a week ago, I guess. Is there a problem?"

"Unfortunately, there is."

"What is it?"

"Scarlett, there's no good way to say this, so I'm just going to say it."

"What happened? You're starting to scare me, Constable." Scarlett shot a look toward the headmaster. His head hung, and there was no way to meet his eye. She turned toward Luther. His eyes welled with tears, then he pursed his lips and looked away.

"Your mother, brother, and sister are dead, Scarlett."

Her eyes shifted between the three somber faces. "Not a good joke, fellas."

"I wish it was a joke. I truly do, Scarlett," the constable responded.

"Did Professor Pinkerton put you up to this? If so, tell him this is a new low, even for him."

The three of them eyed each other. Not a smile between them.

"Okay, I'll bite. How?" she asked.

"Was there anyone who might have wished your family harm, Scarlett? Anyone at all?" the constable asked.

"You two are seriously going along with this?" Scarlett asked, looking between Luther and the headmaster. Neither met her gaze. Scarlett looked down at her hands. They were shaking.

"It's important that you tell me anything you can remember, and it's important you tell me now, Scarlett. Time is of the essence in situations like—"

"I want to see them. Where are they?" she interrupted.

"You can't see them, they're—"

She pushed past him and ran for the door.

"Scarlett!" Luther yelled.

She didn't stop. Scarlett was done listening. She ran out of the Academy, then she ran out of the keep. She ran down the main road and all the way out of Ravenstar. Then, she ran some more.

Scarlett was bawling by the time she hit the main road, but that didn't stop her. She paused several times on the way to the little cabin, but as soon as she'd caught her breath, she was running again. By the time she got to the little plot of land a few miles out of town, her legs were on fire, and she was a wheezing, sobbing mess.

The cabin had been in her family for generations, but they'd only moved here after her father's death. He'd loved the city, but her mother had always wanted to be closer to nature. Scarlett ran down the little pathway that weaved between the trees. Hooves beat on the packed dirt behind her as she slammed into the little green door.

What she saw next would haunt her dreams for the next five years. But it was too painful to relive willingly, at least during her waking hours.

━━━━◄○►━━━━

Thwack. Thunk. Creak.

Thwack. Thunk. Creak.

Thwack. Thunk.

With her left hand, Scarlett reached up and fingered the smooth orb of moonstone woven into the necklace around her throat. Taking it had been an accident, but she'd kept the gem after finding it in her pocket a few days later. The little stone could restart her life someday if she ever needed it to.

Scarlett wiped sweat from her brow and looked toward the setting sun. Her stomach growled.

"Wow, I am absolutely ravenous."

When was the last time I ate? Lunch?

Scarlett left the head of the axe buried in the stump and walked past the compost pile to her cold cellar. She opened the hatch and rummaged around until she had two large cabbages and a few turnips. She whistled loudly, loading Roland's trough with the produce.

Her stomach growled again.

"I got it, I got it," Scarlett said. "Take care of yourself as much as the moose."

The snow crunched under Scarlett's feet as she hauled a load of split wood toward the front door. Roland met her by the gate, gave her a gentle nudge with his big, oval nose, and sauntered over to the feeding trough.

"You have to be the most spoiled moose in all of Darin. You get to graze on willows all day and still come home to sweet veggies."

Scarlett tromped back to the house, unloaded the wood, stoked the fire, then walked back out and closed the gate to the backyard.

"Good night, my big hairy turd on legs," she said, standing on tiptoes and peering over the fence.

The enormous moose raised his head, snorted, then went back to his cabbages.

Scarlett walked back to the front of the house but stopped on the tiny front porch. Her little cabin had one hell of a view. It overlooked the Kihnton jungle, and on a clear evening such as this, she could see all the way to the Divide. She smiled.

It really is stunning.

"Maybe I'll have dinner outside tonight. Watch the stars."

Scarlett had always loved the stars and night sky. She'd studied them at the Academy but had been staring into the heavens long before that. Sirius was already waxing into view overhead, and Huna would be out tonight as well. They were so pretty.

Huna was soft, round, and expansive. Sirius was more of an acquired taste, but Scarlett had always been keen that its frightening countenance was merely a result of volcanic activity on the surface. Aura, though, that was the moon for her. It orbited Sirius, pulling in sunlight like a greedy child and had the power to warp the face of its much larger sister. The black and purple moon was an absolute curiosity, and no one at the Academy could explain it.

There are too few mysteries left in this world.

Scarlett walked back into the cabin and grabbed her biggest pot. She loaded it with snow and hung it over the hearth.

"Soup tonight!" she said with a smile. Her tummy rumbled in agreement.

Scarlett pulled her little chair out onto the porch so she could watch the night sky unfold. She grabbed some vegetables, a knife, and a cutting board, then settled into the chair. The knife tapped rhythmically against the board, slicing through potatoes as she watched the night sky. The three moons were so beautiful, and Aura's glow was just starting to pull Sirius's face into a smile.

15

ELLIS
TEMPERTON

"Who in the hells is running this damn circus?" the stranger shouted.

Ellis quietly pulled his hand away from the ancient tome he'd been shelving: *How Steam Will Power the World*. The title had intrigued him, even if he wasn't allowed to read the pages.

"Good morning to you, too, Gavin," Vincent said.

"What in the hells is going on with that bloody island of yours?" Gavin demanded.

Probably best if I stay behind the stacks for this conversation.

"I presume you mean Seafront?"

"Of course I mean bloody Seafront! How many gods-forsaken islands does the Order own?"

"A few," Vincent said dryly.

"I don't actually care about the rest of your damn islands," Gavin said. "Why am I receiving word from my bloody secretary that Seafront hasn't checked in?"

"We have received no birds," Vincent said. "That doesn't mean—"

"Save it, Vincent," Gavin's voice lowered. "My son is on that island, and *you* convinced me to send him."

"I'm sure the boy is fine," Vincent said calmly. "A contingent has already been dispatched."

"He'd best be."

Ellis peeked over the forbidden tomes.

A tall man in a well-tailored suit was pointing a finger at Vincent.

Is he a noble? Or someone from the Order?

Ellis didn't recognize Gavin, but he'd never heard someone talk to Vincent like this.

He's either very high up or very stupid.

Ellis decided it must be the former since he'd somehow arrived unannounced.

"You fix this, Vincent, and you fix it now," Gavin said, turning away.

Vincent watched calmly, hands folded on his desk, as Gavin strode to the door and gave it a shove.

It didn't budge.

Gavin turned back, expression somehow darkening further.

Click.

The door unlocked as Vincent disengaged the bolt with the mechanism below his desk. "Sorry about that. Slipped my mind."

Gavin's face twitched, then he stormed from the room without a retort.

Vincent let out a long sigh. "You can come out now."

Ellis stepped from behind the bookcase and approached Vincent's desk. "Who was that?"

"Gavin Kemp," Vincent said dryly. "His family has been tied to the Order longer than yours has been tracking its lineage."

Ellis pictured his name, penned on the wall of his family's manor under so many others. There were at least ten generations of Tempertons above him, and the last five had all been OAM members.

"Does he outrank you?" Ellis asked skeptically.

"No, not exactly. But he has substantial influence, and his younger brother shares my title."

"The head Magus in Ardendale?" Ellis asked.

"Yes. Edmond Kemp," Vincent said. "Ardendale isn't quite as important as Norinspire, but Edmond could make life difficult, and I imagine Gavin has even more pull."

"Do you think he'll cause problems, sir?"

"Without a doubt, if we don't get his son back. But Captain Booker is due to arrive at Seafront in a few days. I imagine we will soon receive a report that a sickness simply spread through the rookery."

"You don't think the expedition will be forced to follow the protocol we received, do you?" Ellis asked.

"I hope not." Vincent met his eye. "That artifact has been secure for a long time."

"Aren't you ever curious about them?"

Vincent's eyebrows tightened.

"I mean, not to actually utilize, but from an academic perspective."

"Of course, but put the relics out of your mind, young man. They're trouble." Vincent shook his head, then muttered, "I just hope nothing happened at the Forge."

Ellis knew better than to ask about that. He had no idea what the Forge was, but any questions would only cause Vincent to close up like a clam. The Order loved its secrets, and according to Vincent, they'd been keeping them by any means necessary for over a thousand years. Ellis's gaze shifted to the illegal texts, lining the shelves all the way to the back of the room.

Maybe someday I'll be in a position to read them all.

Vincent cleared his throat. "Ellis, would you be so kind as to prepare some tea?"

"Yes, sir."

"Oh, and have the rookery ready a crow for Windmore. I think it best we prepare a contingency plan in case Booker's trip doesn't go as expected."

16
DAVID TRUEHEART

Torchlight flickered from a window near the top of the Freemen's tower.

Hope whoever owns that ledger isn't still up.

David looked down at his hands. They'd finally stopped shaking, and the Trickster was back behind the clouds.

Thank the gods.

He approached the vine-covered wall, pulling out his grappling hook. A faint glow topped the ramparts, but everything else was pitch black. The clouds shrouding the moons also stopped any starlight from piercing the inky black.

Another stroke of luck.

David drew his arm back and threw. The hook clattered against the wall, then came back down, straight at him.

Shit.

He leapt from the hook's path just before it hit the cobblestone with a clang.

"Damn. That was close," David muttered, then froze and listened.

No alarm bells rang. No horns blew. David twirled the rope, throwing slightly to the side this time. The grapple caught in the vines halfway up, forcing him to yank it out. Again, he threw, and again, it fell. After a few more failed attempts and more than a few muttered curses, the hook found purchase somewhere over the wall. He tested the rope with his weight, then swung back and forth to ensure it would hold before looping it through his belt.

Seems stable enough.

David pulled a machete from his bag and sawed at the thorny vines as quietly as possible. Unfortunately, it wasn't even close to silent. He didn't try to clear everything, just enough to keep his boots from being filled with thorns.

Hand over hand, David pulled himself up, bracing his feet against the wall to keep as much weight as possible off his arms. Every few steps, he clung to the rope with one hand,

131

took out the slack with the other, and cinched down a brake on his belt. The technique allowed him to rest for a bit when he needed to and ensured a fall wouldn't be all the way to the ground.

As long as everything holds.

Each time David engaged the brake, he tested it, took a short rest, and cut new openings for his feet. It was slow work, and all the noise made it risky, but it was the best plan he'd come up with.

No doubt Tanya would've found a better way. But I'm just an am-aaa-teur. David sang the last word.

There was a song in there somewhere.

"The Thief and the Amateur"?

David paused the hacking and scratched his chin.

No, that's no good. "The Guild and the Amateur"?

He considered it.

No, worse. "The Assassin and the Amateur"?

His lips curled into a smile.

There it is.

After another twenty minutes, more sweat than he thought possible, and several new verses of a song, David finally crested the top of the wall. Slanted rooftops butted up to the outer wall inside the compound, forming a little courtyard. A pit surrounded by sand and training implements filled the center of the compound.

The Freemen were well known for training their slaves and only entered them in the Coliseum after they proved their mettle in the pits. They were the most prominent gladiator guild in the city, and any stone placed on their fighters was safer than most.

Apparently, they've taken up banking as well...entrepreneurial gladiators.

The idea nearly made him laugh.

There's a funny ballad somewhere in there as well.

The two men in charge of the guild were ex-gladiators granted their freedom through victory in the arena. Emancipation through violence took at least thirty combats, countless injuries, and years.

Anyone who survives all that must live and breathe carnage.

David unhooked the grapple, stood, and coiled his rope.

Makes sense they'd get back into the business. Peddling death must be easier than dealing it out yourself.

David twisted the rope in the middle twice, then folded it in half and placed it in his bag.

Thankfully, there were no vines on this side of the stone structure. David knelt, crawled backward over the edge, and lowered himself until he hung by his fingertips. He looked down, analyzing the fall one last time.

Less than a span to the shingles below.

The roof was slightly slanted, and the landing would be noisy. David took a deep breath, preparing himself.

His fingers slipped.

Shit.

Air rushed past, and his hands flailed once—

Crash.

David hit the roof, scrambling for a hold as the world lurched. He tumbled down the shingles and off the edge, landing on his back.

Crunch.

Wind sputtered from David's lungs, the back of his head whipped against the ground, and pain lanced through his abdomen. The world dimmed. He blinked, trying to reorient his addled brain. Slowly, the torchlit courtyard came back into focus.

"Otix's bloody belly button," David groaned.

Stunned shock slowly shifted to pain. David sucked in a lungful of air. He suppressed another groan and reached around, examining his back. His hand squished into something moist, soft, and...*grainy?*

My guts? No, not wet enough.

He pulled a fistful of the substance around, squinting in the dim light.

Fucking dirt?

With another groan, David tossed the soil aside and rolled off the mound. Shards of pottery, dirt, and a poor, innocent plant were pressed into a David-shaped outline. He sighed in relief and reached for the back of his head. His fingertips came back wet and spotted with blood.

Damn near brained myself, and just when things were starting to go my way. Oh well, plans only last until the first hand's been dealt.

David flexed his shoulders and looked around. The pavilions surrounding the walls were all covered in bars.

Must be where they keep the gladiators.

He turned, checking the cell behind him. The torches in the courtyard only cast light half a span past the bars.

Uneven footfalls sounded near the gate.

David took a few steps toward the middle of the yard, looked around, then vaulted into the pit. Slowly, he stood and peered over the rim. A guard was bent over, examining the broken pot and breathing heavily.

What're the odds he doesn't raise the alarm?

David scowled.

Slim to none.

He crawled out of the depression and crept forward.

"What in the fuck," the guard muttered.

Sometimes, you gotta get your hands dirty.

His father's words again. David slid his knife silently from its sheath.

The sentry pulled off his helmet, clearly trying to get a better look at the shattered ceramics and scattered dirt.

Maybe I can just knock him out? David glanced at the pommel of his knife. His heart was tap-dancing so loud he could barely hear the guard muttering.

The sentry stood, cracked his back with a groan, and scratched his head. David quickened his pace. The man shifted his weight and started to turn.

David swung.

The pommel hit the stocky guard square in the temple.

He staggered back, mouth opening as he fumbled for the hilt of a sword.

So much for knocking him out. It's him or me now. The thought flashed through David's mind as he flipped his knife around into an overhand grip and stepped in close.

"Hel—"

The guard's cry was cut short as sharp steel slid into soft flesh. The man's life and yell both severed as blood spurted from his neck. He fell back, landing on the broken vase. One hand twitched at the leather strap holding his blade in place; the other clasped at his throat in a futile attempt to stop the bleeding.

His eyes slowly glazed over.

He didn't deserve this...

David took a deep breath.

Sure, the Freemen's Guild peddles in death, but not this man.

Aunt Jocelin used to say the first kill was the hardest. For some reason, it didn't feel that way. The man in the alley had been following David, maybe even trying to kill him.

This guard was only doing his job, probably just trying to make a little stone to feed a wife and kids. David felt sick. He looked away from the man's face, eyes settling on a twitching boot.

Not the time to grow a conscience. Write a lament to the man later.

David took a shuddering breath and turned away from the body. He looked up, accidently meeting the Trickster's gaze.

Bloody bastard's out again and smiling.

David pulled his gaze away from the moon, but it landed back on the guard.

Fuck!

He fixed his eyes on the tower in the corner of the pavilion. The sound of the shattering pot would be louder than his footfalls, but he still stepped softly as he crept through the shadows toward the spire.

David halted as he spotted an enormous man standing at the edge of his cell near the tower. The gladiator's face was pressed against the bars, staring into the night sky as torchlight flickered across his features. David didn't think the prisoner had seen him, but it wouldn't be easy to sneak past the man. His eyes shifted from the gladiator to the tower, then back to the big man.

A wild grin spread across David's face.

The smile faded as he walked back to the dead guard, who was already marinating in a considerable pool of blood. He stepped gingerly around the corpse, trying to avoid it with both eyes and feet. David grabbed the bars of the nearest cell and leaned over. His eyes met the man's cold, lifeless ones. He flinched and quickly averted his gaze upward.

David's eyes locked on the Trickster. "Good fuck. Is nowhere safe to look?"

The sinister moon stared down at him as David blindly groped at the man's belt. Finally, after what seemed like an age, his fingers closed around a loose metal ring. He fumbled with the leather strap securing the iron loop, eventually freed it, then pulled it into the moonlight.

Gods, that's a lot of keys.

David pushed himself off the bars and flipped through the iron ring. He'd always been fascinated by keys. It probably stemmed from his obsession with locks. He used to try to pick the lock on Aunt Jocelin's front door just to prove he could. She always caught him and accused him of being louder than a cat trying to bury shit on a tile roof, but he eventually had got that door open. David found the largest, most intricate key of the bunch.

Good bet you belong to the outer gates.

With a twist, David undid the clasp, removed the key, and pocketed it. He pulled a torch from the center of the yard and approached the nearest cell. It was empty. So was the next one. An old gladiator slumped in the corner of the third.

"Hey," David whispered as loud as he dared.

The man didn't even stir.

"Hey, you." Louder this time.

The old man startled awake, then stilled as his eyes settled on David. He cocked his head to the side but remained seated and silent. David snaked the key ring through the bars, rattled them once, then tossed them toward the gladiator. They landed right in the older man's lap. He looked down at them, then back up at David quizzically.

"You'll have a better chance at freedom if you open the rest of the cells," David whispered as he wedged the torch in the bars and crept back into the night. Keys rattled as the man stood and walked to the cell door.

Not the stealthiest person in Darin.

David smiled.

One more stroke of luck tonight.

He headed back to the tower at the far edge of the pit. The cell to the right of the spire housed the star-gazing gladiator. The one to the left was empty, and the door hung ajar. David slipped inside the empty cell and carefully pulled the door a finger's width from shutting.

Wouldn't want that to latch.

He moved to the darkest corner, hunkered down, and waited.

Two gladiators worked quickly, opening cells simultaneously. Before long, most of the slaves gathered at the front gate.

Torchlight flickered into existence in the tower.

Finally, they're up.

All the slaves were out, and most were trying to open the thick oak door to the street. David fingered the key in his pocket.

The door to the tower burst open, and men poured out. They were likely mercenaries or perhaps retired guards from the city watch.

I wonder how this will play out.

The hired men's best fighting years were behind them, but they were armed and armored. On the other hand, the gladiators had youth and were fighting for their lives.

Wouldn't mind putting a little stone on the gladiators.

As the mercenaries fanned out and encircled the slaves, an older man stepped calmly from the tower. He was lean, muscled, and scarred like a butcher's block.

You must be Odin.

The gladiators formed a tight circle.

The guildmaster moved forward, face tightening as he watched the men who filled his coffers square off with the men who drained them.

David slipped from his cell and slid along the wall behind Odin and into the tower.

A desk sat in the middle of the room, surrounded by fancy couches and a fireplace. Stairs wrapped the outer wall of the building, spiraling up the structure and down into a basement. David bolted up the steps, taking them two at a time. He passed an open door at the first and second landing, but the one on the third floor was shut. He ignored it.

The ledger will be on the highest level, and it's all that matters.

The door to the fourth floor was open. The room contained a large office and living quarters. The clang of steel on steel resonated through the windows from the courtyard below.

Sounds like the gladiators armed themselves. That'll buy me some time.

The stairs ended in a half circle landing on the fifth floor. A solid wooden door framed by two burning torches stood opposite the steps. David gave the doorknob a tentative turn.

Locked.

He pressed his ear to the wood.

Nothing. Not even the clatter of a chip.

David pulled his two lucky lockpicks from his belt and inserted them into the keyhole. They scraped around inside the device. Something moved in the mechanism, and he held that pick in place. He pushed the other pick to the same spot, then slid the first further in. Another pin moved. He twisted the picks, and the lock let out an audible click.

Huh, guess even a blind butler bumbles into the door once in a while.

David turned the handle and pushed the door lightly. It swung inward soundlessly on well-oiled hinges.

Moonlight streamed through a dozen windows, lighting the space. Ornate, clearly custom bookcases curved around the walls between the glass-filled openings, and a giant desk stood in the middle of the room. A plush chair sat behind the desk, with two slightly less extravagant seats opposite it.

Expensive. Glad my debt hasn't been paying for anything frivolous.

David strode to a window overlooking the courtyard at the far end of the room.

Let's see how much time we have left.

The Trickster moon peeked through the clouds, bathing the killing ground in crimson.

Greedy fucker, gotta take in the carnage, don't you?

David's gaze shifted from the moon to the gladiators below. They were losing.

"Guess I really don't know where to hedge my bets," he muttered.

Something creaked behind him.

David instinctually shifted to the right. A club slammed into his left shoulder with a crack. He bent with the blow, absorbing some of the impact with his legs as he sprawled to the floor.

David rolled to his back.

An older man loomed over him. He rippled with sinewy muscle, and scars crisscrossed him like a stack of cards tossed on the floor. David rolled to the left as the club hammered into the carpet with a thud. He sprang up, dodging another swing. The man leveled the club at him like a fencing sword.

Guess I was wrong. You must be Odin.

Odin moved faster than anyone his age had a right to. David leaned back as a hard cross swing clipped the tip of his nose, knocking his head to the side. He barely ducked under the next swing and felt the club graze his curly mop of black hair.

David pulled the knife from his boot and lunged up at the old man's neck. Odin brought the club down, deflecting the blade. The strike skidded off a rib and sank into the flesh underneath. David tried to pull the blade free to strike again, but the club crunched into his side. He lost his grip on the blade and wobbled backward, feet tangling as he twisted. Mortar-lined stone filled his vision, then his head slammed into the wall beneath a window.

Wispy spots danced through David's sight as he grabbed the windowsill and pulled himself onto unsteady legs. His eyes briefly met the Trickster's before he turned back toward the old gladiator. Odin staggered back, knees wobbling. Blood dripped from the pommel of David's blade onto the expensive carpet.

With a flick of his wrist, David flung another dagger from his sleeve. The blade sunk into Odin's left shoulder. Unfortunately, he was wielding the club in his right. Odin stumbled at him with a sudden burst of uncontrolled speed, bringing the club down in a momentous chop. David ducked, springing forward and leaning into the blow. The club shattered the window with a shrill crack. David pushed up, throwing Odin's legs into the air.

The rest was simply a matter of momentum.

The remaining glass shattered as Odin's shoulders crashed through it, and he sailed into the night. David stood, turning just in time to see the man hit the ground near the bottom of the tower with a wet smack. Someone skidded to a halt in front of the body, then vaulted over it and sprinted into the building.

Time to go. He's gonna be up here in no time.

David ran a hand along his ribs and winced. Two of them jutted out at an odd angle.

Dislocated, maybe broken too. At least Jocey taught me how to set 'em.

With all the concentration he could muster, David placed his right palm over his ribs and angled his elbow up toward the wall. With a scream, he threw his weight against the smooth stone, elbow first. His ribs ground back into place with a sucking pop. David fell to the floor, gasping. For a moment, all he managed to do was lie there and groan.

"Damn, Jocey," David moaned through gritted teeth. "Wouldn't have done that if you'd been honest on how much it was gonna bloody hurt."

After what felt like minutes but was probably seconds, David wobbled up. He limped over to the door and locked it, then took the rope from his bag and secured it to the massive desk in the middle of the room. His ribs throbbed as he tossed the coiled rope across the room and turned back to the desk. David pulled open the top drawer and rifled through it. There were pens, letter openers, and a seal, but no green ledger. He moved on to the next drawer. Paper and trinkets.

The bottom drawer was locked.

David jammed his two favorite picks into the mechanism. They bound up. He tried to turn them. They didn't move. He tried to pull them out. They were stuck.

"Son of a monkey's pox."

He glanced at the door, then wrenched on the picks.

Snap. Two little steel tabs protruded from the end of the lock. The rest of his lucky picks lay on the floor.

"Borix's brown butthole!"

David pulled the sword from his belt and jammed the tip between the desk drawer and frame. He pried at the two pieces of wood, using the blade like a crowbar. Pain spiked through his side as a long, drawn-out series of vowels escaped his gritted teeth.

The front of the cabinet broke clean off.

David tore the drawer open. Nothing green, just dark-brown files and folders.

"Fuck, fuck, fuck—bloody fucking fuck!"

Mind racing, David flipped through the documents. The last file slid forward, revealing the back of the drawer but no ledger.

What now?

He looked around the room.

It could be anywhere.

Slowly, his eyes drifted back to the drawer. Past the back of the last hanging file was a sliver of color. Frantically, he ripped out the folders, revealing a green book resting flat on the bottom of the drawer. David let out an audible sigh, then instantly regretted it as his side punished him. He took the green ledger, tucked it into the inside pocket of his jacket, and limped toward the farthest window from the courtyard.

No time for the glass cutter.

David grabbed a book from the shelf and hurled it at the window. It bounced off and came back, hitting him squarely in the head.

"Fuck!" David stomped out a circle, pinching the bridge of his nose. "Cock. Bitch. Evil-titty-gremlin." The curses came out sharp and nasally.

The shooting pain slowly subsided to a dull throb.

David returned to the desk, dragged the most lavish of the three chairs to the window, and smashed its legs into the glass. It broke this time, and once he had a hole big enough to fit through, he shoved the chair out the window. Wood splintered on the cobbles below a few seconds later.

David looped the rope quickly through the belay device on his belt, then backed out of the tower window, rappelling down the stone exterior. The coarse rope flowed through his belt and hand in short bursts as his feet pushed away from the tower wall. Friction slowed his descent, but he didn't have much time, so he let the rope speed through the device.

A hard landing's better than a cut rope and a long drop.

David picked up speed near the midpoint of the tower and cinched the rope tight. His weight and momentum were too much.

The rope slackened, and he began to free-fall.

A loud screech tore through the night as the desk gouged through the floorboards.

He screamed, bracing for the end as the wall came up to meet him.

The desk crashed into the window frame. The rope went taut just as David's feet hit the parapet. Pain lanced up his legs as they took half his weight, while the harness strained against his back, taking the rest.

"Fucking son of a whoring mongrel!"

David's feet were fully nested in the thorny vines at the top of the wall. He tried to lift his right, then his left. Neither budged in the plants' barbed grip.

Something whizzed past David's head, and he let out a little yelp. He frantically looked around. Down in the courtyard, a guard was shouting and pointing as they loaded another bolt into their crossbow.

David pulled the slack out of the rope, yanked his right foot from the thorns with an agonized grunt, and placed it on a bare patch of stone. He did the same with his left, then stepped off the wall. The rope held, and so did the desk above.

No choice but to go fast now. They'll be headed out the front gate soon.

David rappelled in big leaps, avoiding what he could of the thorns. It was no good. They were everywhere. The only thing worse than hitting the wall was when the barbs came free. Each time, pain sang through his feet, causing him to let out a little curse.

"Fuck."

"Damn."

"Bitch."

"Cunny."

"Cocksucker."

"Thundercunt."

His feet hit the ground. David undid his climbing belt and left it hanging as he lurched away from the wall. His boots squished with blood as he ran, each footfall driving embedded thorns deeper into his feet. He started to slow as he got farther from the guildhouse and darted into the first alleyway he found. His vision blurred, swishing around like cloudy water in a dirty fishbowl.

Damn thorns. Damn vines. Damn—

He was having a hard time thinking straight and couldn't come up with something else to condemn to the hells.

Should've learned more about those vines earlier.

Despite a growing lack of awareness, David kept moving. He took alleyways randomly, trying to put more distance between him and the guild. His vision started to fade into a wall of white, and his movements became more of a drunken stumble than anything else. David collapsed face-first onto the filthy cobbles that lined the back alleys of Windmore.

The white wall enveloped him.

17
NATHAN

That night, Nathan dreamt. He dreamt of battles long ago and ancient betrayals. He dreamt of the dull roar of the crowd and the silence that followed. He dreamt of bloody work and death in the night.

Nathan scrambled into consciousness, instinctively reaching for the sword that wasn't strapped to his back. Sweat poured down his face as he blinked away the night's terrors. Nothing tangible told him death was coming to this little village, but he couldn't shake the feeling anyway.

The room was dark, quiet, and still. Nathan sat on a raised platform, pelts bunched around him and a feather-stuffed pillow pressed against the headboard. It felt extravagant after his days in the woods, and he doubted many outsiders would receive this treatment if they stumbled into Trill. Nathan had never heard of the village, but that wasn't surprising when he hadn't heard of anywhere.

By helping these people, will I fulfill a false god's prophecy?

He frowned.

Would the One be all right with that? Maybe not.

Nathan walked over to the washbasin and grabbed a towel.

Why else would the One put me here, though?

He wet the cloth and wiped his face.

Unless They didn't. But if not Them, then who?

Nathan scrubbed off the remaining sweat and grime from the forest as best he could.

No, the One is the only reasonable answer, and They would want me to be a beacon to these folk, no matter who they worship.

Clothes were laid out next to the large bowl. The pants' reinforced knees were wearing through for the second time, and the shirt had clearly seen more than its fair share of hard labor.

Those weren't there when I passed out.

Nathan cocked an eyebrow.

That's a bit unsettling.

He looked down at the shimmering water in the basin. The face staring back was not one he recognized. He had blue eyes, brown hair cropped short, and the beginnings of a beard. His face was scarred, but the white lines were old and weathered.

Guess I'm no stranger to violence.

Nathan squinted, trying to morph the reflection into something he might recognize. It didn't work. He dashed the water with his fingertips, sending ripples across the surface, then dressed and left.

A cool gust assailed him as the door swung open, revealing a sky full of stars.

How long did I sleep? A few hours? Or through a whole cycle of the sun and more?

Nathan scratched his chin.

Only one way to find out.

He stepped into the cool night air and walked up the empty street. The stars brought a modicum of light to the darkness, and all three moons cast their glow across the little village. He'd caught glimpses of the three moons on his trek through the forest, but the canopy had blocked out most of the light, preventing him from getting a complete picture.

The largest of the three moons was a rusty maroon. Small clouds swirled through its atmosphere, bright red lines interlaced the landscape, and ridges built up by wind scraped across the surface. It was immense, full, and cresting over the ridgeline in the distance.

The next moon was considerably smaller than the first, though still large. Yet, it grabbed Nathan's attention far more. It filled the middle of the sky as if it were the centerpiece of the night. Red rivers and pools surrounded black cliffs, jutting outward like thousands of fingers crossed and interlaced. The red lines flowed together, forming a grisly, grinning face.

Well, that's a bit unsettling.

The last of the three moons was much smaller. It was a deep, dark black, and judging by its proximity, Nathan decided it must be orbiting its much larger, fiery sister moon. A violet outline swirled about the third moon, pulling in light from everything around it. The light churned, mingling with the purple before being consumed by the jet-black void in its center. The vortex of a moon not only drank in the reflected light from the sun but also from its sinister sister, bending the expression on its face.

Why don't I remember these moons?

The largest seemed somewhat familiar, but the other two were foreign. Nathan racked his brain, sifting through the knowledge he could access. He knew a single noble house governed each city, and the capital was overseen by a council of three.

How do I remember that and not these moons?

He shook his head. It made no sense.

Nathan looked down from the moons to the surrounding mountains and forests, eventually falling on the streets and buildings closer at hand. Sentries were posted all around Trill. He could tell exactly where they were by the little balls of light bobbing through the night.

Fools. Might as well hang a sign above your heads.

Nathan headed toward one of the torchbearers, making a mental note to talk to the shaman from yesterday about the issue.

What was his name? Something with an R...Relis? Ramolor? Raymis? Nathan racked his brain. He'd been so tired when the man introduced himself. *Rayolour maybe?* That seemed right.

He took a little side path, ended up behind a sentry, and walked up, placing a hand on the man's shoulder.

The guard spun on him, young face twisting into a snarl.

"Oh, didn't see you there." The kid visibly pulled himself together. He had a slight accent, but nowhere near as pronounced as the man who'd tackled Nathan.

He can't be a day over seventeen. What's he patrolling for, and why so jumpy?

"Yeah. Sorry about that. Could you tell me where to find Rayolour?" Nathan asked.

"Ray-o-lour?" The kid sounded out the name slowly, then pursed his lips in a frown. "Oh, you mean Raylor?" The young man took a step back, grip tightening around the shaft of his spear.

"Yeah, that's the one," Nathan said, keeping his voice calm and even.

The kid glanced up at the sky, then back down, eyes meeting Nathan's once more.

The silence stretched as a dozen heartbeats went by.

Nathan raised an eyebrow, then tried again. "You know where he is?"

The kid stared back at him blankly for a moment, then it dawned on him.

"Oh! Raylor. Yeah. He's up the road." The young sentry pointed up the hill. "Well, I mean, his house is. Not real sure where he is, you know? But you might be able to find him there. Big house, on the left, with the porch. Can't miss it."

"You all right?" Nathan asked.

"Yeah. Sorry, it's just this damn moon."

144

"I see three."

"Oh yeah...guess so. But only the one gives me the jitters." He pointed up at the middle-sized moon with the grisly expression. The moon was full, or close enough, and while it did look somewhat frightening, it was still just a moon.

God, are they scared of everything here?

"Looks like a moon to me. What's your name, son?" Nathan tried to keep the condescension from his tone.

"Benjamin, or Ben for short," the kid said, extending a shaky hand.

Nathan reached out and grasped it firmly. The kid's grip was stronger than expected. For a moment, they just stood there hand in hand.

Awkward little bugger.

Nathan was about to say something when Ben finally loosened his fingers. The kid seemed a bit steadier, though, so Nathan decided the odd exchange had probably been worth it.

"What do you call it, Ben?"

"Call what?"

"The moon. The red one."

"Oh! The Trickster?"

"Guess so. How about the other two?" Nathan asked.

"Well, the big one over there is Huna." The kid pointed to the large, rust-colored moon. "And that one's Aura." He pointed to the little black and purple void.

"Well, don't worry about 'em too much, kid. They ain't gonna hurt you," Nathan said as he headed up the street toward Raylor's house.

"I'm not the only one who's afraid o' it, just so you know," Ben called.

Nathan nodded without stopping.

"It's bad luck. Plus, it's full. That's double bad!" the kid yelled after him.

Nathan waved over his shoulder.

It's almost as if these people want to be scared.

He frowned.

Who gains the most if this town lives in fear?

Nathan pondered the question as he walked but came up with no good answers. He rounded the corner near the top of the hill and spotted a big house on the left.

Kid was right about one thing: can't miss it.

The building was about six times larger than the other huts, and sharpened logs jutted from a porch that wrapped three of its sides.

When Nathan got to the front steps, he was surprised to find Raylor already on the porch. The middle-aged shaman stood at a table, surrounded by men and women with bows slung across backs and leaning on planted spears. Nathan approached and nodded a greeting.

"Ah, Nathan! Good to see you finally awake." Raylor's voice boomed a deep baritone, optimistic despite the somber gathering.

"How long was I out?" Nathan asked.

"For quite some time, my friend. You slept through the night and the whole next day. I came to check on you once, just to ensure you were still breathing."

"Guess I needed it," Nathan said.

"I would say you did. You slept well, I trust?"

"Perhaps too well," Nathan lied as dregs of his dreams came swimming back. He looked around the group. They had an air of confidence about them but were visibly relaxed and lacked the discipline of soldiers.

Hunters then?

"So, Nathan, I'm sure you have questions," Raylor began. "What would you know of us and of our little settlement?"

"Why did you cut down the trees around your village? Clearly, you've used some for defenses, but they also appear intentionally thinned."

"Perceptive." Raylor smiled, but the expression quickly faded. The shaman paused, considering his words. When he finally spoke again, his voice was grim, dark, and full of shadows. "For a long time now, we have been besieged...besieged by an evil that is as unpredictable as it is malicious. To answer your question, we thin the trees because it uses them."

"What kind of evil?" Nathan asked.

"Those who have seen its shadowy form say it climbs faster than a man can run. The trees seemed the most logical place to start, so we cut them down to take away its cover. We ended up with more wood than we knew what to do with, so we sharpened them to stakes."

"It stalks your hunters in the forest? Or is it so bold as to come all the way into Trill?" Nathan knew the answer before the question finished leaving his lips.

Jumpy Ben was answer enough.

"It comes all the way into Trill to take our people," Raylor said.

"Has no one seen it?"

"Some, though most who have, are no longer with us."

146

"Killed?"

"Or taken, which we expect is the same thing," Raylor said. "Few people still alive claim to have seen the beast, but those that do speak of a huge, shadowy figure. The sightings are fleeting and often from a distance. Still, there are a few things the witnesses seem to agree on. The creature is extremely fast and usually described as a hulking, shadowy blur. It's been seen walking on two legs or hurtling across the ground on all fours." Raylor's voice was slow, calm, and deliberate.

Despite his tone, the hunters shifted in their seats and glanced around at the surrounding darkness.

Do they think speaking of this creature might possibly bring it forth?

"It's a devourer of hope," one of the hunters cut in.

Well, that's dramatic. It must be a beast, though perhaps a particularly nasty one.

Nathan looked around the group. The abject horror he found there was palpable.

Do they think this thing is something mystical?

He shook his head.

Hard to say. People in the remote parts of the world believe all sorts of folklore.

Something deep in the back of Nathan's mind urged him toward superstition, but he stuffed the feeling down.

"The two or three it takes each month is tragic," Raylor said. "But the loss of hope will eventually destroy us."

"How long has this gone on?" Nathan asked.

"Years, now." Raylor closed his eyes, pinching the bridge of his nose between thumb and forefinger.

Nathan studied the shaman.

Is he the problem? No, I think not. Maybe the man from yesterday? No, not yesterday, two days ago. What was his name? Horin? Something like that—

"The confidence of our people has been lost," Raylor said. "Their confidence in my hunters and their confidence in me. The beast steals not only our women and children but our resolve."

Most of the hunters were nodding, but a few looked at the floor.

This thing takes their friends, their families, their loved ones. Are they really so powerless to stop it? Nathan doubted it, but he was becoming increasingly certain of one thing: *If the One put me here, it's to deal with this. Guess my missing memories will have to wait.*

"If I go to find the beast, who will join me?" Nathan asked.

Silence.

The hunters' eyes were wide, but each looked away as he tried to meet their gaze.

"None of you?" Nathan asked.

A red-hot anger stirred in the pit of his stomach.

Your heads hang in shame. Yet, when someone speaks of action, no one stands to fight?

Nathan let out a deep sigh, tamping the fury back down.

This isn't you. You're a calculating man, and anger will solve nothing here.

Nathan was sure of that, despite being unsure of most everything else. Still, he couldn't shed the distinct desire to shake the fear from them.

"I will follow you to find the creature. I will follow you to find Elrontis." The voice pierced through the dark, and hunters all around the table murmured.

Nathan leaned in, eyes slowly widening.

Raylor was clearly a hunter, but it was just as clear his best fighting years had passed. Between his position, status, and home, he had more to lose than most. What surprised Nathan more than Raylor's resolve, though, was the name he'd called the creature.

Elrontis.

"What did you say?" Nathan wasn't sure why or exactly how, but he recognized the word. It meant darkness and dread. Or literally, the dreaded darkness.

"I said, I'll follow you to find the creature. Together, we will kill it," Raylor explained.

Nathan opened his mouth to ask about the word again, but one of the hunters cut in first.

"I'll join the hunt as well," a tall, muscular woman said, thumping her spear on the wooden deck.

Nathan met her eyes, and she didn't look away this time.

Good. She'll do what needs to be done.

"As will I." A shorter man on Nathan's right spoke. He pounded the haft of his spear into the deck as well.

"We will track it and kill it." A third hunter slammed the butt of his spear into the deck.

"Find its lair and root it out." Another joined the call.

The wooden shafts drummed on the porch, growing to a dull roar.

The dam has loosened, so let the conviction flood.

Nearly all the hunters were pounding their spears into the floorboards now. A small, hesitant smile crept across Raylor's lips, and he gave a nod of respect. Nathan nodded back, then motioned toward the door. Raylor cocked his head to the side, then understanding dawned his weathered face.

"Hunters!" Raylor boomed. "Tomorrow, we will bring the fight to our tormentor. We will turn predator to prey!" A chorus of cheers rose from the men and women surrounding the table. Raylor let them continue for a moment, then raised a hand for silence.

"Tonight, though, let us come in from the cold and rest our weary bones. For tomorrow, we will have vengeance!" Raylor waved toward the house, and the group followed him.

Nathan waited until all the hunters filed in, then entered.

Raylor stood at the far end of a long table, adding fresh spices to a large pot over the hearth. The hunters seated themselves, and soon, Nathan smelled mulled wine and citrus. Raylor tasked one hunter with tending the pot and doling it out once ready, then met Nathan's eye and gestured to a room off the main hall.

Nathan followed Raylor, pushing past some pelts that served as a door. The hunters were in good spirits, and he could still hear their jubilant banter even after the skins waved shut behind him.

Just have to pray their hope in me is well founded.

But even false hope was better than the apathetic despair consuming this town.

Raylor lit a candle, illuminating the room with flickering light. Books, a desk with a map, and various trophies decorated the study's walls.

"How did you come by that name?" Nathan prodded.

"Raylor? I suppose my mother gave it to—"

"No, not that name. Elrontis. Where'd you come by it?"

"You should not speak it so lightly." Raylor's voice remained calm, but there was warning in it.

"You just said it. Do you think saying 'Elrontis' will somehow bring this creature down on us?" Nathan leaned in as he asked the question. He could feel the tightness in his jaw and a boiling in the pit of his stomach.

Calm. You were sent here to help.

"It's superstitious, I know. But the word has brought us nothing but misery."

"You need to say the creature's name. It will control you if you don't."

"I know, but most think it brings death."

"Fear of a word gives it power. That stigma makes your people act like mice instead of men."

"You are right. Still, if you must say it, please keep your voice down. For the sake of the hunters. They have already agreed to follow us, and I would rather keep their spirits high." Raylor met Nathan's gaze, then lowered his eyes and let out a long sigh.

Suddenly, the shaman appeared much older.

"All right, but where did it come from?" Nathan pressed.

"A man named Ishen gave it the name. He was the first of our people to be attacked."

"Where is he now? Did he get a good look at it?" Nathan asked.

"I imagine he did. We found Ishen in his cabin. He'd been living there alone, deep in the forest outside of town. This was before we moved everyone in from the outskirts, you see. Before we built all the barricades, thinned the forest, and relocated the common folk to the center of town."

"Any chance I can speak with him?"

"I'm afraid not. We found Ishen alone, bleeding, and not long for this world." Raylor closed his eyes and shivered.

Is he going to be sick? Nathan wondered but decided not to interrupt.

"What was left of Ishen's innards were spilling from his belly. Most likely, we scared it off since you don't live long with your guts in a pile." Raylor sighed again. "His insides were pulled out intentionally, and the work wasn't clean like a butcher. Instead, his entrails were gnawed, ripped, and chewed upon."

"And he was still alive?" Nathan asked, brow furrowed.

"We didn't think so at first. Ishen was old, but he'd been taking care of himself a long time. When you live the way he did, subsisting on your own, it makes you tough. Plus, I knew the man. He could be a son of a bitch, without a doubt, but there aren't many I would've preferred to have on my side in a scrap." Raylor paused and looked around the room. "I think I need some of that wine."

The shaman stood and pushed past the furs to the other room. A moment later, he returned with two cups, offering one to Nathan.

Not sure I really want this.

Nathan took the wine anyway. The warmth felt good in his hands, if nothing else.

Raylor sat on a low stool and took a long sip from his cup. "I hadn't seen Ishen for a while, but he looked strong still, or like he had been a short time ago. He probably could have held his own against any of us. But this thing, whatever it was, it hadn't even bothered to kill him. It had just started eating...devouring him while he was still alive. All the while, Ishen bashed the hell out of it with his fists. When we looked him over later, we found the bones in his hands were shattered to bits. I don't know how many times a person would have to slam an already broken fist into something to cause that kind of damage, but it must be a lot."

A bit of respect crept into Nathan's heart for these people. A blind man could see how much they feared whatever plagued them, and they truly believed it was some sort of monster.

Yet, they're willing to hunt this thing with me. Their hope and faith are admirable, even if their fear is not.

"So, how was it named Elrontis?" Nathan asked.

Raylor winced at the name but held his tongue.

"When we first approached Ishen, he grabbed a friend of mine by the cloak and pulled him close. Scared the hell out of all of us. Don't know how he was still alive, but he was." Raylor paused for a second, the weight of the memory evident in his eyes. "All he whispered was one word."

"I imagine I can guess what it was," Nathan said.

Raylor nodded.

"We tried asking what tore him open, but those were the last three syllables Ishen ever uttered. He said the word with such fear and dread we could only assume it was the name of whatever did this to him. Later, I wondered if the name was just the nonsensical ravings of the dying."

"The final words of men are seldom bits of parting wisdom," Nathan said.

How do I know that?

"True, but for better or worse, the last rasp of old Ishen stuck with us. That night, in that cabin, Elrontis was born. Perhaps not physically, but in the hearts of our people."

"The name has no other meaning for you?"

"No, it means death as well, but that came after the creature had taken more people than we cared to count." Raylor raised an eyebrow. "Are you asking if we ever heard the name before?"

"Yes! Had you ever heard the name Elrontis before?" Nathan pressed.

Raylor's eye twitched. "No. Later, like you, I decided it must have been the gibberish of a dying man. But at that point, it had stuck, so it wasn't gibberish anymore. Why? Does the word have meaning to you?"

"It does, though I'm not sure why. That seems too much of a coincidence to ignore, though, don't you think?" Nathan paused for a moment, mind racing. "Where did Ishen come from? Was he an outsider?"

"In fact, he was, but he came to Trill nearly thirty years ago when we were still somewhat welcoming to strangers."

"You didn't know anything else about him?"

"Some, but not where he hailed from," Raylor began. "Back then, we were willing to respect someone's privacy too. A lot has changed. I wish I could claim any of it was for the better." Raylor shook his head, then looked up. "What exactly does the word mean to you?"

"Technically?" Nathan asked but didn't wait for an answer. "It means the dreaded darkness. I just wish I could remember how I know that." He pinched the bridge of his nose and muttered, "Elrontis." The name was like a memory tickling at the edge of his mind.

Raylor let out a long sigh. His mouth was tight, eyebrows narrowed.

"What?" Nathan asked.

"The name is not something to be used lightly," Raylor replied. "When it must be spoken, then it must. I used it earlier to show conviction. But saying it merely to yourself, without any cause or warrant? It's simply tempting fate."

Nathan scoffed.

"I can tell I won't convince you, but many of the hunters believe saying the beast's name will bring it forth to pull their loved ones into the darkness."

I have no loved ones, or if I do, they're lost to me now.

Nathan met Raylor's gaze. It was undoubtedly superstitious drivel, but these people had fed, sheltered, and taken him in. He wouldn't fight about it, but neither would he bend to customs that were killing people with fear.

"How sure are you that Elrontis is a beast?" Nathan asked. "Are you positive it isn't a woodsman and a pack of hounds or wolves? I know it seems simple and a whole lot less scary, but the obvious answer is often the right one."

Again, Raylor winced at the name, and again the fury in the pit of Nathan's stomach started to rise.

They're far too scared of this word. About time we changed that.

"You must not say its name!" The objection wasn't Raylor's this time; it came from one of two hunters at the door.

I'm tired of this farce.

"What name? Elrontis!" Nathan bellowed as he stood.

"You must not say it!" the hunter repeated.

Maybe these folk do need to have the fear shaken from them.

"Think of our children, of our loved ones!" This time, it was the tall woman.

"I have no loved ones, and neither will you if you continue on this way. *Elrontis* will take them all from you. It will take *everything*!" Nathan shouted.

The tall woman lowered her head, but the edges of the man's mouth curled in a semi-snarl.

The first signs of violence.

Nathan widened his stance.

Brrrrrroooooooooonnngggggg.

The sound quaked through the walls of Raylor's house, stopping the hunters in their tracks.

What in the hell was that?

The low crinkle filled the night again as it reverberated through the town.

Nathan racked his brain...

The gong.

Slowly, the noise died out, and silence returned.

Nathan held his breath, ears straining.

More silence.

That's when the screams started.

18
RIGEL CROSS

E verything was cold.

Cross would have shivered if it hadn't taken so much effort. He looked up, trying to gauge how much longer he needed to hold on before Elinfall pierced the night sky. It was no good, he would never make it all the way to nightfall. Cross took a deep breath as one chilly evening faded to another.

Cold iron bars left indentations in Cross's cheeks as he searched for the source of the noise. A crash echoed through the yard earlier, and he'd seen a flicker of movement, but only the shifting of shadows since.

If only there were some stars tonight.

Cross glanced toward the place where Elinfall should be. It was covered in clouds.

Did I imagine the movement? Maybe, but the noise too? No, something's happening.

Cross's eyes strained, trying to pick up anything in the darkness.

Maybe it was nothing.

Something metallic clinked nearby, slowly growing louder.

Is that armor? No, smaller. Keys?

Cross's heart skipped a beat as Higrim's weathered face emerged from the shadows.

The older gladiator crept forward, wonder and wariness at war on his face as he inserted a key into the rusty lock.

A trap?

"You ready to get the hells outta here?" Higrim whispered.

Cross nodded eagerly but didn't dare make a sound. A smile crept across the older man's face, and Cross warily returned the expression. Higrim inserted the fourth key in the lock.

Grind, click.

A mechanism released, and the cell door swung slowly open.

"Take this." Higrim handed Cross the key ring. "Free everyone you can. I'll see about getting the gate open."

"Wait." Cross's voice was low but urgent. "How'd you get out?"

Higrim ran a hand through dirty brown hair and shrugged. "A man just showed up. Threw me the keys."

"You think it's a trap?" Cross asked in a hushed tone.

"Might be, but I can't see why the guild would let their gladiators out, even as a test."

Cross bit his lip, decided Higrim was right, then exited the cell. He crept along the wall, nearly tripped over a pot, and stifled a curse. The man in the back of the next cell stood, cocking his head to the side. Cross put a finger to his lips, then began inserting keys into the lock. On the sixth key, he finally heard the familiar grind and click. Cross motioned the man forward.

"Here, take these," Cross whispered, pulling half the keys from the loop and handing them to the man. "It'll go faster with the two of us. Higrim's already working on the main gate."

The gladiator gave a silent nod and stalked off in the opposite direction.

Cross continued around the yard, freeing ten men before passing the other gladiator again. Loud grunts rang out near the main gate. The gladiators were prying at a hinge on the solid oak door with a long metal bar.

Cross's heart sank. They were being far too loud.

Best get the rest of the men out for now.

Cross moved quickly, giving up the pretense of stealth. He finished unlocking the final cell, pointed to the gate one last time, and stopped. Metal plates ground together, audible even through the tower's thick stone walls.

Not long now.

The tower door burst open, and light poured onto the sand. Men emerged wearing armor, sharpened steel, and grim expressions. Cross darted into the nearest cell and crouched in the corner. His chest heaved as rage and adrenaline threatened to take the reins.

Outside the cell, the gladiators gave up trying to pry open the gate and formed a semicircle, preparing to fight. Cross considered joining them, then decided against it.

I'll do more for our escape from here.

"Hold the line!" Higrim shouted through the clatter of metal.

Armed and armored men continued to stream from the tower.

"Take their weapons if you can!"

The gladiators' formation tightened.

"Better to die with a taste of freedom than to the cheers of the Coliseum!" Higrim yelled. He was a soldier before being taken as a slave and talked of it often.

The flow of mercenaries was finally starting to lessen.

The Freemen employed retired city guards and sellswords to watch the gladiators during the day and even housed them in the evening.

All paid with blood money.

Cross's heart slammed, pumping liquid rage through his veins. It was only a matter of time now, like a kettle left over the fire.

Cross had been through enough fights now to know what the flickering fury was capable of. Soon, his hands would clench and his toes would curl. It would seep into his head and make his vision hazy. He would still be able to see, but faces would blur, and the line between friend and foe would become harder to identify. For now, the red haze lingered on the fringes of his vision.

The mercenaries were out of the tower, forming a semicircle of their own. They marched forward, boots clanking against stone paths and pounding into the sand, tightening the noose.

"Hold! Or we all die like bloody fucking dogs!" Higrim yelled.

The armed men passed Cross's cell.

Doesn't look good. Either the gladiators surrender, or more blood would soon soak the already stained sands.

The other gladiators saw it, too, and their morale was flagging.

Need to act soon, or they may give up.

Cross felt his nostrils flare with each inward breath.

Surprise is all I have. Best not waste it.

Despite a growing desire to act, he waited, fists clenched, head simmering with anger.

Finally, as the gladiators were completely penned in and likely about to surrender, one of the two guildmasters stepped into view.

Marius.

The guildmaster often oversaw their training, watching with an obsessive eye for detail. He corrected any misstep with brutal efficiency and an extremely heavy hand. Marius had taken a particular interest in Cross after his first savage show in the pits. He was cold, unrelenting, and profited more than most from the thriving slave trade.

He's just one cog in the mill, but he's a big one.

Cross stared at the guildmaster, eyebrows narrowing, teeth grinding. He let go of the straining beast inside him.

It was like the breaking of a dam.

The haze boiled forth, overflowing Cross's vision as his heart pumped fiery liquid fury through his veins.

"Hold, men! Let's give these insubordinate curs a chance to—"

Slap-slap-slap. Cross's bare feet pounded on stone.

The guildmaster's head whipped around.

"Take him down!" Marius bellowed.

The words barely registered through the fog of wrath.

The gladiators surged forward, engaging the line of sellswords.

The mercenary closest to Cross tried to turn, but his spear was wedged in the line of gladiators ahead. He let go of the shaft, fumbled with the strap of an enormous sword on his back, then gave up and pulled a short steel instead. He was still setting his feet as Cross reached him.

Off balance. Fatal mistake.

They were Marius's words.

Lessons you never should have taught me.

Cross slapped the sword to the side and grabbed the man's wrist. He wrapped his other arm behind the mercenary's elbow and pulled.

Crack.

The noise should have been sickening, but it was a melody. Bones snapped, flesh gave way to a protrusion, and blood followed. The rage controlled Cross now, but he'd learned more civilized combat in the last four years with the Freemen. He let the training guide his fury. The drills and techniques couldn't control the anger, but they could temper it, mold it. The guild had been forging him into a finely honed weapon, and now, he'd turn it back on them.

The mercenary gaped at his broken arm as Cross slammed a palm up into his nose.

Crunch.

The cartilage crumpled musically as he forced it into the man's brain. The mercenary went limp. Without missing a beat, Cross let go of the man's arm, snatching his dagger and short steel as the body fell away. He tossed the weapons toward the unarmed gladiators clustered near the gate. Rage pounded in his ears as he pulled the great sword off the lifeless man's back. The blade was massive, nearly as tall as a normal man.

The line of mercenaries was locked in combat with the gladiators, but a few were breaking free to defend the guildmaster. Cross bore down on the closest one, swinging the massive sword sideways. The guard raised his shield. Steel met steel in a clash of scraping metal. The shield took the brunt of the blow, but the weight of the blade and the force behind it spun the man.

The mercenary stumbled, trying to regain his balance. The greatsword came in low, cleaving through the man's legs. His torso and hips slid from the rest of his thighs and fell to the sand with a thump and a smattering of dust. For a moment the mercenary's legs teetered, then toppled. Cross moved on before the screams even began.

The yard was complete pandemonium. Cross reveled in it. A man charged him. He deflected the blow with a grunt. The smaller blade flew from the mercenary's grip. The man squealed and brought his hands up.

Too late.

Blood sprayed as head and hands fell away together, hitting the ground with a sloppy thump. Cross stepped through the red curtain, wiping viscous fluid from his eyes. He smelled iron, tasted it on his lips and in the air.

Marius was backing up, looking around at the chaos.

The line of mercenaries surged forward as gladiators yanked on spears, creating a break in the wall.

Cross noticed it only absently, eyes never leaving the guildmaster.

Two mercenaries broke free, moving between him and Marius.

Cross's legs started moving again, seemingly of their own accord. He brought the massive sword around counterclockwise as one of the two men moved up to meet him. The mercenary caught the blade in a grinding parry. The two swords scraped together until the crossguards met. The steel held, but the other man's wrist didn't. Bones crunched, and the mercenary's sword fell away.

Cross smashed a fist into the man's bewildered face.

The guard stumbled back and toppled.

Cross stepped in to follow, but the second man was coming on fast. Cross tried to get two hands back on his sword—

Too late.

He pulled his blade to the right to redirect the charging man's blow. The swords connected, and Cross's blade deflected the thrust, but not enough. The strike aimed at his neck sank into his shoulder.

Red-hot pain sang as the blade pierced muscle and scraped along bone.

Cross roared, dropping the massive sword. He grabbed the man's wrist with one hand and ripped the helmet from his head with the other. The first guard was starting to rise, so he hurled the helm at him. The casque clanged into the other guard's temple, sending him back to the dirt. Cross slammed his forehead into the face of the mercenary in front of him.

Crack.

The man stumbled back, letting go of the hilt of the blade. Cross yanked on the man's wrist. The mercenary lost his footing, crashing into the sand. With a howl, Cross pulled the quarter-span of steel from his shoulder and plunged it into the guard's spine as he tried to rise. The body fell back to the sand, leaking blood.

Cross bent, scooped up a fist of bloody sand, and shoved it into his shoulder wound with an agonized grunt.

Thump, thump, thump.

Another guard was charging. Cross hurled the sword at him. The man stumbled, attempting to deflect the blade careening toward him. Too slow. The sword hit the man pommel first, bouncing off boiled leather.

"Fuck!" The mercenary reeled backward.

By the time the guard regained his balance, Cross was rising, hands regripped on the greatsword. The guard screamed, then charged. Cross bellowed right back, bringing the blade around in an overhead chop.

The guard's steel sliced toward him, but Cross's massive sword was already coming down. The blade severed flesh and bone as it tore through the man's shoulder and ribs before finally wedging between his spine and pelvis. The right half of the man's body and the sword he'd been swinging fell away with a slurp, then a clatter. Cross attempted to yank the massive blade free of the corpse, but it wouldn't budge. He tried again.

Stuck.

Cross let go of the blade and stepped over the gory mess. Without breaking stride, he snatched up the short steel he'd hurled at the man. The first guard started to rise, clutching at his broken wrist and clearly still dazed from the helmet blow to the head. Absently, Cross put four fingers of cold steel through the man's neck. The guard fell to his face, letting out a gurgle as his last breaths pushed loose sand across the bloody yard.

Screams echoed throughout the compound as people died. Blood dripped from Cross's hands, face, and nearly everywhere else. The smell of iron, entrails, and bowels hung in the air. His shoulder throbbed dully through the fury.

The yard was a bloodbath. Carnage everywhere. None of it made sense.

Where am I? What am I doing?

The thought echoed through the red fog.

Cross caught a glimpse of Marius, and purpose streamed back into him. One more man stood between the two of them. Cross stepped forward, letting out a bloodcurdling howl.

The mercenary turned to run, but Cross lunged, thrusting the short steel into his side. The blade lodged in the mercenary's ribs as he twisted, pulling it from Cross's grip. He stumbled, then fell, driving the sword deeper with his weight.

The guard began to blubber.

Something about a child?

Cross barely heard it. He stepped around the man, not bothering to retrieve the sword. The guildmaster stood before him, and like Cross, he appeared to have lost his weapon.

Marius didn't turn and run like the moaning man behind Cross, though. The guildmaster squared off, rolling his neck as determination filled his features. His body was rigid and tense, and those blue eyes were as cold as ice. They were the same frigid eyes that observed Cross during sparring. The same icy gaze that watched him fight in the pits. The same calculating stare that Cross had grown to hate.

Confidence. Let's try and fix that.

A low, uncontrolled growl rumbled deep in Cross's chest as he stared Marius down. They were only three paces apart. For a heartbeat, everything around them, all of the violence, all of the death, seemed to stop. It was just the two of them.

Cross lunged forward, throwing the bulk of his weight toward the older man.

Marius stepped to the side at the last second, leaving a leg outstretched as he leaned away from Cross's reaching hands. Cross's foot caught on Marius's toe. He wobbled, then fell, hitting the ground headfirst. For half a heartbeat, his vision swam.

Got to move.

Cross turned to his back.

The old man was falling toward him, right knee leading the way.

Cross tried to roll.

Crack.

Marius's knee connected with Cross's ribs. Pain spiderwebbed through Cross's side. He growled, and another spike of agony spread through his chest.

"I told you to stop charging in. You need to use this, instead of this." Marius pointed from head to heart.

Cross didn't respond. Instead, he pulled his leg up and kicked it back down. His heel connected with the older man's ankle.

Crunch.

Marius went down, landing on top of him.

Cross grimaced at the pressure on his ribs and shoulder, but to hesitate was to die. He grabbed the guildmaster's long white hair and pulled him close. Marius swung a fist at Cross, but it bounced off his bicep. Teeth snapped together a finger's width from Cross's nose.

Cross slammed his free hand into the side of Marius's mouth.

Pop.

The old man's jaw dislocated. With the same hand, Cross grabbed the jawbone and squeezed.

Snap.

The bone gave way.

A blow came in from Cross's right.

He let go of the jaw to block and pulled Marius's hair back, exposing his neck. Cross leaned in, teeth sinking into Marius's throat. He bit down hard, yanking the guildmaster's head back.

Rip.

Hot, sticky blood fountained over Cross's face as the chunk of flesh came free. He pushed the guildmaster's still-flailing body off and spat the hunk of meat into the dirt.

Cross rolled over, got to his knees, and crawled on top of Marius's near-lifeless form. He grabbed the older man's head, pounding it against the hard, packed sand with all his considerable bulk.

"Diiii—"

Once. The skull cracked.

"—iiiiiii—"

Twice. The back of the head shattered.

"—iiiiee—"

Three times. Blood splattered, bits of skull and brain painting the sand.

"—eeee!"

Cross finished the scream as he slammed what was left of the man's head into the ground twice more. He inhaled, sucking in the red mist, then forced himself up. Cross's ribs ached. His shoulder throbbed. Slowly, the world flowed back into focus.

The gladiators were losing. There was no doubt about it. Most still alive had surrendered, and those who hadn't were fighting three-to-one.

This is over.

Cross had no intention of going back to his cell. Death would be better. He considered throwing himself into the remaining mercenaries, then glanced up. Elinfall had pierced the clouds.

Cross sprinted for the door of the tower. Steel rang all around the yard, everything smelled of blood, and somewhere glass was shattering.

I've got to—

Something flashed through Cross's vision.

Smack.

A body hit the sand directly in front of him, glass shards raining down around it. Blood, bones, and innards sprayed Cross. He nearly stumbled, then hurdled over the corpse, barely losing momentum.

I don't know what that was, and I don't care.

Cross burst through the tower door, charging toward the basement. He sprinted down the steps, trying to ignore the blaring throb of his shoulder and ribs. The pain was no longer a dull ache. It was real now and becoming more demanding as the fury subsided. Despite the pain, Cross took the stairs two at a time, ignoring the closed doors at each landing. No doubt the house slaves were in those rooms, but they had ample opportunity to escape every day.

Just gotta get to the basement.

The existence of latrines had amazed Cross when he first arrived at the Freemen's Guild. He'd asked a few of the gladiators how they worked and been the butt of more than a few jokes for weeks afterward. Eventually, they relented and explained how waste ran beneath Windmore.

He remembered laughing at the amount of work it must've taken, all so people could live packed like rats in a can. Cross smiled. He was glad they existed now. The sewers were no doubt built on the backs of thousands of Terran slaves, and it was only fitting they might be his only means of escape.

Hopefully, the mess in the courtyard keeps the Freemen busy for a time.

Marius would've noticed Cross was missing right away, but that wouldn't be a problem anymore. A giddy fear settled deep in Cross's bones.

I might make it out of here. I might be...free.

Cross could hardly wrap his head around the idea.

162

Freedom. The word seemed so fragile, like a star pulled from the sky and held in his palm. He imagined it: bright, delicate, and fleeting, like Elinfall in the morning light.

Cross stopped and sniffed. Something rank hung in the air. He walked to the door on his right and opened it. Human waste assailed his nostrils.

A slave looked up as he entered.

How long has he been down here?

The stone room was rectangular, with a shoot at the far end and a large channel of sludge below it. Cross stepped past the servant, eyeing a horrific broom and shovel propped against one wall.

Perhaps there are worse things to deal than death.

Cross turned back to the middle-aged man.

"I'm leaving. There's chaos in the compound above. If there was ever a time to escape, it's now." Cross's voice came out a rasp. He hadn't realized the full extent of the damage to his ribs, and even talking pulled at the muscles in his skewered shoulder.

The older slave shook his head.

"Why not?" Cross asked.

No response.

"There's nothing left for you here." Cross gestured around the chamber.

The man shook his head again, then opened his mouth. A nub waggled back and forth where his tongue should be.

"They take it?" Cross asked.

The old slave gave a single nod.

"Good chance they're dead now," Cross said, pointing up.

"Ah-ah-ah." The man let out a bellowing laugh, but without a tongue, the sound was off.

"Not coming, then?"

The slave shook his head and made a slicing gesture across his throat.

I guess there's always something left to lose.

"Suit yourself." Cross turned back to the stream of sewage. He took a deep breath, set his jaw, and stepped off the ledge.

The stench hit Cross like a wave. He gagged, choking back bile.

Didn't think the smell could get any worse.

He looked up from the vile sludge that was up to his armpits. An iron grate blocked the stream ahead.

Cross's heart sank.

The metal bars must have been installed to deter anyone as desperate as he was from entering or exiting the Freemen's Guild through the sewers. Cross waded over to the grate and groped around in the muck. Jagged points protruded downward, but there was a substantial gap below them.

Either the metal wore away over time, or someone wanted to ensure it didn't clog.

Cross bit his lip and inhaled through his nose. The stench invaded his nostrils with new vigor, causing him to gag.

I can't imagine this will be good for the hole in my shoulder.

Cross knew nearly nothing about medicine, infection, or disease but realized a soak in this muck wouldn't hasten his recovery.

Oh, well.

With one more deep breath and another choked-off gag, Cross ducked under the surface. He cupped his left hand over his shoulder in a futile attempt to keep it clean and grabbed the bottom of the grate with his right, pulling through the vile muck. The journey was immeasurably disgusting but blessedly brief. Cross emerged on the other side. He tried to hold back a retch, failed, and that evening's dinner came up.

The bile swirled in the rancid liquid, joining the rest of Windmore's bodily fluids. Cross wiped the remaining sludge from his nose and mouth, vomited again, then staggered down the ever-darkening tunnel. The light illuminating the slave's chamber slowly faded as he waded chest-deep into shit, piss, puke, and darkness.

As Cross rounded the first turn, the light disappeared entirely. He continued, fingers sliding along the slime-filled crevices lining the tunnel wall.

Hopefully, if I...no, hopefully, when I get out of here, the stars will be out. Maybe then I can follow Elinfall to the east.

To the east, and to Terra.

19
GERARD STOCKWORTH

The darkness stretched on forever, an endless void. The lantern creaked as it swung back and forth, causing shadows to slink and jump across the dirt walls. Gerard had walked for hours with nothing to do but think. Worst of all, the only thing he could think about was Vigilant.

How could I've been so stupid? Didn't check Jeff's bonds all day.

The rain and foul weather had distracted him, causing him to focus on the wrong things.

Sloppy. Fucking sloppy.

Gerard let out a groan.

Knots loosen when they get wet, for fuck's sake.

Gerard had considered taking his sword to the hatch, but cutting his way out would've taken hours, and Jeff would have been long gone.

I'll never forgive myself if something happens to that horse. The thought made Gerard's skin crawl, but he tried not to linger on it. *Vigilant's worth a lot more alive than at the butcher.*

Gerard turned his attention back to the crawling gloom.

Who built this monstrosity, and why?

He lifted the lantern high, shedding light a little further. It weighed far too little.

How long have I been down here?

Time underground was a funny thing. He checked the oil reservoir.

Less than half an hour left. Better make the most of it.

Gerard began to jog.

Running had its own perils but was less risky than groping through the dark. Once the light went out, his progress would slow to a crawl, and there would be no telling if the tunnel split or slowly changed direction.

Gerard was sweating when the light finally guttered out. He stopped, breathing hard as he waited for his eyes to adjust.

They didn't.

Darkness is so complete underground.

He reached out with his right hand, tentatively stepping toward the wall. After a few shuffling steps, his weathered fingertips brushed coarse, packed dirt. Gerard took a moment to imagine the long expanse stretching out before him. He moved slowly forward until his fingers found a vertical support running up the side of the tunnel. Gerard pointed the lantern away from his body, then shattered the glass against the heavy timber. Carefully, he gathered the pieces and spread them across the tunnel behind him.

With any luck, that'll tell me if I get turned about.

Gerard wasn't sure he'd hear the glass against the stiff dirt, but it was worth a shot. He held one hand against the wall and stretched the other out. He took a cautious step, then another. A third—

His outstretched fingers collided with something coarse, almost bristly. He resisted the urge to recoil and ran his hand along the object.

Rough-cut wood. A low-hanging support—not meant for touchin'.

Gerard bit his lower lip.

No way to move fast anymore. Not if I want to keep my head on straight.

With a sigh, Gerard ducked under the beam and groped his way forward.

Hope they didn't discover any crevasses when they built this place.

Gerard grimaced as an image of Jeff dumping Vigilant in a ditch flashed through his mind. He pushed the notion away and plodded forward, but it was tough not to think about his horse when the only distraction was the occasional timber brushing by his fingertips.

Every ten paces or so, a support ran up the side of the tunnel, but only occasionally were they low enough to force him to duck. He didn't count with any sort of conventional time. Instead, he counted the wooden columns as his right hand grazed them. He finally gave up and slumped down against the dirt wall after feeling the rough-cut grain of number six hundred and thirty-seven.

Gotta remember to turn right when I wake up.

Gerard closed his eyes and exhaled, long and deep.

Right. Right. Right...unless I got turned around already.

No, that was unlikely. His right hand had only left the wall for seconds, and he'd heard no glass underfoot. Still, it had been a long day. Gerard had rode for over twelve hours in freezing rain and spent who knows how long plodding down the tunnel of eternity. He felt his eyes close again, then forced them back open. He groped around, crawling forward until he found a timber column. With a grunt, he jammed his hunting knife into the wooden support, slumped against the wall, and let sleep take him.

Gerard awoke from drowning with a start. Over the next few frantic breaths, the frigid waters faded into the nightmare they'd been.

No matter—dreams are meant to be forgot.

Gerard fumbled around, feeling for his knife. He found the wooden support but no knife.

A jolt of panic hit him.

Shit.

Gerard frantically groped for another column. His fingers found more rough wood on the opposite side of the tunnel. He reached up, hands patting the bristly texture until they closed on something cold and solid.

A little shiver worked up his spine, and he pulled the knife free.

Must've been tryin' to swim outta here.

Gerard oriented himself by putting his right side toward the marked column, then began walking at the same slow pace. His muscles ached, and his hand was raw from scraping along the packed dirt, but the only option was to endure.

An undefinable amount of time passed.

Am I just stumbling deeper into a mine shaft with no exit? Perhaps it's time to turn back.

No, his lips were already cracking, and his mouth was dry.

A shred of light flickered into existence in the distance.

Gerard squinted.

The light vanished.

A trick of the eye?

He was far from sure but trudged down the tunnel anyway. The light reappeared every few minutes, growing larger as he grew nearer.

Before long, Gerard stood in front of something cold and solid. A moment later, soft, even footsteps fell on the other side of the barrier, and a new shred of light illuminated his bootstraps. He looked around, assessing things in the dim light. The cold object turned out to be three fingers of oak inlaid with more thick iron than was any sort of practical. The door had a large slat cut into the wood at head height, a metal plate blocked the opening, and there was no keyhole or handle.

Not lookin' to entertain.

The light faded with the soft footfalls, leaving Gerard in darkness. Heading back to the cabin wasn't an option without more water.

So it's death or the door.

Gerard frowned.

Maybe I just ask nicely? The thought nearly made him laugh.

It was quite some time before the tiny glow reappeared in the corner of the frame. Slowly, the light grew, and more soft footfalls joined it. Old, rusty iron creaked as the source of illumination shifted back and forth. Gerard held his breath, waiting until the light was directly on the other side of the oaken barrier.

He rapped on the wood hard.

The footsteps stopped.

Silence.

Gerard blew out a long breath, then beat on the door again.

No response.

He waited, body rigid, arm poised like a snake, ready to strike at the slat. His thumb moved across his first two fingertips—a nervous tic developed in some lotus house long ago.

Nothing happened for what felt like an eternity. No sounds, no shifting of the light. Even the air was stagnant. Then the slat slid open with an old, tired grind.

Gerard lunged forward, hand breaching the barrier.

Someone gasped.

His fingers opened and closed once, grasping only air, then his thumb and forefinger caught something slimy. Gerard's first instinct was to recoil, but he fought the urge and latched on instead.

Whoever was on the other side of the door yelped as he pulled them tight to the wood. His eyes slowly adjusted to the light, and a face came into focus. A hazel eye was pressed tight to the slat, held there by his pinched fingers. The skin around the eye was expertly shaded with charcoal and had a green streak painted at the corner.

"Open the door." Gerard's voice came out more growl than coherent words.

Whoever was on the other side let out a petrified little shudder, but the door didn't open.

"I'm not gonna hurt you."

Unless you don't open this door.

Silence.

Gerard looped a finger through a lock of stray hair, securing his grip on something more solid than a wet flap of skin.

Cheeks are a slippery business, after all.

He tried again. "I gotta get through here. Someone's life depends on it."

Half a minute crawled by.

Might have to do something drastic. Something—

A bolt clicked, and the door swung slowly inward. Gerard shoved a foot past the threshold, let go of the cheek, and stepped into a narrow hallway.

The full light of the lantern forced him to squint as the form before him slowly took shape. She was young, with a face made up to look much older than it was. The young woman shrank back as Gerard grabbed her shoulder and leaned in.

"Lead me to a room where we won't be disturbed."

"You said you wouldn't hurt me," she whimpered.

"I won't...if you hurry." His voice was soft yet undeniably threatening.

The young woman led him quickly to a room down the hall and opened the door. Gerard bustled her into the space, then let go of her and closed the door behind them. He turned to find her backed into a corner and still clutching the lantern.

Good.

Gerard didn't want to hurt the girl, but scared meant pliable, and pliable meant he wouldn't have to do anything drastic.

He spotted a pitcher on a silver tray, walked over, and downed the contents. Nearly a cup of water ended up on his shirt and the floor, but it was hard to care about that at the moment. Gerard set the clay vessel back on the tray and looked the girl up and down. She wasn't wearing much more than a slip, and one of the straps had fallen off her shoulder.

She's pretty.

Gerard took another two steps forward.

The girl cringed. "Take what you want, just don't hurt me." She pulled her arm from the fallen strap, exposing well-oiled and unblemished skin.

Gerard cocked his head to the side, eyebrows slowly knitting together.

She pulled the other strap down.

"Whoa! Hold on." Gerard grabbed the dainty strap in two meaty fingers, hand brushing against her light brown skin as he pulled it back up. He felt himself stiffen.

Damn, it has been a long time.

Gerard pushed the notion away and took two steps back. The girl was probably an adult, but it was hard to be sure with all that makeup. Besides, even if she'd been ten years older and they'd met in vastly different circumstances, he had a horse to find.

"I appreciate the offer, but someone's life really does depend on me."

The girl hung her head.

"I mean...not to say you aren't pretty," Gerard explained. "You are...I just. Well, I just need some information, is all."

The girl looked up, her face a mask.

"What is this place?" Gerard asked.

The girl remained expressionless.

Dumbfounded? Or terrified?

"Where are we?" he pushed.

She glanced at him sideways and then around the room. He followed her eyes with his own. An enormous bed stood in the corner, surrounded by smooth sheets of hanging silk, and the rest of the furniture was just as plush. He looked back at her and the clothes she wore, or more importantly, the ones she didn't.

The girl must have seen recognition dawn on him, for she finally spoke.

"'Tis a pleasure house, m'lord."

Gerard had visited brothels before, but they hadn't looked anything like this. The room was too fancy, and this girl was far prettier than any night-cat he'd ever seen.

A romp in this place must cost a fortune.

"How'd you get here?" Gerard asked. "And what's the tunnel for?"

The girl shied away from his gaze.

"They hurt you?"

She didn't answer, but she didn't have to. Her eyes were answer enough.

Gerard stepped in, hands out to the sides, maintaining eye contact the same way he'd have treated a skittish horse.

"It's okay. I'm here to help," he stated.

Her eyes darted to either side like she might lash out or bolt.

"No need for that. I'm not gonna hurt you. What's your name?"

She hesitated, met his eye again, then answered, "Ana."

"All right, Ana, how'd you end up here? And why's there a tunnel in the basement of a pleasure house?"

Ana's chest filled as she drew in a deep, quavering breath.

"I w-was the daughter of a farmer," Ana said, slumping into a chair. "We lived outside of Grenisport in a small tan house. My father and brother worked the field on our little plot of land. One morning, after I returned from berry picking, I found the house aflame. As I ran toward the fire, I nearly tripped over my brother's body." Ana exhaled through tight lips. "He was all splayed out. With two deep holes in his back, and covered in blood. I rolled him over. His eyes. They were so wide."

The girl's eyes were wide too.

"I wept. All the while, the house burned." Tears streamed down Ana's face as the words tumbled from her lips. "The next thing I knew, a bag was over my head, and someone was tying my hands behind my back. I screamed. They hurt me for it. I tried to fight. They hurt me worse for that."

"I'm sorry," Gerard said.

Slaves were only supposed to come from Terra, and most people thought they always did, but Gerard had no such delusions. Terra had attacked first in the War of Iron and Blood, but the people of Darin had finished that fight, and truthfully, they hadn't been real civil about it.

The Terrans would've done the same thing if they'd won. Or maybe somethin' worse.

People were mostly terrible in Gerard's experience. A person could be good, but people on the whole...

Rotten.

The slave trade had big problems. The only discernible difference between a Darin and a Terran was their accent, which lasted a generation at most. So, the best way to tell if someone was a slave was to check the brand on their right hand.

And a brand's only as honest as the man holdin' the end of the iron.

He knew some slavers took from this side of the Divide. It wasn't legal, of course, but it was lucrative, and stone had a way of making most any problem disappear. It was a flawed system, all in all, but it kept grain in Vigilant's stall.

Gerard pulled his focus back to the girl. "How'd you end up here?"

"I screamed and fought a lot that day. They struck me for it, but I had a hard time caring. Finally, they pulled the bag from my head. The sun was so bright in the late afternoon. I couldn't even get a look at them before they shoved something over my nose, and I blacked out."

Lotus extract, refined real pure. It wouldn't take much to do that to a child.

Gerard scratched the right side of his neck, trying to think of something consoling to say.

Nothing came.

"When I woke up, I was in a cabin," Ana continued. "Things got a little better after that. The man there was nice to us, but we weren't allowed to leave."

"Us?"

"There were a bunch of us girls in the cabin. A few boys, too, but not as many. The man read stories to us at night, and he was kind. I remember that. We all wanted to go home. Wanted to see our families again." A single tear streamed down Ana's face, and she lowered her gaze. "I guess I was still lying to myself then. Pretending there was a family to return to."

Gerard remained silent despite an itching desire to get to Vigilant.

"A few days later, the bad men returned with more kids. The next day, the old man led us down a long tunnel. I thought you might be that nice old man." She paused again, glassy-eyed and distant.

"How old were you?" he asked.

"Seven."

A vision of Arabella swam through Gerard's mind. A daughter lost long ago. Before the pox took her and her mother, and before the lotus had taken him. He pushed the memory away.

Focus. Got problems here and now.

"How long have you been here?"

"Thirteen years."

Gerard wanted to vomit, but it turned out his stomach was made of sterner stuff.

"All the girls end up here?" he asked.

"Depends on their looks. Some are sold off and end up as chambermaids or some such. They usually sell the boys, too, but some of the real pretty ones stay here. For the more...eclectic clientele."

"Well, that word's certainly worth at least a ru'. You mean some of your patrons are into boys?"

She nodded, and Gerard met her eye.

Don't get attached.

Gerard shook his head.

Ah, hells, I guess it's a little too late for that.

Arabella would've been only a few years younger than this girl.

Gods, I am gettin' too old for this shit.

"Wait here a spell. You never saw me, got it?" Gerard walked to the door.

"You aren't going to hurt anyone, are you?" Ana asked.

"Not if I don't have to."

He turned back. She wasn't crying anymore.

"I know some people in high places. I'll see what I can do about all this," Gerard said.

"I wouldn't mind." Ana hesitated. "That is..."

"You wouldn't mind what?" Gerard asked.

"If you see a wiry man on your way out with a missing nose and a bunch of earrings, I wouldn't mind if he got hurt. Most us girls wouldn't."

He held her eye a moment longer, nodded, then stepped through the door and shut it.

Gerard's mind was a torrent as he walked to the staircase at the end of the hall. He knew slavers branded legal citizens but didn't expect it on such a large scale or in such a highbrow establishment.

Some of the slaves I've brought back to face House Rocktell's justice likely weren't real slaves at all.

The thought didn't sit right, but it was reality.

This place needs dealing with, but I'm not the right man for that job.

Gerard headed up the steps. The banister was fine polished wood, and the walls were lined in velvet.

Where's this place located?

Gerard ran his fingertips along the finery.

Why didn't I ask Ana that?

He shook his head. It was a silly mistake.

Probably just outside of Windmore. Somewhere that won't attract attention.

He had a good sense of direction, but there was no telling where he'd ended up after miles in the dark. Gerard softened his tread as he crested the top step. A luxurious and overly ornate lobby sprawled out beyond an open door. Three couches upholstered with fine imported silks filled the room, surrounded by mahogany trim polished to a brilliant hue.

Polished by little girls stolen from their cribs.

A woman, presumably the madam, was seated behind a small desk, and a man stood before it, chatting with her. He had at least six earrings studded with little sapphires in one ear alone and only half a nose. A chandelier and fireplace lit the room, but no windows let in sunlight.

That desk should face the front door in a typical brothel.

It was a risk, but Gerard had places to be, so he strode toward the door he assumed was the entrance like any other patron. The madam and man stopped their conversation and watched him, and he was halfway across the room before the man spoke.

"Hey! What in the hells do you think you're doing?"

Gerard ignored the question, finishing the last few steps to the door, and opened it. He was greeted by a dark, cloudy sky and the quiet pitter of rain as it pissed onto cobbled streets. Gerard took a deep breath, basking in the tiny bit of natural light.

Nothing like fresh air after a deep dark—

"Hey! I'm talking to you." The man's voice was raised and aggressive.

Gerard ignored the noise, savoring the sweet smell of new rain.

"Not only are we closed, but you're getting dirt all over my carpets."

Two thuds sounded as the man took two steps toward him.

I'm coming, Vigilant. Just gotta take care of one last thing.

"Who's going to pay for this?" the same voice demanded—right behind him.

A hand clamped on Gerard's left shoulder, and something snapped inside him.

He turned. In a flash, two handspans of steel appeared in his right fist. Gerard plunged the blade into the ugly man's gut and twisted. The slaver doubled over, and the hunting knife slid free with a squelch.

"You—you fucking stabbed me!"

"Sure did."

"W-w-why?" All of a sudden, the bravado was gone. Gerard wanted to tell the man he shouldn't force little girls into slavery, that he shouldn't be complicit in the murder of good, honest folk. But he didn't.

"Blood stains worse than dirt," Gerard said instead.

"W-what?" The man clasped his belly as he fell onto one of the plush sofas.

"Now you ain't gotta worry 'bout the dirt on the floor," Gerard explained as he turned and stepped through the open frame.

"You're going to fucking pay—"

The door thumped shut and latched, muffling the man's threats behind a grip of solid oak.

I shouldn't have done that, Gerard thought, but it was hard to regret.

The man had probably done unspeakable things to those girls, and that was plenty enough reason to die in a world as ruthless as this one. Gerard knew he was a son of a bitch himself, but he still had scruples.

Men like him don't.

Gerard looked around. He stood in the middle of Windmore, in an upper-class district, no less. He'd walked this street often and never thought twice about the unmarked and nondescript building behind him. Sex work was only legal for free citizens, but that didn't stop places like this one from existing. It was an odd distinction, but it felt right too.

Clearly, the corruption's extensive, but how deep does it run, and what kind of hornet's nest did I just kick?

Now wasn't the time to worry about that, though. Gerard needed to get back to the cabin and pick up Jeff's trail.

Hopefully, Vigilant was still alive.

Don't be too much *of a pain in the ass, old boy.*

Gerard made his way toward the lower-class part of town in the drizzling rain. He needed to procure another horse to get on the road as soon as possible, and the mounts in this district were far too expensive. He worked through the familiar streets as quickly as possible but was drenched before even arriving in the outer city.

Soon, Gerard found himself in front of the Ancient Bagpipe Inn. Most people just called it the Old Sack, though. The weathered sign over the door was supposed to depict a bagpipe, but it looked more like a burlap sack with a few sticks protruding from the top.

Gerard walked around the back of the inn to the stables and found Tim standing there, shovel in hand. He was a good lad and always took great care of Vigilant.

"Hi, Gerard! Back from one of your jobs?" Tim asked.

The kid was always eager for a story, and usually, Gerard would've indulged him.

"I'm in a hurry, Tim. I need to borrow—"

"Oh, don't you worry about that, sir. Vigilant's aaall ready to go. I've already brushed 'im and fed 'im. Let me just—"

"What'd you say?" Gerard interrupted.

"Your horse, sir."

A familiar whinny sounded from the covered stalls. Gerard ran around the corner. There, at the far end, was Vigilant. He was trotting and hopping in place as he tossed his head about in excitement. Gerard ran to him, wrapping his arms around the big horse's neck.

"I thought I'd lost you, boy," Gerard whispered.

"He came in early this morning," Tim called out. "Looked like he'd been ridden pretty hard, but nothin' a bag of oats an' a good rub wouldn't fix. The man with him was kinda strange, though. At first, he asked me if we bought horses, but he changed his tune when

I asked about you. He said you'd be along and that you'd asked him to bring Vigilant back to town."

"He have another horse with him?"

"Sure did," Tim said. "The piebald's right over there."

Spots stood just two stalls down.

Didn't even see her. Must be losin' my touch.

"I thought it was kinda strange, him comin' into town with two horses and all. But he didn't seem in much mood for talking," Tim explained.

"You know where he went?"

"Not sure. It sounded like he might get a room for the night. But after I asked about you, he said he had some business to attend to, then just kinda limped out of here."

"Ah. Good lad. Well, if he comes back, make yourself scarce, eh? And if you see him walk out of these stables with either of the two horses, call the guards. Got it?"

"Yes, sir!"

"Now, if you don't mind, I'm gonna spend a little time with this fella," Gerard said, patting Vigilant's neck.

Tim excused himself with a smile.

Gerard took a brush from Vigilant's saddlebag and began to comb a very happy beast.

20
SCARLETT REINHOLM

A ll three moons were in their full glory. Sirius was high in the sky, Huna had crested the horizon, and Aura was just starting to peek from behind her sinister sister. As a child, Scarlett had always been fascinated by them. As an adult, she'd studied them. Now, she ached for them. Scarlett felt their power course through her veins. A tiny bit of her hated the three moons, but that part was inconsequential. The rest of her—the part that mattered—loved them more than she loved life itself. There was no denying that, not in the face of the three.

Scarlett's stomach churned. An insatiable, ravenous hunger swelled deep in the pit of her belly. She stood, ingredients tumbling from her lap into the snow. Her rocking chair creaked as she stepped to the edge of the little porch. The voracious feeling started in her stomach, rumbling there for a moment, gathering momentum. Then it spread, rising to her mouth and seeping into her loins. Scarlett ached and began to salivate. Pressure built behind the bridge of her nose, turning to a dull throb. It was only a nudge at first, then slowly grew more insistent, building until she relinquished control.

Dark green eyes rolled back in Scarlett's head, filling with an inky jet black. The world came back into focus, new lines visible despite the darkness. Hairs grew over the back of her hands, enveloping her forearms as muscles buckled. She screamed, equal parts agony and ecstasy.

Foreign muscles knotted across her back as bones fractured and rearranged. A thick coat of fur grew in patches across her body. Her chest expanded, sinewy muscles pulling tight. A series of hideous cracks sounded as her ribs broke apart, grew, and reformed. New muscles flexed, rippling in the moonlight.

Hair follicles dotted Scarlett's body, filling any bare skin with a sleek brown coat. She doubled over in pain and euphoria as her facial features blurred. Fissures split Scarlett's skull as it cracked, widened, and pulled forward into a snout.

Row by row, new teeth formed, pushing incisors and molars from her gums like carrots sprouting through fresh soil. Her canines stayed, growing and curving into vicious spikes as her snout snapped and gnashed at the air. Loose cartilage fell away as new ears formed, tucking back with a flexing of her jaw.

With a jerk, Scarlett's arms stretched out, fingers splaying wide as her whole body racked with pain and pleasure. Her nails grew, extending into long, wicked points. Finger bones snapped and lengthened as powerful hands flexed, gripping the air. Stitches gave way to flesh as new feet tore free of leather. Her calves and thighs ripped through her pants, bursting forth like the final crescendo in a malignant symphony.

The Trickster grinned down at its malevolent creation with love and adoration. Scarlett's long, powerful arms rested in the snow as reformed legs bunched—ready to spring. Dark brown fur covered her entire body, except for a ring of tan running around her eyes, down her back, and to the tip of her tail. Mist rose from her coal black snout.

Scarlett stood, half-human, half-wolverine.

I'm not that, though. I am death.

A churning gurgle rumbled through Scarlett's belly, forcing her eyes from the moons. Her stomach felt tight, wrung out like a dirty washcloth. She needed to devour and somehow knew this hunger couldn't be appeased on the plateau. Wolverine meant glutton in the old tongue, but the name barely began to describe Scarlett's appetite.

She required flesh, and only fields of it would satisfy.

Cold night air wafted into Scarlett's nostrils, and she took it in with two long pulls. A picture slowly unfurled in her mind, like watching an expert painter as they added strokes to a canvas. Soon, Scarlett could smell everything. The water simmering over the hearth. The freshly split wood in the backyard. The faintly sweet willow trees. And Roland.

Scarlett's mouth watered.

No, I don't want moose. Not tonight.

A light breeze drifted up the mountain. It carried the smell of fires, livestock, and the intoxicating scent of human flesh. Scarlett's angular head reared up, taking in the scent with a deep, greedy inhalation. Her black eyes met with the beautiful moon's gaze one last time. A dozen heartbeats skipped by as she basked in its luminous splendor.

Scarlett's stomach rumbled again, pulling her from euphoria, and she started down the mountain. She moved in leaps and bounds across the tundra and down the steep, scree slopes. Before long, she neared the base of the plateau.

Torches shone like fireflies in the distance, revealing the village. She took in the scent, lowered her head, and loped into the tree line. The man camp disappeared, but she took in the succulent scent and followed its sickly sweet trail.

Deep in the woods, Scarlett stopped again. It reeked of human here. She could smell where they rested, where they made a kill, even where they'd relieved themselves. She stood for a moment, upright and inhaling. There were rodents, wolves, and even big cats about.

They shouldn't bother me. Natural creatures are more intelligent than that.

A wolf howled in the distance, and she considered following the sound. A pack of wolves wouldn't be a problem.

They might even sate my hunger.

Scarlett inhaled again. The scent of human was far more robust than the forest life, which meant they were far more...

Delicious? Delightful? Delectable? So many words—so little time.

Scarlett licked her lips. She could taste the wolves on the wind. They were close. Her nose twitched, weighing the options.

No, a meal must be fully appreciated.

After one more appraising sniff, Scarlett dropped back onto all fours and continued toward the village. She bounded along for a time, then slowed to a shambling sideways trot.

Snap.

Scarlett froze, ears perking up into two perfect triangles. She inhaled deeply. The smell of man overwhelmed her nostrils, making her mouth water, but it wasn't the only scent. Her nose slowly painted something new into the picture. It was vague at first—a wash of color, an etching of black. Finally, it took shape.

A murderous growl crawled from her belly.

Silence.

Movement. High in the tree to the left.

Scarlett's keen eyes finished painting what her nose had started. In the same heartbeat, the massive panther leapt. It fell at her, all raking claws and snarling fury. The creature landed on her outstretched claws, and she rolled with the weight of it.

A big one. Maybe bigger than the lions of the Mirrored Basin.

The thoughts passed absently through Scarlett's head as she and the beast tumbled together. Her fingers hooked around bone in the cat's chest. The thing yowled in pain, claws tearing into her. Scarlett was on top when they finally stopped rolling, but that wasn't always good when dealing with cats.

Massive paws latched into her shoulders, pulling her neck toward snapping jaws, while back legs shredded her hips.

Scarlett held the teeth back easily with her claws in its chest. She slid one hand free, grabbing its lower jaw by a colossal canine. Scarlett pulled its mouth wide, moving forward and out of the reach of its flailing back legs. She and the cat were close now, nearly eye to eye.

Close as lovers.

The cat struggled, desperately trying to free its jaw but unwilling to let go with its front paws.

An embrace is fitting.

Scarlett slipped her second claw from the panther's chest, tugging the beast even closer by its jaw. The cat yowled and shook its head back and forth. Scarlett snatched its lolling tongue, pulling the wet muscle taut.

Time for a kiss.

Scarlett tried to say the words, but all that came out was a guttural growl that stuttered and clicked simultaneously. The noise was alien to the creature, and uncertainty filled its eyes.

Soon, that will be fear.

Scarlett sniffed the air, trying to taste the delicious dread.

Not yet, but soon.

With a sloppy gush, Scarlett sank her teeth into the panther's outstretched tongue. The creature's back legs kicked, and its front claws retracted. Scarlett let go of the tongue with her hand and gripped the panther's upper jaw. She had the raspy flesh in her teeth now, and there was no escaping those.

Scarlett pulled the cat's jaws apart as her snout invaded its mouth. Paws scrambled, not even trying to rake her anymore as they frantically searched for purchase.

Bite by bite, Scarlett worked the tongue into her mouth until she was at its base. She bit down, arched her back, and pulled. The tongue stretched. A wet rip filled the air, then a pop as it came free.

Blood fountained from the cat's mouth, spraying Scarlett's face, neck, and chest. It wasn't the blood she craved, but it was blood nonetheless. The raspy bit of flesh fell from her teeth as Scarlett's tongue snaked out, cleaning hot red liquid from her nose and jowls.

There's the fear.

A wave of heady ecstasy washed over her mind and nethers. The cat squirmed furiously in Scarlett's grip, but controlling it was easy with clawed hands on either side of its jaws.

Aren't cats usually the ones playing with their food?

Scarlett giggled, but only clicks echoed through the quiet forest.

Clawed fingers sank into the soft flesh under the beast's waggling stump of a tongue as Scarlett clenched her fist. She pulled with her right hand and pushed with her left. Bones crunched, and tendons tore.

As easy as tearing up an old test back at the Academy.

The cat's mandible dislocated from one side with a pop.

Scarlett released the jawbone, letting it swing by the one tendon still attached. The panther tried to yowl, but it came out an inarticulate slosh. Her head cocked to the side, and her ears perked up as the cat futilely pawed the air.

The fight was quickly draining from the panther. Scarlett looked down. A large pool of blood had formed under the creature. The cat rolled to the side, exposing emaciated ribs as it tried to crawl away.

He was starving. No wonder he attacked something so foreign.

Something tickled at the back of her mind.

Compassion? Sympathy? No, she had none of that.

Scarlett bent, closed her powerful jaws around the creature's throat, and shook hard from the points of her teeth to the tip of her tail. The panther's throat tore open, and Scarlett gulped down the steaming flesh.

A taste. Still, best not spoil my appetite before the main course. Besides, I left the moose on the plateau if I get hungry later.

After the last glimmer of life left the big cat's eyes, she dragged the kill to a nearby tree and climbed.

Carrying a thirty-brick cat up a tree wasn't something Scarlett would've believed possible when she studied at the Academy, but this body managed it with ease. She draped the kill across a few thick branches and took a moment to fuss over its placement. Once Scarlett was sure it wouldn't fall to the ground for scavengers to find, she jumped to the forest floor, looked around one last time, and inhaled deeply. The smell of bark, sage, and fresh fern filled her nostrils.

No predators. The smell of death hasn't attracted anything. Not yet, anyway.

Satisfied her kill would be safe, Scarlett prowled down the hill. Before long, the smell of burning tree sap filled the air, and torchlight flickered through the trees. She pushed to the forest's edge and sat on her haunches, staring down from a little knoll that overlooked the village.

Soon, the carnage will begin.

Her stomach churned, and her eyes glimmered in the moonlight. Sharpened posts protruded from the ground around the man camp, and villagers patrolled the paths weaving through the buildings. It was the same as last time, except there were even more sentries.

That will just make it more fun.

Scarlett stalked down the knoll and crept along the base of the sharpened posts. The soft red light of the moons threatened to expose her, but the shadows were plentiful, and this hunting ground was familiar.

Two men rounded a corner in front of Scarlett. Her muscles bunched as she prepared to pounce. The winding path forked in front of them. Salvation lay to their right; Scarlett lay to their left. They moved forward slowly, without so much as a word of conversation. Both men were alert, but they wouldn't see her.

Not until it's too late.

Scarlett's tail twitched back and forth in anticipation. The watchmen took the right fork, and Scarlett stifled a growl. It was a meal missed, but she would find another.

The more succulent specimens are closer to the center of town anyway.

Scarlett crawled forward, keeping an eye on the two men. They stopped near the edge of the stakes, staring out into the woods they dreaded. Scarlett could smell their fear. The sour, acrid aroma made her mouth water.

Fear truly is nature's ambrosia, but it's also...what's the saying?

Scarlett licked her lips, pondering, then it came to her.

An acquired taste.

"*Such a refined palate,*" someone else thought.

There was that voice in the back of her mind again. Occasionally, it would manifest, and it never appreciated her penchant for fine cuisine. She ignored it. Her belly was much more insistent than a powerless whisper.

Scarlett's ears perked up. The village was noisy tonight. Pottery clinked, and music played. People were yelling, but not in terror.

Are they jovial? They know death is coming, and still they sing?

It was outrageous. Absolutely absurd. Undeniably disrespectful.

Fine, celebrate tonight, but tomorrow, you will mourn.

Scarlett's mouth watered.

If only I could get a whiff of that.

The smell must be glorious.

Perhaps even more delicious than fear.

She sniffed the air, hoping for the new scent, but found only cookfires and filth.

"I've got a bad feeling, Rowan."

Scarlett's ears swiveled, head following.

The two men were on their way back up the path.

Maybe not a missed meal after all.

"Ye always have a bad feeling about it, Ben. So why don't ye do me a favor? Keep yer mouth shut and focus on steppin', eh?" Rowan scolded the younger man, but there was something more than condemnation in his tone.

Fondness?

"No, this is worse. I'm tellin' ya, somethin's wrong."

"Yeah, yeah, I got it. Probably just the Trickster doing what 'e does best, lad."

The young man looked up. The despair that slid across his face was palpable.

"What do you mean?" Ben asked.

"Well, 'e scares ya, but it's only misdirection, smoke and mirrors. Use yer head, lad." Rowan tapped an index finger on the side of his temple.

"No, that's not it. I didn't even see the Trickster till now." Ben looked skyward again, took a deep breath, then turned away and shuddered. "I already knew somethin' was wrong. The Trickster peekin' from the clouds just confirms it. I'm tellin' you, Rowan, it's bad."

"What did I just say, Ben?" Rowan paused for effect.

"You said—"

"I told ye to shut up and keep on steppin'. That's what I fuckin' said. The question was a rhetorical one."

There was a short pause.

Scarlett could smell the young man's confusion.

"That means it's a question not meant for answerin', you twat," Rowan said. "Now, why can't ye seem to shut your mouth and keep movin', eh?"

For a moment, the two sentries were silent. Ben hung his head, and Rowan seemed to consider his words.

"I'm sorry, Ben, it's just..." Rowan looked up at the moons, then shivered. "Well, it's been a while since that thing took someone, and it must be gettin' hungry. I don't like to think about it, let alone voice it."

"Yeah, I know," Ben sighed. "It has been a while."

Rowan nodded, turned, and headed back toward the village, passing Scarlett without even a glance.

Ben stood at the edge of the spikes a moment longer, staring into the night sky. Maybe in another time, in a different village, he could've been admiring the stars. But he wasn't. Scarlett could smell his terror. Her stomach let out a low, bubbling growl.

They're right about one thing. The beast is hungry. But Ben can help with that.

Scarlett scurried silently across the path, snaking into the clump of jutting stakes that separated her and Ben. She climbed through the posts soundlessly, powerful limbs transferring her weight from one to the next until she was directly above the young man. Scarlett balanced there as all three delightful moons peered down.

"Damn chilly night too," Ben murmured. He shivered, pulled the hood of his cloak tight, and turned to walk away.

Scarlett leapt. A soft, chittering sound rumbled from her chest, and time seemed to slow. It was always this way before a kill, the thrill coursing through her veins, the weightlessness of a well-timed pounce.

She slammed into Ben like a ballista shot. His body raked along the dirt, and Scarlett's claws pierced his back, slicing through bone and sinking deep into soft tissue. Air sputtered from his lips. He tried to scream, producing a little squeak.

Like trying to fill a festival-day balloon riddled with holes.

Blood spilled from Ben's mouth in a burble, confirming the boy wasn't about to raise any alarms. Scarlett wasted no time with her first kill of the night; she was too hungry for that. With one claw, she flipped him over, then buried her snout into his soft belly.

Ravenously, Scarlett devoured the pungent flesh and organs. His innards wouldn't fill her, but they'd be enough to clear her head, enough to take the edge off. She'd waited a long time for tonight, and she wasn't about to be satisfied with one boy.

Scarlett stood from her kill and peered over the spikes. Flames bobbed through the night, meandering toward her. No one was running. No one was screaming.

Not yet.

Scarlett hoisted Ben up and tossed him into the spikes the men had placed around the village. His near-lifeless body landed in the points a few rows back, producing a musical slurp. Scarlett could still see him, but she doubted human eyes would.

That should keep my kill safe until I return.

Another rumble emanated from Scarlett's belly, and she turned from Ben, stalking away into the shadows. She climbed spikes and ducked between buildings, often waiting for bouncing torchlight to flicker past. Once it had, she would slip back into the darkened streets or crawl along the posts toward the center of the delicious human filth. Scarlett kept her eyes open as she moved, watching for another kill. She passed plenty of sentries, but they were always close enough together to pose a risk.

I need a straggler to cull from the herd. Something tender. Something succulent. Something near the heart of town.

Scarlett moved deeper and deeper into the village and soon was surrounded by huts. The homes used to be scattered around the settlement and even sprinkled outside, but not anymore. The humans had moved the most tender creatures to the center of town some time ago.

They try to hide the best cuts of meat from me.

The tastiest humans were young, tender, and supple enough that their muscles hadn't fully developed. Diet really was the most critical factor, though, and ideal livestock was fostered on berries or mother's milk.

Though the mothers aren't bad either.

Drool seeped from Scarlett's mouth.

As she reveled in the night's prospects, something pushed against her tantalizing thoughts. She shrugged it away, shaking her head in annoyance and perking up her ears in search of the intruder.

A soft, cheerful sound flitted through the night like a bird in the morning light. Her head cocked to the side as she stalked toward the pleasant notes.

What is that?

Scarlett followed the melody toward its source: one of three huts in a cluster. She sniffed the air, head slowly shifting back and forth. A faint scent wafted from the house on the right. It wasn't the standard human stench, although it contained notes of that. This smelled like rosemary, lavender, and maybe a dash of sage, all wrapped in a smoky shell.

Barbecue.

Scarlett followed her nose around the side of the house to a set of shutters. Light streamed through the angled slats, spilling into the night.

The melody and smells combined in a delightful performance that Scarlett's ears and nose eagerly devoured. She crept forward slowly, not wanting to spook her next meal. The sweet aroma filled her nostrils, causing her to salivate. She peered through the slats and into a dimly lit room. A young woman sat in front of a vanity.

She is...beautiful.

She is...mouthwatering.

Innocent.

Delectable.

She could be our little sister.

She could be our dinner.

The two voices clattered against each other in Scarlett's head, nearly causing her to snarl at the intruder. Noise wouldn't do, though. Not with prey so close.

The tender morsel ran a comb through her hair and sang with the soft voice of a nightingale.

Scarlett licked her lips.

The girl stared into a mirror, emerald eyes shining back.

Eyes like mine. Eyes like my sister's.

Her nose twitched.

No, that's not right. There were no other kits in my litter.

The girl sat there, combing her hair, utterly naive that death lurked just outside the window. She was young, pure, and simple—the perfect picture of innocence. She wore only night clothes, leaving a considerable amount of bare flesh exposed. Scarlett watched her thighs, eyeing the tender meat there. Saliva fell from her jowls, silently dripping onto the windowsill.

The shutters slowly separated as her snout invaded them.

Something slammed into Scarlett's mind.

She staggered back, looking for the carriage that must have crashed into her.

Nothing.

There was no one around, no one attacking her. The small dirt path between the huts was empty, and the only sound resonated from dinner's sweet humming.

Scarlett shook the feeling away and moved forward.

The sensation hit her again, but she was ready for it this time. The force pushed against her mind, but Scarlett pushed back with a gnashing of teeth and a chittering growl. The alien presence faded, clearly forced into submission.

Still baring her teeth, Scarlett sniffed the air, trying to confirm the other was dispatched. Things smelled the same...except the acrid smell of fear had returned.

Scarlett looked back at the window. The girl stood, holding her candle up like a ward against the cracked shutters. Green eyes met black ones, and horror swept across the girl's face. She held out the wax cylinder, frozen except for her quivering arm. Scarlett drank in the terror eagerly through slits in her coal black nose.

Savoring this moment always makes the next so much more satisfying.

Scarlett stalked forward slowly, avoiding sudden movement that might cause the paralyzed prey to bolt. She pulled in air through her nose, practically tasting the herbs this little flower wore as perfume. Her claws weaved through the slats in the shutters, and her nose pushed the panels wide. Hinges squealed as the wood frames parted, and—

A horn blared in the distance.

Scarlett blinked.

What's that about?

Before she could decide, a gong filled the night.

Ah, for me then.

Scarlett focused on the prey.

A dinner bell would be more fitting.

The girl took a step back.

Not much time for supper. The realization was pressing, but so was Scarlett's desire. She put a foot on the windowsill, claws digging into the wood as she prepared to spring.

The girl inhaled as much as her little lungs could hold, then screamed. The sound was ear-piercing but not entirely unpleasant.

Scarlett snarled, reaching into the room and latching onto the sides of the window frame.

Something rammed into her mind again, and she staggered back. She tried to push the intruder away again, but it was insistent. Somewhere, the prey was still bleating, but it took all her will to beat the presence into submission this time.

I can't fight this battle, kill the hunters, and devour the girl all at once.

Scarlett was not afraid of men, but there would be many, and she didn't want to diminish her favorite food source.

This little morsel might be worth it.

She sniffed the air.

They'll be here soon.

Her ears swiveled. Feet pounded on the dirt path.

They aren't far now.

With a broken snarl, Scarlett leapt up the side of the building, clawed her way to the apex of the roof, and sprinted across the beam at its center. At the edge, she coiled, muscles bunching, then sprang forward with one great leap.

Scarlett landed on the next roof, rolled out of the landing, and charged ahead on all fours. Something whizzed by her head, then a point sunk into the right side of her back. She reached around, tore the spear free with a snarl, and tossed it aside without slowing.

More spears flew through the night, but they all landed far behind. Scarlett rushed for the next building, leaping across another substantial gap. She landed on a beam, heard it strain under her weight, then moved on to the next.

In less than a minute, she was out of the little village.

Her ears perked up, listening for anyone following.

They were still searching but would never catch up.

Scarlett worked her way back through the dark forest to the big cat. The idea pained her, but its meat would have to be sustenance enough tonight. She needed to get back up the mountain.

There's still much to do before the human awakens.

21
DAVID TRUEHEART

L ight pierced pink through David's eyelids, and he let out a groan. His head pulsed, his limbs were stone, and something was spread atop him. David slowly opened his eyes. He was in an alleyway, but couldn't say if it was the same one he'd collapsed in...

Yesterday?

David's feet were ragged, and his ribs throbbed with an intensity that made his head feel better only by comparison. He shaded his eyes and rolled to his back. His ribs protested, and trash spilled from atop him, but he clenched his teeth, willing his way through the motion.

A wave of pain hit him. He gasped, amplifying the agony.

David rolled to his uninjured side, curling into a ball of suffering. The shallow breaths that followed were awful but not half as excruciating as the initial lungful of air.

"Who in the hells threw trash all over me?" he whispered. "Animals." His entire body felt foreign, like something he simply wore over his skin. He stretched his neck and groaned.

I know some lotus fiends who'd pay good stone for the toxin in those vines.

David rolled slowly back to his chest and pushed himself to one knee. Pain laced up his leg, sending him toppling sideways onto a heap of trash. He lay there a moment, groaning through gritted teeth. Slowly, his black boots came into focus. He reached down, grimaced, then gave one a hesitant tug.

No dice. They ain't coming off easy.

David lifted one foot and examined it. Broken barbs from the vines pierced through the sole of his boot and into his foot. He undid the lacing. The pain was immense, but what came next would be worse.

"Gods, this is gonna hurt," David groaned. He bit his lip, then yanked the boot off.

"Fuckiiiiing son of a nipple! Apple-whore!" David's voice quavered as the boot slipped off and congealed blood oozed onto the cobblestone.

189

Chunks of flesh were missing from David's foot. Some were actively bleeding from the barbs he'd just pulled free. Others were crusty dots from last night's escapade.

At least my boot took the brunt of the abuse.

David tossed the shoe aside and gingerly reached for the other one.

"Cock-bitch-mother—fuck-of-a-monkey!" David screamed as the second boot came free with a squelch. He wobbled, vision slowly fading to white again. He took a deep breath, steadying himself with one arm, as the world came back into focus.

Over the next hour, David pulled the remaining thorns from his boots and feet. He cursed the gods. He cursed the Freemen's Guild. He cursed Rob, the innkeeper. He cursed Tanya, and most of all, he cursed himself. Then he ripped two lengths of cloth from his cloak and tenderly wrapped his wounded feet in the makeshift bandages.

I gambled big last night. I lost a lot of hands, but at least I took the big pot.

David reached into his coat, feeling for the ledger. The pocket was flat where it should've bulged.

David froze.

Frantically, he shoved a hand into the pocket, groping about as his mind raced.

It has to be here somewhere. No one would've taken it without killing me or at least turning me in.

After nearly a minute of searching and another couple digging through the trash, David leaned back against the alley wall and let out a long, high-pitched groan.

The ledger was gone.

I fractured ribs, punctured my feet, poisoned myself, and for what?

He checked the first pocket again.

No bloody fucking ledger.

A flat crinkle sounded as David pulled his hand free. He paused, head cocking to the side, eyebrows narrowing.

Apprehensively, he reached back into the pocket. Smooth ridges of quality parchment brushed his fingertips. He pulled the paper out. It was one sheet, folded simply into thirds. He opened it. The script wasn't flowery like the original assignment. Instead, the words were scrawled haphazardly across the paper in a short, concise hand.

Report back to Tanya tonight for your last assignment.
Don't be late.

That was all. But by the gods, was it enough.

David inhaled deeply to let out a sigh of relief, but his ribs punished him before he could let the air out. It didn't matter. The ledger wasn't stolen. In fact, it was better than that. He didn't even have to worry about holding onto it anymore.

Things are looking up.

Without thinking, David tried to stand.

"Evintri's unwed-bloody-bedpan!"

David fell back onto the refuse pile with a grunt. After the pain subsided, he grabbed his left boot, took a slow, deep breath, and pulled it onto his foot. A long, drawn-out squeal escaped his gritted teeth. He followed a similar pattern with his other foot. Once both boots were on, David managed to stand. It hurt like the hells, but after a few shaky steps, he was moving.

It'll get easier.

After a dozen quaking, shuffling steps, David decided he'd been wrong.

The trip back to the inn was the most agonizing thing he'd ever experienced. David tried his best to keep a low profile, but even in Windmore, it was uncommon for someone to limp through the streets covered in blood. He stuck to the back roads, and although he got a few odd looks, no one tried to stop him.

When he finally arrived at the Rooster, it was late afternoon.

Right as the place is starting to get busy. Just my luck.

David hoped it wasn't full of people waiting for a show. If so, there would be no way to avoid attention, and he wasn't sure his ribs could take a slap on the back.

What other option is there? Not scaling the wall to my window anytime soon.

David shook his head.

Besides, my rope and harness are still dangling from the Freemen's tower.

Without a better plan, David limped through the front door.

A sweet melody assaulted his ears.

He stopped dead in his tracks.

Wait, this is my *inn.*

Worse yet, the song wasn't half-bad. David nearly laughed aloud.

I should be glad of the competition today.

Most people didn't even look as he entered, and those who did gave a quick nod and returned their attention to the stage. The performer had some talent, without a doubt, but she was putting on a different sort of show too. She had a cute smile that she threw around indiscriminately.

And the pair of tits bursting from that overly tight bodice isn't hurting either.

191

Not that David was complaining. He was happy for the distraction, and like the rest of the patrons, he appreciated the view.

Even if it leaves little to the imagination.

David sighed.

Best stop gawking and take advantage of my fortune while it lasts.

He shuffled over to the stairs, gripped the railing, and climbed. Each step was agony, and his ribs ached with each pull. Still, he hobbled upstairs without attracting much attention and limped down the empty hall to his room.

David spent the next few hours with his feet in a basin. He'd thought pulling his boots off in the alleyway would be the worst of the pain, but the stiff grain alcohol he used to clean his wounds now proved far worse. After nearly passing out twice, invoking the names of all thirteen gods, and inventing some new ones to curse, David finished with his feet. He sighed and moved on to his ribs.

His side was already black and blue, but it appeared he'd set the bones decently last night, and messing with them further would only cause more damage. Pushing them back into place amid everything yesterday was honestly a miracle.

Every once in a while, those winning hands come around. Best use 'em, and weather the duds as they come.

David paused, wondering if the saying was one of his father's or his own.

Harder and harder to tell the difference these days.

With his wounds situated, the bed was starting to look mighty enticing. David stumbled over to it and collapsed. Sleep took him almost as soon as his head hit the pillow.

Not even sleep ended David's suffering.

He dreamt of creeping up behind the guard from the Freemen's Guild. The man turned to yell. David slashed his throat, then stared in horror as the life drained from his wide eyes. Suddenly, the guard was upright, and David was creeping toward him again. He tried to bash the man across the temple. The guard stepped away from the blow, then slit his own throat, the same shocked expression filling his face. The next time, David tried to stop the man from taking his own life, but he couldn't.

Over and over again, David conceived a new plan to stop the guard, and each time, the man would die anyway. Minor details changed in each iteration of the dream. Sometimes, it would be in a new place, or the guard would kill himself with some new implement, but one thing always stayed the same. The guard always wore that same shocked expression, the very look he'd possessed when the light left his eyes the night before.

The room was full of screaming when David awoke, and it took him a minute to realize it was his own. For a moment, he just sat there, blinking and breathing hard in the darkness. The pitter-patter of rain was hard on the Rooster's kiln-fired shingles, and red moonlight danced through the window. David looked out, locking eyes with the nearly full Trickster.

Shit. Gotta get moving.

With a groan, he rolled over and sat up. Everything ached, and the prospect of putting his boots back on made him want to vomit. David's ribs burned, and his feet throbbed, but both felt substantially better than they had earlier. His stomach rumbled. He hadn't eaten all day, and he'd lost a lot of blood.

David's gaze shifted from the full moon to his bag.

Tanya's going to skin me alive.

He stood, hobbled over to his pack, and pulled out a pouch of smoked jerky. It was seasoned with spices from the Preserver's Guild and would've been an incredible indulgence if he'd bought it. Like most anything good, David won it in a game of cards. He'd been saving it for a special occasion. It was a little hard to celebrate the holes in his feet but not so hard to celebrate that his debt would soon be paid in full. He popped a piece of the oily meat into his mouth.

The jerky was savory and salty, with a hint of sweetness, and he wolfed it down greedily. David ate nearly half the bag before managing to stop, then grabbed his water skin and took a swig. Somehow, even the water tasted better than usual, and he drank the whole skin down.

Enough procrastination. Time to move.

David quickly changed the bandages on his feet and padded the bottom of his boots with more cloth. He took a moment to eye them apprehensively, then took a deep breath through gritted teeth and pulled them on. David tied them tight, which made his wounds throb, but it would feel better than loose leather sliding around. He slung a fresh cloak about his shoulders, then hesitated, eyes lingering on his blade. It was best to keep the sword in his pack when possible, as it did attract undue attention. He pursed his lips and frowned, then grabbed the sheath and looped it through his belt.

Better to be prepared than caught with your pants down.

David wasn't sure what they would ask of him, but a sword wouldn't hurt.

Might want me to skewer a bloody chicken or some such nonsense.

He nearly laughed, shouldered his bag, and headed out.

Rain pelted Windmore as David hobbled through the darkened streets. He pulled his cloak tight and soon found himself thinking of Tanya. Something about her intrigued him—something beyond being easy on the eyes. David hoped she wasn't waiting by the fountain in this downpour, even though she likely was. The weather tonight was similar to their last encounter. She'd been limping then and appeared somewhat disheveled, but she'd still been beautiful.

She's tough, but maybe she's sweet under that hard shell.

David smiled.

She's clearly not putting up with my shit either way.

He hobbled along, distracted enough to ignore the pain lancing through his feet. It wasn't long before the Coliseum loomed in the distance, and the fountain materialized from the shadows. David shivered. The rain was coming down in buckets and gave no sign of abating.

At least I get to see her pretty face again.

His smile wavered.

But I might pay for that, too, depending on her mood.

As David got closer, details on the fountain slowly materialized. Water flooded the basin's edge again tonight, drowning desperate faces. He tried to dismiss the image with a shudder, then looked up.

The Trickster smiled back.

Gods! How does that thing shine through a torrential fucking downpour?

The moon's purple sister was peeking from behind it, distorting the Trickster's face and pulling half its smile into something maniacal.

Hate that damn moon—looks like it knows too much.

A dark silhouette stepped from behind the fountain. David reached for his sword, then recognized Tanya and took a deep breath.

Only one more debt to pay, then this is done.

Tanya's features shed their shadows as she swayed into the pale red moonlight. Leather creaked as she reached back, soaked clothes clinging tightly to her shapely form. Wet hair cascaded down her back as she unbuttoned a satchel and produced a letter.

Wow, just wow.

"Back to reality, David!" Tanya snapped her fingers in his face. "You're late, and I'm bloody soaked."

David smiled at her, then took the letter. "This is the last of it?"

"Are you too daft to remember a conversation from two nights ago?" Tanya locked eyes with him for a few seconds then continued. "I'm not privy to your assignment."

"You really never look in the letters?"

"You caught me. I open all the letters." The words dripped with sarcasm. "Then I seal them back up with red wax and the official insignia I carry around in my back pocket."

"Now that's a trick I'd like to see."

Tanya's eyebrows narrowed. "Where's the punchline?" she asked, rolling her hand impatiently.

"Didn't think you could shove anything into the back of those tight pants, let alone wax and a seal." David craned his neck in a mock attempt to see her backside, then looked up with a mischievous smirk.

Tanya crossed her arms. "Got that out of your system?"

"At least someone thinks I'm funny."

"You don't count when it's your joke, you twat."

"Not me," David explained, pointing up. Their eyes followed his finger together. The Trickster's sister moon was in full view, and the half smile David had seen earlier was gone, replaced by a snarling visage.

"Well, that was about as ineffective as it was morbid," Tanya said. "You proud of yourself?"

"Guess not." David paused, eyes still locked with the Trickster's.

"Are you going to open the damn letter?" Tanya asked. "Your banter isn't worth waiting in this rain."

David pulled his gaze from the moons, looked Tanya in the eye, then took the letter and read it. He blinked, trying to make sense of the words.

There's no way she opened this letter.

David glanced up at her, then read the same carefully scrawled cursive silently to himself again, and again, and again. Each time, he believed it less than the last. Still, there it was, penned in the same flowery script as before and reflecting the moonlight.

We ask only one final task of you now, David:
Kill Tanya.
Leave the body in the fountain.

BURN AFTER READING.

David looked at Tanya, hoping his face hadn't already shown his cards. *The Trickster wasn't laughing with me earlier. It was laughing at me.*

22
TANYA RINGHOLDER

The Trickster was a red sliver in a sea of black.

He's not coming.

Tanya stood, hand touching the stitches in her side. She'd waited by the fountain all night for nothing.

Gotta come back tonight too.

Tanya groaned.

If the gods are kind, there won't be any rain.

She nearly laughed.

The gods are never kind.

Tanya left the square, heading toward the guild.

"At least it makes you tough," she murmured.

They were her father's words. Tanya didn't think of him often but occasionally recalled a handful of sayings. She was five when he disappeared and barely a year older when her mother remarried.

Tanya wasn't sure how often she heard those six words as a child, but it must have been a lot since they'd stuck with her. As she got older, Tanya caught herself thinking the phrase often or even accidentally saying it to others. It was almost as if a little piece of her father lived on in her that way, a gift from him, like her thick skin.

Sure isn't from my mother.

Tanya imagined her mother's face, cringing, in their little kitchen.

She'd take a beating before ever standing up for her daughter.

After her mother remarried, she *had* taken a beating. Many of them, in fact. Her mother claimed Father ran off on them, but Tanya never believed it. The lies were a justification—a story meant to make her stepfather look better by comparison. Tanya was pretty sure her father had been callous and full of hard truths, but she'd never seen him lay hands on her mother. That was more than she could ever say for Weber.

Maybe if he hadn't been so brutal, I wouldn't have ended up on the streets, and he wouldn't be in the dirt.

With a wince, Tanya climbed the last few steps to the guildhouse. Her side burned, and the new stitches strained as she took the steps two at a time.

I might not be as tough as my father, but I'm tough enough to take a stab wound. Tough enough to sew it up myself too.

Then again, being tough was seldom an issue for Tanya. The real problem was the little voice in her head. The one that simply *had* to question everything. The voice was easy to ignore on a job, but it was damn insistent in the quiet moments.

Are you cut out to keep up in a circle of cold, hard killers?

Did you climb the ranks on merit alone, or does Reynolds want something else?

Why didn't you save Jack and Ted?

Who is Reynolds yelling at in his office?

Tanya exhaled at the reminder of her most recent blunder, then knocked on the guildhouse door and gave the password. She'd been avoiding Reynolds since peeking into his office yesterday, and their few interactions seemed unusually distant.

Probably on his shitlist.

Three enforcers sat around a table stacked with empty tankards in the middle of the otherwise empty hall. Tanya strode through the room, heading to her chamber.

"Hey, you!" A young man stood from the cluster of three.

Marcus Instem.

Tanya knew the man by ill reputation, but she'd never had the displeasure before.

"Bit past your bedtime, ain't it?" Tanya asked without stopping.

Marcus stepped out in front of her, blocking the path to the stairs. He was a head taller than her and looked a little like Jack might have if he'd grown old enough for his voice to deepen and his chest to widen.

"Wet out there." Marcus traced her with his eyes.

"Who told ya?" Tanya asked, brushing past him.

A hand clamped onto her shoulder, halting her progress.

Always something. Tanya sighed.

"Going to see Reynolds?" he asked.

She turned back. The would-be man reeked of foul liquor and unwashed ballsack.

"Nope, Reynolds doesn't need me to check in after every little task."

Snickers from the two men behind Marcus. He glanced back, and they fell silent.

Probably shouldn't antagonize him. But you can't show fear either, not with the hyenas.

Besides, she never could help herself with idiots.

"Damn, you got a mouth on you, huh?" Marcus began. "Could put it to good use if you're keen. Promise to show you a good time too."

"Honey…" A sympathetic smile slid across Tanya's face as she slowly shook her head. "You couldn't satisfy me with the help of both your friends."

More laughs from Marcus's drinking buddies.

Morons. It's an insult to you as much as him.

Tanya turned away.

"I s-suppose not." Marcus's voice warbled. "Heard you only get on your knees for a promotion anyway."

"Ooooh." More snickering from the hyenas.

The corner of Tanya's mouth twitched into a snarl. She knew some folk whispered Reynolds only made her an agent in exchange for something less than reputable, but no one had been bold enough to say it to her face.

Not till now.

Tanya stilled her lip, turning it up into the sweetest smile. Slowly she pivoted to face Marcus, cocking her head to the side.

"How'd you know?" she said with genuine interest.

Confusion flickered across Marcus's face. His eyebrows narrowed, and he opened his mouth to speak.

"Wh—"

Whatever he said was lost as Tanya's knuckles hit his throat. He clutched at his neck with one hand, reaching for her with the other. She stepped in close, past the grasping fingers, slipped her leg behind his knee, and shoved. He let out a gurgling cough and toppled over her braced leg. The two hyenas cackled, but she barely heard it.

A wheeze as his back hit the floorboards.

Tanya lowered a knee to his solar plexus, slapping his fumbling hands away. She pressed her weight down, not enough to break bone, but enough to make his already sputtering breaths nearly cease. Cold steel was in her hand now, kissing the soft skin under his chin.

He took shallow little gulps of air, fighting to keep the point from piercing his neck.

"Next time you question why someone was made agent, remember this moment." Tanya still wore the same sweet little smile. "Cause if sucking dick was all it took, then you and your friends would all have the same title as I do." She glanced up. The hyenas weren't laughing anymore. "Do we have an understanding?"

Marcus nodded ever so slightly against the tip of her blade.

"Good. Now, if you don't mind, I'm exhausted."

Tanya pushed off the man's ribs, causing him to let out another agonized groan. She took a step away, then stopped and turned back.

"Oh, by the way." She crouched back down, the same little smile tugging at the corner of her mouth. "If I hear one bloody whisper about you doing anything like this again, I'll cut your fuckin' stones off." Tanya gave his crotch a tap with the flat of her blade for emphasis, then stood, spun on a heel, and headed upstairs.

After checking the room and locking the door, Tanya unbuttoned her leather coat and hung it on a peg by the door. She knew she should dry it off with a towel but was too tired to do more work tonight. Instead, she unbuttoned her pants and peeled them off. They felt even more soaked than the jacket, so she hung them up too.

Cold air streamed in the window, chilling her drenched cotton shirt. Tanya shivered. With quaking hands, she tried to pull the shirt over her head. She almost had it off when it got stuck around her upturned arms.

Tanya flailed about, nearly tripped twice, and stumbled into the bedpost.

"Ahhhh!" No real words escaped her lips, just an exasperated cry.

Finally, she wrestled free of the blasted thing and flung it across the room in frustration.

Not my most graceful moment.

She arched her back, craning her neck in an attempt to see her wounded side.

No luck.

Tanya lifted her arm and looked under it, but that didn't work either. She even tried pulling her skin to get the stitches into view but gave up when the threads threatened to break. There was no way to see it without a mirror, but it only itched a little, which was a good sign. She blew out her cheeks, pulled off the last of her rain-soaked clothes, and crawled into bed. Tanya couldn't fall asleep despite how tired she was. It was too cold.

Terrible damn circulation, terrible damn mother for gifting it to me.

Tanya pulled the covers tight, closed her eyes, and shivered until sleep finally took her.

Thump.

Tanya awoke to noise from across the room. She sat up, eyes scanning the chamber.

Nothing.

Tanya slid back down the headboard, took a deep breath, and listened. Sweet silence. She rolled to her side and closed her eyes.

A quiet rushing of air trickled through the room.

Tanya's eyes flicked open again. She shifted to face the door, trying to locate the sound. A draft swirled around the room, slowly growing in volume, but she couldn't pinpoint the source. She glanced toward the foot of the bed and nearly jumped from the covers.

A silhouette stood there, the same one from Reynolds's office, except this time he had a face. He stared at her, but not with eyes—there were no eyes. He watched her through gaping holes, lidless and empty. Slowly, he moved along the foot of the bed. Tanya knew she should run or at least scream. But just like in the hallway, she was frozen.

The man didn't move quickly. He didn't even seem to walk. Instead, he glided evenly across the floor. The bed was tucked in the corner of the room, and after he rounded the bedpost, she'd be trapped. Tanya tried to force motion into her arms and legs, but they were like lead. She barely managed to pull away from the specter and press her back to the wall.

That's when she recognized the face it wore. Weber's face. Her stepfather's face. He gave her a tired smile. The same smile he used to give her mother. The smile that said, "I don't want to do this. I just have to."

"You can't," Tanya trailed off.

The specter leaned in.

"You're dead," she whispered through tight lips.

The face shifted. Weber's sinister smile slid away, replaced with a boyish grin.

David's grin.

He bent to touch her. No, that wasn't right. It was the specter, or maybe not. None of it made sense.

They placed one blackened hand on her shoulder and pulled her close, almost tenderly. Tanya tried to move, but the thing's grip was a manacle. They cupped the back of her head, pulling her lips to theirs. Black smoke billowed from their mouth, nostrils, and eye sockets. The smoke forced her lips apart, pouring down her throat. Noxious vapor filled her lungs and nose, choking her as it consumed her from the inside out.

"Shhhhh," something whispered. "This is the end." The world went foggy.

It's almost over. Tanya wasn't sure if the thought was hers or the thing's.

Tanya sat up, trying to shove the apparition away, but the specter was gone. Reality slowly set in as her slick hands frantically searched for a weapon. Her sheets felt as soaked as her clothes had the night before, and she was just as cold.

Worse yet, the nightmare wasn't over.

The horrid smoking image still plagued the fringes of her vision but vanished each time she tried to focus on it. Tanya took a deep breath, trying to calm her racing heart. The faces it wore were what frightened her the most.

Two men who couldn't be more opposite.

When the image finally faded, Tanya swung her feet onto the freezing floor.

Pirel's bush, why's it so cold in here?

Tanya gritted her teeth and walked to the door, resting a hand on her jacket. It was still damp, so she grabbed dry clothes and slid into them. She didn't have another coat, though.

Oh well. Should be dry by tonight.

Tanya looked down, checking her appearance.

Damn Mother gave me Amara's own curves.

She hated giving men like Marcus Instem any reason to comment, but she wasn't about to sit in her room all day just because her jacket was damp.

"Ah, fuck 'em," Tanya said, exiting the chamber.

She headed downstairs and strode straight through the common room into the open air.

Little booths lined the buildings on each side of the street, and the calls of merchants rang out with propositions and prices. Dew clung to awnings from last night's rain, and the sweet aroma it left behind lingered in the air.

At least something washes this filthy city clean.

Tanya meandered through the busy street until her nose picked up another sweet scent. She stopped, sniffing the air. Something smelled phenomenal. Ahead, merchants were selling satchels and clothing, but a baker had set up a stand past them.

"Ah!" The man behind the counter gave a smile as warm as the sun as Tanya approached. "What can I get for the beautiful lady?"

All kinds of baked goods lined the wooden cart. Some were filled with chocolate, others were flaky with powdered sugar, or even covered in cheese.

"That one," Tanya said, pointing. The pastry's corners were pinched together, and light scorch marks accented the flaky dough.

"The turnover. An excellent choice, m'lady." He picked up the treat and handed it to her with another smile. "Two 'paz, ma'am."

Tanya handed him three topaz shards. "Have a good day," she said, returning the genuine smile.

Tanya picked at the turnover absently as she walked down the street. She had no idea where she was headed, but it hardly mattered. The sun was shining, and the black clouds on the horizon were only a distant threat.

Better to cherish the sun than lament the storms. Another gem from her real father.

Tanya realized there was only one spot she wanted to be—the park. Truthfully, it was more of a large garden these days, but she'd heard it used to be bigger before it got all gobbled up by taverns and the Coliseum.

Who'd have thought the people of Windmore desire blood and ale more than grass and flowers?

Tanya snorted. She understood the draw of the Coliseum and had even attended a handful of times. The spectacle was more exciting than the park, but it had so much less substance and usually left her nauseous.

Nothing quite like watching two men bash each other's heads into the sand.

People were absent all the way to the park's center, where a hedge surrounded a massive tree. The ancient oak twisted, spiraling upward as branches spread like wings. Some old trees could appear scary or ominous, but not this one. Tanya quickly gravitated to the sunny side of the oak and sat down, leaning against the gnarled behemoth.

This was probably the center of town at one point.

Tanya glanced up at the looming Coliseum.

Before the Rocktells built that monstrosity.

As the sun beamed down, Tanya nestled back into the trunk and found it hard to care about politics. Instead, she wished for a good book to read. She'd never been much of a reader, but that came more from a lack of time than any real dislike of the activity.

Might be nice to get lost in a story other than my own once in a while.

Eventually, Tanya managed to accomplish what a book inevitably would have and fell asleep. She slept for a long time and, thankfully, didn't dream again. She awoke to a chilly wind nipping at her.

Groggily, Tanya stood, rubbing the gunk from her eyes.

The sun was barely a golden dot on the horizon.

Damn, it's getting late, and David might actually show up tonight.

Tanya headed back.

The sky was dark when she arrived at the guildhouse, and a quarter-full Trickster peeked through the clouds. The guild was lively, and the scoundrels were out. She felt their eyes on her as soon as she entered.

Animals. Try something and see what happens.

A particularly ugly enforcer who was missing one eye and a chunk of his nose gave her a pointed look but didn't say anything. Tanya ignored it, walking briskly through the room. Trouble from men was easy enough to predict.

Just need to remember how often they think with their cocks.

Tanya returned to her room, grabbed her coat, and threw it over her shoulders. She buckled it up the side and grabbed the satchel with David's assignment. A short time later, she strode back through the common area.

Reynolds was in the corner, talking to a pole of a man in all black she didn't recognize. The tall figure stood as she passed, heading toward the door.

Is Reynolds having me tailed?

The idea seemed far-fetched, but the man choosing that moment to leave was odd. Tanya turned left toward the fountain and ducked into an alley. She crouched, peering back at the door. The tall man stopped under the eve of the guild's roof and looked around. He produced a pipe from his pocket and struck a match.

Tanya sighed, shaking her head.

Just having a bloody smoke. I must be gettin' jumpy.

She looped around the backside of the guildhouse and headed toward the fountain. Tanya kept to side streets and doubled back a few times, weaving through the empty city. Despite not seeing a soul, she couldn't shake the feeling of being watched.

Leather scuffed on stone.

Tanya spun, reaching for a knife as her eyes scanned the shadows.

Nothing moved.

Guess I am getting jumpy.

Tanya frowned, then moved on.

The rain was pouring when she finally arrived at the fountain.

Gonna be another one of those nights, isn't it?

Tanya walked around to the back of the basin, where the shadows were deepest, pulled her cloak tight, and hunkered down. Soon, she was soaked again and shivering in the bloody cold. The wound in her side throbbed, and she looked up, meeting the Trickster's gaze. Aura peeked from behind the larger moon, causing its grin to widen. It was complete horseshit, but sometimes the Trickster seemed to aggravate her aches and pains.

It's only a rock in the sky, nothing more.

Time crawled by as the Trickster grew until it was finally full.

Where's that damn bard?

A man stumbled into the square, but he turned out to be just a drunkard lost on his way home. The second time someone meandered up to the fountain, she dismissed it.

Another drunk, limpin' their way home in the dark.

Tanya watched them from the shadows anyway. The man shuffled awkwardly forward and stood at the basin.

Oh great. Gonna ask the gods where it all went wrong?

She shook her head.

Or worse yet, he might start singing.

That was the last thing she needed. David could show up any minute, and they couldn't have their meeting with this fool belting out "We All Walk Down the Moonlit Fence." The drunk didn't sing, though. He simply wobbled back and forth, hood pulled tight, staring at the fountain. As the man swayed, a sliver of moonlight slid under his hood.

David? Why's he wobbling like a fool?

Tanya's frown slowly shifted to a smile.

Then again, he might actually look good in motley and bells.

She forced back a laugh, then strode from the shadows.

For a moment, David didn't even seem to notice, then he startled, fumbling for the hilt of his sword until their eyes met.

Edgy are we?

He looked tired. Face stretched thin and haggard.

Tanya pulled the letter from her satchel and held it out.

The fool didn't even respond.

"Back to reality, David!" Tanya said, snapping her fingers. "You're late, and I'm bloody soaked." His eyes shifted from her to the letter, and an exhausted smile crept across his face. The expression should have been innocent enough, except it was eerily close to the smoky face from her nightmare.

"This is the last of it?" he asked.

"Are you too daft to remember a conversation from two nights ago?" Tanya asked.

David just looked at her dumbly.

"I'm not privy to your assignment."

"You really never look in the letters?" David asked.

By the gods, he's stupid sometimes.

"You caught me. I open all the letters," Tanya said, voice full of dry sarcasm. "Then I seal them back up with red wax and the official insignia I carry around in my back pocket."

"Now that's a trick I'd like to see." David paused, a sly smile creeping across his face.

Clearly baiting me, Tanya thought. *But all right, I'll bite.*

"Where's the punchline?" she asked, gesturing for him to get on with it.

"Didn't think you could shove anything into the back of those tight pants, let alone wax and a seal." The same boyish grin from the other night filled his face. For a fraction of a second, smoke poured from his mouth and eyes, then vanished.

Tanya stifled the instinct to step back, then shook her head and raised an eyebrow. She waited, drawing out the silence until David appeared adequately embarrassed. "Got that out of your system?" she finally asked.

David sighed. "At least someone thinks I'm funny."

"You don't count when it's your joke, you twat."

"Not me." David pointed up.

The Trickster is always smiling, you nitwit.

Tanya glanced up and realized she was wrong.

Aura was on the bottom side of the Trickster, warping its toothy smile into a grimace.

"Well, that was about as ineffective as it was morbid." Tanya paused. "You proud of yourself?"

"Guess not," David said, still staring up.

"Are you going to open the damn letter? Your banter isn't worth waiting in this rain." Tanya tried to keep her tone light and playful, but she wasn't entirely sure it worked.

We all need a little levity on nights like this one.

Tanya hesitantly glanced up at the moon again. It hadn't changed.

Why'd I do that? Just gotta know, huh?

David took the letter and opened it, eyes scanning the page. His brows narrowed, and he blinked, then his eyes returned to the top of the sheet. He did this several times, a disconcerted expression growing on his face.

A tingle crept up the base of Tanya's spine.

If the Lance gave him a challenging second assignment, that's his problem, not mine.

David struck flint and steel together and cupped a hand over the letter. He let it burn down until the flames licked at his fingertips, then flung his fist about and dropped the scrap of parchment.

Fool.

David stared at the fountain, then slowly shifted his eyes to hers. They were full of sadness. He took a small, shuffling step forward.

"Anything I need to know about in there, David?"

He didn't respond, but his hand rested on cold steel at his waist.

"David?" Tanya asked, reaching behind her back and gripping the hilt of a knife.

"Yes, Tanya. There is," David said, voice laced with hesitation and something else…

Resignation?

"What is it?"

The shadows on David's face swirled into smoke.

Tanya stepped back.

Her heel hit the edge of the basin, setting her off balance.

David bit his lip, smoke seeping from between his teeth.

"This had best not be a bad joke." Tanya kept the fear from her voice, but the light playing tricks made it difficult.

"I'm sorry about this, Tanya. I truly am."

David's sword was out in a flash, and he moved far faster than his stumbling gait should allow.

Tanya pulled her dagger, but he caught her wrist. She grunted as cold steel sliced her side. They wrestled with the dagger, but his grip was stronger than it looked.

David leaned in close, whispering in her ear.

"Sorry—there's no good way to tell you this."

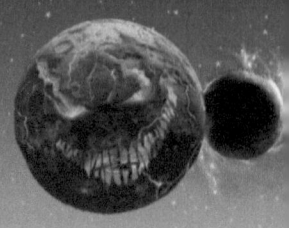

23
JANUS OSGOOD

"He actually got the ledger?" Reynolds looked down at the green book sitting on his desk.

"It seems so."

"Wow. I guess we underestimated our musical friend." Reynolds shook his head.

"Apparently."

"And there was an uprising at the Freemen's Guild last night?"

"Yeah. The rumor is Odin and Marius are dead."

"Dead?"

"Nothing substantiated yet, sir. But there's a lot of talk. I'd be surprised if there wasn't some truth to it."

Reynolds laughed. "This couldn't have gone better." His smile quickly faded. "Well, perhaps it could've gone a little better. Unfortunate business with Tanya."

Janus opened his mouth to ask why she fell out of Reynolds's good graces, then thought better of it. Reynolds would never tell him, and asking as few questions as possible was just good policy.

"You still want me to ensure he follows through with it?"

"Yes, nothing's changed." Reynolds let out a long, tired sigh. "Report back to me as soon as it's done."

"Yes, sir."

"Actually, how about a drink?"

Janus frowned.

Reynolds rarely fraternizes with the agents.

"I've got nothing but time to kill," Janus said anyway.

"Hopefully."

Janus nearly laughed, but the look on Reynolds's face stopped him.

Together, they stood and exited the office, heading to the common room. Reynolds filled two ales for them, and they sat at a table in a corner.

"Those new boots?" Reynolds asked.

"They are. Found a tailor in the Industrial District."

"Really? They look nice. Which outfitter?"

"The Cordovan Cinch."

"You like 'em?" Reynolds asked.

"Love them. Keep my feet dry, even in this weather."

"I'll have to check the place out." Reynolds nodded. "Be careful of David too."

"I will."

He seemed pretty harmless face down in the alleyway yesterday, though.

Janus had dragged the kid to the side of the street, heaped some trash on him so he might live long enough to complete his second assignment, and taken the ledger.

"The first tail we put on him went missing, and we still haven't found the body."

"Who was it?"

"Cohen."

Janus frowned. Cohen was a new agent, but decent by all accounts, and not one to slip up with someone like David.

Could've told me that before you had me follow him.

Janus considered asking why Reynolds withheld that little tidbit, then decided against it. He doubted David had anything to do with the disappearance.

The kid's a pussycat, not a lion.

Reynolds's mood only darkened over the next four ales and two hours.

Tanya finally appeared at the far end of the hall, striding across the room like she owned the place. She had a reputation for getting things done, but Janus had never worked with her.

"Keep your distance. She's more slippery than a sea leech," Reynolds whispered.

Janus nodded. "You know me, sir, no unnecessary risks, no heroics."

"Good." But the look on Reynolds's face was anything but.

Janus stood and followed Tanya out of the Lance. He stopped outside and looked around. She was nowhere to be seen but might watch for a tail if she was as good as they said. Janus stopped under the overhang, lit his pipe, and took a few deep pulls, enjoying the calming leaf. A few minutes later, he knocked the ash from his pipe on the handrail and headed down the main road.

Follow Tanya and ensure David kills her.

Reynolds's words echoed through his head.

Janus didn't know why, and he didn't care. He didn't ask unnecessary questions, which was undoubtedly why Reynolds chose him for the task.

The fountain square was empty when he arrived.

Janus circled the plaza until he found a sturdy drainage pipe on the side of a tailor's shop and used it to climb to the tile roof. The rain showed no sign of letting up, so he tucked his new boots under the hem of his cloak and hunkered down.

Eventually, Tanya showed up, clearly having taken a less direct route. She walked to the other side of the fountain and disappeared into the shadows.

Janus's eyebrows narrowed, then his face slowly relaxed.

She wasn't going anywhere. David hadn't arrived yet, and she'd have to be a magician to leave the square unseen.

Not one of those gray-cloaked bastards either. She'd have to be able to do real *magic.*

Janus forced back a laugh.

A long while went by before David limped into the square.

Even when my note specifically said don't be late.

Janus sighed.

Some people simply cannot follow directions.

David approached the fountain. For a minute, he just stood there, staring at the sculpture like he was daft. Tanya emerged from the shadows. They argued briefly and looked up at the Trickster, then Tanya handed him the letter. David unfolded the parchment and clearly read it but didn't act. The note couldn't be long. "Kill the bitch and leave her in the fountain" could only be written in so many words.

Sure hope I don't need to intervene.

Janus shook his head.

Boy ain't got the stones. Likely never—

David moved in, drawing steel.

Tanya stepped back, but she was tight against the basin. David plunged his blade into her side. Tanya got a dagger out, and Janus was pretty sure she managed to draw blood. The two of them wrestled over the weapon, but David's blade was still in her side, and soon she fell limp in his arms. He held her there momentarily in what could've been a tender embrace. Then, gently, he laid her in the fountain, closing her eyes with one hand.

Did he fall for her?

Janus scratched his chin.

She was pretty, sure. Still, how long had they known each other?

David limped out of the square, sniffling.

Is he crying?

It was impossible to tell with the rain coming down the way it was.

Once David was a few blocks away, Janus moved to the edge of his roof, used the storm drain to descend to the street, and walked over to the basin's edge. Tanya floated near the middle of the fountain, bumping against the statue, arms drifting lazily at her sides. Blood was in the water, but it was hard to tell how much in the red light of the moon and with the churning fountain.

I probably should wade in there and get a pulse...

"Damn," Janus whispered, looking down at his new boots.

Wet feet are the worst.

Tanya's chest was still as stone.

Janus pursed his lips, glanced at the Trickster, then shuddered. It was an ugly one tonight, all scowl, teeth, and laughing eyes.

Janus turned and began the long walk back to guild headquarters.

Time to report back to Will Reynolds.

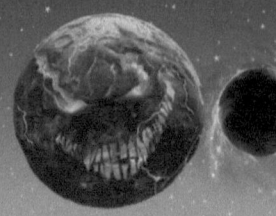

24
NATHAN

"The screams are coming from the inner village," Raylor muttered, almost to himself, then he shouted it.

Raylor's yell echoed in the distance, barely audible over the pounding of Nathan's feet. The screaming was easy to follow, and soon, he was approaching a cluster of huts. He slowed, looking around for backup, but the only thing that managed to keep pace was the darkness.

Nathan shook his head. *Sometimes, quick wits are as much a curse as a gift.*

The cries were coming from the central structure, but he noted no damage to the front door. A path weaved between the huts, leading to the back of the structures. He slipped between the buildings.

Something scraped on wood around the corner, and Nathan halted.

Should've grabbed a weapon. Oh well, wish in one hand, shit in the other.

A chittering snarl echoed from behind the hut, and a shiver wriggled up Nathan's spine. The noise was utterly alien, the stuttering chirp of a hyena but far deeper and full of menace. He took the next turn wide, peering around the corner of the building.

A shadowy form loomed at the window.

It's enormous. The creature was taller than a horse and must have outweighed one.

Nathan took a step back.

The hulking shadow scrambled up the wall.

God, it's fast.

Despite its size, the beast disappeared over the roof's edge with the grace and speed of a cat. Nathan sprinted back around the house. Two hunters approached, clearly trying to locate the screams. He snatched a spear from the closest man.

The beast leapt from the building.

Nathan tracked its trajectory, took aim, and hurled the spear ahead of it.

"Take it down!" Nathan yelled as the spear left his grip. "Throw, damn it!"

Two more grunts and two more spears sailed into the night.

The yelling of hunters grew louder from somewhere, but Nathan didn't turn to look. He held his breath, eyes locked on the weapon. The tip slammed home with a meaty thud.

That'll slow it.

The creature landed on another roof, then reached back and pulled the spear free, tossing it aside with a low growl.

"What!" Nathan snarled, sprinting after the creature as the other two spears fell short.

Why would a beast do that?

He rounded a steep incline, barreling down the hill.

How did it rip a widened tip free with ease?

Sharpened stakes forced him right down a curving path.

Does it have thumbs?

The monster emerged from the darkness, bathed in the red light of the moon, then vanished over the apex of another roof.

Nathan glanced around.

A sharpened stake loomed into view.

He dodged to the left, feet slipping and sending him into a roll. The point caught his arm, cutting a thin line along the skin as he kicked up a cloud of dirt. An instant later, he was up again.

Damn your good-for-nothing defenses.

Nathan took a path on the right, but the creature was widening the gap between them.

At least we should have a decent trail of blood to follow.

The creature leapt through a patch of torchlit ground. Dark brown fur lined its side where parted muscle and blood should be.

Impossible.

Nathan rounded another cluster of huts, nearing the edge of the village.

Perhaps it was just a trick of the light.

A torch was planted in the soil, marking the edge of the defenses. Nathan snatched it up, moving into the cleared ground between Trill and the forest.

No tracks. No blood. No sign at all.

Nathan had to stop himself from charging into the woods alone.

"Damn." *What in God's name?*

A minute later, Raylor and the other hunters caught up.

"Is it...gone?" Raylor asked, chest heaving.

"For now," Nathan responded. "Let's go. The trail's as fresh as it will get, and we have all the warriors we need."

213

"Now?" Raylor asked.

"Of course."

An unfamiliar hunter took a deep breath. "We can't possibly—"

"We can kill it," Nathan cut in. "It's a beast of flesh and blood."

Although perhaps a very unique and deadly one.

He saw no reason to say that aloud, though.

These people have enough to fear.

He looked around the group and was met with a few nods, more scowls, but mostly disbelief.

"We must take the fight to it," Nathan said, voice rising. "This creature has sown fear into your hearts. It does so by raiding your homes and taking your loved ones. Let us return the feeling!"

Nathan paused, locking eyes with Raylor. The man's face was a mask.

"We need to hunt it back to its lair, wait till morning, then smoke it out," Nathan continued. "It gives us reason to fear the night. Let's give it reason to fear the day!"

Only two hunters met his eye, one of which was the man who tackled him.

Nathan's heart sank.

"It'll pick us off one by one," Horinth said. "Even if we manage to find it, we'll all be slaughtered."

"It's a demon, I tell ya," another hunter said. "Sent by the gods to punish us. We men have no place slayin' demons."

Nathan's blood began to heat.

Stubborn cowardice will kill them as sure as the monster, just a bit more slowly.

Nathan found himself nose-to-nose with Horinth without realizing how he got there. He leaned in, fists clenching unconsciously at his sides. Before he could say anything, Raylor appeared, gently pushing them apart.

"Stop this nonsense," Raylor scolded. "This man will cleanse our land of the darkness."

"Not all yer prophecies have come true, Raylor," Horinth said.

"No, but more have come to pass than dwindle away." Raylor slowly looked at each of the gathered men and women. "Do any of you deny it?"

Most of the hunters shook their heads.

"We need to listen to Nathan," Raylor said. "But, Nathan, you must be reasonable as well. We should leave at first light. Its tracks will be easier to follow in the morning. You know this to be sensible."

Raylor paused, clearly waiting for an objection.

No one spoke.

"The hunters need to see their loved ones tonight, and the village needs a chance to count the dead. We can leave tomorrow after a good breakfast and a proper night's rest." Raylor met each hunter's eye. "I will follow Nathan out at first light. Anyone else who wishes to defend their loved ones should join us."

Nathan nodded. It was fair enough. The creature likely had far better night vision than them, and deep down, he knew charging after it in the dark was a blunder.

"Tomorrow, then," Nathan said. "Who will join us?"

Reluctantly, fourteen of the twenty-two hunters stepped forward.

More than half, but not by much.

"Yer all dead. It will devour yer flesh and then yer souls, and if the gods are good, it will save ye for last." Horinth pointed at Nathan. "Then, ye may see the devastation ye have brought upon the rest of us. The beast is not something that can be destroyed. It is something that must be endured." He turned and walked away, seven hunters following close behind.

"Coward," Nathan accused. The insult was pointless, but he couldn't help it.

Horinth turned back, spat on the ground, then continued.

Nathan considered knocking some sense into the man, but it wouldn't change his mind.

More likely to turn others against the cause too.

"We'd best see who the beast took tonight," Raylor murmured, then raised his voice. "I will meet you all in the great hall tomorrow morning. For now, you should all get some rest."

"See you in the morning," Nathan said. "I've slept long enough."

"Where will you go?"

"Back to the hut, where the thing was skulking about. With any luck, whoever was screaming got a better look at it."

Raylor nodded. "Hopefully, the screams mean they are still alive."

Nathan hadn't even considered that possibility.

Hope I'm not walking into a bloodbath.

Light seeped from under the door of the little hut.

At least someone's still alive.

Nathan knocked. Light footfalls moved across the floorboards inside. The door opened a crack, and green eyes peered out.

"Hello?" a feminine voice asked with only the hint of a quiver.

"Hi, my name's Nathan. Could I speak with you for a minute?" He tried to sound calm and soothing, but his voice was raspy and stern, even to his own ears.

She looked him up and down. "Is this about the monster?"

"I'm afraid so. I was the first to arrive at your home and saw it at the window but didn't get a good look before it fled."

"So, you were the one." She hesitated, then opened the door.

Nathan stepped inside.

The modest dwelling contained a table, a few chairs, and a small kitchen. A coatrack stood near the entrance, and two doors led to other parts of the house. A tattered pair of boots sat in the corner, and an old sword hung above the hearth.

Nathan's eyes shifted to the woman. She wore a long jacket that was far too big for her.

Maybe a husband's?

"I'm Nathan," he said, extending a hand.

"You said that already. Plus, I know who ye are." Her accent sounded similar to the rest of the village except mixed with his own. She took his outstretched hand and shook it. Her hand was small but calloused, and the grip was firm.

"My name's Eva," she said as their hands separated.

"I'm sorry to bother you right now, Eva," he explained. Their eyes met, and Nathan paused, noting how deep and striking of a green they really were. "I hate to ask because I know how traumatic tonight must've been. But you see, we're leaving tomorrow morning, and I need to know everything I can about our quarry." Nathan's words were tangling in his treacherous mouth, and he still hadn't asked what he'd come here to. "What I mean to say is...I was wondering if you saw anything. Or rather, did you see it?"

I'm terrible at this. Raylor should've come instead.

Eva shivered.

Great, and now I've upset her.

Nathan felt heat rise to his cheeks.

Some nerve, asking this woman to relive the terror from less than an hour ago.

He looked to the ground, but couldn't help noticing where her coat ended and athletic, shapely legs began. With a snort, he forced his eyes back at the old boots in the corner of the room, took a breath, then met Eva's gaze.

"I-I," Eva paused, looked around the room, then shuddered. Suddenly, the words were spilling like water from a fractured dam. "I don't know what I saw exactly, but its eyes were black—darker than the night. It was watching me...it wanted to *eat* me. I can still see its wet nose pushing through the shutters." Eva shivered. "Hands as big as a skull. Claws as long as a hand. Eyes as hungry as a panther."

Nathan had to hold back from cutting in with more questions.

After a minute, Eva blew out a deep breath. "It was big, nearly as tall as you, and it was crouching." She gestured at Nathan, emphasizing the point.

Nathan stood two hands over the average man but wasn't a giant by any means. Still, the top of Eva's head barely reached his chin, so the thing was enormous compared to her.

"I am so lucky the gong went off, and you all came as quickly as you did. If you hadn't, I'm sure it would've got me. Even after the gong sounded, it nearly came through the window. I could see the hunger in those jet-black eyes. The noise it made..." Eva drew in a breath, shivering it out. "It was unlike anything I've ever heard. An *evil* sound."

"Yeah, I heard it too—"

Thump, thump, thump. Something heavy hit the door.

Nathan almost jumped. "You expecting someone?"

The knock came again.

"Yes, but I don't know why he's knocking," Eva said with a frown.

She moved gracefully to the door, cracked it open, and uttered a greeting to whoever was outside.

A man muttered something low and incoherent.

Nathan craned his neck, trying to see who it was, then caught himself admiring Eva's bare legs again and pulled his eyes away.

Be respectful.

He considered slapping himself.

She's gone through a lot tonight, and she's got a husband, for God's sake—

"No! That can't be right." Eva's voice rose, instantly putting him on edge.

The man said something else, but again, it was incomprehensible.

Nathan took a step closer.

"No, you're mistaken!"

"Sorry" was the only word Nathan made out through the door.

"There must be a mistake. Let me see! I need to see!"

"You can't." The man was louder now. "I'm sorry. I have to go."

Eva turned, eyes squeezing shut as she let out a slow, shaky breath. Her hands curled into fists at her sides. For a long moment, she didn't move. Then, without a word, she crossed the room and sank into a chair, leaving the door open wide behind her.

Not good.

Nathan walked over to the entrance, closed the door, then approached the table until Eva's expression stopped him. Shadows clung to her face, and her shoulders slumped. The heavy jacket she'd been wearing for warmth now weighed on her. Tears streamed down her face, and her chest heaved in and out erratically.

Nathan took a step closer.

"What was—"

"It's nothing. Leave. Please." Eva's words came between shallow breaths, voice quivering like strings on a violin.

Nathan stopped his advance but didn't turn to go.

Tears pitter-pattered softly on the floor as he took another step.

"Leave!" Eva's voice rose, but her eyes never left the floor.

Nathan glanced at the door, then back at her.

She clearly wants to be alone...but she's in pain. Does she have anyone who could help?

His eyes found the boots in the corner again.

Asking about kin might be tactless right now. So, I guess that leaves me.

Nathan took another step forward. No discernible objection filtered through the sobbing, so he closed the distance between them. He put an arm around Eva and crouched. She didn't flinch away, so he wrapped her up in a full embrace.

What should I say? I barely know this woman.

There were no words. Nothing could stifle true loss.

But I can do this.

After another few heartbeats, Eva pressed her face to his chest and wept. She sobbed for what felt like hours. All the frustration, fear, and pent-up rage flowed out of her in the most primal way.

Nathan held her without saying a word, unmoving despite the burning in his thighs.

I'm no stranger to loss, and she just needs someone solid right now.

Somehow, he knew that despite not knowing anything else.

Slowly, her sobs eased, and slurred words began to push through gasping breaths.

"W-why? He was s-such a...I just don't...Elrrrontiss!" She growled the last word without a note of fear.

It wasn't the time for smiles, but one crept across Nathan's face anyway.

This little lady is braver than every hunter in the village. She's willing to say its name, even after it takes her husband and nearly her as well.

Slowly, Eva's sobs subsided.

"I'm sorry." Nathan's voice was gravelly from disuse yet still came out solemn and sincere.

How long did I hold her?

"Are you...going to kill it?" she asked.

"Or die in the attempt."

The expression on Eva's face didn't change as she nodded, wiping away snot on a sleeve.

"Good. That thing deserves death. It's taken *far* too much from us. Far too much from me." Eva's mouth twitched. Nathan wasn't sure if she held back a sob or a snarl, but either way, she held it back.

Tougher than she looks.

"I should go. You asked me to earlier, and I didn't. I'm sorry about that." Nathan stood on aching legs.

"No. Stay. Please. I feel safer with you here. And I want to help kill that thing."

Nathan offered an apologetic smile. "I think you've done enough."

"No, I haven't," Eva said firmly.

Nathan cocked his head quizzically.

"You were the first person here. You scared off Elrontis before it got me. You stayed and comforted me." She swallowed hard. "And now you're going to avenge my brother."

"Your brother?" Nathan asked without thinking. Then, it clicked.

Well, that's what I get for assuming.

"Yes. It took him—just tonight," Eva stammered, then started sobbing anew.

Nathan held her again, but she pulled herself together far more quickly this time.

Eva eventually repeated what she remembered of Elrontis, but it wasn't much more than the first time. She hadn't gotten a good look at it, and her description mostly matched the shadowy figure he'd chased through the village. He offered to leave again once Eva finished describing her encounter with the beast, but once more she insisted he stay.

"What about you?" Eva asked. "I heard you just kinda showed up out of nowhere?"

"I don't know."

"What do you mean you don't know?"

"I don't remember."

"Like amnesia?"

"Yeah," Nathan said. "I know it's strange, but I woke up on the side of a river alone, naked, and with no memory of who I am or where I come from."

Eva cocked an eyebrow. "Completely naked?"

Nathan nodded.

"Sounds like a sight. You can't remember anything?"

"Well, I remember basic concepts, like how to read and write or hold a conversation. But bigger things, like my past..." Nathan sighed. "They're all gone."

"Is that why you talk funny?"

Nathan had nearly forgotten the villager's accent and even found himself accidentally slipping into it on occasion.

Odd. Mimicking an accent so fast can't be normal, but what does it mean?

"I imagine it is," Nathan said with a frown, then stood.

"Where are you going?"

"I should go. We head up the mountain at first light."

"No. Stay."

Nathan looked at her. Tiny emerald wells shone back at him. Her eyes were dry, but that could change at any moment with what she'd been through tonight.

Eva stood, grabbed his hand, and led him to a back room. She pushed aside the furs functioning as a door and pulled him into the chamber. A wolfskin rug sat in the middle of the room, surrounded by a small bed and tiny vanity. Eva sat him down on the bed and plopped down next to him. Before Nathan could object, she curled into his arm and blew out a long breath.

Guess she doesn't want to be alone, and who could blame her after a night like this?

"What's this?" Eva tapped the tattoo between his thumb and index finger.

"A symbol." Nathan hesitated. *She shared with me.* "The mark of the one true God."

"Only one god?" Eva asked. "Sounds a bit boring. How do they manage it all?"

"Manage what?"

"All of it." Eva waved a hand about in a vague gesture.

"I'm not sure they do."

"What's their name?"

"I don't think they have one."

"Seems silly."

"How many gods do you have?" Nathan asked.

"Thirteen."

"Huh. Why so many?"

"Different gods for different things," Eva said as if it made perfect sense. "You know, Pirel for the hunters, Evintri for the mothers, Amara for the lovers."

"Seems like a lot to keep track of."

"You can't keep track of thirteen things?" Eva craned her neck up at him.

Nathan chuckled.

Eva smiled, but the expression quickly fled as her eyes left his.

She's pretty resilient.

"What can you tell me of your one god?" Eva asked.

Is she actually interested? Or just looking for a distraction? Maybe both.

"Well, there's only one," Nathan explained.

"Yeah, I got that. What else? Are they a man or a woman?"

"Neither."

"Oh, like Sasesh then."

"Who's Sasesh?" Nathan asked.

"One of our gods. Sometimes, they're depicted as male, sometimes female. Other times, something in between." Eva nodded as if she was explaining something every child already knew.

"No, not like that."

"How so?"

"Well, they don't really have a gender. Probably don't even look like us at all."

Eva cocked an eyebrow, glancing up at him. "And you say thirteen gods are confusing."

Nathan laughed again. "I guess you're right."

"I know," Eva said, yawning.

Nathan opened his mouth to say something else, then stopped. He wasn't sure how else to describe God. They were hope. They were life. They were everywhere, and They were nowhere.

How can I explain what I barely understand myself?

Nathan stared at the ceiling for a time, trying to organize his thoughts. After a few minutes, he realized that he had more questions than answers on the subject. He looked down. Eva was sound asleep, head resting on his chest, breathing finally even.

Nathan inhaled. She smelled of woodsmoke, herbs, and hard work.

She's strong. If I return from the hunt, who knows what will happen? She just needs someone tonight, though, and I'm happy to help—no strings attached.

Nathan couldn't remember anyone from his past. So, he had no one, but it seemed like neither did she—not anymore.

Maybe we can have each other.

The thought was silly and whimsical, but it was innocent, and it bounced around in Nathan's head as he drifted off.

25
TANYA RINGHOLDER

T anya lay in the basin, still as stone, David's words echoing in her head.

"Don't go back to the guild."

Did he say that first or last?

"You need to play dead."

Water from Argyle Rocktell's hands rained on her face.

"You're gonna have to trust me."

Trust? Now that's a fickle thing.

"I'm gonna lay you in the fountain."

At first, his words hadn't made any sense, but they'd sunk in as she wrestled for control of the knife.

"Wait thirty minutes, then meet me at the northeast gate."

Tanya had fought him for real at first, but Pretty Boy was stronger than he looked.

"If you don't, we're both dead."

David had clearly seen something in the letter. Either it told him to perform this charade, or the Shadow's Lance had betrayed her.

If he truly wanted to kill me, he wouldn't have faked the first blow.

Metal rattled on stone in the distance. Tanya's eyes fluttered open. A shadowy figure was climbing down a drainpipe at the edge of the square.

Well, that's not nefarious or anything. What're the odds he isn't here for me?

Tanya pushed off the fountain's rim with her toe, sending her body drifting toward the middle of the basin.

I'll hear the splashing first if they decide to put a hole in me for good measure.

Tanya cut a line across her left palm, then stowed the blade. Her stitches felt like they'd reopened, and a bit of David's blood was already in the water. As the shadowy outline approached, she closed her eyes and slowed her breathing.

223

Jack's and Ted's lifeless bodies floated through her mind as she held completely still, mimicking the listless forms that haunted her dreams. Eyes were on her. She could feel them. Water rained across her nose, and she accidentally sucked some into her lungs. Tanya nearly sputtered but held in the choking breath.

After what seemed like an eternity, leather scuffed on stone. The footsteps were barely audible through the water in her ears, but they softened as someone retreated. Her lungs burned, aching to push out the moisture.

Heartbeat after heartbeat went by.

The footfalls ceased.

The pain was unbearable. She needed air, or the act wouldn't be a farce much longer.

Tanya gasped, coughing up water and sucking in a shuddering breath. She opened her eyes and looked toward the edge of the square. A tall, gaunt silhouette headed toward the guildhouse.

Did he hear me?

The man didn't turn back.

Either the fountain masked the noise, or he's just not letting on.

The figure slowly disappeared into the shadows.

Coincidence he's headed toward the Lance?

Tanya bit her lip.

Doubtful.

A few minutes later, her teeth started chattering.

Not making a very convincing corpse anymore.

Tanya pulled herself up using the statue in the middle of the fountain. Water poured from her coat, pants, and cloak as she waded to the basin's edge.

Air kissed the cut on her hand for the first time, causing it to sting. The shallow incision was still bleeding, but would soon be just another clean white line. Tanya considered confronting Reynolds and reporting David for abandoning his mission.

No. Not worth the risk.

She chewed her lip.

Damn bard might've been telling the truth. Best hear him out.

If David's answers were unsatisfactory, she could always return to the Lance.

With that in mind, Tanya headed toward the edge of town. She kept to the side streets for a few blocks past the main square, then took the most direct road. At the northeast gate, a hooded man leaned against the wall, holding the reins of two horses in a loose grip.

Before long, moonlight revealed David's angular jaw and mop of coal black hair. He grimaced in the rain but attempted a half-hearted smile as she approached. It was a little grotesque, the sort of grin given when the only choice was to laugh or cry.

"We need to go. Now," David said as soon as she was within earshot.

"We?" Tanya asked.

"Well, you certainly don't *have* to come. But *I'm* leaving. They'll be after me soon, and unless I'm greatly mistaken, they'll be after you too."

"What *exactly* did the letter say, David?"

"It said to kill you and to leave your body in the fountain."

"That's it?" Tanya asked. She already believed him but still needed to hear the words.

"That's kinda all it had to say. I assumed they were watching, hence the little show."

Tanya measured the calm determination in David's striking blue eyes.

If he's a liar, then he's an exceedingly good one.

Reading people was a necessary skill growing up on the streets of Norinspire, and David's face was like a book.

Gods, no wonder he racked up a gambling debt.

Besides, the shadowy figure at the fountain was confirmation enough.

"You're a wanted man now, huh? A gambling debt to the Freemen, a double cross to the biggest guild of assassins and cutthroats in Darin, and now horse robbery?" Tanya asked, gesturing to the two mounts.

"If you've already got half your money in the pot, you might as well go all in." David's voice rose slightly as if reciting the words.

"How profound. Who said that?"

"Dunno. I knew a drunkard who used to say it, but I doubt he came up with it."

"Well, at least you have good role models in your life."

"Had," David corrected.

"What?"

"He's dead."

"Sorry?" Tanya asked, wondering if he expected sympathy.

"Don't be. He was an asshole and a cheat to boot."

David held out a set of reins. Tanya took them, walked around the horse, and swung into the saddle. David put one foot in the stirrup, cursed, then struggled onto the other horse.

"Remind me to check those wounds later," Tanya said.

"Just want to get my shirt off, eh?"

"Wow, you discovered my master plan. Get the musician to try and kill you for an excuse to undress him and tenderly nurse his wounds."

"Sarcasm?"

"Nope, not a lick of it. Now shut your trap and ride, and I'll consider still looking at your injuries when we stop."

They nudged the horses into a trot, and miraculously, David kept silent. They passed under the gate and into the rolling hills surrounding Windmore.

"Care to explain why you used to hang out with a drunk?" Tanya finally asked. "Just curious who I'm throwing my lot in with."

"I hang out with a lot of drunks. Comes with the territory, you know." David pointed to his lute case for emphasis. "But in this particular instance, I didn't have much choice."

"Care to elaborate?" Tanya asked.

"Hard to escape blood."

"Your father?"

"Yeah. Old bastard drank like a fish."

Figures. We're all shaped by our environment, and some have that better than others.

They rode on in silence for a while, and the rain finally let up. The red light of the Trickster bathed the rolling hills as the tall grass swayed in the wind like waves in the ocean.

"So, you got some kind of plan? Or was 'ride off into the sunset' as far as you got?" Tanya finally asked.

"You do realize it's full dark, right?"

"It's a turn of phrase, dimwit."

"If I planned a ride into the sunset at midnight in a torrential downpour, then you'd better worry about who you're ridin' with."

"Oh, trust me, I am. Hence the questions."

"I just saved your bloody life!" David exclaimed indignantly.

"Seems to me that might be the first smart thing you've done in your...eighteen cycles?"

David looked positively aghast at her guess. In truth, she knew he was older than that, but goading him had been pretty fun so far.

"Eighteen? Eighteen!" David repeated with a shake of his head. "I'm twenty-five, I'll have you know. Almost twenty-six. That's the last bloody time I stick my neck out for someone." He grumbled the last part under his breath, but a smile tugged at the edge of his mouth.

"Are you sure you're twenty-five? I've never met a man who still referred to himself as *almost* anything in his twenties." Tanya couldn't help a twitch of a smile as his scowl deepened.

David was silent for a time, leaving Tanya to her thoughts.

Gods, he must be used to saps in search of love or professionals working for stone.

Either way, they wouldn't have much more than dirt between their ears.

Let's see how he handles someone with half a brain.

Tanya glanced over at David. He was rocking in the saddle, a dopey expression plastered on his face.

I'll save him once, so we're square, then ditch him if he's as incompetent as he looks.

"But seriously, let's give you the benefit of the doubt," Tanya said. "Let's say, just for the sake of argument, that you planned to ride off into the sunset. Then what? Don't get me wrong—I'm pretty happy to ride off into the sunset if it's the only plan where I don't end up dead."

David turned to her. "Is that your attempt at a thank you?"

"You expect people to thank you for *not* killing them?"

David's eyebrows narrowed, but he didn't respond. Instead, he backtracked to the previous question. "Honestly, the only plan was to get the hell out of Windmore and put as much distance between us and the bounty hunters as possible. I've been thinking on it, though."

"Oh, that sounds dangerous," Tanya cut in.

"Yeah, I've heard the hunters are no joke."

"No, I'm not worried about them."

"What?"

"You thinking. Sounds dangerous."

"Fuck, Tanya!"

"Sorry. Couldn't resist. You were saying?"

David gave her a sideways glance and sighed. "I was thinking, before I was so rudely interrupted, that we could lie low in Norinspire. You know, sell the horses, maybe find some work, blend into the crowd."

"And you think they won't be able to find the new traveling minstrel in town?" Tanya asked. "The Lance has a guildhouse in the capital, and it's a big one. We might be able to lie low there for a time, but that time would absolutely be limited."

"The Lance?" David asked.

Tanya hesitated, Reynolds's stern face flashing through her mind.

Old habits die hard, I guess.

She pushed the inhibition away.

"The Shadow's Lance." Tanya eyed him skeptically. "You know, the guild of cutthroats and assassins you threw your lot in with because you couldn't pay your debt."

"Great, and now they're after us. Is it possible to pay 'em off?"

"With what money?" Tanya asked. "You gonna borrow some more stone from the Freemen's Guild?"

David pursed his lips, turning back to the road.

He makes that face a lot, doesn't he? Oh well, contemplation is kinda cute on him. Even if it doesn't accomplish much.

"Anyway, they'll do just about anything for enough stone, but they typically contract through the OAM or the noble houses," Tanya explained.

"That sounds promising. If we can just wrangle up the 'phire."

"Sapphire?" Tanya laughed. "Try diamond or 'rald."

"Emerald?" A goofy smile split David's face, stretching from ear to ear.

Kind of a doofy thing, isn't he?

Tanya looked over, cocking an eyebrow as she waited for him to get the picture.

"Oh, gods! You're serious. Tanya, I've never even seen a 'rald!" David moaned.

"It doesn't matter. Even if we had the gravel, once the Lance takes a job, they don't stop till it's done. Reputation is the only thing they value more than stone. You and I? Well, we're a blight on that reputation now. They'll want us dead, diamonds or 'ralds be damned."

"All right, let's think then. Maybe we stop in Norinspire? Off-load the horses? Then we run and keep on running."

"To where?"

"Not sure, but we have some time to figure that out. Maybe up north? What's that little town called?"

"Darkloom?"

"Yeah, that's the one!" David said, snapping his fingers.

"You have any ideas on how to make money on the way to Darkloom?" Tanya asked.

"Well, we can sell the horses," David said again.

"Yeah, when we get there, maybe. What about on the way? You thought about food? Water? Feed for these two?" Tanya gestured to the two beasts.

"I could sing for meals and lodging."

"Ha!" Tanya laughed, looked at David's indignant face, then giggled a little more. "By Pirel's tits, you are naive sometimes."

David frowned, looked away, then muttered, "I'm actually quite good, believe it or not."

"Oh, you misunderstand. I have no doubt your pretty face could feed and lodge us for the night. But the Lance could follow your bawdy songs and ballads to Darkloom without even trying."

"Well, I don't see you coming up with anything. Isn't subterfuge what you're supposed to be good at?"

"Yeah, just wanna see what I'm working with here. You got any other skills? Or have you always sung for your supper?" Tanya couldn't help the full grin that crept across her face this time.

"I'm not half bad with a blade, I'll have you know," David said, patting the hilt of a short sword.

"Well, that's something. I actually think Darkloom might be our best bet, or better yet, Terra. We'd need even more money for that trip, though, and I bet our likeness is posted around the docks soon enough. Let's think on it tonight and make a clearheaded decision in the morning."

David nodded, and they bounced along in silence for a while.

Little pockets of trees dotted the landscape on either side of the road, breaking up the endless sea of grass. Tanya kept an eye on the trees, watching for any sign of movement as she considered their options. None of the plans were very good, but they were plans, and that was something.

They rode the rest of the night through, and Tanya passed the time by asking David about his past. Occasionally, she teased him for not being able to get by without his charm and good looks, but mostly, they simply rode and chatted.

At least he's easy to talk to and takes verbal punishment with a smile.

By the time the sun started rising, Tanya was done laughing. She was nearly falling asleep in the saddle and trying not to think about the riding sores she'd have tomorrow. David led them off the road and up a little hill to a cluster of trees.

No way I'm going to restitch the wound in my side tonight—or rather, today.

The good news was, the rain had stopped a while back, and the ground here wasn't completely soaked. Tanya tied her horse to an oak tree, walked to the other side, and collapsed without bothering to take off her wet clothes or look for a blanket. With a deep sigh, she closed her eyes and embraced the oblivion of sleep.

Something tugged at Tanya's jacket; then it slid away. Half-awake, she reached for her knife. Two fingers of steel slid free before the jacket was replaced with a warm blanket, and thoughts of stabbing were replaced with an exhausted grumble.

Someone mumbled something nonsensical about hypothermia as sleep retook her.

The sun was low when Tanya finally awoke. She looked around. David was nowhere to be seen, but his horse and belongings were still tethered to an old oak. Her coat hung on one of the lower limbs of the tree. She stood, took it, and threw it over her shoulders.

Wow, I must've been completely out for him to get that off without getting stabbed.

Tanya had a vague memory of the event, but nothing more.

Amazingly, the jacket was dry, so she buckled it down the side with practiced fingers, then looked up and frowned.

Is that music?

A faint melody drifted through the air. Tanya followed the pleasant notes up a small hill and found David sitting on a rock overlooking the tree. His hands moved deftly over the strings of his lute, and he didn't look up as she approached.

Completely engrossed. Good thing I'm not a bandit or a Justiseer.

The song was sad, lonely, and surprisingly, rather beautiful.

Dum-dum, diddle-la-da-dum. Da-dum-dum da-dum.

Tanya had only seen David play once before, but that was a bawdy tavern tune. She knew he was decent then. This, however, was something else entirely.

He's honestly quite good. Of course, I can never let him know that, Tanya decided.

"The warrior he was, a hero of old.

Come from the land, of frigid and cold."

David's fingers moved flawlessly, jumping along the frets as he sang in a sad, low tone.

"We called for a general, were given a hero.

Oh where did you go, our hero of old."

Dum-dum, diddle-la-da-dum. Da-dum-dum da-dum.

David was about to start another verse when he looked up and smiled.

"Morning, sleepy." His tone was cheerful and light despite being a wanted fugitive.

"Morning," she said, more gruffly than intended. Just then, Tanya realized how direly she needed to pee. "Excuse me a minute."

"Everything all right?"

"Yep. Gotta piss."

"Anyone ever tell you how ladylike you are?" David called after her.

"All the bloody time. Glad you noticed."

The same sad melody started again as Tanya strode down the other side of the hill toward a small clump of trees. She unfastened her belt, rounded one last tree just to be safe, and pulled her pants partway down. The tip of her foot caught a root, sending her sprawling.

Tanya's arms shot up by pure instinct to protect her face, but she couldn't roll out of the fall with her pants around her knees. She hit the ground, knocking the wind from her lungs.

Tanya wheezed in a single breath.

"Son-of-a-whore," she croaked, sucked in a few more gulps of air, then started laughing.

Ass over the campfire in a heap, with my pants half down to boot. Good thing no one saw that. Certainly not the most dignified thing I've ever done.

Tanya braced her elbows against the ground, pushing up to hands and knees. She shook the hair from her face, blew the last few strands away, then froze. Yellow eyes stared through the tall grass half a dozen spans away as a black tail flicked from side to side.

Not good, the voice in the back of her head whispered.

The panther licked its lips, muscles bunching as the song drifted down the hillside.

Dum-dum, diddle-la-da-dum. Da-dum-dum da-dum.

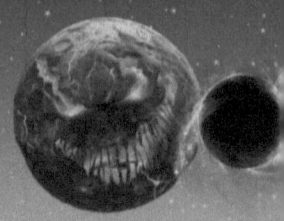

26
RIGEL
CROSS

The sewers were entirely absent of light. Cross had waded through the vile filth for hours. Disgustingly, he'd become somewhat accustomed to the stench. His shoulder throbbed, his ribs ached, and worst of all, he was utterly lost.

Good chance I'll die down here.

Cross ran his fingers along the wall. The trick should eventually lead him out of the labyrinth and minimize the number of times he waded through the same waste. The method would've worked for the rats if only they'd been smart enough to use it.

Then again, I'm no rat, and this is no maze. Not intentionally, anyway.

Hours had passed since Cross put his hand to the wall.

Am I walking in one giant loop?

There was no way to know. Windmore was enormous.

How many people must it take to create this much waste?

Cross remembered the overwhelming feeling of insignificance as they dragged him through the city streets for the first time. There were so many people, all with so little compassion, as if the more humans there were, the less they cared for one another.

He stopped, rolled his good shoulder, and stretched his neck.

Gods, I'm sore.

The pain was easy to ignore during a fight, but later, he was always stiffer than the last stubborn oak stump in an unplowed field. Cross tried to recall the battle in the yard, but the details wouldn't come.

Maybe I'll remember after I sleep.

He plodded on, fingers trailing on slippery stone.

Will I die down here?

Cross scratched his stubbly jaw and felt it clench.

No, I need to see home first.

He imagined Elinfall, piercing the night.

Hopefully it's still dark when I get out of here.

232

If it was, he could follow the star east. There was an ocean between him and Terra, but he'd swim that if he had to. Cross sent a quick prayer to Borix:

Please help me get home. If I die after that, so be it.

Cross didn't know much about the gods, but he knew Borix was the patron of farmers, and he never gave up.

Hopefully, that will be enough.

A quiet trickle reached his ears.

What is that?

Cross stopped his slog through the filth and listened.

Moving water?

He put a finger into the waist-deep sludge and held still.

Something slowly drifted into it.

A current?

Cross followed the sound and lazy drift of the sludge. The trickle slowly grew to a rush. Light painted the wall ahead where the tunnel bent. Cross ran, rounding the corner. Sunlight blinded him. He staggered back, pulled up an elbow to shade his eyes, then took a deep breath. The foul odor still lingered, but the air was fresh and clean by comparison.

A shallow stream ran over his feet, flowing off the edge of a stone ledge a few spans away. Cross stood on an elevated structure, similar to the aqueducts that brought fresh water to the bathhouses.

My very own crap-e-duct.

Cross laughed, took a few steps forward, and peered over the edge. His chuckle ceased. Sewage spattered onto rocks six spans below before flowing into a large pond.

No way to climb down.

He took a few steps away from the ledge and glanced back at the darkness.

No chance I'm going back in there.

Without much more thought, Cross charged toward the end of the structure and hurtled off the end. He tucked, trying to maneuver his uninjured side toward the surface as he plummeted.

Smack.

The world went dark.

A moment later, Cross's head emerged. He gulped in fresh air, wiping the sludge from his eyes. Swimming with an injured shoulder and ribs was excruciating, but he pushed through the pain. As soon as his feet touched the bottom, he stood and washed his wounded shoulder. The water wasn't anywhere close to sanitary, but it had to be better than what he'd been marinating in for hours.

I'll find something cleaner once I'm farther from Windmore.

Cross waded from the water and looked to the sun.

Midday now. How long did I spend in those sewers?

It didn't matter. What mattered was getting away from the city. Unfortunately, he'd been counting on Elinfall for directions. He looked around. A filthy creek flowed toward grassy hills sprinkled with little bunches of trees.

Cross decided to follow it downstream.

A few hours later, the creek joined a river. Cross waded upstream, put his cracked lips to the water, and drank until his stomach hurt. He stood, burped, and looked around. Ahead, the curving river divided the horizon. Grasslands stretched as far as the eye could see on the left, and a thick bayou engulfed the landscape on the right.

Cross rinsed off as much filth as he could and thoroughly cleaned out the wound in his shoulder. It hurt like all the hells, but it was for the best. The wound was itchy, hot to the touch, and already starting to close. He waded to shore and headed downstream.

The river forked a couple of hours later.

Both should flow toward the Great Divide, but which way is quicker?

Cross tried to visualize the map of Darin and Terra he'd seen so long ago. The outline of each continent appeared in his mind, but that was about it. He took a deep breath, then headed left.

Clouds rolled in through the evening, and it was pouring by the time night fell. Cross walked through most of the night, hoping the downpour would lessen or Elinfall would shine through the clouds. The rain never let up, though, and eventually, he collapsed under a tree.

Sleep took him quickly, but he found no peace in it.

◄O►

The towering walls of the Coliseum loomed all around. Cross looked down at his blood-smeared palms. Red slowly enveloped his hands, running down his forearms and dripping from his elbows. The viscous fluid continued to expand, filling the enormous building and forcing him to swim. Soon, he was drowning in it.

———————◄○►———————

Cross awoke with a start, still slumped against the tree. Everything was sore and throbbing. He blinked, shaking the remnants of the nightmare away. The rising sun was low on the horizon, and Elinfall was nowhere to be seen. He got up and continued his trek down the river.

Throughout the morning and into the afternoon, Cross found two little inlets with gathered fish. He spent a little while trying to catch them from shore, but they were too quick. When he saw a third cove, he waded into the river. The fish tried to escape, but they had to swim past him this time. Miraculously, he snagged a small one from the water and ate it raw, waist-deep in the current. The sliminess should've bothered him, or the way it still wriggled, but he found it difficult to care after the last twenty-four hours.

Cross's ribs still hurt, but not as much as yesterday. His shoulder was another story. Pain pulsed through it constantly, and it was hot and itchy. Cross didn't know much about medicine, but he'd seen plenty of slaves put down for less severe injuries after they festered.

May have to risk a trip to a healer once I find a town.

Cross inspected the slave brand on his hand. The mark wouldn't be easy to hide.

Maybe I can wrap the whole limb in a bandage?

The sun was finally setting as Cross crested a small bluff. A distant road wound through hills to the left, and the river he was following eventually veered right into the swamp.

Not good.

The river had kept Cross alive so far, but he'd never see Elinfall if he followed it into the wetlands.

Besides, other dangers lurk in the marshes of Darin.

Cross shook his head, then moved down the slope.

I'll keep to the river until it forces me to choose between it and the bayou. Then—

"Oof!"

The noise came from somewhere to the left.

Cross stopped, looked around, then crept forward. Someone groaned, then cursed. A distant melody drifted in from somewhere. Crouching, Cross peered over the tall grass. A figure was balled up in the dirt, backside hanging in the breeze, and they were...

Laughing?

Cross moved a little closer, staying low. The figure turned out to be a woman, and a fine-looking one by any standard. She caught her breath, got to hands and knees, then pushed the tousled hair from her face. Cross wasn't keen on peeping, but the sight was just too odd to look away.

Clearly, she tripped, but why isn't she getting up?

He frowned.

Being on all fours in the dirt can't be comfortable.

She was frozen, eyes locked straight ahead.

What is she looking at?

Cross scanned the grass.

There.

A patch of black stood out in the tall yellow stalks, something flicking back and forth near the thing's rump.

A big cat? Perhaps from the nearby swamp.

Large cats were dangerous beasts, often captured in the wild and released in the arenas for sport. Cross had never fought one, but he'd seen it done.

Men don't live long in that type of bloodbath. Not unless there are three or more.

The woman reached back with one hand, pulling at the top of her pants. She got them most of the way back up her thighs, but they caught on her bottom. The panther crept a few steps closer, and she stopped trying to pull up her too-tight trousers. With the hand still behind her back, she drew a blade from her unbuckled belt. Cross crept through the grass. He was about ten paces from the lady, thoughts churning through his mind.

I should turn and run.

One step. *I should leave her to the panther and head right back up the hill.*

Two steps. *She and whoever's playing that music might be slavers.*

Three steps. *Or worse, bounty hunters.*

Four steps. *They certainly aren't honest folk, not this far from the road.*

Five steps. *Why am I doing this again?*

Six steps. *Almost there—*

With a yowl, the panther sprung.

Cross burst into motion.

The big cat sailed through the air, and the woman brought her knife around. She didn't look afraid, though she did look a little silly with her pants hung up below her butt. She swung the blade right as Cross hurtled into the cat from the side.

They flew in one tangled mass, hit the dirt, and tumbled down the bluff. They were one ball of bunched muscle, claws, fists, teeth, and fury. Once, twice, three times they connected with the ground as they bounced down the slope, then separated.

Cross pulled himself up, using a tree he'd nearly collided with. The big panther was already on its feet, one eye swollen shut.

Must've got a lucky jab in.

Dozens of new punctures marked Cross's body, but the pain barely registered. The big cat snarled, and Cross roared right back. Then the cat was moving, and so was he. It leapt at him, and he leapt at it. The creature wrapped him up in its claws, sinking huge teeth into his wounded shoulder. Cross screamed wordlessly as they went down in a heap, the cat on top.

Blood gushed from his shoulder, spurting over the panther's face. Cross swung at the cat's head, battering its uninjured eye. His other fist connected with the beast's jaw, cracking a cheekbone. The cat released its hold on his shoulder, teeth snapping toward his throat.

Cross threw an arm up to block the clamping jaws and ended up with a fist down the creature's gullet. Teeth sank into the back of his forearm but couldn't seem to muster the force to break bones.

The panther tried to spit his arm out, but Cross moved with the cat, shoving his fist deeper into the creature's maw. He hadn't intended to put his hand in its mouth, but he wasn't about to release the cat's most deadly weapon either.

Cross thumped the panther across the brow.

The beast dug its claws further into his chest and tried to shake his arm free.

He balled his fist, wedging it in the panther's throat.

Claws pierced Cross's chest, shredding muscle fibers. He let out another guttural scream, palming the creature's head and gouging his thumb into its only open eye. The beast yowled, opening its mouth wide, trying to pull its head away. Cross drove half his arm down the beast's throat, bellowing wordless rage.

The cat's claws raked deeper, shredding flesh in ribbons of red. Cross's thumb found bone, and the eye popped free. The cat threw its head back and forth, furiously trying to dislodge his fist from its throat. Cross was concentrating so hard on keeping his arm in the cat's mouth that he barely saw the enormous paw swipe in from the side.

Too late.

The pain was hot and immediate as the panther batted him across the side of the head.

Cross's vision blurred, fading to white.

Everything went red.

Rage took hold as blood filled his right eye.

He pulled his slimy thumb from the cat's eye socket and reached into its open mouth, latching onto a massive tooth. The cat swung its paw at his face again. He pulled forward and bit down on its jowl with a snarl.

The massive paw grazed the back of his skull.

Cross yanked on its tooth as hard as he could.

It wiggled.

He screamed, wrenching with all his might.

Pop.

Blood fountained as the tooth came free. He flipped the tooth in his grip, point protruding from the bottom of his fist. The cat swiped again, claws catching the arm stuffed down its throat. Cross hammered the tooth into the panther's neck. Blood spurted over his face and shoulders as he tore the sharp point along the side of the creature's throat.

Rip.

With a wet yowl, the cat yanked Cross's arm from its mouth.

His shoulders hit the dirt.

The panther lunged forward, teeth gnashing toward his throat. He grabbed a handful of fur, straining and screaming, as the cat brought its whole weight to bear.

He jammed the tooth into the panther's neck again.

Thunk.

Then its head, then its neck, then its swollen eye.

Thud. Thump. Squelch.

Blood spurted as Cross slammed the tooth into the creature over and over.

Jaws snapped shut a finger's width from his nose.

The beast yowled, spattering his bunched-up face with more blood and saliva. Cross was nearly as blind as the panther now, screaming agonized fury as the monster writhed atop him.

Suddenly, the weight left his chest.

Cross flailed, still screaming, but the tooth only connected with air. He wiped the blood from his eyes. The beast took one more staggering step away, then collapsed. Lifeblood poured from a dozen holes, pooling around the panther and soaking into the dirt.

Rage and adrenaline still filled Cross's veins, so he pulled himself to a sitting position against the side of the old oak. Blood flowed from a dozen wounds, streaming down his body and coalescing with the panther's.

The sun was setting, and a chilly wind swept the plains. Blood clouded Cross's right eye, and he closed the other. A wolf let out a long, lonely howl, and Cross knew, soon, he would be dead.

Seems we're all made of the same stuff in the end.

Cross looked to the sky. Elinfall was nowhere to be seen.

Funny. Only a few days ago, I was just a slave to the ring.

He let out a long sigh. Fighting was all he'd done for so long.

Is that all I am anymore, a weapon?

His vision began to fade.

No, all that violence was for others.

Cross closed his eyes.

Bits and pieces of his life flashed through his mind. A fight in the pits, Wortack killing his father, his escape from the Freemen's Guild.

None of it was any good.

Cross opened his good eye again. He was back on the bluff. His life had been a sad thing and, recently, a bloody one. He was born a slave, and he would die with barely a taste of freedom on his lips.

I guess that's what sticks with you in the end—the real shit parts of life.

Cross chuckled, then coughed.

Maybe I can make it a little longer. Long enough to see Elinfall one last time.

Ambient rays of sunlight still streaked the horizon.

Can I make it to sundown?

Cross doubted it, but he'd give anything for one last glimpse of the star that might've led him home.

At least I died for something pretty.

He chuckled, remembering the bare-assed woman staring down the panther.

Better to die for a lady I never knew than to fatten a noble's purse.

Cross closed his eyes again.

Thuds echoed from somewhere. They were a distant, unimportant thing, but he opened his eyes anyway. A form was running at him, blurry and out of focus.

Guess the cat has friends.

Cross tried to rise and fell back into the dirt.

Someone's hands were on him.

"Fuck, holy fuck of the gods. Fuuuuck!" Something pressed against his wounds, and Cross winced. Blearily, he opened his one eye not filled with blood. It was the gal with the bare bottom. He smiled at her.

"Don't worry about me...pretty lady," Cross said, words slurring. "It was worth it." Something pierced his skin. "Damn cat."

The panther was back, kneading his flesh.

Prick. Pull. Prick.

"David!" the woman screamed. "I need you! Now!"

She was yelling at the gods, but Cross didn't know any gods named David.

"By Usin's fucking beard, I still need to piss...fuck it." The claws stopped prodding his flesh. Leather stretched as something unbuckled, a rustle of fabric, then streaming water.

An acrid smell reached his nostrils.

The river of filth? How did I get back here?

The talons started kneading again.

Prick. Pull. Prick.

"What in the hells are you doing?" A male voice.

Who is that? Never mind, doesn't matter.

Cross's vision was fading to white.

"Stitching him up. What the fuck's it look like?"

Prick. Pull. Prick.

The panther claws were still digging in and out of his skin, but Cross found it hard to care. It was almost over.

"I see that, but why are you bloody havin' a tinkle?"

"Because my *bloody* fucking bladder was about to explode, you twat! Now quit staring at my ass and help me with this!" The woman again.

Prick. Pull. Prick.

The smell of urine was even stronger than the tang of blood.

My bowels and bladder giving up?

That happened at the very end. The arena smelled as much of latrine as it did blood and gore.

"What am I supposed to do with this?"

"Staunch those wounds, you idiot. Or were you planning to sing 'em shut?"

Prick. Pull. Prick.

"Who is he?" the male asked.

The world was entirely white now, and everything was muddled and distant.

240

"Not a fucking clue. Hold that bloody cloth against his shoulder. Now, damnit!"

Prick. Pull. Prick.

"Why are we helping him?"

"He just saved my life. So we're sure as hells gonna try and return the favor," the lady said.

The cat's claws continued to prod.

Prick. Pull. Prick.

It was the last thing Cross felt before everything ceased to exist.

27
GERARD STOCKWORTH

Gerard sat in silence on a stool next to Vigilant's stall. His bow rested across his lap with an arrow nocked but not drawn. Slowly, his eyelids closed. He forced them open and gave himself a light slap on the face.

None of that now. Justice doesn't take naps.

Jeff would be back, as sure as a lotus fiend would return to the smokehouse. The bastard was clearly planning to sell Vigilant and perhaps Spots too.

At least he thinks I'm still trapped in a cellar miles from here.

A shadow drifted across the hall at the far end of the stable. Gerard lifted his bow, drawing back the arrow.

A stray cat wandered in, rubbing against a post on the first stall.

Gerard sighed, let down the arrow, and lowered his bow. The orange tabby meandered over, sat at his feet, and gave a quick meow. Gerard raised an eyebrow. The cat gave one more meow, then rubbed against his boots, purring. He reached down and scratched the cat around the ears. It nuzzled into the motion, purring louder.

"You got a name, little fella?" Gerard asked with a smile.

The cat slipped away, ducking into Vigilant's stall. It weaved around the stallion's legs in a figure-eight pattern, rubbing its body against the horse's fetlocks.

Brave cat. One kick, and it'd all be over. Gerard looked up.

Three men stood at the stable's entrance, Jeff at their center.

Gerard scrambled to his feet, drawing an arrow as steel freed from scabbards. He loosed. The shaft sailed through the air, slamming into the eye of the man on the left. The thug dropped bonelessly to the floor. Jeff turned and lurched into a hobbling run out the door. The third man charged, sword swinging. Gerard sidestepped, deflecting the blade with the tip of his bow. The steel caught on the string.

Twang.

The tension bound up in the wood released all at once. The bow's upper limb slapped Gerard in the face as the bowstring whipped into his assailant's eye. Gerard stumbled backward, clutching his head. He hit a post, spun, and fell to the hay-strewn floor.

"Fucking hells!" someone cursed.

Gerard rolled over. A large gash marked the side of the thug's face, and he was wiping blood from his eye. The man advanced, his one good eye locked on Gerard. The thug raised his sword, bringing it down fast.

Gerard winced.

Nowhere to go.

The sword hit the post with a meaty thunk.

Lucky he's half blind.

Gerard pulled a knife from his boot and flung it. The blade sank into the thug's upper thigh, and he let out a grunt. Wood creaked as the man yanked on his sword, but it didn't come free of the post. He abandoned it and fell on Gerard.

Hands wrapped around Gerard's throat, tightening. He grabbed the thug's wrists, trying to push him off. It was no use; the bandit was much larger, and gravity was on his side. Gerard let go of the man's wrist and landed a solid right hook on his assailant's temple. The bigger man's head twisted, but he didn't let go. Instead, he squeezed harder.

The thug snarled something incomprehensible.

Gerard's lungs strained, vision fading. He fumbled a thumb into the man's mouth, pulling on his cheek, then jammed another finger into his eye. The ruffian reeled back, releasing Gerard's throat long enough to suck in a ragged breath. He tried to take in a second gulp, but the thug was already coming back down, a large knife gripped in both hands.

Where in the twenty-six hells did that come from?

Gerard caught the man's wrists as the knife descended. He stared at the blade's bloody tip as gravity and force slowly brought it down.

Holy hells, it's mine.

Finger by finger, the man's weight and strength came to bear, and the blade quivered closer.

This bloody bastard's gonna kill me with my own blade.

Gerard let out a groaning wheeze. With all his strength, he pushed back, but the man didn't move a finger's width.

Is this really how it ends? Down in the manure?

The thought flashed hot across Gerard's mind as the tip of the knife kissed his neck.

"Time to d—"

Blood, brain, and fragments of skull erupted from the thug's head. Gerard sputtered through the shower of gore, still struggling to keep the knife from his throat. A second later, the strength drained from his assailant, and he pushed the lifeless body away. Blood still spurted from a partial spine and jaw, but everything else was gone. Gerard spat, wiped his mouth, then got to his feet.

Vigilant whinnied, and Gerard's eyes followed the noise. Somehow, the big horse had turned himself around in his stall, and there was a trace amount of blood on his hind legs.

"Well, it's about damn time! Didn't want to get your hooves dirty?" Gerard accused.

Vigilant snorted, tossing his head to the side.

Gerard bent to retrieve his bow. A man-shaped outline stood in relief where he'd shielded dirt and straw from the spray of blood and bone. He looked down and discovered his upper body was entirely covered from the shoulders up in sticky red gore.

Oh, shit. Jeff!

Gerard sprinted into the street, glancing left, then right. A cart was tipped over in the mud on the right. He ran past the wreck, turning at the next alleyway—a beggar huddled in the side street.

"Someone come down here?" Gerard asked.

An open palm was the only response.

Gerard grumbled, dug through his pockets, and hastily dropped a couple of 'paz in the outstretched hand.

The beggar pointed down another alleyway to the left, and Gerard took off. He ran down the back road until it forked again. Fresh footprints marked the wet dirt path to the right, and the smell of urine filled his nostrils. He ran to the end of the alleyway and burst into the main street. He checked each way. The street was mostly empty to the right, but to the left, a hooded man limped along. Gerard ran down the street and was gaining on the man when a carriage pulled out in front of him.

"Outta the way!" a coachman yelled, nearly flattening Gerard. "Watch where you're going."

A moment later, the carriage passed, and the hooded man ducked into an alchemist's shop. Gerard crossed the street, skirting the edge of the buildings as he approached the apothecary. At the front door, he stopped, peering through the slatted shutters.

Shelves lined the shop, filling the walls from floor to ceiling with crushed herbs, spices, and compounds. In the middle of the room, an elderly alchemist stood behind a counter lined with many bins filled with more foreign substances. Another door stood behind the counter. Jeff was pretending to examine something against the left wall.

This could get ugly if he decides to fight. But he could slip out the back if I wait here.

Gerard frowned, then entered the building. The woman behind the counter smiled with a mouth half full of teeth.

"Welcome in, dearie. Let me know if there's anything I can help—" the shopkeeper's words trailed off as she got a better look at his gore-covered shirt and face.

Gerard smiled back, pulled the Justiseer's mark from around his neck, and held a finger to his lips. The elderly woman cocked her head to the side, then slowly looked around the room. He turned away, pretending to examine a jar of herbs. Gerard sniffed some sort of root, tapped a clay pot, and decided against stirring a green powder with his finger as he slowly worked along the outer wall.

Jeff moved from the wall to the main counter, examining some blue powder in the bins.

What in the forty-ninth hell is he looking at?

Gerard got as close as he could ostensibly get, then turned and drew his blade. He moved quickly, not bothering with silence anymore. Right as the shopkeeper was about to exclaim, Gerard wrapped his arm around Jeff's shoulder and drew the knife to his throat. The shopkeeper gasped, put a hand over her mouth, and stepped back.

"Thought you could give me the slip twice, Jeff?" Gerard asked as he pulled the old man's hood back.

Old man?

"Seventeen fucking hells. You're not Jeff!"

"By the gods!" the older man exclaimed. "What are you doing? Unhand me."

Gerard released him and sheathed his blade, quickly brushing some blood and bone off the other man's shoulders.

"Sorry, mistook you for someone else," Gerard tried to explain, producing the Justiseer's sigil again from the chain around his neck.

"Just because you're a lawman doesn't give you the right to harass my customers!" The emboldened shopkeeper squinted at Gerard's necklace.

Gerard backed away, hands held up. "Sorry, only lookin' for a fugitive. I'll leave you both to your business."

"Unbelievable," the woman said, shaking her head.

"Young people these days," the old man chimed in. "They never do seem to get things right."

"Always running about, never thinkin' of the consequences," she agreed.

"Yeah, a lawman needed more than a hunch to act in our day."

Gerard turned away, leaving the shop. He could still hear them chattering about the good old days as the door swung shut and the main road assailed his nostrils. Common folk bustled past as he considered his options.

Keep looking for Jeff 'round here or back to the horse stalls?

Gerard wasn't convinced the trail he'd followed was entirely wrong but wasn't naive enough to think he'd find the man by running around Windmore blind.

Best make sure Jeff didn't double back for the horses. Besides, dead men may not say much, but their pockets often do.

On the way back to the Old Sack, Gerard contemplated how a crippled Jeff managed to give him the slip twice. It was honestly embarrassing. So far, he had nothing to show for either of his bounties, and he'd already spent a considerable amount of stone on the mission.

Kal's head was missing from Vigilant's saddle bags. So, Jeff had either dumped the thing or buried it somewhere on the way back to Windmore. Either way, it was gone. Without a head, Gerard could collect a partial bounty, but those barely paid the bills, never mind setting aside anything for a rainy day.

Gerard arrived at the stables to find Timmy outside, trembling uncontrollably.

"Safe to assume you went in there, Tim?" Gerard asked.

The boy nodded, eyes wide, yet blinking constantly.

Well, fuck. Didn't mean for the kid to see that.

"Sorry about that, my boy...You already call the guards?"

Timmy nodded again.

Better hurry, then. Guards are a toss-up.

Sometimes, they were good, honest folk. Other times, they were greedy scavengers. Pretty much always, they just cocked things up.

Gerard walked past Timmy and stepped over the corpse by the door. The thug had bled a surprising amount through only his eye. Gerard bent and pulled the arrow free of the man's brain. He cleaned the tip on the thug's shirt, tossed the projectile toward his quiver at the far end of the stable, then searched the bandit's pockets. The man had a stone purse, a pipe, and a book of matches. Gerard opened the bag and took the few topaz and one ruby.

Better in my pockets than the city guards.

The matchbook had a gray bird stamped on the outside.

Expensive. And fancier than these thugs should have access to.

Gerard flipped it open.

"The Iron Owl," he read aloud. "Figures. The last place I wanna go." Gerard looked at Vigilant, but the horse wasn't even listening.

Still, it was a lead, so he put the matches in his pocket and proceeded to the other body. Nearly nothing was left of this one's head except a lower jaw and an artist's rendition in the ancient style spattered on the stable wall. Gerard rummaged through the coat, found another stone purse, then his hand closed around a smooth wooden stem.

"Another lotus pipe," Gerard murmured, looking up to get Vigilant's take.

Vigilant chewed on some hay at the back of his stall.

Damn. Might need to check the chimney out.

Gerard shook his head. It had been a long time since he'd visited a smokehouse.

The thug had nothing else out of the ordinary, so he took one last look around the stables. Gerard was searching for any reason not to follow his one lead, and he knew it. He sighed, then spotted something out of the corner of his eye and turned.

A black dome sat atop the hay in the stall next to Vigilant. Gerard walked over, patted the horse, and picked up the object. It was a hat, and a fancy one at that. He examined it, cocked his head, then walked back over to the first thug.

Same hat.

Gerard picked up the second bowler.

Identical, or near enough.

He flipped each lid and looked inside.

Same tailor.

The Needle and Stitch.

"How creative," Gerard scoffed. He'd seen a sign for the place a while back, and it was near enough to the Iron Owl in a rough part of town.

Not too far from here, actually.

Gerard wiped the blood from his face, grabbed a clean set of clothes from Vigilant's saddlebags, and changed. With hat in hand, he grabbed his unstrung bow and exited the stables.

"Tim, my boy."

The kid jolted as if woken from a deep sleep, wide eyes locking with Gerard's calm ones.

"I need to go. But give the guards this if they come by, will ya?" Gerard handed the kid the book of matches. "Tell them you found it on the body."

"Y-yes, sir. Aren't y-you gonna stay and talk to them, though?" Tim's voice was shaky, but he got the words out.

"No, I've gotta follow a lead. Be a good lad and tell them I'll debrief with them later. Actually, tell them I went to the Iron Owl." Gerard pressed a finger to the matchbook.

"Y-yes, sir."

"And Tim...do yourself a favor. Don't go back in there, eh?"

Tim nodded.

Gerard turned to leave, then twisted back and met the boy's eye. "Oh, and one last thing."

"Yeah?"

"Get yourself a woman tonight. The Dainty Doe's a good place to start. Got legal girls there—or boys if that's more your fancy. Get a nice one, and you treat 'em right. Got it?" Gerard pressed three rubies into Tim's hand, closed the kid's fingers around them, then walked away.

Far more than he should need for a night with a woman, but he more than earned it.

"Y-yes, sir!" Tim finally called when he was nearly out of earshot. Gerard looked back. The kid was staring down at the stone cupped in his hand.

Needs to talk to someone, but I'm not the right man for that job.

Molly would have known what to say. She'd always been better suited to just about everything. Gerard glanced down at his hunting knife.

At least everything worth a damn.

Gerard weaved through side streets until he found himself outside the Needle and Stitch. It was a dingy little shop in an even worse part of town than the Old Sack.

I love that little inn, but it sure is seedy.

Gerard twirled the bowler hat on one finger, pushed open the door to the Stitch, and swaggered in.

"Ey, mate!" Gerard changed his inflection, matching the gangs of the slums. A middle-aged man stood behind the counter, and bolts of fabric hung along the walls.

"Ah, welcome, and what can I do for you?" the shopkeeper asked.

"Lookin' for an 'at, y'see. The boss sent me down 'ere. Said you make all da 'ats." Gerard held out the bowler. "Like dis one 'ere."

"Now, come, come. Stinson knows I don't just have those lying around. They need to be made custom to the cranium."

"What 'id you just call me, mate?" Gerard stepped in, pulling the blade across his hip into the open air.

"Whoa, whoa! Stow your steel, good sir. A cranium is just another name for your head."

"Oh! Me 'ead?" Gerard pointed to the side of his skull.

"Indeed."

"Well, why didn't you just bloody say so, den?" Gerard sheathed his steel and looked to the shopkeeper. "Well, I'm gonna need dem 'ats. You know how da boss is. Can't come back with nuffin' t' show for me troubles, now can I?"

"I suppose not." The shopkeeper hesitated. "Well, this is what I can do. I'll take a measurement of your...'ead, and put your order at the top of the list. You can return to the Iron Owl and tell Stinson that your hat will be ready the day after tomorrow." The gaunt shopkeeper addressed Gerard slowly and calmly as if he were a wild animal.

Damn. Seems there's no escaping that chimney.

"Well, 'at'll do nicely, wit'out a doubt. But Stinson ain't gonna be 'appy wit' just one 'at, ye see. 'E needs a 'ole bunch o' 'em. 'E's been givin' 'em out like 'ot cakes."

"Like what?"

"Wat'n you mean, wat?"

"What cakes?"

Poor man didn't grow up in the slums.

"'Ot cakes? Wat'in-na-fuck you think I said?"

"Ot cakes," the shopkeeper repeated in bewilderment.

"Yeah, fuckin' 'ot cakes. 'Aven't you ever 'ad a bloody 'ot cake? They been flying off da shelf, mate. You know w'at, doesn't fuckin' matta'. Point is, it's a turn o' phrase, mate."

"I see..."

You really don't.

"I 'ope fuckin' so. But back to bidness. Stinson needs a dozen 'ats. Make 'em in the usual fuckin' sizes, I don't give a damn. Don't 'ave to be bloody perfect. I'll tell Stins dat we can pick 'em up day after t'morrow. Seeya den, mate." Gerard turned and swaggered toward the door.

"I can't have twelve hats ready by then!"

How unfortunate.

"It wasn't a request, mate." Gerard turned back, narrowing his eyes. "If you can't produce the goods...well, then you and me's gonna 'ave to go for a walk, and you are goin' to 'ave to 'splain it to ol' Stins. Ain'tcha?" Gerard turned and opened the door, then muttered, "He can't explain noffin', doesn't even know wat a bloody 'ot cake is." He laughed, stepped outside, slammed the door, and dropped the swagger.

Well, that should keep him busy. He won't be going to the chimney tonight and telling Stinson he got the order. Not with twelve hats to make. Plus, nothin' wrong with racking up the gang's tab a little.

Gerard chuckled, then sighed as an itch manifested on the back right side of his neck.

Looks like I've gotta visit the Iron Owl, after all.

28
SCARLETT REINHOLM

The door creaked open, and light flooded into the starry night. The smell of iron and sandalwood merged, producing something not entirely unpleasant. Scarlett peered into the little cabin through the small gap between the green door and the frame.

Two candles sat atop a table in the middle of the room. One lay on its side, still burning. The other stood upright, wax overflowing a saucer and spilling onto the table. A toppled chair lay near the center of the room next to a few books strewn across the floor. The two candles were all that lit the space, and the meager illumination only made the shadows darker by comparison.

Scarlett pulled the door open silently.

Don't wanna wake anyone.

She tiptoed across the floor, doing her best to avoid the creaks waiting just beneath the floorboards. Wood shifted underfoot, then squealed, stopping Scarlett dead in her tracks. She grabbed the table for support, eyes flitting around the room. No one rose or even stirred. Scarlett glanced down. Deep gouges marked the table near her hand. Deon must have made a mess when he was playing. Her brother was too rough on things.

Mother always says so.

Scarlett bent and blew out the toppled candle, leaving the other lit so the monsters wouldn't get her on the way to bed. She crept forward, lifting each foot slowly to avoid more creaks from the boards, then leapt the last pace to the mattress.

Always best to jump the last bit to avoid the monsters under the bed.

Scarlett peered over the edge of the frame into the darkness consuming the floorboards. If the monsters had tried to nab her, they'd missed. She slid back and pulled the covers tight around her shoulders. The blanket was cold. No better than the night air still streaming through the cracked door.

Curses.

The door was still open. Scarlett looked to her brother's bunk above.

I could join him. He'd be warm, at least.

No, that wouldn't do. Deon was "too old" for that and said so often.

Maybe I could wake him? Tell him to close the door.

Scarlett considered the idea.

No, he'll only get angry, then tell me to do it myself.

Scarlett could rouse her younger sister Kaylee, but she was in the upper bunk above Mother.

I'll just have to risk the darkness and bed monsters again.

With a sigh, Scarlett tossed her blanket aside and vaulted from the bed. She didn't want to wake anyone, but staying silent wasn't worth getting snatched by the monsters lurking beneath the bunk. The door creaked as a gust of wind billowed in. The remaining candle sputtered. Scarlett stopped in the middle of the room, glancing from her bed to the door. She sure didn't need any more monsters coming in from outside; there were enough under the bed already.

Don't want to get nabbed while shutting the door either.

Scarlett bit her lower lip, then scampered over to the door and pulled it shut with a swish and a thud. The candle flickered again but didn't go out. She looked across the room. Miraculously, neither the pitter-patter of her feet nor the door had woken a soul. She turned back to the beds and took two steps.

Oops. Nearly forgot to lock it.

Scarlett turned and took the two steps back to the door. Then, on tiptoes, she grabbed the deadbolt. A shadow moved outside. Scarlett slammed the bolt home, charged back across the room, and hurtled into Mother's bed. She buried herself in the covers, peering out.

The flickering flame revealed nothing moving around the cabin, inside or out.

Why is it still so cold?

Drip. Drip. Drip.

Is the roof leaking?

Mother's bed was larger than the rest, even with the smaller bunk built atop it. Scarlett scooted closer to where her mother usually lay.

She'll be warm.

Something cold, wet, and slimy dripped onto Scarlett's forehead.

What is that?

Scarlett wormed further toward the center of the bed. Her side slipped through something cold and viscous with a squelch.

"M-m-mom?"

Scarlett turned and reached for her mother. Her hands found a face as cold as the bed.

"Mom!"

Scarlett shook her mother.

No response.

She felt around, hands wrapping around something wet and textured like a sausage casing. She threw the covers off, jumped from the bed, and stumbled backward into the table. Scarlett screamed her mother's name, then her brother's, then her sister's, then she screamed them all some more. She looked down at her hands in the candlelight.

They were covered in blood.

Scarlett screamed again, this time for no one but herself.

The door creaked, swinging slowly open as if she'd not just locked it. A hulking form crouched at the threshold. Cold black eyes locked on her in the dim light. She let out one final scream, releasing all the air her little lungs could hold in one final burst.

Scarlett sat straight up. Sweat streamed down her face in rivulets. Her hair was soaked, the sheets and linens were on the floor, and goosebumps covered her clammy skin. Air came only in short, ragged breaths. She clung to her necklace and focused on her breathing as she looked frantically around the room.

"I'm not in Terra."

A wheeze.

"I'm in Darin."

Another gulp of air.

"On the plateau."

A sharp inhalation.

"There isn't another person for hundreds of miles."

A long, deep sigh.

"Just a terrible dream."

Her breathing was finally starting to calm.

"You're safe."

A small inhalation through only her nose.

"Whoever killed them isn't out here in the middle of nowhere. No one is. Just me and Roland."

Edging to the side of the bed, Scarlett lowered her feet to the floor then yanked them back up immediately. The boards were freezing as if covered in frost. She exhaled through gritted teeth and dropped her feet to the floor again. Scarlett grabbed a thick button-down shirt from a peg on the wall and slipped into it. The frost pulled painfully at the soles of her feet with each step toward the hearth.

The fire was typically coals by dawn, but it looked like it had been out for days.

Strange, I'm sure I lit the hearth before bed.

Scarlett peered out the window. The sun was high in the sky, and it was well after midday.

"Guess all that hauling and chopping really took it out of me."

She rolled her shoulders with a grimace.

Feels like I harvested a whole damn forest, not one tree.

Scarlett threw a few logs on the fire, carefully arranged a bit of tinder under them, then placed a curl of birch bark under the kindling. With flint and knife, she sparked the bark, watching the flames until the tinder caught.

"Still need to skin, draw, and quarter that big cat, or it'll attract predators."

Scarlett wasn't the biggest fan of eating cats from the jungle. Predators usually didn't taste very good, but the meat would fill her belly, and any food on the plateau couldn't go to waste. She used everything from a kill. Teeth she would turn to knives, tendons to sinew rope, and the pelt would make good leather. Scarlett wasn't sure how she went through so many clothes, but they were constantly wearing out or going missing.

Probably all the hard labor that needs doing.

Images and sounds flashed through Scarlett's mind, a cacophony of screams and panic. It was gone an instant later, more a blur of color and feeling than any coherent details. She shook the dregs of the nightmare away. Visions often came after the recurring dream, but they were just part of the nightmare. Still, it often felt like there was more to the dream than she could ever recall.

Scarlett eyed the bed longingly. The warm blankets were enticing, and she could cocoon in them until the fire was blazing.

No, there's too much to do, and I don't want to return to the nightmare.

Scarlett pulled on a pair of trousers, buttoned them, and laced a pair of deerskin boots. Kettle in hand, she retrieved some snow from the porch, setting it to boil on the stove, then slipped on her coat and exited the cabin.

The air was crisp and cool, even though the sun was out, but dark clouds loomed on the horizon. Scarlett's boots crunched in the hard-packed snow. She rounded the cabin's corner and found Roland's big goofy nose resting atop the nearest fence post.

"Hi there, my beautiful boy!"

Roland's antlers shifted back and forth as the moose danced from hoof to hoof on the other side of the fence. Scarlett opened the gate, slipped in, and shut it. Roland's snout nuzzled into her, nearly knocking her over before she could even turn.

"Hold on, big guy. I'm working on breakfast. I just overslept."

Scarlett turned, patted the excited moose on the nose, then rubbed and scratched his snout right where he liked it. Roland closed his eyes, getting weak in the knees from the scritches. Scarlett stopped before he was a puddle in the snow. She touched the side of his head, then walked past the compost pile to her frozen cellar. Brushing away the snow, she retrieved two cabbages, two carrots, and one turnip. It was more treats than usual, but he'd earned them after yesterday's lumber haul.

Roland greedily devoured the vegetables from her hand as she gave him some more scratches, this time behind the ears.

An insistent whistle rose from inside the cabin.

Scarlett glanced at the big cat lying in the snow. It had a large hole in its throat where she'd bled it out the previous day, and the innards were gone.

Processing will have to wait until after tea.

She opened the gate and watched Roland saunter out toward a favorite patch of willows.

He'll be all right out there for a while.

Scarlett returned to the cabin, hung up her coat, and removed her snowy boots. She took the kettle from the stove, dumped some herbs into a mug, and poured steaming water over them. The tantalizing scent of fresh mint and rosemary wafted from the cup. She wasn't sure why, but something about fresh rosemary was simply irresistible.

The mug warmed Scarlett's hands as she padded over to her bookshelf and looked over the old battered spines. She hadn't been able to take much with her when fleeing Terra, and these few books were the only non-essentials to last the trip. Initially, she'd packed more, but necessity had forced her to leave a scattered trail of manuscripts through the desert.

Scarlett regretted that, but the journey had been thousands of miles, and the books weighed nearly as much as water. She'd packed a small telescope, too, but it was heavy and hadn't even made it out of Terra.

She'd always loved the constellations and moons. They were so pretty, but they also had practical uses, like wayfinding and tide prediction. Mostly, though, she loved the stars because they were fascinating, mysterious, and the source of so much wonder.

Hard to imagine a time when I stared at the constellations for a living.

Scarlett's eyes wandered back to the six books. They were nothing compared to the grand libraries of Ramos, Norinspire, or the Academy. But these six books were precious. She read their titles, index finger tracing the spine of each manuscript:

Lunar Cycles, the Cosmos, and a Table of Tides. The last remnant of her old life, a life devoted to science and discovery.

Stalwart and Strong: A History of Stonewood. Her mother's favorite book. She always used to say their ancestors could trace their lineage back to the founders of the little hamlet.

The Prince of Ardendale. A guilty pleasure. Fiction. And a bit smutty, truth be told.

Seed, Spore, and Sprout: An Ecology of Plants and Fungi. An incredibly useful book. Scarlett had read it dozens of times yet still referenced it to identify vegetation and confirm knowledge during the planting season.

The Gray Tome. A survival book. She hadn't needed it as much in recent years, but it had saved her life more than once since she left the Academy. The text contained practical knowledge, such as how to make a fire without matches or find north in a canopy-covered forest.

Greep and Bondel's Folklore and Fairy Tales. One of Scarlett's favorites. It wasn't the most useful book, but it had been her father's. Its pages were filled with numerous tales—some light and fun like stories of the ellen; others dark and morbid with drinkers and eaters. She liked the book on the whole but mostly avoided the more sinister tales.

Too scary, she thought with a shudder.

Scarlett pulled *The Gray Tome* and nestled into the little chair by the fire. With a book in one hand and a mug in the other, she brushed up on her knowledge of skinning and processing. She probably didn't need the book anymore, but reading was a joy, and it was made that much better with tea. So, Scarlett curled up in the chair, sipping between flips of the page.

Once the tea was gone, and she was confident in her ability to dress and skin a panther, Scarlett reluctantly got up. She stoked the fire, laced her boots, and grabbed her jacket. A chill wind buffeted her as she pulled the door open and crunched back into the snow. The sun was far past its apex, the dark clouds had arrived, and big white flakes drifted down lazily.

"Hopefully, I can get the skinning done today," she muttered.

Scarlett took a deep breath and prepared mentally to get elbow-deep in blood. She'd bled out and gutted the cat before hauling it to the cabin...

Yesterday? Scarlett wondered.

Pressure built behind her eyes. She blinked, trying to clear her head. Usually, the only thing that helped with the migraines was to quit thinking and get to work. Today that would be a messy business.

"Processing always is."

The breeze brought a familiar scent to Scarlett's nostrils, and she paused. Something was off, but what? Her ears strained, and her head cocked to the side. Subconsciously, she sniffed the air again.

"Something's wrong."

Scarlett couldn't have said what, why, or how she knew, but she did. She tucked her large skinning knife into a boot and grabbed the axe she used to split wood. Stealth was nearly impossible in the snow, so Scarlett walked boldly back around to the front of the house.

Shadowy figures swayed into view through a thickening veil of snow.

It was hard to tell exactly what the silhouettes were, but they walked on two legs like men, and there were more than a fair few. Scarlett hadn't seen another person in nearly four years, and the idea of confronting one now filled her with dread.

Why are they here? What might they want?

29
RIGEL CROSS

P ain. It was all Cross was.

Is it all I've ever been?

Cross tried to move and found he couldn't.

Am I in one of the hells?

He decided he must be.

But which one?

He wasn't sure. Honestly, he didn't even know how many there were.

Occasionally, voices echoed through the hurt. They were hazy, distant, and far less insistent than the agony of reality.

"We need to take him with us."

"No, we can't. He'll slow us down too much, and we need to make good time. Besides, we only have two horses, and there's no way he's gonna ride with one of us."

"I'll ride with you. We've got to try and save him."

A moment of silence.

"No, it's a waste of time. He's already dead. Look how much blood he's lost."

"I won't leave him. Not after yesterday."

"We can't even sling him across a horse. His wounds will open as soon as the beast begins to trot."

"Then we figure something else out."

Everything faded away.

───────◆───────

The sway of movement was Cross's whole world as his mind returned to focus. Each swing was filled with red-hot pain. His shoulder, sides, chest, and face all blazed with a throbbing ache.

I'm surely dead.

Then, the music came:

Dum-dum, diddle-la-da-dum. Da-dum-dum da-dum.

Why's there music in one of the hells? Cross wondered absently as the world waned.

"I think he might make it."

"Maybe, but let's not count the chips till all the cards are on the table."

"He needs hope. Can't you see that?"

"I'll admit he's doing much better than I believed possible. Seems like you don't want to die, big fella."

Reality slipped away again.

Cloth restricted Cross's arms, and warmth flickered across his back. Crackling merged with soft music, dancing through his ears. The song wasn't the same as before, but it was beautiful. Cross shivered. His whole body was hot, yet everything was cold. He tried to open his eyes, but his lids were heavier than the lead bars they'd trained with at the guild.

The world disappeared.

It was still night when consciousness returned. Or perhaps day had come and gone. No music played.

Something rustled.

Someone tossing in their sleep?

Muffled voices. A stifled cry. Silence.

Cross tried to move. He wanted to ensure no one was injured but was too feeble.

Awareness fled.

Cross woke to deft and calloused hands stabilizing something against his lips. Water poured into his mouth. He gulped it down. The swaying started again. It felt like he might finally be able to move, so he slowly opened his eyes. He lay in some sort of hammock stretched between two horses. A man led the animals, and a pretty face smiled down at him. Cross's skin was cold and clammy. His teeth chattered as he tried to open his mouth for a question.

"Shhhh, sleep. You might just make it out of this," she whispered. Cross couldn't help but oblige such a pretty face.

Threads tickled the tips of Cross's toes, and natural light splayed across a slatted ceiling. He stared at the wooden roof, slowly deciding he might finally be ready to move. Carefully, he turned his head from side to side. There was pain, but nothing like before. He shrugged his injured shoulder. It throbbed dully.

How long was I out?

The remnants of a fever lay just under the surface of his skin, and the bedding smelled of dried sweat. He slowly flexed each stiff hand. They ached, and the strength had gone out of them. He took a deep breath and looked around.

The room was modest at best and contained only two pieces of furniture. One was the bed he occupied. The other was a nightstand, with food and water on it.

Where am I?

Cross tried to lift an arm and found it more akin to swinging a sword than to performing a simple gesture.

He pushed the blanket from his body, then grabbed a hunk of bread and drew it to his lips. With a tremendous effort, he opened his jaw. The muscles in his face screamed on the first bite, then lessened to a dull ache as he slowly chewed the grainy chunk. After Cross was halfway done with the stale loaf, he reached for the water. The liquid tasted stagnant, but he drank it down greedily anyway. He finished the bread, laid his head back into the pillow with a sigh, and closed his eyes.

Cross was covered by the blanket again and sweating. With a groan, he twisted, feebly trying to free himself from the fabric prison. A calm hand fell atop his frantic one. It moved down, pulling the blanket off him with ease. Cross tried to say thank you, but his tongue felt like a foreign object in his mouth.

"Shhhhh, sleep now. You need your rest. There's no need to thank me," a sweet voice assured him as he drifted away.

Warm metal rested against Cross's lips. A strange sensation on his return to the world of the living. Everything smelled of chicken and dumplings, which was oddly pleasant. Some of the warmth was already in his belly. He took another sip, opening his eyes. The same little room appeared, but two people stood before him. The pretty face from earlier pressed a spoon to his lips, and an equally pretty man stood in the corner with arms folded.

"Where am I?" Cross's voice was gravel churned under a cart's wheels.

"Grenisport," the lady said kindly, ladling another spoonful of soup into his mouth.

"Where's that?" Cross asked.

"It's the biggest port town in Darin and sits right on the Divide," the man in the corner said with a sigh. He had chiseled cheekbones, curly black hair, and a cute button nose.

What in the hells am I doing with these two?

Cross looked between them in bewilderment.

They each belong in a painting, not in this dingy little room.

"Who are—" Cross coughed, then cleared his throat.

"I'm Tanya. The sour one in the corner's David."

"I'm not sour, just not sure where else to turn. We can't stay here much longer with the law closing in."

"Sorry about that." Cross's gaze shifted to the brand on his right hand.

"It's not your fault. We have demons of our own." Tanya scowled at David, then turned back. "Is your name Elinfall?"

How does she know about Elinfall?

"No, Rigel Cross, but everyone just calls me Cross."

"Well, it's good to officially meet you, Cross," Tanya said. "If you don't mind me asking...who's Elinfall? You wouldn't stop calling out for them in your sleep, especially during the worst of your fever."

For a moment, Cross wondered if he could trust these two. But they'd saved him, and if they wanted to kill him or turn him in, they would've done it already.

"It's a star. And it points east. My ancestors used it to find their way home."

"A star that points east?" Tanya asked. "I didn't know that was possible."

"Well, one of them does." Cross looked to the window. "I'll show you tonight, as long as the skies are clear."

"Where's home?" David asked.

"Terra."

"Terra's a pretty big place."

"My father said our people were from a place called Creed," Cross offered. "But anywhere in Terra is good enough for now."

"Well, that's the bust," David said. "We've been trying to secure passage, but it hasn't been very effective, seeing as we barely have ten rubies between us."

"How much do they want?" Cross asked.

"Just ten 'phire each," David said.

Cross's heart sank. He'd never even seen a sapphire, let alone held one.

Slaves are bought for less.

"We won't ever make that."

"Ah, at least the big guy's a realist." David uncrossed his arms.

"We might, but not by sitting around here," Tanya interjected.

David looked more than a bit skeptical.

"Could we sneak onto one of the ships? Hide in the hold?" Cross asked.

"I'm pretty sure you're not sneaking anywhere, big fella," David said. "Besides, even if we got into the hold, they'd find us eventually. If they know there's a bounty on our heads, they'll throw us in the brig till they can haul us back to Darin. If not, they'll just slit our throats and toss us in the Divide."

"Either way, we're dead," Tanya added.

"You two can't swim?" Cross asked.

"You're more of a fish than I thought," David said.

Cross wasn't sure what that meant, but fish could swim, so he decided to take it as a compliment despite the tone.

Tanya shot David a nasty look.

"The Divide is massive, Cross," Tanya said. "You'd need to be able to swim for weeks straight to get to Terra. Even if you could, you'd swim in the wrong direction as often as not."

"Gods," Cross murmured. The world was always so much bigger than it looked on that little map. "So, do either of you have another idea?"

"Not a good one." David gave Tanya a pointed look.

"I know it's a long shot, but it's the best plan we've got," Tanya said. "Plus, I don't see you coming up with anything better."

"We could go north," David offered.

"We could hide in Norinspire too. But we both know those are temporary solutions. The Justiseers or the Lance will find us eventually if we stay in Darin."

"They might find us even if we go to Terra."

"What's the other option?" Cross asked, interrupting their bickering. "Also, what's the Lance?"

David looked to Tanya.

"The lion's already out of the trap," Tanya said with a shrug, then turned back to Cross. "The Lance is a guild of mercenaries. Officially, they're contractors for hire, willing to do anything for the right price. Sometimes, they protect precious cargo or work as investigators. But usually, due to their price tag, they're hired for less reputable work."

"Like?"

"Like assassinations, instigating a coup, or poisoning an entire village," David said.

Cross wasn't sure what instigating a coup meant and was itching to find out.

No, I don't want to show ignorance. Save the questions for another time.

"And they're after you two?" he asked instead.

"I used to work for them, and we didn't leave on the best of terms. But that's where the plan comes in. We could travel to Norinspire and pick up a job from the OAM if they haven't been informed of my separation from the guild."

"That's a big if," David interjected.

"Not helping," Tanya said with a scowl. "We could go to Norinspire and pretend to work for the Lance. My old guildmaster told me about an OAM contact there. Apparently, he used to contract with the Lance for all sorts of odd jobs. Reynolds even mentioned sending a group to Norinspire for a job recently. Sounded pretty hush-hush, but I'm sure it paid well. We could pretend to be that group. If the job pays in advance, we can take the money and run."

"And if it doesn't?" David asked.

"Then we complete the job quick and use the stone to book passage to Terra."

"And if the contact knows you aren't with the Lance anymore?" David looked from Tanya to Cross.

"Then we're fucked," Tanya snapped. "But he won't have been told. The Lance would never publicize something like that. They don't want anyone to know there are cracks in the foundation. But that's not the biggest issue."

David raised an eyebrow. "Oh really? What is then?"

"Things get sticky when the real Lance shows up to meet Vincent."

Cross nodded. "That does sound like a problem."

"Yeah, we'll have to ambush the second group," Tanya explained.

"So, we just add murder to our list of crimes?" David asked.

"We already stole horses, David. You know the Rocktells take that way more seriously than the murder of us common folk."

"Doesn't mean I want to do it." David looked away, eyes glazing over for a second.

"Well, we can try to subdue them then," Tanya offered.

"And if that doesn't work?" David asked.

"We improvise!" Tanya rounded on the man, clearly fed up. "You got a better idea?"

"I'm in," Cross said, tossing the blanket off and rising. It hurt like the hells, but a moment later, his feet were on the floor.

"Whoa, whoa, whoa." Tanya put a hand on his chest and pushed. "This is the first time you're coherent. Take it easy."

"It actually sounds kinda doable," David said, scratching the stubble on his chiseled jaw. "Let me look around the docks one more time. I want to try and convince one of these captains to let us work for passage across the Divide."

"I've already tried that, David," Tanya said, still pushing on Cross's chest despite it doing about as much as shoving a stone wall.

"Yeah, I know, but have you seen me? I'm a delight."

"That's what I'm worried about."

30
NATHAN

I t was pitch dark when Nathan awoke, and Eva still curled against his side. He considered rousing her to say goodbye, then decided against it. They'd been up late last night, but he'd slept for a whole day prior.

We'll see each other again if I return from the hunt.

Nathan gently removed Eva's arm from his chest and slid off the bed. It was better this way. She wouldn't have to say goodbye, and he wouldn't have to promise to return tomorrow.

A promise I may not be able to keep.

Nathan slipped out of the room and pulled on his boots. He took one last look around, eyes lingering on the sword above the mantle. Nathan considered borrowing it. Killing the creature with her brother's sword seemed fitting, but he wouldn't take it without permission and wasn't about to wake her.

With a sigh, Nathan exited the cabin.

"I will rid these people of Elrontis or die trying. Hear my words, and hold me to them." Nathan uttered the oath in the predawn light cresting the eastern horizon. He swore it to Eva, he swore it to the people of Trill, and most of all, he swore it to the one true God. Nathan was becoming increasingly sure that ridding these people of Elrontis was the reason he was here.

Why would God deny my memories, though?

He shook his head.

Another good question with no good answer.

Nathan took a deep breath, clearing his head. The morning air was crisp and cool as he hiked the empty paths to the great hall. It was a massive T-shaped building with an entrance at each leg and smoke billowing from a central hole.

Nathan smiled.

At least some hunters didn't lose their nerve.

He ducked into the building, coarse fur brushing against his face.

The hall was vast, large enough to hold the entire village if they crammed in tight. Dozens of tables, chairs, and braziers filled the floor. Horns, antlers, and pelts lined the walls in a collection that must have taken generations to assemble.

Seven hunters gathered around a cookfire near the center of the room. Raylor sat among them, and the corners of his mouth twitched into a half-hearted smile as Nathan approached. The expression fled as the old hunter's gaze shifted back to the somber group.

Nathan stepped up to the edge of the circle, looking around at the gathered men and women. Fear lined their faces, but they were here, which meant they had more courage than most.

"Only seven this morning?" Nathan asked.

"Aye, you make eight," Raylor replied, stirring the fire. "Give it a bit more time. The dawn is only starting to break."

"Right. We need to leave soon, though. Can't afford to waste the light."

"Agreed. The longer we wait, the more likely the elements will destroy the trail. But let's have breakfast. We will need our strength, and perhaps a few more will wander in."

Three more hunters came through the door while they cooked a hearty breakfast of sausage and eggs. As they ate, the hunters introduced themselves. Nathan tried to commit each name to memory, but it was futile with nine relatively new faces.

I'll remember their names as their actions set them in stone.

The gathered hunters were standing when the furs that functioned as a door pulled back, and a young man sauntered in.

"Hurry and grab a bite." Raylor gestured to the food.

The group exited the great hall and headed down the hill, with the young hunter running out shortly after. Nathan looked the kid up and down in the early morning light.

He may not have wisdom yet, but he looks quick and strong.

"Nathan," he stated, extending a hand to the young man.

"Oh...um...Brandon," the boy said between chews of a sausage. He grabbed the link in his teeth, took Nathan's hand in a greasy grip, and gave it a shake.

"Glad you could make it, Brandon." Nathan glanced down at his palm, then wiped the sausage grease on his pants.

Brandon nodded without noticing, concentrating on his food as they walked.

Nathan nearly laughed.

It would seem the self-concern of youth is the same everywhere in the world.

The group worked their way through the winding paths, a somber procession of weapons, grim faces, and reluctant hope. At the edge of the village, they fanned out, searching for any sign of the creature.

"Over here!" someone yelled a minute later.

A woman crouched over a patch of churned ground. Traces of blood marked the soil with no other sign in sight.

"Landed here?" Nathan asked.

The woman nodded.

"Agreed. Good work, Alice," Raylor said from behind. "Let's have a look around. See if we can pick up the trail from here."

The hunters spread out again, and within a minute, a man was shouting over another patch of clawed dirt and blood. The next track was over five spans from the first sign.

It sure can jump, whatever it is.

They proceeded this way for a while. With each print, the blood lessened, finally disappearing after the fifth sign.

So, it heals unnaturally fast or is smart enough to bind a wound. Bad news either way.

Nathan kept the revelation to himself, not wanting to disrupt the tenuous morale.

Over the next hour, the group followed the beast from one patch of clawed soil to another, and Nathan could only marvel at the thing's stamina. Finally, they came to something even more puzzling.

Crimson-filled grooves lined the ground, blood spattered the trees, and the tongue of some great beast lay in the dirt. One creature had pounced on another from above, and they'd fought. The victor hauled the other into a nearby tree, but the kill was missing.

Not sure I want to imagine something strong enough to do that.

A still dread hung over the hunters as they took in the scene.

It was Elrontis, without a doubt. Still, Nathan wished he could picture the thing. The carcass had been stored in the tree for some time, judging by the large pool of gore at the base of the trunk.

Did Elrontis bleed out a kill? That implies a high level of intelligence.

"I think so," Raylor said, startling Nathan.

"Think what?"

"I think it bled the big cat dry."

Maybe he truly is a prophet? Or he simply came to the same conclusion.

Nathan frowned.

A bit unnerving either way.

"Elrontis, you mean?" Nathan asked.

"We do the same thing," Raylor continued, pointedly ignoring the name. "Any good hunter knows to hang a kill. It preserves the meat and lightens the load before you pack it out."

"That's disconcerting." Nathan's brow furrowed. "You ever seen an animal do that?"

Raylor shook his head. "Not a one."

For a moment, they stared at the blood-soaked tree in silence.

"Here, have a look at this," Raylor said, walking around the tree and pointing down the hill. "Seems it made the kill, then continued on toward our village."

"Why would it do that?" Nathan asked. "There's a lot of blood on that tree. It should have been plenty of meat."

"Why, indeed," Raylor said.

"So, it fought the creature first, went down to the village, then doubled back to claim the kill." Nathan's eyes followed the trail of blood from the tree up the hill they were climbing. "Then it hauled the carcass back up the mountain. You think that's where it came from?"

Raylor nodded. "Were you a hunter before you came to us, Nathan?"

"Maybe, but I'm a bit fuzzy on it."

"Well, don't rule it out. You have a keen mind and a knack for tracking. My hunters and I have been doing this our whole lives, and you're seeing the same things we are."

A shrill chirping pierced the morning air, drawing Nathan's gaze upward.

Hunters jumped to attention, readying weapons.

A familiar furry little face poked from a nearby tree's branches, and the group relaxed.

"Ah, you found me again, huh?" Nathan asked.

Another angry little protest chattered above.

"Found who?" asked Raylor, glancing around.

"Steve."

"Steve?"

"Yeah, the little squirrel thingy." Nathan pointed to the tree Steve was defending with angry little squeaks.

"Ah, the forktail?" Raylor asked, looking up.

"I guess so."

"Odd, they're rare and normally avoid humans."

"Yeah, well, I fed the little bugger, and now he considers me his personal chef."

"Huh."

Nathan looked back toward the trail of blood. It lessened as Elrontis continued down the hill toward the village. He decided not to mention whatever had fought Elrontis made it bleed, and within thirty paces of leaving the tree, Elrontis wasn't bleeding anymore.

Nathan raised his voice. "We know which way the beast headed. Let's move."

The hunters drew together, faces tight and reluctant.

"I know this thing unnerves you. It frightens me as well. But it can bleed." Nathan gestured to the burgundy, spattered around the creature's tracks. "That means it can die, the same as us. Spill enough blood, and we leave it in the dirt." He looked around, meeting each hunter's eye. "I won't lie to you. This thing's unlike anything I've ever encountered."

Or at least remember.

"But we can bring it down—together," Nathan continued. "We must, for the entire village and all those we care about. Otherwise, it will just keep coming, and it will just keep taking. Soon, we won't have any loved ones left to protect. I, for one, will give anything to stop that. Even if it means I give my life."

Nathan paused, reading each face around the circle.

The hunters murmured their assent, determination filling their features.

"So, let's go kill this fucker!"

Men and women raised their spears, yelling.

Nathan turned, heading up the hill, and the group fell in behind him.

"Fine speech," Raylor said, stepping up beside him. "I hope our words will be enough when we find it."

"They will. Humans are the most dominant force in Darin for a reason."

"And what might that be?" Raylor asked.

"Two things, actually."

Raylor cocked his head quizzically to the side.

"This." Nathan pointed to his head. "And this." He pointed to his heart.

Raylor considered. "And perhaps these," he said, flexing his fingers with a smile.

Nathan laughed. "Yes, I suppose those too."

They ascended in silence for a while, the forest slowly thinning with the altitude.

"So, Nathan. You spoke of love," Raylor said.

"Did I?"

"Well, in a manner. You said for those we care about," Raylor clarified.

"I suppose I did."

Where are you headed with this?

"Do you remember any loved ones?"

Nathan pursed his lips. He wouldn't call what he felt for Eva *love*. The feeling was too new for that, but she'd kindled something in him, another reason to defend them all. In truth, he would've done it anyway. He was certain of it—something in him needed to protect those unable to do so themselves.

A creed? Or a purpose from God?

Nathan wasn't sure, but Eva was a connection, and his relationships with her and Raylor were the only bonds he could remember. They'd each shown him kindness, and he would rather die than let them come to harm.

My life means little, after all. I can't even remember who I am.

"No," Nathan finally said. "No loved ones for me, but God would want me to help defend your village. Besides, I owe you and your people. Most wouldn't have taken me in, especially with such great troubles of their own."

"Think nothing of it. We need you far more than you need us," Raylor replied.

"Your kind words are appreciated, but I'll remember your kind gestures far longer." Nathan smiled.

Raylor nodded, and the two walked on in amicable silence for a time. They passed a thicket of what Nathan had dubbed mustard berries. He picked a few and threw them to Steve, who was still following them. Raylor watched him, an amused twinkle in his eyes.

Nathan finally broke the silence. "What can you tell me of Eva?"

"The young woman?" Raylor glanced over without turning. "I heard her brother was our only casualty last night. Did you speak with her?"

"I did. She saw the beast, but not much more than I."

"Hmmm, what would you like to know?"

"Just curious. Is she the last of her...clan?"

"I'm afraid so. I knew Eva's father well. He was a hunter, taken by Elrontis nearly three years ago."

"He ever hunt with that sword above their mantle?"

Raylor chuckled. "No, the blade was passed down for generations to hear him tell it. Honestly, I'm not sure he even knew how to swing the thing. Not much use for a blade like that out here. He was a great hunter, though, and brave."

"Sounds like they were forged from the same iron."

"Eva wasn't too shaken up?"

"Oh, no, she was. But she had a hell of a night. So I'd say she more than took it in stride."

"Perhaps it does run in the family." Raylor's gaze shifted toward the horizon. "That's how her old man was. Maybe once this is over, I'll see if she wants to take up the spear."

"I'm sure she could. Seems to have the heart for it."

Raylor nodded, looked over at Nathan, then turned back.

"You two must have spoken at length."

"Yeah, for a while."

There was a pause as Raylor gave Nathan a sideways glance.

"I take it you noticed how pretty she is too?" A smile crept across Raylor's lips.

"Ha! You don't miss much, do you, Raylor? Aye, she's easy on the eyes."

Raylor smiled but said nothing more on the subject as the two of them hiked along.

Soon, the hunters passed the treeline, and a proper horizon stretched out in the distance. Behind them, Trill sat in a bowl, the vast jungle nearly swallowing it. Ahead, mountains loomed above the steep slope. These peaks didn't fill Nathan with awe as the high places could—instead, foreboding spread through his chest.

Almost as if the climb is just creating a greater distance to fall.

Progress slowed on the rocky slope, and the hunters occasionally slipped or sank into loose footing. Thankfully, no one took a tumble down the mountainside as they continued ever upward. Before long, the terrain was too rocky for most plants to survive and the creature would've been nearly impossible to follow without the carcass. They were finding less and less blood smeared on the rocks, though.

After another hour, the loose stone gave way to boulders, forcing the hunters to climb. They scrambled up rocks, working their way higher for a half hour before someone yelled, "Over here!"

Alice hovered over a bloody jawbone wedged between two boulders. Nathan bent, examining the mandible as Raylor stepped up beside him.

"Panther?" Raylor asked.

Alice nodded. "It's been ripped free. See the claw marks?"

"I do," Raylor said.

"How big do you think the cat must've been, judging by its teeth?" Nathan asked.

Alice held up the mandible. "At least forty brick."

"Twice the size of a man?" Nathan asked.

"And a large man, at that," Raylor remarked.

"Oh, it's big, but we've seen much bigger," Alice explained. "Great cats can get at least twice as large."

Nathan nodded. He could picture massive skulls hanging above hearths in a lavish great hall but couldn't recall when or where he'd seen them.

Beasts that size might still roam the remote parts of the world.

271

Nathan checked the sky. The sun was high, nearing noon, but dark clouds were moving in. "Best eat lunch on the go, I think. We may have daylight, but the weather doesn't look promising."

The group stopped, pulling dried meat and hardcakes from bags and pockets.

"We have time for a fire?" Brandon asked, gesturing toward the little forktail creeping toward them.

"No," Nathan said. "And no eating Steve."

"Why not?" Brandon asked.

"Cause he's got a name. You can't eat things with names."

"Well, *I* didn't name him."

"Leave her, Brandon," Raylor said. "She would barely be a mouthful anyhow."

"She?" Nathan asked.

"Yes, I'm fairly certain the forktail is female. See the two white patches of fur on her flank?"

Nathan nodded.

"The males don't have them," Raylor said.

"Huh. Well, her name's Steve now."

A few hunters chuckled around the circle, and Raylor handed Nathan some dried meat and biscuits.

"Let's keep moving," Nathan said. "We only have so much light left."

The hunters ate as they walked, and Nathan threw Steve a few scraps of a biscuit. Not long after, the trail of blood nearly vanished, and their pace slowed to a crawl.

Whatever Elrontis is, it climbed this terrain while dragging almost two of me.

Nathan frowned.

Unless more than one is working together, passing the kill between them?

The tracks didn't support the theory, but he knew wolves sometimes walked single file.

Maybe Elrontis is the same.

Nathan's scowl deepened, and he shook the notion away.

Finally, after another hour, they crested the last rise, and the plateau leveled out. A white crust covered the ground, and new snow drifted lazily down from the sky. A small flake landed on a crisp track pressed in the white ground.

"We need to move quickly," Nathan called back to the group. "The trail of blood is almost gone, and the snow will soon end our ability to track."

"Nathan, look at this!" Brandon approached the tracks in front of them.

Nathan walked over. Two major sections of pads splayed wide, dotted by five toes, and claw marks longer than a hand. Usually, he'd have guessed the track belonged to a species of big cat since they were all over Darin. But this creature clearly walked on two feet, hauling its kill off to one side. The implication was clear enough.

Elrontis can drag something with an arm and not just its jaws.

Nathan's eyebrows narrowed.

So it does have thumbs.

The weather continued to worsen as the hunters forged on, and Nathan jogged ahead, lost in his thoughts.

Perhaps I've been going about this all wrong. What if this thing, whatever it is, isn't simply a dumb animal? What if it's as intelligent as us? Or even more so? We've been trying to track a beast, but what if it isn't an animal? What would I do if a force with superior numbers was hunting me?

Try to separate them as much as possible.

Nathan looked around at the bleak, desolate landscape.

Then, I'd wait for an opportunity. Perhaps once night fell, or the weather rolled in.

Thickening white flakes obscured everything but Brandon.

How could I have been so stupid? Why else would it leave such an obvious trail?

"Hold up," Nathan raised his voice.

"But Nathan—"

"Hold up, I said!"

"But look," Brandon pointed to the sky.

"What?" Nathan asked.

"A fire."

Nathan followed the kid's index finger with his eyes. Sure enough, smoke rose in the distance. The plume was easy to miss in the falling snow but was obvious now that he'd seen it. Their meager trail headed straight toward the source of the flame.

"No natural fires up here," Nathan stated. "Not in the cold like this."

"Let's go!" Brandon smiled.

"No, we need to wait for the others. It was foolish to charge ahead. It'll take all of us to bring Elrontis down."

Some of the eagerness left Brandon's eyes at the mention of the thing's name, and he turned away. They stared at the smoke in silence while waiting for the rest of the hunters.

"Smoke!" Brandon yelled as soon as Raylor was within earshot. The kid pointed to the sky again, and his silly grin returned.

Raylor frowned. "Odd, I wouldn't think our quarry would need a fire. We know it doesn't need to cook its food. Still, I suppose we should investigate."

They continued to follow the faint trail, even though it was becoming clear they didn't need to. The falling snow continued to thicken, and a short time later, the trail was lost. They followed the smoke after that. The white flakes grew denser, and Nathan feared they might soon lose sight of the smoke as well.

Nathan squinted, trying to make out anything through the falling snow. Slowly, an outline emerged from the veil of white, solidifying into a cabin. The structure had a sloped roof, and a fence skirted the back of the building. A woman stood out front, watching as they approached. She had light-brown hair, a lean, muscular build, and held a woodcutter's axe in one hand. She didn't brandish the weapon, but something in her stance said she knew how to swing it.

31
GERARD STOCKWORTH

Light and smoke mixed as they streamed from the shutters of the Iron Owl. Gerard watched the chimney from a nearby alleyway as he restrung his bow. The Owl was a fairly ostentatious building for this seedy part of town. It was three stories with a porch or balcony surrounding each level. A couple of thugs wearing the same round hat from the Needle and Stitch stood outside, fraternizing with a less-than-reputable-looking woman.

How many of these bastards are there?

Gerard noticed a spot of blood on the rim of his bowler, scraped it off with a fingernail, then twirled the hat onto his head with a practiced flourish. He cracked his neck, rolled his shoulders, and sauntered over to the door of the chimney. The slatted half door swung inward as he entered, and blue smoke billowed into his face. The sweet scent filled his nostrils, causing his mouth to water and his neck to itch. He sighed.

Focus.

A large, L-shaped bar lined with stools filled the right side of the chimney, and a common room sprawled out to the left. Couches, tables, chairs, and parlor games occupied the space, with a large hookah on each table. Plenty of people sat at the bar with drinks, but even more occupied the smoke pit. Four chandeliers hung throughout the room, casting candlelight through the smog and illuminating a staircase at the far end of the pit.

The chairs looked familiar, the hookahs...enticing.

Molly's pox-covered face slid into Gerard's mind. For a moment, the image of his dead wife lingered, then a shiver wormed its way up his spine, and he let out an entirely different kind of sigh.

With more than a little effort, Gerard pulled his eyes from the pipes and scanned the room. Two men sat at a table in the back of the smoke pit. One looked a lot like Jeff. More importantly, nearly a dozen men wearing similar hats lounged about the chimney.

This could get sticky.

Gerard considered waiting outside for Jeff, but with a back door and rooms upstairs, there was no telling when or where he might come out.

I could wait here. Bide my time.

Gerard's eyes lingered on the pipes.

Maybe have a puff or two just to take the edge off?

He pulled his eyes away from the hookahs.

No, I can't do that. Act now or risk losing him again.

Pulling his hat low, Gerard meandered across the room. He stopped to watch a few jumps of a game of gorranga and gave a wink to a working gal. She promptly pulled up the hem of her skirt, showcasing her wares. Gerard tipped his hat, then moved on, closing the distance between him and his potential mark. When he was less than a span away, the man finally spoke.

"Left him in a larder under the house. Got no idea how 'e got out. Figured 'ed starve to death." Jeff's normally cold gaze had vanished, replaced with a lazy smile, and he was clearly higher than a festival balloon on Lunar Day.

"Starve to death in a larder?" the other man asked.

"All right, maybe not, but 'ydration shoulda got 'em."

"You mean dehydration..."

"Yeah, 'ats the one." Jeff took a pull from the hookah on their table and laughed.

At least the other man's not wearing a hat.

Gerard pulled the brim of the bowler down, slipping the long hunting knife from the sheath on the back of his belt. He held the blade behind his back and stumbled over to Jeff's table. Leaning onto his free hand, Gerard fell into the accent he grew up with once more.

"Aye! Is that Jeff? 'Aven't seen you in an age, mate."

"Oi, well, I'm back. Is that you, Sully?" Jeff tilted his head low, trying to see under Gerard's tipped hat.

Their eyes met. In a flash, razor-sharp steel kissed Jeff's throat, and Gerard clamped a hand on the back of the man's neck, pulling him close.

"Thought you could escape justice twice and not even skip town, *mate*?" Gerard added the accent on the last word.

Jeff froze, gritting his teeth.

"Now, we can do this the easy way or the hard one," Gerard began. "The easy way is you and I walk outta here right now, and you face justice for your crimes. The hard way is you end up like...what in the eight hells was his name? Calen? Kory, Kelpi—"

"Kal," Jeff provided in a tone as cold as a sheet of ice.

"Ah, yeah, that's the one. Anyway, personally, I'd prefer the easy way. So, what'll it be?"

"Might I present a third option?" the third man interjected.

"Best mind your own business here. I'm an official Justiseer and have a signed bounty from House Rocktell," Gerard said.

"The third option is you let our good friend Jeff go, and I let you walk out of here with your internal organs intact." Gerard tightened the blade to Jeff's throat, turning him to get a good look at the third man.

"And who might you be?" Gerard asked.

"The name's Stinson."

Fuck.

"Ah. Well, that figures." Gerard looked back at Jeff.

A smug little smile tugged at the corner of the man's mouth.

Gerard mimicked the expression, then plunged his hunting knife into Jeff's neck. A little gurgle escaped Jeff's lips, but nothing coherent as the blade sawed back and forth. Gerard was down to the spine before Stinson was on his feet and through Jeff's vertebrae before the boss got a word out.

"Boys!" Stinson yelled.

A symphony of steel rang through the common room, but Gerard was too busy to look.

No easy task, severing a skull from the spine.

The head came free with a squelch, and Jeff's body fell bonelessly to the floor.

Gerard turned, eyes widening. "Well, that's not ideal," he muttered, head dangling by shoulder-length locks in his grip.

At least twelve men in bowler hats stared him down with steel in hand. Stinson had backed up half a dozen paces and drawn a rapier.

Not likely to get in close enough to use him as a bargaining chip.

Gerard frowned.

Besides, anyone who owns a duelin' sword knows how to wield it.

"I'm on official Justiseer business here," Gerard said, projecting his voice across the room and producing his sigil.

The men continued to advance.

Doesn't seem like they care. Oh well, worth a shot.

"I don't suppose we can talk about this?" Gerard asked, glancing at Stinson.

"Kill 'im, boys."

One man charged. It was a foolish move, considering his fellows were slowly drawing the net tight. Gerard swung Jeff's head by the hair. It connected to the thug's temple with a wet crunch. The blow knocked the man off balance, and Gerard plunged his knife into the thug's gut.

Everyone in the chimney burst into motion.

Gerard hurled Jeff's head toward a window and vaulted onto the nearest table. The head banged through a shutter, thudding to the porch outside. Swords buried into wood behind Gerard as he leapt from one table to the next. He kicked a hookah toward two charging men. It collided with one of them, and the man toppled. The vessel shattered in an eruption of foul liquid and glass.

The other thug staggered back, shielding his eyes from the shards. Gerard hopped to another table, grabbing a tankard from a patron as he stood to leave. He hurled the cup at another thug, but the man ducked. Foamy beer sloshed from the mug, spraying him as it clattered to the floor. Another brigand slipped and went down in a heap.

Gerard grabbed a chandelier, swung over another ruffian's head, and landed at the bottom of the stairway. He sprinted up the steps three at a time, unslinging his bow. Men clamored behind him as Gerard reached the landing and spun. He nocked an arrow, aimed for half a heartbeat, then loosed. The arrow sprung from the front thug's throat, his body clogging the stairway. Gerard drew another shaft and shot the next man. The arrow pierced his shoulder, fletching quivering as it lodged in bone. He let another fly, and a second shaft sprouted from the brigand's chest.

A choke point. I can work with—

A bolt whizzed past Gerard's head, clipping his ear.

Shit. The pain came, sharp and immediate.

Stinson's head pulled back, his crossbow's stirrup still poking from behind the banister.

Gerard loosed another arrow at a man as he waded through the dead and dying.

Something dripped onto Gerard's shoulder.

Another bolt fell into the groove of Stinson's crossbow.

Gerard's arrow thudded into the man, but he wasn't paying attention where.

The bolt began to pull back.

Click, click, click.

Gerard let another arrow fly, but the thug ducked.

Four crossbows popped from behind benches and bodies.

Fuck.

Gerard fell to the floor.

Four bolts whined overhead, needling into the wall. Frantically, Gerard crawled around the corner, scrambled to his feet, then charged down the hall. A door cracked on the right, and a man peered out with drawn steel. Gerard kicked the door in. It slammed into the thug, toppling him back into the room. A woman clung to the sheets. For half a second, he considered tipping his hat, but that would've been absurd, and she wasn't what he was looking for.

No exit to the balcony here.

Gerard moved to a door on the other side of the hall, twisting the handle. It didn't move.

Sixty-two hells.

He kicked it once. Pain shot up his leg, but the door didn't budge.

Fuck. Hope I didn't just break my foot.

Thrum.

A bolt took the hat right off Gerard's head, carrying it hurtling down the hall. He nocked an arrow, drew it back, and left it quivering in the crossbowman at the top of the stairs. More thugs in bowler hats pushed past the body as it fell. Gerard ran to the end of the hall, then turned right and sprinted up another staircase.

At the top, Gerard turned and drew another arrow. He held his breath, sighting down the shaft. A black hat rounded the corner. He led the man with the shot, then loosed. The arrow thudded into the brigand's neck, then he barreled into the wall and crumpled to the floor. Gerard readied another shaft. A second thug's head came around the corner, then pulled back as the arrow whined past.

The thug stepped back into view, crossbow at the ready. Gerard turned and dove. The bolt flew, piercing cloth and slicing skin before hammering into the wall. He grabbed his bow, lurched to his feet, and charged down the hallway. Ahead, the corridor ended in the blank face of a wall.

No more stairs. Where's that bloody balcony?

Gerard was at the end of the hallway when the building's layout finally unfolded in his mind. The balcony had to be back near the stairs. He turned. Three brigands rounded the corner. Gerard loosed an arrow. The projectile pierced the crowd, but no one fell, so he hurled himself at the nearest door. It was an ornate thing, and he bounced bodily off it.

Fuck! Why do I keep trying that?

Gerard grabbed the handle, and the door swung open. He darted in, threw it shut, and slammed the deadbolt.

Men and arms collided with the other side of the door.

Gerard checked his wounded side. A thin line of red marked the skin where the bolt clipped him, but that was all.

It can wait.

A large bed draped in silk centered the massive room. A wardrobe took up one wall, a dresser another. All of it was over-the-top luxury.

Reserved for pampered nobility who want a taste of the slums.

Gerard scanned the exterior wall with his eyes.

Damn, no balcony or window.

Someone yelled in the hallway, but the wood was too thick to make out the words.

Once they're through the door, the jig is up. A sword's no good against that many.

Thud. The door shuddered.

Maybe I can hide somewhere? Gerard moved to the wardrobe, opening it.

Crash. The door quaked again.

The cabinet was full of odd outfits, chains, cuffs, and...*insertables?*

Blinking in astonishment, Gerard shut the door.

By the gods. Some people have too much money.

He shook his head.

If I'm to die, it won't be in a closet surrounded by unwashed equipment.

Slam. Gerard glanced back.

Not gonna hold much longer.

He turned to the massive bed.

Could hide under it. But how long will that last?

Gerard spotted the little door of a dumbwaiter by the bedside, and the thrill of possibility rushed through him. He ran to the hatch and opened it. Two taut ropes stretched through the center of a small shaft.

Bang. Another impact.

Gerard pulled a knife and cut one side of the rope. Nothing crashed to the ground below.

The car must already be sitting on the first floor.

Gerard got his head and one shoulder into the opening before the tip of his bow caught on the wall.

Too tight. Bow's not gonna fit.

Boom. The door groaned in protest.

Reluctantly, Gerard dropped his bow, kicked it under the bed, then worked his shoulders into the shaft. He grabbed the end of the cut rope and pulled. It held none of his weight and unspooled from something above. His shoulder hit the wall, and he pushed with his legs, bracing himself against the floor and ledge.

Fuck, must've been a pulley up top. Guess I should've studied bloody dumbwaiters.

Creak. The door visibly strained.

Looks like they found some leverage.

Gerard pushed against each side of the shaft with his palms and pulled his legs into the narrow opening. He grunted with effort, peering down the brick-lined chute.

"I shoulda been a chimney sweep—"

Rip. Wood splintered as the bolt tore through the door frame, and men in bowler hats poured in.

Gerard tried to adjust himself, but his hands slipped, and he plummeted, scrambling at the walls. Twice, his fingers found purchase in the dark, but each time, his grip failed. Wood crumpled beneath him as he hit something solid.

Cold stone pressed to Gerard's cheek. He blinked. A stack of split wood swayed at the edge of his vision, and pans dangled above. With a groan, Gerard sat up and looked around the kitchen. His backside burned like seventy-two hells. He reached around—something sharp and broken protruded from his ass.

Wincing, Gerard grabbed the thing and pulled. Another sharp pain as the object slid from skin and muscle into the light. It was a splinter longer than his forearm, nearly as wide as his index finger, and covered in a handspan of blood. He got to his feet, threw the wooden spike back into the wreckage, and staggered from the kitchen.

The door squealed as Gerard reentered the lounge from behind the bar. Stinson stood in the middle of the room, rapier still drawn. He turned, and their eyes met. Instinctively, Gerard reached for his bow but found nothing. He glanced between the front and back doors of the building. Stinson was closer to both. Gerard eyed the elegant blade in Stinson's hand.

His sword's built for dueling, mine for butchery. Not good.

With a grunt, Gerard pulled his longsword from its scabbard.

"Sure you want to cross blades with me, Stinson? A lot of evidence 'round here says you shouldn't." Gerard gestured to the bodies littering the floor.

"Those look like arrow wounds. Where's your bow? Lose it somewhere?" Stinson positioned his feet purposefully, then shuffled forward. The deadly point hovered at eye level, glittering in the candlelight.

So he has had training, great.

"No arrows in Jeff," Gerard warned. "You don't want to end up like him, do you?"

281

Stinson just smiled, moving closer.

To the sixteen hells with it. He ain't buying it, and it won't be long till his men return.

Gerard lunged forward, closing the distance between them in two steps. He aimed for Stinson's sword, not for the man himself. If Stinson was trained, he'd parry a strike to his body, then put a hole in Gerard's gut before he could bring the heavier blade back around.

The swords rang as they connected, the lighter blade bent against the weight of the heavier. For a second, Gerard thought it might break, then it snapped back. The tip flicked upward, knocking his blade sideways and slicing into his cheek.

Gerard stumbled back.

Stinson advanced, thrusting and jabbing.

Desperately, Gerard defended with little deflecting touches of steel on steel. On the third thrust, Stinson forced the heavier blade wide, sinking a finger of metal into Gerard's chest.

Well, this won't take long.

Gerard brought his sword around, swinging it as hard as he could. Stinson parried, then wrenched the blade from Gerard's grip with a twisting flourish. The longsword clattered to the floor two spans away. Stinson leveled his sword and advanced. It was over, but Gerard continued the dance anyway.

That's the trouble with swords: the better man wins.

Stinson smiled, closing the distance between them. "You killed a lot of my men tonight. It's time to pay for their blood with some of your own."

Gerard's heel caught on something, and he toppled. His back slammed into the floorboards, air fleeing his lungs in a rush.

Crack.

Gerard's vision swam. He blinked, head throbbing as he tried to shake away the stars. Everything was blurry. He looked down. His legs were tangled in a toppled bar stool, and Stinson approached with leveled steel. Distant thumps echoed outside.

Is that rain? Metal? Hail maybe?

Gerard remembered the cabin, noise growing.

Damn story started with bad weather. Now, it'll end with it.

Something was thudding on wood...*somewhere?*

The entire Iron Owl swayed as if located on the deck of a ship. Stinson halted and looked toward the front entrance. Gerard followed his gaze, still fighting to keep the room from swimming.

The door to the chimney swung open, and armed men swarmed in. Gerard's addled brain tried to process what was happening. Then he saw the red lion's head emblazoned on the tabards.

Timmy! By the gods, I could kiss that boy.

Gerard glanced around the room.

Thugs hurried down the stairs, but there were far more guards than brigands. Stinson just stood there, a snarl plastered to his face as his eyes shifted from his men to the city guard.

"In the name of House Rocktell, lay down your arms!" someone bellowed near the back. "You're all under arrest."

Stinson grimaced, turned back to Gerard, and jabbed. Gerard threw his arm at the blade and felt it slice skin as he deflected it. The tip squealed into the cork floorboards. Stinson yanked on it once, but it held firm. He turned, abandoning the blade and his men as he ran for the back door. Gerard pulled a knife from his boot and hurled it at Stinson's back. It hit the man square between the shoulders, hilt first, then clanged to the floor.

Gerard attempted to utter a curse, realized he was too dizzy to think of one, and gave up. He tried to get to his feet, fell back down, then shook away the dizziness and forced his legs to comply. By the time he was up, Stinson was gone, and his men were running back up the stairs with guards in tow.

They'll never catch 'em, not in chain mail.

Then again, that didn't really matter. Gerard was alive, and it may have been the first time he'd ever been happy to see the city guard.

32
DAVID TRUEHEART

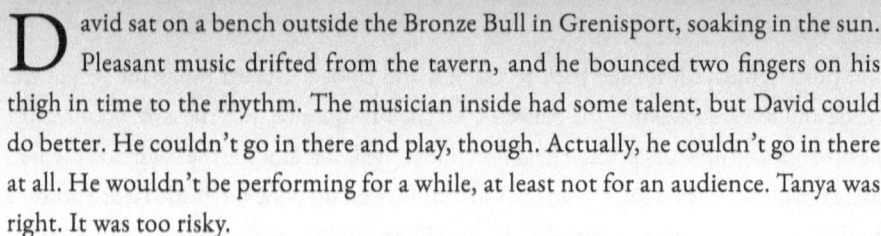

David sat on a bench outside the Bronze Bull in Grenisport, soaking in the sun. Pleasant music drifted from the tavern, and he bounced two fingers on his thigh in time to the rhythm. The musician inside had some talent, but David could do better. He couldn't go in there and play, though. Actually, he couldn't go in there at all. He wouldn't be performing for a while, at least not for an audience. Tanya was right. It was too risky.

Hells, simply sitting outside the tavern is a risk.

David looked longingly toward the door of the Bull. Light, smoke, and a bawdy tavern tune mingled there in such an inviting way.

Life's just a series of wagers. Occasionally, you have to bet against the odds and risk it all. Sometimes, that pays off, and sometimes, it doesn't. But the hall always wins in the end, and in the end, we all end up the same way—in the dirt.

David pictured his father's eyes right before he passed.

Were the last few weeks worth it?

He imagined Tanya sliding on top of him in the middle of the night, and not for the first time.

Yeah, worth it, for sure.

Tanya had been a little odd after that night on the trail, and they'd never talked about it.

Is that because it meant something? Or because it meant nothing?

Somehow, Tanya had smelled of lilacs, even after hiking through the savanna all day. She'd smelled of dirt and sweat, too, but it was the flowers that stuck in his memory. During the act, she hadn't spoken, just stared at him with those beautiful amber eyes.

I need to write a song about those eyes, David thought wistfully. *No one may ever get to hear it, but I can still write it.*

He nearly jumped as the woman herself plopped down on the bench beside him.

"Damn, you're sneaky!" David said, grip loosening from the hilt of his blade.

"Damn, you're jumpy." Tanya smiled at him, then stared off at the docks. "I wasn't terrible at my job, believe it or not. I know it might appear so, considering my employer hired an amateur to kill me."

"Amateur! That's not fair," David said with mock indignation. "I'm pretty sure I could've handled the job."

"Then why didn't you?" Tanya asked.

Silence. It was his turn to stare at the docks.

David turned back to find Tanya deeply contemplating the state of her fingernails.

"I'm not sure taking Cross with us is possible," David began. A look of annoyance flickered across her face. "We already saved him, Tanya, and—"

"He's almost better," she interjected.

"Tanya, he's enormous. He'll stick out like a moonstone in a sea of topaz. No matter what we do, there's no way to hide his size."

"That's precisely why he needs us, David. You heard him. He thinks he can swim across the Divide." Tanya fixed him with a look. "Going to Terra is the best plan anyway, so we might as well help him. I owe him that much, at least."

"Trust me, I get it, but we nursed him back to health. That's gotta count for somethin', right?"

"*I* nursed him back to health, David." Tanya scowled. "He wouldn't have been in such bad shape without sticking his neck out for me either."

"You're right. You did, not me. Still, I don't know how we stay inconspicuous while traveling with him. We can cut our hair and change our clothes, but there's no way to hide him in a crowd. Not ever."

"I get your point, but I'm not leaving him."

David took a deep breath. "Please, Tanya, listen to reason."

"Some of us have to pay our debts, David."

"Now that's not fair."

"Isn't it?" Tanya asked. "Why in the hells do you think I'm still hangin' around with you?"

"Leave then. No one's stopping you."

Another long silence.

"You're right." Tanya stood, turning away. "I think you left your heart back in Windmore, David," she said, heading back toward Grenisport proper.

David watched the now-familiar sway of her hips slowly shrinking into the distance. *Will she look back?*

She didn't.

Seems I'll be traveling with the giant, or I'll be traveling alone.

David knew he was being callous, but he was right too. There was no way to hide Cross once the wanted posters started popping up. The big man would get caught if they stayed in a major city. That left only a couple choices: strike out on his own or get them all out of bloody Darin as quickly as possible.

Well, if I'm to be hunted down like a dog and die in some gutter, then I'd rather do it with a beautiful woman at my side. Plus, that hulk of a man might even keep us alive through a scrap or two.

David sighed, then stood.

Guess I best unpack the old Trueheart charm, then.

He strode down the busy docks, eyes peeled for an opportunity.

There must be a captain willing to lower their price in exchange for some good, old-fashioned hard work.

David could entertain the crew, Tanya knew everything there was to know about knots, rigging, and, well, everything really, and Cross could pull far more than his fair share of the weight.

Unfortunately, they didn't have much money to offer, even if they could offset the cost with labor. The big man hadn't owned any stone his whole life, and Tanya had abandoned her gems in Windmore, which left only the ten rubies David had neglected to pay the Freemen. He had no idea if thirty 'phire was the going rate for passage for three, but he was pretty sure ten ru' would be a hard sell.

Maybe I can find a smaller ship that's shorthanded.

Two midsize vessels were being loaded just down the pier. David smiled and sauntered up. "Oy! You up there," he yelled from the dock.

A bald head poked over the ship's rail. "Can't you see we're busy 'ere?" the sailor yelled, then disappeared.

"Wait! That's what I'm here for."

No response.

"Captain up there?" David yelled.

No one answered.

May as well test my luck.

David walked up the gangplank.

The vessel was bustling with activity. The crew was hauling boxes and using a gantry to lower cargo into the hold. David looked around for someone in charge but didn't see anyone with an overly embellished hat. The aft of the ship had a raised deck built above what was likely the captain's quarters. He strolled over and took the stairs to the upper deck.

Two men argued about something at the top of the steps. They wore more finery than the other sailors but no fancy hats. David considered interjecting himself into their conversation, but in the end, decided interrupting might not be the best way to start begging for a discount. After a few minutes, David gathered one man was the captain, and the other was the harbormaster.

The captain claimed to have prepaid the docking fees when arriving at port. The harbormaster insisted he hadn't. Eventually, the two men agreed to a fifty percent fee. The captain counted out a sum and handed over a rather large bag of stone. The harbormaster disembarked, as the captain muttered that special type of swear that only a man of the sea could produce.

David logged the words for future use.

The captain turned away.

"Uh, sir?" David asked. "Could I borrow a moment of your time?"

The captain stopped, turned back, and looked David up and down.

"What can I do for you, city boy?" the captain asked. "And, who let you on my ship?"

Not the best start.

"Well, sir, I'm looking to barter passage for myself and two comrades. We're willing to work and hope to trade labor for passage. My friend is as big as an ox—"

"Let me stop you there. First off, passage to Terra is negotiated through my first mate." The captain pointed to a man near the bow. "But since you're already here, how much can you pay?"

"Well, I'm a traveling minstrel. I can entertain, and I can help with the rigging. My two comrades are extremely competent as well. One's a giant of a man who could carry two of those boxes at a time." David gestured toward the cargo being loaded onto the boat. The expression the captain wore was not an encouraging one. "My second comrade's handy with a blade, and she knows—"

"Nice qualifications, but that's not what I asked. How much can you pay?"

"Ten ru'," David responded.

The captain's eyes widened, then he burst into a booming laugh. Many members of the crew stopped working to smile and enjoy the show.

David remained silent.

Let him have his fun. I get paid to make people laugh, or I used to.

"Ten whole chips?" the captain finally asked. "Now that *is* a tempting offer."

"We'll work too."

"Mr. Black, do you hear that? We have an offer of thirty chips and help from three people who've never sailed a day in their lives! How could we ever refuse?"

"Not ten each, ten total," David said without thinking the words all the way through.

The captain's smile fell away. "Now you're just wasting my time. Mr. Black! Please see this man off the ship. If he doesn't cooperate, toss him off the docks." The captain turned and walked away. After a few strides, he laughed again. "Ten!" he repeated, then laughed some more.

David cooperated.

I don't want to end up drinking the Divide, after all.

He was a passable swimmer, and the ocean was up. But if a riptide pulled him out to sea long enough for the water to lower, he'd face a sheer wall of slippery rock. Nearly all the coastlines around Darin were cliff faces or enormous bayous. Supposedly, it was because of the rise and fall of the tides, but David wasn't a geographer or a nautical man. Still, as the gangplank creaked underfoot, he couldn't help but hear his father's tired old wisdom:

Once you're in the Divide, you'd be real lucky to get back out.

David spent the rest of the day in a similar fashion. He'd find a boat and someone in charge to talk to, and they would refuse his offer. Sometimes, they'd laugh at him; other times, they'd refuse in a bit more of a cordial fashion, but the answer was always the same. It was near dusk when David finally gave up. He was heading back to the inn to meet with Cross and Tanya when he heard a noise.

"*Psst.*"

David looked around but saw no one. Only when he did a double take did he see a man leaning from the edge of an alleyway.

Was he there a moment ago? David would've sworn he hadn't been.

The short man looked around fifty, had an unkempt bush of a beard, and was all bones and wiry muscle.

"'Ey, over here." The stranger's tone was low and urgent.

David glanced around. He was suspicious, but he was desperate, too, so he walked over.

"I couldn't help but overhear you is lookin' for a vessel to take you to Terra."

"And?" David stepped closer, but not so close that he couldn't draw steel if the scraggly sailor lunged for the ten ruby chips on his belt.

"I'm sure my cap'n would be willing to take ye across for a small sum. That is, as long as yer willing to work, and as long as ye have…flexible morals." The man smiled. "Might ye be interested in such an accord?"

David knew pirates sailed the Divide.

Hells, I even know a few songs about 'em.

According to the songs, the pirates were a pretty notorious bunch. They made their living boarding other ships, killing or ransoming the passengers, and making off with the vessels and cargo. David wasn't sure he wanted to get tangled up with pirates, but they didn't have a lot of options.

"I'm interested." David forced a confident smile across his face.

"Well, I should warn you, our ship's not full of high-class accommodations. But it will get ye across the center o' the world, and for only a modest sum, to be sure." The man reflected David's smile with far fewer teeth.

"How much?"

"That wouldn't be for me to say, ye see. That'd be the cap'n's business. But I'm sure he'd be reasonable as long as ye and yer companions know how to swing a blade." The sailor pointed to the short sword hanging on David's hip.

David looked down at his steel, then back to the sailor. The other man had a little blade of his own, but it wouldn't be much of a match for his longer steel.

"Where's this captain of yours?"

"This way." The sailor turned and walked bowlegged into the alley.

David followed him, keeping a few spans between them.

There's potential for a trap here. Still, gotta ante up if you ever wanna win big.

He wasn't sure if the words were his father's or his own, but they were true.

"Need to move quick now, if ye don't mind," the sailor said, picking up the pace. "The docks get a bit more dangerous after dark."

David looked toward the west. Only ambient light illuminated Grenisport's horizon.

Following the sailor wasn't hard, but it was tiring. He was quicker than he looked and never seemed to slow. Occasionally, he would stop and wait, motioning for David to hurry. By the time he caught up, the sailor was already moving again. This dance continued for a half hour until the sailor stopped in front of a large building. A sign above the door read "Harrid's Shipwright and Supply."

David looked up. The Trickster was half full, winking at him in the dying light. He wasn't sure, but it seemed like this was near their inn.

At least it will be a short walk back.

The bony sailor waited for him to catch up while grinning that same toothless smile. Once David was within a span, the man opened the door.

"Looks like we made it, safe 'n' sound. The cap'n's inside. He's the one you'll be havin' to barter with, but it shouldn't be a problem as long as yer willin' to pull your weight."

Stepping through the door felt like being dealt a good hand while the rest of the table sweetened the pot.

David bit his lip.

Oh, well. In for a chip, may as well be in for a shard.

A single brazier lit the place, casting just enough light for shadows to dance across the walls. A channel split the floor for hauling in a ship during high tide, and a small boat hung by a series of pulleys in the middle of the room. The whole place smelled of sawdust, brine, and lacquer. Three shadowy forms sat around a table near the boat, looking down at something.

Maybe a game of cards? Or dice?

David's heart quickened.

If this doesn't work out, maybe I can win enough money to book passage legitimately.

A thrilling little shiver quivered up his spine.

Something creaked behind David, and he glanced back. The bony sailor had shut the door. David turned to the three people surrounding the table. They were watching him now.

In unison, they stood. Parchment crinkled as one of them took a page from the wood slab. They approached. The brazier lit only their backs, making each appear more like a darkened specter than a man.

David held his ground.

Best not to chum the water with sharks.

"What have you brought us, Gary?" the central man asked.

"Oh, this fella was lookin' for passage across the Divide," the sailor behind David said. "Him and 'is companions don't have a lot of stone, but it sounds like they know how to fight. So, I said you might be interested...Cap'n."

"Oh, that we might, Gary. That we might." The central man held up the parchment, looked at it, then back at David. "Him and how many others are need'n passage?" he asked.

"Two others, sir."

"Two? We might be able to work something out. But how about introductions first? I'm Ericson, but you can just call me Captain if you like."

"Name's Glen," David lied.

"Ah, of course it is." The captain nodded, glancing down at his paper again. "Besides the three sets of strong arms, how much are you offering for a trip across the drink?"

"Ten ruby chips," David responded.

The men to either side of Ericson fanned out.

David's hand wrapped around the hilt of his steel.

Something cold and sharp kissed the stubble on David's throat. He gulped. Foul breath overpowered the pervasive scent of lacquer and brine.

The captain smiled.

"Well, David, let's cut the farce, shall we? Where's Tanya?" Ericson asked, flipping the page around.

On the sheet, drawn by a skilled hand, was an incredible likeness of David. Behind was another page. The illustration on the second sheet wasn't visible, but Tanya's name was scrawled across the top of it. He scanned the paper—twenty sapphire shards for each of them.

It was an absurd sum.

Every bounty hunter and their mothers will be on our trail.

David gulped, then instantly regretted it as the blade pressed tighter to his throat.

33
GERARD STOCKWORTH

The guard captain and a few sentries milled about, surveying the killing ground. The Justiseer's Guild wasn't associated with the city guard, but they were often in the same place at the same time.

What's his name again?

"This your handiwork, Gerard?" The captain gestured around the first floor of the Iron Owl. Two men lay lifeless in a pool of blood at the bottom of the stairs, and Jeff's decapitated body sprawled in the corner. Half the room's chairs were overturned, shattered glass littered the place, and someone appeared to have recently mopped the floor with ale.

Shit. He remembers my name.

"Some of it," Gerard said. "The usual story, you know."

"I'm afraid I don't."

"Aiding and abetting." Gerard twirled a finger.

"Ah. Aiding who?"

"My mark."

"And who might that be?"

"Name's Diego," Gerard lied. "Well, *was* Diego, I s'pose."

"What's he wanted for?"

"Murder and two counts of horse thieving." *Half true.*

"You have the contract on you?" the captain asked.

"No."

"You're supposed to. How do I know you didn't just kill these men over a game of cards?"

"No one carries their contracts around with them. You know that," Gerard explained calmly. "It's on my horse."

"Which one was he?" the captain gestured to the corpses.

"I think I'd rather not say."

292

"That's your prerogative. But if I don't get the whole story, then you and the bodies will have to stick around until we have an account from each witness." A grin crept across the captain's face, but the words sounded rehearsed.

Gerard sighed. "That's him." He pointed to the stiff with an arrow through the eye at the foot of the stairs.

The guard captain looked at two of his minions and nodded toward the body. One was older, the other only a kid.

Must be a new recruit.

The two men sauntered over and flipped the corpse. The kid stared at the shaft protruding from the man's eye, then staggered backward. A second later, his dinner was on the floor.

"Good gods, man," the captain chastised. "You shouldn't sign up for the guard if you can't keep a meal down at the sight of one little body."

"Sorry, sir." The kid wiped his mouth on a sleeve, glanced back at the stiff, then away from it. "Just got a thing about eyes, sir."

"Best get over that quick." The captain shook his head. "Haul that corpse out of here and take it back to the barracks."

"Yes"—the boy retched again—"sir."

The recruit visibly pulled himself together and grabbed the dead man under the arms. Together, the guards lifted, grunting as dead weight left the floor.

"I need that," Gerard said flatly.

Best not ham it up too much, gotta put up just enough fight to avoid suspicion.

"Evidence," the captain stated with the same sly smile.

"Seriously?" Gerard asked.

The guard captain nodded.

"You don't make the rules in Windmore, Gerard. This is our jurisdiction. Justiseers don't keep the peace in the city. We do. Now, get out of here before I decide we need a full report from you at the barracks."

"But..." Gerard trailed off as he met the captain's stern gaze, then let out a long sigh. "You mind if I grab my bow?"

The captain cocked an eyebrow. "Your bow?"

"Yeah. Left it upstairs," Gerard said, pointing to the ceiling.

The captain scratched his chin.

Yeah, it's worth something, but nothing compared to the bounty, you greedy vulture.

"Be quick about it," the captain said.

Gerard hurried upstairs, passing some guards who were coming up with reasons to interview the working girls. He retrieved his bow from under the bed and pulled arrows from dead men on his way back downstairs. Gerard whistled as he snatched the last shaft from a corpse on the ground floor. He looked up, eyes locking with the captain.

Shit, I'm supposed to be properly dismal.

Gerard forced himself to scowl.

"You done?" the captain asked.

Gerard nodded, then left the Iron Owl.

The night air was cold as he strolled around the porch of the chimney. Gerard looked down at Jeff's head, then back inside. The captain stood in the middle of the room, practically counting his stone. He'd find out soon enough there was no bounty for a "Diego." But Gerard would be long gone by then. The lie might cause problems down the trail, but any retaliation from the captain would be through bureaucracy.

It's not illegal to lie, after all. Gerard snorted. *Not yet, anyway.*

Fortunately, most guards were more brawn than brain.

Otherwise, the good captain might've asked why the body in the corner was missing a head.

Gerard pulled a sack from a belt pouch and shook it loose.

Always need a bag big enough for a head.

He grabbed Jeff's head by the hair and stuffed the proof into the burlap sack. Whistling, he turned from the chimney and sauntered into the night.

It took a little over an hour to get to the Justiseer's base of operation in Windmore, and it was late as he ascended the stairs of the guildhouse. Inside, a salty old fellow he'd worked with a few years back called to him.

"Gerard. It's been an age."

"James. How's tricks?" Gerard asked, approaching the man's table.

"The same."

"Any luck with your..."

"Brewery?" James asked.

"Yeah, that's the one."

"None, hence why I'm back here. Looks like you bagged something, though, eh?"

Gerard held up the bloody sack as it dripped on the floor. "That I did. Finally."

"Tough job?"

Gerard nodded. "Just came to throw this in the icebox until tomorrow."

"I think Alex is still in." James took a swig of his ale. "Said he'd some paperwork to finish up."

"Really?"

"Yeah, stealing the Trickster's light tonight."

"Huh, guess I better see him before I ruin any more hardwood." Gerard lifted the bloody bag again and turned to leave. "Good luck with the alehouse."

James waved him off. "Turns out no one wants ale made from corn."

Can't blame them for that.

"Should get your hands on some lotus. Mix that in, and you'll have to fight off the junkies with a stick."

"Huh." James bit his lip, then took a swig.

Gerard walked away, scratching the back of his neck.

Soon, he stood in Alex's office. Alex was his main point of contact in Windmore, a term the guild typically referred to as a handler. Gerard had another handler in Norinspire if things slowed down, but Windmore seldom did. Between escaped slaves, all the debauchery in the city, and the harsh laws of the Rocktells, business was booming.

At two hands over a span, Alex was a tall man and muscular despite sitting behind a desk for as long as Gerard had known him. At some point, he'd been a hunter. The guild was good about promoting from within, and all its staff served at least a little time on the trail.

"What in the hells are you doing here, Gerard?" Alex asked. "Couldn't you have come in the morning? Like a sane person?"

"Technically, it is morning." Gerard smiled.

Alex appeared skeptical.

"I had a run-in with the city guards," Gerard said. "They thought to get clever and poach one of our bounties. Didn't want to give 'em a chance to find out I pulled a switcheroo and come lookin' for the proof."

"Good thing those scavengers don't know their ass from a hole in the ground." Alex laughed. "Still, best be careful with the guard right now."

"Oh, yeah? Why's that?"

"You been livin' under a rock?"

"No, just got back in town. What's the news?"

"Someone knocked off Robert last week."

"Robert?" Gerard asked, raising an eyebrow.

"Rocktell." Alex pinched the bridge of his nose. "Robert Rocktell."

"Any relation to the duke?"

"His bloody son, Gerard. You have been livin' under a rock."

"Sorry, try to stay outta politics."

"So do I. But I still know who Robert bloody Rocktell is."

"All right, all right. I'll be careful with the guards," Gerard conceded.

Alex met Gerard's eye, his face a mask of skepticism, then exhaled. "Who do you have for me?"

"Meet...Kal?" Gerard said, holding up the bloody bag. "Err...I mean, Jeff. Sorry, Alex, it's late, and this job took a bit of a toll." Alex pulled a desk drawer open and quickly flipped through some files. He pulled out a pamphlet: the original bounty for the two men.

"What of Jeff?" Alex asked as he read the flyer.

"You mean Kal."

"Yeah, whatever you said. The other one."

"He's dead. But, like I said, this one was a little rough. Had his head but lost it."

Alex looked up from his papers with a raised eyebrow. "You been writing poems?"

"What?" Gerard asked.

"Doesn't matter. Do I want to know why the job went south?"

"Honestly? No. But he's dead. Put him to bed with my own two hands."

Alex cocked another eyebrow.

"Put him in the bloody dirt. What's wrong with me? How many words rhyme with dead anyway?" Gerard sighed. "I guess it's just late."

"Fair enough." Alex chuckled. "No chance to recover the proof, eh?"

"Not likely. Probably been in the ground for a few days."

They both knew a head could be unrecognizable after just a few hours in the dirt.

"I take it you want to close the bounty without proof, then?" Alex asked.

Gerard nodded.

"All right, so half the bounty for Jeff there and another quarter for Kal in thirty days, as long as no one else comes in with the head."

Always with this same song and dance.

"Yeah, typical contract."

"Same as always," Alex said. "You'll have to pay back the 'phire if someone comes in with the bounty or proof that Kal's alive."

"Yeah, yeah, yeah, I know the rules."

"Then you know I still gotta say it, right?" Alex asked, looking up.

Gerard rolled his eyes.

Stickler.

"How do you want it? Pebbles or boulders?" Alex asked.

"A little bit of both."

Alex nodded, then opened a drawer and rummaged around. He plunked a sapphire shard onto the table, then counted out eight ruby chips and twenty topaz flakes.

"Well, here you are. Sign here and here," Alex said, spinning the contract 'round and sliding it and a quill across the table.

Gerard wet the quill in the blood-soaked bag, signed next to Jeff's name, and pulled a small knife from his belt. He made a quick incision on his left thumb, watched the blood well up in the cut, then wet the quill and signed again next to Kal.

The cut stung, but the red line would soon be just one more white one. Confirmation was a somewhat barbaric tradition, carried over from the first contracts signed so long ago. Gerard wiped the blood on his already red-stained shirt and met Alex's gaze.

"Here you go." Gerard slid the contract back and handed the bloody bag over. Alex took it and pushed the gems across the table. Gerard scooped them up and deposited them in a nearly empty belt pouch.

Gonna be hard for us to afford that little vineyard at this rate.

"Oh, and one more thing," Gerard said with a snap of his fingers. "There's a group smuggling illegal slaves into Windmore, and they're operating out of a pleasure house in the Noble District."

"Really?" Alex asked.

"Yeah, I've got reason to believe they're killing citizens of Darin and forcing their children into slavery." Gerard studied his handler's face.

Not as surprised as I might've hoped.

"This pleasure house got a name?"

"It's an unmarked building. The front lobby could've been any other legitimate business, but they're bringing in slaves from the countryside. Mostly young girls."

"Sounds nefarious," Alex stated dryly.

Is he not even listening?

"I killed one of them," Gerard said, keeping his voice as calm as still water.

"What!" The shock and dismay in Alex's voice were palpable.

So he is listening.

"You killed one of the girls?" Alex accused.

"No, not the girls. The man with half a nose," Gerard explained.

"Half-a-what?"

"Well, most likely, I suppose."

"You killed a man with half a nose?" Alex asked, voice rising.

"Most likely," Gerard corrected.

"Yeah, whatever. What do you mean, you *most likely* killed the man with half a nose?" Alex pointed a finger across the desk.

"Well, I stabbed him. I'm pretty sure he was abusing the girls."

"You're pretty sure? Also, they're bloody slaves, Gerard. They can do whatever the hell they please with them."

"Not sex work, you know that," Gerard said. "Besides, that's the whole thing. They shouldn't be slaves in the first place, and even slaves are people. We like to pretend they're not, but we all know they are. Wasn't the original idea to work off the taxes they couldn't pay in Terra?"

"You know it was, but you also know full well that's not how life works. Either way, that's beside the point. You can't just go around stabbing legitimate business-men, Gerard."

"He wasn't legitimate."

"That's not for you to decide."

"I know." Gerard sighed. "You'll take care of the illegal slave ring, though, right?"

"I'll run it up the chain. And I'll do my best to clean up the mess you made."

Gerard couldn't help but notice the lack of commitment.

Best not push my luck after such an obvious break in protocol.

Alex shook his head, chewing on his lower lip.

That thought looks worth interrupting. "You got any spicy contracts for me?"

Alex met Gerard's eye, paused for a dozen heartbeats, then spoke. "As a matter of fact, I do. Though I should probably give them to someone else at this point."

Gerard gave the handler his most apologetic smile despite not feeling an ounce of remorse for killing the abusive slaver.

Alex sighed. "You're lucky that you're one of the best."

Got him. Gerard's fake smile shifted to something more genuine.

"Two horse thieves stole a couple of beasts and headed out of town last night. One of them's suspected of murder as well." Alex still tried to sound reproachful, but excitement was weaved through his words.

"What's the take?" Gerard asked, eyebrows slowly rising.

"Well, that's where the job gets interesting. The offer's twenty sapphire each."

"Two diamond a head? That's a hell of a lot of stone for a couple of horse thieves."

"Yes, it is, and I've been asked to ensure it gets done quick. These two offended someone pretty bad, and I've got it on good authority that the Justiseers aren't the only ones lookin' for 'em. Plus, the paperwork doesn't say it yet, but there's rumbling 'round the campfire that these two had something to do with Robert's death."

"Who?" Gerard asked.

Alex gave him a sideways look.

Gerard chuckled. "Just foolin'. Any leads?"

"Yeah, they were spotted heading out the north gate toward Norinspire, or maybe Grenisport. But you know as well as I they could be headed anywhere, especially if they were smart enough to double back."

Alex slid the paperwork across the table.

Gerard took the slips.

"You got any other contracts I should be on the lookout for?"

"Yeah. Three others. Two private and one from the city. But Gerard, don't focus on those. We need the first two, and we need 'em quick. You get a chance to collect a head while lookin' for the main bounty, so be it. But don't follow a lead or go out of your way for these others, got it?"

"Of course," Gerard said.

Not only did the guild get a third of the profit, but the high-profile jobs were excellent for their reputation. Alex dug in his top drawer and produced three more contracts.

"We have an escaped prisoner from the city, a merchant who dug himself a deep debt with the Weavers, and finally, an escaped slave from the Freemen's Guild." Alex slid each paper across the table as he described them. Gerard took the paperwork, reading each of the five names as he studied their faces:

Eldon Remis. Jana Stormwind. Rigel Cross. David Trueheart. Tanya Ringholder.

34
TANYA RINGHOLDER

Deep down, Tanya knew David was right. Staying with Cross was a terrible idea.

I should leave them both.

It would be the most rational course of action, but they had each saved her life to their own detriment. Every day, she considered leaving them, and every day, Jack's and Ted's cold, lifeless eyes stared back at her.

So, she couldn't leave. She owed them each a life debt. Tanya hated being in debt. It was probably one of the reasons she initially thought so little of David. But it was hard to judge a debt of stone when she owed two of blood.

Saved by two dumb men. One of whom I might even be falling for.

That's why Tanya left David back there without a second glance. Honestly, she wanted to look but hadn't let herself. Just as she hadn't let herself act differently after their little bout of intimacy.

Love is a fairy tale. Anyone who says otherwise is selling something.

Tanya rounded a corner, then circled back, staying out of David's sight. He wandered toward the docks, strolling like a man in the park. He was clearly determined to secure passage despite knowing she'd already tried.

Best follow him.

David was irrational and prone to idiotic acts of bravery.

I'm living proof of that.

Tanya shook her head.

Singing heroic songs for years must've addled his brain.

He was a fool.

A funny, idiotic, beautiful fool.

Tanya followed him, keeping to the side streets. She had a feeling David was about to take things into his own hands again.

He really does have excellent hands.

She sighed.

His hands were never the problem, though—the head guiding them was another story.

Not good for much more than eye candy.

David strolled down the docks, not a care in the world.

His blind confidence is impressive. Absolutely unjustified, but impressive.

Tanya spotted a poster at the edge of the alley. She walked over, examining the familiar face sketched in black ink. It was her, and she didn't have curly golden locks, an overly powdered face, or puffed-up lips.

WANTED: Tanya Ringholder
KNOWN CRIMES: Horse thieving, murder, and
aiding in the assassination of Robert Rocktell

Those double-crossing pricks.

Tanya knew the Shadow's Lance didn't have many scruples, but she'd never considered betrayal through an assignment they'd given her. She gritted her teeth and read on.

WANTED: David Trueheart
KNOWN CRIMES: Horse thieving, murder, and
complicity in the assassination of Robert Rocktell

The picture was of David, but he was wearing a coachman's uniform.

He wasn't even there. Bastards.

It was a new low, even for the Lance. Tanya ground her teeth, then tore down both pages, stuffing them into her coat.

Best stay with the fool, in case someone recognizes him.

Tanya spent most of the day following the musician and tearing down every bounty poster she could get to without being too obvious. David went from ship to ship, trying the same old song and dance each time. It should've been clear it wouldn't work after he was turned down at the first vessel, but apparently, it wasn't. Even a persistent man should've known the endeavor was folly after two or three failures. Tanya stopped counting David's attempts after ten captains rejected his offer.

Persistence is attractive in a man, Tanya mused. The thought fully registered, and she had to hold back the urge to slap herself. *Gods! Pull yourself together, woman, and stop thinking with your twat.*

Tanya looked up from her fingernails, letting her eyes linger on David's easy smile as he chatted up a pretty girl with a fishing net.

He's a boy, not a man, and this is simply a little fling.

The sun was low on the horizon, and shadows clawed into the side streets when David finally appeared discouraged.

About bloody time.

Tanya's feet were sore from tailing him through half of Grenisport.

David stopped, looked around, and said something.

Who in the hells is he talking to?

Suddenly, the fool was headed into an alleyway, following a skinny man.

Dumbass. No one willing to take you across the Divide needs to meet anywhere but the docks.

Tanya followed anyway.

The two men moved quickly, but Tanya managed to keep up while maintaining distance and stealth. After about thirty minutes, she rounded a corner and watched as the wiry man opened the door to a shipwright and gestured inside. They entered, and the man pulled the door shut behind them.

Each time she gained a little respect for David, he had to go and do something absurd.

Almost as if he enjoys blundering from one crisis to the next.

Tanya circled the building and found some fishing nets hanging on the wall. She scaled them, pulling herself onto the roof. Three glass skylights that must have cost a fortune formed a line in the center of the building.

Maybe the price is offset by less lantern oil during working hours?

Tanya knew that wasn't important right now, but the damn little voice never stopped questioning. The skylights sat in rusty iron frames and looked like they might open to let in fresh air.

Interesting and useful to dry a freshly lacquered hull.

Tanya rubbed away the cloudy scum from a pane of glass and peered into the building.

Four men gathered around David. One held a knife to his throat from behind, and another held a pamphlet in front.

Bounty paperwork. At least things haven't turned violent.

Without warning, the one on the right struck him. Tanya let out an involuntary gasp, and Jack's swollen face filled her mind. They'd beaten him bloody before they slit his throat and threw him in the Channel.

Something tugged at her heart, pulling at it like a puppeteer on Lunar Day.

"Evintri's bloody swollen belly," Tanya muttered.

Don't have long. Silly boy will crack after just a few hard questions.

35
DAVID
TRUEHEART

David had attempted to convince the four men that his real name was Glen. He'd tried and tried, but it hadn't made a difference. They had his likeness. They knew he was trying to book passage. He'd even admitted to traveling with two others, and unfortunately, his captors weren't near as daft as they looked. Shortly after their initial conversation, he was forced into a chair and secured to it.

"Where is she?" Ericson asked.

"Where's who?"

"Don't play dumb. You're a smart fella." One corner of Ericson's mouth pulled tight. "Eh, smart enough, anyway."

David just stared at him.

Ericson glanced at the man on his left, then raised his chin. David sucked in a breath, clenching his stomach right before the fist connected. The bonds stopped him from doubling over in pain, so he sputtered, coughed, then tried to retch.

Fire coursed through David's abdomen, and his jaw throbbed. After a few heartbeats, the newest impact subsided. His eyes fluttered open. A long trail of spittle hung from his lower lip, nearly touching an indistinguishable pile on the floor. He blinked the substance into focus. It was only his lunch.

"This will get a lot easier once you cooperate. So, where is she?" Ericson paused, then sighed. "Don't make me ask again, kid."

"Where's who?" David groaned.

The backside of a hand connected with David's temple, and twinkling white spider-webs enveloped his vision. Slowly, the webs faded, revealing the dingy little warehouse. Ericson let out another long sigh, but he was smiling.

It's just an act. He's enjoying this.

"I'm gonna give you one more chance to answer the question. If you don't..." Ericson paused, clearly for dramatic effect. "Well, then I'll have to do something drastic—something I really don't want to do."

That's a blatant lie.

"We all gotta do things we don't like from time to time," David said. "But I'd be willing to swap places with you, just this once."

"Funny. You should've been a fool instead of stealing horses and getting tangled up with the Rocktells."

"The Rocktells?" David asked.

What do they have to do with this?

Ericson paused, studying him for a moment. "Good liar too. Too bad it won't help you tonight."

"What in the name of Amara's enormous bloody backside are you talking about?"

Ericson chuckled. "You've got a dramatic flair. I'll give you that."

David tested his bonds for what felt like the hundredth time. They were well tied and tight. His hands were secured behind his back, and his ankles were bound to the chair's front legs, leaving him rather exposed. He tried to push the implication of the position from his mind.

I should've fought, even with a knife to my throat.

It would have been a one-in-a-hundred shot at best, but those were better odds than what he faced now.

"Last chance," Ericson warned.

"You know what I find with flies?" David began. "Honey tends to work better—"

A knife slammed down between David's legs. He flinched, sucked in a breath, and held it. He waited for immeasurable pain to blossom in his nethers, but it didn't come. Slowly, David opened his eyes. Two hands of steel were stuck into the wood, less than a finger's width from his stones.

"You didn't actually think I'd cut your balls off with a dirty knife, did you?" Ericson asked. "You're worth a lot less to me if you bleed out or die of infection on the way back to Windmore."

David barely heard the man. He was too busy staring at the sharp edge between his legs.

"Gary! Heat up my knife, will ya?"

The knife creaked as the bony man pulled it free and disappeared behind the chair. There was a clink of metal on metal as Gary presumably found somewhere to rest the blade over the brazier.

"Once that knife's heated, you'll start talking, or we're really gonna get nasty." Ericson's gaze slowly leveled with David's own. "I think I'll start with a few toes. Once that's done,

I'm going to castrate you. If you still haven't given her up...well, you're the musician, right?"

David remained silent, and for a moment, he thought Ericson would hit him again. The man turned to his bony compatriot instead.

"Gary, is this the one that plays the lute?" Ericson asked.

David heard a paper crinkle.

"Yep, sure is."

"Ah, that's what I thought. So, after we cut your balls off, we'll work on your fingers. I'll start with your left and alternate between each hand."

A sickening sensation built in the pit of David's stomach. He pictured his lute and the inscription on the back. An image of his father quickly replaced the lute—one hand outstretched, begging for stone.

That'll be me soon if I'm lucky enough to live that long.

David shuddered, then retched again. Nothing but bile came up.

I can't let this pig of a man have the satisfaction.

"Fuck you," David spat, bits of saliva and bile spraying Ericson's face. The man wiped his cheek, then looked at his hand, fingers curling as his mouth formed a snarl. A fist crashed into the side of David's head, and everything went dark.

———— ◀O▶ ————

David awoke to someone pulling off his boot. His jaw throbbed and felt like it had been forged into something else.

A horseshoe?

With a groan, he looked up. Ericson strolled around him, wearing a leather glove and clutching a red-hot knife. He stopped in front of David and went to one knee.

Their eyes met.

"Where is she, David?" Ericson asked, calm as still water.

"I don't know who you're talking about."

"Wrong answer."

The blade seared through the flesh on David's right foot. He tried to hold in the cry but couldn't.

"Son of a fucking badger's snatch. Bitch—whore—waffle!" David screamed.

"Whoa, look at the mouth on him, boys!" Ericson jibed. "What do you think, fellas? With a mouth like that, maybe we ought to feed him what we're cuttin' off?"

Gary and the other two goons chuckled, but David barely heard it. He was too busy staring at the seared meat where his little toe should curl. He tried to wiggle it, but the little lump of flesh remained motionless.

Funny how such a small thing can feel so important.

A hollowness filled David's chest.

These men are just getting started, and what they take next will be far worse.

An image of his one-handed father flashed across David's mind again. He shivered, gulped, clenched his jaw, and met Ericson's gaze.

"Gary, do us a favor and toast this little toe, will ya? The man should have his meal cooked. We're not barbarians, after all."

Gary snatched up the toe from the floor and disappeared behind David. Footsteps thudded on wooden planks, then a sizzling started as something was placed over the brazier. A moment later, a sickly sweet smell invaded David's nostrils.

Why does it smell like pork?

David wrinkled his nose, until the red-hot knife brought him back to the present.

"Had enough? It's your balls next." Ericson let the words sink in, knife hovering over the next toe on David's right foot.

David gritted his teeth.

"All right. Have it your way."

"Wait! Wait! Wait!"

Ericson hesitated.

Heat wafted off the knife a mere finger's width from David's toes. He rocked his head back and forth a few times, lips moving as he counted out a silent rhythm.

"What in the hells are you doing?" Ericson asked.

"Just savoring the moment."

"What?"

"Tap dancing," David provided.

"Tap dancing?" Ericson asked skeptically.

"I think he cracked, boss," Gary said from behind.

"Just remembering my favorite tap dancing song. I do so love to tap-dance, and I won't be able to s—"

The red-hot knife sunk into David's next toe, and he screamed. The cry slowly morphed into a single vowel and finally transformed into hysterical laughter. David opened his eyes. The two nameless thugs were backing up.

"Guess...he doesn't...like...music," David said between half laughs, half sobs.

"Gary, is that toe done yet?" Ericson yelled.

"Uh...toe?" Gary asked. "Oh yeah, the toe."

The sizzling stopped.

"Give it here. And cook this one up. Let's see if he's still laughing when I feed him what's his." Ericson brought the toe around on the tip of his knife.

The smell should have been repulsive, but it wasn't.

It's just a piece of meat, no longer part of you, David reminded himself.

Heat radiated off the knife as it moved toward David's lips. Black scorch lines marked the toe from whatever dirty grate Gary had found to lay atop the brazier. David took a deep breath, then did the only thing he could think of. The only thing they wouldn't expect. He bit down on the toe, yanking it greedily from the knife.

"Amara's bloody baby maker," said a thug to his left.

"What in the fuck's wrong with him?" asked another voice to the right.

"I think this one's broken, boss," Gary chimed in.

"'Uck, 'ot," David said as his tongue knocked the toe around his mouth.

"What?" Ericson asked.

David spat the scalding bit of flesh and bone out. "Fucking hot." He glared at Ericson. "Good thing the four of you didn't go into business as cooks. You'd burn the roofs of your patrons' bloody mouths on the first night! Let alone the flavor. No herbs? No gravy?"

The four of them looked between each other, but none met David's eye.

Think I'm madder than a junkie tryin' to kick the lotus.

Unfortunately, the act would only buy him a little time, and the bounty hunters had all bloody night.

"Funny man, eh?" Ericson asked. "Let's see if you're still laughing when your balls are cookin' in the brazier." He approached again, this time, with the knife lowered.

Crash.

The captain stopped his advance.

Was that thunder? It isn't raining—

The three men whirled toward the door.

A hulking shape filled the frame as the door creaked on a single hinge. The silhouette's shoulders rose and fell with the rhythmic pattern of short, even breaths. Ericson and two of the thugs took a few steps toward the newcomer.

Where'd Gary go? Still back by the brazier?

David craned his neck, trying to see the bony little man.

"Can I help you with something?" Ericson asked, voice raising, as the two other men pulled blades.

The only reply was the same steady breathing.

David's captors hesitated.

"What are you doing here?"

No response.

"This is none of your business, mate. Now, if you'd kindly be on your way, this won't have to get messy."

Silence.

David spotted Gary skulking along the darkened wall. He was nearly beside whoever was in the doorway and had replaced his razor with a shortsword.

Wait, that's my sword.

David opened his mouth to yell a warning, but it was too late. Gary sprung from the shadows, and he was quick.

As it turned out, so was the massive figure. It was hard to imagine someone so large moving so fast, but they did. As Gary lunged, the form caught his wrist, spun the smaller man toward the other side of the frame, then pulled him back. The movement looked more like a well-choreographed dance on Lunar Day than fighting.

Gary stared down at his belly, gulping for air and clutching at the silhouette of David's blade buried to the hilt. The brute kicked Gary free of the blade with a wet, sucking sound, and the small man collapsed to the floor. Even in the dim light, David saw something spill from the bony man's belly.

The shadowy form stepped over Gary. The smaller man whimpered, trying to stuff whatever had fallen from his stomach back in. The three remaining bounty hunters took a step back.

I don't blame them. I'd rather eat another toe than face that.

The hulking figure lurched into motion, not circling as a hunter might, but in a full-out charge.

He's trying to engage all three of them at once.

It was an insane plan. Then again, getting surrounded was even worse.

"Korinth's bloody ball sack," David muttered, realizing he was simply watching the skirmish unfold and not doing a damn thing.

David pulled desperately at his bonds, but they only tightened. He looked up as the first of the three hunters was impaled on a blade. The thug had his sword raised to strike, but he was already dead. David glanced from the sword in the man's gut to the imposing figure's face.

It was Cross.

Holy fuck, was it ever Cross. David gaped at the big man. He'd seen him plenty over the last few weeks, but never like this.

"Amara's swollen cooter. He's huge," David whispered.

At well over a span in height and spattered with blood, Cross appeared more monster than man.

All lean muscle and motherfuckin' fury.

David found himself cheering like a kid on his first trip to the Coliseum. That was until he noticed Cross's eyes. They were glazed over as if the man didn't care who or what he was killing, only that he was killing. David's elation mixed with dread. On one hand, he wanted to scream with delight; on the other, he felt a deep need to soil his britches.

David's thoughts vanished as the second thug thrust a sword at Cross. The big man dragged the mercenary's comrade into the blow, then lifted the first thug from the ground by the sword in his gut and threw him. Somehow, Cross made it look as easy as tossing chips into the pot.

The nearly dead man landed on Ericson, and they went down in a tangle of limbs. The last standing thug and Cross circled each other. Somewhere, someone started screaming for their mother.

I didn't know people actually did that.

Ericson grunted, trying to stand, but the thug Cross had thrown clung to his leg, screaming.

Cross and the other man finished their half circle, putting the mercenary closer to the door. The man dropped his steel, turned, and bolted. Cross flipped David's short sword in his hand, caught it by the blade, and hurled it like another man might throw a dagger. The steel careened through the air, end over end, and plunged into the thug's back. The brigand sank to the floor, clearly not long for this world, but that didn't seem to matter to Cross. He leapt after the thug like some sort of beast.

Unoiled hinges let out a squealing protest from somewhere, and the whole building groaned as Cross landed on the man. He took the bounty hunter by the hair, pulled his head back, and brought it down on the oaken planks with a sickening crunch. He repeated the process again, and again. David looked away, but the wet smacks still echoed off the shipwright's high walls.

Ericson stabbed the man latched onto his leg and pulled himself free.

David glanced toward Cross. The monster of a man was stalking toward them, clutching David's sword in one hand, a mop of hair and skin dangling from the other. Bits of bone and brain still clung to the scalp as it swayed back and forth with each heavy tread. Cross's face was covered in gore, but he didn't even seem to notice. David gritted his teeth, straining against his bonds as the big man grew closer.

Cross turned toward Ericson, and David let out a sigh of relief.

Ericson looked between the two men then dropped his sword and lunged behind David's chair. For the second time since sundown, steel pressed against David's throat.

Cross stopped in his tracks.

"Fuck! That thing's still hot," David protested. "Don't get *me* involved in this!"

"I'll kill him. I will," Ericson said, ignoring David.

Ericson's hand shook, and David smelled stubble singeing as the knife tapped unsteadily against his neck. Cross looked from one man to the other, then took another step forward.

The knife tightened around David's throat.

He sucked in a deep breath.

Lilacs?

Suddenly, a hand was on Ericson's wrist. Sharpened metal slid into soft flesh with a squelch, then hissed as it was pulled back out. Warm liquid sprayed across the side of David's face, the tang of rust and iron overwhelming the more subtle fragrance of lilacs.

Ericson went limp, toppling like a stack of cards.

"You all right?" a familiar, breathy voice whispered in David's ear. "I followed you. I'd say I'm sorry, but..." Tanya trailed off, gesturing to the carnage. "You just can't help but get into trouble, can you?"

36
RIGEL CROSS

"Wow, opulent," David remarked once the door shut.

Two tapestries decorated the walls, a crystal chandelier hung from the ceiling, and a heartwood table shone like a mirror in the center of the room.

"More like decadent," Tanya corrected.

"Same thing."

"Not quite."

"What does opulent mean?" Cross asked.

"Too rich," Tanya said.

"And...deck-uh-dent?"

David rolled his eyes. "Same thing."

"Just rich," Tanya said, pointedly ignoring him.

Disgusting. And this is only the waiting room. How many slaves suffered for this?

Tanya and David settled onto a small bench with deep-blue upholstery and silver stitching.

Cross stood in protest, inspecting an enormous tapestry of the realm. The little cities were detailed, and someone had taken the time to embroider each mountain, river, and tree. Flowery letters marked the map, and colored fabrics differentiated each type of terrain.

After studying the tapestry for quite some time, Cross gave up and walked to the plainest chair in the room. He tried to pull off the leather cushions, but they were fastened to the wood, so he blew out a breath and sat instead. The room was well lit by an exterior window, yet two oil lamps hung in the chamber. The woman at the desk said their contact would be in shortly, but that was hours ago.

What had his name been? Something with a V.

Five books sat on a table in the center of the room. Cross stared at them with a mix of suspicion, wonder, and jealousy. Tanya passed the time, flipping through one of the books with amazing speed. David sat beside her, occasionally glancing over her shoulder at the page before looking away. It was clear that he could read, yet, for the most part, chose not to.

To have so much knowledge at your fingertips and care nothing for it? Insane.

"You want one of these?" Tanya asked.

Cross pulled his eyes from the books.

Tanya looked at him expectantly.

She must've seen me staring.

"Wouldn't do much good," Cross said.

Tanya cocked her head to the side. She and David were relatively naive when it came to slavery. It was a nice reminder that not everyone in Darin owned slaves.

"Why not?" Tanya asked, pursing her lips. Realization slowly dawned, and sympathy washed her features. "They never taught you?"

"A waste of resources." Cross folded his arms. "Well, that's what they told my father, anyhow."

For a moment, Tanya seemed to consider. "Well, I don't know if we have time right now, but I'll teach you when we have a chance. If you want?"

"You'd do that?"

"Of course."

"I would," Cross said, a grin slowly parting his face. "Like that, I mean."

Tanya really was nice, despite how tough she was. She was extremely competent and knew far more than any single person had a right to. She and David excelled at nearly everything. They created things Cross could barely imagine and did so with so little effort. Sometimes, it made his head spin.

My only gift is destruction. But if I could read...well, maybe I could change that.

Cross's father had known a few letters. Their family had passed them down from generation to generation through scribbles in the dirt. He hadn't known how to write Rigel but had taught Cross how to draw their last name in the sand. That was ultimately why Cross chose the name. He could write it down, and it honored his father as well.

"I'll help too, big man," David chimed in. "I'm not near as quick as Tanya with letters, but I've scrawled out a song or two in my day."

David wasn't half as perceptive as Tanya when it came to emotions, but he was always willing to jump in and help. It was something Cross was beginning to deeply appreciate in the sometimes-rash musician. David took out his lute and began picking at the strings as if talk of writing songs had suddenly inspired him to play one.

Cross liked them both a lot. They were charming, witty, and funny, even if they had bickered all the way to Norinspire. Thankfully, the journey had been relatively uneventful after the first night. They'd cauterized David's wounds, stolen a third horse, and helped the squealing musician into the saddle. Cross hadn't known how to ride, but his time around horses on the Rocktells' farm helped keep him on the thing as they galloped out of town.

The journey to the capital had taken nearly a week, and they'd managed to make it all the way to Norinspire without being recognized. Now, they waited in the OAM's Citadel. Cross had heard of the OAM before but laughed when David and Tanya explained that it stood for the Order of Appropriate Magic.

Tales of magic were reserved for folklore and fairy tales, yet an organization with limitless resources existed to hunt it down. It was hard to believe but even harder to deny sitting in a building worth more than the Rocktells' entire estate.

"So, let me get this straight," Cross said. "The OAM decided that all 'magic' should be illegal, right?"

"You got it." David gave his lute a light strum.

"But none of us have ever seen magic," Cross said. "I mean, tales of it are for children, right?"

"Correct!" David said, playing louder.

Tanya scowled, but there was a playful twinkle in her eye.

She's enjoying this as much as I am.

"So, this massive, well-funded organization hunts down and protects us from what?" Cross asked. "Oh-so-dangerous and completely non-existent magic?"

"Now you've got it, big man," David said, fingers dancing across the strings.

"What sense does that make?"

David glanced up at Cross, cocked an eyebrow, smiled, then began to play.

"Decree and decree, the gray-cloaks proclaim."

Strum.

"All to dictate, a world in their name."

Thrum.

"They hem and they haw, but nothing does change."

Strum.

"When the taxes are due, no one finds it strange!"

Thrum.

All three of them laughed, and David stood and gave a little bow. Then he took a deep breath and positioned his left hand on the frets of the lute.

"David, it's really not the time or the place," Tanya warned.

"Oh, c'mon, we've been here for hours. What are the odds they appear now? If they did, it might be the first real magic we've ever seen. Eh, Cross?"

"Maybe so, but I don't think they'd appreciate your—"

The door opened, and a young man clad in plain gray robes strode in. He was probably too young to be the high-ranking OAM member, but it was hard to be sure with a group as upside down as this one.

"The Magus will see you now," the young man announced.

Cross and Tanya stood.

"Well, we best not keep the *Magus* waiting." David gave Cross a wink.

Tanya brushed past him.

"Ouch! You stepped on my foot," David complained.

"Oops. Clumsy me." Tanya looked back and shrugged.

The three of them followed the acolyte down a long passage lined with doors, each more elaborate than the last. Finally, at the end of the hall, they stopped in front of an ornate slab of wood.

The acolyte knocked.

"Come in." The voice was barely audible through the thick heartwood slab, but Cross could tell the man on the other side was nearly yelling by the pitch.

The young man turned a knob, and the door swung soundlessly inward.

Good hinges, those, Cross thought as they entered.

The office made the previous room look like a slave's hovel by comparison.

Light streamed in through high windows, revealing walls lined with dozens of bookcases.

I didn't know the entire world held so many books.

Occasionally, a frame or other ornament interrupted the shelves, but mostly it was books. There were volumes of all sizes, colors, and shapes. Most stood on end, but some laid flat. Occasionally, one was left open on an overly embellished stand.

Cross ran his tongue over his teeth, noticed his mouth was open, and consciously shut it.

A massive desk carved from some sort of marble sat in the center of the room. Etched runes spiraled up each leg in patterns that looked more like art than writing. Behind the desk sat a well-groomed man with a salt-and-pepper beard and intense blue eyes.

"Please, sit." The older man gestured to three chairs in front of the desk without getting up.

David and Tanya each took a seat.

Cross stood there, gaping at the chamber.

No way anyone could ever read all these books. They must just be for show. Even if one person could read them all, they'd forget half the knowledge by the time they were halfway done.

A soft thumping pulled Cross from his thoughts.

Tanya was patting the empty chair to her right. The motion pushed Cross's brain into action, and his feet followed shortly behind. He sat, vaguely aware that this chair was even softer than the previous one, but it was hard to pull his eyes from the walls long enough to care.

"As I'm sure you've guessed, my name is Vincent," the man behind the desk said. "Oh, and Ellis, you may leave us. Please ensure we are not disturbed."

The acolyte in the gray robes gave a short bow and exited the room, closing the door behind him. Vincent reached under his desk, and a bolt slid into place somewhere in the door with a click.

That's a neat trick. Magic?

Cross looked from the desk to the door.

Would they really use it so commonly when a few steps could accomplish the same thing?

"A pleasure to meet you, Vincent," Tanya said. "Reynolds speaks very highly of you."

Vincent nodded, then smiled.

"I'm Valerie," Tanya said. "This is Kole." She gestured to Cross. "And this is Ashley." She pointed to David.

David shot her a dirty look but quickly smoothed it into a smile.

"Ah, an unusual name. But these are unusual times," Vincent responded. "Well, I'm glad Reynolds sent you. Truthfully, I didn't expect you until tomorrow. But I'm grateful, for we have no time to waste in this matter. I'm afraid I must ask to see your insignia, though."

Tanya pulled out her necklace and presented it to Vincent. It was a circular pendant, about three fingers wide, with a silver lance etched into a field of black.

"Ah, good," Vincent said. "You will have to excuse the formalities, but we do love our protocols in the Order."

"Actually, you'll have to excuse us," Tanya said. "We weren't given much information about the job. Reynolds said you'd provide the details. Hush-hush, and all that."

"Indeed. Even Reynolds is not privy to the specifics of this particular contract, though. We simply negotiated a fee. I believe we did agree on six members, however. Did the rest of your group get waylaid?"

"Oh, no, they're coming," David cut in. "Reynolds sent us ahead on horseback. Said getting here quickly and getting the particulars was important. Plus, sounds like we should only tell them what is necessary. Even the Shadow's Lance has cracks."

"Makes sense. I'm always pleasantly surprised by Reynolds's ingenuity," Vincent said.

Ingenuity? Cross opened his mouth to ask what it meant, then decided not to interrupt Vincent. *I'll ask later.*

"That explains your prompt arrival. We will make accommodations for your mounts here at the Citadel." Vincent jotted a quick note on a piece of parchment at the top of a neat stack. "Well, let's get to business then, shall we?"

"Yes. You did mention time is of the essence." Tanya smiled.

"It certainly is. We need the Shadow's Lance to do a little reconnaissance for us. That, and retrieve a relic."

"Recon-a-what?" Cross asked.

"Scouting," Tanya clarified. "Sorry, you'll have to excuse Kole. He's one of our blunter instruments. But he's exceptional in that role and loyal beyond question." She smiled at Vincent, then turned to Cross. As their eyes met, her smile slid away, replaced with a glare.

Oops.

"I understand. Different tools for different tasks," Vincent said. "Hence, our relationship with the Lance. In any case, an OAM facility has failed to make contact for the last two months. We've hired you to investigate the matter."

"How often do they typically report?" David asked.

"Every two weeks."

"So, they missed the last four rendezvous?" Cross asked. All three of them turned to him. "What?"

"You know a word like rendezvous and not reconnaissance?" David asked.

"I like rendezvous. It's fancy, and my dad used to say it."

David rolled his eyes. "Doesn't matter. Please continue, Vincent."

"I should warn you. The Order already sent one contingent," Vincent said solemnly.

Cross opened his mouth to ask what contingent meant, but Tanya shot him a look, so he clamped it shut.

"What happened to them?" Tanya asked, turning back to Vincent.

"They did not return. That's when we decided to enlist the help of the Lance. Your organization is known for its discretion and ability to handle..." Vincent trailed off, searching for a word. "Delicate situations."

"So, where's this outpost?" David asked.

"Ah, good question. But to answer that, we must first attend to some paperwork." Vincent opened a drawer, produced three stacks of white paper, and slid them across the polished stone.

Very formal writing decorated the top page in the cleanest script Cross had ever seen. The paper didn't have a single wrinkle, tear, or crease either. Cross checked his hands, making sure they were clean, then reverently took the stack. Of course, he couldn't tell what a single word meant, but that was beside the point.

"Feel free to read them over, but they are the standard OAM–Lance disclosure accord," Vincent explained.

"What's that?" Cross asked.

"Essentially, they say that the three of you, and your other compatriots, will not share any details of the following mission or what might occur on it with anyone other than myself or an OAM member of equal rank."

"There's a lot of words for just that," Cross murmured, staring at the stack of pages.

"Indeed. It goes on to discuss payment information and states that any unlawful information shared from this mission will be considered an act of sedition."

Cross wasn't sure what sedition meant, but it didn't sound good.

"Got it. Do the mission, return and report, then forget the mission," Tanya said.

"Exactly." Vincent smiled.

Tanya turned over the first page of her stack and signed the back. David did the same. Cross flipped the front sheet, picked up the wooden pen, and put it to page. Vincent took each stack of papers and lifted the first sheet. He wafted it in the air to dry the ink, read the signature, and replaced it on the stack.

"Valerie Shipwright...Ashley Smith...and...Cross?" Vincent looked up at them in confusion.

Silence.

Tanya and David glanced at each other.

David's hand silently glided to the hilt of his sword.

"Oh! I forgot to mention," Tanya interjected. "Kole doesn't have his letters. Some of our more humorous initiates taught him to write Cross instead of an X, you know." Tanya drew two diagonal lines in the air with her finger, then laughed. It was a high-pitched, twinkly noise and sounded fake to Cross, but he'd heard the real thing.

"Ah. Humorous indeed," Vincent said, but his tone held no amusement.

"I can write his name if it's preferable," Tanya offered.

"No, Cross will do," Vincent said. "Now, let's go over the details. You'll have to excuse the paperwork, but this outpost is more than a bit secret. It's an island located off the coast named Seafront."

"Do you have a map?" David asked.

"No need. The OAM has chartered a ship for you. Only two captains are trusted with the island's exact location, and one went missing with the first expedition. His name is, or perhaps was, Captain Booker. We require the Lance to investigate three things at Seafront. First, check on the settlement and determine why they have not reported in. Second, discover what happened to Booker and the contingent sent to the island." Vincent paused, took a sip of water, and cleared his throat.

"And the third?" David asked.

"The final, and most important piece of the mission, is to retrieve a relic."

"A relic?" Cross asked.

"Yes," Vincent said. "A sword, to be precise."

"Any idea where we might find it?" Tanya asked.

Vincent opened a drawer and flipped through some files, eventually producing a document. He slid it across the desk slowly, one finger pinning it to the polished stone.

Tanya took it.

"You will need to make your way to the center of town." Vincent reached across the desk and touched an illustration of a fountain circled on the map. "Then, enter the barracks." He pointed to a building adjacent to the fountain. "You should find a short staircase at the far end of the armory. You will need to break through a wall there to access it."

"Wait, what?" David asked.

"You will need to break down a wall," Vincent said again. "I imagine Kole will be up to the task. Once you are through the wall, you are on your own."

"What do you mean we're on our own?" David asked. "You don't know what's behind the wall?"

"We do not. We know there will be a vault, and I would not be surprised if it is full of...dangerous situations. But somewhere deep in the vault will be a sword. That is what you must retrieve."

"So, you know the sword's in the vault, but nothing else about it?" Tanya's eyebrow raised ever so slightly.

"Correct. The relic was buried in Seafront some time ago, and it would appear whoever entombed it also destroyed whatever information we had on it."

"Why?" Cross asked.

"I'm not entirely sure. If I am completely honest, none of us even knew of this vault's existence until the fort failed to make contact. We have protocols in place for events such as this. One of these protocols informed us of the relic, the need to retrieve it, and where to start the search."

"Why all the secrecy?" David asked. "If the blade's so important, why didn't you keep it here and put it in a safe or something?"

"Items of true power need to be separated, and metal boxes are not enough to keep them from the hands of men," Vincent said. "As long as someone knows where to find them, a relic is never truly safe. Items like the blade need to be locked away and forgotten. As you can see, though, we have measures in place in case of a breach."

"Are you saying this sword is magic?" Cross asked. "Like, real magic?"

"I am. When you find it, you must not draw it. Not under any circumstances. Is that clear?"

The three of them nodded.

"You should avoid touching it with your bare hands as well," Vincent warned. "I recommend not even looking at it longer than necessary."

"What happens if someone does draw it?" Tanya asked.

"You must not. That is paramount. Magic is inherently evil. It corrupts, and it will annihilate you." Vincent locked eyes with each of them. "Destroying and controlling the arcane is the entire reason the OAM exists. Do not presume to know better than an organization that's controlled this force for a thousand years."

"So, once we've got this sword, what do you want us to do with it?" David asked. "Throw it in the ocean on our way back? No one will find it then."

"You think the Order hasn't tried such measures in the past?" Vincent's words dripped with condemnation. "No, you must bring it here. The blade must not go unaccounted. Relics have a way of resurfacing in the world when not under strict lock and key."

"Even from the bottom of the ocean?" David asked skeptically.

"Even from the deepest places in the world," Vincent said.

"So, find out what happened to Seafront, try to locate Captain Booker, and retrieve a relic," Tanya said.

"Seems easy enough." David leaned back, weaving his fingers together behind his head.

"And do not draw the blade," Vincent reminded. "Retrieval of the relic is the single most important part of this mission. If you do gather it up, do not linger in Seafront. Take whatever information you have on the captain and the outpost and return here immediately. Is that understood?"

"Got it." Tanya looked from David to Cross.

David nodded.

Cross wasn't sure how he felt about the whole thing but nodded anyway.

"When do we leave?" David asked.

"Your ship is ready to set sail as early as tomorrow. However, we didn't expect you today, so the vessel can wait for your companions until the day after."

"Great! We'll wait for the rest of the Lance, then be on our way in the morning," Tanya said. "You boys have any other questions?"

David shook his head, and again, Cross joined him.

"Well, let's secure some rooms for the evening then," Tanya said.

"Hold on. You will need this." Vincent produced a stone from the pocket of his gray robes and slid it across the table.

The stone was perfectly round and could easily fit in Cross's palm. Hundreds of narrow ovals were etched into its surface in a repeating circular pattern. The craftsmanship was incredible.

How would someone even consider making such a thing?

Tanya picked it up. "What's this for?"

"That will get you onto the ship," Vincent explained. "It will also pay for your rooms and meals tonight at the Golden Lamb down the street. Just show them the insignia, and they will charge the Order's account."

"Thank you," Tanya said with a smile. "The Lance is always grateful to work with such a professional organization. What was the name of our ship again?"

"The *Warden*. Simply show that stone to Captain Caldwell. He will take care of the rest," Vincent explained.

They all stood.

"It's been a pleasure, Vincent," David said, extending a hand. Vincent grasped the outstretched hand and shook, then repeated the gesture with Tanya and Cross. They turned toward the door, and it clicked again as they approached. Cross pulled the heavy thing open and held it for Tanya and David.

"Kole, hold back a minute, will you? I would have a word."

The name Kole barely registered, and Cross only stopped walking because Tanya stood in his path, nodding back toward the Magus.

Gods, I'm not good at this sneaking and lying.

Cross turned back and took two steps into the room.

"If you would be so kind as to close the door, Valerie," Vincent said.

Cross looked back. Tanya's brows knit together, and her mouth twitched as if she was trying to come up with something to say. Instead, she took a deep breath and swung the door shut. The door latched with a soft click, and Cross turned to Vincent.

"Kole, you strike me as a man of action, not words. Am I correct in this presumption?"

Can't I be both?

"Yes, I suppose I am, sir," Cross said.

"Then let us speak bluntly. I couldn't help but notice the slave brand on your right hand."

Cross's muscles tensed. He glanced down. The paste Tanya had applied to his thumb earlier this morning had smudged, exposing the mark.

Must've been when I was fiddling with that pen.

Cross took one step toward Vincent.

I don't care how powerful and bookish this man is. I'll strangle the life from him before I go back to the Freemen.

"You strike me as a man who can get things done, Kole. A man of his word," Vincent said confidently. "I am a man of my word too. So, if you and your friends return the blade to me, I'll officially grant your freedom and have that mark erased." Vincent pointed to Cross's right hand.

"You can do that?" Cross asked, stopping his slow advance.

"I can, and I will. You have my word."

"Why?"

"Call it an insurance policy," Vincent said. "Relics...well, they can be tricky things. They corrupt, especially those with not enough incentive."

"Incentive?" Cross asked.

"It means reason." Vincent smiled. "If anyone from the Lance decides they'd rather have the blade than the OAM's funds...well, I'm simply giving you a bit more motivation."

Vincent's smile was the same as a hundred smiles before. It was the same smile the older kids wore when they'd played games as boys. The same smile on a master's lips right before they made him clean the pigsty. The same smile Wortack wore as he'd told his father not to drop the stones. It was always the same look, and it always meant the same thing:

I'm better than you, and I will always win.

Cross's face relaxed.

And maybe he just has.

"Deal," Cross said, spitting into his palm and extending the hand. It was an old custom, supposedly from Terra, but Cross had only seen it used between slaves.

A flicker of disgust flashed across Vincent's face but disappeared in a heartbeat.

The Magus spit into his own palm and clasped hands with Cross. Their eyes met, and after a moment, Vincent winced. Cross glanced down, realized he might be gripping too hard, and released. He nodded to the man, then turned to the door.

"See you soon, Vincent," Cross said, looking back. The Magus still wore that same self-satisfied smile.

"I do hope so, Kole. I truly do."

37

SCARLETT REINHOLM

Twelve specters drifted through the veil of ivory. It was difficult to make out details through the falling snow, but they clearly carried weapons. As the silhouettes slowly solidified, a lithe grace revealed their true nature.

Predators.

Subconsciously, Scarlett sniffed the air.

Man. Somehow, she knew that.

Her fingers twitched, tightening around the axe handle, even though fighting twelve was impossible.

I'm a scientist playing woodsman, not a brawler.

Still, they'd seen her now, and her choices were quickly diminishing.

They're not carrying all those sharp points for a nice debate.

She considered running.

No, I can't leave Roland.

The big moose was likely grazing on willows somewhere around the house, but Scarlett could no longer see him through the falling snow.

That's a blessing, at least.

Features and details slowly materialized on the encroaching silhouettes. They were barely six spans away now.

Maybe there's a diplomatic way out of this? I've got nothing to hide, after all.

"Greetings," Scarlett called through the falling snow.

"Hello." An older man stepped forward. He wore animal skins that left too much flesh exposed to the elements, and bones pierced his ears and clattered in his hair. The rest of the group fanned out surrounding her. The movement wasn't exactly hostile, but it wasn't friendly either. They all carried spears and bows, but the weapons were slung across backs or used as walking sticks.

For now, at least.

"I don't get much company up here. You mind telling me what brings you to my door?" Scarlett asked, voice rusty from disuse. It had been a long time since she'd talked to anyone other than Roland or herself.

"We are on a hunt," the man with the bones said.

"A hunt? You come from the jungle?" Scarlett asked.

"We do." Bones smiled. "What gave us away?"

Interesting. Civilization is far closer than I thought. The revelation made Scarlett want to pack up and move, but she had roots here now, and it was hard to consider doing it all again.

"A long way to come for game," Scarlett said. "Especially when there's more down in the jungle."

A few of the hunters muttered to each other.

"You hunt in the forest often?" a man to the right of Bones asked. He looked serious and didn't fit in with the other hunters. Everyone else had oddly light skin, numerous piercings, and thick accents.

Not from around here, that's for sure.

Scarlett had heard the man's dialect before but couldn't quite place it.

It isn't Terran. So where in Darin?

"I hunt in the jungle occasionally," Scarlett answered. "Usually only in winter when game is scarce on the plateau."

"You all alone up here?" the same man asked.

Norinspire, Scarlett decided after hearing the accent again. *Not sure I like that question.* Still, lying seemed like a useless endeavor.

"Yep, just me," Scarlett said. "Kinda the way I prefer it, if I'm honest."

"Long way from any sort of civilization." Norinspire's eyebrows narrowed.

Not as long as I'd like, apparently.

A few hunters were shivering, and the falling snow was only getting thicker.

"Yeah, like I said, that's kinda the point," Scarlett provided. "Still, the storm doesn't look like it will let up anytime soon. Why don't we go inside? My place isn't really big enough to harbor you through the storm, but we can at least warm you up and have a cup of tea."

"That would be most kind of you," Bones said.

Scarlett nodded, then turned to the door and opened it. She held it wide as the twelve hunters crammed into her little cabin.

"Please remove your shoes, if you don't mind," Scarlett said as her undesired guests entered. "I don't get much company out here, and wet boots aren't good for the floors."

The hunters pulled off cloth wraps and shoes as they entered and found a place to sit or stand. Scarlett grabbed the kettle, refilled it, then closed the door. She watched visible relief spread across each face as the warmth of the fire crept into them.

"I'm Raylor, by the way," Bones said, gesturing to himself. "This is Nathan." Raylor pointed to Norinspire.

"Scarlett," she said, placing the kettle over the fire. "Hope you don't mind sharing. Not sure I have enough cups for the lot of you."

"It won't be a problem," Raylor said with a warm smile. "You're already being far more gracious of a host than expected."

Scarlett tried to smile back but could tell it didn't entirely take.

"So, what're you hunting?" she asked. "Must be something extravagant to bring you all the way up from the jungle—and with twelve spears, no less." The hunters looked from her to each other, but no one answered. "Hoping to bring home the pelt of a great bear?"

"What is a bear?" Raylor asked. "Similar to the big cats we have down in the jungle?"

"Mmm, a little, except much larger. Nearly ten times the weight for a big one and easily triple that for a great bear."

Raylor scratched his chin. "It could be—"

"Describe it," Nathan cut in. Scarlett and Raylor stopped and looked at him. Nathan blinked, then added, "If you'd be so kind."

"Well, like I said, they're quite large and strong, but they're fast too. Not in the same way as a panther per se, but you won't outrun them."

"Do they stand on two legs like a man?" Nathan asked.

"Well, they can, but they tend to prefer all fours."

"Sound familiar?" Nathan asked, turning to Raylor.

"It does indeed. Do they attack humans?"

"Not usually. The few times I've seen one, they wanted about as much to do with me as I did with them."

"That sounds a bit less promising," Raylor said.

"I've only seen one a handful of times, but I've read a bit about them," Scarlett explained. "Apparently, they aren't usually interested in people but become a problem once they've established humans as a source of food."

"You mean once they eat one of us?" Nathan asked.

"Yes and no," Scarlett said. "The book I read explained it usually happens when people leave out carcasses or other things that smell good. A bear has a good nose and may come 'round looking for an easy meal. If they get one, then they'll be back. After that, it's only a matter of time until someone gets attacked."

"That sounds too much a coincidence to ignore," Raylor said.

Nathan nodded.

The kettle began to whistle and quake on the stove. Scarlett grabbed it and bustled through hunters to her kitchen counter. Something rustled near the door, and she glanced back. Nathan was leaning over, whispering to one of the hunters. Scarlett grabbed a handful of loose herbs, sprinkled some into her four cups, and poured the water. The cabin door creaked, there was a crunch of snow, then another creak as the door shut.

"Not real safe going out in a blizzard," Scarlett said to no one in particular.

"Just needed to relieve themselves," Nathan explained.

"Oh, well. More tea for the rest of us, I suppose." Scarlett looked down at the four cups and considered lacing the tea with lotus leaf. Something about these hunters didn't sit right. She'd gathered some of the blue flowers on the way through the desert years ago. Originally, she'd planned to use it as a sedative for a severe injury, but she hadn't needed it yet. Still, not all of them would drink the tea, and even if they did, then what? She'd have a bunch of sleeping hunters and no idea what to do with them.

I could tie them up. But what then? I'm not going to kill them.

Scarlett dismissed the whole idea and doled out the four cups. She offered the first two cups to Nathan and Raylor. Nathan turned it down, and Raylor said maybe after his hunters had their fill. The remaining eight men and women shared the cups between them. They took turns holding the warm vessels and sipping. The tea was clearly not something they were used to, and they savored the bold tastes.

"So, are you folk having bear trouble down in the jungle?" Scarlett asked.

"It would seem so," Nathan responded.

"We're not sure, truth be told," Raylor added. "People have been taken in the night, and we know the beast is powerful, but few have seen it."

"I don't think they particularly like the climate down in the forest. Though I can't be sure, mind you. Most of my knowledge on bears is theoretical."

"Do you know where one might make its home up here?" Raylor asked.

"Well, if I had to guess...I'd say they'd be looking for a den to hibernate."

"High-ber-nate?" Raylor repeated it slowly. "I am not familiar with this term."

"It means to sleep through the winter," Nathan offered.

Raylor cocked his head to the side. "You never cease to surprise, Nathan."

What's that about? Are these two less familiar than it appears?

Scarlett looked back and forth between the two men.

"That's not quite right, but it's close enough," Scarlett said.

"How so?" Nathan asked.

"Well, hibernation doesn't really mean sleep, but that doesn't matter," Scarlett explained. "The main thing is that bears do hibernate up here on the plateau. In a warmer climate, they likely wouldn't. If one's down in the forest, there's a good chance it doesn't feel the same need to sleep the winter months away."

The cabin door opened, and a cold wind gusted in with the two hunters. They didn't remove their shoes.

Gone too long to simply be relieving themselves, and not removing your shoes is just—

"Have you seen anywhere a bear might hibernate?" Raylor interrupted Scarlett's thoughts.

"There's a cave not far from here. I'm not sure there's a bear inside, but it could fit one."

Nathan ignored their conversation, listening instead to the hushed tones of the two hunters by the door. Scarlett leaned in, trying to hear what they were saying. Nathan looked up, and their eyes met.

"You know a lot about bears," Nathan said. "Where'd you say you were from?"

"I didn't. And I don't know a whole lot," Scarlett explained. "I've seen a few and done more than my fair share of reading. But again, most of my knowledge on the subject isn't practical."

"You happen to have that book?" Nathan asked.

"I do, actually." Scarlett stepped toward the bookshelf, faltering as Nathan's hand fell to a knife at his hip. She kept moving, pretending she hadn't noticed the agitated movement. Scarlett bent, carefully pulling the worn book from the shelf while still keeping an eye on Nathan. His muscles were tense, his knees bent.

Ready to spring into action. Something spooked those three.

Scarlett's gaze shifted to the hunters by the door.

What could it be? Did they find bear tracks outside?

"May I see the book?" Nathan asked.

Scarlett approached him slowly, trying to appear casual, as she held the book out. Nathan took the *Gray Tome* and began flipping through it.

"Page ninety-six, I believe," Scarlett provided.

Nathan looked up, eyebrows raising. "You know the page number?"

"Not a lot to do up here. As you said, we're a long way from civilization."

"Hmm." Nathan's raised eyebrows narrowed. He held the book up nearly level with his face, watching her while rifling through the pages.

Something's amiss.

Finally, Nathan stopped flipping the pages and cocked his head to the side, squinting.

"It's pretty close. But what I saw was leaner." Nathan handed the open book to Raylor.

"Perhaps the artist took some liberties?" Raylor suggested.

"It could be a different species or genus as well," Scarlett provided.

"I'm not sure what a genus is. Are you saying not all bears look alike?" Raylor asked.

"Yes, sorry, old habits die hard," Scarlett said.

"So, where do we find it?" Nathan asked.

"I'm not sure. But if it decided that your people were its food source, I doubt it would be all the way up here. Predators usually stay close to where they hunt."

There was a long pause. Nathan stared her down, jaw tightening.

"Is everything all right?" Raylor asked.

"I'm done with the games. Where is it?" Nathan growled.

"Excuse me?" Scarlett asked.

"I said, where is it!"

Scarlett took a step back. "What are you talking about?"

"Where did the panther in your backyard come from?" Nathan demanded.

The panther? What does this have to do with the bear?

Scarlett just stood there, trying to puzzle it out.

Where did that thing come from? Did I hunt it? Or did I find it?

A pressure built behind Scarlett's eyes. She blinked, trying to clear it, but it was no use. She took a deep breath, staring at the floor as she tried to stop thinking about the cat.

Need to focus on right now.

Scarlett looked up. All twelve hunters watched her, clearly waiting for an answer.

"I found it up on the plateau near my cabin," Scarlett said, though she wasn't entirely sure that was accurate. She tried to remember again, but the pain in her head returned, and her stomach churned in protest.

When was the last time I ate? she wondered.

Nathan's unreasonable questions were upsetting her. That was all.

An empty stomach makes nearly every species more aggressive.

Scarlett tried to shake the feeling away.

"When?" Nathan demanded.

When did I find it? Yesterday? The day before?

Scarlett tried to remember, but the details were foggy. It had been lying in the dirt somewhere, or had it been snow? She tried to recreate the scene in her mind but found she couldn't. Scarlett's growing migraine pulsed with a tenacious insistence, and she decided any answer would do.

"Uh...the day before yesterday. I think." Scarlett squinted, pinching the bridge of her nose.

"You *think*? Cut the shit! Where's the bear?" Nathan might as well be yelling now. Fear joined the nausea.

"What are you implying?" Scarlett asked through clenched teeth. She was starting to regret not lacing their tea.

"I imply nothing. I am stating that you know where it is." Nathan took a step toward her. His upper lip crept into a snarl as his fists clenched.

Two of the telltale signs of violence.

Raylor stepped between them. "Nathan, are you saying there's a jungle cat in the backyard?"

"I am. And she knows it. She's hiding Elrontis!"

"What? What is an...El-ron-tis?" Scarlett sounded out the word.

"Don't play coy with me," Nathan accused.

"I'm not sure it is wise to say that name, Nathan," Raylor said. "I know you don't believe it has power. But the creature came down on us right after you shouted the name last night."

Murmurs of assent filled the room.

Scarlett's stomach churned audibly.

When did I kill that cat?

"Let's go out back. Maybe she can explain the panther's corpse!" Nathan pointed toward the door.

"I think that is a fair place to start. Don't you, Scarlett?" Raylor's tone was calm, but he wasn't really asking.

Scarlett did think it was a fair place to start, but something was wrong. Her head was pounding, her stomach burbled again, and she thought she might be sick.

"Y-yes, let's go," she stammered.

Maybe the snow will clear my head.

Getting the hunters back in their boots was a bit of an affair. But once they were on, the group herded Scarlett around the back of the house. They didn't quite push her, but she had no illusion of choice in the matter. She didn't even have her axe now, and they were all still armed.

At least I still have my knife.

The steel pressed against Scarlett's calf, warm and reassuring. Still, if these men and women decided she was somehow involved with this bear creature, they'd kill her.

I'm innocent, of course, but this world's seldom fair, and those with power rarely take pity on the weak.

Nathan had already clearly made up his mind, and Scarlett figured his and Raylor's judgment was about as close as she might get to a trial in this less-than-civilized part of the world.

They bustled her around the corner of her cabin and into the fenced backyard. The circle of hunters opened around the big cat, then reformed to surround her and the carcass. One of the hunters bent and wiped the new-fallen snow away from the cat's head. Scarlett glanced at her cold storage behind the woman, eyes lingering on the compost pile.

"See, its lower jaw is completely missing," the middle-aged woman stated. She was strong, lean, and spoke confidently.

"How do you explain that?" Nathan pointed toward the remains.

Silence.

How did that lower jaw come off?

It wasn't something she would have done to process the animal, and she never took anything as a trophy. Scarlett's stomach churned and burbled again, and she let out a belch. Bile and rancid meat filled her nostrils.

Disgusting. Some of the vegetables I used in the soup must've turned.

"I may have taken the lower teeth to make knives," Scarlett said, swaying.

"You may have?" Raylor asked.

"Yeah, or maybe it was like that when I found it?" Scarlett wobbled unsteadily.

Gods, my head hurts. Why am I so dizzy?

The hunters, the fence, and even the compost pile blurred in and out of focus.

"Enough! Raylor, she's far beyond giving the benefit of the doubt," Nathan said.

Heads nodded all around the circle. Scarlett turned, fell to her knees, and retched.

"Raylor, there's something wrong with her," someone said. "She's either sick or hiding something."

"I agree with Nathan," another muttered.

Scarlett stared at the yellow bile eating into the snow.

When was the last time I ate?

"You were the one that prophesied him. Shouldn't we listen?" Another hunter. *Female?*

I am ravenous. The thought came to Scarlett in a haze. Then, she was being hauled up from the snow. Her eyes met Norinspire's, then drifted back to the compost pile again. This time, he followed her gaze.

"What are you looking at?" Norinspire asked.

Why am I always staring at that thing? I never even till the little patch of ground, yet it always seems freshly turned.

"Brandon, check that refuse pile," Nathan growled, pointing toward the compost, then turned back to Scarlett. "Where is Elrontis!" Nathan shouted, grabbing her by the shoulders and shaking. The movement didn't help her upset stomach.

A young hunter snatched a shovel from the side of the cabin and hurried over to the compost.

Norinspire's grip tightened.

He's strong, Scarlett thought blearily.

Scrape. The wooden implement met loose dirt.

Suddenly, there was bile covering Norinspire's chest.

How did that happen?

Scarlett's head swam. Then she was back on all fours in the snow, the cold, wet flakes jutting between her fingers.

"Holy hells!" the kid yelled. "That's a bloody rib cage."

"And a skull," someone else chimed in.

"More than one. What in Pirel's name..."

Something pressed to Scarlett's side.

A boot?

It rolled her onto her back. Her eyes moved up the shaft of a spear as Norinspire leveled its razor-sharp point to her throat.

"Last chance, Scarlett. Tell us where to find Elrontis."

38
TANYA RINGHOLDER

"**D**avid! Put that thing away."

"What?"

"We're lying in wait here, not kicking up our feet in a bloody tavern." Tanya shook her head.

David stowed his lute with a sigh. Cross sat on his haunches, staring ahead. They huddled behind a small outcropping of trees off the main road to Norinspire. The sun was down, and the Trickster was barely a quarter full.

"I told you not to bring it," Tanya said. "We're trying to set an ambush, and you're set on twiddling your tool."

"Twiddling my tool?" David cocked an eyebrow. "Interesting choice of words."

"I'm just saying, we're trying to keep a modicum of stealth here. So, unless you can entice them to dance themselves to death, I think a bit of silence might serve us best."

"Modicum?" Cross asked.

Both she and David stopped to look at him.

"What does it mean?" Cross clarified.

"It means a little bit," Tanya explained.

"Modicum," Cross repeated, mouthing the word over and over. For a moment, there was a bit of silence.

Sweet silence.

After far too short a time, David turned, a devilish grin splitting his face.

Tanya sighed. "What?"

"You want to twiddle my tool while we wait?"

"If you aren't careful, I'll twiddle something," Tanya threatened.

"You two know I'm here, right?" Cross said.

"I don't mind an audience." David smiled.

"For fuck's sake." Tanya pinched the bridge of her nose.

333

"I'm not interested in watching," Cross muttered, staring straight ahead.

"But I'm actually quite good! You might even learn a thing or two."

Tanya scoffed.

"Just save the twiddling for back in town," Cross said. "When I'm not around, please."

"You don't like my music?" David pointed to his lute.

"Your music?" Cross asked.

"Yeah! What in the hells were you two talking about? Need to get your minds outta the slums."

"You know exactly what we were talking about," Cross told him.

"I'm a performer! I do enjoy an audience."

"Shhhhh." Tanya glared at them.

David opened his mouth for a retort, then clamped it shut as their eyes met.

Tanya pointed down the road. "Those are Lance members, but there's more than six." She pulled a looking glass from her bag and peered through it. The group walked in a tight cluster, all wearing the same garb. She counted them and came up with eight, then counted again and got nine.

"How many?" David had the good sense to whisper for once.

"Nine. I think."

"Nine's a lot," Cross said. "I liked six better."

"Yeah, me too. But if they get to Vincent, this dance is over. The OAM will put out contracts for stealing government secrets, and trust me, they pay even better than the Rocktells."

"I don't think we can take nine," David said. "We might be able to get a few arrows lodged in 'em before they're on us, but that still leaves six or seven. They'd surround us. Not good."

"Just get me up close," Cross said in a low, even tone.

"Not counting you out, big guy, but nine's a lot. Even for you."

They all sat in silent contemplation for a moment.

"New plan," Tanya said with a smile. "David, get your lute back out. You're gonna get Cross a personal introduction."

"How in the hells do you suggest I do that?" David asked.

"Put on your charm. Twiddle that tool of yours," Tanya suggested.

"I'm not sure they'd appreciate my tool..." David trailed off, looking down the road.

"No one ever does. But that's never stopped you from pulling it out and playing with it before."

Cross laughed, realized it was a little too loud, and shut his mouth.

"You aren't coming with us?" David asked.

"With nine of them? No, there's a good chance someone will recognize me."

"Damn!" David said. "Nine on two's worse than nine on three."

"I'll be there. Just get Cross in close. Go before they see you double back to the road."

"Fuck, all right. But..." David paused, searching for something clever, then gave up. "Fuck!"

The three of them broke apart. David and Cross took the small path back to the main road as Tanya crept south through the tall grass. Before long, music and laughter broke the night's silence behind her. Near the edge of the grass, Tanya stopped and looked back. David and Cross were walking along the road toward her. Her eyes flicked between the two groups.

Should meet right about here.

Carefully, Tanya unslung the bow she'd taken from one of the thugs back in Grenisport and nocked an arrow. She wasn't an expert shot but could hit the straw targets in the Lance's training range.

The bow was about the only weapon Cross hadn't taken from the dead men. He'd looked like some sort of walking armory until Tanya showed him how to hide a few knives. He was still armed to the absolute gills, but the sight of him wasn't quite so obscene on the road.

As David drew nearer, Tanya recognized the bawdy tune. It was a popular song about an innkeeper's wife who slept with nearly every man that came through their tavern. In the silly story, the innkeeper constantly chased men naked from the inn, yelling and screaming obscenities. Tanya counted the members of the Lance as she listened to the approaching melody.

Shit.

There were eleven.

Shit.

Tanya counted again and came up with the same number.

Shit.

She shook her head.

Too late to change course now.

The eleven assassins approached David and Cross, clearly unconcerned with their presence. It always paid to be cautious on the road at night, but these were trained killers, and no one would be dumb enough to try to fight them two on eleven.

No one but us, anyway.

David staggered closer to the group. "Hoy there! A ruby for a song, my good men?" He slurred the words, rocking back and forth between each foot. The song was still discernible, but the chords were fumbled.

Didn't know he could act. Maybe he's more than just a pretty face.

David wobbled, nearly pitched headfirst into the dirt, then righted himself without taking his hands from the strings.

Was that real? Maybe he's stumbling from those missing toes.

David had complained incessantly about the injury all the way to Norinspire, and Tanya had caught him stumbling even when he didn't know she was watching.

"Not sure it would be worth it," one of the men responded.

"Sounds like we're getting one for free anyway," a woman remarked.

"And it's not very impressive," another man added.

"Ah, c'mon. How about just a 'paz?" David slung the instrument across his back and pulled out a cup. He held it out, lost his footing, and stumbled into the middle of the group. They parted to get out of the way, and Cross ran forward, catching him by the shoulder before he could topple headfirst into the dirt.

"Don't mind him. He's far too deep in his cups for this lute," Cross apologized.

The surrounding Lance members laughed.

"You two should be more careful out here. Some on the road might take advantage of a situation like this."

Anytime now, Tanya thought, fingers stroking the arrow's fletching.

"You look familiar." The woman cocked her head to the side, studying David. "Do I know you from somewhere?"

"That's 'cause I'm bloody famous." David swayed, pointing lazily at her.

Tanya pulled the bowstring back.

"Oh yeah?" a man asked.

"Yeah! Most famous bard in all o' Norinspire. No, no, all of Darin!" David turned his finger skyward.

"Really? What's your name?" the woman asked.

"Keevner! Keevner the Great!" David was barely comprehensible through the slurred words.

"Never heard of you," another man said.

The woman studied David's swaying form.

"No, I know you. Aren't you that bard from Windmore?" she asked, squinting.

David stiffened.

For a terrible moment, everything was still, then everyone burst into motion.

Cross pulled a sword from a shoulder strap and brought a hand axe from behind his back. He plunged the blade into one man's throat and hacked another's knee clean through with the axe.

David hurled a dagger at the woman who'd accused him. It sank into her chest. She grunted but didn't go down.

Tanya released the arrow. It wobbled once, then hammered into a man's shoulder.

Steel sang as nine members of the Lance freed swords from scabbards.

Cross left his weapons in the men he'd downed, unslinging a massive double-bladed axe.

The quickest rogue swung at David. The blow was about to connect when Cross's axe cleaved the man in half.

Tanya nocked another arrow, pulled it back, and loosed. The point slammed into the chest of the same Lance member she'd hit before, and he went down in the blood-spattered grass.

Not who I was aiming for. Tanya dropped the bow.

David thrust a short steel into the eye of a man who was still getting his blade up. *Six left.*

Two men swung at Cross. He blocked one blow, but the other scored a cut along his bicep. He grunted, retreating. Two more swords lashed out at David. He danced away without trying to block or parry. They weren't surrounded yet, but that wouldn't last long.

The four harried Cross and David while two fanned out, working their way around the sides. They took a couple of superficial stabs, obviously meant to keep the two men at bay. David reached behind his back and hurled a dagger forward. His target sidestepped, and the blade vanished into the tall grass.

Cross lashed out with the big axe as they retreated, but the assassin pulled away from the blow. The injured woman sliced Cross's exposed forearm. The big man grunted and took another step back. Two of the Lance nearly had them surrounded. Thankfully, they hadn't had time to consider why one of their comrades had two arrows in them.

C'mon, just a little closer.

The two killers closed the circle.

One was almost at the edge of the road.

Tanya lunged from the grass, driving her short steel through the flanking thug's back with a rasp, then a squelch.

Cross screamed, tackling a man into the dirt. The injured woman and another rogue pushed in on David. That left Tanya with two as well. They came at her, swords a storm of steel. She parried two strikes, stepping back as a third cut her across the thigh.

"Ack! Fucking son of a—" David cursed somewhere as steel clashed together.

Tanya considered risking a glance, then decided against it as she was forced to parry strikes from either side. The two black-clad killers harried her, and she had no choice but to retreat. She blocked blow after blow, dodged a cut, then a blade skidded across the buckles of her coat. Both assassins were trying to flank her, and the moment they did, the fight was over.

Tanya gave ground, separating herself further from her comrades. The closer of the two thugs came on in a rush. She blocked two blows and stepped to the side as she stabbed him in the shoulder. Her sword caught on something, pulling her around as he staggered past. Tanya yanked the blade free, but it was too late. Steel whizzed through the air behind her. She spun reflexively, raising her sword.

The two blades connected, steel grinding. First, their crossguards locked together, then their eyes did the same. Tanya recognized the grizzled old man but couldn't recall his name. He snarled at her, yellow teeth bared, spittle spraying from the corners of his mouth. Tanya snarled right back, her newer muscles straining against his grizzled old ones.

I don't have time for this.

The second assassin must be up by now and right behind her before long. The shoulder wound might kill him slowly, but it wouldn't stop her from joining him. Tanya tried to headbutt the older assassin, but he leaned back, bringing his lower body closer. She kneed him in the balls, and he doubled over with a squeak.

Grass rustled as someone moved behind her.

Tanya frantically tried to untangle her sword.

Come on, come on, come on!

Tanya gave up, dropped the blade, and turned. It was too late. Steel arced down. Desperately, she reached for his hands, trying to stop the blow.

A loud hollow twang splintered the night.

The thug collapsed mid-swing.

David stood behind him, holding the neck of his crumpled lute. The wreckage of wood swayed by the strings connected to the piece in his hand. Tanya snatched the sword from the fallen killer in front of her, then turned back to the man doubled over in the dirt. He was rising, so she stepped in and put four fingers of steel through the side of his neck.

Tanya turned, surveying the killing field. Cross had the last member of the Lance bent over, one arm wrapped around his head, and was repeatedly plunging a blade into his gut. Tanya stabbed the other man who lay on the ground in front of David, then sprinted back toward Cross. The last thug's lifeless form hit the dirt before she got there.

Everyone from the Lance is dead.

Tanya looked between the three of them. They had a dozen cuts between them, but nothing life-threatening.

A bloody fucking miracle.

Tanya hadn't thought it possible, not with eleven on three, but their only real casualty appeared to be David's lute. He still just stood there, holding the instrument in a loose grip. She followed his gaze down to the pitiful, crumpled wreck.

"Lost my sword in one of those two." David pointed back toward Cross, eyes never leaving the instrument. "Cross came and helped me, and you looked like you needed a hand too...I know I did."

"Thanks," Tanya tried to keep the word soft, but it wasn't easy. Her heart was still racing, and this had been a bloody fuckin' win. Tanya glanced back. Cross was stabbing someone on the ground repeatedly.

"No problem," David responded, still staring at the tangle of strings and splintered wood.

"Wasn't that your dad's or something?" Tanya asked.

"Yeah...doesn't matter, though. Thing's busted." David took one last look at the tattered instrument, then tossed it into the tall grass. "I'd do it again in a heartbeat. It's not like I can play it anymore, anyhow. That thug recognized me. Bet she wouldn't have if I hadn't been playin' the damn thing."

"Maybe not," Tanya said, but her practical side knew David was right. Her eyes drifted back to the lute. It looked pathetic, just a mangled pile of wood and strings nestled in the weeds.

It's far beyond repair, and there are plenty of lutes in the world.

"We'll get you another one when we get to Terra," Tanya said.

"I'll hold you to that." David cracked a smile. "You hear that, Cross? Tanya owes me a lute!"

Cross grunted.

Tanya looked back. Apparently, he was done stabbing and was now pulling numerous armaments from the flesh they'd been left in. He wiped the blood from a blade and slammed it back into a sheath. He cleaned an axe on a fallen man's cloak, then a sword.

Gods, how many weapons did he use?

Tanya wasn't sure, but six was a conservative guess.

The man's an absolute butcher.

Tanya felt her shoulders relax a little.

At least he's our butcher.

"Let's pull these fellas off the road," Tanya suggested. "We don't have time to dig eleven graves, but with any luck, the lions and hyenas will take care of the rest."

Cross nodded, already moving.

"Sounds like a plan," David said, gaze shifting upward.

Tanya followed the look. The Trickster was nearly full, staring down at them with those malignant eyes. David was always looking at that damn moon. She didn't believe the Trickster held any power, but it was hard to ignore how ominous it was amid a sea of corpses and swaying grass.

Cross already had one body slung over his shoulder as David and Tanya grabbed the hands and feet of another. They lifted and carried the man toward the only little outcropping of trees in sight, then dumped him. By the time they were done hiding the dead, it was deep in the night.

Tanya stitched up their wounds and applied a salve. Cross swapped out a few weapons for ones he liked better among the dead. David searched the men and found three dozen topaz flakes, nineteen ruby chips, and one sapphire. It was nowhere near what they needed for a boat, but it would go a long way if they decided to go to Darkloom instead of Terra. The three of them scuffed the blood from the road, ripped out any grass that had been obviously soaked, then fluffed up the stalks trampled during the skirmish.

Once they were done, Tanya stepped back and surveyed their work.

All in all, it looked pretty good for eleven people in the dirt.

The three of them changed clothes and headed back to the Golden Lamb. Surprisingly, people were still eating and drinking in the common room.

They each got a meal and laughed about the absurdity of the night long after they should have been in bed. David regaled them with stories that grew grander with each flagon of ale and every booming laugh from Cross. He made several comments about their luck starting to turn, and Tanya found she couldn't help but agree.

Even if luck is a fallacy.

No one spoke of the gruesome work from just a few hours earlier.

Long after midnight, David stood, pushing his chair out with dramatic finality. He'd kept up with Cross in his cups and was thoroughly drunk. In his defense, so was Cross, and he was nearly twice David's size.

"Good night, Mystery-Hips," David said with an unsteady bow and an attempt to kiss Tanya's hand.

"Mystery-Hips?" she asked dryly, keeping the hand in her lap.

"Do you prefer Mystery-Tits?"

"How old are you again?" she asked. "Also, where in the hells did that come from?"

"Don't let her do anything I wouldn't, Cross!" David said, turning away.

"Well, that doesn't rule out much, now does it?" Tanya teased as he stumbled toward the stairs.

"Not much." David turned. "Except pissing off highly sophisticated networks of insurgents so much they want to gut you."

Cross lurched mid-gulp, trying and failing to cover his nose before ale sprayed the table.

Tanya scowled, considered mentioning David had done precisely that, then decided against it.

Don't need him running his mouth anymore than he already has.

She shook her head. At least the inn was nearly empty.

Still, not a lick of damn sense.

"At least Cross can't ask me to be subtle," Tanya said.

"Indeed!" David walked backward. "Now, if you'll excuse me, a pillow and a chamber pot are calling my name upstairs."

"Sounds like one of your songs," Cross bellowed.

"And perhaps it will be one day!" David shot back. He gave a little showman's bow to each of them, took one more step backward, then turned and tripped over a bucket. "Fucking—"

Tanya and Cross burst into laughter as he sprawled onto his face.

"Came outta nowhere," David mumbled. He pulled himself up, wobbled once, then grabbed the banister and headed upstairs.

My gods, how did I ever become attracted to that? Tanya wondered, wiping the tears from her eyes.

Cross and Tanya continued drinking and laughing deep into the night. Mostly about David. She liked him. A lot, if she was honest. He made her laugh, and he was good. Relatively speaking, anyway. Soon, Cross began to slump, nearly sliding off his seat.

"Come on, you," Tanya said, putting a shoulder under his arm.

Bloody hells, he's heavy.

With more than a little difficulty, Tanya helped Cross upstairs, got him to his room, and watched him flop onto a bed that barely fit him. She shut the door and headed to her own room, shaking her head at the night's absurdity.

Tanya stopped at David's door, raised a hand to knock, then lowered it.

It's too typical. He saves your life by breaking something dear to him, and you decide it's time for a fuck? No, not now. Normal relationships might work that way, but those seldom pan out. Plus, we've got a job to do. Best not complicate it more than I already have.

Tanya continued down the hall and unlocked her room. She quickly removed her clothes, shedding them in a heap of leather and cloth, then fell into bed. She was out almost as soon as her head touched the pillow.

39

ROLAND

R oland loved willows. The bittersweet juice of the saplings was delectable. There really wasn't anything better. Maybe Scarlett. He loved Scarlett more than willows, but it was a close thing. That wasn't saying anything bad about Scarlett, though. On the contrary, comparing one to willows was about the highest form of compliment that could be given.

A sound echoed on the wind, causing Roland's ears to twitch.

The cabin door shutting?

Scarlett, probably. She was always running about doing something. Usually something useless, truth be told. Breaking trees, pulling trees, banging metal against wood, digging dirt; it was always something. Sometimes, Scarlett did things that Roland appreciated, though. Digging in the dirt was one of them. Sometimes, when Scarlett would dig, her hands would come back up with something very tasty. Like a Carrot. A Carrot was a long, cone-shaped thing, and it was bright. Almost as bright as new snow.

Come to think of it, Carrots are far better than willows.

Roland's ears swiveled up. Voices on the wind. Slowly, he chewed the willow leaves, ears flicking.

Is that Scarlett? Maybe she has a Carrot now?

Roland sniffed the wind.

If Scarlett had a Carrot now, she'd have a Carrot once the willows were gone, and it would be just as sweet then as it was now.

Carrots are great. The best, actually.

Roland chewed at a willow.

Better than Scarlett? he wondered.

No, that was silly. Scarlett was Carrots, and Carrots were Scarlett. They were inter-changeable; you couldn't have one without the other. Roland decided if he absolutely had to choose, Scarlett was better. She'd nursed him back to health, and Roland would do anything for her.

Who knows? Maybe Scarlett will dig in the ground someday and pull out something better than a Carrot.

It was hard to imagine anything better than a Carrot, though.

Impossible, probably, but you never know with Scarlett.

She was always running around doing something silly.

Why couldn't she invent something even better than a Carrot?

Roland chewed, then swallowed. It certainly was hard to imagine something better than a Carrot. It wasn't hard to imagine Scarlett creating it, though. She could do anything.

Voices drifted through the air again.

Is that Scarlett? Roland wondered, and not for the first time.

It sounds like her.

Roland looked back at the willow. All the good parts were gone.

How long has it been since Scarlett opened the gate and let me out?

Roland turned back toward the house—a foul smell hung in the air. Something was wrong. The big bull moose sauntered back toward the cabin. He couldn't see it through the falling snow, but he knew where it was.

The voices grew louder as he approached. Sometimes, Scarlett jabbered aloud to him but never in tones like the ones he heard now. These were sharp, short...agitated. Scarlett's voice was always soothing and calm or high and playful. Nothing like these.

A blurry fence came into view, and smudge-like shapes formed a circle in the backyard. Someone was in his enclosure, and something in his blood told him they were aggressive.

Why? Not enough Carrots to go around? No, it's not possible. Scarlett has so many Carrots, and no one can be angry if they have a Carrot.

Roland couldn't even be angry while looking at a bright, scrumptious Carrot, and Scarlett was never angry while holding one.

One of the men stepped to the side, revealing someone lying in the snow.

Scarlett?

She was a bit blurry, but it was certainly her. Roland sniffed the air to make sure.

Yep. The smell confirmed it.

What are they doing to her? Are they hurting her?

Roland studied the situation for a moment.

They are hurting her.

Roland's blood was getting hot.

Scarlett threw up into the snow. She was clearly unwell, and they were hurting her.

They're worse than a pack of wolves!

Roland lowered his head and snorted. His big hoof scraped the top of the snow as mist poured from his huge nostrils.

40
GERARD STOCKWORTH

What a mess.

Gerard stood from his inspection of the last corpse. Isaac Ericson lay face down next to a chair, body twisted as if he'd been yanked to the side while falling. A knife lay on the ground near his right hand.

Someone must've pulled him by the arm as they made the incision.

Ericson had shit himself, too, but that had likely come later.

This kill is far more precise than the other three.

Isaac's assailant had clearly been unknown to him, and Gerard was willing to bet they were professional. One clean cut to the shoulder, simultaneously piercing muscle and one of the largest arteries in the body. Not only would Isaac have bled out in a matter of seconds, but he'd also have immediately lost all mobility in the arm.

"I said, don't touch that," Gerard said to the two guards who were grabbing the hands and feet of the Justiseer apprentice by the door.

"Sorry, sir. Cleanup cart's here, and the captain told us to load the bodies as soon as it arrived," the guard responded.

"Hold on for just one bloody second, then." Wooden planks creaked as Gerard crossed the shipwright's warehouse. "I swear, captains care less and less about the truth every day."

"Just maintaining the peace."

"Yeah, yeah."

Gerard dug through the clothes of the slim Justiseer initiate. He was one of two stabbed in the gut. Both men had bled out real slow—until someone cut their throats. The slight man had nothing of any use. That itself was a clue, but not a great one.

"All right, fellas, go ahead and take the evidence if you must," Gerard said.

"Sorry, sir. Orders an' all. You know how it is," the middle-aged guard apologized.

"Not really. But I understand. Not your call and all that." Gerard turned to the corpse closest to the door.

The head was almost entirely missing. Someone appeared to have bashed the skull into the wooden floorboards until there was nothing left but pulp.

Clearly not done with the same precision as Isaac, Gerard decided, crouching over the corpse. *Think I'd prefer the stab to the neck if forced to choose.*

He searched the body.

Nothing here either. Damn...

Gerard stood. A gruesome mop of hair and skin lay halfway between the chair and the man whose skull had been juiced like some sort of fruit. Gerard watched his feet, stepping around the pools of blood and scalp as he moved to the last corpse. He wanted to preserve the evidence, but more importantly, he didn't want to lose his footing.

Slippery business, scalps.

Thump. Axles squeaked as the first body hit the wagon's wooden deck. The two guards laughed as they sauntered back into the shop.

"Did you see Jimmy with the barmaid last night?" one asked.

Gerard checked the third man over. His throat was slit, but someone also put more than three hands of steel through his abdomen.

"Yeah," the other guard said with a laugh. "Poor kid had no idea what to do!"

There was one slight difference between the kills. The last man had been stabbed in the gut. Here, someone had rammed a blade straight through two of the lower ribs.

Now, that takes some force. Then again, so does braining a man on a wooden floor in just a few blows.

"I know! The barmaid was all over him, sitting on his lap, calling him honey. Nearly laughed my ass off."

No clues on this kid either.

Gerard turned back to Isaac, walking over to the dead Justiseer.

Someone grunted from the other side of the shipwright.

"This one's bloody heavy for not havin' a head," one guard groaned.

Isaac wasn't a bad fellow, Gerard reflected.

He'd only met the man in passing, but the hunters' trade was a tight-knit community. Word was the Justiseer had been a little on the blunt side but got results. Apparently, he liked to pick up strays down on their luck and teach them the craft too.

I'd heard Isaac was changing lives for the better.

Gerard looked from one stiff to the next.

Not these three, though.

Another thump as the guards loaded the second corpse onto the wooden wagon.

Gerard reached down and rifled through Isaac's coat. He'd clearly been searched as well.

"Fucking hells, Sven! You got brains all over my bloody coat."

"Casualties of the trade!" someone yelled back with a laugh.

Isaac had nothing of use on him.

There must be something around here.

Gerard stood and walked over to the chair. Cut ropes lay around each leg and dangled from each arm. Two distinct blood spatters colored the floor near the chair's left leg, and a toe lay near one of the spray marks.

"Did you see Jimmy's face? Basically gettin' a lap dance, and he had no bloody clue how to react. He just sat there, slowly blushin' redder and redder. I swear, his face was more flush than a freshly spanked bottom!"

Where's the other one? Gerard wondered as he looked around. He spotted it, sitting nearly two spans away on the floor. *How in the hells did you get over there?*

"I know! Damn funny shit. That girl wasn't even half ugly, eh?"

Gerard approached the toe, picked it up, and examined it. Black scorch marks lined it. *Singed? Why? How?* He glanced around the room and spotted a brazier by a workbench. Gerard stood and approached it.

There were more groans and heavy footfalls as the guards lifted the third corpse and carried it toward the front of the room.

Flesh and gristle dotted a set of tongs lying near the brazier. Gerard hovered his hand over the ashes. A slight warmth still radiated from them.

Someone was cooking last night. Any significance?

Clearly, the Justiseer and his unlucky apprentices had been using fire to ply information.

But why'd they need the information? And why did they toast the toe...

"I'd pay good money to see it again! That's all I'm saying."

Gerard grabbed the tongs and stirred the brazier. Wispy ash fluttered atop a more solid bed of coals.

Something light and feathery above thicker fuel. Paper? But who burned it, and why?

Gerard looked around the room, then licked his finger and held it up.

"Well, maybe you can. Might be high time we all chip in and get Jimmy a proper woman!" The two guards laughed together.

Wind kissed Gerard's fingertip.

Too much air, even for a drafty warehouse.

Gerard glanced up and spotted an open skylight.

Now, that's odd. Let's see if the wind saved any evidence.

Gerard reached down and scooped up some of the light, silky ash from the top of the brazier, then tossed it in the air and watched as it drifted toward the workbench. He followed it, looking high and low. There, wedged between the wall and the head of a hanging mallet, was a small scrap of singed paper. He took it tenderly between thumb and forefinger and pulled it free. Scorch marks surrounded four letters:

—eart.

"I think you might be right. Perhaps we take him down to the Quack for a roll and a romp?" The two guards laughed uproariously again as they bent to pick up Isaac.

Gerard pulled out his contracts and matched the lettering on the scrap to David's paperwork.

Trueheart! Gotcha.

"They have boys at the Quack?" Gerard asked, striding past the two guards.

"Boys! What in the hells are you implying?" the stockier guard asked indignantly.

"I think he figures you bugger boys, Sven!" the skinny one said with a laugh.

"Not for you," Gerard explained. "For Johnny. Or Jay. Or whatever in the thirty-seven hells his name was."

"Jimmy?" Sven asked.

"Aye, that's the one," Gerard said.

"What about him?" Skinny asked.

"He likes boys. So, if you mean to buy him something, make it a fellow, eh? Or better yet, just leave the kid alone." Gerard continued to the door.

Silence.

"You think—" the bigger guard started.

"Oh!" Gerard snapped his fingers. "I nearly forgot. Any other crimes of note last night?"

"Uhhh."

Clearly, the idea of a comrade swinging to the left has addled their brains a bit.

"Horse thievin'," Skinny provided.

"How many?" Gerard asked.

"Just one."

"Which stable?"

"The Singing Shield."

"Where?"

"West side of town, near the gate. Can't miss it."

"Thanks," Gerard said with a nod, then opened the door to leave.

"Wait! How'd you know that 'bout Jimmy?" the bigger guard asked.

"I don't. Just a hunch. Take it easy on him, eh, boys? If I'm right, he's got it hard enough right now." Gerard walked out, breathing in the fresh sea air.

There's not a much worse mix of smells than salt water, blood, tar, and shit.

The sunlight warmed Gerard's face as he wove through the city toward the west gate. He found the Singing Shield Inn and popped into the stables for a quick chat with the girl tending horses.

The stable girl stood outside, shoveling piles of manure into a bucket.

"Fun job," Gerard said, walking up.

"At least it's not pigs," the girl grunted.

Gerard laughed. "Things could always be worse."

"Not much worse than pigs," she said with a shake of her head.

Gerard considered pursuing the question, then decided against it. "Heard you had a spot of equiecy last night."

"You mean horse thievin'?"

"Yeah."

"Well, ain't that a fancy word."

"I suppose it is. Can you tell me about it?"

"You're a little late. Guards came by hours ago."

"I'm not with the guards." Gerard pulled out his necklace and let it dangle.

The girl squinted at it. "What in the hells is that supposed to be?"

"Justiseer."

"Oh," the girl looked up without halting her shoveling. "Thought you were offering me a bribe."

A long silence stretched out between them.

"Would it help?"

She shrugged. "Wouldn't hurt."

Gerard stepped forward and drew out two topaz.

The girl's eyebrows rose skeptically.

Little extortionist.

He pulled out three more, placing the five flakes in her outstretched palm.

"Boris was gone this morning," she said, pocketing the stone.

At least she knows his name, though I'm not sure how helpful that is.

"Got a description?"

"Big, even-tempered, brown-and-white gelding." The girl finally smiled. "He's a sweetheart."

"That's it?"

"Yeah, no one saw anything."

"Seriously?"

"I did happen to hear the guards talking, though."

Gerard waited for her to go on.

She didn't.

Slowly, the girl's empty hand rose again.

With a sigh, Gerard reached back into his pouch and pulled out two more flakes. The girl's eyebrows started to rise again—

"This is it now, you plucky little swindler."

"Can't blame a girl for trying, don't want to be scraping pig shit forever." She smiled again, taking the stone. "The guards mentioned three people were spotted riding out of the west gate toward Norinspire late last night."

"That's all?" Gerard asked, eyeing the girl's hands to make sure they stayed by her side.

"Yep," she said with a shrug.

It wasn't a lot to go on, but it was a description and a direction.

"Good luck with the pig shit," Gerard said, turning.

"Thanks, but these are horses."

I know what they are, you cocky little shit.

Gerard smiled. Arabella's face filled his mind for a moment. She'd been the same, always looking for an angle.

At the city gates, Gerard stopped and checked the bounty board. His two marks were on there, but the posters stated David and Tanya were wanted for the murder of Robert Rocktell.

So it's official. Why such a high price on them before, though?

Gerard frowned.

Maybe the Rocktells were trying to keep it quiet? If so, what changed?

One more piece of the puzzle, but one that didn't quite fit the whole.

Gerard found himself whistling a jaunty tune as he rode out of town. It was just nonsensical noise, but Vigilant always seemed to enjoy it.

it

"We're close to our quarry, old boy," Gerard said aloud. "They'll either be riding fast, or they'll head off the road and try to cover their tracks. If we try to match their pace, we risk losing 'em on a double back. If we go slow, they get farther ahead."

Silence.

"What do you think? Speed? Or certainty?"

Vigilant snorted.

"Yeah, I think so too. It's too early to go charging headlong into danger. These two have proven a bit sloppy and more than a bit dangerous. Let's see if they make another mistake."

Gerard sat back and let Vigilant set the pace at a nice, even trot.

41
TANYA RINGHOLDER

L ight streamed into the little room, and Tanya let out a groan.

Why was I excited about the glass windows yesterday?

Tanya shut her eyes and rolled over, dragging a pillow over her head. Blocking out the light almost worked until her head began to throb. The pounding had only increased a few minutes later, so she rolled out of bed, rubbing her temples. She dressed, shouldered her pack, and headed downstairs.

The common room was bustling with activity. Servers weaved around tables as patrons called for breakfast and chatted. David sat at the table in the corner of the room, close to a woman playing a flute. His feet were propped up on the beautiful hardwood slab, and he nodded back and forth to the horribly high-pitched notes she was producing. Tanya sighed and worked her way into the bustle. She passed merchants, a group of clearly successful artisans, and someone who might've even been nobility. David grinned up as she pulled out a chair.

"Morning!" he said with far too much cheer.

"It's too early for your shit."

"What?"

"My head hurts. I need something in my stomach. Gods, did you have to pick the spot right next to the flute?"

"Music lover." David smiled apologetically.

A barmaid scooped up David's plate and hustled away.

"Can I get some breakfast and an ale?" Tanya called after her.

"Of course, dear," she said, turning back.

"And another coffee."

"Coffee, breakfast, and an ale coming up."

"Double that, and add another breakfast, please," Cross said, thumping into an empty chair.

"Three breakfasts, two coffees, and two ales. That right?"

"Yeah, but let's make it three coffees," Tanya added.

"Thanks, Cross, but I already had breakfast," David said.

"Those two are for me," Cross clarified.

The server eyed them with a touch of bewilderment.

"You had it right," Tanya explained. "Unless shutting up that flutist is on the menu."

"Three breakfasts, three coffees, and two ales?" the server asked, cocking an eyebrow. "Sorry, I don't control the music. If I did, we'd get Danton in here." She smiled.

"Who's Danton?" David asked.

"Oh, he's..." The server paused, staring off toward the bar. "Mmmm, well. His face looks like it belongs on a ship's bow, and he plays the lute. Anyways, let me go put your order in," she said and walked away.

"You hear that? *She* likes a man who twiddles his tool." David waggled his eyebrows.

"Yeah, too bad you broke yours, huh," Cross said.

"Yeah, too bad." David sighed, clearly appreciating the barmaid's backside as much as lamenting the loss of the instrument.

"Gods, do you men ever even *try* to hide your ogling?" Tanya asked.

"Hey, don't lump me in with that. I wasn't looking," Cross said defensively.

"I'm not hurting anyone. Just admiring. She has a nice bum." David shot Tanya a wicked smile.

"She is pretty, I guess," Cross agreed.

"So you *were* looking! Both of you," Tanya accused.

"I looked, but I didn't...og-ley? What did you call it?" Cross asked.

"How do you know you didn't if you can't even say it?" Tanya pinched the bridge of her nose. "Gods, why does it feel like there's a team of horses galloping around in my skull?"

"'Cause I saw David, and I didn't do that! So, if he was googling, then I didn't," Cross stated, weaving meaty forearms across his chest.

"Sound logic," David said, maintaining eye contact with Tanya as he shot a finger in Cross's direction.

"Besides, I'm allowed to say someone's pretty without being attracted to them. You and David are pretty. Doesn't mean I'm googley for you."

"Thanks, buddy," David said, bobbing his head back and forth in time with the tune. "Maybe we unpack that later, though, eh?"

"So, what's your excuse, then?" Tanya rounded on the smug bard with a scowl.

"We're already fast friends," David said. "She wouldn't mind."

"So, you don't mind if I point it out to her when she comes back?" Tanya asked.

"No, not at all! If jealousy demands you do something irrational and uncouth, well, knock yourself out, I suppose," David said.

"Uncouth?" Tanya's eyebrows rose. "Maybe. But you've lost your bloody mind if you think I'm jealous."

Gods, he's infuriating.

David shrugged.

"Uncouth?" Cross asked.

"It means crass," David explained.

Cross cocked an eyebrow at him.

"Ummm." David scratched his chin.

"Uncivilized or barbaric," Tanya provided.

"Why do we have so many words that mean the same thing?" Cross asked.

"Because of bards like him." Tanya pointed in David's direction.

"I don't make up the words. I just use the words," David said, still swaying with the tune of the flute.

"I like them, even if they *are* a little silly." Cross looked around the room, mouthing his two new words.

"Big man likes big words," David said, an enormous grin plastered to his face.

Steaming hot plates slid across the wood, and tankards thumped down in the center of the table. The server removed three little saucers and cups from the top of the two ales and set them down with a click.

"Anything else I can get for you three?" she asked, giving David a wink.

Tanya opened her mouth to ask if the server minded David staring at her ass, then decided better of it.

"No, I think we're good," David said. "Thank you, dear."

"You're welcome, cutie," she responded with a warm smile, then turned. Tanya watched the two men as the barmaid walked away. David's eyes followed her again, but Cross was already shoveling food into his mouth despite the steam wafting from it.

"I think she likes you," Cross said between mouthfuls. "You might not even need your lute."

"Yeah. You might be right." David sighed. "But, so many bums, so little time."

Tanya scoffed. "You're repulsive."

"You wound me!" David clutched a hand over his heart dramatically. "Eat up. We gotta head to the ship soon." He slid the second plate of eggs, bacon, and toast to Cross.

"Repulsive?" Cross asked.

"Gross, buddy. It means gross," David clarified. "But she doesn't mean it. She's just tired of unwanted attention." David flashed Tanya a wicked smile.

Cross tore into a piece of bacon, nodding as he muttered the new word between bites.

"I can't deal with you before breakfast," Tanya said, grabbing her fork.

For a short while, she and Cross enjoyed their meal while David enjoyed the music. Cross ate one whole plate, downed the ale in one pull, then moved on to the second breakfast. Tanya ate half of hers and had a few swigs of ale before switching to the coffee. David simply sat, happily tapping his knee and listening to the flutist. Tanya ate a bit more, then pushed her plate aside.

"Done with that?" Cross asked.

"Yeah." Tanya leaned back.

Cross pulled the plate close, then practically inhaled the rest.

Gods, he can eat.

"Ready?" Tanya asked.

"Yep," Cross said with a belch.

David looked remorsefully at the flutist, then around at the rest of the bar. He let out a long sigh and nodded. "Let's go."

They checked on their tab with the innkeep, but the etched stone from the OAM apparently covered everything, so they headed out. The Golden Lamb was in the most affluent part of town, and they would need to travel through the Severance Quarter to get to the wharf. They could go around, but it would add hours to the trip, and a boat was waiting on them.

"Best stow anything valuable in your bag," Tanya said as they approached the Severance Quarter. David stopped and put all their money in his bag, and Cross considered stowing some weapons, then decided against it.

Walking through the neighborhood she grew up in was odd. The streets felt cramped, and buildings that once loomed over the quarter now seemed short. Still, Norinspire had clearly grown, and the sprawling metropolis stretched far beyond what she remembered.

So much smaller, yet the city on the whole is much larger.

As Tanya took in the sights, orphans crept from the alleyways, slowly surrounding them.

"Are you new to the city, ma'am?" a little girl asked.

"Not new, just back," Tanya said with a smile.

"You're sooo pretty!"

A little hand entered one of Tanya's pockets.

"And so are you! But your friend should learn to lighten up his touch," she scolded without dropping the smile.

The little blond girl returned her smile nervously, then shrugged.

Some things never change.

Tanya looked back at the dirty little urchin trying to fleece her. His expression shifted from concentration to the abashed apology only youth could produce as he pulled the hand from her pocket. They continued on, and the little circle of urchins walked with them.

Three little boys eyeballed Cross, trying to decide if getting close was worth the risk. Three more children surrounded David, asking about his trade.

"How'd you get so big, mister?" a little boy finally asked.

"Dunno. Ate lots of food, I guess," Cross said.

"Didn't you get full?" another little boy asked as he picked his nose.

"Is the meal over when you're full?" Cross asked.

"Sometimes. That is, when there's a meal at all," a little girl commented.

Cross frowned, dug through his pockets, and came up empty-handed. "Guess I don't have much to help with that." His frown deepened. "Wait!" He pulled a short sword from a sheath and knelt, holding the weapon out hilt first. "Here. This should buy you each a few meals."

The girl jumped back. Her eyebrows briefly narrowed, then she tentatively stepped forward and took hold of the grip. Once she had both hands on it, Cross let go. The tip hit the ground with a clang.

The little girl wrestled with the little blade and got it up on one little shoulder, then smiled as big as the Trickster.

"We don't even need to sell it! We can just take what we want now!" one of the boys yelled.

"Now look what you've done," Tanya said but couldn't keep the smile from her lips. The children ran circles around them, cheering and whooping as the little girl held up the wobbling sword for all to see.

It wasn't long before the little girl was riding on Cross's shoulders, and the rest of the children knew half a dozen dirty songs from David. They were still singing one about a farmer in love with a pig when they got to the edge of the Severance Quarter, and it was time to say goodbye. Cross reminded the young girl not to put the pointy end of the sword into anyone unless they tried to hurt her, David corrected one last lyric, and Tanya drew out a topaz flake for each of the children from her bag.

Near the edge of the Quarter, where the Severance met the docks, Tanya stopped in front of a dilapidated, burned-out house. Sunlight streamed through the collapsed roof, revealing scorched brick walls.

Amazing, no one's taken the time to clear the rubble and make it their own.

Tanya's hand moved subconsciously to the back of her neck as she stared through the charred frame. A stain marked the sidewall, but this one wasn't made from soot or fire.

Suddenly, she was back in that kitchen. Twenty-some odd years ago.

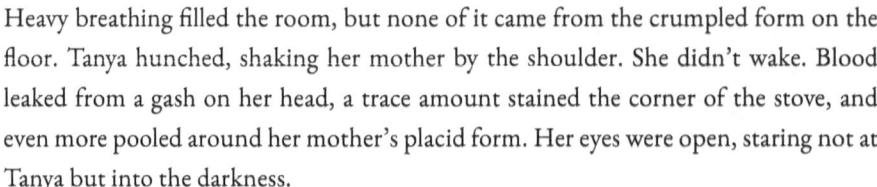

Heavy breathing filled the room, but none of it came from the crumpled form on the floor. Tanya hunched, shaking her mother by the shoulder. She didn't wake. Blood leaked from a gash on her head, a trace amount stained the corner of the stove, and even more pooled around her mother's placid form. Her eyes were open, staring not at Tanya but into the darkness.

She's dead. Even at six, Tanya knew that.

Quivering, Tanya stood, face scrunching as her hand found the only knife they could afford. The hilt was smooth, worn by many hands over many years. She looked at Weber, jaw tightening as she forced back a sob. He slumped against the wall, breathing even.

Not a care in the world.

A bottle of grain alcohol lay on its side near his hand, a puddle soaking into the floorboards. The stench of it...no, the stench of *him* made her sick. Blood marked the corner of the bottle.

Tanya had heard them shouting; then she'd heard them stop.

No more shouting now.

She stumbled forward, plunging the knife into Weber's gut with a scream. His eyes fluttered open, and suddenly, his screams joined hers. Blood bubbled over her little hands, covering them in burgundy.

Never mind, no more shouting soon.

She pulled the knife free with another cry and plunged it back in.

Weber screamed again.

Roaring with all the fury her little lungs could muster, Tanya pulled the knife out and sank it in for the third time.

Movement flashed at the edge of her vision, then Weber's hand connected with her temple. Her feet left the floor, her back slammed into something, then she slumped. Tanya tried to get up, but the floorboards moved and shifted beneath her as the whole world lurched.

Thump. Thump—thump. Leather hit unevenly on the wooden floorboards.

Tanya rolled over. Weber staggered forward, form blurring as wisps of white danced through her eyes. She glanced at the knife lying near the puddle of alcohol.

I'll have to get through him to reach it.

He took two more steps, wobbled, then collapsed in a heap. She scrambled over to the knife, clutching it as her whole body shook. Weber's uneven breaths stilled. The knife fell from her grip, clattering to the floorboard. Tanya stared down at it. Slowly, her quivering, blood-soaked hands came into focus. She dropped to the floor, chest heaving, as she curled into a ball and shook.

Now I'm entirely alone. The realization hit her harder than Weber ever had.

Tanya cried for what seemed like forever.

She watched her mother's lifeless eyes, willing them to move. She watched her own blood-soaked hands, trying to still their shaking. She watched the floorboards as the red glow of the Trickster slowly shifted to the white light of morning.

Eventually, Tanya stood and walked over to the stove, stoking it just the way Mother taught her. She opened the metal door, heaped the remaining logs on the floor, and gathered the grain alcohol. She wiped most of the blood from her hands, then poured the rest on the logs.

Tanya's eyes met her mother's one last time. They were as lifeless now as they'd been all night. She looked away, focusing on Weber, and felt her quivering lip curl into a snarl.

Hands unwavering, she lit the bonfire.

"Everything all right?" David asked, pulling her from the memory.

Tanya looked from him to her fingernails. The blood was still there, gathered in the cuticles. She'd scrubbed it away so many times since that day, but the red stains never really came off. Not completely.

The first time's always the hardest.

359

Tanya wasn't sure where she first heard the words, but they'd proven true.

"Yeah. Just a shame, really." Tanya's eyes lingered on the stain.

"A shame?" Cross asked.

"Yeah, all those homeless children, yet buildings like this one remain vacant." Tanya sighed. "No one in the city ever takes the time to clean things up and make 'em right."

"How do you know it's been empty for a long time?" David asked.

"Just a guess," Tanya lied, then turned from the house and headed into the Waterfront District.

Once she was facing the other direction, Tanya wiped a single tear from her cheek. She didn't much care if the house was abandoned, but she didn't want anyone else rooting around in her past any more than she wanted to do so herself.

Best let devils lie dormant.

The docks of Norinspire sprawled along the Savage Channel, but most folk just called it the Channel. The quarter-mile-wide river skirted the capital's western edge and served as both passage to the sea and freshwater supply for the city.

The skies were clear, and the sun was out. The smell of fish guts, fresh tar, and barnacles filled the air. Sailors bustled about yelling as they lugged cargo along the docks. After nearly twenty minutes, Tanya spotted *WARDEN* painted in bold, unadorned letters across a ship's hull.

"A bit of an ominous name for a boat hauling three fugitives," Tanya muttered.

Cross nodded, and for once, David had the good sense not to burst into song about the situation.

The boat was clearly designed for the sea, with rails standing over four spans above the dock. Tanya hadn't spent any time on the ocean but knew seafaring vessels needed the extra height and hull to withstand extreme weather and dock at low tide. The tides didn't affect the Channel very much, but a true port would have accommodations to deal with the six-span rise and fall of the ocean from a stationary wooden dock.

Big boat for three of us.

Cross stepped around her and headed up the gangplank. She followed, slatted planks creaking as David stepped on behind her. Tanya thought she felt his eyes on her momentarily, but when she glanced back, he was looking up toward the quarterdeck.

Just paranoid.

Truthfully, Tanya didn't mind David looking, but that was beside the point. Just because he had a pretty face didn't mean he could *googley* whoever he wanted. Tanya shook her head, smiling again at the mispronunciation.

"Hoy," someone called out. "What's your business, mate? This is a private vessel."

"A pirate vessel?" Cross bellowed back.

"No. Pri-vate vess-el!" the sailor yelled.

"We're here on OAM business!" Tanya interrupted.

A head poked over the side rail, studying them.

"Aye, sorry, miss," the sailor lowered his voice. "You just don't look like typical OAM passengers. Come aboard, and I'll get the captain." The man's head disappeared as he stepped away from the railing.

Once they were all up on deck, Tanya looked around. The ship was large, with three masts, and could likely carry a hundred people in relative comfort. Ballistae lined the boat's sides, mounted on pedestals that could be swiveled and aimed in battle.

The Warden must be an old battleship left over from the War of Iron and Blood, Tanya decided. There were probably a lot of ships like this one when the nations of Darin and Terra fought, but most were likely decommissioned long ago.

Odd that this one hasn't been. Maybe it hunts down pirates when it's not fulfilling OAM contracts?

A tall man emerged from the cabin near the back of the boat and approached them. He was wiry, with gray hair pulled back in a short tail and sleeves rolled to the elbow. His clothes were made of fine material but cut and tailored practically, allowing for efficient movement.

"Captain Caldwell, at your service," the man said, offering his hand.

"Valerie," Tanya lied, shaking the proffered hand.

The captain looked down at their clasped hands and seemed to consider. He tightened his grip slightly, almost as if he initially thought he might break her, then decided better.

"Ashley," David said as Caldwell turned to him.

"Excuse me?" the captain asked, and Tanya had to force back a snicker.

"Yeah, very unkind parents," David said, shooting Tanya a contemptuous side-eye.

"Indeed," Caldwell said, turning to Cross.

"Cross. Err...I mean Kole," Cross said, taking the captain's hand. Caldwell winced, glancing down at the big man's grip. The captain's eyes widened for an instant, then returned to still water. Cross looked down and loosened his grip, apologizing as their hands parted.

Gods, David's right. Subterfuge is really not that man's strong suit.

"Is it Cross or Kole?" Caldwell asked, flexing his hand.

"Kole," Cross repeated. "Cross is my last name."

"Well, good to meet you, Kole Cross. Do you have the pass?" he asked. Tanya produced the stone. Captain Caldwell took it, pulled out a jeweler's loupe, and inspected the symbol. "Everything appears to be in order."

Tanya gave him half a smile.

"When do you think the rest of your party will arrive?" Caldwell asked.

There was a short pause.

"Oh, they won't be joining us," Tanya said. "They ran into some trouble on the road."

"Are we to sail with only the three of you, then?" Caldwell's eyebrows rose slightly.

"Yes," David said. "Unfortunately, there's an urgency to our mission, as I'm sure you've been told."

"Indeed." The captain looked between them, considering something. "I'll have my midshipman show you to your quarters. Seward!" The captain's voice boomed across the deck. A young woman perked up and hustled over.

"Oh, and one more thing," Caldwell began. "Please make yourself at home on our ship. We're a contract vessel that works almost exclusively with the Council of Darin and the OAM. We're not slavers or pirates, and we have nothing to hide. However, please stay out of the crew's way while we are at sail. They have a job to do, and they need to move quickly. Finally, welcome aboard. Any questions?"

Tanya looked at her comrades. Cross stared at the captain, eyes slightly narrowed, and David was smiling at the approaching woman. Tanya shook her head.

"Then I'm afraid I must excuse myself. Much to do to get underway. You're in good hands with Seward." With that, the captain turned on a heel and strode back toward the aft of the ship, yelling orders to his officers.

"Odd he mentioned not being a slaver," Cross muttered, eyes following the captain.

"You screwed up your name, then he saw your brand," Tanya whispered. "He was trying to put you at ease. We'll talk it through later."

Cross's brow furrowed, but he didn't say anything else.

"Seward, at your service," the young woman said with a salute. She was straight-backed, with a serious face, and was dressed in the same formal wear as the rest of the officers.

Tanya liked her immediately.

"Hello, Seward. Pleasure to meet you," Tanya said.

"You as well, ma'am. May I show you to your quarters?" Seward asked.

"Yep." Tanya nodded. "But you can drop the ma'ams and sirs."

The girl smiled in a way that said, *we'll see about that*, then led them toward the bulkhead. Their quarters were located directly under the captain's cabin. Each contained a personal hammock and a trunk bolted to the floor. Tanya knew private quarters on a ship were usually held for important or honored guests, but this ship was quite large and apparently had been chartered to ferry just the three of them. Seward showed them the mess hall, then to her quarters in case they had any questions, and finally, to the privy.

"You may be needing this once we hit the open ocean," she warned, pointing to a hole off the stern of the ship.

"I've spent a little time on the water," David said with a smile.

"I'm sure you'll be fine, then." Seward returned the smile, but Tanya was positive the girl didn't mean the words.

The following two weeks were a nice reprieve: Tanya, Cross, and David played cards, enjoyed the scenery, and got to know the crew. Tanya borrowed a book from the captain and started teaching Cross how to read. On the fifth day, Seward offered them her croix set, and Tanya taught Cross and David the game's rules. David insisted he already knew how to play, but Tanya wasn't so sure after their first match. She trounced him three more times before he finally gave up and decided to watch her and Cross battle it out.

After that, David pretended not to be interested in the game but always found an excuse to hang around while they went to war. Tanya caught him watching as pieces moved across the board more than once and teased him for not simply losing gracefully. Cross was even worse than David at the game, at least at first. However, he was voracious in his appetite for it and turned out to be a quick study. It wasn't long before she had to try to best him, and less than a week before he won his first match.

They all played silly games and laughed together during those first two weeks, but mostly, they finally got some rest. New wounds began to fuse together, and old, tired ones finally got a chance to finish healing.

When they weren't playing croix, David and Cross spent time with the crew. They listened to stories of tavern brawls, drowned men being brought back to life, and other tall tales of the sea. David was clearly using the stories as song material, and Cross ate them up as if they were facts that might someday save his life.

As their journey continued, Tanya became increasingly curious about how the vessel would sail upriver. It turned out it didn't. The crew would push oars from the hull when they were going against the current and pull them in when they went downriver. They would use the wind when it was at their backs, and they would reef the sails when it wasn't.

Sometimes, their travel was slow, and other times, they sped along at a quick pace. Always, they continued west, toward the coast of Darin.

They sailed through the lakes surrounding Ardendale, and even entered a canal carved from the rock. The crew happily hooked up to a team of oxen, which pulled the vessel for a day.

As the *Warden* snaked across Darin, Tanya found herself wishing David still had his lute. He pined for it often and with very little subtlety. One night, she crept into his room, waking him from a deep sleep. They lay together for hours afterward, but Tanya slipped away before sunrise. They were all in good spirits for the next few days.

Until they hit the open ocean.

It turned out Seward was right. The waves and swell of the tide made all three of them sick, and they spent the next two days puking over the rails or in the privy. More than once, Seward explained the ocean was relatively calm and the feeling would pass. On the third day, they all started to feel slightly better. That evening, the captain turned them away from shore, and they began to follow a colorful wall of coral into deep water.

"Why do we follow the reef?" Tanya asked Seward the next day. "Why not head straight for the island?"

"Well, sailors are a superstitious lot. They fear the open ocean on the edge of the world," Seward explained as her eyes fixed on the horizon.

"Why's that?" Tanya asked.

"There are stories...things in the depths."

"Like?"

"Things that would make this ship look like a barrel of apples bobbing in the waves."

"But nothing real, right?"

"To be honest, I'm not rightly sure, ma'am," Seward said. "But I'd say it's nothing substantiated. Just men muttering and dockside tavern tales from sailors deep in their cups."

"Well, that doesn't seem like much evidence."

Seward shrugged. "It's not."

"So why not head straight for the island?" Tanya asked again.

"Well, following the coastline comes with practical benefits as well. It keeps us close enough to shore in case we need to seek an emergency port in a storm. It also allows us to gather supplies or even cut down a tree and fashion a new mast in a pinch."

"Well, that makes sense. So why follow the reef?"

"The reef serves two purposes, ma'am."

"Like what?"

"It's pretty hard to get lost while following the reef," Seward explained.

"And reason number two?" Tanya asked.

"It keeps the sailors happy. Seeing something besides black, inky depths is good for the crew's spirits. Bad morale can sink a ship as easily as a storm or a ship full of cutthroats," Seward said, almost as if she'd rehearsed it.

"Sounds like pretty good reasons to me," Tanya said. "How long have you been a midshipman? That is the correct term, right?"

"Five years, and it is, ma'am. I know it's midship-*man*," Seward explained, "but it's the same term for us gals. Probably just because there aren't too many of us on the open sea. Not sure why. I love it out here. It's so beautiful."

"It sure is that. Though, I'm not sure I could handle that sickness for the first few days of each voyage," Tanya said with a smile.

Seward smiled right back, then laughed. "You get used to it. I haven't been swell sick for years now."

"Is the water this shallow in the Divide too?" Tanya asked, pointing at the reef below. *We'll be crossing that soon, hopefully.*

"Yeah. The Divide is fairly shallow in most parts. Enough that sailors aren't concerned with creatures of the deep. But it comes with its own set of difficulties."

"Like?" Tanya prompted.

"Pirates, storms, and coral that can rip a hull to shreds," Seward explained. "The tides create an ever-changing landscape in the Divide. There are areas you can sail right over at high tide, but the tide can bring you right down on a rocky outcropping or a reef if you're not quick enough."

Tanya nodded.

Good things to watch out for. Let's hope we don't have to deal with that.

"Ma'am? You mind if I ask why you do that?" Seward asked, pointing.

Tanya tore her eyes away from the cuticles on her right hand. She'd only been distantly aware that she was examining imaginary blood.

"Do what?" Tanya asked.

"Look at your hands like that. I've seen you do it a few times, and you never seem real happy about it."

"Oh, really? Just thought I saw some dirt," Tanya lied.

"Oh." Seward frowned, clearly considered pursuing the question, then decided against it.

She's sharp. Her mind's wasted at sea. Then again, is the path I chose any better?

The two women spent a lot of time together over the next few days. Seward taught Tanya a little bit about navigation and the stars. Tanya even learned the star Cross was always going on about couldn't actually be a star. Seward explained that no star could point east or west, citing some reason about how the planet was spinning.

Tanya asked what the star was, but Seward was unsure on that point. It was an interesting revelation but one she had no intention of sharing with Cross. The big man spent many an early evening staring at the damn thing, and learning Elinfall wasn't a star might crush his spirits.

On the sixth day of ocean travel, an island came into view. At first, it was only a speck on the horizon, but soon, stone walls stood ominously atop battered cliffs. Tanya had followed their journey on a map Seward was kind enough to share and knew Seafront wasn't on it.

As they sailed closer, Tanya spotted flags snapping on the ramparts. They were sun-bleached, tattered, and hadn't been lowered or cleaned in some time. As the *Warden* sailed closer, Tanya found herself staring up at enormous cliffs. They were at least twenty spans tall and loomed over even the highest point of the *Warden's* crow's nest.

Soon, the island's shadow swallowed them, filling Tanya with an odd sense of dread.

42
GERARD
STOCKWORTH

Vigilant snorted and pulled, trying to break into a canter.

"What is it, boy?" Gerard muttered, pulling back on the reins. He looked around, then sniffed the air. Something stank.

Decay? Perhaps a lion made a kill, then abandoned the carcass.

They were only a few hours outside Norinspire. Over the past week, Gerard had stopped at a dozen patches of trampled grass or other signs of travel off the road. Each time, someone was merely stopping to make camp or relieve themselves.

Still, any lead is worth checking at this point.

Gerard dismounted, bent, and scuffed the road with his boot. The top layer of sand was fresh and loose, but it wasn't an obvious thing. The road was made of stone, and sand was always strewn across it. There was more of it here, though, and it appeared a bit intentional. Gerard bent, blowing the remnants of the dusting away. Below the fresh sand was a dark red stain.

Blood.

Gerard cocked his head, looking around. A few hills defined the horizon, a backdrop to the sea of yellow grass shifting in the wind. Ahead, six great oaks marked the road where it bent to the left. The tall grass wasn't all leaning the same way, and patches didn't bend with the breeze. Gerard walked over to the side of the road, examining the vegetation. White lines ran horizontally across the stalks as if they'd been bent then straightened again. Gerard pulled the plants aside, inspecting the root.

More blood, and lots of it.

Gerard walked over to Vigilant and stepped into the saddle. The horse trotted forward, eager to get away from the putrid smell. Gerard dismounted again, close to the small outcropping of trees. He held up a fist, making sure the horse could see it.

Vigilant shook his head, pawing the ground.

"Patience, boy, I don't like the smell any more than you." Gerard drew his bow and waded into the tall grass, circling wide around the little copse of trees.

Don't want to surprise a lion amidst a meal.

The smell of death grew stronger, and prairie flies began to dot the air. As the tangle of branches grew closer, the flies swarmed thicker. Soon, keeping the barrage of insects from his face became a constant battle. One flew up his nose mid-breath. He gagged and coughed, finally spitting the fly—still buzzing—from his mouth. Gerard spent the next few moments hacking repeatedly, trying to rid his mouth of whatever filth the disgusting creature had been rooting in. He almost sucked in a couple more flies before clamping his mouth shut and slowly raising his eyes.

Ahead, a large black-and-green pile sat on the far side of the trees. Gerard didn't need to get any closer to know it was human remains.

How many though?

He hesitated, swatting half a dozen flies away from his face. The pile was two paces wide in each direction and heaped nearly the height of the waist-high grass.

Ten at least.

Gerard's scowl deepened.

By the gods, I hate bloody flies.

With a deep breath, Gerard gathered his resolve and shouldered his bow. He clamped a calloused hand over his mouth and waded into the thick cloud of insects. The corpses were clad all in black and dark green.

Gerard inhaled once more through his cupped hand, then grabbed a body by the shoulders and pulled it from the pile. Thousands of fly eggs sprawled across the corpses beneath. Gerard felt his stomach turn, but luckily, the eggs hadn't hatched.

I bloody hate flies, he thought again, slowly forcing his eyes back to the heap.

Died just yesterday. Otherwise, they'd be swarming with maggots.

Gerard alternated breathing into the crook of his elbow and pulling bodies away from the heap. He stopped often to swat flies from his face and nearly lost his breakfast more than once as he deposited each stiff in a line. There were ten men and one woman among the dead. They all had old scars and looked to have been cold, hard killers in life.

They'll be mud and maggots soon enough.

Gerard mentally noted the cause of death for each.

A stab to the gut, a leg severed at the knee, something sharp through an eye socket. There was no shortage of different wounds, but one thing was clear: each of them died in combat. Whoever walked away from this had a lot of skill, superior numbers, or were the luckiest devils in Darin.

Gerard looked them over again. Based on their garb, they were one unit, and he didn't see any freshly tilled graves.

Whoever killed these men and women had no casualties? Or maybe they took their dead with them? Only one died from arrows, which rules out the proper way to carry out this sort of butchery.

Gerard looked back toward the site of the ambush and imagined archers popping up from the grass on either side of the road.

Could this have anything to do with—what were their names? Tina and Daniel?

Gerard shook his head.

No, not unless they met up with twenty friends in Norinspire.

Still, it was an oddity, so best to be sure. He patted down a corpse and found a necklace emblazoned with a silver spear on a field of black.

The Lance.

The hairs on the back of Gerard's neck stood, and so did he, eyes scanning for any sign of movement. The tall grass swayed, moving in unison without revealing any obstruction. Gerard let out a breath, turning back to the bodies.

These weren't thugs or roadside bandits; they were trained killers.

Gerard checked the necks of the rest. All except two wore the pendant. Dark patches unbleached by the sun marked many belts and sections of leather bunched or buckled from carrying constant weight.

Someone took a lot of weapons.

Any stone they possessed had clearly been pilfered, but Gerard searched their pockets anyway. He nearly vomited after the second handful of unhatched maggots but forced himself to push on.

Results often spring from the oddest places.

After inspecting the front of each assassin, Gerard began rolling them to their backs. Something rustled as he flipped the sixth corpse over. He stopped, head cocking to the side, then patted down the man's sides and belt pouches.

Where'd that noise come from?

Gerard searched the man again. Nothing. He checked the cloak for pockets. Nothing. The boots. Nothing. He frowned, unclasped the cloak, and pulled it free to get a better look at the tall, gaunt man.

The same crisp sound crinkled from the cloak.

Gerard ran his fingers along the inside of the fabric, feeling the palm-sized patch before he saw it. The square scrap of cloth was the same material as the garment, and whoever did the stitching knew how to weave directly into the original fabric.

Perhaps he needed more practice with a blade and less with a needle.

Gerard walked away from the worst of the flies and spread the cloak on the grass. He drew his razor-sharp hunting knife, then carefully cut the patch's stitches, one by one. A dry, coarse square of parchment brushed his fingertips. He pulled it free and flipped it over. A note was penned on the outside of the folded page.

Janus Osgood.

The lettering was clear, but it scrawled out sideways informally across the paper.

A note from you? Or are you Janus? Don't suppose you'll tell me.

Gerard unfolded the page, revealing a partial map of Norinspire with a cluster of buildings circled in red ink. He studied it for a spell, located the Justiseers' guildhouse, and used that to orient himself.

I know this building.

The Citadel. Headquarters of the OAM in Norinspire. He'd seen the towers many times, but never as circles and lines on a map. Gerard had his own opinions on the organization, but they were hardly relevant. The Order paid their bills on time, and they paid well.

That's really all that matters. Even if they are a bunch of puffed-up bureaucrats.

"Vincent," Gerard read the name scrawled across the map.

Who in all the eighty-six hells is Vincent?

Gerard began the trek back through the tall grass toward Vigilant.

Is this lead even worth checking?

He didn't think so. It couldn't be his marks, not with eleven members of the Lance feeding the vermin.

Maybe if the horse thieves' trail runs dry.

Twang.

Gerard's foot hit something, and he went ass over the campfire into yellow stalks. He let out a long groan and checked his nose. It wasn't broken. Tentatively, he rolled a few joints to ensure everything else was intact, then got to his knees.

"What in fuck's name was that?" Gerard cracked his neck to either side, then reached back. Something sharp stabbed his finger. "Forty-eight hells!"

Gerard yanked his hand away. A tiny spot of blood welled from his index finger.

Did something just bite me?

Gerard got to his feet, took a step away from the thing, then turned. Something brown and shiny lay in the dirt. It didn't look alive, it looked...

Broken?

Cautiously, Gerard took a step forward, bending at the waist.

Yep, broken. It didn't bite me. It poked me.

Gerard took hold of the splintered object, more carefully this time, raising it to eye level. A mass of tangled strings and wood dangled from his fingertips.

A lute? What in the seventeen hells are you doing out here?

Gerard rolled it in his hand, carefully inspecting the body of the instrument. Letters were etched into the wood, but the message split where the instrument fractured. Gerard gently folded the two pieces back together and read the inscription:

For Trueheart, a man as faithful as his name implies, and the absolute love of my life.

Gerard stared at the note a moment, then read it again.

Trueheart.

That was the name of his man; he was sure of it.

But how'd it bloody get out here?

Gerard looked around again, but the landscape was as desolate as before.

Are these two far more dangerous than I thought? Or perhaps they have dangerous friends?

He frowned, considering the possibilities.

Well, it's a lead, but it appears the quarry might warrant a bit more caution.

Gerard pulled his knife, marred the inscription, and tossed the lute back into the tall grass. He walked to the road and joined Vigilant, who was irritably snapping at flies. Vigilant broke into a canter before Gerard's ass was even in the saddle.

They'd arrive at the capital in a few hours if they kept a good pace, so Gerard let the horse have his head. They galloped away from the bodies for a short while, but before long, Vigilant slowed and began to alternate between trot and canter.

"In a hurry, huh?" Gerard asked. "You know there's a roof and an oat bag waiting for you at the capital, eh?"

Vigilant didn't even bother to snort in response.

The gates were open when they arrived, and they entered the city through a large portcullis. The walls of Norinspire were massive, standing at least eight spans high. Gerard wasn't certain when they were built, but the last time they were relevant was in the War of Iron and Blood.

The war between Darin and Terra was over a hundred years ago, and the two nations hadn't fought since. Terran nobility were responsible for the war, and the noble houses of Darin had only enslaved their families at first. But it turned out free labor was in high demand, and the Darins soon found less egregious acts to justify the slave trade.

The OAM headquarters were close to the center of the sprawling metropolis, and Gerard slowly worked his way up the main road. It was bustling with activity, but common folk moved aside as Vigilant approached. It was illegal to trample folk within the city limits, but it still happened, and no guard would follow up on a broken leg.

The sun was well past its apex as Gerard arrived at the Citadel. An enormous, walled structure surrounded three massive towers sprouting in a triangle from a sea of steepled roofs. Each spire had been built many years apart, a fact made clear by the weathering of stone.

Probably the Magus who commissioned each structure attempting to outshow their predecessor in some sort of generational dick-measuring contest.

Gerard dismounted and wrapped Vigilant's reins around a rail by the stables.

"You want me to put him up, sir?" a small chestnut-haired girl asked as she rounded the corner.

"No need. I won't be long. I'm sure he'd appreciate some oats and a brush, though, if you have the time."

"Yes, sir. He's magnificent!"

"Hear that, old boy?" Gerard asked, patting Vigilant on the neck. "It's been a long while since someone called you magnificent."

Vigilant snorted derisively.

"I know, I know. You ain't old. You're in your prime, buddy." Gerard turned to the stable girl. "What's your name, kid?"

"Dina," the girl said. She approached Vigilant from his front right side, making clear eye contact while speaking sweet nothings.

"Thanks, Dina." Gerard tossed the girl a ruby mark.

"No, thank you, sir!" Dina called back, catching the ruby without taking her eyes off the horse.

Gerard decided she knew her trade well enough and headed up the steps. He looked back as he reached the top of the stairs. Dina had retrieved a bag of oats for Vigilant and was combing the horse down.

Good kid, Gerard thought, opening the door and stepping into the confines of the Citadel.

It turned out Gerard was wrong, and getting an audience with Vincent took some time. He was apparently a high-ranking member of the Order, and like any government organization, the OAM moved at a snail's pace. So, Gerard wasn't all that surprised when he spent the next four hours waiting on an overly plush cushion in a chamber where guests were sent to be forgotten. Near the end of the fifth hour, he finally found himself in a room with the middle-aged official.

The office was clearly designed to make him feel small and portray Vincent and the Order as something larger than life itself. There were more trinkets, baubles, and wealth than anyone had good reason to display. And then there were the books. There were more of those than anyone could ever read in one lifetime. The message was clear enough: the OAM has forgotten more knowledge than you will ever know.

Too bad they probably need a diagram from one of those books to tie their bloody boots.

"Always a pleasure to receive contact from the Justiseer's Guild," the man behind the desk said, interrupting Gerard's thoughts.

"Likewise. I mean, for the OAM, that is." Gerard extended a hand. "The name's Gerard."

"Vincent." The official stood, taking his outstretched hand. "Though I suppose you already knew that. My secretary said you asked for me directly and that it was a matter of some urgency?"

Vincent gestured to the seat opposite his own, and they both sat.

"Yes, I'm afraid I may have some bad news."

"Oh, really? Do tell." Vincent steepled his hands and leaned forward.

"Were you waiting for a contingent from the Shadow's Lance?"

Vincent frowned, brow narrowing. There was a long pause as he studied Gerard.

"What makes you say that?" the official finally asked.

"Well, I thought you should know they won't be showing up," Gerard said.

"And why might that be?"

"They're dead."

Another long pause.

"What makes you think I have anything to do with them?" Vincent asked.

Gerard pulled the folded map from his pocket and tossed it. The parchment landed on the man's oversized desk and slid across, spinning until it stopped a finger's width from the edge. Vincent stared down at the paper, carefully read the name on the outside, then opened it. He looked at the map, running a finger under the lettering of his name. His face scrunched up, then he let out a breath and rummaged around in a desk drawer until he produced a letter. He set the page on the desk, comparing the handwriting between the two names.

Smart...smarter than I'd expect from a learned man.

"Where did you get this?" Vincent asked incredulously.

"From eleven dead Lance members."

"Eleven?"

"Yeah, eleven. I mean, technically, it came off one, but you get the point."

"I see..." Vincent trailed off. "That's impossible, though."

"I've got eleven liquifying, maggot-infested stiffs that would disagree if they still could."

"Are you sure there were eleven? Not just three?"

"I may not have gone to a fancy school like you, sir, but I can sure as shit count." Gerard knew he should keep the exasperation from his tone, but after weeks on the road and a four-hour wait, his patience was all used up.

"Indeed." Vincent looked Gerard in the eye, clearly studying him. Slowly, his expression shifted. "It's not possible because I met with three members of the Lance only yesterday and have reports confirming they boarded a ship this morning."

"Three?" Gerard asked.

"Yes. Three. They were to meet up with three more members from Windmore."

"Oh, I'd say they met. Though that sounds like too small a number. Are you sure it was just three?" Gerard asked.

"I'm most certain that I can count as well." Vincent's face was a blank mask.

"Three on eleven, though? Those aren't odds I'd bet on, not even with the element of surprise on their side."

"I would tend to agree."

"Sir, if you don't mind, could you describe the three you talked to?"

"Certainly. There were two men and a woman, all in good shape. One man was slight, the other enormous. The woman wore a black coat and had bright, brown eyes. I remember thinking she was the leader."

"Did they look like this?" Gerard pulled out two sheaves of paper and slid them across the table.

"In fact, they did. They didn't give these names, though." Vincent studied the page. "Are you telling me they're wanted criminals?"

"That's exactly what I'm saying. Can you tell me where they went?"

"I'm afraid I cannot."

"Cannot, or will not?"

"Take your pick," Vincent said.

Gerard's eyebrows narrowed. "They're wanted fugitives. Whatever they're doing for you, they won't hold up their end of the bargain."

Vincent pursed his lips, drumming his fingers on the desk.

"Gods...what a mess," Vincent finally said, sitting back in his chair. He stared off into space for a moment, then blew out a breath and set his jaw. The Magus opened another drawer and rifled through it, producing a small stack of paper. "Here, sign this, and be quick about it," he said, sliding the document across the desk.

"What is it?" Gerard asked, scanning the page.

"Standard disclosure accord that we use with the Justiseer's Guild. Sign it."

"It has some heavy language."

"Sign it." Vincent's tone made it clear there was no room for debate, not anymore.

He's already said too much. Best sign it before he does something rash.

Gerard scrawled his name across the page in an uneven and scratchy hand. He'd never had much use for writing, despite the need to read it often.

"Good," Vincent said, snatching the pages back from Gerard. He looked back down at the bounty tickets. "So, it appears you're already contracted to acquire two of them. All I ask is that you finish the task with one small caveat. Bring them to me first. Oh, and if they have a sword, I will need that as well."

"There are a lot of swords in the world," Gerard said.

"I am quite certain you will know it if you see it. Either way, bring me them or their heads, and the OAM will quadruple the bounty."

"Quadruple?"

Vincent nodded.

Gerard did the math.

We're talking emeralds now. That's some serious stone.

He'd only seen an emerald once, let alone held one. Typically, they were reserved for business between nobles and more often used for jewelry than currency.

The only gem worth more than 'ralds is moonstone, and those are unobtainable.

"You're serious?" Gerard asked.

"Four times the bounty. Plus, you can still turn them in after you show them to me."

"What's the catch?"

"No catch," Vincent said. "They lied to the Order. That cannot be tolerated, and they must not abscond with the blade."

"No, we mustn't allow that," Gerard said with a nod. All he could see, though, was the start of a little estate and rows of grapevines lining a hillside that might someday turn to wine.

Vincent and Gerard talked for a long while.

They spoke of an escaped slave named Kole, a small sailing vessel, and a silent island, but most of all, they spoke of a blade.

43
TANYA RINGHOLDER

Sea water sprayed Tanya's face as the *Warden* bobbed through the waves. The ocean was choppy and only worsened as their vessel neared the island.

"Mr. Bolis, get us as close to the cliffs as you can without dashing the *Warden* on those rocks, if you please," the captain boomed.

The first mate yelled orders so fast that Tanya had a hard time keeping up with all the nautical terms—something about reefing the sails and a mizzenmast.

Sailors scurried about, and the ship pulled to the side, skirting along the enormous cliff.

"Keep us close, Mr. Bolis," the captain said as two sailors let out a rope on the starboard side.

"Tighten that line!" Mr. Bolis yelled. "Gotta kiss the cliffs, so we don't leave our ass hanging in the breeze."

Tanya felt heat rise to her cheeks.

Cross stood two spans away, staring wide-eyed at the passing cliffs. They never had talked about the circumstances of the panther encounter, and if Cross made the connection now, he gave no sign of it.

The two sailors wrestled with the rope, wrapping it around a wooden pin they'd been calling a thumper.

It was a tricky balance. Too far away and they risked being seen from Seafront. Too close, and they risked the *Warden's* hull smashing on the rocks. Tanya gripped the ship's rail hard enough to juice one of the old, crusty limes in the galley below.

Seward's right. The ocean is pretty, but I can't say I'll miss sea travel.

The plan was to be back on the boat tomorrow morning so they wouldn't have much reprieve from the bobbing waves.

If everything goes according to plan.

The ship rounded a large pillar of rock, revealing the mouth of a vast cavern.

"Take us in, nice and slow," the captain bellowed.

The helmsman adjusted his wheel, pointing the bow straight at the cave's mouth. A whistle blew, and sailors scurried about, taking down two of the three sets of sails. The *Warden* slowed, gliding into the enormous cavern. Huge stone teeth hung from the ceiling, and Tanya now understood why the captain had circled the boat while they waited for the tide to ebb. Planks and cargo littered the cavern walls, and pieces of sail flagged about in the stalactites above.

Captain Caldwell and his officers directed the ship to an outcropping of rock at the far end of the cave. As they cut through the water, the debris wedged in the cavern walls grew denser. The captain ordered the crew to slow even further, and they dropped the last of the sails. Oars jutted from the side of the hull, and soon, they moved with only the power of arms and the current. The captain approached Tanya on the main deck as sailors jumped to a slippery slab of stone to moor the boat.

"What do you think happened here, Captain?" Tanya gestured around vaguely.

"Hard to say for sure, but it appears the tides rose and smashed the *Divinity* into the ceiling." Caldwell took a deep breath and looked around the cave. "Why Booker and the crew would simply wait for that to happen is beyond me, though. In any case, are you ready to depart? I have no intention of subjecting the *Warden* or my crew to the same fate."

"We just hit low tide, right?" David asked from Tanya's left.

"Correct, my good man. We should have some time, but I'd rather not tarry. If I had to guess, it was probably that type of assumption that got Booker into trouble."

"When can we expect you back?" Tanya asked.

"We'll return at the first low tide each morning for three days." The captain flipped open a pocket clock as if the thing wasn't a mechanical marvel. "Tomorrow's low tide will be at approximately five thirty. The following day at six twenty. The day after at seven." He snapped the lid of the little clock shut. "We'll circle the cavern once. If we don't see you on shore, we'll head back to the reef and set anchor until the next morning."

Tanya jotted down the times on a small notepad she'd picked up in Norinspire after her old one had been thoroughly soaked in Windmore's fountain. She glanced at her handiwork to ensure the numbers were correct:

Ship docks:
5:30, 6:20, 7:00

"You wouldn't happen to have an extra one of those, would you?" Tanya asked, gesturing to the captain's pocket clock. The captain's face scrunched as he considered the trinket in his hand, then he held it out by a short leather strap.

"You know how to read it?" he asked as Tanya carefully took it. It was a fair question. Most people had never even seen one, let alone knew how to use the thing.

"I do," Tanya said.

I also know it's worth more than anything else on this ship.

"Well, it looks like you'd best teach your comrades," Caldwell said, eyes shifting from Cross to David. They were each staring at the clock with a mix of fascination and awe. "Just in case something happens to you while you're on the island," the captain clarified. "Well, let us not tarry. I'm already quite certain I'll be hearing whispers of sea monsters for a year after this expedition."

"It's been a pleasure, Captain," David said. "We'll see you in a day or two."

"Indeed, and you as well, young man. I hope to see you on the morrow." Caldwell looked around and spotted Seward standing nearby. "Oh, one final thing. If you need an emergency pickup prior to our scheduled arrival, then you'll need a flare."

Seward held out a package nearly the length and width of a forearm. The cloth-wrapped bundle smelled of pine and tar, and a length of twine spiraled around it in concentric loops.

"Thanks," Cross said, taking the flare.

"Simply light it in an emergency. If we see black smoke, we'll be on the way, but it will take some time for us to get to shore. We won't be able to enter the cave at high tide, but if the water's low enough, we'll deploy longboats to pick you up. Still, you may have to be patient. Please adhere to the schedule unless things are truly dire. I'd rather not risk my crew in a longboat unless it's absolutely necessary."

"Got it," Tanya said, then turned and headed up the gangplank. Waves dashed the cliffs, and mist sprayed. A huge swell hit the sheer wall as she stepped off the slippery ramp.

"Damn it all in a bloody barrel of cod shit!"

Tanya turned back. David was halfway up the ramp, completely soaked and muttering more nonsensical curses.

Dramatic, as usual.

Cross got misted as he headed up the gangplank but avoided most of the roiling ocean. Soon, the three of them stood together, staring up at steps carved directly into a stone slab.

The whole world still seemed to sway despite being on solid ground.

Sailors pulled in the gangplank and unhitched the mooring holding the ship in place. Their only means of escape began to float away. With a deep inhale, Tanya turned and started up the slippery steps. She glanced back a final time before the top of the entrance blocked her view.

The *Warden's* white letters slowly disappeared around the side of the cave.

Stranded on a mysteriously abandoned island, with only wreckage left from the previous voyage...great start to this mission.

She turned back and headed up the stairs.

Oh, well. What did I expect?

Tanya caught up to Cross just as David finished lighting a torch. The steps were straight at first, then wound upward in a slow spiral through solid rock. As they climbed, the stairway slowly narrowed, and the steps were barely wide enough for two people to walk abreast when they finally reached a doorway. David approached first, pushing the iron handle. The heavy wood swung inward freely with the slightest creak.

Unlocked? Is that a good sign or a bad one?

The chamber walls were lined with weapons and armor, and a pot was staged over a stocked firepit. Tanya lifted the lid and took a whiff. The smell of pitch, tar, and animal fat invaded her nostrils. The keep's inhabitants must have planned to dump it down the stairs and light it during an invasion.

But why? Who would assault an island that's not even on the map?

"Let's keep moving," Tanya said. She itched to know what happened to the OAM stationed here but doubted they'd make any discoveries in this little armory. David turned from some chain mail he had been inspecting, and Cross pulled a massive sword from a rack as he turned back to her.

"Holy fuck, Cross, that thing's bigger than me," Tanya said. "You know how to use it?"

"Not positive, but I'm pretty sure you put that pointy end in 'em," Cross said, gesturing toward the tip of the blade. "Or perhaps they happen to fall onto one of these sharpened bits." The big man ran a finger down the blade's edge. "Either way, might be useful. Never know who we might run into up here. At least it won't be a sea monster."

"Oh, gods, you're as bad as the sailors. You know there are no sea monsters, right? They're as fake as fairies or ellen."

"I'm not sayin' there are. But we don't know what ripped that boat apart, so let's not rule it out."

"There are more logical explanations than myths and fairy tales. Right, David?" Tanya prompted.

"I'm with the big man," David said. "Seems to me those sailors would've been out of the cavern quick if the tide was rising and their mast was headed toward those spiky rocks. Either they abandoned the boat, or there was something real scary in the open water."

"You two are more superstitious than a couple of soothsayers," Tanya said. "But I suppose there's still shit in this world we don't understand."

This island being a prime example.

"Let's head for the vault first and try to get the relic," Tanya continued. "We can figure out what happened to these people once we have the damn thing."

"Sounds like a plan," David agreed.

Cross nodded, replacing a large axe on his back with the enormous two-handed sword. They left the room through a wooden door and found themselves on a cobblestone street.

By the look of it, Seafront was once a prosperous and modern town...but not anymore.

"Rula's holy fuckin' backside," David whispered through quivering lips. "It's a bloody fuckin' massacre." It was the greatest understatement Tanya could imagine, yet she had no better words for the spectacle.

About three-quarters of the buildings were rubble. Debris littered the streets, and human remains were...well, they were everywhere. The air reeked of blood, bile, excrement, and bird shit.

Countless crows and seagulls filled the street. Some hopped from one bloody mass to the next, picking at the most tender bits. Others stood vigil atop piles of rubble or lampposts. The birds must have been feasting for some time because they no longer fought for scraps.

Someone retched to Tanya's left, and she turned to see David bent at the waist. Cross was covering his nose, looking skyward. Tanya just stared at the carnage with horrified fascination.

"What could've done this?" Tanya murmured, stepping toward a jelly-like smear spread across the cobblestone. It was probably human once, but it was hard to be sure.

Even their bones appear pulverized. Maybe a boulder from a siege weapon?

Someone vomited again behind her.

But then, where's the boulder? Something massive did this.

"Let's go," David said queasily. "The quicker we get the sword, the quicker we get the fuck outta here."

Pretty boy may be a delicate flower, but he's not wrong.

"Agreed." Tanya stood. "Judging by the birds, it seems whatever did this is long gone. Still, let's step softly on the way to the vault, just in case."

They continued through the streets in silence, tramping through a solid handspan of what felt like mud but was far too red. Most likely, it was a mix of congealed blood, guts, and bird droppings. Tanya didn't see any good reason to point that out to the others, though.

They passed intact homes, half-demolished structures, and piles of rubble. Tanya could find no rhyme or reason to the destruction. Some buildings looked like they'd been ripped apart from the outside, while others collapsed inward.

Whatever did this, it came in hard and fast. Seafront never had a chance.

The placement of corpses was also odd. Most were ground into the stone streets, but others lay crumpled on rooftops or smashed into the sides of houses. One corpse was even impaled on a column below a collapsed balcony.

Thrown? Or did he fall?

Tanya decided it didn't matter.

Dead is dead.

Piles of rubble were as prevalent as the corpses, and lifeless limbs often protruded from between wooden beams and wreckage. However, only the squawks of birds accosted them as they moved toward the center of town.

"This is it," Tanya whispered as they entered the square.

"Are you sure?" David peered over her shoulder, trying to get a better view of the map.

"Yes, I'm bloody sure. Look, there's the butcher and the barracks," Tanya scolded, pointing at two buildings surrounding the town center. "Plus, three roads into the square."

"Well, yeah, but where's the fuckin' fountain?" David asked.

A crater filled the center of the square where a fountain should flow.

"Siege weaponry?" Cross offered.

They stepped closer, peering down into the hole. There was no boulder, no projectile of any kind. Simply a crater, all the way down to bare dirt.

"Fascinating," Tanya said, staring.

"That's one fucking word for it," David muttered.

Cross grunted in assent, giving no clue as to who he agreed with.

"Maybe they were in the midst of a construction project?" Tanya wondered aloud.

"Maybe," David said. "Does it matter? Let's just get this done."

Across the square was the armory. A giant hole yawned where the door used to be. The entrance to the vault was marked on the map at the back of the sleeping quarters. As long as the structure's interior wasn't caved in, they should be able to access it.

The square was littered with flattened bodies, but unlike the others, these were armed and armored. Weapons were strewn about, and the men and women appeared to have been crushed while still inside their armor. Near the door, a gray robe of the OAM clung to a body that was more puddle than person. Tanya was reasonably sure the pool of flesh was once human, even though some of the remains had washed away and birds had picked at the rest.

They entered the building through the collapsed entrance, stepping around a massive hole in the floor. The structure was half-destroyed by whatever transpired here, and the remaining supports appeared as if they might give way at any moment. Tanya hurried them to the far end of the room. Someone had cleared the rubble from the door to the sleeping quarters and left it ajar.

Cross went through first, and Tanya followed, careful not to disturb anything lest the whole place collapse. Daylight streamed in through a caved-in portion of the roof on the right side of the room. The chamber was otherwise relatively intact, and surprisingly, there were no bodies. A brick wall was ripped open at the far end of the rows of bunks, exposing a set of stairs.

"Someone's already been here, and they exhumed the vault," David stated the obvious as usual.

"Exhumed?" Cross asked.

"Dug it up or exposed it," Tanya provided. Cross muttered the word a few times as they walked to the staircase.

It was dark, even at the top of the steps, so Tanya took a torch from the wall and lit it with flint and steel. The flickering light held the darkness at bay as they descended. The stairway started straight, then slowly curved, like the passage from the cavern. Tanya counted the steps. When she hit a hundred and five, the smell of brine permeated her nostrils. It was another twenty-eight before the floor leveled out into a long chamber.

The room was nearly six spans long and ended in a flat wall. Three openings lined each side of the corridor, snaking into the darkness. The walls were tall, smooth, and glossy. Tanya ran her finger along the stone, and it came away slimy. She looked up. The whole wall was covered in the same slick, viscous coating.

Something splashed to Tanya's left, and she spun.

"For fuck's sake!" David said, shaking water from his boot. "I can't stay bloody dry today." He took out a torch and lit it as Tanya approached. A sea urchin sat on the bottom of a small pool, and a few small fish darted about in the shallows.

"Outside water gets in here somehow," Tanya said. "There's no way these creatures live their whole lives underground in this one pool." She looked at the walls again.

They're smooth from the seawater, and the slime is algae.

Then it dawned on her.

"Nobody move—"

Click. The noise echoed behind her.

Tanya turned. Cross was staring down at his feet a little farther down the hall.

A deafening grind filled the chamber.

Slam.

A massive pillar of stone hit the floor, blocking the staircase.

Well, that's not good.

"Fuck! We're stuck," David moaned, splashing over. "Cross, what did you do?"

"I dunno. Something sank underneath me, but it looked just like the rest of the floor."

Tanya walked over and crouched. "Pressure plate. Well made and well hidden." She ran a finger along the nearly seamless edge of the trap. "Nothing for it now. Best get moving. We don't have much time."

"What do you mean we don't have much time?" David asked.

"How tall do you think the ceiling is in here?" Tanya asked, heading straight to the end of the hall.

"Hmmmm...wait! Where are you going?" David asked.

"About four spans," Cross said, with a hand raised.

"Gods, I forget how big you are sometimes," David said. "Can you really reach two spans?"

"Not quite. Almost, though."

"Okay, so four spans, and how long do you think it's been since we got off the boat?" Tanya asked. The two men splashed through puddles.

"An hour? Maybe a little more," David guessed as he caught up to them.

Tanya checked Caldwell's pocket watch and turned right at the end of the passage. The hall continued straight for six spans, then curved to the left. "Then we have about an hour until we're swimming," Tanya said, still walking.

"Swimming!" David protested. "Oh, shit."

Tanya glanced back. Realization had spread across David's face, but Cross was still working it out.

"One hour until we're swimming, about four till we run out of air, and that's if we can swim for three straight hours." Tanya got to the end of the hallway—the passage split, curving left and right.

Gods, there are a lot of fuckin' paths, and we're just getting started.

"Go right," David chimed in. Tanya eyed him skeptically. "It's a maze, right? We need to go straight as often as possible, and then if the maze forces us to turn, we always go right."

"And how in the hells do you know that?" Tanya demanded, heading right. Another short hallway lay ahead of them with two more passages on the right.

"My dad took me to a hedge maze as a kid. The gardener whispered the trick to me before we entered. We got lost, but I led my father through with that method."

"Oh, it's a maze!" Cross said with a little too much exuberance. "And the tide's meant to drown us. So it's a maze with a natural time limit. Very clever."

"You got it, buddy," David said, but Tanya could practically hear his eyes roll.

Good thing that man's better than half a regiment in a fight.

Tanya rubbed at her temple.

Then again, he's not stupid. He grabs onto knowledge and consumes it voraciously. He's just been sheltered in the worst possible way.

"Voracious," Tanya said.

Silence. Tanya looked back. Cross and David both stared at her, heads cocked to the side.

"Another word for you."

"Oh!" Cross said excitedly. "That sounds like a good one."

"What's it mean?" David asked.

Tanya laughed. "Stumped the bard at his own game, did I?"

David scowled. "Never claimed to know *every* word."

"Hungry, like really hungry," Tanya said, continuing straight past a hallway on the right.

They tramped through small pools of water and were forced to turn at the following right. They passed another hall and headed straight.

Click.

Fuck!

Tanya ducked down on pure instinct.

No bolts or darts flew overhead. No spikes or blades punched from the walls. Slowly, she got up and looked around. They stood in a hallway with five other exits. She stepped back and watched the plate squeal back into position. Her surroundings seemed familiar. She looked up and to the left. Two small seams outlined the stone pillar that had just locked them in.

Damn. Back where we started.

"You were saying, David?" Tanya asked, pointing.

"I told you, we have to go straight, then..." David trailed off as his eyes settled on the column of stone. "Well, we're fucked then. I guess whoever made this maze was smarter than the gardeners of Ardendale."

"Yeah, that's what I was thinking," Tanya said.

"You've been to Ardendale?" David asked.

"No, the 'we're fucked' bit," Tanya clarified. "Anyone got any other good ideas?"

"I don't think the straight thing works," Cross said.

"What do you mean?" Tanya asked.

"I think we need to take every turn in one direction we can. Like, put your hand to the wall and keep it there," Cross said.

"How do you know about mazes?" David asked.

"Rats."

Tanya blinked. "What do you mean, 'rats'?"

"Used to make mazes for rats when we were kids," Cross said. "Guess we're the rats now."

"Very profound," Tanya said dryly. "I'm not sure we have time to unpack the philosophical significance of that right now, though."

"Profound?" Cross asked, then before Tanya could answer, "And fill-uh-what?"

Tanya ignored the questions and looked at David skeptically.

"I don't have any better ideas," he said, frowning.

"All right, but let's try to go around the edge this time," she suggested.

Tanya led them back to the stone pillar blocking the entrance, then took an immediate left turn. As they followed the gentle curve of the passage, she became increasingly confident it must be the perimeter of the labyrinth since the only exits were on the right. Dozens of holes of varying sizes dotted the smooth surface of the wall, and water was starting to dribble near the floor.

So that's how the ocean gets in.

They hugged the left wall as often as possible, but more than once, they came to a dead end and were forced to double back and take a passage they'd passed on the right. Eventually, Cross's trick always brought them back to the hole-filled wall. Cross hounded her about the words as they walked until Tanya finally tried to explain them. "Profound" was easy enough, but "philosophical" turned out to be a bit more challenging.

The water was halfway up Tanya's calves when they finally came to something new. A black mass was piled on the floor in front of them. The heap was wider than a span in each direction and nearly up to Tanya's waist. Cross unstrapped his enormous sword as they approached.

Gods, that thing's massive.

She shook her head.

If another man carried it, I might think he was compensating for something.

Tanya knew Cross wasn't, though. She'd played nursemaid for weeks on the trip to Grenisport and in the city.

"Poke it," David prompted.

Cross looked at Tanya.

She shrugged.

The big man prodded the mass with the tip of his blade. The pile twitched. Then, part of it separated, wiggling free. Three shadowy forms slithered toward them through the shallow water. Each was longer than an arm and wider than a hand. David stamped on the first one, then stabbed it. Cross skewered another. Tanya tried to step on the last one, but the creature snaked away at the last second and latched onto her calf.

"Ouch!"

Pain blossomed from what felt like a hundred needles.

Tanya lifted her leg, cutting the tail off the thing with her short steel. Cross grabbed the writhing tentacle, yanking it free. Even with half its body removed, it curled upward, trying to latch onto his arm. David caught it behind the mouth, and together, the two men held the thing still long enough to get a good look at it. The severed tail writhed, spraying blood into the air and water.

The creature was a slimy, inky black, and it had no eyes. Its maw opened and closed methodically, searching for purchase as it flexed. Each time the creature's mouth opened, it revealed row after row of concentric, razor-sharp teeth spiraling down its gullet.

"That thing's disgusting." Tanya sliced it in half again between the two men's grip. Cross dropped the rest of the tail, and David tossed the gaping mouth back into the water a span from them. The maw opened and closed as it sank to the bottom, somehow still alive.

At least it can't seem to swim without its tail.

"What in the hells was that?" Cross asked.

"I think it was a sea leech," David said.

"What in the everliving fuck is a sea leech?" Tanya asked.

"Never seen one, but there's a line in a song about one. I thought they'd be bigger, though, based on the ballad."

"Bigger? That thing was fucking enormous!" Tanya said. "Once we get you a new lute, I fully expect you never to play that song in my presence. Deal?"

"Deal," David agreed.

"Voracious little buggers," Cross said, watching the still-twitching mouth.

She and David laughed, but it sounded a little grim.

Tanya's eyes slowly settled on the water.

"You don't think those are more sea leeches, right?" David asked.

Spindly red clouds spread through the water. Tanya's brows narrowed as she searched for the source.

Tendrils of red dissipated into the shallows from her leg, and the leech, like ink, dropped into a clear pool. Lazily, the current pulled the red toward the slimy black mound.

The mass squirmed.

"Time to go." Tanya stepped backward.

One by one, the sea leeches slid away from the greater whole. Tanya took another two steps, but it was too late. The leeches fell from the heap, slowly revealing tattered gray robes. There must have been over a hundred wriggling, black tendrils feasting on the flesh of the bloated OAM member.

Not anymore. Looks like they want new blood.

Tanya turned to run.

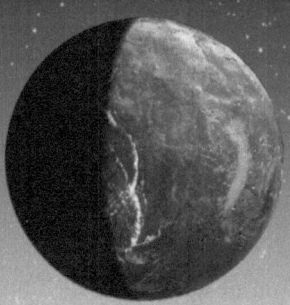
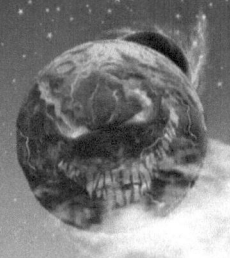

44
NATHAN

Nathan set his jaw, pressing the tip of his spear against Scarlett's chest.

If she's not with us, then she's with it.

A swell of sound echoed through the storm.

What was that? Nathan looked up.

A brown form thundered through the snowy haze. Brandon shoved Raylor as something bowled into the circle.

Nathan leapt sideways.

Men and women flew in all directions. One fell to the ground, trampled under stamping hooves. Another was shouldered aside, collapsing in the snow. Huge antlers caught Brandon under the ribs, carrying him across the yard.

The enormous beast slowed as it approached the fence, lowering its head and depositing Brandon in the snow before circling wide. Nathan rose. The creature was well muscled, with a bulbous head and a pair of antlers over a span wide. It ran on four legs, was covered in thick brown fur, and stood head and shoulders above a horse.

Nathan ran to Brandon.

Blood streamed from two massive holes where antlers punctured skin, broke ribs, and pierced the organs beneath. He took the kid's hand, watching as the pure white snow turned burgundy.

"Hold on, Brandon." Nathan knew the words were hollow before they even left his lips.

Kid's not long for this world.

"Take it down!" Nathan yelled, then looked back at Brandon.

There was nothing to be done. Blood spurted from the kid's chest in time with his heart as the red stain spread. Brandon grasped Nathan's hand and looked into his eyes, pleading without uttering a word.

Punctured lungs? Probably.

A moment later, the strength left Brandon's grip. A single tear tracked down Nathan's cheek as his eyes found the beast. It had turned around and backed into a corner, shaking bloody antlers back and forth. The hunters encircled it, spears leveled. Nathan's upper lip curled into a snarl as anger sank its claws into him.

Not now. I need wits to deal with this creature.

The ugly cross between a horse and a cow scraped the ground with its front hoof, throwing up snow and clods of dirt. Condensation poured from its nostrils, dissipating into the falling snow. The creature swung its antlers back and forth menacingly as Raylor and the hunters drew close. One man prodded the monster in the side with a spear, drawing blood.

The beast turned, antlers slashing. The spear wedged between two bony points and was ripped from the man's hands. The antlers caught the hunter's shoulder on the backswing, knocking him off his feet. Another man moved behind the beast, stabbing the creature's flank.

Nathan hurled his spear, running after it.

"Bring it down!" Raylor yelled.

The spear sank into the monster's ribs.

"Kill Elrontis!" someone shouted to Nathan's left.

The beast let out a bellow, not unlike a cow. The noise echoed through the yard, loud and guttural, full of fright and determination.

An arrow whizzed by Nathan's head, thumping into the creature's shoulder.

"Nooo!" A scream of pure anguish came from somewhere behind.

The beast kicked out with a back leg. The hoof connected with a hunter bracing a spear in the beast's flank. One moment, the man had a head; the next, he did not. The hunter fell bonelessly to the ground, revealing a fence splattered with blood, brain, and bits of skull. Two more hunters moved in, sinking their spears into the monster's ribs. Nathan stalked forward.

Something hit him in the back, sending him sprawling.

He rolled, raising his hands defensively, but no one loomed over him. Nathan leapt up. A wooden bucket lay nearby. He glanced back at the house. Scarlett snatched up a rake and hurled it at another hunter. The red-hot iron in Nathan's gut nearly made him turn on her instead of dealing with the monster.

No, that's what she wants. The creature's the real threat here, not this wiry woman.

Nathan looked back at the beast, then around at the hunters. Five spears and half a dozen arrows jutted from its body. Alice was near Scarlett, sending shaft after shaft from her bow.

"Take her, Alice!" Nathan yelled, pointing to Scarlett.

Alice stopped shooting, eyes following Nathan's finger. Scarlett picked up a hammer. Alice dropped her bow and pulled a knife, moving toward the other woman. Nathan turned back to the beast. Raylor and another man rammed spears into the monster's side.

"Together now!" Raylor yelled.

As one, the hunters pushed the beast toward the fence.

"Stop! He didn't do anything!" Scarlett's bloodcurdling screams echoed through the snow, even over the grunting and yelling.

"Hold it!"

"Steady!"

"Watch its feet!"

Nathan pulled two hunting knives from his belt, ducking spear shafts as he moved in. A hoof lashed out, and Nathan rolled to the side.

I was made for this.

Nathan was sure of it. He was made to fight. Made to struggle. Made to protect those unable to do so themselves.

This is who I am.

Lightning quick, he slipped under the beast's massive head, knives darting. Steel met fur and muscle, parting flesh. Blood poured from an artery. The creature swung its huge head sideways. He ducked. Antlers tore through a spear shaft, goring a woman in the shoulder and tossing her across the yard.

Nathan stood, burying a knife in the monster's massive neck. Distantly, he heard a sinuous tearing sound and glanced up. The hunters were taking turns plunging their spears in and out of the creature.

"Yes, bleed it out!" Nathan yelled, pulling his knife free and thrusting it back in.

A front hoof struck out at him, and Nathan pulled to the side. The tip of the hoof clipped his hip, spinning him. Nathan stumbled away from the beast, entirely focused on keeping his feet from getting tangled. He looked up. A wooden shaft loomed into view, then connected with his forehead.

He went down with a thump in the snow.

The world fuzzed.

Nathan blinked up at the spiderweb of latticed spear shafts. He shook his head and took in a deep breath of cold mountain air, then forced himself up with a groan. Five hunters held the creature in a cage of spears, and two more sent a constant barrage of arrows into its side.

Blood poured from the monster's neck, and it faltered.

Just gotta hold now.

"Brace!" Nathan yelled.

The great beast teetered.

"It's coming down!" he shouted.

The monster's front legs buckled, then it collapsed in a heap. A great snort filled the yard as blood poured from enormous nostrils. The beast looked past Nathan and let out a long, sorrowful bellow.

A complex emotion?

The creature's chest heaved as it pulled in a massive breath, then sank as it let out one more melancholy note.

Nathan listened, increasingly confident that this creature felt as much as any of them.

"We killed it!" one of the hunters yelled. The man took one hand from his spear to pump a fist in the air.

"Elrontis is dead!" another hunter cried.

"We did it!"

"Our village is saved!"

"Elrontis is no more!"

The echoes of victory spread through the hunters like wildfire. Euphoria seeped into Nathan's bones as the frenzy of battle slowly faded. Relief washed over him, even though the beast had killed three hunters and injured two others.

It could've been so much worse.

The wet ripping continued as if they stood in a butcher's shop.

Where's that sound coming from?

Nathan glanced around through the thickening snow. No one stabbed the corpse in triumph. No one was trying to skin the beast. No one attempted to claim a trophy.

"But that wasn't Elrontis," he muttered.

This isn't over.

Tendrils of terror slid into Nathan's gut.

The hunters were celebrating, but nothing explained that sloppy rending. Nathan scanned the perimeter, ears straining, trying to locate the source of the sound. The noise was sickeningly familiar, like bones crunching and flesh tearing during a battle. The sound seemed to bounce around the little yard as thick flakes of snow drifted down.

A loud, high chirping drew Nathan's attention to the peak of the cabin's roof. Steve was making a racket, screaming down at something.

Nathan followed her gaze.

Alice slumped against the wall, a hunting knife stuffed into her right eye. The noises weren't coming from her, though—they were coming from Scarlett. More accurately, they were coming from what was left of the lean woman.

Nathan stared in horror as bones popped and flesh fissured across a growing set of bulging muscles. Meat and skin weaved and knitted back together in a wholly unnatural way as something emerged from the woman. Fur grew across the hulking form, and Scarlett let out a chittering yowl. The noise was utterly foreign, a cross between a hyena's laugh and the roar of a lion echoing through the falling snow. Nathan only watched the atrocity unfold for seconds before realizing he was wasting precious time.

"Elrontis!" Nathan shouted, eyes never leaving the creature.

The hulking ball of fur splayed out, corded muscles racking as snow drifted around it.

"Is not—"

A sloppy gnashing of teeth filled the air.

"—dead!"

Claws churned snow and frozen ground.

"Hunters!"

Hair filled in, and two tan stripes bleached down either side of its back.

"To me!"

Another chittering roar.

"Hurry!"

Green eyes rolled back, returning as glass-black pools of hate.

"To *me!*"

The monster's arms unfurled as it stood to full height.

Nathan pulled his spear free from the downed beast, glancing back at Elrontis. The creature's hands flexed, revealing razor-sharp claws, each longer than a hunting knife.

Nathan pulled back the spear.

Elrontis met his eye, upper lip curling into a snarl as saliva dripped from long fangs.

He hurled the weapon.

The monster was nearly twice the height of a man and well over twice the weight.

The spear sailed through the air, on target.

Pure black eyes never left him as Elrontis swatted the tip away. The weapon spun, landing near Brandon's corpse in the freshly fallen snow. For a moment, Nathan thought he saw recognition in those smoldering eyes.

Of what, though?

The labored breaths of the hoofed creature behind him ceased.

The yard erupted into chaos.

Elrontis leapt, landing on one of the two remaining archers, six spans away. Bones crunched as they went to the ground. Elrontis sank its claws into the woman's chest, opened her ribcage like a book, then bounded off again. Nathan grabbed a machete from the headless hunter and unslung his own.

God, I wish I had a sword, Nathan thought, running forward.

The last hunter loosed an arrow at Elrontis mid-flight. The shaft clipped the beast's arm before it bore him to the ground. With a stuttered snarl, Elrontis grabbed the archer's head, slamming it through powdery snow and into the packed ground. It lifted him by his skull, holding him out like a rag doll.

The man blinked, gulping in air through a wide mouth—a fish out of water. The monster yanked the dazed man to the side, putting him between it and a thrusting spear. The other hunter tried to pull back, but the pike sank into the disoriented man's gut with a wet squish.

Elrontis moved with him, swinging the man around by the head. It bludgeoned the hunter to the ground with the other man's body, then brought the human flail down on the prone hunter.

Once.

Bones snapped, but from who was impossible to tell.

Twice.

Blood splattered across the white snow.

Three times.

There was a pop as the head Elrontis was holding pulled free from the body.

The creature was a blur of motion. Mere seconds had passed, and three hunters were dead, but Nathan was nearly on it now. Raylor was on his left, two other hunters on his right, and one more just behind. The power and speed of this thing were like nothing Nathan had ever seen. It bludgeoned a man to death with another human in the time it took to run three steps.

Elrontis faced their charge, still holding the man's severed head. It whipped its arm around, hurling the skull forward with another chittering roar. Nathan tried to dodge, but the head hit him square in the chest. He staggered back, felt his heel catch something, and toppled. Gasping for breath, he struggled to his knees.

Raylor thrust his spear at the monster.

Elrontis caught the tip, breaking it off.

Three more spears darted in. The beast dodged one and narrowly ducked another, but the last sank into its side.

The monster turned, snarling.

Nathan got to his feet, coughed, sucked in a lungful of air, then he was moving again.

Elrontis brought its claw down, cleaving through the shaft of wood embedded in its side. The tip of the spear fell away, and the creature lunged forward. Raylor rolled to the side as the monster shouldered into a hunter. She hit the ground, torso plowing through the snow for spans. Elrontis's enormous jaws closed on the collarbone of another hunter.

The man's feet left the ground as the monster shook from tip to tail like a dog with a rat. He flailed for a moment in its maw as bones crunched and dislocated. Then, with one more sickening snap, he went limp. There was a crunch, and the man fell to the ground, a massive hole where his shoulder should've been. Elrontis opened its mouth, letting the mass of blood, bone, and meat fall onto the hunter below. The final hunter faced down the beast. Her arms quivered, yet she held resolute.

Nathan was only five paces away.

The monster stalked forward, closing on the last hunter. The woman held her spear steady, planting it for the charge. Elrontis stopped short of the tip and grabbed the shaft, ripping it from her grasp. The beast snarled, bearing down on her.

Raylor jumped on the creature's back, sinking a knife into its shoulder.

Elrontis hurled the spear at Nathan, forcing him to duck and roll. The last thing he saw before his vision turned to churning snow was Raylor pulling another knife and planting it between the creature's shoulder blades.

Nathan righted himself, wiping wet flakes from his eyes just in time to see the last hunter hurtling toward him. The woman collided with him, and they went down in a heap. Nathan tried to stand, but his leg was trapped under her torso. Elrontis grabbed Raylor's wrist and threw him into the cabin wall. The old hunter slammed into the logs with a crack and collapsed in the snow.

The leader's knife was still lodged in Elrontis's back, but the thing didn't even seem to notice. It took one lunging step forward, grabbed Raylor by the neck, and hoisted him into the air. Nathan and the last hunter were up now, charging Elrontis as one.

Nathan screamed, trying to get the thing's attention.

Raylor flailed once.

With a snarl, Elrontis grabbed a shovel from the wall and plunged it into Raylor's belly.

There was a loud squish as the shovel parted muscle and bone, then a thud as it embedded into the wooden wall. Raylor screamed, hands clasping around the haft, feet dangling several hands above the snow.

Nathan heard the other hunter peel away.

Probably the smart move.

The monster bled from half a dozen wounds but wasn't slowing.

This may be a doomed effort, but what else is left?

Elrontis turned right before he got to it. Nathan slashed with his left blade, and the creature caught his wrist. It roared at him, canines dripping with bloody saliva a hand's width from his face. His right blade came around and scored a cut on its abdomen. It wasn't a killing blow, but it was a start. The creature yelped, but its iron grip didn't loosen. Out of the corner of his eye, Nathan saw Raylor struggling against the shovel, suspending him by his ribcage. He brought his right blade back around—

Something hit him in the head.

A moment of weightlessness, then Nathan's shoulders were plowing through snow. Stars took his vision, and a high-pitched ring filled his ears.

Nathan blinked, trying to clear the white twinkling lights. His head swam, and the world swayed. Falling snow shifted in and out of focus, blending with the stars. Blearily, he spotted the final hunter running. Nathan didn't blame her. This thing was more than a force. It was...

Unstoppable. At least it's still bleeding.

Everything was spotted and blurry.

Or are those snowflakes?

He couldn't tell. It didn't matter.

This is over.

Elrontis landed on the back of the woman, seizing her shoulder in its teeth. It lifted her and shook its head, then smashed the hunter to the ground. It did it again, and again, and again. Over and over. All the while, Elrontis watched him. The woman was dead by the second shake and smash, but that didn't seem to bother the creature. It growled and chittered as it mangled the hunter's flailing corpse.

The woman who'd been shouldered aside earlier rose behind the beast. She wobbled.

Must've taken a blow to the head.

Nathan blinked and watched as she considered attacking the creature's back. She thought better of it and turned, making a break for the gate.

Elrontis's ears perked up. It dropped the body it was bludgeoning, turned, and leapt after the woman. A claw closed around her ankle. She tripped, then was pulled into the air. For a few heartbeats she dangled—struggling, screaming. It raised its arm, cracking her whole body like a whip. The woman slammed into the ground headfirst.

Nathan tried to rise, but his legs betrayed him, and he wobbled backward into the snow. Elrontis stood at its full height, the woman hanging upside down in one clawed hand. It grabbed her other leg, ripping it free, the same way a human might pull a thigh from a chicken. The pain brought some coherence back to the hunter, and she began to scream and wiggle.

With a groan, Nathan wobbled up. Something hit his shoulder, nearly causing him to topple again. He glanced down. The hunter's leg lay in the snow at his feet. He looked back up at the creature. Elrontis stepped toward him, still holding the squirming, screaming woman. It ripped her arm free and tossed it underhanded at him, clearly not even meant to destabilize. The beast tore her other arm free. The limb landed at his feet a second later, near a spear. Nathan snatched up the weapon.

The screaming stopped.

The monster grabbed the hunter by the neck and pulled her last leg free, tossing it at him as the dismembered torso fell to the snow.

Elrontis slowly crouched until it was eye to eye with Nathan and let out another broken roar. Blood and saliva sprayed the yard, and foul breath filled his nostrils. The bellow seemed to go on forever, initially all rage and bestial fury, but slowly turned to a whimper.

Nathan glanced around. The place was a battlefield, not a backyard. Only eleven people had died here, but it looked like a hundred.

Likely to be twelve real soon.

"And what in the fuck do *you* have to be sad about?" Nathan snarled, leveling the spear. He had to lock his knees to keep from falling over but wasn't willing to go down without a fight.

Even if it won't be much of one.

Elrontis hunched, then bounded forward. Before he could even tell what was happening, the spear flew from his hand, and a claw clamped around his throat. Nathan's feet left the ground, kicking reflexively for purchase, but found none. He glanced down to find he was suspended nearly a span above the snow. He tried to pull the monster's hand from his throat, but the beast's grip was more solid than a manacle.

Elrontis let out a deep, guttural growl.

Nathan flailed, swinging for the monster's head, but its arms were far longer than his. Its teeth gnashed menacingly.

Why aren't you killing me? he wondered, face darkening.

Nathan brought fists down on Elrontis's forearm, blow after blow.

Its upper lip curled into a snarl, nostrils flaring as it took a deep whiff.

"Just fucking end it," Nathan tried to roar, but all that came out was a tiny rasp. He continued to hammer the creature's forearm, but each hit seemed more ineffective than the last.

Elrontis chittered, bared its teeth, then took one last sniff.

45
TANYA
RINGHOLDER

"**R**un!" Tanya yelled.

All three of them turned, splashing back the way they'd come in a dead sprint. Water churned as leeches thrashed through the shallows behind them. They took a passage on the right, rounded a left corner, then ran down a straight hall. Tanya glanced back. Tails whipped about, spraying froth as leeches writhed over and around each other in a tangled mass of slimy flesh.

Fuck, why'd I even look?

They took a turn, then another. A third. A fourth. Tanya soon lost count. She focused on staying near the exterior wall and prayed each turn wouldn't reveal a dead end.

Two vertical lines on the wall caught Tanya's attention. She stopped, sucked in a great breath, and glanced around a familiar chamber. She stood in a short hall, wider than the rest, with six exits.

Damn, back at the start of this wretched labyrinth.

Tanya turned to fight, studying the roiling surface as it slowly calmed.

Nothing moved except the slightly foamy and steadily rising seawater. Someone let out an audible sigh to her left. Tanya looked around. Cross and David were thankfully still with her.

"Well, I'd say we avoid that whole hallway," David remarked.

"Agreed," Tanya said, "but I counted six offshoots we didn't go down, and who knows how many times those hallways split. We may have to explore them, but we can try others first."

"So we're just going to wander aimlessly?" David asked.

"You got a better idea?"

"Well, no…"

"All right then, lucky for you, someone's been paying attention," Tanya said, pulling out her notebook. She flipped past the page with the *Warden's* pickup schedule and began to draw. "The maze is curved. It's subtle, but it's clearly round." Tanya drew half an oval on the blank sheet. "I think we should try again. This time, hugging the right wall. David, can you keep track of our steps? Drawing this thing to scale could be important."

"On it!" David said.

"I'll try to draw the maze as we go. I think we took around six hundred steps before encountering those leeches."

"You think that corpse was from the previous expedition?" Cross asked.

"Must've been," David said. "Or nothing would have been left of that body."

"Focus, fellas!" Tanya scolded. "Water's rising, and we don't have much time."

"Sorry," Cross said.

"No need for apologies. Let's just get moving. Cross, can you use one of your blades or that hammer and mark the passage we came from with an *S*?" Tanya asked.

Cross nodded and quickly etched three lines in the stone. The mark looked more like a backward *Z*, but it would suffice, and hopefully, it would prevent them from running into those sea leeches again.

"All right, David's counting steps. Cross, you mark each passage we go down from now on with an *X*, and I'll try to draw this gods-forsaken place. You know how to write an *X*, right?"

"Yes, ma'am," Cross said.

"Then let's go."

The three of them headed out, hugging the right wall this time. The water was still rising, and Tanya noted it was most of the way up her calf. Holes dotted this curving wall, too, letting in streams of water. They walked for a while and only passed one offshoot, then the maze forced them into a curving left turn that ended in a stony point. Tanya peeked around the point and noted the exterior wall arced back to the right.

So, not entirely round.

"Let's keep to the wall. How many steps, David?"

"Three hundred-ish."

"Ish?" she asked.

"Got distracted once looking for leeches," he said.

Tanya considered scolding him, but her eyes had been shifting between the frothy water and her notebook since she pulled it out.

Lucky there was another expedition recently. If the leeches hadn't been latched onto that body, they'd likely be spread throughout this place, looking for prey. An image of spiraling teeth filled Tanya's mind. She shivered and tamped the thought down with a shudder.

They followed the exterior wall past two more openings on the left. Tanya stopped, holding up a hand. Another black-and-gray mass jutted from the water ahead. This one was almost entirely submerged, and the leeches clinging to it floated around it like fat, slimy strands of hair.

"How many steps now?" Tanya asked, backing up. They were nearly ten spans from the corpse, but that wasn't any reason to take chances.

Those things will be much harder to outrun with the water lapping at our knees.

"Six hundred-ish," David said as they retreated.

Once the body was out of sight, Tanya turned and leveled her pad and pencil. "So, that must be the same corpse." Tanya closed the loop on the drawing and presented the paper to Cross and David.

For a few moments, they all stared at it in silence.

"Looks a bit like a bum," David said with a smile.

"Gods! Why are you so obsessed with ass? Death is closing in from every bloody side, and that's all you can think of?"

"Nothing wrong with a nice bum," Cross chimed in.

"Don't you join in too!" Tanya warned, stabbing a finger toward the big man.

Cross shrugged.

Tanya shook her head. "You two want the good or the bad news first?"

"The good," David blurted out.

"The bad," Cross said simultaneously.

"The bad news is this whole thing's round. Well, round-ish," Tanya explained.

"I think hedge mazes always have entrances and exits on the perimeter, though," David said. "How would you possibly get out, otherwise?"

"I'm not sure." Tanya paused, considering. "Maybe the sword's somewhere in the middle? But if that's the case, we'd need to get to it and back out in..." She pulled out the pocket watch and checked it. "Forty minutes."

"The cheese is in the center then," Cross said.

Both Tanya and David turned to look at him.

"Following one wall only works if the cheese is through an exit at the edge, not in the middle," Cross explained.

She and David stared at the big man a moment longer, then looked at each other.

"Rats, remember," Cross said.

"Oh, yeah. Rats." Tanya ran a hand through her hair.

"Well, what's the bloody good news?" David asked.

"The good news is that we know something new," Tanya explained. "We need to get somewhere in the center of the maze. We've been—"

"That's the bloody good news?" David moaned. "Fucking Korinth's hairy sagging bloody fuckin' ball sack. I thought you were about to tell us you knew the way out, and we just had to get there. Fuck! We're gonna bloody die in here, aren't we?"

Tanya fixed David with a glare and waited until he finally met her eye.

"Got that out of your system?" she asked dryly.

"Yeah...I think so."

"Good, 'cause it's not helping," Tanya said. "Plus, I'm not sure invoking the sea god's name right now is wise."

David looked at the floor and nodded, properly chastised.

"Now, as I was saying," Tanya tapped her pen on the page. "We've been taking paths that lead us toward the edge as much as possible, but I think we need to do the opposite. Hopefully, that'll get us to the relic."

"I'm not sure I can swim with a torch," Cross said. They each looked up at the flickering flames, then down at the rising water.

"If the light goes out, and we have the blade, then we swim until we find a long, sloping wall with holes. Hopefully, we can follow that to the entrance." Tanya pointed at the map, drawing her finger along the exterior wall.

"So, let's say we get the bloody blade and swim back in the bloody dark, and we manage to get past the bloody sea leeches. How in bloody fuck are we gonna bloody get through that bloody stone pillar?" David asked.

Good question.

The two men watched her expectantly.

Tanya racked her brain, but nothing came.

"Well, bloody fucking fuck!" David exclaimed.

Cross just frowned.

"I think we're going to have to figure that one out when we get there, boys," Tanya said. "Who knows, maybe retrieving the blade lifts the pillar. For now, all I know for sure is that we need to move." Tanya glanced down at the water lapping at the middle of her thigh.

Not good. We're wasting time and don't have much left.

They turned away from the passage to the bloated body, hurried back the way they'd come, and took the first offshoot on their right. The hallway led them into a large room with a central, oblong pillar and eight exits. As they explored the passages, Tanya drew them. Slowly, an image resembling a butterfly emerged on the page. The central pillar was the body, and the paths formed the wings.

Most of the passages led back to the same central room, except the one that nearly spit them out on the same leech-ridden corpse. Luckily, they were able to back slowly away without disturbing the creatures. They explored the rest of the area but wasted almost fifteen minutes with only some scribbles to show for it.

Tanya studied the map. "Well, it's either brave the leeches or head back the way we came...again."

"That's an obvious choice," David stated emphatically, then began wading back toward the entrance.

Tanya looked down at the water. It was halfway up her ass now and rising nearly a finger a minute.

They traveled back the way they'd come, trying to force their way toward the center of the labyrinth. It wasn't long until the curving passage dumped them into a triangular-shaped room with a round column and too many exits. Tanya circled the pillar, drawing exits as she counted them.

"Fourteen choices," she finally whispered.

"Four-fuckin-teen!" David moaned.

"It is a bit uncouth of whoever made this place," Cross declared.

Tanya couldn't help but giggle. Things were starting to feel a little desperate and getting to the point where the only choice was to laugh or cry.

Plus, Cross trying his new words is cute, even in our dire circumstances.

"This is unbelievable," David whined. "There's no fucking way we're getting out of here!"

"Not with that attitude." Tanya stared down at her notepad. The water churned behind her, then David was peering over her shoulder.

"Gods! We've only explored about a quarter of it," David practically wailed.

"Not even," Tanya said.

The map was a mess. She was doing her best, but keeping things to scale had turned out far more difficult than anticipated. Each time she thought a whole area was penciled in, they'd discover another passage that needed to somehow fit on the page. "Let's go this way," Tanya said, pointing at a cluster of five passages.

"Why that way?" David asked.

"They're headed toward the center," Tanya explained. "I don't think we'll have time to explore the whole maze."

The bloody place is probably designed that way.

"Good enough for me," Cross said as he scored another *X* near the pathway they'd come from.

David sighed but seemed to have the good sense not to complain further without offering a better suggestion. The central passage of the cluster looped back around in a U-shape and spat them out of one of the remaining four entrances in the same group.

Scrape, scrape. Cross added another *X*.

Lucky. Two exits down in about thirty seconds.

They took the middle passage of the remaining three. It led down a small hallway, then split into three more. Tanya looked down at each passage. The ones on the left and right headed back the way they'd come.

"Cross, mark these two off, will you?" Tanya asked, scribbling on the map. She couldn't see the end of the passages, but they probably led back to the column where fourteen paths converged. They headed straight into another long, curving hallway. After a few minutes, it doubled back the way they'd come.

What a waste of time.

Tanya looked down at the frothy salt water that was already halfway up her stomach.

There were two paths in front of them. Tanya was reasonably sure the left one led back to the room with fourteen exits, while the one on the right headed deeper into the maze. She took the right path, and soon, it split as well. Tanya took the next right, heading further into the heart of the labyrinth. The hallway spiraled inward, and she became more and more certain it would drop them into the center of the maze.

"We must be close," she muttered.

"Why do you say that?" David asked, a tinge of hope entering his frantic voice.

"If this loop goes in a full spiral, there can't be another way to enter the center of the maze. Otherwise, their paths would have to intersect."

"Intersect?" Cross asked.

"It's when two things meet," David provided. "Kind of like the two lines you have been carving to make an *X*."

Cross nodded.

The passage continued to curve hard. The water was nearly chest deep, forcing Tanya to bounce through it to keep pace. She landed, prepared to jump again, and froze.

Tendril-like tails waved out in every direction, less than three paces ahead.

The closest one twitched.

Another clot of leeches, and we'll never outrun them in the high water.

Tanya planted her feet, trying to take a step back.

Something bumped into her from behind.

"Hey! C'mon, we gotta go," David accused with dire impatience.

Tanya teetered forward on the balls of her feet, nearly dunking the map into the water as she frantically reached for the walls. The fingertips of her free hand scraped stone, applying the slightest bit of friction.

Her map hand reeled, desperately trying to keep her body vertical. Tanya let go of the wall, reaching back, hand grasping for anything.

Nothing...nothing...there.

Tanya's fingers found purchase on a mound of fabric, tightening into a death grip and yanking hard.

"Oooo," David squeaked. "Those are my bloody balls. I knew you'd—"

"I don't give a flying fuck what they are," Tanya growled. "Don't bloody fucking move. Don't talk, and don't you dare push me again."

A hand clamped over Tanya's shoulder, pulling her upright. She released David's stones and slowly backed away, pushing the two men trying to peer past her. When they finally made it back to the start of the spiral, Tanya let out a sigh of relief.

"How in the hells are we gonna get past that?" David asked.

"We aren't," Tanya stated. "It's a dead end. That OAM member must've been doing the same thing we were when they got cornered."

Again, Tanya found herself thanking the gods that someone else had gone through this leech hive first and baited the creatures to a few locations.

"I thought you said we were close?" David said.

"I was wrong." Tanya held the map above her head and peered at it in the flickering light. "If my drawing's accurate"—*and I'm not sure it is*—"then that path went in a nearly complete circle. That leaves space for one small hallway next to it. If we can find that passage, it should lead to the center."

The relic could be somewhere else, but something in Tanya's gut told her it had to be in the middle.

Why else would the map look like this? Could the middle really just be a circular room with nothing in it? Why not, though? We've come to plenty of dead ends already.

Tanya pushed the idea away. It was the only plan, no matter how desperate it was starting to feel.

"David, let's try your trick now, except with a small variation," Tanya said.

"Yeah? What's the change?" David's eyes lit up, clearly hearing the hope in Tanya's voice.

Cross had his mouth open as if to ask a question, then he smiled and mouthed the word "variation," apparently figuring it out for himself.

"We aren't gonna go straight. We are gonna go right every chance we get," Tanya explained as they looked at the map.

"I think that's Cross's trick, and it doesn't work here," David said. "We would've gone around in one big circle over and over if we'd used it. I paid attention to that."

"It doesn't work when the cheese is in the center," Cross repeated. "Plus, all these walls that aren't attached to anything screw up the whole idea."

"Yeah, I know, but hopefully, now that we're away from the exterior wall, it will take us closer and closer to the center of the maze." Tanya tapped the little, circular chamber outlined on the map.

"It seems like as good of a plan as any," Cross said.

"I'm gonna keep drawing, but I'm afraid it's not long till our map gets wet," Tanya said grimly. The water was mid-chest now and would be over her head in less than ten minutes.

They took a hall to the right. The maze forced them to travel toward the entrance again as it snaked back around. After a short while, it converged with four new paths.

What if this doesn't work? What if we're headed in the wrong direction?

The thought was useless, but Tanya never could control that little questioning voice.

"Cross, take this," Tanya said.

The big man waded over and took the parchment. Tanya began to swim. The two taller men hopped along behind her as she led them down another long hallway, still drawing in her head. It wouldn't be very accurate, but it was all she had. The passage split again, and Tanya took the map back from Cross. She scribbled their rough path onto it against the wall, handed the notebook back, and took the hallway to the right.

They were still headed away from the center of the maze.

Soon, David was forced to alternate between swimming one-handed and bouncing slowly along, holding his torch aloft. Cross was the only one tall enough to push through the water with any speed, and all that thick muscle and metal he was carrying helped to keep his feet on the ground. They passed two passages on the left. Tanya ignored them and swam to the end of the hall. There, the maze doubled back.

Finally, heading toward the center again.

"We're going the right way now," Tanya called back

Well, the right way to get to that circular room, anyway.

The passage opened into a little room with free-standing corner walls. The ninety-degree columns divided up the chamber, making it look like a bunch of small passages that wove in and around each other. Cross trudged in last with the torch and map held aloft.

Once he's forced to swim, it won't be long till we're all bloated corpses. Tanya pictured herself covered in leeches, then tried to push the mental image away. She could still barely touch the bottom, but it wasn't efficient to move that way.

It'll be nearly impossible to swim with our packs and heavy clothes for long, and Cross isn't gonna make it more than half a dozen spans or so with all the heavy steel—

"Ouch!" Cross yelled.

He reached under the water, hand coming up with nothing. He passed the map to his torch hand and ducked his head under the frothy surface. The torch tipped, water sloshing into the bowl.

The flames sputtered out.

Cross emerged, holding a leech, its mouth twitching. It tried to latch onto his face. He swung it away, but the thing clamped onto his bicep. Steel scraped on steel as Cross unsheathed a knife and severed the leech's mouth from its body. The tail fell away, revealing teeth still tearing through flesh from the backside of its gullet.

Blood ran down Cross's elbow into the churning water. With a grunt, the big man ripped off the mouth that was still trying to bleed him dry and tossed it across the room. It smacked the wall, then splashed into the water.

"You're bleeding a lot," Tanya said. "They'll be coming."

"Time to go!" David chimed in.

"Cross, leave the hammer. David, give him your torch," Tanya instructed.

"Don't drop it, big guy." David handed over their only remaining source of light.

Cross let the hammer fall into the water. Then she and David were swimming, and Cross was doing his best to keep up while bouncing along. They took the first exit on the right.

"Ouch!" Cross yelled again behind them.

Tanya latched on to the end of a wall.

"Grab my foot!" she yelled, dangling a leg back.

Cross put the map between his teeth, grabbed her foot, and pulled himself past. David was already ahead, holding on to the next corner. Tanya swam ahead of him, then stopped and looked back. Cross grabbed onto David's leg and pulled. Midstep, the big man let out another grunt.

Flames danced over the water's surface, illuminating Cross and a small area around him. Two thick, black strands were latched onto his right leg, visible even through the froth.

If we stop to remove them, they'll just overwhelm us.

Tanya grimaced, then turned and swam ahead.

The end of the next wall was a long way off, so Tanya swam to the narrowest part of the hallway. She rotated until perpendicular to the passage and pressed her hands and feet against opposite sides. The walls were slippery, but Tanya managed to form a somewhat rigid shape between them. David swam under her and on toward the end of the hallway, where the passage turned.

Cross grabbed her coat, pulled himself close, then ducked under, passing the still-blazing torch and map over her side. He pushed off her back, propelling himself forward. Tanya released the tension in her muscles and swam up behind him again.

Something brushed her leg. Frantically, she kicked it, and the thing fell away.

With the help of David's dangling leg, the three of them rounded the switchback. Tanya didn't have her map, but she was fairly certain the path was taking them farther from the center again.

I have no idea what to do if we get there anyway. Besides becoming leech food.

The dark thought flashed unbidden through Tanya's mind.

Oh, well, we're out of time for other options.

They proceeded down another passage, and Cross grunted two more times. Tanya got to the end of the curving hallway first. Another passage headed back to the right, paralleling the one they'd come from. She visualized the map in her mind. It looked like it would lead to the central point of the spiral.

"Hurry!" Tanya yelled, looking back and tightening her grip on the end of the wall. "We're almost there."

Water lapped at Cross's grimacing face as he grabbed Tanya's leg and pulled past her. His movements were growing sluggish.

He's not going to make it.

Tanya bit her lip, considering leaving them both. She would have a better chance on her own, especially with them lagging behind as bait. It was the smart move. The sensible choice. The right play in a game of croxix.

An image of Jack and Ted face down in the Channel flashed through Tanya's mind.

Not today.

"Cross! Lose as much of that steel as you can," Tanya yelled. "David. Help me. Now!"

Tanya dove under the surface.

Bubbles clouded the water, and the salt stung her open eyes. Six slimy tails drifted from the big man's calf, hamstring, ass, and back. David appeared next to her, frantically looking from the leeches to her. Sharpened steel fell around them as Cross unloaded armaments into the churning water. He was still walking, but his movements were as slow as tree sap.

Four leech tails drifted about lazily. The other two were wrapped around Cross's body, latching on with more than teeth. Tanya snatched a shortsword as it sank past, cut the first leech free, then ripped the mouth from Cross's calf. David grabbed a blade and cut another off the big man's back. They each got one more before they were forced up for air.

Tanya sputtered, gasping for breath.

David's head broke the surface a moment later, but she was already diving.

Another leech was already latched onto Cross's calf. Tanya skewered it and pulled it free, then cut into one of the two wrapped around the big man's legs. The thing was latched on tight, and slicing through the creature without accidentally cutting Cross was risky at best.

David's face emerged from the bubbles, and his fingers wormed their way around the leech. He used his freakishly strong grip to pry the thing away, and Tanya gutted it, pulling the mouth from Cross's leg. Together, they wrenched the last sinuous tail free and cut it in half.

A mouth snaked from the darkness, filling Tanya's vision with teeth. She maneuvered to the side, grabbing the thing and plunging her knife into its maw. Blood erupted, clouding the water. She left her knife wedged in the oscillating teeth, then resurfaced, wheezing and gasping for air.

"—et's go!" David was saying. "Time to swim!"

"The map!" Cross said, pulling it from his mouth.

"We'll figure it out later." Tanya snatched it from his hand, stuffing it down the front of her jacket. It was wet there, too, but pressing the paper between leather and skin might keep it intact enough to salvage later.

If we ever get a chance to try.

"Lose that hammer." David pointed to the only weapon still strapped to Cross's back.

"No, we might need it." Cross started trying to swim with one hand while holding the torch aloft in the other.

"You can't swim with the light, big guy, and speed's more important than sight now!" David yelled. "Besides, if this passage doesn't lead outta this nightmare, then we're leech food. Time to embrace the darkness!" David took the torch from Cross's hand and looked to Tanya, a crazy twinkle in his eye.

Dread coiled in Tanya's belly like a sack of snakes, but she set her jaw and nodded.

David dumped it.

Everything went dark.

Frantic splashing filled the space.

David cursed behind her.

Cross grunted somewhere to her right.

Her hand hit a wall, sending shooting pain up her arm.

"Fuck!" Tanya yelled, but all that came out was a burble as water filled her mouth.

Hope that's not broken. Doesn't matter now—might never matter.

Something latched onto Tanya's leg, and she kicked it off. Her hands continued to bang into a sloping wall.

More splashing, all around her.

Something collided with her head.

A foot?

A rope-like appendage constricted around her leg. Tanya kicked at it, but it clung on. Sharp barbs sank into her thigh.

She kicked at it again.

It held fast.

Fuck it.

Tanya kept swimming. The thing weighed on her leg, but it was swim or die, so she swam. The wall continued to turn, her skinned knuckles the only thing guiding her.

We have to be nearly at the center of—

Something brushed Tanya's other leg. She kicked it off. It wriggled back, spinning around her ankle. She flung her foot about, but it was useless.

Sharp points sank into flesh. Tanya thrashed through the water, legs weighed down by the creatures. A thud echoed ahead of her.

A deep voice cursed.

Slimy strands slid through her hands every few strokes, like swimming through a patch of river weeds.

Moving, biting, fucking river weeds.

The sound of churning water echoed off the walls, seemingly from everywhere.

"You bloody fucks are—" the voice behind her transformed into a gurgle.

The wall continued to wrap and spin further. Another leech latched onto her leg. The creatures wriggled all around her. The walls fell away, and Tanya put forth one last burst of speed. She crawled through the churning mix of water and slime-covered flesh, hands grabbing slick, writhing rope as often as they scooped seawater.

Her fist slammed into a wall.

A dead end.

Another leech wrapped around her waist, constricting as it tried to burrow through her jacket.

Tanya fumbled about, searching for something, anything.

Wait, that's not a wall...

Tanya groped at it. Some of it was horizontal, some of it was vertical, all of it was slimy, and like everything else in the dark, it was as hard as stone.

46
SCARLETT
REINHOLM

The Nathan dangled in Scarlett's grasp as she inhaled his scent. Sweat and musk filled her nostrils, yet there was no fear. That was surprising and one of two reasons he was still alive. The other was a faint smell she couldn't quite place. Slowly, her nose painted the picture her eyes couldn't. Whatever she recognized was faint, obscured by the falling snow and tang of blood. Fists continued to bounce off her forearm, but Scarlett barely noticed. She breathed in deep through her nose. Green and a touch of silver flooded her mind.

Sage! And...

Another deep whiff.

More green. A dash of purple.

Rosemary and...lavender? Where did I smell those recently?

The whole picture coalesced, working its way from the soft membranes of her snout to her brain.

The girl from the village. The tasty one.

The young woman's face swam through Scarlett's vision. The one called Nathan had lain with her.

She must be his mate.

Scarlett looked back at Roland. He wasn't breathing, and there was no doubt he was dead. The other didn't care, but Scarlett did, and today, they did this together. She vaguely recalled other terrible things it had done.

No, that's not right. Things I've done.

Scarlett shook the thought away. It didn't matter—not right now. What mattered was making these men pay. For the rest of the hunters, their lives would have to be enough. But not for the one she held, still wriggling. The Nathan. This one had been their leader, he and the Raylor. The old man still sputtered up blood and clutched at the shovel, pinning him to the side of the house. She'd ravaged his hunters, each and every one. Even

412

better, she'd forced him to watch. That would have to be enough for him, but not for this...Nathan.

"He gave the order to murder Roland, and he delivered the killing blow," a voice whispered in Scarlett's head. She snarled, turning her ire back on the squirming man. Roland was the only thing left in this world she loved.

Or...had loved.

This man took him from her, so now she would take everything he loved. She would make him suffer.

"I will kill her!" Scarlett tried to scream, but all that came out was a stuttered growl.

He doesn't understand. Can't understand. So, I'll have to show him.

Scarlett tossed the man aside.

The throw wasn't hard, yet his head slumped to the side as he crashed into the fence. She watched him, ears perking up, listening for a breath. Once he pulled in a lungful of air, she was off. Vaguely, Scarlett noticed her wounds weren't healing and understood that was unusual despite never inhabiting this body before.

That's not quite right. I've never been conscious *before. I've been here, though. Many times, I think.* The thought made Scarlett want to vomit, but she was only half in control, and the other half wasn't the slightest bit queasy.

Scarlett leapt the fence, heading along the familiar path she'd unknowingly taken so many nights before. The presence of the other turned out to be a constant thing, lurking just beneath the surface. As Scarlett bounded down the hill, she became increasingly certain it was always with her, just as she had always been with it. Even in her waking moments, it rode along behind her like a passenger on the back of a horse. During the day, it was typically dormant, but not now.

Between leaps and bounds, oddities in Scarlett's life clicked into place. She reasoned out strange occurrences in her past. The big cat in the backyard was the most recent event, but similar things had been happening for years, even before she'd built the cabin on the plateau. Scarlett racked her brain, trying to piece together connections between events in her life.

Last night, all three moons were full...could it be that?

Scarlett reflected on other abnormalities.

Were they around the full moons? They might've been.

She'd always been fascinated by the moons and studied them extensively at the Academy, but she doubted simply staring at them could cause this kind of transformation.

"Now is not the time for analysis. Now is the time for blood!" The same voice in her head. Not quite her own, but not entirely foreign either. She tried to resist.

A big peanut-shaped head flooded into her mind's eye.

Roland.

The big dopey moose bled from dozens of holes into the pure white snow. The voice was her anger, her fury, her hate made manifest. But deep down, Scarlett knew it was her voice. She could blame no one else for the things it—

No. The things we will do in the name of hate.

Soon, the little village sprawled out ahead. Scarlett tasted the breeze as a chilly wind blew down from the plateau. She smelled bits of Nathan. He was easy to pick out, as her nose already stored his scent.

So, he's on the way. Good.

He was fast.

Not fast enough, though.

Scarlett loped along on all fours as the trees gave way to open ground. The village had plenty of activity, but no sentries were posted. She walked along the trickle of a stream rolling in from the highlands, then up a hill. As she crested the rise, a small group of women came into view. They chatted and laughed, filling buckets of water from the stream before it was contaminated with the human stench.

"Feast," said the voice in Scarlett's head.

No, they're not who we're here for.

Scarlett was so angry. She considered unleashing the creature on anything and everyone with even a shred of responsibility for Roland's death, but most of these villagers weren't to blame for that. Her and the presence were of one mind when it came to making Nathan and everyone he loved suffer, though.

"We need to feed. That's their purpose. Cattle, for the slaughter."

No. They're humans, the same as us...well, mostly the same, anyway.

"They killed your animal."

Scarlett skirted around the villagers, weaving through a row of spikes like a spider through a web.

Our animal—and his name was Roland. Besides, these people didn't kill him, their hunters did. These women are just washing their clothes.

"They should pay."

No. He should.

"He is them. They deserve it. They need it!"

414

There was a gasp, then a scream. Scarlett glanced back. One of the villagers washing clothes was pointing at her.

"*Devour!*"

A force pushed against Scarlett's mind. Suddenly, her legs were no longer her own. She tried to shove back, but whatever had thrown her from her own mind was strong. She slammed her consciousness into it. The assault was primal, instinctive, as intuitive as breathing. Scarlett couldn't wrestle control from the other, but her body stopped moving forward. The women were all screaming now.

"*Let us feed!*"

Not—on—them. The thought felt strained, like trying to talk while hauling a log.

The presence would not relinquish control again, but together, they turned from the fleeing women and slunk back through the spikes. Scarlett lifted her head, nostrils flaring. She was looking for the cabin from the other night, but the memory was hazy, and they'd never seen this place during the day.

Suddenly, Scarlett was in control again. She couldn't have said when it happened. For a while, they'd ridden in tandem, then in the space of a breath, the reins were hers again. The presence remained but had seamlessly receded, granting her full use of her limbs once more. Scarlett tasted the breeze, trying to pick up the scent of lavender, rosemary, or sage.

A gong rang in the distance.

Then again...and again...and again.

They'll be coming.

"*This is your fault. They should have died silently.*"

The village was abuzz with activity. Feet pounded on dirt paths, doors creaked open and slammed shut, and townsfolk wailed. The fear was palpable. Scarlett crept around the back of a hut as a mother shuffled two children out the front.

"Where are we going?" a little boy asked.

"To the great hall. Now be quick about it," the mother chided.

"Why's the gong going off?" a little girl asked. "The gong's only for nights."

"I know, dear. They'll explain what's happening at the top of the hill. For now, stay close and be quick." Their voices trailed off as they continued up the path toward the enormous hall looming over the settlement.

Scarlett crept through dirt paths, searching for the cabin from last night. Another five minutes passed before she picked up the scent of sage. Soon, rosemary and lavender joined it, and she followed the alluring bouquet to a little hut off the main road.

The cabin was quiet, the front door ajar. Scarlett crept around to the back of the structure and pushed the shutters wide. No one was inside, so she invited herself in, crawling over the sill like a fox entering the henhouse.

The aroma of lavender, sage, and rosemary permeated everything here. But there were other scents too. Scarlett could smell Nathan on the bed, mingling with another tantalizing flavor. Scarlett inhaled it greedily.

Woodsmoke and succulent sweat, only masked by herbs.

The girl's true scent.

Scarlett crept into the living area. The girl's aroma permeated everything here, but there was a banquet of other smells as well.

Something...familiar.

Scarlett found an old pair of boots by the door. They were the strongest source of the fragrance. Something about it reminded her of last night.

It dawned on the other first. *"He was delicious."*

The young sentry we killed.

"His sister is younger. She will be even more tender. More..."

The other paused, rooting around in her memory for the right word.

"Exquisite," it finished, with far too much satisfaction.

The girl's scent led out the door. Scarlett stalked from the house, moving silently through the empty streets. Her nose twitched, informing her that nearly all the humans were in the center of town.

What should I call you?

"Whatever you like. You are me, and I am you."

You must have a name, though.

Silence.

Could it truly have no name?

"You may call me...El-ron-tis." The presence sounded the name out in their head as if saying it aloud for the first time.

How did the hunters know your name?

"They did not, and neither did I. El-rontis is new. But the name inspires fear, and fear is ambrosia."

The voice in Scarlett's head was a constant, terrifying reminder that she was not in control. But, a small part of her was relieved by its existence.

Perhaps all this violence is not entirely my fault.

Despite the horror of it all, a small piece of her was even a bit fascinated. She'd spent so many years studying at the Academy and had never heard of anything like this.

Scarlett climbed the roof, peering over the apex. People streamed into the meeting hall, packing together like lambs in a flock. Sentries patrolled the hilltop, and delicious dread seeped from the great hall.

All the courage already headed up the mountain to find me.

"*To find us.*"

Right. Us.

"*Let's go. It's time to dine.*"

There are a lot of them, and we're not healing. We best wait for an opening.

"*No, the time is now. Our mouth waters.*"

Indeed, it was. Saliva dripped from Scarlett's canines onto the roof, dribbling down the thatch. A voracious hunger churned in the pit of her stomach, and she could not deny the deep desire to gorge herself on anything and everything.

Most of these people have done nothing wrong. They don't deserve us.

"*They do not matter. They are cattle. They are scrumptious.*"

I can't let you. I won't let you.

Elrontis remained silent.

Movement pulled Scarlett's gaze to the tree line. A man emerged from the woods. Even at this distance, she recognized him.

Nathan.

Scarlett let out a low growl. The man slowed momentarily, catching his breath, then sprinted toward the village. Roland's face flashed through her mind, and her blood boiled. Darkness crept around the edges of her vision. Her upper lip quivered then curled into a snarl.

The first signs of violence.

The darkness encroached, curling around Scarlett's perception like an aperture on a telescope.

Where are the stars?

The inky black enveloped her in a malevolent, cradling, sinister, devoted embrace.

Elrontis leapt from the building, landing on another roof, then she was off to the next. Two sentries spotted her and began sending shaft after shaft in her direction. As she neared, they finally called for help. One arrow whizzed by as she landed on a roof adjacent to the meeting hall.

She pounced.

The sentry dropped his bow, fumbling with a spear as gravity brought her down. One of her claws hewed through the man's wrist as she landed on him, spear clattering to the ground. Her other claw tore through ribs, skewering his heart. Elrontis ripped it free, wolfing it down.

"A delicacy," she thought as the heart slipped down her gullet beat by beat.

The second archer dropped his bow and pulled a spear. Elrontis roared, arms spread and fingers flexed in challenge. He dropped his weapon, turned, and ran. With one great leap, she landed behind him, cleaving his right leg off at the knee with one claw and raking him across the back with the other. Blood spurted as he wobbled on one leg, kneecap dangling, then toppled.

"He'll be dead in moments, and there are much juicier morsels inside."

Elrontis moved to the front doors, clawing the furs to the side. A jumble of tables and chairs blocked the entrance. Six arrows flew at the door from inside the hall. Four thumped into the makeshift barricade. The other two hissed through gaps in the furniture. One went wide. The other clipped the top of her shoulder, drawing blood. She snarled, dropped the flap, and stalked around the side of the building.

She heard the two men skulking around the perimeter before she saw them. They leveled spears and charged, stabbing in unison. Elrontis reared up on hind legs, swatting the metal tips to the side. She leapt past the points and fell on the two men, driving her claws through each bag of flesh and into the wooden planks below. Her teeth sank into the neck of the one on her right, tearing out his trachea with a snarl. She gulped it down as the other man screamed.

Red-hot pain flashed across her left bicep, and she turned to the source. The man had managed to draw a knife and was bringing it around for another stab. She pulled her claw free and slapped the insolent fool across the face.

He dropped the dagger mid-swing, eyes rolling. The blade clattered away on wooden boards. Elrontis tore him open, buried her snout in his belly, and began to feast. A moment later, someone screamed, then fists were hammering on the back of her head. The blows were inconsequential. Her snout was buried in warm, savory flesh, and she was in the throes of ecstasy.

Something pulled on her senses. At first, she paid it no mind, but it tugged again. Soon, it became too insistent to ignore. Elrontis shivered as she snapped back to reality.

She raised her head. Why had the other interrupted her feast? Reluctantly, she stood and walked away from the man as he tried to stuff chewed entrails back into his belly.

"Fuck—why—Pirel help us!" the man screamed.

Elrontis stopped listening as she climbed the great hall's roof.

Smoke poured from a central hole in the thatch. Together now, they approached the opening and peered inside. Getting a clear picture through the gossamer veil was impossible, but she could see villagers packed in tight, like books on a crowded shelf.

Six braziers lit the hall, and barricades blocked the three entrances. Archers stood in the center of the room, sighting down shafts trained at each barricade. Elrontis couldn't make out the face of her quarry in the crowd, and smoke shrouded the girl's smell.

"The time for subtle pleasantries is over. The banquet is about to begin."

They dropped silently through the hole.

Carnage ensued.

47
DAVID TRUEHEART

F*uck!*

It was getting harder and harder to swim.

Fuck. Oh, fuck. Oh, fuck!

David saw nothing, heard too much, and felt everything. Slimy ropes tightened around his body, and churning water echoed through the deafening din. Some of the splashing was him, some was his companions, but most was undoubtedly leeches.

He'd counted the bites at first but had given up after six. David had no bloody idea how many of the things were latched onto him, but even more wriggled through the water. His right forearm slid along a slimy, writhing rope. Something curled around his thigh, constricting. He plunged a hand into the water. Slippery flesh squirmed where liquid should be. He grabbed onto it anyway, using it as leverage to thrash through the writhing soup.

The whole thing was a useless endeavor. David had lost track of Tanya and Cross in the chaos and could only pray they were still in front of him.

Not that it matters. There's no way out. We're gonna be bloated, floating corpses—

Thump.

Pain sang through David's head and neck, his vision somehow blurring even in the complete darkness.

Another damn wall.

A new leech wrapped around his forearm. David winced, expecting teeth.

"Fucking cocksucker!" David yelled as sharp points sank into his left butt cheek.

There they are...but that's the wrong place.

The thing tightened around David's forearm, hauling him upward.

Airborne?

A moment later, solid ground was underfoot.

Gods, I could kiss it.

A frantic, scraping sound filled the darkness. Something grabbed his cock in a vice-like grip, yanked once, then groped around. David's stomach lurched, but the pain wasn't quite enough to double him over.

"Fuckin' hells," he squeaked. "What in bloody fuck are you doing?"

Scrape, scrape, scrape.

Sparks shattered the darkness, illuminating the bare outline of Cross's face for an instant.

"You said one was on your cock," the big man said. "Just trying to help."

David reached back and ripped the flapping leech from his ass.

Scrape, scrape, scrape.

Sparks lit the room again. An image of leeches wriggling over the stone floor burned into his retinas, then everything was gone again. He thought back, visualizing the scene.

No, not the floor.

They stood on stone, and somehow, Tanya was two heads taller than him.

Stairs?

"Fuck it." Tanya's more feminine voice was a contrast to Cross's cavernous baritone.

Something clattered, like winnings pulled across a table. David blew out a breath, lips flapping, then started tugging leeches off his calves and arms. Oddly, pulling the bastards free hurt less than the initial bite, but the fuckers were strong, and there were a lot of them.

Bloody tenacious bastards.

David strained, trying to pull another free.

Glug, glug, glug.

The unmistakable sound of wine poured from a bottle.

But why? Guess I could use a drink.

"Up here," Tanya said.

A large hand clamped onto David's shoulder, pulling him. He stumbled up the first couple of steps, but the hand kept him upright, and his feet soon found the cadence.

Scrape, scrape, scrape—

Sparks flew, setting the writhing ground ablaze.

High-pitched squeals echoed off towering walls.

Burn, fuckers.

The three of them stood on a staircase carved directly into stone. It spiraled up into darkness and down into…David wanted to call it water, but the thrashing puddle of leeches contained more flesh and blood than brine.

421

David glanced back up the steps. Tanya was tucking flint and steel into a jacket pocket. She bent and picked up a half-empty bottle of lantern oil from the steps, corked it, and placed it in her bag.

With a shudder, David looked himself over in the burning light. Two of the disgusting creatures still clung to him. He yanked the first off quickly but struggled with the second wrapped around his leg.

Cross bent, grabbed hold of the leech, and tore it free like it was nothing. The thing wriggled, gaping mouth searching. The big man tossed it onto the steps below, still slick and burning. The leech quickly joined the screeching chorus of its fellows.

Serves you right, fucker.

David watched the writhing creature briefly before turning to Tanya, who was still digging around in her pack. Cross turned and looked up the stairs past her. A sea leech still dangled from the big man's ass.

"Hold still," David said, grabbing the creature and pulling with all his might.

The thing came free with a pop, and David's head spun, suddenly woozy. He tossed the leech backward, and his equilibrium went with it. His arms began to windmill, icy panic sinking its teeth into him. He tipped backward toward the fiery steps and thrashing water.

Cross reached out, snatching one of his flailing arms and pulling him upright.

"Damn this place, damn the OAM, and damn these fuckin' leeches!" David yelled once he was fully upright. "They didn't know there would be a maze down here? They didn't know about the traps? They didn't have a bloody map of this fuckin' maze? They didn't know about the fucking, blood-sucking, bloody fucking parasitic fucking leeches?"

Glug, glug, glug. Tanya was pouring something again.

"Does seem a bit crass of them," Cross remarked.

David stopped yelling, a smile slowly spreading unbidden across his face. "By the gods, big man. Sometimes, the shit you say."

Cross raised an eyebrow. "Maybe they gave their only map to the first group?"

Scrape, scrape, scrape.

Sparks flew again, and soft lantern light pushed away the worst of the darkness.

"Maybe this vault is so old that records of it were lost or destroyed," Tanya suggested. "Kinda sounded like the OAM meant to lock the relic up and bury the key." She lifted the lantern and headed up the stairs.

"Could be," David said, following behind her. "They sure spent a lot of time and money building this place, though."

"Taxes explain that," Tanya said. "Don't forget, the OAM needs to justify its existence. Projects like this one rationalize their need for funding."

"Yeah, but they could've just tossed the relic in the ocean," David protested. "Or took it deep into a mine, then collapsed the damn thing. Seems like they spent a whole lotta time and money to get fuck all."

"Not sure I can disagree with you there," Tanya said. "It does seem a bit wasteful. But Vincent did mention that they've tried tossing relics into the sea and burying them. I've only dealt with the Order a few times, and I can't say they ever seemed frugal or even practical, but they were always prudent."

Cross opened his mouth to say something.

"Careful with money and being smart," David provided.

The big man closed his mouth and nodded, visibly committing the words to memory.

The stairs led to a narrow hallway that opened into a small chamber. Six sconces lined the walls. Four held torches, but two were conspicuously empty. The room was otherwise unadorned, except for another passage at the far end. David walked over and took a quick peek. The hallway continued straight until the darkness swallowed it.

"Let's catch our breath here for a minute," Tanya suggested. "I want to see how much damage these leeches caused. The bites don't hurt anymore, but they may have a similar numbing agent to their freshwater cousins."

Tanya rolled up a pant leg, inspecting the calf where one of the creatures bit her. David walked over and joined her. Dozens of little holes marked her pants, but the leather had stopped a good portion of the injury, and the teeth only pierced far enough to draw blood. Tanya took out a salve and began rubbing it into the punctures.

"It doesn't look that bad," David remarked.

"I don't think it is, but we should treat them for infection anyway," Tanya said. "We need to eat something too. I have a feeling we lost a lot of blood."

David dug through his soaked backpack, pulled out some hardtack and jerky, then dumped the rest of the contents across the floor.

Hopefully, it'll dry out a little.

Tanya finished applying the salve to all the wounds she could reach, then removed her coat and lifted the back of her shirt.

"Get my back, will you?" Tanya held out the small container.

"I'd been wondering when you'd ask me to put my hands all over you."

"Shut up and get to work." Tanya turned away, but not quick enough to hide the smile that danced across her lips.

David took the tub and applied the paste to all the wounds on her back, then got to work on his own. It stung like the thirteen hells, and he was covered in far more bites than Tanya. Eventually, she scooped up some salve and began rubbing it into unreachable places in what seemed like the least gentle way possible.

"Ouch!" David said.

"Quit whining." Tanya shook her head. "A little sting just makes you tough."

"Tough for what?" David asked.

"Life."

"Overrated."

"Life?" Tanya's eyebrow slowly raised.

"No, being tough."

"Says the one squealing at a little salve."

David was about to retort when she jammed more of the paste into another set of punctures, causing him to wince.

"Damn, that hurts!"

"You're hopeless," Tanya chastised, but David could hear the amusement in her voice, so he let it lie.

Cross managed to pull three of the wall-hung torches from their sconces and dropped them into the center of the room with a clattering of steel.

"Me next!" the big man said, stripping completely naked.

"Good gods, man! You didn't have to take it all off," David objected.

"Actually, I think he did," Tanya observed.

Hundreds of punctures covered Cross's body from dozens of bites.

"How are you still standing, buddy?" David asked, eyes widening.

"Dunno, guess I don't want to die in the dark."

"What?"

"Hand me that salve, David." Tanya held out a hand. "And give Cross some of that food."

David passed her the tub, then went to get the hardtack and a bit of the jerky. He turned to find Tanya rubbing the paste all over the big man's naked body.

A slight twinge twisted through David's chest.

Jealousy?

David pushed the feeling away. He'd encountered many a jealous man as a musician, and it was never a good look.

Most of the time, it has the opposite of the desired effect anyway.

424

So, David plastered on a smile and handed Cross the rations.

After a few more minutes, Tanya finished lathering the big man up, and soon, he was clothed again. David lit the only torch still attached to the wall and doused the lantern. They ate, hung spare clothes by the torch to dry, and rested. David slumped against the stone wall and nodded off.

Click.

Tanya slid the pocket watch into her jacket pocket.

"How long was I out?" David asked, realizing he might just feel like a real human being again.

"Couple hours," Tanya said.

"So, what's the plan? Head off down the dark tunnel?" David stood with a groan.

"Well, we have a few hours before the next high tide, and another six until they're low again," Tanya explained. "We'll want to wait until the water's down before trekking back through the maze."

"So that gives us around nine hours to explore the tunnel, find the blade, and get back here," Cross calculated.

Tanya nodded.

"We know two OAM members ended up as leech food, right?" David asked.

"Correct," Tanya said. "But there were likely more. We only explored a little over a third of the maze, if my drawing was at all accurate."

"Yeah, so there could be a few more corpses behind us," David said. "But I imagine they brought a sizable group. You think it's safe to assume that some of them made it this far?"

"Yeah, judging by the two empty sconces." Tanya gestured to the metal tabs bolted to the wall.

"Well, I hate to state the obvious," David began.

"That's never stopped you before," Tanya cut in.

David fixed her with a glare.

Tanya smirked.

"I think we can assume they made it here, and we know they didn't make it back to the mainland," David said.

"So, we know that path's not filled with rainbows," Cross offered, pointing down the hall.

425

"Precisely."

Cross's brow furrowed, head tilting to the side. "It means you agree?"

"You got it, big guy."

A smile split Cross's face.

"It can also mean to be very detailed," Tanya added. "But you don't need to use all these fancy words. David only likes them because he's a *baaard.*"

"What's wrong with bards?" David demanded.

"Nothing, they just tend to be a teensy bit full of themselves, is all." Tanya held up a tiny gap between thumb and forefinger as a smile played across her lips.

"I am not full of myself!" David protested.

Cross let out a booming laugh.

"Don't you side with her now!"

"Oh no, I didn't mean you, David. I meant the other bards." Tanya gave Cross a wink.

The big man doubled over, laugh echoing about the chamber.

"Well, I'm glad I could be the butt of your joke," David said.

Tanya shrugged. "Stare at something long enough, and you're bound to become it."

David's mouth dropped open. *Well, ain't that some shit.*

Cross fell to the floor, still roaring with laughter.

David scowled, but Tanya only grew more smug.

"Oh, gods, I'm crying," Cross wheezed.

"You two are just delusional from blood loss," David grumbled, thrusting one of the two torches at Cross. "Let's go."

The big man stood, wiping tears from his eyes. He accepted the torch and led the way down the hall. After quite some time, they came to a set of stairs leading down.

"Why don't you let me go first, big guy," David said, squeezing past Cross. He stepped gingerly, trying to ensure the stone didn't depress before putting his full weight on each foot.

I hope the OAM made it this far. It'd be lucky if they sprung some traps ahead of us.

But as they descended, David found no gray-robed corpses, pressure plates, or pitfalls. After two flights, the staircase ended, and a short hallway opened into a much larger chamber. The room was nearly eight spans across and lined with statues slowly disappearing into the inky black.

David stepped forward.

"Stop!" Tanya exclaimed.

David froze.

Tanya slid past him.

He risked a glance at her backside.

Exquisite.

David smiled.

Round, supple, firm. Confident. Is that right? Could an ass be confident?

He took another look at hers.

Sure can.

Tanya ran a hand along the stone wall near the end of the hall, then held her torch aloft, staring at the ceiling.

"Another stone pillar?" David asked, squinting upward.

"I think so," Tanya said absently, continuing to examine.

"What's that smell?" Cross asked.

David sniffed. A soggy, rotten stench hung in the air.

"Not sure. Rotting, bloated gray-cloaks, I'd wager," David said.

"More leeches?" Cross asked.

"I bloody hope not." David shuddered, suddenly feeling slimy flesh wriggling against his skin again.

Tanya got down on all fours and crawled slowly forward, brushing the floor with light and precise fingertips. David's eyebrows crept upward, unable to pull his gaze away. Deep down, he was pretty sure Tanya wouldn't mind, but he preferred to avoid a tongue-lashing whenever possible.

She glanced back, and David quickly averted his eyes.

"I don't feel a pressure plate, and I'm not about to crawl through this whole damn hall," Tanya said. "Not while you stand there twiddling your thumbs and staring at my ass, anyway."

"Me?" David asked, putting on his most innocent smile. "I wouldn't dare."

"How did you know?" Cross asked.

"C'mon, you're supposed to be on my side, big guy!"

"Just a feeling," Tanya said. "You can sense eyes if you're used to people watching."

"People watch me all the time," David said. "I can't feel 'em."

Tanya gave David a pointed look. "The other half's knowing your audience."

"Sorry, sorry. I know. It's just..." David paused. "It's like asking an artist not to admire a masterpiece."

"A masterpiece, huh?" Tanya stood and turned away. "I'll take that. Still...you? An artist? Now, that's a bit of a stretch." She turned enough to give David a wicked grin.

427

"Hard to imagine, right? Maybe I simply haven't found my muse." David widened his eyes. "Wait, is that you?"

"Seriously?" Tanya asked dryly.

"Yeah. I mean, can't you feel the inspiration flooding in?" David paused for dramatic effect. "I can hear it even now." He cupped a hand to his ear. "'The Ballad of the Bottom!'" David belted out the brand-new title in a cavernous baritone.

Deep laughter swelled through the chamber.

"No, please don't, I can't take anymore," Cross pleaded, tears already welling in his eyes.

"How about 'The Ballad of the Bloody Blade'?" Tanya suggested. "That's what *all* of us are here for, not bottoms."

"Hmmm." David scratched his chin. "That does have a nice ring to it. Could you write that down for me, Tanya? Then again, how do we justify all the rhymes with ass I already came up with? Maybe we dedicate just one verse to Tanya's bottom? What do you think, Cross?"

The man was laughing hysterically and in no shape to reply.

"Ass, mass." David counted out the words on his fingers.

Tanya stared at him, a single eyebrow slowly rising.

"Pass, gas." He couldn't help the devious grin from spreading across his face as his third and fourth fingers went up.

"David," Tanya warned. "If you write a song about me, and it has even one fart joke...I swear—"

"Don't be crass. It's just some sass." David chuckled.

A smile tugged at the corner of Tanya's mouth, but her eyes were full of menace.

David looked from Tanya to Cross, who was rolling on the floor.

Can I really stop with such a captive audience?

He met Tanya's gaze one last time.

Yes, I can.

"C'mon, buddy," David lowered a hand. Cross took it and pulled. David felt his back strain. "Durno's enormous saggy testicles," he groaned through gritted teeth. "How many bloody brick are you?"

Cross got his weight over his own two feet and shrugged. He clapped David on the back with a blow that nearly knocked him over, then turned to Tanya.

"You two got that out of your system?" Tanya asked. "Ready to get back to work?"

"Yeah, David's not wrong, though, Tanya. You do have a nice bottom," Cross said, tone purely factual.

"Cross!" Tanya scolded. "I expect that sort of behavior from David, but not from you."

The big man's cheeks flushed, visible even in the torchlight.

"Sorry, just saying. Besides, David has a nice bottom too. It's just a fact. Doesn't have to be weird."

"Thanks, big guy! I work real hard on it, and it so rarely gets the attention it deserves."

"You two are insufferable," Tanya said, still smiling. "There's no pressure plate here, so let's go. Follow right behind me, now, and only step where I step first. Oh, and David?"

"Yeah?"

"Keep your eyes on my feet, eh? Don't need you getting distracted and setting off something catastrophic." Tanya moved forward with a deft precision David could never hope to match. He followed behind her, and even though he did, on occasion, sneak a peek at her backside, he kept a closer eye on the placement of her feet.

As they moved farther into the room, more statues loomed from the darkness, and the stench worsened.

Crunch.

David felt the noise under his boot. Apprehensively, he raised his foot and lowered the torch. Something was ground into the stone.

What is that? A crab?

David scanned the floor. Tiny, lifeless crustaceans littered the rough stone.

Where did you all come from?

His gaze finally settled on the statues. Each figure wore a robe with the cowl pulled back and was locked in a different pose. The statue on his left appeared to be female. She stood, hands clasped and head bowed. The one on his right was male. He had one hand tucked into the flap of his robe, the other extended as if trying to shake hands.

In greeting? Or trying to make a deal?

David nearly reached out and took the hand, then decided against it.

A gray-clad mound lay on the floor behind the next statue.

At least there are no leeches on this one.

"Think I found the rest of the gray-cloaks." David took a step toward the lifeless pile.

"Careful," Tanya warned. "There's probably a good reason he died in that spot."

David looked around but didn't see any murder holes or pressure plates.

The gender of the statue nearest the dead man was rather ambiguous. They held the hilt of a sword, the blade embedded deep in their gut. David bent, examining the stone-carved weapon. Underneath the blade, a key jutted from the stone.

No, that's not quite right.

There was a handle that belonged to a key, but the hole had no notch at the bottom, like a keyhole should.

A key that can't be removed? Curious.

David grabbed the statue's stone hood and leaned over the corpse. He wedged the tip of his right toe under the body, then flipped it. The corpse rolled, and the man's gray hood slid from his face.

Except there was no face. The soft flesh of his eyes, nose, and cheeks had been thoroughly picked clean. Beyond the man's empty eye socket, the lifeless form of a crab lay still, buried deep in his skull.

David's stomach did a flip, then a twist. Suddenly, the jerky and hardtack were coming up.

"Damn acrobatic belly," David moaned.

With a groan, he wiped his mouth on a sleeve, then risked another glance at the dead man. Bile filled the eye socket. Visually, it was an improvement. Still, David didn't let his eyes linger.

"Looks like our friends ran into some trouble with crabs," David called out.

"Crabs?" Cross asked. "The room's bone dry."

"So was the corpse."

"It's been dry here a while," Tanya said. "Otherwise, those crabs would still be feasting. There's plenty of meat left on these fellows."

"There are more?" David asked.

Tanya stood in front of an enormous door at the far end of the room. Six more statues lined each side of the hall, casting shadows clawing up the walls in the flickering light.

That makes sixteen, eight on each side.

"Yeah, looks like six gray-cloaks made it through the maze," Tanya said.

"All strewn about and stinking," Cross added.

David rose and walked back to the center of the room. The monk opposite the one with the sword in the gut had feminine features and was cupping a cloud held aloft by three jagged pillars.

A storm cloud?

He looked right then left, examining the statues as he passed. Each one was unique and seemed to have a deeper meaning. Some were clearly men, some distinctly women, others somewhat in between. Each had the same unremovable key embedded in their torso.

David took mental notes of the different statues.

Left: A man adjusting a sundial.

Right: Someone gripped a mirror, holding it toward the room. Torchlight reflected off it, dancing up the walls as David passed.

Left: A woman, head in her hands. *Weeping?*

Right: Hands cupped, holding a sculpted flame.

Left: A bearded man clutching a candle.

Right: A woman with an index finger held over pursed lips.

Ooh! A bit naughty, are we? Want to tell me your secret?

Left: Someone contently cradling a baby.

Right: A man grasped a stone bowl.

Left: A woman clutched a heart that looked like it had been recently extracted from someone's chest.

Right: A waterfall of gemstones poured from the statue's mouth, pooling in their cupped hands. Most of the gems were carved from the rock, but a few real stones inlaid the piece.

Left: A man holding a scratched and pitted orb.

Right: The last statue held an open book but wasn't reading it. Instead, she smiled at him. Even after passing her, David couldn't shake the feeling he was still being watched.

How in the hells did the sculptor do that?

David reached the end of the chamber and stood before a massive iron door set in a sturdy metal frame. Despite its size, the heavy iron slab resembled something that belonged on a noble's safe rather than in this cold stone room.

A central wheel protruded from the door at nearly chest height. Five complex hinges connected the wheel to five different rods. Each rod was spaced evenly along the door frame, reminding David of a hand with fingers splayed wide. The rods passed through several iron loops bolted to the door and disappeared into heavy housings cast directly into the frame.

"That's some vault," David murmured. "How'd they even get the bloody thing in here?"

"Not sure. Looks like it's got five individual locks, though," Tanya said without even glancing up. She stood off to the side, near the clasp at the far left of the frame.

"How much do you think this is worth?" Cross pointed to the statue spewing gemstones.

"Probably the same amount as the stones embedded in it," David said. "But I doubt they're easy to pull out."

"You don't think the whole statue's worth anything?" Cross asked.

"Maybe. The mason clearly had some talent. But I can't imagine who'd want the damn thing. Plus, it can't be easy to remove."

"It wouldn't be too hard. The gemstones aren't even attached to the mouth they're coming out of," Cross said.

"How in the hells would you get it out of here—"

"Don't touch it," Tanya cut in. "Something's funny here. They may have left something tempting like gemstones as bait."

Cross stepped closer, squinting at the sculpture's neck. "The head is a separate piece, made after the initial cut of stone."

"Makes sense," David said. "It would be nearly impossible to get detail on the back of the head with that hood in the way."

"I guess that's true," Cross muttered.

David walked over to Tanya and peered over her shoulder. She was staring at three lines of text etched directly into the stone with her torch tight to the wall.

> You can keep it, but never own it.
> You can break it, but you can't touch it.
> It's fleeting by nature, yet rarely is it complete.

"A riddle?" David asked.

"Looks like it." Tanya sighed. "I hate bloody riddles."

"Really? Seems like they'd be right up your alley. That is, with you being so smart and all."

Tanya shot him a glare. "Don't get me wrong, part of me likes them, but they drive me crazy if I can't figure them out. Almost as much as you do."

I drive you crazy, huh?

David opened his mouth to voice the thought as suggestively as possible.

"I love riddles!" Cross boomed.

"You?" David asked in astonishment. "You can't even spell riddle, big guy."

"Riddles aren't about spelling," Cross protested. "They're about puzzling. Let me read it."

There was a short silence as Cross stared at the words.

"I guess I meant, read it to me, please," Cross corrected.

"Oh yeah, sorry. I forgot," David said. "You can keep it, but never own it. You can break it, but you can't touch it. It's fleeting by nature, yet rarely is it complete."

"What does fleeting mean?" Cross asked.

"It means to flee or to run away, kind of," Tanya responded.

Gods, he won't be any help here. Doesn't even know the words.

David examined the door again. Three lines of text were carved in the stone at the end of each lock. He turned away from the wall and walked back along the side of the room as Tanya pulled out her notebook and started scribbling.

I'm surprised that thing's dry. Maybe the papers near the center stayed intact?

"An open book, a fountain of gemstones, a stone bowl," David muttered, pausing at each statue. "A severed heart." He stopped.

Hearts mean love.

David looked at the rest of the row: *a flame, a mirror, a sword to the gut, and a handshake.* "Tanya, read that passage aloud, will ya?"

"You can keep it, but never own it," Cross's deep voice filled the hall. "You can break it, but you can't touch it. It's fleeting by nature, yet rarely is it complete."

"You memorized that whole thing?" Tanya asked.

Love fits.

Cross grunted.

The tide will be going out soon, and we need to be on the way out of this bloody death trap when it does. Time to ante up.

"It's love!" David shouted. "You can't own it, but you can keep it, and you can't touch it, but you can break it." He turned the key.

A grinding sound emanated from the statue, followed by a series of clicks. The monk's head slammed backward, thudding into the stone hood as water poured from the thing's neck.

Boom.

The stone column crashed to the floor at the far end of the hall, blocking them in.

"Fuck!" David yelled as water fountained onto him. "I just can't stay bloody dry today."

The chamber began to fill.

48
EVA
ERENHART

The sun was high in the sky when Eva finally awoke. Her hands slid across the bed, looking for Nathan. The furs where he should lay were cold. Her fists clenched, and she breathed out a long sigh. She wasn't even really looking for him; she was just looking for someone. Anyone, really. Her father's cold, dead eyes filled her mind, slowly morphing into her brother's.

Her chest constricted as yesterday's tears threatened to make a reappearance.

"No," she told the darkness. "Not today."

She'd shed more tears over the last two years than she could count and none of them had done the slightest good.

I'm done crying.

Eva sucked in a long quivering breath, gathered herself, and stood.

She padded over to her vanity, ran a bone comb through her hair twice, then headed to the main room without changing her clothes. Eva walked swiftly to the front door, pointedly keeping her eyes away from the boots in the corner. She grabbed her shoes, slipped them on, and shouldered through the door into the afternoon light.

Eva didn't bother to shut the front door. Her brother had always nagged her to close it, and her father before him.

Not anymore...

Her throat tightened, and she forced back another wave of tears. She almost turned around to slam the door, but managed to stuff all the feelings down instead.

The path to Aram's forge was familiar, and her feet took her there without thinking. Smoke billowed from the room as she pushed the front door open, and the blazing heat wrapped her in an embrace.

Aram's eyes widened a fraction as he looked up from the crucible he was tipping into a mold.

Eva nodded and grabbed her leather apron by the door, fastening it around her waist.

"You all right?" Aram asked as she walked over.

So he's heard.

Eva nodded.

Aram eyed her skeptically. "Really?"

"I need this."

Aram bit his lip, then nodded. "We always need more axes," he said, pouring the rest of the molten metal into another rectangular mold.

Eva watched the iron solidify, trying to concentrate on only the cooling metal.

Tongs in hand, she dislodged the ingot from the mold and moved to her anvil.

Clang. Her hammer narrowed one end of the ingot, shaping it into something new.

Bang. She breathed, hands tightening around the wooden handle.

Clang. Creating something new felt good. Forging something pliant into something resilient. Taking something with no purpose and giving it one.

She flipped the metal over, losing herself in the familiar rhythm as she worked the other side.

Occasionally her brother's face would creep in from the edges of her vision. She pushed it away, focusing instead on anything she could. Mostly she thought of the work, but she let her mind wander to Nathan as well.

She was glad he'd stayed, even if she'd asked him not to. He was a little intense but genuinely seemed to want to do the right thing.

Even if he does have a funny accent.

The thought brought a reluctant smile to her lips.

She'd have thrown him out the door if he'd pushed for anything more. But he hadn't. He'd ignored her first request to leave but had otherwise been a perfect gentleman and precisely the distraction she'd needed.

The red, curving axehead slipped from her tongs. Eva dropped the tool and reached for it. She came to her senses before her hand touched the molten metal.

She shook her head and blew out a breath.

Need to focus.

Eva picked up the tongs, pinched the half-formed axe head off the ground, and returned it to the anvil. She tapped either side, knocking off the dirt, and went back to work.

She lost herself in the rhythm again.

Eva considered Nathan's single, silly god, wondered where the man had come from, and found herself hoping Raylor was right about him. Hopefully, he would deliver them from the darkness as the prophecies foretold.

Hours passed, and Eva finally gave the metal one last quench before stepping outside. She wiped sweat from her brow and ladled up some water from Aram's rain bucket.

The water was crisp, and the breeze felt good after hours in the forge.

She looked up, checking the sun. It was low on the horizon, but they still had a bit of light—

The town gong rumbled through the air.

The ladle fell from Eva's grip.

She looked around.

The breeze sent a shiver up her spine.

It can't be. It's far too soon.

49
DAVID TRUEHEART

A series of clicks reverberated through the long hall.

"Damnit, David! Love isn't fleeting!" Tanya yelled. "What kind of bloody bard are you?"

"The kind who knows love is for songs and fairy tales!" David shouted as he tried to force the monk's head back down. Hinges kept the head in line, but he couldn't get a good grip with the hood in the way, and the water pressure was far too great anyway.

"Time to focus, you two," Cross bellowed.

David glanced over. Cross had wedged his torch in a bar and was wrenching on the wheel at the door's center. The big man's muscles rippled, but the handle didn't budge.

"Did one of the locks open?" David yelled.

Cross stopped straining and looked up. "No."

David glanced around the room. The water streaming from the statue's neck was already up to his ankles.

"All right, riddle master! We've got an orb. A storm. A candle. A secret. Depression? A sundial and someone praying?" David had to yell to be heard over the rushing water.

"What's a sundial?" Cross asked.

"It tells time!" Tanya and David yelled in unison. Their eyes met. "Time!" David shouted.

Tanya ran to the statue holding the sundial and turned the key. Its head hinged backward into its hood as water gushed from it. Another series of clicks shook the room.

"Did the lock move?" Tanya hollered.

"No." Cross ran over, stopping at the sculpted monk with hands outstretched. "Trust?"

David was at the statue in an instant, pinching the key.

"Wait-wait-wait!" Cross said. "You can keep it, and you don't own it. You can break it, and you certainly can't touch it. But is it fleeting by nature?"

David took his hand off the key.

"It is rarely complete," Tanya added.

"I mean, it's a good guess," David said. The water was already mid-calf, and the ceilings were less than three spans high.

Gods, we'll be swimming again soon. Then, this gets a lot harder.

David's eyes landed on the hooded figure with hands clasped in prayer.

Prayer? Belief?

David repeated the riddle in his head:

Keep it, never own it. Yes break it, no touchy. Fleeting by nature, rarely complete.

"I fucking hate riddles!" Tanya cursed.

"Hold on. Hold on," David said.

Faith. You can keep faith. You can break faith. It can be fleeting, and it's seldom complete.

"Faith! It's faith!" David yelled, pointing toward the statue.

Tanya looked at him, followed his gesture to the statue at her side, then grabbed the key.

"Is it fleeting by nature, though?" Cross asked.

"Sometimes!" Tanya yelled. "We need to hurry, and it's a good guess." She turned the key. The head of the monk tilted back, slamming into the hood as water erupted from his neck.

David groaned.

A loud scrape echoed through the room as the clamp on the top right corner rolled on rusty hinges. The mechanism released the bar attached to the main wheel, and the same loud clicking reverberated through the room.

"We bloody got one!" David yelled in triumph.

"Yeah, but apparently, even the right answer still tries to drown us," Tanya called back.

Cross ran back over to the door and tried the wheel again. It didn't budge.

"What's the next one?" Tanya yelled over the rushing water.

"I don't know," the big man grunted, still wrenching on the handle.

Tanya muttered something, splashing over to Cross.

The water was nearly up to David's knees now. Something bumped into him from behind. He whirled, drawing steel. The floating corpse of a gray-cloak drifted in the current, new crabs feasting as they scuttled across it.

"He might light up your world, but it would be the shadow of the real thing. You've seen his face, but never his darker side. He's as cold as ice, yet you wouldn't know it by his appearance," Tanya shouted.

David looked around, eyes settling on the woman holding her head. Her hands were flexed, fingers straining as if in pure anguish.

"How about her?" David pointed to the statue. "She's got a darker side."

"No, she's not lighting up anyone's world," Tanya shot back. "What about the storm cloud?"

David ran the riddle through his head again.

"I think it fits!" Tanya shouted. "We may need to outrace the puzzle at this point. So, if this one's wrong, just turn all the keys before this place fills up." Tanya waded over to the statue and turned the key.

Water spurted from the neck, and there was another grinding sound, followed by a loud bang.

Click.

David looked at the door.

"Just try another one!" Tanya yelled.

"What in the fuck was that?" David asked. "Did we get one right?"

Click.

"No, it didn't open. In fact, the one we had open shut again," Cross boomed.

"Son of a whore on a barley barrel!" David yelled, splashing back over to Faith and turning the key.

Nothing happened.

Click.

Shit.

David tried again.

Nothing.

"Not good!" he yelled.

The clicking stopped.

David tried one more time. The clamp creaked open, and the clicking restarted. The water was mid-thigh now. "There's a timer on the puzzle!" he yelled.

"Yep, not gonna be able to brute force our way through," Tanya hollered. "Did you try fire?" she asked, pointing to the statue holding flame.

"What's the bloody riddle again?" David asked.

"Fire's not cold!" Cross yelled, climbing the door and wedging a torch between the highest iron loop and the bar. He repeated the riddle as he yanked on the clamp.

"He might light up your world, but it would be the shadow of the real thing." *Clang.* Cross hit something on the door with his fist. "You've seen his face, but never his darker side." The big man's words came through clenched teeth. "He's as cold as ice, yet you wouldn't know it by his appearance."

Gods, how does he remember all that?

Cross took a knife and tried to wedge it under the clamp.

I don't think pure strength will get us through that door, though.

The frothy seawater lapped at David's waist.

At least the torch is high up.

"I bloody fuckin' hate riddles!" Tanya repeated to no one in particular.

"The mirror!" David exclaimed. "The answer's yourself."

"Don't get cocky!" Tanya shot back.

"No, seriously. You only ever see your front, and the surface is cold, yet sometimes it looks warm and inviting," David explained.

"That works," Cross bellowed.

David moved to the hooded figure holding the mirror.

You're a genius, he thought, giving his reflection a little wink. He turned the key.

There was another grind, a spray of water, and a bang as the one open mechanism slammed shut.

"Fuck!" David yelled, diving toward the praying monk. He waited for the clicking to subside, then turned the faith key, opening the mechanism again.

"It's the moon," Cross boomed. "Not sure why I didn't see it before."

"It fits! But I don't see the Trickster staring down at us, Cross," David shouted over the pouring water.

"It's not the Trickster. It's Huna!" Tanya yelled, diving toward the scratched and pitted orb. Another grinding click echoed through the chamber as the lock on the upper left side of the door unlatched, and more water fountained into the room.

"We don't have much time!" David yelled.

Tanya swam over to the door, climbing the bars toward the next riddle.

"Get the one on the lower right," Cross called down from his perch.

Good thinking. We'd have to dive for that riddle soon.

Tanya dropped back into the water and read aloud. "They cast a shadow in the midday sun, yet you cannot hold them. They can fill a chamber, yet you cannot touch them. They can come from within, but more often from without."

Before David even had time to consider, Cross yelled, "Fire! It's the flame."

David dove for the third statue from the door and turned the key.

Creak. Bang. Creak. Bang. The locking mechanisms clamped shut again.

"Isidri's dried-up bastard vagina," David spat.

Seven statues poured water into the ever-rising tide.

"Sorry. I guess fire doesn't really cast a shadow at midday," Cross said.

David and Tanya each swam for the two correct statues. Tanya turned her key, and David waited for the clicking to stop to turn his. The water was chest deep and rising.

"What do we have left?" Cross asked.

"Trust or a handshake. A sword to the gut. A secret. Gemstones. Or an open book," David yelled.

"Pain, maybe?" Cross said without much conviction.

David swam over to the monk with the sword.

"Wait. What do you have, Tanya?" Cross asked.

"I have sadness or something," Tanya began. "A bowl, a bloody fucking baby! Gods, David, that's obviously love, not the disembodied heart!"

"Not helping," David yelled back.

"And a candle," Tanya spat.

For a moment, the only sound was the rushing water.

"Light!" they all yelled at once.

Tanya dove to the candle. The latch on the door farthest to the right opened as she turned the key, and more water flooded in from the statue's neck.

Click...click...click.

David wedged his torch into the hood of a sculpture, swam to the door, then climbed to the upper right side of the frame.

"We inspire hope in some, yet disdain in others. Children have us, yet it's the old who need us most. You can lose us, but no one can take us from you," David yelled.

Water churned through the silence as the words churned through his mind.

"What does disdain mean?" Cross asked.

David looked down. His hands were shaking.

Don't panic. Lose your nerve, lose your life. The old lyric resounded through his head.

David took a deep breath, fists clenching as he tried to steady himself.

"It means to look down on someone, kind of like a slave master might," Tanya yelled.

Cross tensed, head cocking to the side. "It doesn't make any sense."

"It's a fucking riddle. They never do!" Tanya shouted.

The water was nearly over Tanya's head. She started pulling off her coat and gear, abandoning them before she was forced to swim. It was getting hard to see the objects in the hooded statues' hands underneath the churning surface.

Water lapped into Tanya's torch, and it went out.

Mine's next.

David glanced at his guttering flame.

Not good.

He read the riddle again silently:

> *We inspire hope in some, yet disdain in others.*
> *Children have us, yet it's the old who need us most.*
> *You can lose us, but no one can take us from you.*

David's torch went out. The only light remaining was the one Cross wedged into the mechanism near the top of the door. David took a deep breath and tried to imagine the remaining objects in his mind:

A handshake...trust? Or a deal? Trust kind of works.

The sword in the gut...maybe pain?

He went over the riddle, compared it to pain, and decided it didn't fit.

A bowl? What in the fuck's a bowl have to do with it?

A monk spewing gemstones from his mouth. Greed? No, greed doesn't work.

The book? Knowledge? No. Doesn't fit the children's line.

It must be trust.

"Trust? The hand-shaking monk," David yelled, but he wasn't sure.

"Maybe. Love works too," Tanya called from across the room.

"Try love," Cross shouted. Tanya dove and turned the key on the figure cradling the baby. The eruption of water from the statue's neck pushed her back as the locks slammed shut.

"Fuck the OAM, and fuck their bloody relic!" David screamed. The water was rising at an alarming rate, and they had less than a span of air left. "Time to reset." David slipped off his gear and lowered himself into the water.

"Wait, try trust before we reset," Tanya yelled.

"You're a bloody genius!" David shouted. "Why didn't I think of that?"

Cross dumped his pack, then dove into the water from the top of the door. He was in front of the monk statue an instant later, turning the key. Water pushed him back as he swam for the surface.

The door's locks remained shut. *Click...click...click.*

"Cock on a cracker," Tanya spat. "Damn these riddles and damn the smegma-filled heads that came up with them." The string of curses would've made the Ivory Gauntlet's roughest patrons proud.

"Just open the right ones again," Cross boomed. "We've only got one or two more tries."

Each of them swam to the three statues they knew were correct.

David ducked under the water for moon.

Click...Click...Click.

Tanya dove for faith.

Click...Click...Click.

Cross plunged under for light.

Once they were done, David glanced at the statues on Tanya's side, then swam to the door. They had a little over half a span of air left.

David reread the riddle:

We inspire hope in some, yet disdain in others.
Children have us, yet it's the old who need us most.
You can lose us, but no one can take us from you.

David compared them with the answers he was inferring:

Despair, a secret, pain, a bowl, greed, and knowledge.

"None of them make any fucking sense!" David yelled. He looked at Cross.

The big man was shaking his head.

David looked at the mechanism on the door again.

Something's off.

The lock was set up a bit like a compass. Each bar, clamp, and corresponding riddle was about forty-five degrees apart. David laid a compass over the whole thing in his mind. West, northwest, north, northeast, and east. They'd solved the riddle at the east lock, and it had opened the east lock. The same was true with the northwest lock. But the first riddle they'd solved was written at the west lock, and it opened the northeast.

"What was the answer to the first riddle?" David asked.

"Faith," Cross replied.

"Bloody hell, we fucked ourselves. This one's faith!" David yelled.

They both just looked at him.

"We inspire hope in some yet disdain in others. Children have us, yet it's the old who need us most. You can lose us, but no one can take us from you," David said.

"You're right!" Cross replied. Tanya was already diving. She came back up a few seconds later.

"You can keep it, but never own it. You can break it, but you can't touch it. It's fleeting by nature, yet rarely is it complete," Tanya repeated the first riddle.

A quarter span of air left, and the water lapped dangerously close to their only source of light.

"It could be despair," David yelled. Tanya started swimming. "Wait, wait, wait. It could also be a secret...or pain...or knowledge."

"We only have time for one guess here. We won't be able to reset, and we still have one lock left after this."

Rushing water filled the silence between them.

"I think despair!" Cross yelled.

"I don't know. My despair's pretty fucking complete right now!" Tanya shouted.

"How about a secret," David suggested, swimming out toward the middle of the room.

"I don't think secrets are fleeting by nature, and they can be complete if taken to the grave." Tanya squinted toward the statue, holding an index finger against their lips. Her head cocked to the side then she frowned. "You bloody fucking doll-faced fool of a bard! That statue doesn't mean secret. She's shushing you!" Tanya swam for it. "I shouldn't be surprised. You never did understand the idea of shutting your bloody mouth."

Tanya dove.

For a moment, David chewed on her words.

"Silence," Cross provided.

Another grind filled the room as the far west lock opened, and the clicking ticked through the little remaining air. Tanya surfaced, glanced at the door, then at each of them.

Water sloshed around them as their heads bumped into the ceiling.

"The good news is, the only lock left is at the top of the door," Cross said.

"But we have one shot at getting it right," David groaned.

"And we don't have much time to puzzle it out," Tanya added, swimming for the door.

"Then read, woman!" Even David could hear the panic in his voice.

Tanya scowled but read the last riddle aloud anyway. "She bestows life to some families, yet she wrecks others. She is quick to anger but seldom without warning. She can carry you, but you cannot restrain her."

The three lines echoed through the quickly shrinking pocket of air. David couldn't even see the statues anymore.

"Despair, pain, a bowl, greed, or knowledge," David recited the clues from memory.

Water licked at the bottom of Cross's torch.

We'll have to go for the statue blind, and worse yet, not one answer makes a fucking lick of sense.

Water spilled into the torch, and everything went dark.

50
GERARD STOCKWORTH

Wind tossed Gerard's cloak about as the *Warden* came into view. The ship was enormous compared to their little schooner, the *Swale*.

The journey was finally near its end. The first half had been spent on rivers and lakes, the second half on open water. A few days ago, the first mate had spotted the reef, and they'd followed it for some time. The two sailors had kept the *Swale* directly over the spine-like ridge with a fervor that would've made a zealot proud.

Avoiding the darker depths.

Everything was just as Vincent described so far.

Everything except the ocean.

Gerard had sailed the Divide in his younger years, but the day they found open water had been the day he lost his breakfast. Thankfully, he recovered in a couple of hours, but those few hours felt like a trip to one of the hells. The two sailors had assured him his recovery was impressive, but it hadn't felt that way.

Twenty days, all in all, but the quarry is finally in sight.

Metal squealed as a pulley spun on an unoiled pin. Gerard glanced back to see the two sailors raising a scrap of sail up the *Swale's* mast.

"What's that?" he asked.

"Flag of parley," Joe said.

Joe was technically the captain of the *Swale*, but the title didn't quite fit the man. It wasn't as if the boat was illegitimate—she was small but fast and seaworthy. Still, Gerard doubted Joe and his partner, Sam, often took jobs on the open ocean.

Apparently, scruples get tossed right out the window when the OAM starts rattling stone.

Gerard could almost hear the gravelly sound of gems churning in a leather pouch.

Mine certainly did.

"What's it for?" Gerard asked.

"Typically used if you're in a spot of trouble. Short on supplies, a broken mast, or whatnot." Joe waved his hand about as if a broken mast was a trivial matter. "Should facilitate a conversation."

"Should?" Gerard asked.

"Yeah, but you never know. There's a code out here on the open ocean, but things are a bit less civilized than in Darin."

"So, sometimes the flag's ignored?"

"That would be the best case if they don't feel like talking." Joe reached into his coat, pulled out some dried leaf, and packed it into a pipe.

"And the worst?"

Joe hunched, sheltering the pipe from the wind, and lit it. "Well, you see those big ballistae on the main deck?" He took a couple of deep puffs to get the fire started.

"Ah, point taken," Gerard said.

Joe laughed, blowing smoke. A second later, Sam joined him.

"What's funny?" Gerard asked.

"I didn't know you had a sense of humor. I do enjoy a good pun."

Gerard thought back, then chuckled. The wordplay wasn't intentional, but that only made it better.

Ballistae swiveled as the little schooner pulled up beside the *Warden*. The big boat was anchored in the shallows, within the safety of the reef. Joe and his first mate maneuvered the *Swale* expertly and dropped the sails one at a time until the two vessels nearly kissed hulls.

A whistle pierced the air above, soon joined by thudding feet. Weathered ropes flew over the *Warden*'s rails, thumping into her hull. A moment later, men were sliding onto the *Swale* and mooring the two vessels together. A rope ladder rolled out from above and came to a clattering halt half a span above the deck.

"Wait here," Gerard said.

"Not sure I've much choice in the matter," Joe muttered, repacking his pipe.

You're probably right on that count.

Eight sailors had boarded their little vessel. No weapons were brandished, but they all carried knives or cutlasses.

Gerard turned back to the ladder and began to climb. Near the top, two sailors grabbed him by the arms and hauled him up. They let him go as soon as he was over the rail, and Gerard flopped onto the main deck. He blinked, a pair of polished black boots nearly touching his nose.

"Seward, if you'd be so kind." The voice was commanding, yet not harsh.

A hand extended, and Gerard took it, pulling himself up. He found himself facing a young woman and an older gentleman. Both were dressed well, but it was the man who held his attention. He had a sprinkling of gray through his hair and wore plain clothing with the sleeves rolled up. He was clearly in charge yet looked ready to pull a line or fire a ballista if the occasion called for it. Gerard liked the cut of his jib immediately.

"Gerard," he said, extending a hand.

"Captain Caldwell." The middle-aged man grasped the proffered hand firmly.

"Are you the captain of the little schooner?" Caldwell asked.

"No, but I did ask for the parley on behalf of Vincent Willcrest."

One peppered eyebrow rose. "You have my attention."

"You transported known fugitives, Captain Caldwell," Gerard explained. "Unknowingly, of course," he added. Gerard handed the captain a sealed letter from Vincent, then the bounty tickets for his two marks and the escaped slave.

"Well, this is quite irregular," Caldwell responded. He examined the seal, then cracked it open and quickly scanned the page. "I must admit, I'm a little taken aback. Still, the documentation appears to be in order." The captain looked up, meeting Gerard's eye. "Vincent gives explicit direction to assist you in any way possible and explains that you intend to bring these fugitives to justice."

"Excellent. Are they aboard?"

"I'm afraid not."

"On the island, then?"

"Indeed. We're scheduled to make port at first low tide each morning."

"When did you drop them off?" Gerard asked.

"Earlier today. You and the *Swale* must have been on our tail for the last few weeks."

"Perfect. Let's stick to the plan and dock tomorrow morning. If they try to board, let them. We can take them when they do."

"And if they don't show?" Caldwell asked.

"Then I'll disembark and have a look around. Vincent hoped I could work out what happened to the settlement. The next morning, I'll let them board the ship peacefully and follow them on. Do you have a brig?"

"I do."

"Good. Does it hold three?"

"Four cells," the captain stated, all business.

"Excellent. We can take them into custody and use your brig to hold them on the return journey."

"Seems simple enough."

"The best plans usually are." *Until everything goes to shit.*

"Indeed, less to go wrong," Caldwell stated, as if reading his mind.

Gerard nodded and walked over to the edge of the vessel.

"Joe! Captain Caldwell will take it from here," Gerard said. "When the OAM debriefs you, please report we made contact with the *Warden*."

"Yes, sir," Joe yelled back. "It's been a pleasure. I hope we meet again someday, Gerard!"

"Likewise," Gerard said with a quick wave.

"Mr. Bolis, if you'd be so kind as to help the *Swale* disembark," Captain Caldwell boomed.

Seconds later, everyone was in motion, reversing the mooring they'd just completed. In a matter of minutes, the *Swale* was gliding away from the *Warden*.

The sun was starting to set, and the captain invited Gerard to dine with him and the officers. Gerard accepted, and a few hours later, they were being served roast bird. The cook called it pheasant, but Gerard was reasonably sure it was a gull of some kind. Still, it and herb-covered potatoes were the best food he'd eaten in weeks.

The captain and the officers were good company, too, all sharp men and women with quick wits and no-nonsense attitudes. Gerard was becoming increasingly sure the return trip would be one of the better sea voyages of his life. The officers told tales of trips gone wrong, and Gerard regaled them with a few botched bounties. After dinner, Seward showed him to his quarters. Before long, he was fast asleep.

Gerard awoke to the creak and rock of the hull.

Already in motion, then.

He got up, dressed, and headed to the main deck. The crew was mooring the boat to a small spit of rock in an enormous cavern. Sails, planks, and bits of cargo littered the craggy walls. The sailors went about their business, clearly doing their best not to look at any of it.

As if that might make it all disappear.

Gerard approached the captain. "What happened here?"

"We aren't rightly sure," Caldwell said. "The crew whispers of creatures from the depths, of course, but I imagine something else forced the captain to leave his ship here while the tide rose."

Gerard glanced up. Debris and sails were wedged into the stalactites above.

Sound reasoning.

"Either way, we aren't keen to stay long," Caldwell explained. "We'll wait for an hour at low tide. If they don't show up, we'll anchor near the reef again."

"Seems like a good plan. I'll wait and see if they show. If they don't, then I'll see you tomorrow morning."

"Seward, bring me another flare, if you would be so kind," the captain said.

The young woman hurried away.

"Seems sharp," Gerard remarked.

"She is, though she's taken a lot of work." The captain paused, looked around, then continued, "She's my brother's girl. Family's always tough to train, yet the bond there is usually strongest in the end."

Gerard wasn't sure about all that but nodded just the same. They stood in amicable silence for a moment until Seward returned with a sea flare.

"If you run into trouble, light that up," Caldwell stated. "If we see smoke, we'll head back to the island and attempt a rescue."

Seward handed Gerard the bundle.

"I don't need to tell you that lighting the flare will endanger my crew, right?" Caldwell asked.

"Consider me advised." Gerard strapped the flare to the top of his pack. "Oh, and Captain, a piece of advice in return. If the fugitives board your ship, no half measures. You'll want lots of men with crossbows at the ready."

"I imagine my entire crew will be sufficient to the task."

"I'm sure they will. Still, I've got good reason to believe these three are extremely dangerous, even to a force with superior numbers."

"I appreciate the tip. We'll be ready," the captain assured. "Oh, and Gerard, good luck and gods-speed, man."

"Thanks. Can't say I've ever been real lucky, though."

"Nor can I."

The two of them chuckled and shook hands.

"Now, if you'll excuse me, there's another matter I must attend to." The captain walked toward his cabin, yelling, "Mr. Bolis, you have the deck."

After an hour, the fugitives hadn't shown, so Gerard disembarked, and watched the *Warden* oar back out to sea. He started up the stone steps. As he ascended, the stairs narrowed, then spit him out into a small armory.

Gerard decided not to linger and walked out into the streets.

Carnage, massacre, butchery.

The words swam through his mind, but none of them did the place a bit of justice.

Blood.

There was so much blood. So many bodies. That was if you could even call them bodies. They were more pulp than human remains, as if someone had juiced them against the cobbles. The gore pooled and flowed lazily through mostly clogged gutters, and oil lampposts lined the streets. Some of the posts were toppled, and most of the ones still standing were draped with entrails and splattered in blood.

No doubt the birds redecorated the place.

The winged creatures were everywhere. In an apparent demonstration, a gull swept down, grabbed a piece of intestine, clipped it off, and took to the air again. It landed on a nearby chimney, swallowed half of the morsel, and left the rest hanging.

Most of the buildings on the main street were in similar disarray. Only a wall or two had caved in on some, while others were reduced entirely to rubble.

Is there enough stone in the world to justify this trip?

Gerard nearly laughed.

There's enough stone in the world to justify anything.

With a deep breath, he unslung his bow and headed up the street, carefully avoiding as much gore as possible.

Slippery business, gore.

If Vincent's directions were correct, he'd find the city square and barracks at the top of the hill. The three criminals should be there or still in the vault. Gerard had no desire to descend into the depths of this island. Instead, he'd planned to wait for the fugitives near the barracks. If they weren't back up in two days, he'd head down and retrieve them, or at least their heads. The prospect of waiting around in this massacre was feeling less appealing by the minute, though.

The bowels of this place might not be any better, and I still need to find out what happened here.

Cause of death was usually the best place to start when it came to murder. This was far more than that, though. This was the elimination of an entire town. Still, there were similarities in the dead. Most appeared to have died from blunt force trauma or had been pulverized into a slurry of meat and bone.

Best focus on the ones that still have some...substance.

Gerard spotted a body slumped against the wall in an alleyway and walked over. The birds had done some damage to the corpse, but she'd mostly been intact when killed. He bent down, running a finger along her bones.

Ribs are broken for sure.

Gerard rolled her over.

The back of the head was flat where it should be round. He ran a finger down her spine.

Broken. And in more than one place.

Gerard inspected the wall. Cracks fissured through the stone. Something had thrown her hard enough to damage masonry with flesh and bone.

That's a lot of force.

He ran his fingers across the foundation of the building, then pulled his knife and rapped on the wall with the pommel.

A dull, hollow thud resounded.

Either pulled from a river or the sea.

Water had seeped into the stone, eroding it over centuries. The rock wasn't as solid as granite, but cracking it would still require a tremendous impact. Men-at-arms weren't strong enough to cause that type of damage with brute force and violence.

If not by human hands, then what? Some sort of construct?

Gerard scratched his beard.

Who has the funding to create something like that?

The OAM was the only name that came to mind, but that seemed improbable.

Unless they were testing something?

No, it didn't fit.

The OAM would use slaves or send whatever did this to Terra.

Gerard decided it couldn't be the gray-cloaks. Seafront had clearly taken an absurd amount of money to build, and the OAM had no good reason to destroy it.

But who else has the resources to create something capable of this?

He stood from his examination of the corpse.

No one.

Gerard continued on.

Whatever caused this devastation demolished these buildings as easily as it broke that woman's back.

Ahead, most of the structures were simply destroyed, but one building caught his eye.

A large crater pitted the center of the wreckage, and the only remaining wall threatened to collapse at any moment. The demolition of a structure wasn't odd for a city under siege, but parts of it were suspiciously absent. There was no sign of the roof, which must have collapsed, and too little rubble was scattered about the crater in a circular pattern.

If the structure was hit by siege equipment, debris should be everywhere.

"Huh." Gerard scratched his beard.

Looks more like the building pulled in on itself, then vanished.

He wasn't used to being stumped, but nothing added up.

This is something new.

Before long, Gerard approached the town square. It was a mess here, too, but less so than down the road. It appeared rain and time had washed much of the remains to the lower parts of the city, but the bodies here wore weapons and armor.

Maybe some sort of resistance? Not much of one, though.

Gerard inspected each corpse, which wasn't much more than a mash of human mulch. They all wore the same uniform with the same OAM insignia. Weapons littered the ground, many not even near a body, and there wasn't a single aggressor among the dead.

Another oddity. Maybe the invaders took their casualties with them?

No, opposing armies always failed to account for someone in the chaos.

Why would this place be any different? Unless they had no casualties? He dismissed the idea. Both sides would always take losses in a full-scale invasion.

Near a gaping hole in the barracks, Gerard noticed a body that wasn't armed or armored. The most discernible thing about the corpse was that there was nothing to discern. They could've been man or woman, old or young. They weren't simply flattened like the others either. They were a puddle.

Gerard tried to roll the body over with a toe, but his boot sank into the mass of flesh instead. He looked around, spotted a halberd on the ground, and scooped it up.

It's no shovel, but it'll do.

The metal head of the axe scraped along the stone cobbles, pushing around the gelatinous flesh. It took a few scoops, but he managed to turn the remains over, bit by bit.

At least there aren't flies.

Wiggling maggots filled Gerard's mind, causing his stomach to twist. The halberd hooked on something, and he tugged at it. A gray robe slid free of the pooling flesh.

Just more gray robes and gray matter.

Gerard started to turn, then stopped. Something caught the sun's light. He turned back to the corpse and knelt. A small object glinted in the center of the pulverized flesh. Gerard frowned, then pushed thumb and forefinger into the congealed remains. His fingers closed on something cold, hard, and slippery. He drew it forth, flicked the gore onto the ground, and held it up to the light.

A signet ring? Curious.

Brushes and scrolls surrounded the letter *K* etched on the golden loop's face.

Odd for a member of the OAM to have a signet ring.

A house sigil was usually reserved for members of a greater noble house, but occasionally, minor nobility used them.

Still, strange to find one on a gray-cloak.

Gerard wiped the ring on the cleanest patch of robes he could find, then pocketed it.

There's something to all this. I'm just not looking hard enough.

He glanced at the barracks.

Best focus on the marks for now. They could come out of the vault anytime.

Gerard circled the building.

The few remaining windows were barred, and the only other entrance had collapsed into an impassable pile. Gerard walked back around to the front. A two-story building that still seemed structurally sound stood opposite the barracks. He walked over and opened the door. A desk sat in the middle of a room filled with scroll racks, and a staircase wrapped three of the walls. He climbed the steps to a mezzanine and found a table surrounded by bookshelves.

A balcony door overlooked the square with a good view of the barracks. Gerard's gaze lingered on what should have been the fountain. The sculpture wasn't destroyed like the rest of Seafront, it was entirely absent.

Another oddity. Intriguing, yet disconcerting.

A flicker of movement near the edge of the square caught Gerard's eye. He pulled back into the door frame, then slowly peered back out. A small form skulked from one pile of rubble to the next in complete silence. Suddenly, they stopped, head turning toward the balcony. Gerard ducked back in cover, waited a dozen heartbeats, then peeked back out. A scraggly mop of hair disappeared into the first floor below him.

Gerard unslung his bow and nocked an arrow as he returned to the mezzanine. He drew the arrow back, sighted down the shaft, and focused on the bottom step. A tangle of grimy yellow hair bobbed into view from under the overhang. He moved the iron arrow tip with the figure as they took two steps and stopped. They looked left, then right, turning.

The intruder froze, frantic eyes locking on him. They were small, long-haired, and grimier than a seedy brothel.

Looks like they've been through all ninety-two hells and back. Twice.

As they stared at each other, the slight frame and more feminine face became obvious.

A young girl?

"Don't move," Gerard said calmly.

Her eyes shifted from him toward the door.

"Don't try it," Gerard warned. "Don't want to send this arrow through your heart, but I will if you move."

The girl's eyes darted toward him again, but thankfully, she didn't bolt.

"Need you to come up the steps now. Real slow, got it?"

The girl said nothing, just stood there frozen. She glanced once more between him and the door, then slowly started up the stairs.

"All right, far enough," Gerard said as she got to the landing between floors. "What's your name?"

No response.

"I'm Gerard. You a survivor?"

Silence.

"You mute?"

Still no response.

"I'm gonna need you to answer some questions, then maybe we can get you off this rock. Would you like that?"

The girl nodded.

"Okay, so you understand, then?"

The girl nodded again.

Hells, why's it always gotta be difficult?

"All right, then. Come on up here—nice and slow—and keep those hands wide." Gerard motioned with the tip of his bow to the next landing, a span or so from where he stood.

The girl took the steps one at a time, painfully slow. When she finally got to the top step, Gerard shouldered his bow.

"Stand still, now. I don't want to hurt you, but if you move, I'll have to assume you are tryin' to hurt me. Got it?"

She stood there for a moment, eyeballing him, then nodded.

Carefully, Gerard patted her down, all the while watching her hands. She winced at his touch, but her arms remained rigid. She was clearly young, but how young was impossible to say in her savage state. He felt something hard in the right pocket of the garment that might've once been a dress. Gerard reached in, pulled out a handspan of sharpened steel, and tossed it down the stairs.

"What happened here?" Gerard asked, taking a step back.

Still no response.

Gerard sighed, then reached into his bag and produced some trail rations. He held out a hardened biscuit. "Hungry?"

The girl eyed the stale ration warily, crept forward, then snatched it. She sniffed it once, then tore into it with the fervor of a fanatical priest.

"Guess so."

Gerard let her eat, then tried again.

"What's your name? I'm Gerard."

The girl watched him warily from behind her biscuit, still chewing.

"All right, not much of a talker, I can respect that. My best friend's the same way." Gerard scratched his chin. "You live in this town before...well, before whatever in the eighty-six hells did this to the place?"

She nodded, dirt-caked strands of blond hair swaying.

"What in the hells am I gonna call you?"

No response.

Gerard looked her up and down. The only thing that stood out was her filthy yellow hair.

"Blondie?"

The girl shook her head, scowling.

"Lemon?"

She considered this one, then shook her head once in an oddly definitive way.

"Hmm, Buttercup?"

She chewed her lip a moment, then nodded.

"All right, you seen any other survivors, Buttercup?"

She shook her head.

"How old are you?"

She frowned, considering his words. Slowly, she held up all ten fingers, then lowered them and held up another five.

"Fifteen? A little small for your age, huh?"

Her mouth pulled into a snarl.

"Whoa, all right. A good size then."

Her eyes narrowed, but the words seemed to mollify her.

Looks like I struck a nerve. Still, at least she's got a little fire left.

Gerard sighed, then glanced over his shoulder toward the square and barracks.

No sign of them yet.

"I've gotta take care of something, but I've got a boat, and after I'm done, we'll get you out of here." Gerard turned back to the girl. "Can I trust you to wait down here while I take care of business?"

Buttercup nodded.

"All right, stay quiet and be still. It won't do for someone to hear us." Gerard produced another trail ration and held it out.

The girl snatched it, much more boldly this time then settled into the corner of the upper landing.

With a shake of his head, Gerard exited onto the balcony and looked back.

Good, can't see her from outside.

Gerard examined the wall of the building. The construction of the eave looked solid. He gave the railing a shake. The metal didn't budge. He leaned against the wall and got his feet on the handrail. Gripping the roof joists, he worked his hands onto the overhang above. With a little hop and a climbing technique called a mantle, he pushed and pulled himself onto the tile roof.

A good spot.

He had a clear view of the barracks and the surrounding area. Gerard unslung his bow, walked to the apex of the roof, and crossed to the other side. He shuffled down the slope, got to his belly, and peered over the peak. Anyone who came out of the barracks would have a tough time seeing the small profile of his head, but he'd have a great view of them.

And now, we wait.

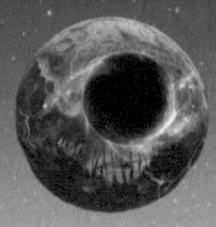

51
RIGEL
CROSS

D arkness consumed everything—a starless night.

Maybe dying under that old oak would've been better.

Water lapped at the bottom of Cross's chin as he mouthed the three lines over and over:

She bestows life to some families, yet she wrecks others.

She is quick to anger, but seldom without warning.

She can carry you, but you cannot restrain her.

Some of the lines matched a few of the clues, but none fit them all. It didn't matter. They would never feel their way to the answer in the pitch black, and Cross had already tried to force the iron handle at the door's base.

"It has to be greed," David said, voice laced with desperation.

"That doesn't make any sense." Tanya still somehow sounded calm and collected.

"We've got to do something! Let's just try it. Maybe whoever came up with this riddle was daft."

"There's no way it's greed, David."

"I'm not going to sit here and drown! We have to—"

Someone sputtered then spit, clearing water from their mouth.

"Try something," David finished.

"How are you gonna find the statue in the dark?" Tanya asked. "You'd be swimming in the current blind."

"You got a better plan? 'Cause I don't want to end up as crab cuisine like these OAM fucks!"

Cross considered asking what cuisine meant, but now wasn't the time, and it had to be some sort of food. The bar and final clamp felt cold. He pulled on the heavy steel cuff with one hand and the bar with the other. The clamp didn't budge a finger's width, but the bar wiggled.

There were only a couple of handspans of air left.

Cross ducked under the water, shifted his grip on the bar, then pulled. It flexed but didn't come free of the iron cuff. He surfaced again.

"I'm going to try to bend it," Cross said calmly. "See if you can give me a hand."

"Bend what?" Tanya asked.

"The bar."

It's a long shot. But it's the only shot we have left.

"What do you need?" David asked eagerly.

Cross unslung his war hammer and prodded David with the handle. "Got it?" Cross asked as the weight lessened.

"Yep, now what in the hells do I do with it?"

"See if you can put more strain on the metal," Cross said. "Tanya, try to help me pull. If we make any headway, wedge something in there so I can adjust my grip."

"Got it," she said.

"What in the hells does putting strain on the metal mean?" David asked.

"Hit the bar. Vibration can help the metal bend. Like a blacksmith."

"Gods, this thing is heavy. How'd you swim with—"

David's words dulled as Cross let the weight of his few remaining weapons pull him under the water. He kept his right hand on the clamp and slid his left down till it touched the first iron circlet.

If the bar flexes at all, it'll do so here.

He moved both hands to the central point, placed them in an opposing grip, and set his feet flat on either side of the bar. Cross pushed against the door with his legs and pulled with his back and arms.

The bar flexed. He felt Tanya join him, adding her strength to his.

Bang.

The iron hummed even underwater, sending tremors through Cross's elbows and shoulders.

Bang.

It bent a little more, and they managed to stop it from bouncing back.

Bang.

Vibration trembled through the bar, and it flexed a finger's width. Cross felt Tanya slip a leg under the bar and brace. He let go, adjusted his grip, then pulled with all his might. Tanya brushed against his arm as she slipped out to join him.

Bang.

It moved another finger.

459

Bang.

Half a hand.

Bang.

The bar gave way with a screeching protest.

Cross's head hit the ceiling before his mouth found air. He tilted his head back, panicking until his nose touched stone, and his lips broke the surface. Seafoam spilled into the side of his mouth as he tried to suck in the air. He sputtered, spit, then took in another shuddering breath. Water lapped in his ears, muffling the gasps of the others. Cross pulled in one last lungful of air, then let the weight of his armaments take him under again.

Using the broken bar, Cross guided himself down until his feet touched the ground. He reached out, fumbling for the wheel.

There.

Cross grabbed the handle in both hands, wrenching it to the left. It didn't move. He tried right. It was just as solid. Cross pictured the wheel in his mind.

The buckles needed to hinge left to pull the bars from their locks. Cross tried again, muscles straining. A grinding creak thrummed through the water as rusty metal fought ancient bonds, but the handle moved less than a finger. He wrenched on the wheel one more time with all his might.

It didn't budge.

Cross considered going up for more air, but it would be long gone by now. He yanked on the wheel, trying to break it free with frantic jerks.

It remained still as stone.

This is it. It's over. Never gonna see Elinfall again. Never going to see Terra...

Another hand slid onto his. It felt its way across his fingers, then latched onto the iron beside his. Then another. Two more. Cross twisted one more time with all his weight, strength, and rage.

The handle gave way, spinning.

Buckles creaked as bars pulled toward the center of the door. A series of clicks and squeals echoed through the water as a mechanism worked on the other side of the iron barrier.

A current snatched Cross, sweeping him away from the others.

He pushed down the urge to suck in a breath.

His legs hit something, sending him spinning.

Pain erupted in his back as he was dragged along a series of bumpy outcroppings.

Cross couldn't help it anymore. He opened his mouth, letting the water invade his lungs.

No, not water...air. Well, mostly air.

Cross sputtered, coughed up liquid, then groaned. Water rushed all around him, filling the darkness with noise.

No one else coughed or sputtered, though.

David! Tanya!

Cross scrambled to hands and knees, groping through the dark for his friends. His fingers brushed something cold and slick. Desperately, he groped at it.

Metal. A buckle from Tanya's coat.

Cross flipped her over and fumbled around for her face. It was cold. He didn't know nearly as much about healing as Tanya, but he'd heard of the breath of life. The sailors on the *Warden* all had stories of someone having life breathed back into them after drowning. He put his lips to hers and blew.

Nothing.

Cross took a great breath and pushed more air through her lips.

Nothing.

Again.

Nothing.

Cross pounded a fist against her chest in frustration. He was about to hit her again when she gurgled. A rattling cough filled the darkness. Cross groped through the dark for David. His fingers weaved into something wet and curly, then found David's cold face.

Cross placed his lips against the bard's, filling the man's lungs with his own.

David sputtered and took in a strangled breath.

With a deep sigh, Cross leaned back. For a short time, labored breath and rushing water were the only sounds.

Something clattered.

Glug, glug, glug.

Scrape, scrape, scrape.

Blinding light flooded the small passageway. Cross blinked, eyes slowly adjusting.

David was on his hands and knees, looking as if he might spit up. Tanya was shading her eyes from the unbearable glow.

Thank the gods they're all right.

They sat on steps that rose for another span, then leveled out. Water still rushed from the riddle room, draining through a massive grate at their feet. Cross got up, offering David a hand.

"If I never see salt water again, it'll be too bloody soon." David took the hand.

"We do have a long boat ride ahead of us," Tanya croaked. "That's assuming we get out of here."

David groaned, then fell into another fit of coughing.

Tanya stood, lantern in hand, and headed up the stone steps. David pushed himself up, following close behind her, and for once, the bard didn't seem to stare at her ass. A short hallway led away from the landing, ending in a plain yet solid door. Tanya took the lead, creeping along and lightly pressing on the floor in search of traps before finally stopping in front of the heartwood slab. She ran a finger along the riveted iron bands, inspected the seams around the frame, then pulled the handle.

The door swung open soundlessly despite its ancient hinges.

"Why would someone spend good stone on heartwood no one will ever see?" David asked.

"It wasn't even locked..." Tanya trailed off as she stepped into the room.

Cross and David followed.

An impossibly smooth stone pedestal rose from the floor at the center of a circular chamber. A sword sat within a groove carved so precisely that it was hard to tell where metal ended and stone began. The only exception was two shallow pockets at either end of the scabbard that were unmistakably meant for hands.

Almost looks like it's on display.

Cross frowned.

But display for who?

The scabbard was unadorned dark brown leather but appeared well made, and the stitching was clearly done with a practiced hand. The hilt was another story entirely. The pommel was a deep, dark purple orb, the inside of which seemed to swirl with black liquid in the lantern's light. Two lions carved from some sort of blackened alloy crouched back-to-back, reaching outward with raking claws to create the crossguard. The big cats' faces were fixed in matching snarls, and their tails twisted together and spiraled up the grip. Behind the tails, a red backdrop that looked like corded muscle stretched tight over the hilt.

What must the blade look like?

"By the fucking gods," David breathed.

462

"It is...something," Tanya whispered.

"'Something' doesn't do it a lick of justice," David said. "That's bloody moonstone in the pommel! That piece alone is worth way more than the OAM will ever pay us."

"How much?" Cross asked.

"Ten thousand 'phire?" David suggested, turning to Tanya for confirmation.

"Maybe for the gem alone," Tanya said. "Probably much more for the sword if the craftsmanship on the blade matches that hilt."

"We still need to bring it back to Vincent," Cross said with more warning than intended.

"Buddy, this sword has to be worth ten times what they're gonna pay us," David explained without taking his eyes off the weapon.

"More like a hundred," Tanya interjected.

"Maybe, but Vincent said he'd get rid of this." Cross held up the slaver's mark, turning it toward David.

They were all quiet for a moment.

"With the money we'd get from that blade, we could pay off all our debts, get the best tattoo artist in the realm to cover your mark, and still buy a whole bloody estate!" David said, finally breaking the silence.

"That might be a bit of a stretch," Tanya responded. "Still, hard to be sure without seeing the blade."

"It wouldn't be legal, though," Cross said with determination. "They could still come for me anytime. Plus, Vincent warned us not to draw the blade."

"Yeah, that's true," David agreed. "But Vincent also failed to mention the maze full of flesh-eating leeches and the fact we needed a scholar's background in riddle craft to keep from drowning to death." David threw his arms in the air. "I say fuck Vincent! His lack of direction nearly got us killed time and time again."

"I think I'm with Cross," Tanya said. "As much as I want to see what's inside that scabbard, it's probably best not to betray the OAM."

"Really?" David asked. "I expected you, of all people, to be on my side here. We could clear our debt and pay off whoever needs to be silenced."

"Yeah, but even if we could get the Freemen's Guild and the Lance to stop hunting us, the OAM would put out new bounties," Tanya said. "They're tenacious and have the type of funding the guilds can only dream of." She paused, staring down at the sword. "But we could draw the blade...just to see what we are dealing with. It would give us some options. Let us make an educated decision."

Cross shot her a look. The glimmer of curiosity in her eyes was unmistakable. She wanted to know what was under that veil of stitched leather.

So do I, but not enough to disregard Vincent.

"I know they said it was a powerful relic," Tanya said. "But let's be honest. Magic doesn't exist. Can we still agree on that?"

Silence. The three of them looked between each other.

"We're not drawing it, and we're not selling it," Cross said with finality.

David let out a long-suffering sigh, then his face lit up, and he snapped his fingers. "Tell you what. I'll roll you for it." The musician shook two cubes from a small leather pouch and rattled them around in his hand with a smile. "High roll decides what we do with the blade. Then we roll again to see who carries it outta this hellhole."

Cross wasn't sure he was willing to accept either David's or Tanya's plan if they won the roll, but he didn't see another way to convince them.

Plus, I have as good a chance as they do, right?

And if you don't win? a little voice in the back of his head nagged.

I'll take that path when it comes.

Cross wouldn't trade his freedom for any amount of stone, though, and that was a fact. So, he just set his jaw and nodded.

"Let me see those!" Tanya snatched the cubes from David's hand. He tried to pull back, but she was too fast. Tanya shook them, rolled them in her hand, then tossed them in the air a little. "Rigged. Pull out the real set, you little shit."

"Can't blame a bloke for trying," David said with a crooked smile, then produced a second set of cubes from a wet sleeve.

Where had those come from?

Tanya inspected them. "These are on the level," she said, handing them back to David.

"Can I have the others back?" he asked.

Tanya shot him a look. "Once we're done...maybe."

David sighed, then rolled. The dice bounced along the stone floor and off the side of the pedestal. Cross didn't know the rules but still held his breath.

I really don't want to have to do something drastic.

Cross was pretty sure he'd be willing to look at the blade if Tanya won, even if he didn't think they should.

But if David wins...

Cross glanced at the brand on his right hand.

"Nine!" David proclaimed, smiling from ear to ear.

Apparently a good roll.

Tanya grabbed the dice and examined them one more time. Once she was satisfied they hadn't been swapped, she rolled as well.

"Shit," Tanya cursed, then looked at Cross and clarified. "Three."

Cross felt a modicum of fury twitch inside him as the first tendrils of anger slithered behind his eyes. He tried to push the feeling away as he scooped up the dice.

There's still a chance...I think.

Cross wasn't sure if there was a technique to it or how exactly it worked, so he shrugged, shook the two cubes in his hand, then tossed them. They danced across the ground, spinning and bouncing until finally coming to a stop. He held his breath, staring at the symbols without understanding.

"Fuck!" David spat.

Tanya was smiling, but clearly more at David's dismay than any luck of her own.

"What'd I get?" Cross whispered to Tanya.

"Eleven," Tanya said, on the verge of laughter.

"Good, so we take the blade back to Vincent," Cross said.

"All right, all right. But we still need to decide who carries it." David grabbed up the dice again and tossed them. "Ha, ten!" he exclaimed, passing the cubes to Tanya.

She shook, then threw.

"Seven," David said gleefully as the dice came to a stop.

Cross took them up and tossed them. The dice came to a rattling halt, with the same symbol shown on each. He looked at Tanya.

"Two," she said.

David snatched the dice back up.

"We may have to give the sword to Vincent. But I get to carry it!" David declared triumphantly.

"Don't listen to him," Tanya said. "It's a consolation prize. The addict is just excited he got to shake his little toys."

David frowned for a second, but his grin returned in a heartbeat. "You have an open invitation to play with my toys, too, just so you know."

"Consolation?" Cross asked.

"It means it wasn't the real prize," Tanya said, pointedly ignoring David. "Kinda like something given out to just make you feel better."

"So, you don't want to give 'em a shake?" David persisted.

Silence.

"No?" He rattled the pouch suspiciously close to his crotch.

"Who are you even talking to?" Tanya asked.

"Anyone who wants to listen!" David's grin was enormous. "I don't discriminate. Cross, if you want to handle my dice, all I ask is that you're gentle."

"Don't listen to him." Tanya leaned in close, voice lowering to a conspiratorial whisper. "He likes the abuse," she said, still loud enough for all to hear.

"I do not!" David protested. "Also, it's not a consolation prize. You just can't abandon me in the dark while I have it. Plus, who knows what'll happen by the time we get back to the mainland? You two might change your minds."

"Speaking of the dark," Tanya said. "We don't have a lot of oil left. I think I can navigate the maze, but not without this lantern."

"All right," David said, turning back to the pedestal. He reached for the blade, then stopped short. A look of apprehension slid across his face. "You don't think something horrible will happen when I take it, do you? Like the door slams shut, and the ocean floods this chamber? Or the whole place starts shaking, and the roof comes down on our heads?"

"Not sure. But you won the roll. So, *you* get to take the sword," Tanya said cheerfully.

Cross moved to the door, pushed it all the way open, and braced.

Just in case.

David removed his cloak, put his hands in the pockets, and reached into the two stone slots, grasping the scabbard through the fabric.

Cross held his breath, back pressed to heartwood.

David pulled the blade free of the stone.

Silence.

Nothing moved, nothing shook, nothing even creaked.

David started laughing.

Cross exhaled and heard Tanya do the same.

"I'm not gonna lie—that had me a little worried," David said.

"Me too," Cross chimed in.

Tanya nodded. "Let's get the fuck out of this dark hole."

David wrapped his cloak around the sword, tying it with twine at each end. He tucked the hood over the grip and slung it over his shoulder. The hilt was clearly still accessible by pulling back the fabric.

Intentional or coincidence?

Cross decided it didn't matter as long as David didn't draw the blade.

Nothing horrible happened as they left the room, and Cross was starting to feel like they might be in the clear until the faint rushing of water trickled into his ears.

"You hear that?" Cross asked.

They all stopped and listened.

"Run!" David yelled.

Cross reached the top of the stairs first, taking the steps three at a time. Torches and dead OAM members were deposited on the grate below, and water still flowed into the drain. They all slowed, looking into the room. Water still poured from the statues' necks, though with far less pressure than before, and the stone pillar at the far end of the room was up. Cross turned and blew out the lantern.

"Hey!" Tanya said.

"Shhh, I think someone's coming."

"Why?" David asked.

"The pillar's up. Someone on the other side must have reset it, right?" Cross guessed.

They sat in silence for a minute, but no light appeared at the far end of the hall. Water rushed down the grate, but the sound was coming from his left and right, as well.

Scrape. Scrape. Tanya's lantern illuminated the hall again.

"You hear that?" she asked.

David and Cross nodded.

Tanya headed back up the steps, running her fingertips along the wall. She stopped, cocked her head to the side, then pulled. The stone hinged inward, revealing a passage. Tanya motioned for them to join her. Cross walked back up the stairs, peering through the opening into an enormous chamber. A catwalk ran from the doorway into the open air, fading into the darkness. Water rushed over surrounding retaining walls.

"What in the hells are we looking at?" David asked.

"I think this is the inner workings of the trap that nearly killed us," Tanya said, looking around. "Whoever set this was a master."

"How so?" Cross asked.

"Well, I can't be certain without more time to study, but I bet this chamber fills up at each high tide." Tanya pulled out the pocket clock. "Looks like that was almost thirty minutes ago."

"So, what does it do?" Cross asked.

"Well, the tide fills this chamber, providing the water pressure to power the trap when someone springs it. I bet if we wait a little longer, the tide will stop filling the reservoir, and those statue heads will drop back into position."

She was clearly excited, but Cross still had no idea what it meant.

"Tanya!" David exclaimed. "Get to the bloody point already. The rest of us don't have your fetish for the unexplained."

Tanya scowled at him. "Well, what it means is—"

"Fetish?" Cross interrupted.

"Don't worry about it, buddy," David said, grinning.

Cross looked to Tanya for answers.

Her light-brown skin was slightly rosy.

A blush? But Tanya never blushes.

"What it means," she continued, "is that the tides are resetting the trap, and this whole labyrinth functions without any human interaction, maintenance, or manual force."

"How's that possible?" David asked.

"Well, the tide fills this chamber at its peak, providing the water pressure needed to fill the riddle room. If the door remained shut and we drowned, there wouldn't be enough pressure to keep the statues' heads open anymore. I bet it resets the trap once they drop back into position."

"What about the stone pillar?" Cross asked. "Also, what's a fetish?"

"Damn you, David," Tanya muttered.

"It's Ashley, actually, and you're welcome," he quipped.

"Some sort of huge float could explain that," Tanya said, still ignoring Cross's question about the fetish. "If you chained the pillar to something buoyant enough, the tide could raise it."

"Well, wasn't it near high tide when we were in that infernal room?" David asked.

"Yes," Tanya said.

"Then why wasn't the pillar opening and letting all that bloody water out?"

"I don't know. We could go have a look," Tanya said, eyes glimmering in the torchlight.

"Maybe it had a locking mechanism tied to the opening of the door?" Cross ventured.

"Could be, but it would have to be tied to the statues, too, in case we never made it through, like the OAM."

"That all makes my head hurt," David said. "Let's just get the fuck outta here."

"For once, you're right, even though I'd love to see how this thing works," Tanya said.

The seawater had nearly stopped spilling over the retaining wall, and the reservoir was almost empty. The three of them headed down the stairs, stepping over OAM corpses covered in fresh crabs.

Water still trickled from each statue's neck as they entered the riddle room. When they were halfway down the hall, the flow stopped entirely, and a series of clicks and whirring sounds filled the room. Hooded heads refastened to stone necks, and the massive, rusty door ground shut behind them. Metal squealed as the wheel turned, pushing rods back into place as clamps slammed shut.

"Incredible," Tanya whispered.

As they headed through the chamber, Cross looked at each statue, finally stopping in front of the hooded figure holding the bowl. A crustacean milled about in the seawater. Cross cocked his head to the side, then turned back toward the door. He couldn't read the riddle, but he remembered what it said:

She bestows life to some families, yet she wrecks others.
She is quick to anger, but seldom without warning.
She can carry you, but you cannot restrain her.

Cross's booming laugh echoed about the chamber.

"What's funny?" Tanya asked.

"The ocean."

"The ocean's funny?" David asked. "That's the last bloody thing I find funny today."

"No, that's the answer. The ocean."

"The answer to what?" David asked.

"The riddle!" Tanya exclaimed.

David stomped back to the door and read the riddle aloud. "You've got to be fucking kidding me! That's cheating. There was no ocean in that bowl till the room was halfway full! Cross, where is that bloody hammer of yours? I'm gonna break this fuckin' bowl." David returned, craning his neck as he tried to locate the tool.

"Don't do that. This little guy won't live much longer. We should at least leave him his water." Cross pointed at the crab, biting his lip. "I'm gonna take him with us."

"That thing's gonna pinch the shit outta you," David warned.

"Nonsense," Cross said, pulling a tin cup from his bag and scooping up the little crab. It tried to crawl out, but he wrapped a cloth around the top of the cup and held it down. Cross glanced back at the rusty door.

"Leave them," Tanya said, placing a hand on his shoulder. "They have a way out. They can go down that drain and find whatever water source the grate dumps the ocean back into."

Cross nodded, deciding it made sense.

They journeyed back up the steps to the small room, took the last torch from the wall as a backup, and headed down the stairs toward the maze. They found more water after a few steps, and Cross tossed the crab into it.

He'll have a chance, at least.

They doused the lantern to preserve the fuel. In the dark, David and Tanya jibed and bickered with each other as they waited for the tide to fall. Cross mostly tuned them out, occasionally laughing if one of them got in a good quip. Mostly, though, he imagined Elinfall and Terra. Soon, if everything went according to plan, they would be on their way to his homeland...

Together.

The thought of living somewhere without David and Tanya was becoming less and less appealing. He really liked them, and they were beginning to feel like family. They could never replace the one he'd lost, but perhaps they could be a new one—a family...and one not born into the bonds of slavery.

Freedom.

The concept was still barely comprehendible.

What will I even do with it? Become a farmer?

No, farming had never been Cross's true calling.

He let out a long sigh.

My only talents lie in blood.

Cross didn't like the idea. He was tired of fighting, tired of killing, tired of feeling empty.

Blood is all I know. But does it have to be?

Over the last few weeks, Cross had learned so many things. How to play croxix. To read a little. So many new words. He drummed a hand on the wall.

No, I'll leave the blood behind in Darin. He wasn't sure what he would do instead but decided it would be something else.

The comical bickering had stopped some time ago, and someone finally scraped life back into the lantern. Light flooded the passage, revealing David's head resting on Tanya's lap. Cross had been sure David was interested in her for a while, but he was surprised to see Tanya had allowed it.

She checked the time, then roused David. They gathered themselves and descended the steps back into the maze. There was virtually no water left at the bottom of the stairs, and the leeches had apparently gone looking for prey. As Tanya led them through, they encountered no bloated corpses and only got turned around once. When they neared the entrance to the maze, she reminded them to keep a wide berth of the pressure plate. Finally, they were climbing the original stairs to the barracks.

"Let's camp here," Tanya suggested once they were on the surface.

"Not down by the landing?" David asked.

"I thought you were scared of sea monsters?" Tanya rolled her eyes.

David bit his lip.

"This is the least-destroyed part of the city we found, and it has far less blood and gore than the streets," Tanya explained. "Plus, it has beds!"

"You think it's safe?" David asked.

"We can take watches," Tanya suggested.

"Seems frugal since everyone on the island was murdered," Cross said.

They both just stared at him.

Cross searched his memory. "I mean prudent."

"Ha, there you go, big guy."

Tanya shook her head. "I'll take first watch."

Cross awoke to a singular beam of sunlight streaming through the hole in the roof. David still lay in a bunk near him, and Tanya was slumped in the corner of the room. A sword lay across her lap, and the leather strap of Caldwell's watch dangled from her limp hand.

Clearly, she hadn't made it through the night, but it was hard to blame her for that. Cross hurt everywhere, and the small punctures across his entire body ached. Quietly, he stood, muscles protesting as he crept over and checked the watch. He didn't fully understand the thing but had learned enough to read the hour.

Ten something.

Cross couldn't remember exactly when the boat was supposed to arrive, but it had been before ten. There was no point in waking the others, so he spent the next hour or so eating some trail rations and relaxing. He was absolutely famished, and even their soggy hardtack tasted good.

"By the gods, I'm sore," David moaned, then stretched. "Let's get the hells out of here, big man."

"Can't. We missed the boat," Cross said, cheerfully chewing.

471

"Well, fuck. I know I mentioned never wanting to see the ocean again, but I was quite looking forward to being off this bloody island."

Tanya stirred, blinked, then groaned and rolled her shoulder.

"Shit. Guess I fell asleep, huh?" she asked.

"Yep, but we're all fine," Cross said. "Besides, I think we needed the rest."

Tanya raised the watch. "Way past our appointment with the boat."

"They'll be back tomorrow," Cross said through a mouthful of dried meat.

David turned to him. "Is that my jerky?"

"Yeah. I had a fetish for it!" Cross exclaimed.

Both David and Tanya looked at each other, then burst into laughter. They laughed until they were crying, and David actually fell to the floor.

So, not quite right then.

"One of you gonna tell me what it means?" Cross asked once they'd finally stopped.

David's and Tanya's eyes met again.

"That's on you, David. You taught him the word."

"It means to like something a lot," David explained. "Like a lot, a lot."

"Well, then I do have a jerky fetish 'cause this stuff's amazing," Cross boomed. They both lost it again. He waited patiently for them to stop, but each time one slowly settled, the other would lose it again.

Cross smiled.

At least we can laugh again. Much better than the grim place we were in yesterday.

Finally, the two of them calmed enough to catch their breath.

David paused, visibly gathering himself. The corners of his mouth twitched, but he managed to say, "Like, in a sexual way."

"Oh," Cross said, eyes widening. It was his turn to laugh.

After breakfast, they raided the armory. Tanya took a new bow and quiver, David found two knives he liked, and Cross replaced most of the weapons he'd abandoned in the maze. Once resupplied, they exited the barracks.

The square was just as awful as Cross remembered.

The smell of blood and iron permeated everything, and the constant squawking of gulls was disorienting.

"We've got till tomorrow morning to discover what happened here," Tanya said. "After that, we're boarding the *Warden* with the blade, and we aren't even going to look back as we leave this wretched fuckin' island."

472

"Wretched?" Cross asked, then clarified, "It's not sexual, right?" They all chuckled, but laughing too hard in their current surroundings was difficult.

"No, not sexual. You can look to David for those words," Tanya said, shooting the musician a scowl. "It means evil or kind of hopeless."

"Good word for this place," Cross said, looking around the square. The crater in the center caught his eye and seemed as good a place to start as any. He walked over and slid down the short slope to sift through the rubble. A pile of tiny rocks that might have been part of a fountain sat at the bottom, but they weren't enough to make up the whole thing.

Very strange.

Cross climbed out of the pit and looked around. More destruction led away from the fountain, so he followed it. David and Tanya trailed behind him, talking and pointing at things. He walked past a few destroyed buildings before finally spotting a large pile of rubble.

"There," Cross said, pointing down the street.

"What in the hells is it?" David asked, squinting at the wreckage.

"It's the fountain," Cross said. Bits and pieces of statues were all jumbled together in a pile of chiseled body parts.

"Well, I see that. But what in the name of Atheia is it doing all the way over here?" David asked.

Tanya passed Cross, approaching the pile.

"I'm not sure that's a good idea," David called after her.

"It's only masonry, David," she shot back. "Don't tell me you're afraid of a little stone. Plus, we're supposed to find out what happened here."

Cross glanced down alleyways on either side of the road. Even off the main street, the buildings were all mangled and torn apart.

What in all that's sacred could cause destruction like this?

To the right, Cross heard Tanya digging through the rubble. He turned to see David closing the distance between them.

I don't like this. Something feels off.

"There's something in the center!" she yelled.

"Tanya, I think you need to stop!" David shouted. "How in the hells did the fountain get over here?" He ran toward her.

"It's just rock! Maybe it was a siege weapon?" she guessed. "I can almost touch it...T here!"

A loud hum rippled through the air.

Cross spun.

Something tore from the rubble next to Tanya, lifting into the air. It was covered in blood, dirt, and pulverized rock dust, and it glowed a deep, dark purple.

52
NATHAN

White light faded into falling snowflakes as the world came into focus. Nathan let out a low groan. Everything hurt, and his head swam.

Where am I?

Nathan drew in a ragged breath.

The tang of blood and iron was palpable, and a constant low gurgle droned in the background. With gritted teeth, Nathan stood. The yard was an absolute bloodbath. Corpses sprawled in the snow, dismembered limbs littered the place, and blood spattered the blanket of white.

A wet sputter pulled Nathan back to the present. He turned, searching.

Raylor hung on the wall, suspended by the shovel in his gut. He'd gripped the handle tight, holding himself steady, not struggling. Blood dripped from the wooden shaft, pooling below him. Nathan walked over and looked the old hunter up and down.

No saving him.

"So much for that prophecy, huh?" Nathan asked, pushing down the serpent coiling in his guts.

Mourn later, act now.

Raylor gurgled something, blood dribbling down his chin.

"You make it up?"

Another incomprehensible attempt at speech, then Raylor nodded.

"Thought so. You want me to end it?"

More blood spilled from Raylor's lips as he mouthed something.

"I reckon that's a yes." Nathan took a deep breath.

Raylor nodded, hands clenching around the handle of the shovel.

Nathan took another step forward, picking up Raylor's knife from the snow. A mix of rage and regret filled him as he placed a hand on the old hunter's shoulder and raised the blade.

"You weren't wrong to lie to them—just so you know. They needed hope more than they needed truth," Nathan told him.

Raylor's chest heaved. His mouth twitched. Tears welled in his eyes.

A flicker of a smile? No, probably not.

Tears streamed down Nathan's face as he pulled the sharp edge across Raylor's throat. Blood spilled, but not nearly as much as a throat should produce. Nathan stayed with Raylor for a few seconds. That's all it took for shallow breaths to cease and eyes to glaze.

Nathan let out a long sigh, wiped his eyes, then turned from the man who'd shown him nothing but kindness. He cleaned Raylor's blade, then gathered up three spears and a plethora of other knives from the killing ground. He gave the mercy of steel to two more hunters on his way out of the backyard, then began to run.

He sprinted down the mountainside, taking ledges in leaps and bounds instead of climbing as they had during the ascent. On more than one occasion, he almost tripped and careened off a cliff, but quick reflexes barely saved him each time. He wasn't sure why Elrontis hadn't killed him, but a sinking feeling in the pit of his stomach told him where the creature was headed.

In less than an hour, he was in the forest, and before long, trees gave way to the rolling hills surrounding Trill. He'd run down what had taken nearly eight hours of hiking in little more than one. As the village came into view, Nathan stopped to catch his breath. No one moved about the settlement, and a dull silence hung over the place.

Where's the thud of axes? The clanging of smiths?

An enormous plume of smoke rose from a hole in the great hall's roof.

The villagers are still here, and they aren't screaming. Not yet, anyway.

Nathan took a long, ragged breath, then ran toward the silent village.

Need to check on Eva first, then organize a defensive position.

The settlement became no less desolate as Nathan moved through it, and the silence only deepened. The uneasy feeling twisted about in his gut, growing worse all the way to Eva's cabin.

The front door was ajar.

A shiver quivered up Nathan's spine as he pulled Raylor's knife and cautiously entered. Huge, dirty paw prints weaved through the room. He followed them, creeping silently across the wooden planks. The tracks circled an old pair of boots, then trailed back toward their point of origin: Eva's bedroom.

Nathan closed his eyes, took a shuddering breath, then pushed the door inward. Muddy prints were everywhere, but there was no sign of Eva or bloody entrails. Nathan let out a sigh of relief.

Why did Elrontis come back here?

Most of the tracks surrounded the bed and a mirror adorned with hanging herbs.

Unless...

Nathan's blood went cold.

An image of an enormous snout pulling in great gouts of air filled his mind.

It must have caught her scent. I put Eva in grave danger by comforting her.

Nathan sank to his knees, the revelation hitting him like a galloping horse.

This is my fault. I'm the reason this—

A cry rang out from somewhere outside.

Nathan was on his feet in an instant.

Hate yourself later. Save these people now—save Eva.

Nathan ran back into the main room, darted over to the fireplace, and pulled the sword from the mantle. The metal sang as it left the sheath, and he charged out the door, discarding the scabbard in the grass. The sword was heavy and cold in all the right ways, and the balance felt good. As his hand tightened around the hilt, a piece of himself seemed to click back into place.

I can unpack that later, Nathan decided, sprinting toward the great hall.

The screams started once he was halfway up the hill. They were all terror and panic at first but soon mingled with wails of grief and the blubber of the dying. The villagers were calling out to their false gods, but no help would come from them.

If you sent me here, some assistance wouldn't go unnoticed, Nathan prayed as he crested the hill. A fire blazed on the left side of the great hall, and the screaming had only grown in volume.

Nathan tried to duck past the skins on the door and ran into something solid. Furniture and people were packed tight against the other side. He craned his neck, trying to see through the crowd, but all he could make out was smoke and blood spattered across the rafters. Yanking the pelts from a set of nails, he grabbed a chair and ripped it into the open. The crowd on the other side didn't even appear to notice him.

"Help me, God damn you!" Nathan yelled through the barricade.

People screamed and shoved each other but didn't turn.

"Push that furniture through to me!"

Still, they ignored him.

They were all facing away, bodies pressed tight like sheep. Nathan crawled through the small hole he'd made, shoving his way into the crowd.

A shoulder hit his chest as a man collided with him, wide eyed and frenzied. The crowd surged, and the man was gone.

Like cattle, after the first steer's been slaughtered.

A woman fell with a scream, disappearing underfoot.

Someone shoved Nathan into the barricade, slamming his spine into a chair leg. Nathan punched the man in the face, and he fell away, lost under trampling feet.

It freed up just enough space for Nathan to turn and shove a couple more pieces of furniture through the barricade. He grabbed a woman's shoulders and pushed her through the gap. Then a man. A child. Slowly, the villagers took notice. Suddenly, the dam of people broke, and everyone was scrambling and clawing at each other to get out.

Nathan quit shoving people from the building and pushed into the crowd. His eyes darted around, frantically scanning the screaming masses for Eva as he shouldered through the press. Suddenly, he was churned into open space. He stared into the hysteria for a few more seconds, then turned to the other end of the hall. The sight of the place stopped him in his tracks.

Massacre.

It was the only word that fit, yet it seemed wildly insufficient.

A tipped brazier lay near the hall's middle entrance. Thick black smoke billowed from the fiery barricade, forming a veil in the center of the room before streaming out the hole in the roof.

The haze obscured the other half of the hall but not the carnage on this side. It was a slaughterhouse. Some villagers were impaled on the horns and antlers of beasts they'd so proudly displayed as trophies, others were slumped over chairs or furniture, and even more were strewn about the floor. Dozens of men, women, and children had been slaughtered indiscriminately, and Nathan could only see half the room.

His stomach churned, but he forced himself to look at each face. None were Eva.

Where is she?

Nathan stepped around a torso hanging by its intestines from the rafters and nearly slipped on the blood-coated floor.

How did that even get up there?

Nathan looked at the woman's dead eyes.

Not Eva.

A sinking feeling grew in the pit of his stomach as he scanned the room for her face.

Is this fear for love? Or responsibility?

Nathan stood before the thick veil of smoke. Screams and carnage filled the space behind him. A wet ripping, smacking echoed through the hall ahead. With a deep breath, he stepped into the billowing black.

Dread filled Nathan as the haze swallowed him. Screams echoed all around him through the black fog. His stomach twisted.

This thing decimated an entire hunting party, and I'm just one man.

He exhaled, pushing the dread from his mind.

Lose your nerve, lose your life.

The haze parted, and Nathan took in the other side of the hall with terrible clarity. His twisted stomach dropped away. He hadn't thought it could get any worse, but he'd been wrong before.

Elrontis crouched on a long table near the end of the hall. Bodies piled around the creature in a circle. Some were hunters who'd stayed behind. Most were townspeople. None had stood a chance. Nathan couldn't tell how many had been slaughtered due to the pieces they were in, but dozens felt conservative.

A sickly sweet odor, like crispy pork, wafted through the air.

At the far end of the room, two bodies burned in a large brazier. Innards and intestines dangled from the rafters, almost as if Elrontis had disemboweled these innocents and flung their entrails about purposefully.

Maybe it did.

The carnage looked far too intentional to be anything but spectacle.

"You set this up for me." The words echoed through Nathan's mind long after he uttered them aloud.

The slurping stopped, and Elrontis raised its blood-drenched maw. It pushed whatever it had been eating forward.

Eva's head flopped back over the edge of the table.

Lifeless green eyes stared with glassy condemnation. Her hands, covered in bloody gashes, fell listlessly to either side. Shards of pottery littered the ground and dotted the fur on Elrontis's head and shoulders.

It ate her alive. All while she smashed dish after dish against its skull.

Elrontis let out a long and chittering wheeze.

It's laughing at me.

53

DAVID TRUEHEART

T he boulder vibrated and hummed in the air.

Tanya paused, clearly transfixed by the spinning stone.

"Run!" David screamed, stepping back.

For a moment, Tanya hesitated, then turned to run.

The boulder pulsed.

Something tugged at David's pant leg. He reached down to yank it free of whatever snagged it but found only air. The force pulled at his limbs as he grabbed a nearby lamppost and yelled, "Hurry!"

The pole creaked, flexing against the pull.

Thank the gods the OAM is overfunded.

Tanya was nearly to him, wading through the air like mud. David wrapped one arm around the lamppost, extending the other toward her. She reached, face tightening with effort, but their fingers were still a pace apart.

Fuck it.

David lifted a leg, hooked it around the lamppost, and let go with his other hand. His whole body pulled toward the torrent of energy. Tanya reached—stretching, straining, grasping. Their fingers met, intertwining and locking together. David's other hand seized her wrist in a vice-like grip, and Tanya did the same.

All that music was good for something, David thought, forearms bulging.

Tanya's feet lifted from the ground, and her whole body pulled parallel with the cobblestone. The iridescent purple glow throbbed as the boulder ripped and tore at its surroundings. Rubble from the fountain crashed into the huge stone, followed by a pile of human mulch and bits of the surrounding building. A seagull flew too low, squawked, then plummeted toward the crystal. Each added to the mass, sticking like flies in honey.

The stone pulsed again, then again, and again.

With each pulse, the pull increased.

"Hold on!" David screamed, but even the words were lost to the vortex.

My grip won't last forever.

He looked around frantically.

Cross crept toward them but stopped as the stone started to pull at him. Fire burned through David's hamstring and calf, straining to hold their combined weight. His leg slipped a finger's width. He glanced back, teeth clenching, willing it to stay put. The leg slid farther.

Tanya's grip loosened.

David looked at her, eyes widening.

She stared at him, jaw set with determination.

"Let go," Tanya mouthed.

David's lip quivered. His grip was failing.

"I can't go on without you!" he tried to scream.

The words were lost.

Tanya's lips were quivering, too, but the determination hadn't left her eyes.

"Goodbye, David," she mouthed.

With a scream, he flung his right leg backward, hooking knee and foot together and cinching them tight around the pole.

The maelstrom pulled at them with no sign of ending.

David glanced back at his locked legs.

Where in the hells did I learn to do that? Maybe I saw someone do it in a bar—

Suddenly, everything was falling.

David hit the ground, air knocking from his lungs. Distantly, he heard rocks, debris, and all manner of other things clatter to the cobblestone. He coughed and gasped, then someone was hauling him to his feet.

"What in the absolute fuck was that?" David wheezed.

"You all right?" Tanya asked, meeting his eyes, then glancing over her shoulder.

She really does have such pretty eyes—

Tanya shoved him. They went down together in a heap.

A metallic rip squealed overhead.

Tanya rolled off him into a crouch. David followed her gaze. A hulking form loomed over them.

Fists the size of card tables connected to massive arms that propped up a torso made of rubble and debris. A pile of pieces vaguely resembling a head rested atop the torso, with a gaping hole for a mouth. Black smoke billowed from two pitted sockets on either side of the twisted jumble. Playful, childlike faces peered from the rubble locked in mocking stone.

The OAM commissioned the only happy mason in all of Darin to chisel that fountain.

The lamppost that was their lifeline a moment ago was bent in half in the thing's grip. Without taking her eyes from the monstrosity, Tanya extended a hand. David took it, pulling himself up.

The hulk roared, bits of stone flying from its mouth in a gravelly cascade. David clamped his hands over his ears, wincing and weathering the noise. Slowly, the sound died off, then the monster was moving.

A hand was on his chest, pushing him.

David stumbled back as Tanya dove in the opposite direction. The creature's fist smashed into the ground between them. David's feet tangled as his shoulder collided with a half-demolished structure, and a shower of stone peppered his back.

He pushed off the wall, turning as the behemoth's huge open fist swiped across the ground. The claw-like hand ripped up the stone street as it raked along, tossing shards of rock into the air. David danced back, retreating through a cloud of dust. An arrow whizzed past, bouncing off the monster's head. He looked back as Tanya nocked another shaft. The beast let out a roar, dragging its body forward.

"We need to get the fuck out of here!" David yelled.

Cross barreled in from the side, leaping onto the thing's back.

The big man scaled the creature, wielding his war hammer like a climber's pick. He crested the beast's shoulders, grabbed onto a metal bar protruding from its head, and rained down blows.

The fiend steadied itself, then swatted at Cross. The big man ducked under the first sweeping strike. The next fist came in hard, trying to squash him against its head. Cross hooked his hammer around the bar, ducked down, and leaned back. The creature's fist connected with its head in a grinding smash. It lurched to the side, off balance, ready to topple.

What in the bloody hells should I do?

David looked around.

Tanya sent arrow after arrow into the creature, but it was clearly useless.

David glanced over his shoulder at the cloak-covered pommel of the sword.

Should I draw the blade?

The monster regained its balance and swatted at Cross again.

Like a drunkard trying violently to deter a fly.

The absurdity of it would've made David laugh if circumstances hadn't been so dire.

Then again, the big man's doing about as much damage as a fly—

A piece of the fountain chiseled free of the monster's head, and it let out a grinding bellow. Cross locked his knees around a statue for stability, raised the war hammer in both hands and brought it down on the bar he'd just held.

Once.

Twice.

Three times.

The thing roared louder with each blow, then placed both hands on the ground and drew itself tight. Rubble bunched together, like the flexing of muscle.

Cross dropped the hammer and grabbed onto the bar.

The monster shook, shoulders swaying like a wet dog.

Cross clung on, legs whipping about twice, then he was airborne. He hit a nearby wall with a smack, slid to the cobblestone, and stilled. The behemoth turned toward the big man as one of Tanya's arrows flew through the rubble and connected with the crystal at its center. The beast screamed, turning its gaze on her.

"Run!" David yelled. "To the docks."

For bloody fucking once, Tanya listened. She turned and sprinted down the main street, and David followed suit. Soon, they ran side by side, ground quaking as the creature clawed after them.

David risked a glance over his shoulder.

The thing was seven—no, six—actually, make that five spans behind.

David pulled Tanya around the corner as they entered the square. "Quick! We can hide in the entrance to the vault!" he yelled, pointing to the barracks.

The behemoth barreled into view. It clearly saw them, but momentum carried it past into the plaza. With another deafening roar, it crashed into the barracks, and the entire building caved in around it.

Tanya's eyes widened in a mix of exasperation and horror. "You just had to fuckin' say something."

"Shit," David muttered. "Never mind. To the docks!"

They sprinted down the blood-filled street. David risked a glance back, nearly slipping as the monstrosity emerged from the cloud of rubble that was once the barracks.

We've got a bit of a lead, but it won't last long.

Birds hopped about in the street, squawking in protest and scattering before them. Tanya glanced over her shoulder once, then twice. David was about to venture a look when she yanked him into an alleyway. The behemoth careened past them, stone hands scrambling on the gut-smeared cobblestone. Rotting gore splattered birds as they rose from the carrion or were crushed under the creature's bulk.

I hope Cross is all right.

David decided the big man was probably the safest of all of them right now.

As long as he's still alive.

Tanya pulled David farther into the alley. The creature's head and arms tore into the side street, ripping through the buildings. Tanya yanked him down another street on the right. The ground quaked as the thing clawed around the corner, closing the distance. They passed another pile of rubble, a purplish stone glimmering within. Another turn, this time to the left.

"Holy fuck...there are more...of those things?" David shouted between labored breaths.

"At least we...solved the mystery...of Seafront," Tanya yelled.

Buildings collapsed as the monster squeezed through the alley behind them.

"Not that anyone...will bloody...believe us," David wheezed.

"Can you...blame them?" Tanya asked.

"Let's worry about...convincing them...later."

"Just shut up...and run...you beautiful...fuckin'...idiot!"

David risked another glance back.

A boulder was hurtling through the air toward them. David leapt, tackling Tanya as the enormous stone sailed overhead. They scrambled up. The monster lowered its arm and lumbered forward, torso grinding through the gore and stone beneath.

It's never gonna stop. It will—

Tanya grabbed David's hand and dragged him back into the carnage of the main street.

"This way," David yelled, running toward the docks.

The hulking brute crashed through the buildings on either side of the alley like they were nothing more than gambling chips. It spotted them, roared, then clawed down the street toward them. They had a lead on it, but in the open, it closed the distance.

Another dozen steps, then Tanya tugged David into one of the few side streets not blocked with rubble. They ran to the end, took a right, then skidded to a halt. A horse-sized purple stone stood amidst a pile of wood and debris, blocking the way.

"Shit," Tanya hissed.

They turned, running back the way they'd come. The beast rounded the corner, hands gripping the buildings on either side of the alleyway. Slowly, it lowered its head to their level. Black, soot-like trails drifted from its eyes, and a purplish light pulsed through the side street.

Cornered. No way out.

David glanced back at the stone. If they tried to slip past, it would undoubtedly awaken another horror. His hand found Tanya's and squeezed.

"I think this is it," David murmured, then pulled her close and brought his lips to hers.

"Fuckin' hells, David!" Tanya protested, pushing him off. "This is *not* the time!"

The monster slowed, almost as if it understood they were trapped. Unhurried, it tore down the buildings on either side of the street, creating a clear path for its torso.

Like a cat who's already cornered a mouse.

"This might be the only time we have left, Mystery-Hips," David whispered, eyes shifting from the monster back to Tanya.

A tremendous roar split the morning air.

David winced.

Cross surged over the thing's shoulders, bellowing a cry more bestial than human. He grabbed the iron bar he'd hammered into the behemoth's neck, levering it back and forth. Stone cracked and shifted, and the beast let out a howl as it reached for the big man.

Tanya grabbed David's wrist, pulling him through the gap under the thing's raised arm. They darted back onto the main street, and David risked a look. The fiend had given up trying to reach Cross and was throwing its back toward a wall instead. Its shoulders hit first, shattering stone and sending Cross through the side of the structure.

"Fuck," David cursed through clenched teeth. He considered turning back, but no one could survive being smashed through the side of a fucking building.

"What?" Tanya asked, still pulling him toward the docks.

David was starting to slow, his sides ached, and his breath was labored. "Nothing. Just move," he wheezed.

A moment later, the creature rounded the corner, something clutched in a clawed fist. It pulled back the arm, then threw. David yanked Tanya to the side as a boulder the size of a small carriage crashed into the cobbles where they'd just stood. The stone bounced past, kicking up gore in a red wake.

The projectile finally rolled to a stop in a pile of blood, bone, and entrails near the dock's entrance. David and Tanya sprinted toward it and were nearly there as the thunderous scraping behind them resumed.

"Just gotta...get to the—"

The boulder lifted into the air.

They each turned, fighting to stop their momentum.

The stone hummed, then pulsed. Everything started vibrating toward it. They scrambled back up the street as the pull began to assert itself on David's limbs. The first creature lurched toward them as another was born behind.

David glanced between the two monstrosities.

How in the hells are we gonna deal with two?

"We need to split up," David said.

The ground quaked as the fountain monster lumbered toward them.

"I'll head left. You go deeper into the city," Tanya said with a nod.

"All right, go!"

They each sprinted toward alleyways on opposite sides of the street. The gravelly rumble behind David lessened. He slowed, looking back. The creature was following Tanya. Past the main street, in the direction she'd run, loomed the city walls.

A weight settled in David's stomach, reminding him of times he'd left the Ivory Gauntlet with pockets as full as the Trickster.

There's no way that alley doesn't end in the blank face of the exterior wall.

Tanya was trapped, and it wouldn't be long before the beast ripped its way to her.

David crept back out of the alleyway.

The other humming stone had formed a nightmarish colossus of blood, bone, and squawking birds. Tendrils of black smoke drifted from the beaks of two crows positioned where eyes should sit.

The creature's mouth opened, and a wet, sticky roar shook Seafront.

Apparently, it's as unhappy to be reborn as I am to be unborn.

It was an intrusive thought, cynical, and not helpful.

David's heart leapt as Cross stumbled from an alleyway up the street.

Holy fuck, how's he still alive?

The big man was limping badly and bleeding from at least a dozen wounds.

Looks like he's been run over by a bloody carriage.

David's gaze shifted from Cross to each of the two monsters. Something deep in his psyche screamed at him to run, but he stuffed the feeling down.

Did she lead that thing down the alley, knowing there was no way out?

Tanya was anything but dumb and had the best sense of direction he'd ever seen.

She bought me time, and I'm wasting it. I shouldn't let her sacrifice be in vain.

David looked over his shoulder at the blade wrapped in layers of cloak.

"Sometimes, when all the chips are on the table, you just gotta go all in, my boy."

Sage advice from a washed-up, one-handed musician.

Everything seemed to slow. The lumbering horror approached from the docks. The monster clawed and bellowed at Tanya, and Cross limped down the street toward him.

Too bad I don't know how to use this thing.

David unslung the blade from his back.

But I know someone who does.

"Cross! Catch!" David yelled, tossing the sword toward the big man.

"You aren't very bright, are you?"

The first words Tanya ever said to him.

I suppose not.

With that, David did the dumbest thing he could think of. He ran at the monster, closing the distance in a few long strides, and scrambled onto the thing's back. Stone shifted as the creature reached for Tanya, and David nearly lost his fingers more than once.

Just like climbing a rock wall—a living, moving, autonomous rock wall.

David crested the monster's shoulders, grabbing hold of the iron bar in the thing's back. The steel rod went all the way down to the purple orb at its core.

"You!"

David screamed with an animalistic fury he'd never possessed.

"Will!"

He yanked the bar to the right.

"Leave her!"

David pulled the bar to the left.

"Alone!"

He twisted it.

"You fucking!"

He wrenched on it.

"Bloody piece!"

He pushed the metal with all his might.

"Of inanimate!"

Crack. The sound reverberated through the stone, ringing through the morning air.

"Scrap!" David shouted as he levered the bar back and forth one more time.

The monster bellowed and stood.

Shit. What have I got myself into now?

David stopped yanking on the bar and looked down. His forearms bulged, with a grip so tight it would've crushed the neck of his father's old lute.

An image of the inscription flashed through his mind:

For Trueheart, a man as faithful as his name implies, and the absolute love of my life.

54
NATHAN

The beast roared and leapt into the air.

Nathan pulled out of his charge, stepped to the side, and swung Eva's sword.

Elrontis's claws slashed forward. Instead of carving through flesh, they met the tip of the blade. Steel parted sinew and bone, sending two fingers careening through the air. Elrontis landed and let out a stuttered howl. Its muscles bunched, then it sprang.

Nathan dodged out of the way, leaving the sword outstretched. The creature flew by as the blade scored a long line in its side, but a claw caught Nathan in the shoulder. The blow spun him like a top. The pain came a moment later, and with it, blood. Nathan gritted his teeth, turning back to the other side of the hall.

Elrontis was gone.

Somewhere beyond the screen of smoke.

With a grunt, Nathan took a step forward and readied his blade.

The beast materialized.

One instant, it was a shadow in the curtain of smoke; the next, it was hurtling toward him.

Nathan fell prone.

Teeth gnashed overhead, claws tore through his shirt, and something crashed into the long table. He rolled. Plates, cups, and Eva's lifeless body flew across the room. Elrontis staggered up, shaking its head. Nathan leapt to his feet, transferred the sword to his left hand, and unslung a spear. He aimed for the creature's neck and threw.

The spear sailed through the air, on target.

Come on. Please, God.

Elrontis turned.

The spear skidded across the side of the monster's head, tearing through skin and cartilage before clattering to the floorboards.

With a chittering yowl, Elrontis stalked forward, missing jowl revealing half its teeth.

Guess it's done leaping around.

Nathan gripped the sword in both hands, widening his stance as molten fury coursed through his veins.

Elrontis shouldered through the hanging entrails, baring the rest of its teeth. The creature was a little over a span away, yet it towered over him. A low growl rumbled from its chest as it circled slowly closer.

Nathan turned with the beast, sword up and ready.

Elrontis slashed down.

He parried the blow with his blade, leaving a bloody trail down the creature's hand and forearm. A raking claw came from the other side. Nathan tried to sidestep, but the blow caught him full in the ribs. Bones crunched as his feet left the floor.

His back slammed into something. Air fled his lungs. He sputtered and scrambled up to his knees, preparing to stand. Something wet and viscous dripped onto his face.

Nathan froze.

Slowly, he turned his head. Elrontis crouched over him, grisly muzzle hovering a hand above his head. Another trail of bloody saliva dripped from its ruined jowl onto his temple. Elrontis let out a low growl. The sound was almost musical, in a horrific sort of way.

This is it.

Nathan's teeth clenched.

Maybe it'll leave the rest of these people alone after I'm dead.

An arrow thudded into the creature's back, and a spearpoint hammered into its flank. Elrontis turned, claws raking toward him. Nathan dropped to his belly as the razor-sharp points tore through the wall above. He pulled Raylor's knife and sank it into the back of the monster's calf as the creature sprung. It hurtled wide to the right.

Another chittering growl filled the room.

Nathan looked around frantically.

Eva's family sword lay on the ground a few paces away. He scrambled over to the blade, grabbed it, then he was up.

Elrontis was elbow-deep in Horinth's chest, holding him aloft by the spine. Arrows pierced the man as Elrontis flung him about like a shield and moved toward two more hunters who refused to go up the mountain.

Nathan charged.

Elrontis threw Horinth at one of the archers, and they went down in a tangle of blood and bone. With its wounded right hand, it grabbed the other archer by the head, lifting her from the floor. She let out a single, muffled note of a scream before her head collapsed. Skin, skull, blood, and brain pressed through clawed fingers like the pulp of a juiced fruit.

As the body fell, Nathan's sword came down.

Elrontis's hand flew from its forearm, blood fountaining. With a yowl, the creature brought its left claw around, but Nathan was already spinning around it like a post in the training yard. Its arm swiped past, cleaving through air.

His blade sliced across a hamstring, and Elrontis fell to one knee. He thrust his sword at its side, but it turned, and the blade scraped across ribs instead of piercing vital organs. The back of its remaining hand struck Nathan, sending him tumbling. He collided with a brazier, a sea of embers spilling onto him.

Nathan rolled from the fiery mess.

Sparks drifted down as Elrontis stared at him from several spans away. He could feel the malice in those black pools. The beast gripped the end of its right forearm, stanching the flow of blood.

Smoke swelled behind the creature as it stood to full height.

How? Why won't you die?

Elrontis took a tentative yet determined step toward him on the leg he'd left Raylor's hunting knife embedded in. Pain swept across its face in a wave, and it snarled.

An arrow hammered into its shoulder. A couple fingers higher, and it might have been a killing blow. The woman nocked another shaft. Elrontis bared its teeth, eyes shifting from her to Nathan.

The arrow thudded into its chest.

Nathan grabbed his sword, using it to push himself up.

Elrontis snarled, chin raising.

Nathan followed its gaze.

The creature's muscles tensed as it stared up at the smoke hole in the roof.

"No!" Nathan yelled, starting to run.

Another arrow hammered into the creature's side.

Then, Elrontis was airborne, surging toward the opening in a lopsided leap.

It's not going to make it.

Nathan prayed, charging forward.

The creature's left hand latched onto the ledge of the roof.

Nathan slashed at its dangling foot and scored another cut along its already-injured calf.

An arrow hit it in the thigh.

With one arm, it pulled upward, its back legs scrambling on the rafters. Blood from its right stump spattered Nathan across the face. He jumped, swinging blindly through the red veil. His blade caught nothing. Another arrow whizzed by, thudding into a roof joist.

Elrontis's feet disappeared into the smoke.

"No!" Nathan screamed into the billowing void. He sprinted back toward the door, wincing as he passed Eva's lifeless form.

Should I check, just to make sure?

No. She was long past helping.

All I can do now is avenge her.

The back entrance was clogged with bulky furniture, but rage still boiled behind Nathan's eyes. He ripped away pieces of the barricade until he had a hole large enough to fit through, then was out the door. He scanned the rooftops clustered below the great hall.

Where is the demon?

Nathan caught a glimpse of movement and focused on it. Elrontis limped into the open ground between the forest and Trill. It moved on two legs, clutching its right arm and disappearing into the trees.

"Damn, it's fast," Nathan whispered, then took off. He weaved through the village as fast as he could with a set of broken ribs and a multitude of smaller wounds. By the time he got to the edge of town, he was wheezing, and his throbbing side was nearly unbearable.

Nathan looked back.

The town was ablaze, and screams still filled the air.

My fault...

The thought was unproductive, but no less true for that.

It would never have caused this destruction if not for me.

Nathan's eyes moved from the burning village to the sun low on the horizon, then finally to the sizable trail of blood disappearing into the forest.

Nothing to be done for them anymore, except perhaps a little vengeance.

Nathan took a deep breath and staggered into the dark.

55

TANYA RINGHOLDER

*T*rapped. *Like a fat rat in the Severance Quarter.*

The horrific monstrosity scraped toward her. Tanya chose this alleyway because one side was a tower on Seafront's exterior wall. The stone would be thick and would hopefully slow the behemoth.

Tanya knew there was no way out of the narrow street, but at least David would escape. He'd saved her life, time and time again. In reality, she knew she'd done the same. Still, he wouldn't be in this mess if it wasn't for her. After he'd kissed her in a sweet acceptance of death, Tanya decided she couldn't let him die. He was a stupid bastard sometimes, but she'd grown fond of the superficial, loveable idiot.

So here she stood, backed into an alleyway with nowhere to go. A massive hand clawed toward her, trying to break through one of the most reinforced structures in the city. The stone head of a wailing child stared up at her from the monster's middle finger. It wasn't the first disturbing detail she'd noticed from the remnants of the fountain.

But it might be the last.

The thing opened its mouth in a tangled mass of childish stone limbs.

Why are statues always so grisly and—

"Cross! Catch," David yelled from somewhere behind the monster.

Why? You stupid, stupid man! Just run, damn you.

Tanya decided to keep the thought to herself.

Whatever the fool's doing, words won't stop him.

Besides, a small part of her still held out hope for survival. She'd willingly sacrificed herself in a fit of valorous stupidity, but that didn't mean she had lost all instincts for self-preservation.

A moment later, David's head appeared over the creature's. He grabbed the iron bar Cross had hammered into the monster and twisted it with a scream.

"Leave, you idiot. You aren't Cross." Tanya meant to yell the words, but they came out a whisper.

David levered the bar back and forth, yelling something incomprehensible.

What is he saying? Bloody-fucking something or other—

The monster roared.

Run, you stupid fool.

The creature reached up and batted at David. He nearly let go of the rod, barely dodging the stone hand. The monster swatted at him several times, then shifted back and forth, throwing David's legs about as he clung to the bar. It reminded Tanya of a stable master on an untamed stallion. But David was no stable master, and the rubble monster had to be about a thousand times stronger than a horse.

This is going to end soon—and not well.

David screamed something nonsensical again from the creature's back.

I've got to do something. But what?

Tanya looked around, frantically searching for something that might hurt the creature.

Nothing presented itself.

She unslung her bow, nocked an arrow, and took aim.

David's legs flew back and forth, mimicking the tattered flags on the distant battlements. His forearms bulged, the only thing securing him to the colossus. Tanya couldn't get a clear shot as the creature shook David about like a rag doll.

More likely to hit him than to hurt the thing.

Tanya kept her sights trained on the creature as David bucked back and forth. Out of the corner of her eye, she saw a figure limp into view.

Cross? How's he even breathing?

The big man pulled the hood of David's cloak back from the hilt of the blade, then yanked the sword free of the scabbard.

For an instant, the huge man froze.

Black smoke seeped from the pommel of the blade, snaking around his wrists.

Suddenly, everything was happening all at once.

David's grip failed, sending him flying. He hit the side of the tower with a smack and fell to the ground.

The hulk turned and swiped at Cross.

It always surprised Tanya how fast the big man was with a weapon in hand. The way he moved now, though, was something else entirely.

Whatever limp Cross had a moment ago vanished. He ducked the monster's swipe and used the same momentum to barrel forward. A feral roar split the air as Cross threw all his weight into a slash aimed at the monstrosity's wrist.

Why? You clearly need to stab the core of it, or—

The sword cleaved straight through stone.

Tanya's mouth fell open.

The hulk let out a gravelly scream, showering Cross in fragments of masonry as it lifted its severed wrist. Cross screamed right back. The creature's other hand came down from above. Cross dove to the side, rolling as the monstrous palm slammed into cobblestone. Dust, dirt, and blood erupted on impact.

In one fluid motion, the big man stood from his roll, turned, and hacked through the monster's other wrist. It screeched and lifted the arm, leaving the severed hand embedded in the street. The creature brought the stump down.

Cross sidestepped. The stump smashed into the ground where he'd just stood. The huge man leapt impossibly high, grabbed the creature's shoulder, and pulled himself onto its back. He took one great step across the shifting stone, bringing him in range of its head. Chunks of rock and building material rained down as Cross hacked pieces from the whole.

Tanya shook her head, clearing it.

Stones fell all around her as she ran for David. She grabbed him by the collar and pulled with all her might. The torso of a statue smashed into the ground where he lay a moment ago. Something struck her head. Tanya fell backward, David slumping into her lap. Her vision swam, and her ears rang as her back pressed against something. Frantically, Tanya fumbled for David's neck.

Thump. Thump. Thump.

The rhythmic beat of his heart was a stark contrast to the frantic pounding of her own. Slowly, her vision cleared. Tanya stared down at her beautiful idiot. David stirred. She brushed a lock of coal black hair from his face, then looked up.

Cross hacked two more chunks from the thing's head. The monster swiped at him with its left forearm. He chopped through the arm, then sliced through what might have constituted a neck.

The head of the beast sloughed away.

Cross flipped the sword around, lifted it, then drove it down into the monster's body. The sword sank through the stone like it wasn't there at all, finally hitting something solid at the core of the beast.

Light bathed the alleyway in an iridescent purple pulse. Cross ripped a piece of stone from the creature's back, raised it high, then brought it down on the sword's pommel.

Crack. The light flickered.

Bang. The monster wobbled.

Slam. The light went out, then flickered back into existence.

Cross dropped the stone, grabbed the sword in both hands, and twisted. A sound like a thousand panes of glass shattering reverberated through the alleyway. The colossus teetered, then toppled. Cross ripped the blade free as he rode the wave of rubble to the ground. He was on it again before Tanya even took a breath.

Cross was a storm.

He moved faster than Tanya could have ever imagined, cutting piece after piece from the monster, all while bellowing wordless rage.

A moment later, the big man was at the center of it, chopping into the stone like a woodcutter. The sphere in the center cracked, then parted, falling into two equal halves. Black mist dissipated into the air with a hiss.

The rest of the monster crumbled away, all the inanimate pieces suddenly forced to adhere to the natural laws of gravity once more. The smoke had coiled up Cross's forearms to the elbow like some sort of shadowy bracer. The inky black tendrils writhed and constricted in time with his labored breaths.

"What in the hells happened?" David groaned.

Good, he's awake, Tanya thought, sweeping black strands of hair from his eyes.

"You pulled a dumb stunt. Now keep quiet and wait here." Tanya slipped out from under him, grabbed her bow, and moved into the main road.

What she saw shouldn't have surprised her, yet it was the most abhorrent thing she'd ever seen. The monster resembled the first behemoth, except it was made more of blood, bone, and sinew than anything else. It had stopped advancing, yet was clearly unwilling to back down.

Apparently, it can assess a threat... Why though? Has it ever even seen one?

"What an abomination," Tanya muttered, nocking an arrow.

"Abomination," Cross grunted, but Tanya understood it was a question.

"An ugly, evil thing," she explained with a snort and a shake of her head.

Tanya watched Cross's lips move as he silently commit the word to memory, then with a bestial roar, he charged. He splashed through blood and guts, kicking up gore as he neared the monster made of the same stuff. Tanya drew back the string and let the arrow fly. The monster screamed, and her arrow hammered home in its open mouth. The creature didn't even recoil. Instead, it started slamming its fists into the ground like an enormous ape. It brought one meaty hand overhead right as Cross came within range.

"I will intersect you!"

The fist came down.

"You repulsive!"

The blade split through the center of blood, bone, and stone.

"Uncouth!"

A shower of sinew parted around Cross.

"Crass!"

The hulking monstrosity yowled, pulling back an arm split down the middle.

"Exhumed!"

Cross moved in as the thing tried to lean away.

"Abomination!"

One of Tanya's arrows thudded into the creature's head.

"With a voracious!"

The thing let out a bloodcurdling scream.

"Fetish!"

Cross moved in, hacking and slashing.

"For human flesh!"

Another arrow hit the monster.

The hulk's other hand swept in. Cross turned his sword to the side, spearing the palm. The blade sank through the meat and stone like paper, then the hand slammed into him.

Another arrow thumped into the creature.

Cross hurtled through the air, colliding with a building on the other side of the street with a tremendous smack. It was the type of sound one didn't get back up from.

Tanya let another arrow fly, skewering a squawking bird on the thing's head.

I need that blade. It's the only thing doing any permanent damage.

The monster turned to her, apparently understanding Cross was out of the fight.

Tanya gritted her teeth, dropped her bow, and ran for the sword.

With a wet scream, the creature moved to intercept her. It was closer, and it was faster. A moment later, the thing stood between her and Cross.

Tanya skidded to a halt and took a couple of steps back. The creature lumbered forward slowly, clearly in no hurry to chase.

Does it understand that the blade is the most important thing?

Impossibly, Cross stood, stalking forward as if he hadn't even taken a blow.

His back should be broken...

Tanya took another step away.

Cross plunged the sword into the creature's back. The monster turned on him, meaty claw swinging. The beast's rotation peeled it about the middle like Tanya's mother used to peel an apple.

As the claw came around, Cross yanked the blade from the creature's center and raised it. The hand hit him right as the sword fell on its wrist. The enormous fist liquified, swallowing Cross in a wave of gore.

Tanya sucked in a breath.

One heartbeat went by.

Two.

Three.

Cross stepped from the tide of blood and bone.

He moved in on what was left of the creature, screaming and carving his way toward its center like a seasoned butcher. Slurping chops joined the cacophony of squawking birds far above them as he disappeared into the mass of flesh.

A moment later, the monster toppled, a puff of black smoke dissipating into the cool breeze. Bits and pieces of the gory abomination sloughed away, revealing Cross's hulking form. He was entirely coated in blood and butchery, breathing hard, like some sort of ancient hero reborn.

The spirals of blackened smoke had worked their way up his biceps, and the purple stone stood before him, sundered in two.

"Did we win?" David groaned from behind her. He hobbled out of the alleyway, clutching what must have been broken ribs.

"I think we did," Tanya said with a smile, then walked over and put a shoulder under David's arm. He winced at first, then rested his weight on her. Tanya helped him down the street toward Cross.

David slipped away from her as they got close.

You big bloody faker, Tanya thought with a shake of her head.

"Amara's enormous, beautiful, bloody backside!" David yelled, stepping into the remnants of the gory construct. "Do you see this?"

Tanya considered explaining that it wasn't okay to objectify even the goddess of love, but instead just laughed and said, "A blood-covered rock?"

"No, what's underneath. Look!" David wiped the blood off a flat edge of the stone, where the blade had hewn straight through.

"Fuck, David, don't touch the bloody thing," Tanya cautioned.

"It's dead. See?" He poked it for emphasis.

"Still."

"And we're bloody fuckin' rich!" David wiped away the blood again. A glowing purple hue emanated from the stone, even through the red coat of gore. "Where's a game of bloody cards when you need one."

Tanya was about to say his gambling days had best be over since he clearly wasn't any good, then she recognized the violet glow for what it was. "Is that...moonstone?"

"Enough to buy a fuckin' castle."

"Uh, guys," Cross said.

"More like a kingdom," Tanya murmured.

"Cross, come see this! It's incredible," David marveled.

"Guys," Cross repeated.

"I hate to say I told you so, but I was damn right about that sword. Never would've made it without it."

"Even a blind dog finds a bitch once in a while," Tanya said with a laugh.

"Guys!" Cross yelled.

They stopped gawking and turned to the big man.

The ropes of smoke had finished spiraling up his arms and were wrapping around his neck.

How long has it been since he pulled the blade? Minutes?

Cross held the sword as far as he could from his chest while still gripping the hilt.

"Just let go of it," Tanya warned.

"I can't!" Cross sounded frantic.

Tanya had never seen the big man shaken.

The smoke slowly finished circling his neck. The strands spiraled together, forming a column of midnight. The tendril curled in front of Cross's face, then reared back like a snake coiling to strike. Tanya pried at the big man's fingers, but they were iron around the blade's hilt.

The gossamer tendril rushed forward, slamming into Cross's mouth and forcing itself down his throat. Wisps of it curled away, billowing up his nose, snaking into his ears, and slithering into the crevices around his eyes.

Tanya and David tried to brush it clear. It didn't work. They tried to grab it, but there was nothing to hold. They tried to cover his mouth, but the black mist pushed through their fingers.

Suddenly, it all felt horrifyingly familiar. Tanya stood, backing away with a shudder.

Cross convulsed as the smoke poured into him. His eyes rolled back, and he fell to his knees. The smoke that originated from the sword's pommel finished its spiral up his arms, then vanished into his mouth and other orifices. His eyes snapped shut, and his whole body seized.

"Cross! C'mon, big man! Stay with me now!" David yelled, trying to steady him.

"David..." Tanya said. "It's time to go."

He stared at her, blinking.

"Now!" Tanya yelled, still backing up.

David took a few steps away from the big man.

The seizure stopped.

Slowly, Cross stood, cracked his neck to each side, then rolled his shoulders.

"Cross?" David asked, voice pleading.

A series of pops filled the silence as Cross flexed each hand. The unfamiliar gesture sent a shiver down Tanya's spine. Cross was covered from head to toe in blood. Bits of bone and sinew clung to him like the tattered clothes of the urchin that so recently sat happily on his shoulder.

Normally, it was easy to forget how large and imposing Cross really was.

Now, it was impossible to ignore.

He towered over both of them, easily twice Tanya's weight and at least three hands taller than David.

"Cross, it's not funny, big guy," David warned. "You're scaring us!"

The big man's eyes opened. They were pure, oily, jet black.

Cross had always been fast, if a little clunky. He'd been even faster once he'd drawn the blade. He moved now with the cool grace of a trained killer, and there was no doubt he would be fast.

A stark contrast to the charging rhino I'm used to.

Wordless, Cross stalked toward her, the tip of the sword hovering just above the cobbles.

David moved between them.

"Run, Tanya!" he yelled, squaring off with the big man.

"Not a chance." Tanya set her jaw and nocked another arrow.

Only three left.

Tanya bit her lip.

Three should be enough for one man.

Her amber eyes met his jet-black ones.

Hopefully, it will be enough for Cross.

David held a shortsword in his right hand, a dagger in a reverse grip in the other. Cross leveled the blade between them. The sword was nearly as tall as David, and the big man vastly outclassed him in reach, weight, and power.

Not to mention the fucking magic sword.

The odds were beyond long, but the fool would bet on anything.

Suddenly, David did just that. He swatted at the tip of Cross's steel with his short sword and stepped forward in a clear attempt to get in close. It was the best bet with brawler weapons and the only shot of subduing Cross without killing him.

The much longer blade didn't move at all when David's sword hit it. Instead, a handspan of steel fell away, clattering to the ground. David's face twisted as momentum carried him forward, too late to correct. The tip of the leveled blade pierced his shoulder, sinking through muscle and bone as if they weren't there at all. With a grunt, David pulled back, freeing himself from the weapon.

Cross cocked his head to the side, then brought the blade around in an arc.

David ducked, then sprang forward, trying to get in close again.

Tanya loosed an arrow.

Cross's blade whipped back up, deflecting her shot. In the same motion, he kicked David in the gut, sending the much smaller man sprawling.

An impossible counter. Tanya nocked another arrow.

Two left.

Cross took a step forward, raising the sword over David for a killing blow.

Tanya let the arrow fly. It thudded into Cross's bicep. David rolled away from the overhead chop, but not quick enough. The blade cleaved through his right wrist and sliced half a span into the cobblestone.

David screamed.

Cross pulled the blade up as if it were wedged in butter rather than interlocked stone. He glanced at the arrow in his bicep, then turned to Tanya and charged.

David scrambled to his feet, blood spurting from the stump of his right arm.

Tanya loosed her last arrow.

Cross deflected it, but not quite far enough. The tip clipped the top of his shoulder, drawing blood but missing vital organs. The big man was nearly on her.

Tanya leapt to the side, throwing her bow at Cross and unsheathing a knife.

The bow bounced off his chest as his steel arced through empty air.

Tanya slashed at his side.

Somehow, Cross's blade met hers.

A shoulder slammed into her sternum.

The pieces of Tanya's blade clattered to the cobblestone just before her back hit the ground. With a grunt, she reached for a dagger. A boot forced her wrist down, pinning it to the stone. She drew another blade with her other hand as Cross's sword pulled back for the killing blow.

No way out, but I can at least buy David a little time.

Tanya buried her blade in the big man's calf as the sword swung down toward her chest.

Something crashed into Cross, and the weight on her wrist disappeared.

Tanya raised her head.

David and Cross were tumbling down the street in a clattering mass of limbs, steel, and blood. They rolled through the river of gore, finally coming to a stop thirty strides away.

Tanya scrambled up.

David had come up on top and threw a punch with his remaining hand.

Cross caught the smaller man by the wrist.

David headbutted him.

Cross didn't even flinch as David reeled back, blood fountaining from his nose.

Tanya unsheathed a blade and started running.

Cross slammed a fist into the side of David's head. Even without the big man's weight behind the blow, it knocked David off, spinning him like a top. He landed between her and Cross with a groan.

They were both on their feet by the time she was halfway to them. Tanya's heart hammered in her chest. Time seemed to slow. David glanced back at her. He spit blood and teeth from his mouth, then gave her a half-hearted smile. Gaps stood where pearly whites once conveyed such annoying charisma. David gripped his stump of a hand and said:

"Tanya...I love—"

A blade arced down from above, cutting clean through the bard, from right shoulder to left hip.

Before Tanya could say anything, Cross was brushing past the body. At his touch, David slid apart, each half falling to Seafront's blood-soaked street. Soon, his body would be bird food with all the rest of the human waste.

"No!" Tanya screamed. It was primal, animalistic, more emotion than words. It was love and loss. It was rage and regret.

Cross ran at her, and if the dagger in his calf or the arrow in his arm bothered him, he showed no sign of it.

His sword flashed, a horizontal blur of steel.

She ducked, tumbling through the blood and slashing him across the back.

Without even a grunt, Cross turned, swinging.

The sword blurred through the air. She bobbed under it and came up with a dagger aimed straight at the big man's eye.

Tanya sucked in a lungful of air.

What is that? Tanya felt like she needed to burp.

Slowly, she looked down. Nearly a span of steel was buried in her sternum.

How'd that get there?

In a half-hearted attempt, Tanya brought her dagger down. Cross caught her wrist in an iron grip and squeezed. The blade fell away, clattering to the blood-soaked cobbles.

Tanya could feel her heart slowing, beat by beat.

David's face flashed through her mind.

Such a good face.

Smoke poured from his beautiful eyes and mouth. It came for her. Tanya tried to scream but found she couldn't. In an instant, David's face was all smiles and cheer again.

No missing teeth.

Tanya's vision started to fade, white slowly encroaching from the edges of the world. Her eyes locked with Cross's inky black ones, pleading.

For what, though?

She wasn't sure.

A spray of blood hit Tanya in the face as an arrow blossomed from the big man's chest. Cross finally let out a grunt and turned away from her. Vaguely, Tanya realized she was falling. Blood splashed as her temple thudded to the uneven stone, and the whole world turned ninety degrees.

An image of Jack and Ted, floating face down in the Channel, swam through her mind. She dismissed it. The Channel was a thousand miles from here.

Tanya brought her hands up, squinting at them through the white. They were covered in blood.

Not just in the cuticles.

She watched Cross sprint away, white closing in around him.

Why is he sideways?

Tanya blinked, trying to decipher what she was seeing.

That doesn't make any sense at all.
The white wall took her.

56
GERARD STOCKWORTH

T *hunk.*

The sound of the arrow slamming into the big man's back reverberated up the street. Gerard had almost left after they awakened the first creature, but the monsters were dead now, and so was his quarry.

What was his name? Ronald? Doesn't matter. Whatever it was, he's dead now.

Gerard shouldered his bow.

The big man turned.

What in the bloody eighth hell?

The monster of a man charged.

Gerard's bow was back in hand in an instant.

At least he's still thirty spans away.

An arrow left Gerard's grip. A second later, another shaft was in the air. The big man's sword twitched to the side, knocking the first arrow wide. The second sank into his neck with a squelch. Gerard wasn't putting his bow away this time, though. He loosed another shaft at...

What's his name? Rinfold?

The man cut the projectile in half as it headed for his chest.

Twang.

Or Ragdol?

The arrow sank into the man's kneecap. Muscles bunched as if he might go down, then the shaft snapped.

Thrum.

The man was halfway to Gerard and showed no sign of slowing.

Ristis?

Metal met wood, deflecting the arrow.

Whirr.

505

Gerard's teeth clenched.

Whatever the fuck his name is.

The arrow hammered into an enormous shoulder.

Rinfold, Gerard decided.

Goose fletching brushed Gerard's cheek, then sped away. The big man tried to block the shot, but it went wide, clipping his ear.

At least he brought the blade up.

The following shaft slammed into Rinfold's thigh.

Gerard sent arrows high and low. At the throat, then the groin. The head, then the leg. He spread the shots, trying to avoid the impossible deflections, but as Rinfold closed the distance, the plan started to feel pretty desperate.

Another arrow thudded into Rinfold's chest, and the juggernaut finally began to slow. He had six of Gerard's arrows in him, one more from his friends, and a knife in his leg, yet he was still running. Gerard loosed three more shafts. The big man deflected the first, the second crashed into his gut, and the third sank into his leg.

He was on Gerard now, swinging. The blow was clumsy, nothing like the strength, speed, and precision from earlier. Gerard stepped to the side, letting Rinfold's momentum carry him stumbling past.

Gerard nocked an arrow and sent it into the man's back. Then another.

Rinfold turned as another projectile thudded into his neck.

Fucking some bloody number of hells, just die!

The man looked like an old scarecrow, twelve shafts protruding like battered blades of straw. Rinfold took another staggering step forward and swung, still a pace away from striking distance.

The blade wobbled through the air ineffectively.

Gerard sent two more arrows at the man's chest—the first hammered home. Rinfold caught the second, throwing it back as he fell to his knees. The shaft hit Gerard, fletching first, then tumbled to the blood-slick cobbles. Rinfold's chest heaved, life pouring from a dozen holes. He gripped the sword in his left hand, using his right to hold himself above the grimy street.

No chances.

Gerard stepped to the left and unloaded arrow after arrow into Rinfold. The first slammed into his exposed side, right where a kidney should be. The next sank into his right buttocks. Then another into the side.

Hopefully, the liver.

An arrow pierced Rinfold's right elbow, and he collapsed. Gerard reached back for another shaft, fingers closing on empty air instead of fletching. He pulled the bowstring back and loosed. *Twang*. He reached again. *Twang*.

Finally, Gerard's mind caught up with his hands. He sucked in a lungful of air and had to forcibly stop his hand from searching for another shaft.

Dead?

Gerard's heart pounded furiously.

He must be. Impossible to still be alive.

Then again, he'd seen a lot of impossibilities today.

Gerard shouldered his bow and drew his sword. Tentatively, he kicked the cross-guard of Rinfold's blade, sending the weapon skittering across the cobblestone. He'd seen what the edge did to metal and masonry and didn't care to test it on his foot.

Dare I approach the downed beast?

Black smoke poured from Rinfold's mouth, eyes, and nose.

Gerard jumped back, stabbing the body with the tip of his blade. His sword sank into flesh as the smoke streamed out, swirling about in all directions. A tendril snaked out, wrapping around Gerard's ankle. He shook his foot, but the smoke clung on.

Shit, shit, shit.

Gerard danced back.

The smoke tightened.

Should I take the leg?

He gritted his teeth, looking around.

A spiral of midnight found the hilt of Rinfold's blade.

Gerard raised his sword, hands shaking.

A rush of air filled the morning as all the questing tendrils streamed toward the pommel. Seconds later, the smoke was gone, almost as if it had never been in the first place.

Gerard stood there, heart racing, hands shaking, breathing irregular. Slowly, he gathered his wits, sanity, and resolve. With one last deep breath, he stepped forward and put his sword through the big man's chest, right where his heart should be.

"If he ever had one," Gerard muttered, looking down the street toward his other marks.

He pulled the tip of the blade back out, then stabbed the body through again, then again. Mostly satisfied, he left the sword in place as he crouched down next to the corpse. Gerard unsheathed his hunting knife, pulled the man's head back by the hair, and went to work. Before long, he had a head. He pulled out a burlap sack, dumped the bounty in, and filled it with salt.

Gonna be a long trip home, and I don't need you stinking up the place.

Gerard wiped his bloody hands on the big man's shirt, then checked his paperwork.

Huh, guess his name was Rigel. Where in the eighty-six hells did I get Rinfold from?

He frowned.

Oh, well. Doubt he's much concerned with the name anymore.

Gerard headed to the other two corpses, glancing at the big stone they'd gathered around.

"Nine holy hells," Gerard muttered, eyes widening.

Visions of the Stockworth Vineyard swam through his mind.

Maybe I could settle down. Get a good woman.

Gerard glanced at the stone again.

Maybe a few?

Molly's face, unmarred by the pox, blotted out the Vineyard. He pushed the image away. She was long dead, and no amount of stone would change that.

No way in all the thirty-seven fucking hells I'm going to touch that rock.

Truthfully, Gerard wasn't sure how many hells the priests claimed there were, but thirty-seven sounded like plenty to condemn all the sinners like him.

Forcibly, Gerard pulled his eyes from the enormous moonstone and approached the two bodies. The woman lay temple to cobbles, wide eyes still staring up the street. He rolled her with the tip of his toe. Half her face was covered in blood, but it was clearly Tanya. Gerard took her head. It was gruesome, bloody work, but the sooner it was over, the sooner he would be off this wretched island. He sauntered down to the last of them. The man was face up.

Well, half of him, anyway.

It was a little hard to be sure with the broken nose and missing teeth, but the kid looked enough like the pretty boy on Gerard's paperwork.

Hopefully, the head isn't too mangled to collect.

Gerard bent and put his knife to work once more. In less than a minute, another head dangled by a mop of coal black hair. He glanced up the street. Buttercup peeked out from behind a pile of rubble, watching him.

Oops, didn't mean for her to see that.

He looked around at the bloodbath that was Seafront.

At least I won't be responsible for all her nightmares.

Gerard bagged the last head, gathered up the scabbard, and returned to the blade. Blood pooled around it, gleaming in the morning light. Some of it was from its bearer; most was from the countless dead before him.

Slippery business, blood.

Gerard bent, lining up the sheath's mouth with the blade. He tried to push the two together, but the tip caught on the edge of the scabbard and spun. He repositioned and tried again. Again, it rotated.

"Fucker." Gerard let out a long-suffering sigh.

He tried again, but once more, the sword resisted.

"Bloody, butt-buggering blade."

After nearly a dozen more attempts, Gerard finally got the tip into the sheath. Wiping sweat from his brow, he tossed a sack over the handle and pulled the blade into the blood-soaked leather.

Carefully, Gerard wrapped the sword back up in the same cloak his three marks had concealed it in, then dug through each of their packs. He took what little stone they had, pilfered a pocket clock that couldn't belong to them, and lit the pitch flare from Tanya's bag.

The flare let off the pleasant smell of pine and wood smoke, but more importantly, it put out an immense, billowing cloud of black soot. If anything was still alive on the island, it would see the plume rising from the main street.

Best get out of here before something else comes to life.

"Come on, time to go!" Gerard hollered. "And watch your step. Blood's a slippery business."

Buttercup scampered up, bare feet squishing through the gore-coated street. Together, they headed toward the rendezvous point. She watched her step as they walked, clearly more concerned with Gerard's advice than the human sludge between her toes.

Gods, poor thing will be fucked in the head after this.

Gerard felt his face tighten.

How does a little girl deal with something like this?

Molly would've known what to do, what to say, but she'd always been better at such things.

Can't just buy her a woman...right?

Gerard glanced back at the stone one more time.

Maybe a few?

He shook his head and headed into the armory.

The tide stopped them from descending all the way to the dock. But after a few hours, they stood on the shore at the bottom of the stairs. A longboat fought a riptide at the cave's mouth as it waited for the tide to lower enough to enter.

"No need to rush!" Gerard yelled.

His words echoed through the cave, mixing with crashing waves.

No way they heard me.

Instead of yelling more, Gerard simply waited, trying to maintain as much calm as he could manage. It wasn't easy. Little aftershocks of adrenaline still pulsed through him, every noise made him jump, and he still felt the distinct desire to fight or flee. He took a deep breath and slowly let it out.

Don't need them capsizing that boat.

Gerard had lit the flare because getting off the island before another creature awoke seemed prudent. However, now that half a league of rock separated him and Buttercup from the purple stones, he'd prefer the crew not endanger themselves.

As they waited, Gerard found himself staring at the slowly receding tide and the churning water that obscured the cave's depths. He didn't believe in sea monsters, but that didn't stop the unsettling feeling from bedding down in his stomach or the hairs from standing on the back of his arms.

I don't believe in rubble monsters or magic swords either, but here we are.

Gerard pulled his gaze from the water and busied himself by unslinging his pack and strapping the wrapped blade to the back of it. Buttercup didn't even look at him; she just stared at the boat bobbing in the waves. Gerard bundled the remaining pitch flare around the sword's hilt at the top of his pack. It wasn't the most convincing thing in the world, but it would hide the blade at first glance.

Besides, if they aren't more curious about the disheveled teen covered in blood, then there's something wrong with 'em.

Gerard slung the pack over his shoulder and sat down on the final step of weathered stone. Soon, the longboat rowed into the cavern. Gerard watched, waiting for an enormous serpent to emerge or a massive tentacle to writhe from the depths, but neither appeared.

"What in the hells happened to you?" one of the sailors asked as they docked.

"Long story. Let's just get to the *Warden*."

They eyed him and Buttercup skeptically but held the boat steady against the jagged rock.

Gerard helped Buttercup into the vessel and then climbed aboard himself. As soon as he was in, the men began to row. A scrap of sail drifted down as they neared the mouth of the cave. Gerard reached out, catching the cloth between thumb and forefinger.

Normal weathered sail.

Gerard looked up. More debris clung to the cavernous ceiling, but nothing nefarious lurked there.

Once on the open ocean, the *Warden* pulled around and lowered a hoist to scoop them up. Soon, they were on deck. A ballista sat near the rail, clearly removed to make way for the hoist.

Captain Caldwell strode across the deck, yelling orders. "Make ready to set sail! Secure the longboat! Reinstall weaponry!"

Sailors scurried about, preparing to make way.

"A success?" the captain asked. He eyed Buttercup, then looked Gerard up and down skeptically.

Gerard glanced at the girl, then down at himself. She was a little ball of grime and gore. He was completely covered in blood from the knees down and spattered with red well past his waist.

What a mess.

"Some minor setbacks, but a success all in all," Gerard said, nodding toward the three bloody sacks hanging from his bag.

"Ah, no need for the brig, then?" Caldwell raised an eyebrow, eyes shifting subtly toward Buttercup.

"No, I don't think so. She's a survivor. Probably needs a warm meal and a hammock more than anything else. Had to improvise with the others, and things got a bit messy, but it all worked out in the end."

"I see. A pity. The *Warden's* brig sees so little use these days—but I digress. You two must be eager to get cleaned up, and I imagine you'll be hungry. I'll have the cook ready a meal. We have no more business in Seafront, I take it?"

"No, and thank the bloody gods for that," Gerard said.

"Mr. Bolis," the captain called to his first mate. "If you would be so kind as to get us underway, I do believe we've lingered on the edge of the world quite long enough."

Caldwell's officers each took to their tasks, directing different parts of the crew. Gerard heard something about a mizzenmast and lowering the sails, but everything was starting to feel a whole lot less important as his capacity to remain upright faded.

"I don't normally care to comment on another gentleman's appearance," Caldwell remarked. "But I imagine you'd like to get out of your traveling clothes and into something a bit more...untarnished? Perhaps a short rest is also in order, but I do hope you'll join me for dinner and share anything you might be allowed."

Caldwell looked him up and down again, and Gerard was suddenly very aware of the sheath pressed between his shoulder blades. He rubbed his thumb and forefinger together, noticed the tic, and forced his hand into his pocket. It brushed the warm metal of the clock.

"Oh," Gerard said, pulling out the watch. "I nearly forgot. Found this on one of my marks. Yours, by chance?"

Caldwell ceased his examination, locking on the watch instead.

Gerard held it out.

The captain reached forward, hand closing around the device almost tenderly.

"You have no idea how much I appreciate this," the captain whispered. "Is there any way I can repay you?"

"That dinner should do it." Gerard smiled. "Though heading to my quarters would probably be best for now."

"Good, good." Caldwell nearly laughed, blew out a breath, then boomed across the deck. "Seward, would you please get this girl a wash bucket and be so kind as to lend her an old set of clothes?"

The midshipman approached.

"Hi, I'm Seward," she said, extending a hand.

Buttercup pulled back, eyeing the hand reproachfully.

"Not much of a talker," Gerard explained. "Still, I imagine a wash bucket and some clothes is the first step toward fixin' that."

Seward pulled her hand back and smiled, then turned and walked confidently across the swaying deck toward the aft of the ship. Gerard and Buttercup wobbled over the shifting wood and down the stairs after her. It turned out the girl was unwilling to leave his side, but she eventually allowed Seward to clean her up and get her into a fresh set of clothes, provided Gerard stayed in sight. He kept his back turned during the process and worked on his own appearance with a wet rag.

After the washing was done, the two of them looked a bit more like real people. Seward tried to give the girl a room, but again, she refused to let Gerard out of sight. Eventually, they gave up trying to convince her and brought her back to his room. He tried to give her the hammock, but she wouldn't touch the thing. Seward brought them extra blankets and a pillow, and Buttercup happily curled up in the corner between the trunk and wall.

Gerard propped his bag and the sword in another corner.

Should I put it somewhere safer?

He glanced from his bag to the chest bolted to the floorboards at the end of the hammock.

Not gonna fit in there.

Gerard looked around the room. There was nowhere else to store it. He was exhausted and found he had little energy left to care.

Buttercup peered out from her nest of blankets.

"I'm not going anywhere," Gerard said. "Now get some sleep."

He glanced at the blade one more time.

It'll be there tomorrow.

With that, Gerard slipped into the hammock's soft embrace and let oblivion take him.

57
SCARLETT REINHOLM

Blood spilled from Scarlett's mouth, dripping onto the floor. She knew she should savor the meal but couldn't. It was too succulent, too scrumptious, too divine to hold back in the slightest. Instead, her teeth tore into the uncooked meat, ripping and shredding like there was no tomorrow. All three of them had screamed at first but fell silent long ago. Pieces of the male lay scattered about the cabin, the majority heaped near the kitchen table.

The woman lay a span away, throat torn out, a red pool of gravy slowly growing across the floorboards. Scarlett currently enjoyed the youngest of the three but would get to the others eventually. The meat was tender, clean, and supple, with barely a hint of game.

Clearly a vegetarian.

Scarlett raised her head, wolfing down another slippery hunk.

Lifeless eyes stared back at her. The eyes of her younger sister, Kaylee.

⬥

Scarlett let out a scream and sat straight up, gasping. Her body was slick with sweat, and foliage clung to her naked form. She tried to inhale, but invisible hands tightened around her windpipe. Breath by breath, she sucked air past them, clinging to the cord around her neck with quaking arms. Her heart thumped ballistically, trying to free itself from the cage of bone that held it so unreasonably in place.

It didn't help that Scarlett could still see her sister's eyes.

A groan of protest emanated from her belly, and in that moment, Scarlett remembered...

Everything.

Roland's face swam through her mind first, then an image of him covered in holes, leaking blood into new snow. She remembered the consuming utter helplessness, the rage, and the insatiable need for revenge.

I killed the hunters. I killed the villagers. I killed them all.

Scarlett shuddered.

I feasted on that poor girl while she was still alive...

Her stomach twisted.

Gods. What have I done?

The thoughts swam through Scarlett's mind unbidden, unwanted, and no longer just a nightmare.

She retched.

What came up wasn't fully digested and apparently hadn't been chewed a great deal. She turned away from the putrid remains and retched again. Scarlett continued to hyperventilate as she tried to vomit up every bit of the previous day. After only bile dripped from her lips, she shoved a finger down her throat, forcing up more acrid fluid.

Once it was all up, Scarlett curled into a ball and started to shake uncontrollably. She grabbed hold of her necklace, clutched the pendant woven within it, and tried to calm her breathing. It didn't help. Her vision shifted first from Kaylee's lifeless eyes to Roland's lifeless form, then to the rest of yesterday's carnage.

Tears streamed down her face.

She didn't bother to wipe them away.

Vaguely, Scarlett remembered her fight with the man who killed Roland. He'd hurt her physically and emotionally, and she'd returned that pain.

All for petty vengeance.

"*Vengeance is not petty. Vengeance is del—*"

"Shut up!" Scarlett screamed into the cool morning air. "You have done enough!"

She waited for a retort, but the thing inside her remained silent.

More memories from the backyard flooded in. Scarlett pictured the woman who tried to restrain her while they stabbed Roland to death. She'd tried everything to escape, even kicking and biting to get to Roland. It had all felt so futile. Scarlett's grip tightened around her necklace as Roland's dying bellows echoed in her mind.

That's when I released control to the other.

Scarlett sucked in a breath.

I may not have killed them all, but I released it, and together, we did terrible things.

She blew snot from her nose.

Impossible, unfathomable, unforgivable things.

She took a shuddering breath, then retched again.

Nothing came up.

Scarlett looked down at her hands. Her breathing was finally starting to calm.

Didn't Nathan cut one of them off?

Yes, she was sure he had, but there it was like it never happened. Scarlett flexed her fingers and found everything in working order. Slowly, her eyes moved down her body, searching for any sign of damage.

There was none. It should have been a relief, but it wasn't. She'd taken so many lives, killed off entire families, and torn others asunder. The village would never be the same—might not survive at all.

Yet I don't have a scratch on me.

Scarlett reached for her knife in anger. Her hand slapped the naked hip where it usually hung. Frantically, she looked around. She sat in a little clearing, the morning sun barely cresting the treetops. Blood spattered the ground, and arrows jutted from fallen leaves.

Apparently, I ripped them out? Odd. Why don't I remember that?

Scarlett scrambled over the wet ground and grabbed an arrow. It had no tip. She tossed it aside, groping through the leaves in search of another. Her fingers found a second shaft. She grabbed it, hand clenching around the barbed tip. A trickle of blood ran down her quivering forearm as she slowly brought the wobbly point to her throat.

Birds chirped overhead as Scarlett sat on her heels in the little clearing. Light filtered through the canopy, hitting her naked heaving chest. Scarlett let out another sob, and the arrowhead drew a prick of blood.

"Do it!" she yelled into the still morning air. "Just do it, you coward." Scarlett pressed the point deeper, willing her quivering hand to pull it across her throat. For what felt like an eternity, she knelt there, shaking in the pale dawn light, unable to perform this final act of violence.

The arrow fell to the dirt at her side.

"Coward," Scarlett accused, softer now. Defeated.

Elrontis stopped me. It was Scarlett's first thought, but she knew it wasn't true.

No, I'm just a coward. Simply an animal with an instinct for self-preservation.

"Naathaan!" Scarlett screamed in a long, drawn-out wail.

I can't do the deed myself—I don't have the courage. Maybe he can do it for me. It was far easier to yell his name than to drag the point across her throat.

"Nathan!" Scarlett screamed again.

The only response was a fluttering of wings as small birds took to the air at the edge of the clearing.

"Now what?" Scarlett asked no one in particular. She'd never been a particularly fervent follower of any of the thirteen gods or even of the newer single one. Instead, she'd always put her faith in science. She prayed now, though.

Please help me.

Silence, save for the birds.

How can I be rid of this?

No response.

Why have you cursed me?

Scarlett prayed to the old gods and the new. She called out to everything in this world and the stars above. Then she waited, eyes wide, watching for a sign.

Please answer. Someone...anyone.

Silence.

"Fine. Fuck you too!" The words came out half snarl, half sniffle.

With gritted teeth, she rose.

I'm a scholar. I'll figure this out. I don't need help, especially not from some entity that would let this atrocity occur in the first place. An entity that would let me occur...

Scarlett nearly sank back to her knees at the thought. Instead, she took a deep, shuddering breath.

That's enough of that. Either end it or march forward and figure this shit out. Pull yourself up by your fucking bootstraps, woman!

Scarlett sifted through her memory.

Where have I heard of this type of affliction before?

"*It is not an affliction. It is a gift.*" The other reverberated through her mind—half words, half formless realization.

Scarlett's lips curled into a snarl.

I told you to shut up! You have done enough!

No response.

"I will purge you! Whether you are a sickness of my blood, essence, or mind. I will root you out!"

The darkness remained silent.

Scarlett racked her brain. She'd heard tales of humans wearing an animal's skin before. But where? Scarlett looked around, eyes landing on a patch of blue-spotted mushrooms.

A fairy tale! The conclusion came in a rush.

Eaters were close, though she'd never heard of an eater that looked quite like her. They were old legends, used mostly to scare the children of Terra. *Greep and Bondel's Folklore and Fairy Tales* had a story about them, but she'd always avoided it, as it was rather scary.

Where did that tale originate?

Somewhere up north, Scarlett decided. She'd always thought the legends had come from humans wearing pelts to scare other humans or perhaps as a metaphor for the temperament of each clan.

Maybe those tales were based on a darker, more sinister truth.

She'd never considered the possibility before, but she sure as hell did now.

Why is it manifesting hundreds of years later, though? And why in me?

They were good questions, but not ones with any answers.

I'm not likely to get them sitting here either.

Scarlett stood, then hesitated, imagining her little cabin and the life she built on the plateau.

Roland's face filled her mind again.

Her lip quivered. She bit it, pushing the image away. The only thing worth going back for was long gone, back to the dirt in the brutal cycle of life.

Everything else is just stuff.

Scarlett looked around the glade.

Well, I can't stay here. It would never be safe for what remains of that settlement.

Scarlett couldn't remember hunting the villagers, but no doubt she had. Through the same logic, her recurring dreams must be much more than nightmares. Deep down, part of her must have always known. The same part that subconsciously convinced her to leave the only people she loved behind in Terra.

Behind...or in the dirt.

Scarlett pushed the thought away with a shudder.

Why else come to the middle of nowhere? Why else build a cabin where no one lives for leagues? Why else live for years in this desolation?

The questions danced through Scarlett's head, but she knew the answer.

I may be too much of a coward to end things here, but I won't simply allow Elrontis to have what it wants.

Scarlett glanced up at the sun, then checked the moss on the trees for confirmation. It would be a long trip, but there was only one way to start one of those, and that was one foot after the other. She took a deep breath, then took the first step. It was the first step into the next chapter of her life, the first step toward discovery, and the first step toward

Terra. It was the first step toward a lot of things, but most of all, it was the first step toward home.

58
GERARD
STOCKWORTH

S　moke billowed from the huge man's eyes and mouth as he charged. Gerard reached
for an arrow, but his fingers grasped nothing.

"Well, at least you were able to recover the heads," Vincent finished.

With a silent shudder, Gerard snapped back to the present. He'd been seeing things ever
since Seafront. Usually, they were flashbacks, but oftentimes, the details were changed.
Running out of arrows before Rigel Cross collapsed on the cobbles was a common dream
at this point.

"And some information, despite how absurd it sounds in the retelling," Gerard said.

"Unbelievable indeed. Still, in my line of work, the unbelievable is sometimes the only
rational explanation." Vincent paused, reflecting for a moment. "Does that sound a bit
unhinged to you, Gerard?"

"Honestly?" Gerard asked.

Vincent nodded.

"It sounds fucking crazier than a lotus junkie quitting the habit mid-pull of the pipe."

Vincent let out a short bark of a laugh. "I'm sure it often does when you're on the
outside looking in. Unfortunately, that's how magic usually shows its hand in the world."

"Do you mind if I speak freely, sir?" Gerard asked.

"Please do."

"If someone told me magic was real a month ago, I would've laughed in their face. In
fact, if someone had asked me what I thought of your organization, I might have said you
were a bunch of puffed-up bloody quacks who were milking the people's teat for all the
stone you could manage. No offense intended, of course."

"No, none taken. None at all. The fact most believe magic doesn't exist is something
I take great pride in. It means we at the OAM have done our job well. Perhaps too well,
if you read the accounts of some, but I digress...Gerard, I'd like to offer you another job,
one direct from the Order. To be clear, this would not be through your handler or the
Justiseer's Guild."

"About that. I do have one more piece of information for you and a request."

"And what might that be?" Vincent asked.

"Well, I've already described the monsters made of rubble and refuse to you. What I didn't mention is that at their center is a moonstone bigger than you or I."

"Truly?"

"At least the two I encountered," Gerard said with a nod. "In any case, when the creatures finally went down, the crystal split. I'm not going to lie to you, Vincent. I thought long and hard about chiseling off as much as I could carry and making a new life for myself."

"Intriguing. If you're not exaggerating, those would be the biggest moonstones we've ever discovered, and by quite some margin."

"I thought they might be of particular interest to the Order. So, I didn't disturb the crystal once the creature fell."

Plus, there's not enough stone in the realm to justify fighting one of those things. Don't need to burden the OAM with trivial details, though.

"That was considerate of you," Vincent said. "The Order will be sending a contingent to retake Seafront and recover the pieces of one of these monsters. But that is another matter. So tell me, Gerard, what's your request?"

"Well, seeing as I left all that stone sitting there for the Order. I was hoping the OAM might raise their rate."

Silence.

"Nothing outlandish, mind you, but perhaps a bonus." Gerard bit his lower lip. The request rang hollow even in his own ears.

"I'm afraid I can't adjust the rate." Vincent paused, meeting Gerard's eye. "It was pre-negotiated, you see, and even I have superiors to answer to. If I change the rate on a job that's already done...well, they'll ask why I'm paying more for something we have already bought. You understand. Now, if you'd been able to retrieve the blade, that might have been different, but alas, we are where we are."

Gerard nodded. He'd assumed the answer would be no. It would have been his answer, too, if he'd sat in Vincent's chair.

"But you will, of course, still receive your stone from the first bounty, and I took the liberty of rounding up Rigel's to match the other two." Vincent slid three sparkling emeralds across the top of his desk.

That's a hell of a roundup.

Unlike smaller currencies, the emeralds were cut immaculately and polished to a tantalizing shine. Gerard took them gingerly, wrapped each in cloth, then placed them in a pocket. It was more money than he'd ever possessed, let alone carried.

"Now, Gerard, I have a question for you," Vincent said, the corner of his mouth turning up in a mild smile.

"Shoot."

"What do you desire most in the world?"

"That's a bloody open-ended question. What do you mean?" Gerard asked.

"You are a semi-wealthy man now. What will you do with it?"

"I suppose I'll save it."

"Really? For what, might I ask?" Vincent inquired.

"Honestly? I always wanted to start a little vineyard. Maybe make some wine, let Vigilant live out his elder years in comfort."

Gods, why does that sound so stupid when finally said aloud?

Vincent studied him.

Because you're a bloody bounty hunter, not a vintner, you twat.

"Vigilant?"

"My horse."

This just gets better and better, eh? The winemaker and his horse. He's got to be laughing at me.

"I see..." Vincent trailed off, still watching Gerard. "What if I told you the OAM would be willing to fund this venture of yours?"

"What?"

"Fund it? It means to pay for it."

"I know what it means. Why, though? What's the catch?"

"No catch. Not really."

"Sure sounds like the start of a catch," Gerard said.

"You are certainly perceptive," Vincent said with a smile. "I can see why you are so good at what you do. Your discerning personality could make you a great winemaker someday as well."

"Perceptiveness pays the debts in my line of work. Plus, a lack of it'll almost always get you killed."

"Indeed, then let us pull away the veil and speak plainly. If you complete this last job for the Order, we will not only grant you fertile lands outside Norinspire but also subsidize the entire endeavor."

So the job's the catch. What in the actual fuck-of-a-job would justify this sort of negotiation, though?

Gerard thought back to the whole town of Seafront, built in secret.

This is just a wave in the ocean for them.

"What exactly is the job? And what in the sixty-four hells does subsidize mean?"

Vincent laughed. "It means to fund the entire project from the ground up. You can pay back the cost of the facility with a percent of your profits. Think of it like a loan, except free from the counting house's usual interest, of course."

"Of course." Gerard barely held back an eye roll.

"There will be contracts and terms, but let's skip the semantics for now."

Sure, let's skip the details on the offer that's far too good to be true.

"The job?" Gerard asked warily.

"Simply help an associate of the OAM track down a mysterious beast and kill it. We have reason to believe it's headed to a place called Stonewood."

"Why's the OAM involved?"

"It may be magical in nature."

"Magical like the...Vortex Stones?" Gerard asked.

"Vortex Stones? No, no, no, we'll have to come up with a better name than that."

Our taxes, so frugally spent as usual.

"The beast is likely similar in origin, though thoroughly different in manifestation," Vincent explained.

"So, magical, but not a semi-mindless killing machine that's nearly indestructible by its very nature?" Gerard asked.

"Not indestructible, by your own account."

"True, I suppose."

Though I did leave out the part about the magic fuckin' sword.

Gerard still wasn't entirely sure why he'd done that. Maybe it was because the blade seemed far too powerful on its own, let alone in the hands of a world-encompassing organization like the OAM.

Or maybe it's just because I like the way it shines.

The thought nearly made Gerard laugh. "Isn't Stonewood in Terra?"

Vincent opened his mouth to speak—

Thump. Thump. Thump.

"Come in!" Vincent yelled.

The door swung open, and Vincent's assistant ushered in a tall, lean, muscular man. He had brown hair cropped short, a freshly shaved face, and approached Vincent's desk with the graceful gait of a predator.

"I'm Nathan," the man stated, extending a hand.

"Name's Gerard." He stood and gripped the newcomer's well-calloused hand.

A climber? Or a swordsman? Maybe both.

The two men sat down in the overly embellished seats.

"Nathan's been hunting this creature all the way from the jungles in the south. Nathan, I believe Gerard will accompany you to Terra in search of this...Elrantis?"

"Elrontis," Nathan corrected. "The transport's nearly packed and ready to leave. They're loading the horses now."

"What do you say, Gerard? One more bounty before you and your horse enjoy a better life?" Vincent asked. The bloody bureaucrat was smiling, and it made Gerard a little nervous.

Why do I get the feeling I'm stepping from the melee into a cavalry charge?

Yet he couldn't shake the vision of Vigilant grazing in a big paddock. Maybe even with a little foal running around the yard. Gerard took a deep breath.

"I'm in."

"Excellent. Gerard will be an invaluable asset to our expedition, Nathan. He has proven himself not only capable and resilient but also quite tenacious." Vincent rummaged around in his desk, produced a contract, and slid it across the table to Gerard. "Ellis, please draft up an offer of subsidization for Gerard. Installments of twenty-five percent of profit against the principal until paid in full and a flat five percent interest to the OAM upon completion."

"Very generous, sir," Ellis responded.

"We're not in need of opinions, Ellis, we're in need of quick hands," Vincent chided.

"Yes, sir." Ellis bowed and exited the room.

"Ellis will join the two of you on the ship with your copy of the contract within the hour," Vincent stated.

"He's joining the expedition?" Gerard asked.

"Indeed he is. This particular mission requires that I get updates on the state of Stonewood," Vincent explained.

"And why might that be?" Gerard asked.

"Oh, we got so busy talking about contracts that I forgot to mention the second part of your mission," Vincent said.

How convenient, considering I already agreed.

"And that is?" Gerard asked.

"Stonewood has experienced a rash of grisly murders recently, and the OAM member stationed there has requested aid."

"So hunt and kill this Elrontis, discover who's behind the murders, and save the people of Stonewood?"

"If you can. Stonewood should be a second priority. The OAM has a specific purpose, and we need to stick to it, but we also like to help the people when our goals align."

"Got it."

The OAM was supposed to be impartial, but it was common knowledge that they cared more for the people of Darin than Terra.

"Anything further?" Vincent asked.

"No, let's go. We need to be underway in an hour," Nathan said, standing.

Gerard stood as well. "I think I've got the general idea."

The two men said their goodbyes to Vincent and exited the Citadel.

As they walked down the steps, Vigilant let out a whinny and began hopping back and forth in excitement. Buttercup took a step back from the horse, smiling, as an uncontrollable grin split Gerard's face.

"Damn, he always this excitable?" Nathan asked.

"No, steady as a sea-walled cliff. But it's been a while."

Gerard approached Vigilant and patted the big horse on the side of the neck. The stallion nuzzled him, nearly pushing him off his feet. Then he breathed in deep and let out a big snort. As soon as Nathan was within reach, the big horse moved his head from Gerard and pushed his nose into Nathan as well.

"Huh. Think he likes you," Gerard said.

"He's not usually friendly?" Nathan asked. "I do seem to have a way with horses."

"Indifferent is what I'd call it."

"Huh. Well, I'll take that as a compliment, I suppose."

"I wouldn't."

"No?"

"Not at all." Gerard glanced at Nathan. "He typically only likes stable hands and salty old bastards with bad tempers."

They both chuckled.

The stable girl led a magnificent all-black mare with a thick coat and shining mane around the corner.

"Don't get any ideas, Vigilant. We gotta earn that paddock before you can fill it," Gerard whispered to the stallion.

Vigilant just snorted.

The two men mounted up, and Gerard pulled Buttercup onto the back of Vigilant's saddle.

"And who's this?" Nathan asked.

"A stray I picked up on the edge of the world."

They nudged the horses into a walk.

"The stray got a name?"

"Probably, but she ain't keen on sayin' it. I've taken to callin' her Buttercup."

The name had turned out to be pretty fitting for her dirty blond hair once they'd finally washed all the blood and filth from it. She hadn't spoken the entire trip back, and Gerard often caught her staring off into the vast ocean or distant horizon.

"She's coming with us?" Nathan asked skeptically.

"Yeah. She's got nowhere else to go, and I couldn't think of any suitable work for a mute."

"All the orphanages are full?"

"Nah, I couldn't do that to her."

"Not sure Stonewood is the right place for a young girl, though—" Nathan broke off, and Gerard turned in the saddle.

Buttercup's mouth was twisted into a snarl, and she was giving Nathan a stare that would have made the Trickster proud.

"Yeah, I don't think she much likes being called young or little. Can't really blame her, with the horrors she's seen. Only fifteen, and been through more than most will in a lifetime. She's quick, though." Gerard pointed to his head.

"Yeah, and she's got mettle too, eh?"

"Yeah, more than she ought to, probably the only reason she's still alive."

"What happened out there?" Nathan asked.

"Well, that's a long story...maybe a tale for the boat if you're looking for new nightmares."

"Ohhh, ominous," Nathan said with a smile.

"I suppose that was a bit dramatic, eh?" Gerard laughed.

"Just a touch."

Gerard had barely returned to Norinspire and was already on his way out again.

At least Vigilant's comin' along this time, and if everything goes to plan, this will be our last job for guilds and orders.

"Next stop, Grenisport. Then, off to the other side of the world," Gerard said with more enthusiasm than he felt.

"Yes...and vengeance," Nathan muttered with a steely resolve.

"Ohhh, ominous," Gerard said with a smile.

They both had a chuckle at that.

EPILOGUE
RIGEL CROSS

R age, blood, bone, and regret. Silence, darkness, and pain.

Fear, blood, bone, and relief. Silence, darkness, and pain.

Conviction, blood, bone, and sorrow. Silence, darkness, and pain.

Jealousy, blood, bone, and regret. Silence, darkness, and pain.

For what seemed like an age, this was all Cross experienced.

How many days has it been? Or has it been months? Years, perhaps? Impossible to know.

At some point, Cross became aware that he was not alone in the void. Occasionally, another presence would seep into his consciousness. It would flood in like the water in the riddle room, yet unlike the room, there was no escaping this hell. Mostly, the presence was angry. It had far more rage than even Cross could fathom and a plethora of pain.

That's odd. How do I know those words? They aren't ones David or Tanya taught me.

But the question disappeared as soon as it materialized, just like everything else in the void. Everything but the presence. The malignant attendant lingered, anger red hot like the iron rod they'd used to cauterize David's toes. But given enough time, it always retreated, back to its corner of the void.

Vaguely, Cross remembered killing David. He remembered cutting the man in half. He even remembered plunging the blade into Tanya's chest. Her face was etched in his memory. First, there was shock, then bewilderment, and finally surprise as an arrow punched through his chest.

Cross wanted to blame himself, even though he knew those actions were not his own. He wanted to cry and grieve but found he couldn't. It wasn't because he didn't care. He'd cared about them far more than anyone since his father's death. But emotions only existed in the void briefly, and even then, the void seemed to determine what those emotions could be. The one exception was the other's rage and anguish. That was a constant, and the only thing on which Cross could reasonably rely.

528

Occasionally, something would brush against Cross's shapeless form, a presence that didn't exude the fury and suffering of the other.

How many of them are there? One? Two? More?

It went on for an immeasurable amount of time, giving new meaning to the word eternity.

Another word I shouldn't know. Odd, but inconsequential.

Finally, after what seemed like an age, or perhaps even a few, something new happened. It started as a slow pulling sensation, then slowly grew until it felt as if his soul was being shredded. The pain made the anguish of the other pale in comparison. Cross's perception faded from the black of the void to a pure, featureless white. Slowly, even the white receded, revealing a yellowish green. Tiny bubbles danced upward through Cross's vision as a blurry new world worked its way into focus.

The room was dimly lit, a dull green hue emanating from a few dozen cylindrical tanks. The vats surrounded a central mass of iron and a metal that might be bronze. Circular protrusions snaked out from the metal cluster like great serpents intertwining through the chamber. Some were small, around the size of Cross's finger. Others were nearly the size of his waist. The snake-like metal twisted and coiled about the room with no discernable pattern.

Cross noted the green light was all around him as well. Some sort of curved glass encased him, and he was submerged in liquid.

I'm in one of these tanks...

Curved glass on this magnitude was impossible. Then again, none of this should be possible. Cross knew he was dead. He'd felt his body shudder its last breath and something akin to a soul flee that lifeless form.

An iron door studded with rivets creaked open on the other side of the room. A man much smaller than Cross in both height and stature walked in. He wore a gray shirt with buttons up the center, black trousers, and a soot-stained leather smock. White hair sprouted from either side of a tired cap, and a complicated contraption rested on the tip of his nose.

Something black shifted in one of the tanks near the door, gathering like mist on a cool winter morning. The black fog coalesced into a vaguely humanoid shape, moving toward the edge of the tank.

The man spoke to it, but the words were too far away to hear through liquid and glass. Something in the tone sounded kindly, though, and reminded Cross of soft words spoken to a sleeping child.

"This is a mistake. I shouldn't be here. I'm still alive!" Cross screamed, hammering his fist into the glass. No sound came out, though, and nothing slammed into his glass prison. Cross looked down at his hand.

There was no flesh to speak of. Floating in front of him was just dense, soot-colored smoke in the shape of a hand. In horror, he brought it closer to his face, then pressed it gingerly against the wall of the glass. It connected, but he couldn't feel the touch. As he pushed harder, his hand gave way. He tried to gasp, but no sound escaped his lips. He pulled the appendage back, and it reformed a second later. Cross looked down, frantically checking the rest of his body. It was all a swirling collection of jet-black mist. He expected to feel his heart flutter as he came to the realization, but of course, it didn't.

I have no heart...

Cross reached into his own chest and confirmed the fact.

No heart, no lungs, no bones.

Panic gripped him.

Did I just trade a dark void of rage and pain for one of iron, glass, and grief?

It would be better without the other but not by much. Not if he was stuck in a perpetual state of smoke and left only to grieve for the actions of his final moments...

Forever.

Something brushed against Cross's mind. No, that wasn't right. Something brushed against the very fibers of his being.

My essence. Another term he knew, with no recollection of how.

Cross looked around, frantically trying to find the source of the touch.

The metal mass in the center of the room hummed to life, and new yellow light flickered into existence. The man near the sprawling metal monster turned something.

A wheel?

Creak. Creak. Creak.

He pulled on some sort of lever. There was a clunk, then a scraping sound as something moved near Cross's feet.

If I had feet.

The metal monstrosity in the middle of the room whirred and bellowed, but the shorter man didn't jump away.

With a grind, iron slats uncurled at the top of the glass prison.

Then the pressure came, forcing Cross upward. He tried to resist, but his ethereal form proved utterly insufficient to the task. The green liquid disappeared as he was pulled into the hole at the top of the vessel.

Cross tasted black and purple as the world faded away.

Authorial Intrusion 2

I hope you enjoyed reading this book as much as I enjoyed writing it.
I hope you felt for the characters and felt their loss, as I did.
Writing the major deaths was incredibly hard for me.
Yet, it pales in comparison to the real loss we all experience sooner or later.
If you haven't experienced it yet, I wish you many years without it.
If you have, then please accept my deepest condolences.
Please know you are not alone.
We all grieve, but hopefully, like most things in life, we can do it together.

Thank you all again for all your time and for all your support.
This novel would not have been completed without a huge support structure and a lot of love.
Moreover, the series could not continue without readers like you.
If you would like to contribute further and help get this story into more hands, sharing your opinions is the best way. You can do so here:

Or go to:
https://andrewpmeritt.com/books

This was *Ballad of the Blade* -
One story of many in *A Serenade of Smoke*.

Appendix

Or go to:

https://andrewpmeritt.com/appendix

The Great Houses

Nobles of Darin

House Lochling
Sigil: Stag
Location: Darkloom
Flag: Red stag on black fading downward to gray
Other notes: The second largest source of iron in the realms, though a much harder area to mine than Creed due to the frozen ground.

House Elintis
Sigil: Bear
Location: Ardendale
Flag: Green bear on checkered cloth of red and gold
Other notes: A magnificent town surrounded by lakes, ancient architecture, vast gardens, and old money.

House Morison
Sigil: Crocodile
Location: Riversplit
Flag: Green crocodile on a field of gray intersected with a black X.
Other notes: Small settlement on the edge of one of the great bayous. Leather is their main export, and traveling through here is the safest way to Darkloom.

House Willfort
Sigil: Raven
Location: Norinspire
Flag: Silver raven on a black field
Other notes: One of the three great houses that governs the capital. Their house is known for shrewd negotiation.

House Bowman

Sigil: Tree
Location: Norinspire
Flag: White tree with green-and-black diagonal stripes
Other notes: One of the three great houses that governs the capital. Their house is known for incredible patience.

House Duvan

Sigil: Bull
Location: Norinspire
Flag: Black bull on a field of purple fading to yellow
Other notes: One of the three great houses that governs the capitol. Often at odds with House Bowman, as they are a bit more rash and eager to get things done.

House Talamer

Sigil: Scarab
Location: Blackbarrow
Flag: Yellow scarab on a field of black
Other notes: Blackbarrow has recently been taken by the blight. So far the scientists of Darin do not know the source of the tainted ground and vegetation. The Academy would love to get a sample of the vegetation for testing.

House Hibarb

Sigil: Shark
Location: Grenisport
Flag: White shark fin and waves on a field of blue
Other notes: Largest port town in Darin. Nearly all import and export of goods to and from Terra, including slaves, go through their harbor.

House Rocktell

Sigil: Lion
Location: Windmore
Flag: Red lion's head on a field of black, dotted with seven white stars
Other notes: Largest importer of slaves and home to the Coliseum. The Rocktells are known for ruthlessness and a savvy business sense.

House Lawlen
Sigil: Anaconda
Location: Ellisfjord
Flag: Green snake on checkered red and gold
Other notes: The second biggest port town in Darin. Most importers and exporters do not go through here unless they carry something less reputable, as the bayou discourages honest trade by its very nature.

House Stolle
Sigil: Wolf
Location: Swordbreak
Flag: Black pack of wolves on an orange field
Other notes: A militant people who mostly abstain from realm politics. Swordbreak is surrounded by steep cliffs and has a single mountain pass for an entrance. House Stolle has historically stayed out of realm wars, and Swordbreak has never been taken in recorded history, even during the War of Iron and Blood.

Former Nobles of Terra

House Ruxnor
Sigil: Wolverine
Location: Stonewood
Flag: White wolverine on a plain black field
Other notes: A small settlement with major exports of lumber, precious metals, and coal. They do have large deposits of iron as well, but it is much easier to extract from Creed.

House Dristwell
Sigil: Boar
Location: Ravenstar
Flag: Silver boar on black-and-white checkers
Other notes: The town mostly revolves around the Academy. Students come from all over, even Darin, to learn at the Academy. House Dristwell put a lot of value on knowledge and money into the Academy before the War of Iron and Blood.

House Calidis
Sigil: Stallion
Location: Ramos
Flag: White horse on a plain green background
Other notes: One of the three great houses that governed Ramos. House Calidis used to be the glue holding the Darin nobility together, and they led the initial conquest into Darin.

House Orilen
Sigil: Hawk
Location: Ramos
Flag: Purple bird on a field of black
Other notes: One of the three great houses that governed Ramos. They were known for opposing the war initially, but that did not spare them at the end of it.

House Valenstar
Sigil: Rhinoceros
Location: Ramos
Flag: Gray rhino on a red field with a cross of orange
Other notes: One of the three great houses that governed Ramos. House Valenstar was known for their involvement with infrastructure and city planning. They can be traced back to the origins of many of the great features and ancient structures filling the city.

House Kilmond
Sigil: Badger
Location: Ebonstall
Flag: Metallic black badger on a field of black
Other notes: Ebonstall is home to the greatest temple to the thirteen gods. House Kilmond has always been extremely militant and provided much of the force that initially invaded Darin. Massive black walls ten spans in height surround the city and were built even before the Academy was diligently recording history.

House Wynmar
Sigil: Octopus
Location: Lancaster

Flag: Purple octopus on a field of white

Other notes: The town of Lancaster was nearly reduced to rubble during the War of Iron and Blood. It has since been rebuilt but is nothing compared to its former glory.

House Coben

Sigil: Leopard

Location: Creed

Flag: A golden leopard on a field of black fading to green from left to right

Other notes: Major production has always come from mining. Creed was often engaged in the numerous wars between Terra and Darin and was historically the source of fighting between the two realms.

House Estiger

Sigil: Hippopotamus

Location: Swiftbell

Flag: Metallic gray hippo on yellow-and-black checkers

Other notes: Swiftbell, also known as the Emerald in the Sand, is home to the largest flourishing desert town. The river and lake provide much of the resources needed for life.

House Lockney

Sigil: Ant

Location: Brineveil

Flag: White ant hill on blue field intersected by a yellow cross

Other notes: House Lockney always worked very closely with House Estiger. The two of them were of the same mind on most political issues, and they often mistrusted anyone not from the sands. Neither Lockney nor Estiger participated in the War of Iron and Blood, and their respective noble houses were both spared.

Pantheon

The Thirteen Two-Faced Gods

Aethia: God of Judgment
Gender: Female **Facets:** Justice/Vengeance **Symbol:** A bird perched atop a set of scales
Depiction: A woman with high cheekbones and a proud face. Her light side is blindfolded and carries a set of scales. Her dark side has empty sockets and a falcon on an arm.
Typical worshippers: Rulers, Justiseers, city guards, and law-abiding citizens

Amara: God of Love
Gender: Female **Facets:** Love/Lust **Symbol:** A flower
Depiction: An extreme portrayal of the feminine form. Her light side is often depicted with a baby in hand. Her dark side is clad in very little and suggestively posed.
Typical worshippers: Common folk of all types, brothel workers, and anyone looking for love

Borix: God of the Sun
Gender: Male **Facets:** Driven/Stubborn **Symbol:** A plow tethered to a water buffalo
Depiction: A large man with long hair pulled back and a scraggly beard. His light side is usually shown working alongside his buffalo, Kargo. His dark side is typically portrayed riding on Kargo's back and wielding a scythe.
Typical worshippers: Farmers, botanists, and hard-working common folk

Durno: God of the Forge
Gender: Male **Facets:** Protection/Jealousy **Symbol:** A hammer and anvil
Depiction: A man with a close-cropped beard. His light side is often portrayed as an artisan wearing a leather apron. His dark side is clad in plated armor with a warhammer in hand.
Typical worshippers: Blacksmiths, carpenters, masons, glaziers, and laborers

Evintri: God of Hope
Gender: Female **Facets:** Hope/Denial **Symbol:** A harp
Depiction: A beautiful woman proportioned more realistically than Amara. Her light side is often sculpted or painted with a swollen belly. Her dark side holds a harp and wears a knowing smile.
Typical worshippers: Bards, common folk of all types, and anyone looking to get pregnant

Isidri: God of Faith
Gender: Female **Facets:** Kindness/Weakness **Symbol:** A candle
Depiction: A woman wearing the long, flowing robes of a priest and always with face covered. Her light side keeps her head bowed in respect. Her dark side looks outward with shrouded features.
Typical worshippers: Priests, common folk, merchants, and slaves

Korinth: God of the Ocean
Gender: Male **Facets:** Confidence/Arrogance **Symbol:** A net and spear
Depiction: A bare-chested man with well-toned muscle, clean shaven, and always smiling. His light side carries a spear. His dark side holds a net.
Typical worshippers: Fishers, sailors, privateers, and merchants

Malthean: God of War
Gender: Male **Facets:** Honor/Wrath **Symbol:** Shield crossed by sword and spear
Depiction: A man clad in light plates of armor. His light side holds a spear and a plain unadorned helmet. His dark side holds a two-handed sword, and his helm is covered in spikes.
Typical worshippers: Soldiers, politicians, and privateers

Otix: God of the Moon
Gender: Male **Facets:** Cleverness/Deceit **Symbol:** Sirius
Depiction: A plain-looking man, clean shaven. He typically wears a well-cut suit, and nothing changes between his light and dark side except perhaps his expression.
Typical worshippers: Aristocrats, thieves, assassins, and anyone else who is more than they let on. Otix is often worshipped in secret, and therefore, it is hard to judge the full

extent of those who follow him.

Pirel: God of the Hunt
Gender: Female **Facets:** Courage/Abandon **Symbol:** A bow nocked but undrawn
Depiction: A wiry woman draped in furs and a painted face. Her light side holds a bow. Her dark side holds a hunting knife or occasionally just clutches an arrow by the shaft.
Typical worshippers: Hunters, tanners, and common folk

Rula: God of Law
Gender: Female **Facets:** Truth/Derision **Symbol:** A book and gavel
Depiction: A tall, thin woman in a clean suit. Her light side wears spectacles and carries a book. Her dark side needs no glasses and carries a large gavel.
Typical worshippers: Government officials, Justiseers, guards, and law-abiding citizens

Sashesh: God of Ambition
Gender: Ambiguous **Facets:** Success/Complacency **Symbol:** A multifaceted gemstone
Depiction: They are depicted as a well-dressed noble with high cheekbones and prominent features. Their light side is often shown in deep conversation. Their dark side is usually shown with arms crossed in condemnation of overindulgence.
Typical worshippers: Nobles, merchants, slaves, and anyone who is trying to climb the social ladder

Usin: God of Weather
Gender: Male **Facets:** Prudence/Pessimism **Symbol:** A storm cloud
Depiction: An older bearded man typically wearing traveling gear. His light side is calm and collected and carries a walking stick. His dark side wears a cynical gaze and bears a ball and chain.
Typical worshippers: Common folk of all types, farmers, desert cultures, and travelers

The Cult of the One True God

Less is known about the one true God. The cult sprung up during the War of Iron and Blood. They opposed slavery and were condemned as witches and heretics after the Death of the Warrior. They still exist to this day but are hunted and often either forced into slavery or killed if they are discovered. The only cities where they are allowed to worship openly are Brineveil and Swiftbell.

The Moons

Huna

A large reddish-orange moon, Huna rotates the planet on a monthly basis. Ridges mark its surface, and it exhibits some volcanic activity. The presence of Huna and her two sister moons has caused nocturnal predators to thrive on Terra and Darin, and most scholars believe the three moons are also responsible for the planet's unpredictable tides. The water usually fluctuates about six spans, but records indicate swells of seven spans, three hands, and two and a half fingers.

Sirius

Also known as the Trickster by the general populace, this moon has what looks undeniably like a face etched into its surface, and most consider it bad luck to stand under Sirius when it is full. This moon orbits the planet at the same speed that the planet rotates, locking it over the continents of Terra and Darin. This causes it to always be overhead and to wax into existence each night and then wane away in the morning. Sirius has much more volcanic activity than its larger sister Huna, and the lava flow is responsible for its somewhat frightening countenance. Due to the volcanic activity, the moon's surface is always shifting, causing its face to distort and change slightly. This phenomenon is exacerbated by Aura, the third and final moon.

Aura

A small blackened moon with a purple hue emanating from its edge, Aura orbits Sirius and seems to absorb light from its larger volcanic sister. This phenomenon is what causes Sirius's face to shift and change by the hour. Not much is known about Aura, and the question of whether or not it is a moon at all has been the source of some debate.

Nomenclature

Systems of Measurement

Fingerspan: the average width of a finger, often just referred to as a finger
(~1 in. or ~2.5 cm.)

Handspan: the average width of a hand, often just called a hand
(~ 4 in. or ~10 cm.)

Stride or Pace: the average distance of a step, or half a span
(~2'-9" or ~0.8 m.)

Span: the average height of a person
(~5'-6" or ~1.7 m.)

Story: the average height of a single floor of a dwelling, or about two spans.
(~11'-0" or ~3.4 m.)

Brick: based on the average weight of a brick used by a mason in the realms.
(~10 lb. or ~4.5 kg.)

Monetary Increments

Topaz flakes
Typically used for food, a room for the night, small goods, etc.

Ruby chips (worth 10 flakes)
Typically used for larger goods and services such as tools or weekly wages

Sapphire shards (worth 10 chips)
Typically used for horses, farming equipment, and other more expensive goods

Diamond fists (worth 10 shards)
Typically used for homes or other large expenditures

Emerald crystals (worth 10 fists)
Typically used for business transactions between the extremely wealthy and jewelry for nobles

Moonstone orbs (worth ~100 crystals)
Typical uses are unknown; moonstone is nearly unattainable. Small pieces have been hoarded by nobles, but most have been lost over the centuries.
Note from the translator: (There is another sentence written here that has been scribbled out entirely.)

About the Author

Andrew Meritt grew up in Fairbanks, Alaska, where he began telling stories around the campfire. Work has taken him from Alaska to Minnesota, Ohio, and California. He is now settled in the San Francisco Bay Area with his wife, Annika, and their two dogs, Zagreus and Alyeska. He spends his weekends rock climbing, snowboarding, woodworking, and working on *A Serenade of Smoke*.